THE
BEDFORD
READER

By X. J. Kennedy and Dorothy M. Kennedy

Knock at a Star: A Child's Introduction to Poetry, 1982
The Bedford Reader, 1982; Third Edition, 1988
The Bedford Guide for College Writers, 1987

By X. J. Kennedy

Poetry
Cross Ties: Selected Poems, 1985
Hangover Mass, 1984
French Leave: Translations, 1984
Three Tenors, One Vehicle (with James Camp and Keith Waldrop), 1975
Emily Dickinson in Southern California, 1974
Celebrations After the Death of John Brennan, 1974
Breaking and Entering, 1971
Bulsh, 1970
Growing into Love, 1969
Nude Descending a Staircase, 1961

Fiction and verse for children
Brats, 1986
The Forgetful Wishing Well: Poems for Young People, 1985
The Owlstone Crown, 1983
Did Adam Name the Vinegarroon? 1982
The Phantom Ice Cream Man, 1979
One Winter Night in August, 1975

Anthologies
Tygers of Wrath: Poems of Hate, Anger, and Invective, 1981
Pegasus Descending: A Book of the Best Bad Verse (with James Camp and Keith
  Waldrop), 1971

Textbooks
Literature: An Introduction to Fiction, Poetry, and Drama, 1976; Fourth Edition,
  1987
An Introduction to Fiction, 1976; Fourth Edition, 1987
An Introduction to Poetry, 1966; Sixth Edition, 1986
Messages: A Thematic Anthology of Poetry, 1973
Mark Twain's Frontier (with James Camp), 1963

THE
—BEDFORD—
READER

THIRD EDITION

EDITED BY

X. J. Kennedy & Dorothy M. Kennedy

A Bedford Book

ST. MARTIN'S PRESS • NEW YORK

Publisher: Charles H. Christensen
Associate Publisher: Joan E. Feinberg
Managing Editor: Elizabeth M. Schaaf
Production Editor: Mary Lou Wilshaw
Copyeditor: Marianne L'Abbate
Book Designer: Anna Post
Cover Designer: Volney Croswell
Cover Photo: John Pearson

ACKNOWLEDGMENTS

Maya Angelou, "Champion of the World." From *I Know Why the Caged Bird Sings* by Maya Angelou. Copyright © 1969 by Maya Angelou. Reprinted by permission of Random House, Inc. Excerpt from "Work in Progress" by Sheila Weller. Reprinted by permission of the author.

Suzanne Britt, "Neat People vs. Sloppy People." Reprinted by permission of the author.

William F. Buckley, Jr., "Why Don't We Complain?" Reprinted by permission of Wallace & Sheil Agency, Inc. Copyright © 1960, 1963 by William F. Buckley, Jr. First published in *Esquire*. Excerpt from Introduction to *A Hymnal: The Controversial Arts* by William F. Buckley, Jr. Reprinted by permission of G. P. Putnam's Sons. Excerpt from *Overdrive: A Personal Documentary* by William F. Buckley, Jr. Reprinted by permission of Doubleday & Co., Inc.

(*Continued on page 700*)

PREFACE
FOR INSTRUCTORS

The best teachers, a wise man has said, make themselves progressively unnecessary. If you accept this bit of wisdom, you will probably agree that the best textbooks are those that, similarly, show the student a path, then beat a retreat. We want the third edition of *The Bedford Reader* to be that kind of book. For students of writing, the best path we know is to read good and lively writing, get stirred up, and want to say something. "A writer," says Saul Bellow, "is a reader moved to emulation." Yet the book offers more than model essays. It tries to demonstrate how effective writing is written—not just theoretically, but in the working practice of some of the best writers in the English and American languages.

In arranging these essays according to familiar methods of writing (narrating, describing, explaining, persuading), we recognize that such classifications are merely ways to get going. As we suggest in the Introduction, these rhetorical modes may be regarded not as machines to feed with verbiage but as natural forms that assist in various tasks. Like waves in the sea, they rise, take shape, and disintegrate in the flow of a writer's prose. It is not as formulas but as methods of invention and fruition that this book presents these modes and tries to show students their usefulness. Many instructors familiar with both rhetorical tradition and the findings of recent composition research are well aware that they can prompt student writers to discover much more to say. We think a good writer doesn't choose a method, then set out mechanically to follow it. Instead, such a writer probably keeps on thinking and feeling and discovering all along the way.

In choosing essays, we allowed none that we did not enjoy reading and wouldn't want to teach. Some essays (good old Thurber and Catton!) will seem as familiar and trustworthy as Otis elevators, and the instructor can rely on them to lift a class discussion to a higher floor. Other essays, we believe, are likely candidates to rouse a class and inspire good writing, though they may have first seen print only a few months ago. Our choices have been neither whimsical nor arbitrary. Many students have used the questionnaire at the back of the book to send us their opinions. Some 172 instructors who taught from the last edition found certain essays highly effective, or counterproductive, and they have told us so.

THE STRUCTURE OF THIS BOOK

Instructors familiar with *The Bedford Reader* will find its structure little changed since its previous incarnation. At the start of each chapter, we set forth each writing procedure: what it is (The Method) and how to use it (The Process). These rhetorical methods are offered not as inexorable molds but as ways to approach definite tasks. It is worth reminding the student that a writer may well do different things—describe, give examples, compare and contrast—all in the same essay. Let them know that when writers write a definition or write persuasively, they are especially likely to use all or any of these methods.

Then follows a pair of paragraphs showing the method in action. Then come the selections, in which, if we have done our jobs, the method will be apparent. Following each selection appear more questions than you will probably care to ask, grouped as Questions on Meaning, Questions on Writing Strategy, and Questions on Language. These last include, besides matters of style and diction, any vocabulary words in an essay that might cause trouble. In the questions, terms in SMALL CAPITAL LETTERS refer the student to the glossary, Useful Terms.

Besides the Suggestions for Writing that follow each essay, there is a list of Additional Writing Topics at the end of each chapter. If you don't assign specific topics but let students develop their own, this list may simply be pointed out, to start them on the road to discovery.

If you don't see eye to eye with us, or you wish to take up the rhetorical methods in a different order, nothing will hinder you. If you want to ignore rhetorical methods and instead organize your course by subjects, themes, or genres, please see the list, Essays Arranged by Subject.

A brief discussion of every selection appears in the instructor's manual, now called Notes and Resources for Teaching and bound with this book's Instructor's Edition.

WHAT'S NEW?

Familiar though it may seem, the third edition commits itself to newness—not, we trust, mere novelty. The contents are half new: Twenty-seven of our fifty-four selections were not in the book before—one or more new faces in every chapter. Why have we altered so much?

Although nearly all of the 172 instructors who commented appeared well satisfied with nearly all the old selections ("Don't change a thing," some said), it seemed to us that the book would only regress if it stood still. After mulling the instructors' advice, we sought room to improve. Now there are more minority writers and more leading women writers—among them Alice Walker, Suzanne Britt, Joyce Carol Oates, Gretel Ehrlich, Ursula K. Le Guin, Barbara Ehrenreich. Other writers often requested by instructors—Robertson Davies, Garrison Keillor, Stephen Jay Gould—are now represented. Now you should find more material to appeal directly to eighteen-year-olds, and more to engage nontraditional students as well.

Other innovations may strike you. The arbitrary line sometimes drawn between literature (or *belles lettres*) and other, supposedly humbler kinds of writing has long seemed to us a kind of Berlin Wall in need of taking down. To bridge the gap and to supply, perhaps, still more chances to enliven and illuminate, *The Bedford Reader* has made a radical move. In the opening chapter, "Narration," we now include a classic modern short story, Ernest Hemingway's "Hills Like White Elephants." In Chapter 2, "Description," you will now find two richly descriptive poems: D. H. Lawrence's "Snake" and Emily Dickinson's "A narrow Fellow in the Grass." At the very least, you and your students may enjoy distinguishing such kinds of writing from the book's essays (of which there is still a full complement in both chapters). So-called imaginative writing, we suspect, often includes much nonfiction prose.

In the past, instructors who have used *The Bedford Reader* have differed sharply when asked whether the book should admit any student writing. Opponents of the idea have replied, "If I want to teach student writing, I'll just run off some of my own student papers." Still, we have felt troubled lest our book suggest (by all its examples) that professional writers are the only writers to admire and learn from. This time, a majority of instructors who responded to the question were in favor of the idea, so we have listened to them. We have represented student writers with two selections: Todd Alexander Senturia's "At Home in America" and Linnea Saukko's "How to Poison the Earth." Both are among the best-received essays in the first compilation of winners of the Bedford Prizes in Student Writing—the text-anthology *Student Writers at Work: The Bedford Prizes*, edited by Nancy Sommers and Donald McQuade (Bedford Books, 1984). Admittedly, these are not run-of-the-mill student papers, but they originated in freshman writing classes. Perhaps they may serve as examples of what student writing can be.

Now there are twice as many paragraph examples: two for each method of writing. The first illustrates writing for a general audience. All of these examples are about television; we have replaced some of our last edition's examples with contemporary ones. The second paragraph example, taken from a textbook in a nonliterary field, illustrates writing for a specialized audience. In these, the academic disciplines practically span the curriculum. Examples have been drawn from anthropology, art history, astronomy, biology, economics, environment, geography, history, and psychology.

Rewritten with the intention of making it work harder, the Introduction now centers on Joan Didion's "In Bed," an essay that in the past proved a favorite with both instructors and students. Two chapters, besides, have been thoroughly revised in light of what we learned from writing *The Bedford Guide for College Writers*. In "Division and Classification," we trust that matters will now be even more clear. In "Argument and Persuasion," subtitled "Appealing to Reason and Emotion" in the previous edition, we discussed persuasion as being either logical or emotional. This dichotomy bothered some instructors, and us. Any effective argument, we now suspect, enlists both reasoning and feeling. And so we divided this chapter, in the third edition, into two parts that may be more objectively defensible: (1) stating an opinion and (2) stating a proposal. The essays in this chapter now illustrate each kind of writing. For those who wish attention paid to inductive and deductive reasoning, logical fallacies, and the simple method of reasoning recently set forth by British logician Stephen Toulmin, we have added an unobtrusive "Note on Reasoning" (page 501).

Our section "For Further Reading," which in the past may have seemed a mere attic in which to store odd pieces, now focuses in depth on three writers: George Orwell, E. B. White, and Joan Didion. An essay by each writer appears earlier in the book, and this section now adds another two essays by each, in case you want to live with these outstanding writers a little longer. *Suggestions for Writing* is a new feature in this section, too.

But the most noticeable new feature in the third edition is Writers on Writing, which deserves a few words.

WRITERS ON WRITING

Following the questions on each selection, you will usually find a short statement by its author about writing. By and large, these statements are much briefer than the Postscripts on Process that were contained in the previous edition, and there are many more of them. Not just one to a chapter, they now number forty-one strong. To make them more useful in class (or outside of class, for writing assignments), we accompany each with questions: For Discussion.

Some of these comments focus on problems of vital interest to the student: finding a subject, writing, and revising. In a few instances the writers' concerns go far beyond strategy, such as Barbara Ehrenreich's complaint about the tacit censorship she finds in American magazines, and A. M. Rosenthal's memoir of how, as a cub reporter, he learned about the First Amendment.

To discover pertinent comments on how writing is written (or how it ought to be), we combed interviews, prefaces in which the writers state their aims, stray magazine articles, and other sources. A few of these comments were written especially for the last edition of *The Bedford Reader* and have been saved; some were written especially for the third edition. A few writers, though, had little or nothing to say about writing, as far as we could learn.

ACKNOWLEDGMENTS

Debts accumulate with interest, and it is clear that we could not have done the third edition without the help of those scores of instructors, students, and friends whom we have named before. Besides, we now owe thanks to many others, among them Karen R. Dhar, Deborah Kuhlmann, and Helen Neumeyer, who made generous suggestions, and to Paul Fussell, who corrected and rightly attributed a quotation from Jonathan Swift. We are greatly indebted to Sonia Maasik of the University of California, Los Angeles. For one of the book's new features, the additional paragraph in each chapter showing how a method of writing may be used in an academic discipline, she suggested an array of illustrations from textbooks in many fields, and we chose what seemed the most pertinent.

Instructors who, at the invitation of the publisher, wrote their detailed comments on the last edition and rated the effectiveness of the essays were Annette Andre, R. Antonio, Brian Barbour, Judith E. Barlow, Robert L. Barth, Lona Bassett, Ferne Baumgardner, James N. Beard, Mary Bednarek, Sue Belles, Reginald Berlica, Renee J. Berta, Charles Biggs, Ted Billy, Martin L. Bond, Norman Bosley, Anne L. M. Bowman, Kathleen Bridge, William R. Brown, Elizabeth Buckmaster, Arline Burgmeier, John Canateson, Kathy Chamberlain, Cynthia Chapman, Elizabeth A. Chitester, Ruth M. Christ, M. Thomas Cooper, Jimmy C. Couch, James A. Cowan, Bruce Alban Crissinger III, Vicki L. Cromwell, Carol A. Cunningham, Terliko Daniel, Virginia Davidson, Mary A. DeArmond, Lee Deibel, Natalie V. (Mykyta) Dekle, Ed Demerly, Emily Dial-Driver, Marcia B. Dinneen, Emanuel diPasquale, Ruth Dorgan, Stelio Dubbiosi, Patricia G. Duckworth, Margaret Duggan, Lynn H. Dunlap, Kate Duttro, Robert P. Ellis, Laurie Eynon, Cheryl Fish, Joyce S. Fisher, Richard J. Follett, Eleanor Galbreath, Richard Gambrell, Dennis Goldsberry, Diane Goodman, Lee F. Graf, Hannah S. Gray, P. C. Hall, Mary Hanna, Ted Hansen, Bernice Harris, Andrea Havistar, Lynn Flint Hicks, Philip R. Hines, Patty Hoovler, Kate Hulbert, Isabelle Hutton, Rich Ives, Donald Johns, Norma Johnsen, F. A. Kachur, Fred Kai, Mary M. Katzif, Michael J. Kelly, William C. Kenney, Karen Kerr, F. R. Kestler, Joseph L. Kolpacke, Jacqueline Krump, Ralph H. Latham, Lee Leonard, Wallis Leslie, Lis Leyson, Paul Lindholdt, Bernadette Flynn Low, John Low, Gerald F. Luboff, G. Robert McCartney, Billie McClanahan, Horace T. McDonald, Marcia A. McDonald, Michael McDowell, Carmela McIntire, Sue McKee, Janice C. McKniff, Iris M. Maron, Rebecca Martin, William B. Martin, Sue Mayer, Jim Meyer, Deanne Milan, Michael Miller, Gary Mitchner, Toby R. Moore, Gail L. Mowatt, Melanie Moye, William A. Neville, Richard Newby, Peter Oppewall, Jhe Paine, Jeff Park, Sue Park, Richard Pepp, Ruth Perkins, Paul E. Perry, Elizabeth Petach, Betty C. Pex, Paul Pierson, Katherine R. Pluta, Simone Poirer-

Bures, Judith K. Powers, Jane Purcell, June Purdom, Daniel S. Quibb, Katherine Rankin, Mark Riley, Lucinda H. Roy, John Ryan, Jules Ryckebusch, Ted Schaefer, Susan F. Scott, Marlene Sebeck, Janet Seim, Helen G. Smith, John T. Smith, Kathy O. Smith, Mary Steffancin, Virginia L. Stein, Sandra W. Stephan, Ely Stock, Lorena L. Stookey, Sandy Stratil, William Sullivan, Don Swanson, Gregory M. Thomas, Vivian Thomlinson, Marilyn Throne, Mike Tierce, Mary L. Tobin, Edwina Trentham, Judy Turner, Margaret A. Udler, Lynne Vallone, Lyle Van Pelt, Kathleen Vollmer, Eleanor von Dasson, Mary Ellen Walsh, K. J. Walters, Laura Waters, Pam Watts, Dorothy White, John Alfred White, William W. Whitt, Mary Louise Willey, Anita C. Wilson, Julie Wosk, Steve Yarbrough, Helen Zucker, Jack Zucker, and Sander Zulauf.

This time, as always, we relied on generous editorial aid, which goes beyond what any authors have a right to expect, from Bedford Books. Charles H. Christensen, Publisher, suggested new essays and rediscovered E. B. White's "A Boy I Knew." Julie Shevach spent days in the Boston Public Library tracking down statements by writers on writing and won the battle for permissions. When a medical emergency threatened to bog us down, Ellen Darion drafted notes, questions, and writing topics for ten selections, and most of her work stands unscathed. Matthew Carnicelli orchestrated messengers between Bedford Books and Bedford, Mass. Marianne L'Abbate edited copy. Elizabeth M. Schaaf and Mary Lou Wilshaw made the book happen. Joan Feinberg supplied ideas and inspirations; she also worried with us (and for us) every step of the way.

We remain grateful to former students at Ohio University, the University of Michigan, the University of North Carolina (Greensboro), and Tufts University for letting us work with them on their own essays. We thank, too, the five past, present, and future college students in our immediate family for their knowing advice and for reminding us again and again how students look at things.

X. J. Kennedy and Dorothy M. Kennedy

CONTENTS

3 EXAMPLE: Pointing to Instances   155

4 COMPARISON AND CONTRAST:
Setting Things Side by Side **201**

Face to face at Appomattox, Ulysses S. Grant and Robert E. Lee clearly personified their opposing traditions. But what the two Civil War generals had in common was more vital by far.

As children play near the crumbling walls of a notorious concentration camp, a visitor contrasts the calm scene of the present day with the memory of vanished horrors.

With sardonic wit, the writer, whom *Time* called "Queen of the Muckrakers," details the stages through which a sallow corpse becomes a masterwork of American mortuary art.

9 DEFINITION: Tracing a Boundary 429

Starting with the assumption that the English language is in trouble, Orwell urges action to rescue it. Here is a classic attack on smoke screens, murk, and verbosity in prose.

An essayist, perhaps the finest essayist America has produced, paints an unvarnished word-portrait of his most unforgettable character: "a boy I grew up with and nowadays see little of."

When the author's pig fails to show up for his meal, the alarm spreads rapidly. In one of his most praised essays, White shows how a pig's fate and a man's can be inextricably bound together.

"Our notebooks give us away," declares this leading contemporary writer, facing a painful truth about her compulsive notebook-keeping. In so doing, she reveals much of the process by which she writes.

What part have Cuban people played in the recent history of Dade County, Florida? Didion reports objectively on the frictions and misunderstandings between newcomers and long-time Miami residents.

INTRODUCTION

WHY READ? WHY WRITE?
WHY NOT PHONE?

In recent years, many prophets have forecast the doom of the written word. Soon, they have argued, books and magazines will become museum pieces. Newspapers will be found only in attics. The mails will be replaced by a computer terminal in every home.

Although the prophets have been making such forecasts for decades, their vision is far from realized. Books remain more easily portable than computer terminals and television sets — cheaper, too, and in need of less upkeep and energy. The newspaper reader continues to obtain far more information in much less time than the viewer of the six o'clock news. Most business is still conducted with the aid of paper. A letter or memorandum leaves no doubt about what its writer is after. It is a permanent record of thought, and it lies on its recipient's desk, expecting something to be done about it.

The day may come when we will all throw away our pens and typewriters, to compose on the glowing screens of word processors and transmit paragraphs over cables; still, it is doubtful that the basic methods of writing will completely change. Whether on paper or on screens, we will need to arrange our thoughts in a clear order. We will still have to explain them to others plainly and forcefully.

That is why, in almost any career or profession you may enter, you will be expected to read continually, and also to write. This book assumes that reading and writing are a unity. Deepen your mastery of one and you deepen your mastery of the other. The experience of carefully reading an excellent writer, noticing not only what the writer has to say but also the quality of its saying, rubs off (if you are patient and perceptive) on your own writing. "We go to college," said poet Robert Frost, "to be given one more chance to learn to read in case we haven't learned in high school. Once we have learned to read, the rest can be trusted to add itself *unto us*"

For any writer, reading is indispensable. It turns up fresh ideas; it stocks the mind with information, understanding, examples, and illustrations. When you have a well-stocked mental storehouse, you tell truths, even small and ordinary truths, and so write what most readers will find worth reading instead of building shimmering spires of words in an attempt to make a reader think, "Wow, what a grade A writer." Thornton Wilder, playwright and novelist, put this advice memorably: "If you write to *impress* it will always be bad, but if you write to *express* it will be good."

USING *THE BEDFORD READER*

In this book, we trust, you'll find at least a few essays you will enjoy and care to remember. *The Bedford Reader* features work by many of the finest nonfiction writers, past and present.

The essays deal with more than just writing and literature and such usual concerns of English courses; they cut broadly across a college curriculum. You'll find writings on science, history, medicine, law, religion, women's studies, mathematics, sociology, education, child development, natural resources, music, sports, farming and ranching, politics, the media, the minority experience. Some writers recall their childhoods, their families, their own college days, their problems and challenges. Some explore matters likely to spark controversy: drug use, the threat of nuclear war, funerals, sex roles, race relations, class distinctions, bilingual schooling, conservation, the death penalty, a report that rock music is going to the dogs. Some are intently serious; others, funny. In all, these fifty-four selections reveal kinds of reading you will meet in other college courses. There are even a short story and two poems. Such reading is the usual diet of well-informed people with lively minds — who, to be sure, aren't found only on campuses.

The essays have been chosen with one main purpose in mind: to show you how good writers write. Don't feel glum if at first you find an unbridgeable gap in quality between E. B. White's writing and yours. Of course there's a gap: White is an immortal with a unique style that he perfected over half a century. You don't have to judge your efforts by comparison. The idea is to gain whatever writing techniques you can. If you're going to learn from other writers, why not go to the best of them? You want to know how to define an idea so that the definition is vivid and clear? Read Tom Wolfe on "pornoviolence." You want to know how to tell a story about your childhood and make it stick in someone's memory? Read Maya Angelou. Incidentally, not all the selections in this book are the work of professional writers: As Todd Senturia and Linnea Saukko will prove, a student, too, can write an essay worth studying.

This book has another aim: to provoke your own thinking and so nourish your own writing. Just mulling over the views these writers advance, working out their suggestions, agreeing and disagreeing with them, sets your mind in motion. You may be led to search your own knowledge and experience (or to do some looking up in a library) to discover ideas, points to make, examples you didn't expect to find.

As a glance over the table of contents will show, the essays in *The Bedford Reader* illustrate ten familiar methods of writing. These methods aren't classroom games; they're practical ways to generate ideas, to say what you have to say, and to give shape to it. To begin with, of course, you'll need something worth saying. The method isn't supposed to be an empty jug to pour full of any old, dull words. Neither is it meant to be a straitjacket woven by fiendish English teachers to pin your writing arm to your side and keep you from expressing yourself naturally. Amazingly, these methods can be ways to discover what you know, what you need to know, and what you'll want to write about. Give them a try. See if they don't help you find more to say, more that you feel is worth saying. Good writers believe their own words. That is why readers, too, believe them.

Suppose, for example, you set out to write about two popular singers — their sounds, their styles, their looks, what they are like offstage — by the method of comparison and contrast. With any luck, you may find the method prompting you to notice similarities and differences between the two singers that you hadn't dreamed of noticing. At least, hundreds of teachers and tens of thousands of students have found that, in fact, these rhetorical methods can help you to invent and discover. Such little miracles of creating and finding take place with heartening regularity.

Reading the essays in *The Bedford Reader*, you'll find that some writers will stick to one rhetorical method all the way through. Narration is the single method in Maya Angelou's "Champion of the World," since the writer tells a story from first word to last. But in the flow of most expository prose, methods tend to rise, take shape, and disperse like waves in a tide. Often you'll find a writer using one method for a paragraph or two, then switching to another. In "The Black and White Truth about Basketball," Jeff Greenfield mainly compares and contrasts the styles of black and white players, but he begins with a paragraph that follows another method: giving examples. Later, he gives still more examples; he briefly describes famous players in action; he defines the terms *rhythm*, "*black*" *basketball*, and "*white*" *basketball*. Clearly, Greenfield employs whatever methods suit his purpose: to explain the differences between two playing styles.

In truth, these rhetorical methods are like oxygen, iron, and other elements that make up substances in nature: all around us, but seldom found alone and isolated, in laboratory-pure states. Analogy, the method of explaining the familiar in terms of the unfamiliar, is obviously central to Lewis Thomas's "The Attic of the Brain," even though Thomas traces his analogy only in the first part of his essay and departs from it in the last five paragraphs. In this book, don't expect an essay in a chapter called *Description* or *Process Analysis* to describe or analyze a process in every single line. We promise you only that the method will be central to the writer's purpose in the essay — and that you'll find the method amply (and readably) illustrated.

Following every essay, you'll find questions to help you analyze it and learn from it. In some of these questions, certain terms appear in CAPITAL LETTERS. These are words helpful in discussing both the essays in this book and the essays you write. If you'd like to see such a term defined and illustrated, you can find it in the glossary at the back of the book: Useful Terms. This section offers more than just brief definitions. It is there to provide you further information and support.

We have tried to give this book still another dimension. We wanted to break out of the neatly swept classroom and go into a few workshops littered with crumpled sheets and forgotten coffee cups, where some of the better professional writing actually takes place. Accordingly, we collected statements by most of the writers represented, revealing how they write (or wrote), setting forth things they admire about good writing. Some of these statements were written especially for this book; others are taken from articles or interviews. You'll find "Maya Angelou on Writing" (and the other writers on writing) after the questions and the "Suggestions for Writing" at the end of each selection. From what some of these writers say, you can take comfort and cheer: You aren't the only one who ever found writing tough work.

READING AN ESSAY

Whatever career you enter, most of the reading you will do — for business, not for pleasure — will probably be hasty. You'll skim: glance at words here and there, find essential facts, catch the drift of an argument. To cross oceans of print, you won't have time to paddle: You'll need to hop a jet. By skimming, you'll be able to tear through a pile of junk mail, or quickly locate the useful parts of a long report. You'll keep up with the latest issue of a specialized journal aimed at members of your trade or profession: *Computer Times*, perhaps, or the *Journal of the American Medical Association*, or *Boarding Kennel Proprietor*.

But reading essays, in order to learn from them how to write better, calls for reading word by word. Your aim is to jimmy open good writers' writings and see what makes them go. You're looking for pointers to sharpen your skills and help you put your own clear, forceful paragraphs together. Unless with one sweeping, analytic look (like that of Sherlock Holmes sizing up a new client) you can take in everything in a rich and complicated essay, expect to spend an hour or two in its company. Does the essay assigned for today remain unread, and does class start in five minutes? "I'll just breeze through this little item," you might tell yourself. But no, give up. You're a goner.

Good writing, as every writer knows, demands toil; and so does analytic reading. Never try to gulp down a rich and potent essay without chewing; all it will give you is indigestion. When you're going to read an essay in depth, seek out some quiet place — a library, a study cubicle, your room (provided it doesn't also hold two roommates playing poker). Flick off radio, stereo, or television. What writer can outsing Michael Jackson or Luciano Pavarotti, or outshout a kung fu movie? The fewer the distractions, the easier your task will be.

How do you read an essay? Exactly how, that is, do you read it analytically, to learn how a good writer writes, and so write better yourself? Let's look at an actual essay, Joan Didion's "In Bed." It won't be the easiest in this book, but it will be worth your time. In it you will meet a few difficulties, and find out how to get over them.

Before you even start to read this — or any — essay you'll find clues to its content and to its writer's biases. Notice:

The Title. Often the title will tell you the writer's subject, as in George Orwell's "A Hanging" or Gail Sheehy's "Predictable Crises of Adulthood." Sometimes it immediately states the THESIS, the main point the writer will make: "I Want a Wife." It may set forth its thesis as a question: "Why Don't We Complain?" Mark Hunter clearly sums up his thesis (and promises to demonstrate it) in the title of his essay: "The Beat Goes Off: How Technology Has Gummed up Rock's Grooves." Some titles spell out the method a writer proposes to follow: "Grant and Lee: A Study in Contrasts." A title may also reveal TONE, the writer's attitude toward the material. If a work is named "A Serious Call to the Devout and Holy Life," the title gives you an idea of the writer's approach, all right; and so does that of an informal, lighthearted essay: "Oops! How's That Again?" or "Shy Rights: Why Not Pretty Soon?" The reader, in turn, approaches each work in a different way — with serious intent, or set to chuckle. Some titles reveal more than others. In calling her essay "In Bed," Joan Didion arouses, and then defies, our expectations. The essay isn't about sex, or sleep, or lolling around in the sack all day eating chocolates. Didion's opening sentence arrests us with a touch of IRONY as we sense a discrepancy between what we expected and what we find. Whatever it does, a title sits atop its essay like a neon sign. Usually, it tells you what's inside — or makes you want to venture in. To pick an alluring title for an essay of your own is a skill worth cultivating.

Who Wrote It. Whatever you know about a writer — background, special training, previous works, outlook, or ideology — often will help you guess in advance, before you read a word of the essay, the assumptions on which it is built. Is the writer a political conservative? Expect an argument against more federal aid to the underprivileged. Is the writer a liberal? Expect an argument in favor of more such aid, and fewer nuclear missiles. Is the writer a black activist? A feminist? An internationally renowned philosopher? A popular television comedian? By who

writers are, you will know them; you may even know before-
hand a little of what they will say. To help provide such knowledge, this book supplies biographical notes. Here is one on Joan
Didion.

> A writer whose fame is fourfold — as novelist, essayist,
> journalist, and screenwriter — JOAN DIDION was born in 1934
> in California, where her family has lived for five generations.
> After graduation from the University of California, Berkeley,
> she spent a few years in New York, working as a feature editor
> for *Vogue*, a fashion magazine. She now lives in Los Angeles.
> Didion has written four much-discussed novels: *River Run*
> (1963), *Play It As It Lays* (1971), *A Book of Common Prayer*
> (1977), and *Democracy* (1984). Recently, *Salvador* (1983), her
> book-length essay based on a visit to war-torn El Salvador,
> also received wide attention. With her husband, John Greg-
> ory Dunne, she has coauthored screenplays, notably for *True
> Confessions* (1981) and the Barbra Streisand film *A Star is Born*
> (1976). *Miami*, a study of Cuban exiles in Florida, was pub-
> lished in 1987. (A self-contained section from this new book
> appears on page 663.)

Evidently, this note suggests that Didion is a sophisticated Cali-
fornian able to write both popular entertainments and serious
"think" pieces about politics. If after reading the note you guess
that "In Bed" will be thought-provoking yet enjoyable and readily understandable, you will be right.

Where the Essay Was First Published. Clearly, it matters to a
writer's credibility whether an article called "Living Mermaids:
An Amazing Discovery" first saw print in *Scientific American*, a
magazine for scientists and for nonscientists who follow what's
happening in science, or in a popular tabloid weekly, sold at supermarket checkout counters, that is full of eye-popping sensations. But no less important, finding out where an essay first
appeared can tell you for whom the writer was writing. In this
book we'll strongly urge you as a writer to think of your readers
and to try looking at what you write as if through their eyes.
Knowing something about the original readers of the essays you
study will help you to develop this ability. (After you have read

the sample essay, we'll further consider how having a sense of your reader helps you write.)

When the Essay Was First Published. Knowing in what year an essay was first printed may give you another key to understanding it. A 1988 essay on mermaids will contain statements of fact more recent and more reliable than an essay printed in 1700 — although the older essay might contain valuable information, too, and perhaps some delectable language, folklore, and poetry. In *The Bedford Reader*, we try to tell you, in a brief introductory note on every essay, when and where the essay was originally printed. If you're reading an essay elsewhere — say, in one of the writer's books — you can find this information on the dust jacket or the copyright page.

"In Bed," the essay you're about to read, was written in 1968 and was collected in a book of Joan Didion's essays, *The White Album* (1978). Although Didion's subject is a medical one, she isn't writing as a scientist for an audience of specialists but as an ordinary citizen describing her personal experience to any willing and capable reader. This fact will alert you that her language will contain only a few technical terms. Because Didion writes, though, for an educated audience — buyers of hardcover books — she sees no need to avoid a few large words when they seem necessary. If you meet any words that look intimidating, take them in your stride. When, in reading a rich and complicated essay, you run into an unfamiliar word or name, see if you can figure it out from its surroundings. If a word stops you cold and you feel lost, circle it in pencil; you can always look it up later. (In a little while we'll come back to the helpful habit of reading with a pencil. Indeed, some readers feel more confident with pencil in hand from the start.)

On first reading an essay, you don't want to bog down over every troublesome particular. Size up the forest first; later, you can squint at the acorns all you like. Glimpse the essay in its entirety. When you start to read "In Bed," don't even think about dissecting it. Just see what the writer has to say. Even nonsufferers from the paralyzing illness Didion describes will find her account vivid and arresting.

· Joan Didion ·

In Bed

Three, four, sometimes five times a month, I spend the day 1
in bed with a migraine headache, insensible to the world around
me. Almost every day of every month, between these attacks, I
feel the sudden irrational irritation and flush of blood into the
cerebral arteries which tell me that migraine is on its way, and I
take certain drugs to avert its arrival. If I did not take the drugs,
I would be able to function perhaps one day in four. The physiological error called migraine is, in brief, central to the given of
my life. When I was 15, 16, even 25, I used to think that I could
rid myself of this error by simply denying it, character over
chemistry. "Do you have headaches *sometimes? frequently?
never?*" the application forms would demand. "Check one."
Wary of the trap, wanting whatever it was that the successful
circumnavigation of that particular form could bring (a job, a
scholarship, the respect of mankind and the grace of God), I
would check one. "*Sometimes,*" I would lie. That in fact I spent
one or two days a week almost unconscious with pain seemed a
shameful secret, evidence not merely of some chemical inferior-
ity but of all my bad attitudes, unpleasant tempers, wrongthink.

For I had no brain tumor, no eyestrain, no high blood pres- 2
sure, nothing wrong with me at all: I simply had migraine headaches, and migraine headaches were, as everyone who did not
have them knew, imaginary. I fought migraine then, ignored the
warnings it sent, went to school and later to work in spite of it,
sat through lectures in Middle English and presentations to advertisers with involuntary tears running down the right side of
my face, threw up in washrooms, stumbled home by instinct,
emptied ice trays onto my bed and tried to freeze the pain in my
right temple, wished only for a neurosurgeon who would do a lobotomy on house call, and cursed my imagination.

It was a long time before I began thinking mechanistically 3
enough to accept migraine for what it was: something with
which I would be living, the way some people live with diabetes.
Migraine is something more than the fancy of a neurotic imagi-

nation. It is an essentially hereditary complex of symptoms, the most frequently noted but by no means the most unpleasant of which is a vascular headache of blinding severity, suffered by a surprising number of women, a fair number of men (Thomas Jefferson had migraine, and so did Ulysses S. Grant, the day he accepted Lee's surrender), and by some unfortunate children as young as two years old. (I had my first when I was eight. It came on during a fire drill at the Columbia School in Colorado Springs, Colorado. I was taken first home and then to the infirmary at Peterson Field, where my father was stationed. The Air Corps doctor prescribed an enema.) Almost anything can trigger a specific attack of migraine: stress, allergy, fatigue, an abrupt change in barometric pressure, a contretemps over a parking ticket. A flashing light. A fire drill. One inherits, of course, only the predisposition. In other words I spent yesterday in bed with a headache not merely because of my bad attitudes, unpleasant tempers and wrongthink, but because both my grandmothers had migraine, my father has migraine and my mother has migraine.

No one knows precisely what it is that is inherited. The $\quad$ 4 chemistry of migraine, however, seems to have some connection with the nerve hormone named serotonin, which is naturally present in the brain. The amount of serotonin in the blood falls sharply at the onset of migraine, and one migraine drug, methysergide, or Sansert, seems to have some effect on serotonin. Methysergide is a derivative of lysergic acid (in fact Sandoz Pharmaceuticals first synthesized LSD-25 while looking for a migraine cure), and its use is hemmed about with so many contraindications and side effects that most doctors prescribe it only in the most incapacitating cases. Methysergide, when it is prescribed, is taken daily, as a preventive; another preventive which works for some people is old-fashioned ergotamine tartrate, which helps to constrict the swelling blood vessels during the "aura," the period which in most cases precedes the actual headache.

Once an attack is under way, however, no drug touches it. $\quad$ 5 Migraine gives some people mild hallucinations, temporarily blinds others, shows up not only as a headache but as a gastrointestinal disturbance, a painful sensitivity to all sensory stimuli, an abrupt overpowering fatigue, a strokelike aphasia, and a crippling inability to make even the most routine connections. When I am in a migraine aura (for some people the aura lasts fifteen minutes, for others several hours), I will drive through red lights, lose the house keys, spill whatever I am holding, lose the ability to focus my eyes or frame coherent sentences, and generally give the appearance of being on drugs, or drunk. The actual headache, when it comes, brings with it chills, sweating, nausea, a debility that seems to stretch the very limits of endurance. That no one dies of migraine seems, to someone deep into an attack, an ambiguous blessing.

My husband also has migraine, which is unfortunate for   6
him but fortunate for me: perhaps nothing so tends to prolong an attack as the accusing eye of someone who has never had a headache. "Why not take a couple of aspirin," the unafflicted will say from the doorway, or "I'd have a headache, too, spending a beautiful day like this inside with all the shades drawn." All of us who have migraine suffer not only from the attacks themselves but from this common conviction that we are perversely refusing to cure ourselves by taking a couple of aspirin, that we are making ourselves sick, that we "bring it on ourselves." And in the most immediate sense, the sense of why we have a headache this Tuesday and not last Thursday, of course we often do. There certainly is what doctors call a "migraine personality," and that personality tends to be ambitious, inward, intolerant of error, rather rigidly organized, perfectionist. "You don't look like a migraine personality," a doctor once said to me. "Your hair's messy. But I suppose you're a compulsive housekeeper." Actually my house is kept even more negligently than my hair, but the doctor was right nonetheless: perfectionism can also take the form of spending most of a week writing and rewriting and not writing a single paragraph.

But not all perfectionists have migraine, and not all migrain-   7
ous people have migraine personalities. We do not escape heredity. I have tried in most of the available ways to escape my own migrainous heredity (at one point I learned to give myself two daily injections of histamine with a hypodermic needle, even though the needle so frightened me that I had to close my eyes

when I did it), but I still have migraine. And I have learned now to live with it, learned when to expect it, how to outwit it, even how to regard it, when it does come, as more friend than lodger. We have reached a certain understanding, my migraine and I. It never comes when I am in real trouble. Tell me that my house is burned down, my husband has left me, that there is gunfighting in the streets and panic in the banks, and I will not respond by getting a headache. It comes instead when I am fighting not an open but a guerrilla war with my own life, during weeks of small household confusions, lost laundry, unhappy help, canceled appointments, on days when the telephone rings too much and I get no work done and the wind is coming up. On days like that my friend comes uninvited.

And once it comes, now that I am wise in its ways, I no longer fight it. I lie down and let it happen. At first every small apprehension is magnified, every anxiety a pounding terror. Then the pain comes, and I concentrate only on that. Right there is the usefulness of migraine, there in that imposed yoga, the concentration on the pain. For when the pain recedes, ten or twelve hours later, everything goes with it, all the hidden resentments, all the vain anxieties. The migraine has acted as a circuit breaker, and the fuses have emerged intact. There is a pleasant convalescent euphoria. I open the windows and feel the air, eat gratefully, sleep well. I notice the particular nature of a flower in a glass on the stair landing. I count my blessings.

8

When first looking into an essay as rich and complex as "In Bed," you are like a person who arrives at the doorway of a large and lively room, surveying a party going on inside. Taking a look around the room, you catch the overall picture: the locations of the food and the drinks, of people you know, of people you don't know but would certainly like to. You have just taken such an overview of Didion's essay. Now, stepping through the doorway of the essay and going on in, you can head for whatever beckons most strongly.

Well, what will it be? If it is writing skills you want, then go for those elements that took skill or flair or thoughtful decision on the writer's part. Most likely, you'll need to reread the essay more than once, go over the difficult parts several times, with all the care of someone combing a snag from the mane of an admirable horse.

In giving an essay this going-over, many students — some of the best — find a pencil in hand as good as a currycomb. It concentrates the attention wonderfully. These students underline (and perhaps star) the main idea in an essay (if the book is theirs); they underline any idea that strikes them as essential. They score things with vertical lines; they bracket passages. They vent their feelings ("Bull!," "Says who?," "Hear! Hear!"). They jot notes in the margins. Such pencilwork, you'll find, helps you behold the very spine of an essay, as if in an X-ray view. You'll feel you have put your own two cents into it. While reading this way, you're being a writer. Your pencil tracks will jog your memory, too, when you review for a test, when you take part in class discussion, or when you want to write about what you've read. (In *The Bedford Reader*, by the way, paragraphs in essays are numbered, to help you refer to them.) Some sophisticates scorn pencils in favor of markers that roll pink or yellow ink over a word or a line, leaving it legible. (But you can't write notes in a margin with such markers.) Whether you read with close attention and a pencil, or with a marker, or with close attention alone, look for the following elements.

1. Meaning. "No man but a blockhead," declared Samuel Johnson, "ever wrote except for money." Perhaps the industrious critic, journalist, and dictionary maker was remembering his own days as a literary drudge in London's Grub Street; but surely most people who write often do so for other reasons.

When you read an essay, you'll find it rewarding to ask, "What is this writer's PURPOSE?" By purpose, we mean the writer's apparent reason for writing: what he or she was trying to achieve. A purpose is as essential to a good, pointed essay as a destination is to a trip. It affects every choice or decision the writer makes. (On vacation, of course, carefree people sometimes climb into a car without a thought and go happily rambling around; but if a writer rambles like that in an essay, the reader may plead, "Let me out!") In making a simple statement of a writer's purpose, we might say that the writer writes *to narrate*, or *to describe*, or *to explain*, or *to persuade*. To state a purpose more fully, we might say not just that a writer writes to narrate, but "to tell a story to illustrate the point that when you are being cheated it's a good idea to complain," or "to tell a horror story to entertain us and make chills shoot down our spines." If the essay is an argument meant to convince, a fuller statement of its writer's purpose might be: "to win us over to the writer's opinion that San Antonio is the most livable city in the United States," or "to convince us to take action: write our representative and urge more federal spending for the rehabilitation of criminals."

"But," the skeptic might object, "how can I know a writer's purpose? I'm no mind reader, and even if I were, how could I tell what Jonathan Swift was trying to do? He's dead and buried." And yet writers living and dead reveal their purposes in what they write, just as visibly as a hiker leaves footprints.

What is Joan Didion's purpose in writing? If you want to be exact, you can speak of her *main purpose* or *central purpose*, for "In Bed" fulfills more than one. To be sure, Didion keeps us interested. Her recollections of her case history are lively enough: She tells how she "threw up in washrooms, stumbled home by instinct, emptied ice trays onto my bed. . . . " But is her uppermost purpose simply to entertain? This might be a perfectly good purpose for some essays, but certainly Didion's isn't pure fun to read. Parts of it, such as the passage about throwing up in washrooms, might leave us wincing. By the time we finish reading "In Bed," Didion has fulfilled at least three purposes:

a. To define migraine. She does so by explaining how the illness affects its victims. She sets forth its possible causes (family history, a personality type) and what doctors can do for it.

b. To tell the story of her own case. She starts with her first migraine attack in grade school during a fire drill. She relates how she bore up (or was crushed down) under migraine while in college and on the job. And in the end she explains how her attitude toward her malady has changed.

c. To show that she accepts her illness as beneficial. We think her major purpose is this last, even though it becomes clear only in her conclusion, in the last two paragraphs. But it is the main idea she leaves us with.

How can you tell? Ask: What is the THESIS of this essay — the point made for a purpose, the overwhelming idea that the writer communicates? Some writers will come right out, early on, and sum up this central idea in a sentence or two. George Orwell, in his essay "Politics and the English Language," states the gist of his argument in his second paragraph:

> Modern English, especially written English, is full of bad habits which spread by imitation and which can be avoided if one is willing to take the necessary trouble. If one gets rid of these habits one can think more clearly, and to think clearly is a necessary first step towards political regeneration.

Orwell's thesis is obvious early on. Sometimes, however, a writer will state the main point only in a summing up at the end. Other writers won't come out and state their theses in any neat Orwellian capsule at all. Even so, the main point of a well-unified essay will make itself clear to you — so clear that you can sum it up in a sentence of your own.

Didion's essay hold its main point for the end. A sentence in the middle of paragraph 7 stands out. It seems her important final idea. Speaking of her illness, she affirms, "And I have learned now to live with it, learned when to expect it, how to outwit it, even how to regard it, when it does come, as more friend than lodger." That is the first indication we get that this essay will take an unexpected final twist. And in that sentence, Didion sums up her thesis for us. You can state this main idea in many ways; one might be: Migraine, for all the suffering it causes, has a positive value; the terrible monster is in truth a friend.

Having such a clear-cut purpose in mind when you write an essay gives you a decided advantage. You're heading toward a goal. The reader may not know it yet, but you do. You thus control the progress of your essay from beginning to end. The more exactly you define this purpose, the easier you'll find it to fulfill. Of course, sometimes you just can't know what you are going to say until you say it, to echo the English novelist E. M. Forster. In such a situation, your purpose emerges as you write.

2. *Writing Strategy.* Here's another element to look for in an essay, and to learn from. STRATEGY is an inclusive name for whatever practices make for good writing. Because Joan Didion holds our interest and engages our sympathies, it will pay us to ask: How does she succeed? You'll notice that Didion keeps involving her readers by referring to common, or uncommon but intriguing, experiences. The details she gives involve us. Didion's account of her symptoms (when the period of "aura" begins) is convincingly, unforgettably specific and particular. "I will drive through red lights," she says, "lose the house keys, spill whatever I am holding. . . . " And at the end, Didion leaves us aware of the definite, specific joys of having survived a migraine attack: "I notice the particular nature of a flower in a glass on the stair landing." In her wonderful, and wonderfully specific, last paragraph, Didion sets forth her main point once more: that life is worth cherishing despite migraine attacks, perhaps even because of them.

The structure of Didion's essay, with its surprise ending, is worth admiring. Reading "In Bed," we learn right away that migraine headaches are a living curse. But the final idea the writer leaves us with is more interesting. There's a reason for this method of gradual unfolding. By first showing us the terrors and sufferings of migraine, Didion achieves a much greater and more surprising effect when she finally declares that the headache is her friend. Few readers expect, when they begin the essay, that it will end in a strong, vivid account of how a migraine attack is useful; how it leaves the writer refreshed, joyful, thankful, and serene.

3. *Language.* To examine this element is often to go much more deeply into an essay and how it was made. Didion, you'll notice, is a writer whose language is rich and varied. It isn't entirely bookish. Many arrays of common one-syllable words, many expressions from common speech lend her prose style vigor and naturalness: "Three, four, sometimes five times a

month," "Why not take a couple of aspirin." But consult a dictionary if you need help in defining *lobotomy* (paragraph 2), *vascular, contretemps, predisposition* (3), *contraindications* (4), *gastrointestinal, aphasia* (5), *compulsive* (6), *euphoria* (8). We assure you that, while questions in this book point to troublesome or unfamiliar words, only you can decide if they are worth looking up. We don't expect you to become a slave to your dictionary, only a frequent client of it. As a writer, you can have no trait more valuable to you than a fondness for words, an enjoyment of strange ones, and a yen to enlarge your working word supply.

Besides commanding a vigorous, well-stocked vocabulary, Didion is a master of FIGURES OF SPEECH: bits of colorful language not to take literally. (For a rundown of the different kinds of figures of speech, see Useful Terms, page 677.) One such vivid example is her memorable SIMILE (or likening of one thing to another): "The migraine has acted as a circuit breaker . . . " (paragraph 8). Speaking in paragraph 1 of the "circumnavigation" of a job application form, Didion uses a METAPHOR. In paragraph 7 she introduces another: Daily life is sometimes "not an open but a guerrilla war." Sometimes she resorts to deliberate exaggeration, the figure of speech called HYPERBOLE: She "wished only for a neurosurgeon who would do a lobotomy on house call" (2). Exaggeration lets her make a point with force: "Tell me that my house is burned down, my husband has left me, that there is gunfighting in the streets and panic in the banks, and I will not respond by getting a headache" (7). Sometimes, on the other hand, she resorts to UNDERSTATEMENT, drily remarking, "That no one dies of migraine seems, to someone deep into an attack, an ambiguous blessing" (5). (What would that idea be if stated directly? Perhaps "When I'm in the middle of an attack I wish I might die.") These playful and illustrative uses of language — the colorful comparisons, the under- and overstatements — give Didion's writing flavor and life.

In reading essays, why not ask yourself: What am I looking for? Information? Ideas to start my own ideas for writing? Unfamiliar words to extend my vocabulary? A demonstration of how an excellent writer writes?

It never hurts to wonder: What's in this essay for me? Joan Didion, among the other writers in this book, has much to offer. Besides explaining how wonderful ordinary life can be (when the petty concerns and stresses have been swept away), she suggests that we might more keenly relish life. In her rich, beautifully ex-ampled essay, Didion seeks not merely to explain migraines (which, after all, no one completely understands). Her audience isn't only the fellow migraine-sufferer; it's everybody. She wakes us up to our blessings, as if to make us more poignantly alive.

Throughout this book, every selection will be followed by "Suggestions for Writing." You may not wish to take these sug-gestions exactly as worded; they may merely urge your own thoughts toward what you want to say. Here are two possibili-ties suggested by "In Bed."

SUGGESTIONS FOR WRITING

1. Write a paragraph in which, referring to your own experience, you familiarize your reader with an illness you know intimately. (If you have never had such an illness, pick an unwelcome mood you know: the blues, for instance, or an irresistible desire to giggle dur-ing a solemn ceremony.)
2. Demonstrate, as Joan Didion does, that an apparent misfortune can prove to be a friend.

1

NARRATION

Telling a Story

THE METHOD

"What happened?" you ask a friend who sports a luminous black eye. Unless he merely grunts, "A golf ball," he may answer you with a narrative — a story, true or fictional.

"OK," he sighs, "you know The Tenth Round? That night-club down by the docks that smells of formaldehyde? Last night I heard they were giving away $500 to anybody who could stand up for three minutes against this karate expert, the Masked Samurai. And so . . ."

You lean forward. At least, you lean forward *if* you love a story. Most of us do, particularly if the story tells us of people in action or in conflict, and if it is told briskly, vividly, and with insight into the human heart. *Narration*, or storytelling, is therefore a powerful method by which to engage and hold the attention of listeners — readers as well. A little of its tremendous power flows to the public speaker who starts off with a joke, even a stale joke ("A funny thing happened to me on my way over here . . ."), and to the preacher who at the beginning of a sermon tells of some funny or touching incident he has observed. In its opening paragraph, an article in a popular magazine ("Vampires Live Today!") will give us a brief, arresting narrative: perhaps the case history of a car dealer who noticed, one moonlit night, his incisors strangely lengthening.

At least a hundred times a year, you probably resort to narration, not always for the purpose of telling an entertaining story, but usually to explain, to illustrate a point, to report information, to argue, or to persuade. That is, although a narrative can run from the beginning of an essay to the end, more often in your writing (as in your speaking) a narrative is only a part of what you have to say. It is there because it serves a larger purpose. In truth, because narration is such an effective way to put across your ideas, the ability to tell a compelling story — on paper, as well as in conversation — may be one of the most useful skills you can acquire.

The term *narrative* takes in abundant territory. A narrative may be short or long, factual or imagined; as artless as a tale told in a locker room, or as artful as a novel by Henry James. A narrative may instruct and inform, or simply divert and regale. It may set forth some point or message, or it may be as devoid of significance as a comic yarn or a horror tale whose sole aim is to curdle your blood.

A novel is a narrative, but a narrative doesn't have to be long. Sometimes an essay will include several brief stories. See, for instance, William F. Buckley's argument "Why Don't We Complain?" (page 570). A type of story often used to illustrate a point is the *anecdote*, a short, entertaining account of a single incident. Sometimes told of famous persons, anecdotes add color and life to history, biography, autobiography, and every issue of *People* magazine. Besides being fun to read, an anecdote can be deeply revealing. W. Jackson Bate, in his biography of Samuel Johnson, traces the growth of the great eighteenth-century critic and scholar's ideas, and, with the aid of anecdotes, he shows that his subject was human and lovable. As Bate tells us, Dr. Johnson, a portly and imposing gentleman of fifty-five, had walked with some friends to the crest of a hill, where the great man,

> delighted by its steepness, said he wanted to "take a roll down." They tried to stop him. But he said he "had not had a roll for a long time," and taking out of his pockets his keys, a pencil, a purse, and other objects, lay down parallel at the edge of the hill, and rolled down its full length, "turning himself over and over till he came to the bottom."

However small the event it relates, this anecdote is memorable — for one reason, because of its attention to detail: the exact list of the contents of Johnson's pockets. In such a brief story, a superhuman figure comes down to human size. In one stroke, Bate reveals an essential part of Johnson: his boisterous, hearty, and boyish sense of fun.

An anecdote may be used to explain a point. Asked why he had appointed to a cabinet post Josephus Daniels, the harshest critic of his policies, President Woodrow Wilson replied with an anecdote of an old woman he knew. On spying a strange man urinating through her picket fence into her flower garden, she invited the offender into her yard because, as she explained to him, "I'd a whole lot rather have you inside pissing out than have you outside pissing in." By telling this story, a rude *analogy* (see Chapter 7 for more examples), Wilson made clear his situation in regard to his political enemy more succinctly and pointedly than if he had given a more abstract explanation. As a statesman, Woodrow Wilson may have had his flaws; but as a storyteller, he is surely among the less forgettable.

THE PROCESS

So far, we have considered a few uses of narration. Now let us see how you tell an effective story.

Every good story has a purpose. Perhaps the storyteller seeks to explain what it was like to be a black American in a certain time and place (as Maya Angelou does in "Champion of the World" in this chapter); perhaps the teller seeks merely to entertain us. Whatever the reason for its telling, an effective story holds the attention of readers or listeners; and to do so, the storyteller shapes that story to appeal to its audience. If, for instance, you plan to tell a few friends of an embarrassing moment you had on your way to campus — you tripped and spilled a load of books into the arms of a passing dean — you know how to proceed. Simply to provide a laugh is your purpose, and your listeners, who need no introduction to you or the dean, need be told only the bare events of the story. Perhaps you'll use some vivid words to convey the surprise on the dean's face when sixty pounds of literary lumber hit him. Perhaps you'll throw in a little surprise of your own. At first, you didn't take in the identity of this passerby on whom you'd dumped a load of literary lumber. Then you realized: It was the dean!

Such simple, direct storytelling is so common and habitual that we do it without planning in advance. The *narrator* (or teller) of such a personal experience is the speaker, the one who was there. (Three selections in this chapter, by Maya Angelou, George Orwell, and James Thurber, tell of such experiences, narrated in the first person, *I*.) Of course, a personal experience told in the first person can use some artful telling and some structuring. (In the course of this discussion, we'll offer advice on telling stories of different kinds.)

When a story isn't the narrator's own experience but a recital of someone else's, or of events that are public knowledge, then the narrator proceeds differently. Without expressing opinions, he or she steps back and reports, content to stay invisible. Instead of saying, "I did this, I did that," he narrates an event or events in the third person: "The dean did this, he did that." The storyteller may have been on the scene; if so, he will probably write as a spectator, from his own *point of view* (or angle of seeing). If he puts together what happened from the testimony of others, he tells the story from the point of view of a *nonparticipant* (a witness who didn't take part). He sets forth events *objectively*: without bias, as accurately and dispassionately as possible.

For this reason, the narrator of a third-person story isn't a character in the eyes of his audience. Unlike the first-person writer of a personal experience, he isn't the main actor; he is the cameraman, whose job is to focus on what transpires. Most history books and news stories are third-person narratives. (In this chapter, the selection by Calvin Trillin illustrates third-person narration.) An *omniscient* narrator, one who is all-knowing, can see into the minds of the characters. Sometimes, as in a novel or any imagined story, a writer finds it effective to give us people's inmost thoughts. Whether omniscient narration works or not depends on the storyteller's purpose. Note how much Woodrow Wilson's anecdote would lose if the teller had gone into the thoughts of his characters: "The old woman was angry and embarrassed at seeing the stranger. . . ." Clearly, Wilson's purpose was to make a point, not to explore psychology.

Whether you tell of your own experience or of someone else's, you need a whole story to tell. Before starting to write, do some searching and discovering. One trusty method to test your memory (or to make sure you have all the necessary elements of a story) is that of a news reporter. Ask yourself:

1. *What* happened?
2. *Who* took part?
3. *When*?
4. *Where*?
5. *Why* did this event (or these events) take place?
6. *How* did it happen?

That last *how* isn't merely another way of asking what happened. It means: In exactly what way or under what circumstances? If the event was a murder, how was it done — with an ax or with a bulldozer? Journalists call this handy list of questions "the five Ws and the H."

Well-prepared storytellers, those who first search their memories (or do some research and legwork), have far more information on hand than they can use. The writing of a good story calls for careful choice. In choosing, remember your purpose and your audience. If you're writing that story of the dean and the books to give pleasure to readers who are your friends, delighted to hear about the discomfort of a pompous administrator, you will probably dwell lovingly on each detail of his consternation. You would tell the story differently if your audience were strangers who didn't know the dean from Adam. They would need more information on his background, reputation for stiffness, and appearance. If, suspected of having deliberately contrived the dean's humiliation, you were writing a report of the incident for the campus police, you'd want to give the plainest possible account of the story — without drama, without adornment, without background, and certainly without any humor whatsoever.

Your purpose and your audience, then, clearly determine which of the two main strategies of narration you're going to choose: to tell a story by *scene* or to tell it by *summary*. When you tell a story in a scene, or in scenes, you visualize each event as vividly and precisely as if you were there — as though it were a scene in a film, and your reader sat before the screen. This is the strategy of most fine novels and short stories — of much excellent nonfiction as well. Instead of just mentioning people, you portray them. You recall dialogue as best you can, or you invent some that could have been spoken. You include *description* (a mode of writing to be dealt with fully in our next chapter).

For a lively example of a well-drawn scene, see Maya Angelou's account of a tense crowd's behavior as, jammed into a small-town store, they listen to a fight broadcast (in "Champion of the World," beginning on page 33). Angelou prolongs one scene for almost her entire essay. Sometimes, though, a writer will draw a scene in only two or three sentences. This is the brevity we find in W. Jackson Bate's glimpse of the hill-rolling Johnson. Unlike Angelou, Bate evidently seeks not to weave a tapestry of detail, but to show, in telling of one brief event, a trait of his hero's character.

When, on the other hand, you tell a story by the method of summary, you relate events concisely. Instead of depicting people and their surroundings in great detail, you set down what happened in relatively spare narrative form. Most of us employ this method in most stories we tell, for it takes less time and fewer words. A summary is to a scene, then, as a simple stick figure is to a portrait in oils. This is not to dismiss simple stick figures as inferior. A story told in summary may be as effective as a story told in scenes, in lavish detail.

Again, your choice of a method depends on your answer to the questions you ask yourself: What is my purpose? What is my audience? How fully to flesh out a scene, how much detail to include — these choices depend on what you seek to do, and on how much your audience needs to know to follow you. Read the life of some famous person in an encyclopedia, and you will find the article telling its story in summary form. Its writer's purpose, evidently, is to recount the main events of a whole life in a short space. But glance through a book-length biography of the same celebrity, and you will probably find scenes in it. A biographer writes with a different purpose: to present a detailed portrait roundly and thoroughly, bringing the subject vividly to life.

To be sure, you can use both methods in telling a single story. Often, summary will serve a writer who passes briskly from one scene to the next, or hurries over events of lesser importance. Were you to write, let's say, the story of a man's fiendish passion for horse racing, you might decide to give short shrift to most other facts of his life. To emphasize what you consider essential, you might begin a scene with a terse summary: "Seven years went by, and after three marriages and two divorces, Lars found himself again back at Hialeah." (A detailed scene might follow.)

Good storytellers know what to emphasize. They do not fall into a boring drone: "And then I went down to the club and I had a few beers and I noticed this sign, Go 3 MINUTES WITH THE MASKED SAMURAI AND WIN $500, so I went and got knocked out and then I had pizza and went home." In this lazily strung-out summary, the narrator reduces all events to equal unimportance. A more adept storyteller might leave out the pizza and dwell in detail on the big fight.

Some storytellers assume that to tell a story in the present tense (instead of the past tense, traditionally favored) gives events a sense of immediacy. Presented as though everything were happening right now, the story of the Masked Samurai might begin: "I duck between the ropes and step into the ring. My heart is thudding fast." You can try the present tense, if you like, and see how immediate it seems to you. Be warned, however, that nowadays so many fiction writers write in this fashion that to use the past tense may make your work seem almost fresh and original.

In narration, the simplest method is to set down events in *chronological order*, the way they happened. To do so is to have your story already organized for you. A chronological order is therefore an excellent sequence to follow unless you can see some special advantage in violating it. Ask: What am I trying to do? If you are trying to capture your reader's attention right away, you might begin *in medias res* (Latin, "in the middle of things"), and open with a colorful, dramatic event, even though it took place late in the chronology. If trying for dramatic effect, you might save the most exciting or impressive event for last, even though it actually happened early. By this means, you can keep your readers in suspense for as long as possible. (You can return to earlier events by a *flashback*, an earlier scene recalled.) Let your purpose be your guide. In writing a news story, a reporter often begins with the conclusion, placing the main event in the *lead*, or opening paragraph. Dramatically, this may be the weakest method to tell the story; yet it is effective in this case because the reporter's purpose is not to entertain but rather to tell quickly what happened, for an audience impatient to learn the essentials. Calvin Trillin has recalled why, in telling a story, he deliberately chose not to follow a chronology:

> I wrote a story on the discovery of the Tunica treasure which I couldn't begin by saying, "Here is a man who works as a prison guard in Angola State Prison, and on his weekends he sometimes looks for buried treasure that is rumored to be around the Indian village." Because the real point of the story centered around the problems caused when an amateur wanders on to professional territory, I thought it would be much better to open with how momentous the discovery was, that it was the most important archeological discovery about Indian contact with the European settlers to date, and *then* to say that it was discovered by a prison guard. So I made a conscious choice *not* to start with Leonard Charrier working as a

prison guard, not to go back to his boyhood in Bunkie, Louisiana, not to talk about how he'd always been interested in
treasure hunting — hoping that the reader would assume I
was about to say that the treasure was found by an archeolo-
gist from the Peabody Museum at Harvard.[1]

Trillin, by saving for late in his story the fact that a prison guard
made the earthshaking discovery, effectively took his reader by
surprise.

No matter what order you choose, either following chronology or departing from it, make sure your audience can follow it.
The sequence of events has to be clear. This calls for transitions
of time, whether they are brief phrases that point out exactly
when each event happened ("Seven years later," "A moment
earlier"), or whole sentences that announce an event and clearly
locate it in time ("If you had known Leonard Charrier ten years
earlier, you would have found him voraciously poring over
every archeology text he could lay his hands on in the public library").

In *The Bedford Reader*, we are concerned with the kind of
writing you do every day in college; writing in which you generally explain ideas, or organize information you have learned.
Unless you take a creative writing course, you probably won't
write fiction — imaginary stories — and yet in fiction we find an
enormously popular and appealing use of narration, and certain
devices of storytelling from which all storytellers can learn. For
these reasons, this chapter will include one celebrated short
story by a master storyteller, Ernest Hemingway. As Maya
Angelou does in her true memoir "Champion of the World,"
Hemingway strives to make the people in his story come alive
for us. He does, however, do some things that nonfiction narra-
tors ordinarily do not do: He writes his story mainly in dialogue,
letting conversation advance the story. Unlike a historian, a fiction writer may not be interested mainly in exterior, observable
events. In fiction, an author may pay as much attention to a

---

[1]"A Writer's Process: A Conversation with Calvin Trillin," by Alice Trillin, *Journal of Basic Writing* (Fall/Winter 1981), p. 11. Trillin's story, "The
Tunica Treasure," appeared in *The New Yorker*, July 27, 1981.

change of feelings, or a sudden realization, as a historian pays to a decisive battle. Sometimes, and this is certainly true of Hemingway's "Hills Like White Elephants," what matters most is what happens inside the characters' minds and how they feel.

Most storytellers, though, whether they write fiction or nonfiction, whether they write to entertain or to make an idea clear, follow certain common practices. One familiar technique is to build a story toward a memorable conclusion. In a story Mark Twain liked to tell aloud, a woman's ghost returns to claim her artificial arm made of gold, which she wore in life and which her greedy husband had unscrewed from her corpse. Carefully, Twain would build up suspense as the ghost pursued the husband upstairs to his bedroom, stood by his bed, breathed her cold breath on him, and intoned: *"Who's got my golden arm?"* Twain used to end his story by suddenly yelling at a member of the audience, *"You've got it!"* — and enjoying the victim's shriek of surprise. That final punctuating shriek may be a technique that will work only in oral storytelling; yet, like Twain, most storytellers like to end with a bang if they can. The final impact, however, need not be so obvious. As Maya Angelou demonstrates in her story in this chapter, you can achieve impact just by leading to a point. In an effective written narrative, a writer usually hits the main events of a story especially hard, often saving the best punch (or the best karate chop) for the very end.

NARRATION IN A PARAGRAPH: TWO ILLUSTRATIONS

1. Using Narration to Write about Television

Oozing menace from beyond the stars or from the deeps, televised horror powerfully stimulates a child's already frisky imagination. As parents know, a "Creature Double Feature" has an impact that lasts long after the click of the OFF button. Recently a neighbor reported the strange case of her eight-year-old. Discovered late at night in the game room watching *The Exorcist*, the girl was promptly sent to bed. An hour later, her parents could hear her chanting something in the darkness of her bedroom. On tiptoe, they stole to her door to listen. The creak of springs told them that their daughter was swaying rhythmically to and fro and the smell of acrid smoke warned them that something was burning. At once, they shoved open the door to find the room flickering with shadows cast by a lighted candle. Their daughter was sitting up in bed, rocking back and forth as she intoned over and over, "Fiend in human form . . . Fiend in human form . . ." This case may be unique; still, it seems likely that similar events take place each night all over the screen-watching world.

COMMENT. This paragraph, addressed to a general audience — that is, most readers, those who read nonspecialized books or magazines — puts a story to work to support a thesis statement. A brief anecdote, the story of the mesmerized child backs up the claim (in the second sentence) that for children the impact of TV horror goes on and on. The story relates a small, ordinary, but disquieting experience taken from the writer's conversation with friends. A bit of suspense is introduced, and the reader's curiosity is whetted, when the parents steal to the bedroom door to learn why the child isn't asleep. The crisis — the dramatic high moment in the story when our curiosity is about to be gratified — is a sensory detail: the smell of smoke. At the end of the paragraph, the writer stresses the importance of these events by suggesting that they are probably universal. In a way, he harks back to his central idea, reminding us of his reason for telling the story. Narration, as you can see, is a method for dramatizing your ideas.

2. Using Narration in an Academic Discipline

The news media periodically relate the terrifying and often grim details of landslides. On May 31, 1970, one such event occurred when a gigantic rock avalanche buried more than 20,000 people in Yungay and Ranrahirca, Peru. There was little warning of the impending disaster; it began and ended in just a matter of a few minutes. The avalanche started 14 kilometers from Yungay, near the summit of 6,700-meter-high Nevados Huascaran, the loftiest peak in the Peruvian

Andes. Triggered by the ground motion from a strong off-
shore earthquake, a huge mass of rock and ice broke free from
the precipitous north face of the mountain. After plunging
nearly one kilometer, the material pulverized on impact and
immediately began rushing down the mountainside, made
fluid by trapped air and melted ice. The initial mass ripped
loose additional millions of tons of debris as it roared downhill. The shock waves produced by the event created thun-
derlike noise and stripped nearby hillsides of vegetation. Although the material followed a previously eroded gorge, a
portion of the debris jumped a 200–300-meter-high bedrock
ridge that had protected Yungay from past rock avalanches
and buried the entire city. After inundating another town in
its path, Ranrahirca, the mass of debris finally reached the
bottom of the valley where its momentum carried it across the
Rio Santa and tens of meters up the opposite bank.

COMMENT. This paragraph of vivid narration enlivens a college textbook, *The Earth: An Introduction to Physical Geology*, by
Edward J. Tarbuck and Frederick K. Lutgens (Columbus:
Charles E. Merrill Publishing Co., 1984), p. 177. To illustrate
the awesome power of a landslide, the writers give this one-para-
graph example, choosing one of the most horrendous such catastrophes in history. Not all landslides are so spectacular, of
course, and yet this brief narrative serves to set forth traits typical of landslides in general: sudden beginning, fast movement,
irresistible force. This paragraph shows another way in which
narration can serve: as a memorable example, making the point
that landslides concern people and can cost lives, and as a
means to enlist the reader's immediate attention to a discussion
that otherwise might seem dry and abstract.

· Maya Angelou ·

MAYA ANGELOU was born Marguerita Johnson in St. Louis in 1928. After an unpleasantly eventful youth by her account ("from a broken family, raped at eight, unwed mother at sixteen"), she went on to join a dance company, star in an off-Broadway play (*The Blacks*), write five books of poetry, produce a series on Africa for PBS-TV, act in the television-special series "Roots," serve as a coordinator for the Southern Christian Leadership Conference at the request of Martin Luther King, Jr., and accept several honorary doctorates. She is best known, however, for the five books of her searching, frank, and joyful autobiography — beginning with *I Know Why the Caged Bird Sings* (1970), which she adapted for television, through her most recent volume, *All God's Children Need Traveling Shoes* (1986).

Champion of the World

"Champion of the World" is the nineteenth chapter from *I Know Why the Caged Bird Sings*; the title is a phrase taken from it. Remembering her childhood, the writer tells how she and her older brother, Bailey, grew up in a town in Arkansas. The center of their lives was grandmother and Uncle Willie's store, a gathering place for the black community. On the night when this story takes place, Joe Louis, the "Brown Bomber" and the hero of his people, defends his heavyweight title against a white contender.

The last inch of space was filled, yet people continued to wedge themselves along the walls of the Store. Uncle Willie had turned the radio up to its last notch so that youngsters on the porch wouldn't miss a word. Women sat on kitchen chairs, dining-room chairs, stools and upturned wooden boxes. Small children and babies perched on every lap available and men leaned on the shelves or on each other.

The apprehensive mood was shot through with shafts of gaiety, as a black sky is streaked with lightning.

"I ain't worried 'bout this fight. Joe's gonna whip that   3
cracker like it's open season."

"He gone whip him till that white boy call him Momma."   4

At last the talking finished and the string-along songs   5
about razor blades were over and the fight began.

"A quick jab to the head." In the Store the crowd grunted.   6
"A left to the head and a right and another left." One of the listeners cackled like a hen and was quieted.

"They're in a clinch, Louis is trying to fight his way out."   7

Some bitter comedian on the porch said, "That white man   8
don't mind hugging that niggah now, I betcha."

"The referee is moving in to break them up, but Louis fi-   9
nally pushed the contender away and it's an uppercut to the
chin. The contender is hanging on, now he's backing away.
Louis catches him with a short left to the jaw."

A tide of murmuring assent poured out the door and into   10
the yard.

"Another left and another left. Louis is saving that mighty   11
right . . . " The mutter in the Store had grown into a baby roar
and it was pierced by the clang of a bell and the announcer's
"That's the bell for round three, ladies and gentlemen."

As I pushed my way into the Store I wondered if the an-   12
nouncer gave any thought to the fact that he was addressing as
"ladies and gentlemen" all the Negroes around the world who
sat sweating and praying, glued to their "master's voice."[1]

There were only a few calls for R. C. Colas, Dr. Peppers,   13
and Hires root beer. The real festivities would begin after the
fight. Then even the old Christian ladies who taught their children and tried themselves to practice turning the other cheek
would buy soft drinks, and if the Brown Bomber's victory was a
particularly bloody one they would order peanut patties and
Baby Ruths also.

Bailey and I laid the coins on top of the cash register. Uncle 14
Willie didn't allow us to ring up sales during a fight. It was too

---

[1]"His master's voice," accompanied by a picture of a little dog listening to
a phonograph, was a familiar advertising slogan. (The picture still appears on
RCA Victor records.)—Eds.

noisy and might shake up the atmosphere. When the gong rang for the next round we pushed through the near-sacred quiet to the herd of children outside.

"He's got Louis against the ropes and now it's a left to the 15 body and a right to the ribs. Another right to the body, it looks like it was low . . . Yes, ladies and gentlemen, the referee is signaling but the contender keeps raining the blows on Louis. It's another to the body, and it looks like Louis is going down."

My race groaned. It was our people falling. It was another 16 lynching, yet another Black man hanging on a tree. One more woman ambushed and raped. A Black boy whipped and maimed. It was hounds on the trail of a man running through slimy swamps. It was a white woman slapping her maid for being forgetful.

The men in the Store stood away from the walls and at at- 17 tention. Women greedily clutched the babes on their laps while on the porch the shufflings and smiles, flirtings and pinching of a few minutes before were gone. This might be the end of the world. If Joe lost we were back in slavery and beyond help. It would all be true, the accusations that we were lower types of human beings. Only a little higher than apes. True that we were stupid and ugly and lazy and dirty and, unlucky and worst of all, that God Himself hated us and ordained us to be hewers of wood and drawers of water, forever and ever, world without end.

We didn't breathe. We didn't hope. We waited. 18

"He's off the ropes, ladies and gentlemen. He's moving 19 towards the center of the ring." There was no time to be relieved. The worst might still happen.

"And now it looks like Joe is mad. He's caught Carnera with 20 a left hook to the head and a right to the head. It's a left jab to the body and another left to the head. There's a left cross and a right to the head. The contender's right eye is bleeding and he can't seem to keep his block up. Louis is penetrating every block. The referee is moving in, but Louis sends a left to the body and it's an uppercut to the chin and the contender is dropping. He's on the canvas, ladies and gentlemen."

Babies slid to the floor as women stood up and men leaned 21 toward the radio.

"Here's the referee. He's young. One, two, three, four, five, 22
six, seven . . . Is the contender trying to get up again?"

All the men in the store shouted, "NO." 23

" — eight, nine, ten." There were a few sounds from the au- 24
dience, but they seemed to be holding themselves in against tremendous pressure.

"The fight is all over, ladies and gentlemen. Let's get the mi- 25
crophone over to the referee . . . Here he is. He's got the Brown
Bomber's hand, he's holding it up . . . Here he is . . . "

Then the voice, husky and familiar, came to wash over us — 26
"The winnah, and still heavyweight champeen of the world . . .
Joe Louis."

Champion of the world. A Black boy. Some Black mother's 27
son. He was the strongest man in the world. People drank Coca-
Colas like ambrosia and ate candy bars like Christmas. Some of
the men went behind the Store and poured white lightning in
their soft-drink bottles, and a few of the bigger boys followed
them. Those who were not chased away came back blowing
their breath in front of themselves like proud smokers.

It would take an hour or more before the people would leave 28
the Store and head for home. Those who lived too far had made
arrangements to stay in town. It wouldn't do for a Black man
and his family to be caught on a lonely country road on a night
when Joe Louis had proved that we were the strongest people in
the world.

QUESTIONS ON MEANING

1. What do you take to be the author's PURPOSE in telling this story?
2. What connection does Angelou make between the outcome of the
   fight and the pride of the black race? To what degree do you think
   the author's view is shared by the others in the store listening to
   the broadcast?
3. To what extent are the statements in paragraphs 16 and 17 to be
   taken literally? What function do they serve in Angelou's narrative?

4. Primo Carnera was probably *not* the Brown Bomber's opponent on the night Maya Angelou recalls. Louis fought Carnera only once, on June 25, 1935, and it was not a title match; Angelou would have been no more than seven years old at the time. Does the author's apparent error detract from her story?

QUESTIONS ON WRITING STRATEGY

1. What details in the opening paragraphs indicate that an event of crucial importance is about to take place?
2. How does Angelou build up SUSPENSE in her account of the fight? At what point were you able to predict the winner?
3. Comment on the IRONY in Angelou's final paragraph.
4. How many stories does "Champion of the World" contain? What are they?
5. What EFFECT does the author's use of direct quotation have on her narrative?

QUESTIONS ON LANGUAGE

1. Explain what the author means by "string-along songs about razor blades" (paragraph 5).
2. How does Angelou's use of NONSTANDARD ENGLISH contribute to her narrative?
3. Be sure you know the meanings of these words: apprehensive (paragraph 2); assent (10); ambushed, maimed (16); ordained (17); ambrosia, white lightning (27).

SUGGESTIONS FOR WRITING

1. In a brief essay, write about the progress and outcome of a recent sporting event and your reaction to the outcome. Include enough illustrative detail to bring the contest to life.
2. Write an essay based on some childhood experience of your own, still vivid in your memory.

Maya Angelou on Writing

Maya Angelou's writings have shown great variety: She has done notable work as an autobiographer, poet, short story writer, screenwriter, journalist, and song lyricist. Asked by interviewer Sheila Weller, "Do you start each project with a specific idea?" Angelou replied:

"It starts with a definite subject, but it might end with something entirely different. When I start a project, the first thing I do is write down, in longhand, everything I know about the subject, every thought I've ever had on it. This may be twelve or fourteen pages. Then I read it back through, for quite a few days, and find — given that subject — what its rhythm is. 'Cause everything in the universe has a rhythm. So if it's free form, it still has a rhythm. And once I hear the rhythm of the piece, then I try to find out what are the salient points that I must make. And then it begins to take shape.

"I try to set myself up in each chapter by saying: 'This is what I want to go from — from B to, say, G-sharp. Or from D to L.' And then I find the hook. It's like the knitting, where, after you knit a certain amount, there's one thread that begins to pull. You know, you can see it right along the cloth. Well, in writing, I think: 'Now where is that one hook, that one little thread?' It may be a sentence. If I can catch that, then I'm home free. It's the one that tells me where I'm going. It may not even turn out to be in the final chapter. I may throw it out later or change it. But if I follow it through, it leads me right out." ("Work in Progress," *Intellectual Digest*, June 1973.)

FOR DISCUSSION

1. How would you define the word *rhythm* as Maya Angelou uses it?
2. What response would you give a student who said, "Doesn't Angelou's approach to writing waste more time and thought than it's worth?"

· George Orwell ·

GEORGE ORWELL was the pen name of Eric Blair (1903–1950), born in Bengal, India, the son of an English civil servant. After attending Eton on a scholarship, he joined the British police in Burma, where he acquired a distrust for the methods of the empire. Then followed years of tramping, odd jobs, and near-starvation — recalled in *Down and Out in Paris and London* (1933). From living on the fringe of society and from his reportorial writing about English miners and factory workers, Orwell deepened his sympathy with underdogs.

Severely wounded while fighting in the Spanish Civil War, he wrote a memoir, *Homage to Catalonia* (1938), voicing disillusionment with Loyalists who, he claimed, sought not to free Spain but to exterminate their political enemies. A socialist by conviction, Orwell kept pointing to the dangers of a collective state run by totalitarians. In *Animal Farm* (1945), he satirized Soviet bureaucracy; and in his famous novel *1984* (1949) he foresaw a regimented England whose government perverts truth and spies on citizens by two-way television. (The motto of the state and its leader: "BIG BROTHER IS WATCHING YOU.")

A Hanging

Orwell's personal experience of serving in the Indian Imperial Police in Burma in the 1920s provided the memorable story he unfolds in "A Hanging." As in virtually all of his political writing, Orwell here displays a profound sympathy for the victim, the downtrodden. Be sure to notice the specific details that lend color and conviction to this narrative, later gathered into the collection *Shooting an Elephant and Other Essays* (1950).

It was in Burma, a sodden morning of the rains. A sickly   1
light, like yellow tinfoil, was slanting over the high walls into the
jail yard. We were waiting outside the condemned cells, a row of

sheds fronted with double bars, like small animal cages. Each cell measured about ten feet by ten and was quite bare within except for a plank bed and a pot for drinking water. In some of them brown, silent men were squatting at the inner bars, with their blankets draped round them. These were the condemned men, due to be hanged within the next week or two.

One prisoner had been brought out of his cell. He was a   2
Hindu, a puny wisp of a man, with a shaven head and vague liquid eyes. He had a thick, sprouting mustache, absurdly too big for his body, rather like the mustache of a comic man on the films. Six tall Indian warders were guarding him and getting him ready for the gallows. Two of them stood by with rifles and fixed bayonets, while the others handcuffed him, passed a chain through his handcuffs and fixed it to their belts, and lashed his arms tight to his sides. They crowded very close about him, with their hands always on him in a careful, caressing grip, as though all the while feeling him to make sure he was there. It was like men handling a fish which is still alive and may jump back into the water. But he stood quite unresisting, yielding his arms limply to the ropes, as though he hardly noticed what was happening.

Eight o'clock struck and a bugle call, desolately thin in the   3
wet air, floated from the distant barracks. The superintendent of the jail, who was standing apart from the rest of us, moodily prodding the gravel with his stick, raised his head at the sound. He was an army doctor, with a gray toothbrush mustache and a gruff voice. "For God's sake, hurry up, Francis," he said irritably. "The man ought to have been dead by this time. Aren't you ready yet?"

Francis, the head jailer, a fat Dravidian[1] in a white drill suit   4
and gold spectacles, waved his black hand. "Yes sir, yes sir," he bubbled. "All iss satisfactorily prepared. The hangman iss waiting. We shall proceed."

"Well, quick march, then. The prisoners can't get their   5
breakfast until this job's over."

---

[1]A native speaker of one of the southern Indian languages. — Eds.

We set out for the gallows. Two warders marched on either 6
side of the prisoner, with their rifles at the slope; two others
marched close against him, gripping him by the arm and shoulder, as though at once pushing and supporting him. The rest of
us, magistrates and the like, followed behind. Suddenly, when
we had gone ten yards, the procession stopped short without
any order or warning. A dreadful thing had happened — a dog,
come goodness knows whence, had appeared in the yard. It
came bounding among us with a loud volley of barks and leapt
round us wagging its whole body, wild with glee at finding so
many human beings together. It was a large woolly dog, half
Airedale, half pariah. For a moment it pranced around us, and
then, before anyone could stop it, it had made a dash for the
prisoner, and jumping up tried to lick his face. Everybody stood
aghast, too taken aback even to grab the dog.

"Who let that bloody brute in here?" said the superintend- 7
ent angrily. "Catch it, someone!"

A warder detached from the escort, charged clumsily after 8
the dog, but it danced and gambolled just out of his reach, taking everything as part of the game. A young Eurasian jailer
picked up a handful of gravel and tried to stone the dog away,
but it dodged the stones and came after us again. Its yaps echoed
from the jail walls. The prisoner, in the grasp of the two warders,
looked on incuriously, as though this was another formality of
the hanging. It was several minutes before someone managed to
catch the dog. Then we put my handkerchief through its collar
and moved off once more, with the dog still straining and whim-
pering.

It was about forty yards to the gallows. I watched the bare 9
brown back of the prisoner marching in front of me. He walked
clumsily with his bound arms, but quite steadily, with that bobbing gait of the Indian who never straightens his knees. At each
step his muscles slid neatly into place, the lock of hair on his
scalp danced up and down, his feet printed themselves on the
wet gravel. And once, in spite of the men who gripped him by
each shoulder, he stepped lightly aside to avoid a puddle on the
path.

It is curious; but till that moment I had never realized what   10
it means to destroy a healthy, conscious man. When I saw the
prisoner step aside to avoid the puddle, I saw the mystery, the
unspeakable wrongness, of cutting a life short when it is in full
tide. This man was not dying, he was alive just as we are alive.
All the organs of his body were working — bowels digesting
food, skin renewing itself, nails growing, tissues forming — all
toiling away in solemn foolery. His nails would still be growing
when he stood on the drop, when he was falling through the air
with a tenth-of-a-second to live. His eyes saw the yellow gravel
and the gray walls, and his brain still remembered, foresaw, reasoned — even about puddles. He and we were a party of men
walking together, seeing, hearing, feeling, understanding the
same world; and in two minutes, with a sudden snap, one of us
would be gone — one mind less, one world less.

The gallows stood in a small yard, separate from the main   11
grounds of the prison, and overgrown with tall prickly weeds. It
was a brick erection like three sides of a shed, with planking on
top, and above that two beams and a crossbar with the rope
dangling. The hangman, a gray-haired convict in the white uniform of the prison, was waiting beside his machine. He greeted
us with a servile crouch as we entered. At a word from Francis
the two warders, gripping the prisoner more closely than ever,
half led, half pushed him to the gallows and helped him clumsily
up the ladder. Then the hangman climbed up and fixed the rope
round the prisoner's neck.

We stood waiting, five yards away. The warders had formed   12
in a rough circle round the gallows. And then, when the noose
was fixed, the prisoner began crying out to his god. It was a
high, reiterated cry of "Ram! Ram! Ram! Ram!"[2] not urgent and
fearful like a prayer or cry for help, but steady, rhythmical, almost like the tolling of a bell. The dog answered the sound with
a whine. The hangman, still standing on the gallows, produced
a small cotton bag like a flour bag and drew it down over the

---

[2]The prisoner calls upon Rama, incarnation of Vishnu, Hindu god who
sustains and preserves. — EDS.

prisoner's face. But the sound, muffled by the cloth, still persisted, over and over again: "Ram! Ram! Ram! Ram! Ram!"

The hangman climbed down and stood ready, holding the lever. Minutes seemed to pass. The steady, muffled crying from the prisoner went on and on, "Ram! Ram! Ram!" never faltering for an instant. The superintendent, his head on his chest, was slowly poking the ground with his stick; perhaps he was counting the cries, allowing the prisoner a fixed number — fifty, perhaps, or a hundred. Everyone had changed color. The Indians had gone gray like bad coffee, and one or two of the bayonets were wavering. We looked at the lashed, hooded man on the drop, and listened to his cries — each cry another second of life; the same thought was in all our minds; oh, kill him quickly, get it over, stop that abominable noise!

Suddenly the superintendent made up his mind. Throwing up his head he made a swift motion with his stick. "Chalo!"[3] he shouted almost fiercely.

There was a clanking noise, and then dead silence. The prisoner had vanished, and the rope was twisting on itself. I let go of the dog, and it galloped immediately to the back of the gallows; but when it got there it stopped short, barked, and then retreated into a corner of the yard, where it stood among the weeds, looking timorously out at us. We went round the gallows to inspect the prisoner's body. He was dangling with his toes pointed straight downwards, very slowly revolving, as dead as a stone.

The superintendent reached out with his stick and poked the bare brown body; it oscillated slightly. "*He's* all right," said the superintendent. He backed out from under the gallows, and blew out a deep breath. The moody look had gone out of his face quite suddenly. He glanced at his wristwatch. "Eight minutes past eight. Well, that's all for this morning, thank God."

The warders unfixed bayonets and marched away. The dog, sobered and conscious of having misbehaved itself, slipped after them. We walked out of the gallows yard, past the condemned

[3](Hindu) "Drop him!" — Eds.

cells with their waiting prisoners, into the big central yard of the prison. The convicts, under the command of warders armed with lathis,[4] were already receiving their breakfast. They squatted in long rows, each man holding a tin pannikin,[5] while two warders with buckets marched around ladling out rice; it seemed quite a homely, jolly scene, after the hanging. An enormous relief had come upon us now that the job was done. One felt an impulse to sing, to break into a run, to snigger. All at once everyone began chattering gaily.

The Eurasian boy walking beside me nodded towards the 18 way we had come, with a knowing smile: "Do you know, sir, our friend" (he meant the dead man) "when he heard his appeal had been dismissed, he pissed on the floor of his cell. From fright. Kindly take one of my cigarettes, sir. Do you not admire my new silver case, sir? From the boxwallah,[6] two rupees eight annas. Classy European style."

Several people laughed — at what, nobody seemed certain. 19

Francis was walking by the superintendent, talking garru- 20 lously: "Well, sir, all has passed off with the utmost satisfactoriness. It was all finished — flick! Like that. It iss not always so — oah, no! I have known cases where the doctor wass obliged to go beneath the gallows and pull the prissoner's legs to ensure decease. Most disagreeable!"

"Wriggling about, eh? That's bad," said the superintendent. 21

"Ach, sir, it iss worse when they become refractory! One 22 man, I recall, clung to the bars of hiss cage when we went to take him out. You will scarcely credit, sir, that it took six warders to dislodge him, three pulling at each leg. We reasoned with him, 'My dear fellow,' we said, 'think of the all the pain and trouble you are causing to us!' But no, he would not listen! Ach, he wass very troublesome!"

I found that I was laughing quite loudly. Everyone was 23 laughing. Even the superintendent grinned in a tolerant way. "You'd better all come out and have a drink," he said quite

---

[4]Policemen's wooden clubs. — Eds.
[5]Small pan or dish. — Eds.
[6]Merchant of jewelry boxes. — Eds.

genially. "I've got a bottle of whiskey in the car. We could do with it."

We went through the big double gates of the prison into the road. "Pulling at his legs!" exclaimed a Burmese magistrate suddenly, and burst into a loud chuckling. We all began laughing again. At that moment Francis' anecdote seemed extraordinarily funny. We all had a drink together, native and European alike, quite amicably. The dead man was a hundred yards away. 24

QUESTIONS ON MEANING

1. What reason does the superintendent give for wanting Francis and the other jailers to hurry? What is the real, unspoken reason?
2. In what ways is the appearance of the dog (paragraph 6) "a dreadful thing"? What, exactly, makes its presence disturbing to the men who accompany the prisoner?
3. How does the condemned man's stepping aside to avoid a puddle trigger a powerful new insight for the author?
4. Explain why the men react as they do to the prisoner's rhythmic "crying out to his god."
5. How do you account for the animated talking and laughing that follow the hanging?
6. What PURPOSE other than to tell an absorbing story do you find in Orwell's essay?

QUESTIONS ON WRITING STRATEGY

1. What order does Orwell follow in his narrative? Where in his account does he depart from this order?
2. Orwell makes no mention of the crime for which the prisoner has been sentenced to death. Had he done so, would his essay have been more effective?
3. Devoting your attention to just one of the characters in "A Hanging," list the concrete details and IMAGES that lend vividness to Orwell's characterization. Share the list with your classmates.
4. Where in the essay does Orwell come closest to declaring his views about capital punishment? What are they? How do you know? (When you have read H. L. Mencken's essay, "The Penalty of

Death" in Chapter 10, try setting Mencken's views and Orwell's side by side.)

QUESTIONS ON LANGUAGE

1. Use a dictionary if you need help defining the following words: warders (paragraph 2); pariah (6); gambolled (8); servile (11); reiterated (12); abominable (13); timorously (15); oscillated (16); garrulously (20); refractory (22); amicably (24).
2. Notice the SIMILES in the first paragraph: the light "like yellow tinfoil," the cells "like small animal cages." Are these FIGURES OF SPEECH merely decorative, or do they add something vital to your perception of the scene Orwell draws? If so, what?
3. Point to other similes in Orwell's essay that seem to you especially apt. Where does the author use METAPHORS to achieve an effect?
4. Point to a few sentences in which the author uses UNDERSTATEMENT. What, in each case, does this figure of speech contribute to the sentence's EFFECT?
5. What does the author mean when, at the end of paragraph 10, he speaks of "one world less"?
6. Explain the force of the phrase *dead silence* in paragraph 15.

SUGGESTIONS FOR WRITING

1. In an essay, recall an unforgettable public event you have witnessed or taken part in, one that gave you some insight you didn't have before. Such an event could be a wedding, a funeral, a graduation, an accident, the dedication of a monument, or another that you can think of. Make clear what caused the event to stick in your memory.
2. Write several paragraphs in which you agree or disagree with Orwell's attitude toward capital punishment. Be sure to include your reasons for believing as you do.

George Orwell on Writing

Don't miss George Orwell's "Politics and the English Language," a famous argument for more accurate, less pretentious writing, reprinted in full in this book (starting on page 624). Speaking more personally, Orwell explains the motives for his own writing in another essay, "Why I Write" (1946):

"What I have most wanted to do throughout the past ten years is to make political writing into an art. My starting point is always a feeling of partisanship, a sense of injustice. When I sit down to write a book, I do not say to myself, 'I am going to produce a work of art.' I write it because there is some lie that I want to expose, some fact to which I want to draw attention, and my initial concern is to get a hearing. But I could not do the work of writing a book, or even a long magazine article, if it were not also an esthetic experience. Anyone who cares to examine my work will see that even when it is downright propaganda it contains much that a full-time politician would consider irrelevant. I am not able, and I do not want, completely to abandon the world-view that I acquired in childhood. So long as I remain alive and well I shall continue to feel strongly about prose style, to love the surface of the earth, and to take a pleasure in solid objects and scraps of useless information. It is no use trying to suppress that side of myself. The job is to reconcile my ingrained likes and dislikes with the essentially public, nonindividual activities that this age forces on all of us.

"It is not easy. It raises problems of construction and of language, and it raises in a new way the problem of truthfulness. Let me give just one example of the cruder kind of difficulty that arises. My book about the Spanish civil war, *Homage to Catalonia*, is, of course, a frankly political book, but in the main it is written with a certain detachment and regard for form. I did try very hard in it to tell the whole truth without violating my literary instincts. But among other things it contains a long chapter, full of newspaper quotations and the like, defending the Trotskyists who were accused of plotting with Franco. Clearly such a chapter, which after a year or two would lose its interest for any ordinary reader, must ruin the book. A critic whom I respect read me a lecture about it. 'Why did you put in all that stuff?' he said. 'You've turned what might have been a good book into journalism.' What he said was true, but I could not have done otherwise. I happened to know, what very few people in England had been allowed to know, that innocent men were being falsely accused. If I had not been angry about that I should never have written the book.

"In one form or another this problem comes up again. The problem of language is subtler and would take too long to discuss. I will only say that of late years I have tried to write less picturesquely and more exactly. In any case I find that by the time you have perfected any style of writing, you have always outgrown it. *Animal Farm* was the first book in which I tried, with full consciousness of what I was doing, to fuse political purpose and artistic purpose into one whole. . . .

"Looking back through the last page or two, I see that I have made it appear as though my motives in writing were wholly public-spirited. I don't want to leave that as the final impression. All writers are vain, selfish, and lazy, and at the very bottom of their motives there lies a mystery. Writing a book is a horrible, exhausting struggle, like a long bout of some painful illness. One would never undertake such a thing if one were not driven on by some demon whom one can neither resist nor understand. For all one knows that demon is simply the same instinct that makes a baby squall for attention. And yet it is also true that one can write nothing readable unless one constantly struggles to efface one's own personality. Good prose is like a window pane. I cannot say with certainty which of my motives are the strongest, but I know which of them deserve to be followed. And looking back through my work, I see that it is invariably where I lacked a *political* purpose that I wrote lifeless books and was betrayed into purple passages, sentences without meaning, decorative adjectives, and humbug generally."

FOR DISCUSSION

1. What does Orwell mean by his "political purpose" in writing? By his "artistic purpose"? How did he sometimes find it hard to fulfill both purposes?
2. Think about Orwell's remark that "one can write nothing readable unless one constantly struggles to efface one's own personality." From your own experience, have you found any truth in this observation, or any reason to think otherwise?

· James Thurber ·

JAMES THURBER (1894–1961), a native of Columbus, Ohio, made himself immortal with his humorous stories of shy, bumbling men (such as "The Secret Life of Walter Mitty") and his cartoons of men, women, and dogs that look as though he had drawn them with his foot. (In fact, Thurber suffered from weak eyesight and had to draw his cartoons in crayon on sheets of paper two or three feet wide.) As Thurber aged and approached blindness, he drew less and less, and wrote more and more. His first book, written with his friend E. B. White, is a takeoff on self-help manuals, *Is Sex Necessary?* (1929). His later prose includes *My Life and Hard Times* (1933), from which "University Days" is taken; *The Thirteen Clocks*, a fable for children (1950); and *The Years with Ross* (1959), a memoir of his years on the staff of *The New Yorker*.

University Days

Ohio State University in World War I may seem remote from your own present situation, but see if you don't agree that this story of campus frustration is as fresh as the day it was first composed. Notice how, with beautiful brevity, Thurber draws a scene, introduces bits of revealing dialogue, and shifts briskly from one scene to another.

I passed all the other courses that I took at my university, but I could never pass botany. This was because all botany students had to spend several hours a week in a laboratory looking through a microscope at plant cells, and I could never see through a microscope. I never once saw a cell through a microscope. This used to enrage my instructor. He would wander around the laboratory pleased with the progress all the students were making in drawing the involved and, so I am told, interesting structure of flower cells, until he came to me. I would just be standing there. "I can't see anything," I would say. He would begin patiently enough, explaining how anybody can see through a microscope, but he would always end up in a fury, claiming that I could *too* see through the microscope but just pretended that I couldn't. "It takes away from the beauty of flowers anyway," I used to tell him. "We are not concerned with beauty in this course," he would say. "We are concerned solely with what I may call the *mechanics* of flars." "Well," I'd say, " I can't see anything." "Try it just once again," he'd say, and I would put my eye to the microscope and see nothing at all, except now and again a nebulous milky substance — a phenomenon of maladjustment. You were supposed to see a vivid, restless clockwork of sharply defined plant cells. "I see what looks like a lot of milk," I would tell him. This, he claimed, was the result of my not having adjusted the microscope properly, so he would readjust it for me, or rather, for himself. And I would look again and see milk.

I finally took a deferred pass, as they called it, and waited a year and tried again. (You had to pass one of the biological sciences or you couldn't graduate.) The professor had come back from vacation brown as a berry, bright-eyed, and eager to explain cell-structure again to his classes. "Well," he said to me, cheerily, when we met in the first laboratory hour of the semester, "we're going to see cells this time, aren't we?" "Yes, sir," I said. Students to right of me and to left of me and in front of me were seeing cells; what's more, they were quietly drawing pictures of them in their notebooks. Of course, I didn't see anything.

"We'll try it," the professor said to me, grimly, "with every adjustment of the microscope known to man. As God as my witness, I'll arrange this glass so that you see cells through it or I'll give up teaching. In twenty-two years of botany, I — " He cut off abruptly for he was beginning to quiver all over, like Lionel Barrymore,[1] and he genuinely wished to hold onto his temper; his scenes with me had taken a great deal out of him.

So we tried it with every adjustment of the microscope known to man. With only one of them did I see anything but blackness or the familiar lacteal opacity, and that time I saw, to

[1]A noted American stage, radio, and screen actor (1878–1954). — EDS.

my pleasure and amazement, a variegated constellation of flecks, specks, and dots. These I hastily drew. The instructor, noting my activity, came back from an adjoining desk, a smile on his lips and his eyebrows high in hope. He looked at my cell drawing. "What's that?" he demanded, with a hint of a squeal in his voice. "That's what I saw," I said. "You didn't, you didn't, you *didn't!*" he screamed, losing control of his temper instantly, and he bent over and squinted into the microscope. His head snapped up. "That's your eye!" he shouted. "You've fixed the lens so that it reflects! You've drawn your eye!"

Another course that I didn't like, but somehow managed to   5
pass, was economics. I went to that class straight from the botany class, which didn't help me any in understanding either subject. I used to get them mixed up. But not as mixed up as another student in my economics class who came there direct from a physics laboratory. He was a tackle on the football team, named Bolenciecwcz. At that time Ohio State University had one of the best football teams in the country, and Bolenciecwcz was one of its outstanding stars. In order to be eligible to play it was necessary for him to keep up in his studies, a very difficult matter, for while he was not dumber than an ox he was not any smarter. Most of his professors were lenient and helped him along. None gave him more hints in answering questions or asked him simpler ones than the economics professor, a thin, timid man named Bassum. One day when we were on the subject of transportation and distribution, it came Bolenciecwcz's turn to answer a question. "Name one means of transportation," the professor said to him. No light came into the big tackle's eyes. "Just any means of transportation," said the professor. Bolenciecwcz sat staring at him. "That is," pursued the professor, "any medium, agency, or method of going from one place to another." Bolenciecwcz had the look of a man who is being led into a trap. "You may choose among steam, horse-drawn, or electrically propelled vehicles," said the instructor. "I might suggest the one which we commonly take in making long journeys across land." There was a profound silence in which everybody stirred uneasily, including Bolenciecwcz and Mr. Bassum. Mr. Bassum abruptly broke this silence in an amazing manner.

"Choo-choo-choo," he said, in a low voice, and turned instantly scarlet. He glanced appealingly around the room. All of us, of course, shared Mr. Bassum's desire that Bolenciecwcz should stay abreast of the class in economics, for the Illinois game, one of the hardest and most important of the season, was only a week off. "Toot, toot, too-toooooot!" some student with a deep voice moaned, and we all looked encouragingly at Bolenciecwcz. Somebody else gave a fine imitation of a locomotive letting off steam. Mr. Bassum himself rounded off the little show. "Ding, dong, ding, dong," he said, hopefully. Bolenciecwcz was staring at the floor now, trying to think, his great brow furrowed, his huge hands rubbing together, his face red.

"How did you come to college this year, Mr. Bolenciecwcz?"   6
asked the professor. "*Chuffa* chuffa, *chuffa* chuffa."

"M'father sent me," said the football player.   7

"What on?" asked Bassum.   8

"I git an 'lowance," said the tackle, in a low, husky voice,   9
obviously embarrassed.

"No, no," said Bassum. "Name a means of transportation.   10
What did you *ride* here on?"

"Train," said Bolenciecwcz.   11

"Quite right," said the professor. "Now, Mr. Nugent, will   12
you tell us — "

If I went through anguish in botany and economics — for   13
different reasons — gymnasium work was even worse. I don't even like to think about it. They wouldn't let you play games or join the exercises with your glasses on and I couldn't see with mine off. I bumped into professors, horizontal bars, agricultural students, and swinging iron rings. Not being able to see, I could take it but I couldn't dish it out. Also, in order to pass gymnasium (and you had to pass it to graduate) you had to learn to swim if you didn't know how. I didn't like the swimming pool, I didn't like swimming, and I didn't like the swimming instructor, and after all these years I still don't. I never swam but I passed my gym work anyway, by having another student give my gymnasium number (978) and swim across the pool in my place. He was a quiet, amiable blond youth, number 473, and he would have seen through a microscope for me if we could have got

away with it, but we couldn't get away with it. Another thing I
didn't like about gymnasium work was that they made you strip
the day you registered. It is impossible for me to be happy when I
am stripped and being asked a lot of questions. Still, I did better
than a lanky agricultural student who was cross-examined just
before I was. They asked each student what college he was in —
that is, whether Arts, Engineering, Commerce, or Agriculture.
"What college are you in?" the instructor snapped at the youth
in front of me. "Ohio State University," he said promptly.

It wasn't that agricultural student but it was another a   14
whole lot like him who decided to take up journalism, possibly
on the ground that when farming went to hell he could fall back
on newspaper work. He didn't realize, of course, that that would
be very much like falling back full-length on a kit of carpenter's
tools. Haskins didn't seem cut out for journalism, being too embarrassed to talk to anybody and unable to use a typewriter, but
the editor of the college paper assigned him to the cow barns,
the sheep house, the horse pavilion, and the animal husbandry
department generally. This was a genuinely big "beat," for it
took up five times as much ground and got ten times as great a
legislative appropriation as the College of Liberal Arts. The agricultural student knew animals, but nevertheless his stories were
dull and colorlessly written. He took all afternoon on each of
them, on account of having to hunt for each letter on the typewriter. Once in a while he had to ask somebody to help him
hunt. "C" and "L," in particular, were hard letters for him to
find. His editor finally got pretty much annoyed at the farmer-
journalist because his pieces were so uninteresting. "See here,
Haskins," he snapped at him one day, "why is it we never have
anything hot from you on the horse pavilion? Here we have two
hundred head of horses on this campus — more than any other
university in the Western Conference except Purdue — and yet
you never get any real lowdown on them. Now shoot over to
the horse barns and dig up something lively." Haskins shambled
out and came back in about an hour; he said he had something.
"Well, start it off snappily," said the editor. "Something people
will read." Haskins set to work and in a couple of hours brought
a sheet of typewritten paper to the desk; it was a two-hundred-
word story about some disease that had broken out among the

horses. Its opening sentence was simple but arresting. It read: "Who has noticed the sores on the tops of the horses in the animal husbandry building?"

Ohio State was a land grant university and therefore two years of military drill was compulsory. We drilled with old Springfield rifles and studied the tactics of the Civil War even though the World War was going on at the time. At 11 o'clock each morning thousands of freshman and sophomores used to deploy over the campus, moodily creeping up on the old chemistry building. It was good training for the kind of warfare that was waged at Shiloh but it had no connection with what was going on in Europe. Some people used to think there was German money behind it, but they didn't say so or they would have been thrown in jail as German spies. It was a period of muddy thought and marked, I believe, the decline of higher education in the Middle West.

As a soldier I was never any good at all. Most of the cadets were glumly indifferent soldiers, but I was no good at all. Once General Littlefield, who was commandant of the cadet corps, popped up in front of me during regimental drill and snapped, "You are the main trouble with this university!" I think he meant that my type was the main trouble with the university but he may have meant me individually. I was mediocre at drill, certainly — that is, until my senior year. By that time I had drilled longer than anybody else in the Western Conference, having failed at military at the end of each preceding year so that I had to do it all over again. I was the only senior still in uniform. The uniform which, when new, had made me look like an interurban railway conductor, now that it had become faded and too tight made me look like Bert Williams in his bellboy act.[2] This had a definitely bad effect on my morale. Even so, I had become by sheer practice little short of wonderful at squad maneuvers.

One day General Littlefield picked our company out of the whole regiment and tried to get it mixed up by putting it through one movement after another as fast as we could execute

15

16

17

[2]A popular vaudeville and silent-screen comedian of the time, Williams in one routine played a hotel porter in a shrunken suit. — Eds.

them: squads right, squads left, squads on right into line, squads right about, squads left front into line, etc. In about three minutes one hundred and nine men were marching in one direction and I was marching away from them at an angle of forty degrees all alone. "Company, halt!" shouted General Littlefield. "That man is the only man who has it right!" I was made a corporal for my achievement.

The next day General Littlefield summoned me to his office.   18
He was swatting flies when I went in. I was silent and he was silent too, for a long time. I don't think he remembered me or why he had sent for me, but he didn't want to admit it. He swatted some more flies, keeping his eyes on them narrowly before he let go with the swatter. "Button up your coat!" he snapped. Looking back on it now I can see that he meant me although he was looking at a fly, but I just stood there. Another fly came to rest on a paper in front of the general and began rubbing its hind legs together. The general lifted the swatter cautiously. I moved restlessly and the fly flew away. "You startled him!" barked General Littlefield, looking at me severely. I said I was sorry. "That won't help the situation!" snapped the General, with cold military logic. I didn't see what I could do except offer to chase some more flies toward his desk, but I didn't say anything. He stared out the window at the faraway figures of co-eds crossing the campus toward the library. Finally, he told me I could go. So I went. He either didn't know which cadet I was or else he forgot what he wanted to see me about. It may have been that he wished to apologize for having called me the main trouble with the university; or maybe he had decided to compliment me on my brilliant drilling of the day before and then at the last minute decided not to. I don't know. I don't think about it much any more.

QUESTIONS ON MEANING

1. In what light does Thurber portray himself in "University Days?" Is his self-portrait sympathetic?
2. Are Bolenciecwcz and Haskins stereotypes? Discuss.

3. To what extent does Thurber sacrifice believability for humorous EFFECT? What is his main PURPOSE?

QUESTIONS ON WRITING STRATEGY

1. How do Thurber's INTRODUCTION, his TRANSITIONS, and his CON-CLUSION heighten the humor of his essay?
2. Criticize the opening sentence of the story Haskins writes about horse disease (quoted in paragraph 14).
3. Thurber does not explain in "University Days" how he ever did fulfill his biological science requirement for graduation. Is this an important omission? Explain.
4. Do you find any support in Thurber's essay for the view that he is genuinely critical of certain absurdities in college education?

QUESTIONS ON LANGUAGE

1. Be sure to know what the following words mean: nebulous (paragraph 1); lacteal opacity, variegated (4).
2. Explain how Thurber's word choices heighten the IRONY in the following phrases: "like falling back full-length on a kit of carpenter's tools" (paragraph 14); "a genuinely big 'beat' " (14); "the decline of higher education in the Middle West" (15).
3. What is a land grant university (paragraph 15)?
4. Where in his essay does Thurber use colloquial DICTION? What is its EFFECT?

SUGGESTIONS FOR WRITING

1. How does Thurber's picture of campus life during the days of World War I compare with campus life today? What has changed? What has stayed the same? Develop your own ideas in a brief essay.
2. Write an essay called "High-School Days" in which, with a light touch, you recount two or three anecdotes from your own experience, educational or otherwise.

James Thurber on Writing

In an interview with writers George Plimpton and Max Steele, James Thurber fielded some revealing questions. "Is the act of writing easy for you?" the interviewers wanted to know.

"For me," Thurber replied, "it's mostly a question of rewriting. It's part of a constant attempt on my part to make the finished version smooth, to make it seem effortless. A story I've been working on — 'The Train on Track Six,' it's called — was rewritten fifteen complete times. There must have been close to 240,000 words in all the manuscripts put together, and I must have spent two thousand hours working at it. Yet the finished version can't be more than twenty thousand words."

"Then it's rare that your work comes out right the first time?"

"Well," said Thurber, "my wife took a look at the first version of something I was doing not long ago and said, 'Goddamn it, Thurber, that's high-school stuff.' I have to tell her to wait until the seventh draft, it'll work out all right. I don't know why that should be so, that the first or second draft of everything I write reads as if it was turned out by a charwoman. I've only written one piece quickly. I wrote a thing called 'File and Forget' in one afternoon — but only because it was a series of letters just as one would ordinarily dictate. And I'll have to admit that the last letter of the series, after doing all the others that one afternoon, took me a week. It was the end of the piece and I had to fuss over it."

"Does the fact that you're dealing with humor slow down the production?"

"It's possible. With humor you have to look out for traps. You're likely to be very gleeful with what you've first put down, and you think it's fine, very funny. One reason you go over and over it is to make the piece sound less as if you were having a lot of fun with it yourself." (*Writers at Work: The Paris Review Interviews, First Series* [New York: Viking Press, 1957].)

On another occasion, Thurber set forth, with tongue in cheek, some general principles for comic writing. "I have established a few standing rules of my own about humor," he wrote, "after receiving dozens of humorous essays and stories from strangers over a period of twenty years. (1) The reader should be able to find out what the story is about. (2) Some inkling of the general idea should be apparent in the first five hundred words. (3) If the writer has decided to change the name of his protagonist from Ketcham to McTavish, Ketcham should not keep bobbing up in the last five pages. A good way to eliminate this confusion is to read the piece over before sending it out, and remove Ketcham completely. He is a nuisance. (4) The word "I'll" should not be divided so that the "I" is on one line and " 'll" on the next. The reader's attention, after the breaking up of "I'll," can never be successfully recaptured. (5) It also never recovers from such names as Ann S. Thetic, Maud Lynn, Sally Forth, Bertha Twins, and the like. (6) Avoid comic stories about plumbers who are mistaken for surgeons, sheriffs who are terrified by gunfire, psychiatrists who are driven crazy by women patients, doctors who faint at the sight of blood, adolescent girls who know more about sex than their fathers do, and midgets who turn out to be the parents of a two-hundred-pound wrestler." (What's So Funny?" in *Thurber Country* [New York: Simon & Schuster, 1949].)

FOR DISCUSSION

1. By what means does Thurber make his writing look "effortless"?
2. Is there any serious advice to be extracted from Thurber's "standing rules about humor"? If so, what is it?

· Calvin Trillin ·

CALVIN TRILLIN, distinguished commentator on American life, was born in 1935 in Kansas City, Missouri, where he grew up. After earning his B.A. from Yale in 1957, he worked as a reporter and writer for *Time*. In 1963 he joined *The New Yorker* as a staff writer and ever since has been a contributor to that lively weekly magazine. From 1978 until 1985 Trillin wrote a column on political affairs for *The Nation*, a liberal review, and in 1986 became a syndicated newspaper columnist. Some of his political commentary has been gathered in *Uncivil Liberties* (1982) and in *With All Disrespect* (1985). *If You Can't Say Something Nice* (1987) collects some of his essays. Trillin has also written (with appetite) about food and drink in *American Fried* (1974) and *Alice, Let's Eat* (1978).

It's Just Too Late

This essay first appeared as one of a series called "U.S. Journal," which Trillin contributed to *The New Yorker* until 1982. The author has since included the narrative in *Killings* (1984), a collection of factual chronicles of violent death in America. The book, says Trillin, "is meant to be more about how Americans live than about how some of them die. . . . A killing often seemed to present the best opportunity to write about people one at a time."

Knoxville, Tennessee
March 1979

Until she was sixteen, FaNee Cooper was what her parents sometimes called an ideal child. "You'd never have to correct her," FaNee's mother has said. In sixth grade, FaNee won a spelling contest. She played the piano and the flute. She seemed to believe what she heard every Sunday at the Beaver Dam Baptist Church about good and evil and the hereafter. FaNee was not an outgoing child. Even as a baby, she was uncomfortable when she was held and cuddled. She found it easy to tell her parents that she loved them but difficult to confide in them. Particularly compared to her sister, Kristy, a cheerful, open little girl two and a half years younger, she was reserved and introspective. The thoughts she kept to herself, though, were apparently happy thoughts. Her eighth-grade essay on Christmas — written in a remarkably neat hand — talked of the joys of helping put together toys for her little brother, Leo, Jr., and the importance of her parents' reminder that Christmas is the birthday of Jesus. Her parents were the sort of people who might have been expected to have an ideal child. As a boy, Leo Cooper had been called "one of the greatest high-school basketball players ever developed in Knox County." He went on to play basketball at East Tennessee State, and he married the homecoming queen, JoAnn Henson. After college, Cooper became a high-school basketball coach and teacher and, eventually, an administrator. By the time FaNee turned thirteen, in 1973, he was in his third year as the principal of Gresham Junior High School, in Fountain City — a small Knox County town that had been swallowed up by Knoxville when the suburbs began to move north. A tall man, with curly black hair going on gray, Leo Cooper has an elaborate way of talking ("Unless I'm very badly mistaken, he has never related to me totally the content of his conversation") and a manner that may come from years of trying to leave errant junior-high-school students with the impression that a responsible adult is magnanimous, even humble, about invariably being in the right. His wife, a high-school art teacher, paints and does batik, and created the name FaNee because she liked the way it looked and sounded — it sounds like "Fawn-*ee*" when the Coopers say it — but the impression she gives is not of artiness but of soft-spoken small-town gentility. When she found, in the course of cleaning up FaNee's room, that her ideal thirteen-year-old had been smoking cigarettes, she was, in her words, crushed. "FaNee was such a perfect child before that," JoAnn Cooper said some time later. "She was angry that we found out. She knew we knew that she had done something we didn't approve of, and then the rebellion started. I was hurt. I was very hurt. I guess it came through as disappointment."

Several months later, FaNee's grandmother died. FaNee   2
had been devoted to her grandmother. She wrote a poem in her
memory — an almost joyous poem, filled with Christian faith in
the afterlife ("Please don't grieve over my happiness/Rejoice
with me in the presence of the Angels of Heaven"). She also
took some keepsakes from her grandmother's house, and was
apparently mortified when her parents found them and explained that they would have to be returned. By then, the
Coopers were aware that FaNee was going to have a difficult
time as a teenager. They thought she might be self-conscious
about the double affliction of glasses and braces. They thought
she might be uncomfortable in the role of the principal's daughter at Gresham. In ninth grade, she entered Halls High School,
where JoAnn Cooper was teaching art. FaNee was a loner at
first. Then she fell in with what could only be considered a bad
crowd.

Halls, a few miles to the north of Fountain City, used to be   3
known as Halls Crossroads. It is what Knoxville people call
"over the ridge" — on the side of Black Oak Ridge that has always been thought of as rural. When FaNee entered Halls High,
the Coopers were already in the process of building a house on
several acres of land they had bought in Halls, in a sparsely settled area along Brown Gap Road. Like two or three other
houses along the road, it was to be constructed basically of huge
logs taken from old buildings — a house that Leo Cooper describes as being, like the name FaNee, "just a little bit different."
Ten years ago, Halls Crossroads was literally a crossroads. Then
some of the Knoxville expansion that had swollen Fountain
City spilled over the ridge, planting subdivisions here and there
on roads that still went for long stretches with nothing but an
occasional house with a cow or two next to it. The increase in
population did not create a town. Halls has no center. Its commercial area is a series of two or three shopping centers strung
together on the Maynardville Highway, the four-lane that leads
north into Union County — a place almost synonymous in east
Tennessee with mountain poverty. Its restaurant is the Halls
Freezo Drive-In. The gathering place for the group FaNee

Cooper eventually found herself in was the Maynardville Highway Exxon station.

At Halls High School, the social poles were represented by the Jocks and the Freaks. FaNee found her friends among the Freaks. "I am truly enlighted upon irregular trains of thought aimed at strange depots of mental wards," she wrote when she was fifteen. "Yes! Crazed farms for the mental off — Oh! I walked through the halls screams & loud laughter fill my ears — Orderlys try to reason with me — but I am unreasonable! The joys of being a FREAK in a circus of imagination." The little crowd of eight or ten young people that FaNee joined has been referred to by her mother as "the Union County group." A couple of the girls were from backgrounds similar to FaNee's, but all the boys had the characteristics, if not the precise addresses, that Knoxville people associate with the poor whites of Union County. They were the sort of boys who didn't bother to finish high school, or finished it in a special program for slow learners, or got ejected from it for taking a swing at the principal.

"I guess you can say they more or less dragged us down to their level with the drugs," a girl who was in the group — a girl who can be called Marcia — said recently. "And somehow we settled for it. It seems like we had to get ourselves in the pit before we could look out." People in the group used marijuana and Valium and LSD. They sneered at the Jocks and the "prim and proper little ladies" who went with the Jocks. "We set ourselves aside," Marcia now says. "We put ourselves above everyone. How we did that I don't know." In a Knox County high school, teenagers who want to get themselves in the pit need not mainline heroin. The Jocks they mean to be compared to do not merely show up regularly for classes and practice football and wear clean clothes; they watch their language and preach temperance and go to prayer meetings on Wednesday nights and talk about having a real good Christian witness. Around Knoxville, people who speak of well-behaved high-school kids often seem to use words like "perfect," or even "angels." For FaNee's group, the opposite was not difficult to figure out. "We were into

wicked things, strange things," Marcia says. "It was like we were
on some kind of devil trip." FaNee wrote about demons and vul-
tures and rats. "Slithering serpents eat my sanity and bite my
ass," she wrote in an essay called "The Lovely Road of Life," just
after she turned sixteen, "while tornadoes derail and ever so
swiftly destroy every car in my train of thought." She wrote a lot
about death.

FaNee's girl friends spoke of her as "super-intelligent." Her   6
English teacher found some of her writing profound — and disturbing. She was thought to be not just super-intelligent but
super-mysterious, and even, at times, super-weird — an introverted girl who stared straight ahead with deep-brown, nearly
black eyes and seemed to have thoughts she couldn't share. Nobody really knew why she had chosen to run with the Freaks —
whether it was loneliness or rebellion or simple boredom. Marcia thought it might have had something to do with a feeling
that her parents had settled on Kristy as their perfect child. "I
guess she figured she couldn't be the best," Marcia said recently.
"So she decided she might as well be the worst."

Toward the spring of FaNee's junior year at Halls, her prob-   7
lems seemed to deepen. Despite her intelligence, her grades were
sliding. She was what her mother called "a mental dropout."
Leo Cooper had to visit Halls twice because of minor suspen-
sions. Once, FaNee had been caught smoking. Once, having
ducked out of a required assembly, she was spotted by a favorite
teacher, who turned her in. At home, she exchanged little more
than short, strained formalities with Kristy, who shared their
parents' opinion of FaNee's choice of friends. The Coopers had
finished their house — a large house, its size accentuated by the
huge old logs and a great stone fireplace and outsize "Paul Bun-
yan"–style furniture — but FaNee spent most of her time there
in her own room, sleeping or listening to rock music through
earphones. One night, there was a terrible scene when FaNee returned from a concert in a condition that Leo Cooper knew had
to be the result of marijuana. JoAnn Cooper, who ordinarily
strikes people as too gentle to raise her voice, found herself losing her temper regularly. Finally, Leo Cooper asked a counsellor

he knew, Jim Griffin, to stop in at Halls High School and have a talk with FaNee — unofficially.

Griffin — a young man with a warm, informal manner — 8 worked for the Juvenile Court of Knox County. He had a reputation for being able to reach teenagers who wouldn't talk to their parents or to school administrators. One Friday in March of 1977, he spent an hour and a half talking to FaNee Cooper. As Griffin recalls the interview, FaNee didn't seem alarmed by his presence. She seemed to him calm and controlled — Griffin thought it was something like talking to another adult — and, unlike most of the teenagers he dealt with, she looked him in the eye the entire time. Griffin, like some of FaNee's friends, found her eyes unsettling — "the coldest, most distant, but, at the same time, the most knowing eyes I'd ever seen." She expressed affection for her parents, but she didn't seem interested in exploring ways of getting along better with them. The impression she gave Griffin was that they were who they were, and she was who she was, and there didn't happen to be any connection. Several times, she made the same response to Griffin's suggestions: "It's too late."

That weekend, neither FaNee nor her parents brought up 9 the subject of Griffin's visit. Leo Cooper has spoken of the weekend as being particularly happy; a friend of FaNee's who stayed over remembers it as particularly strained. FaNee stayed home from school on Monday because of a bad headache — she often had bad headaches — but felt well enough on Monday evening to drive to the library. She was to be home at nine. When she wasn't, Mrs. Cooper began to phone her friends. Finally, around ten, Leo Cooper got into his other car and took a swing around Halls — past the teenage hangouts like the Exxon station and the Pizza Hut and the Smoky Mountain Market. Then he took a second swing. At eleven, FaNee was still not home.

She hadn't gone to the library. She had picked up two girl 10 friends and driven to the home of a third, where everyone took five Valium tablets. Then the four girls drove over to the Exxon station, where they met four boys from their crowd. After a while, the group bought some beer and some marijuana and reassembled at Charlie Stevens's trailer. Charlie Stevens was five or six years older than everyone else in the group — a skinny, slow-thinking young man with long black hair and a sparse beard. He was married and had a child, but he and his wife had separated; she was back in Union County with the baby. Stevens had remained in their trailer — parked in the yard near his mother's house, in a back-road area of Knox County dominated by decrepit, unpainted sheds and run-down trailers and rusted-out automobiles. Stevens had picked up FaNee at home once or twice — apparently, more as a driver for the group than as a date — and the Coopers, having learned that his unsuitability extended to being married, had asked her not to see him.

In Charlie's trailer, which had no heat or electricity, the group drank beer and passed around joints, keeping warm with blankets. By eleven or so, FaNee was what one of her friends has called "super-messed-up." Her speech was slurred. She was having trouble keeping her balance. She had decided not to go home. She had apparently persuaded herself that her parents intended to send her away to some sort of home for incorrigibles. "It's too late," she said to one of her friends. "It's just too late." It was decided that one of the boys, David Munsey, who was more or less the leader of the group, would drive the Coopers' car to FaNee's house, where FaNee and Charlie Stevens would pick him up in Stevens's car — a worn Pinto with four bald tires, one light, and a dragging muffler. FaNee wrote a note to her parents, and then, perhaps because her handwriting was suffering the effects of beer and marijuana and Valium, asked Stevens to rewrite it on a large piece of paper, which would be left on the seat of the Coopers' car. The Stevens version was just about the same as FaNee's, except that Stevens left out a couple of sentences about trying to work things out ("I'm willing to try") and, not having won any spelling championships himself, he misspelled a few words, like "tomorrow." The note said, "Dear Mom and Dad. Sorry I'm late. Very late. I left your car because I thought you might need it tomorrow. I love you all, but this is something I just had to do. The man talked to me privately for one and a half hours and I was really scared, so this is something I just had to do, but don't worry, I'm with a very good friend.

Love you all. FaNee. P.S. Please try to understand I love you all very much, really I do. Love me if you have a chance."

At eleven-thirty or so, Leo Cooper was sitting in his living 12 room, looking out the window at his driveway — a long gravel road that runs almost four hundred feet from the house to Brown Gap Road. He saw the car that FaNee had been driving pull into the driveway. "She's home," he called to his wife, who had just left the room. Cooper walked out on the deck over the garage. The car had stopped at the end of the driveway, and the lights had gone out. He got into his other car and drove to the end of the driveway. David Munsey had already joined Charlie Stevens and FaNee, and the Pinto was just leaving, travelling at a normal rate of speed. Leo Cooper pulled out on the road behind them.

Stevens turned left on Crippen Road, a road that has a field 13 on one side and two or three small houses on the other, and there Cooper pulled his car in front of the Pinto and stopped, blocking the way. He got out and walked toward the Pinto. Suddenly, Stevens put the car in reverse, backed into a driveway a hundred yards behind him, and sped off. Cooper jumped in his car and gave chase. Stevens raced back to Brown Gap Road, ran a stop sign there, ran another stop sign at Maynardville Highway, turned north, veered off onto the old Andersonville Pike, a nearly abandoned road that runs parallel to the highway, and then crossed back over the highway to the narrow, dark country roads on the other side. Stevens sometimes drove with his lights out. He took some of the corners by suddenly applying his hand brake to make the car swerve around in a ninety-degree turn. He was in familiar territory — he actually passed his trailer — and Cooper had difficulty keeping up. Past the trailer, Stevens swept down a hill into a sharp left turn that took him onto Foust Hollow Road, a winding, hilly road not much wider than one car.

At a fork, Cooper thought he had lost the Pinto. He started 14 to go right, and then saw what seemed to be a spark from Stevens's dragging muffler off to the left, in the darkness. Cooper took the left fork, down Salem Church Road. He went down a hill, and then up a long, curving hill to a crest, where he saw the Stevens car ahead. "I saw the car airborne. Up in the air," he later testified. "It was up in the air. And then it completely rolled over one more time. It started to make another flip forward, and just as it started to flip to the other side it flipped back this way, and my daughter's body came out."

Cooper slammed on his brakes and skidded to a stop up   15
against the Pinto. "Book!" Stevens shouted — the group's equivalent of "Scram!" Stevens and Munsey disappeared into the darkness. "It was dark, no one around, and so I started yelling for FaNee," Cooper has testified. "I thought it was an eternity before I could find her body, wedged under the back end of that car. . . . I tried everything I could, and saw that I couldn't get her loose. So I ran to a trailer back up to the top of the hill back up there to try to get that lady to call to get me some help, and then apparently she didn't think that I was serious. . . . I took the jack out of my car and got under, and it was dark, still couldn't see too much what was going on . . . and started prying and got her loose, and I don't know how. And then I dragged her over to the side, and, of course, at the time I felt reasonably assured that she was gone, because her head was completely — on one side just as if you had taken a sledgehammer and just hit it and bashed it in. And I did have the pleasure of one thing. I had the pleasure of listening to her breathe about the last three times she ever breathed in her life."

David Munsey did not return to the wreck that night, but   16
Charlie Stevens did. Leo Cooper was kneeling next to his daughter's body. Cooper insisted that Stevens come close enough to see FaNee. "He was kneeling down next to her," Stevens later testified. "And he said, 'Do you know what you've done? Do you really know what you've done?' Like that. And I just looked at her, and I said, 'Yes,' and just stood there. Because I couldn't say nothing." There was, of course, a legal decision to be made about who was responsible for FaNee Cooper's death. In a deposition, Stevens said he had been fleeing for his life. He testified that when Leo Cooper blocked Crippen Road, FaNee had said that her father had a gun and intended to hurt them. Stevens was bound over and eventually indicted for involuntary manslaughter. Leo Cooper testified that when he approached

the Pinto on Crippen Road, FaNee had a strange expression that he had never seen before. "It wasn't like FaNee, and I knew something was wrong," he said. "My concern was to get FaNee out of the car." The district attorney's office asked that Cooper be bound over for reckless driving, but the judge declined to do so. "Any father would have done what he did," the judge said. "I can see no criminal act on the part of Mr. Cooper."

Almost two years passed before Charlie Stevens was brought to trial. Part of the problem was assuring the presence of David Munsey, who had joined the Navy but seemed inclined to assign his own leaves. In the meantime, the Coopers went to court with a civil suit — they had "uninsured-motorist coverage," which requires their insurance company to cover any defendant who has no insurance of his own — and they won a judgment. There were ways of assigning responsibility, of course, which had nothing to do with the law, civil or criminal. A lot of people in Knoxville thought that Leo Cooper had, in the words of his lawyer, "done what any daddy worth his salt would have done." There were others who believed that FaNee Cooper had lost her life because Leo Cooper had lost his temper. Leo Cooper was not among those who expressed any doubts about his actions. Unlike his wife, whose eyes filled with tears at almost any mention of FaNee, Cooper seemed able, even eager to go over the details of the accident again and again. With the help of a school-board security man, he conducted his own investigation. He drove over the route dozens of times. "I've thought about it every day, and I guess I will the rest of my life," he said as he and his lawyer and the prosecuting attorney went over the route again the day before Charlie Stevens's trial finally began. "But I can't tell any alternative for a father. I simply wanted her out of that car. I'd have done the same thing again, even at the risk of losing her."

Tennessee law permits the family of a victim to hire a special prosecutor to assist the district attorney. The lawyer who acted for the Coopers in the civil case helped prosecute Charlie Stevens. Both he and the district attorney assured the jurors that the presence of a special prosecutor was not to be construed to mean that the Coopers were vindictive. Outside the court-

room, Leo Cooper said that the verdict was of no importance to
him — that he felt sorry, in a way, for Charlie Stevens. But
there were people in Knoxville who thought Cooper had a lot
riding on the prosecution of Charlie Stevens. If Stevens was not
guilty of FaNee Cooper's death — found so by twelve of his
peers — who was?

At the trial, Cooper testified emotionally and remarkably   19
graphically about pulling FaNee out from under the car and
watching her die in his arms. Charlie Stevens had shaved his
beard and cut his hair, but the effort did not transform him into
an impressive witness. His lawyer — trying to argue that it
would have been impossible for Stevens to concoct the story
about FaNee's having mentioned a gun, as the prosecution
strongly implied — said, "His mind is such that if you ask him a
question you can hear his mind go around, like an old mill
creaking." Stevens did not deny the recklessness of his driving
or the sorry condition of his car. It happened to be the only car
he had available to flee in, he said, and he had fled in fear for his
life.

The prosecution said that Stevens could have let FaNee out   20
of the car when her father stopped them, or could have gone to
the commercial strip on the Maynardville Highway for protection. The prosecution said that Leo Cooper had done what he
might have been expected to do under the circumstances —
alone, late at night, his daughter in danger. The defense said
precisely the same about Stevens: he had done what he might
have been expected to do when being pursued by a man he had
reason to be afraid of. "I don't fault Mr. Cooper for what he did,
but I'm sorry he did it," the defense attorney said. "I'm sorry the
girl said what she said." The jury deliberated for eighteen minutes. Charlie Stevens was found guilty. The jury recommended
a sentence of from two to five years in the state penitentiary. At
the announcement, Leo Cooper broke down and cried. JoAnn
Cooper's eyes filled with tears; she blinked them back and continued to stare straight ahead.

In a way, the Coopers might still strike a casual visitor as an   21
ideal family — handsome parents, a bright and bubbly teenage

daughter, a little boy learning the hook shot from his father, a warm house with some land around it. FaNee's presence is there, of course. A picture of her, with a small bouquet of flowers over it, hangs in the living room. One of her poems is displayed in a frame on a table. Even if Leo Cooper continues to think about that night for the rest of his life, there are questions he can never answer. Was there a way that Leo and JoAnn Cooper could have prevented FaNee from choosing the path she chose? Would she still be alive if Leo Cooper had not jumped into his car and driven to the end of the driveway to investigate? Did she in fact tell Charlie Stevens that her father would hurt them — or even that her father had a gun? Did she want to get away from her family even at the risk of tearing around dark country roads in Charlie Stevens's dismal Pinto? Or did she welcome the risk? The poem of FaNee's that the Coopers have displayed is one she wrote a week before her death:

> I think I'm going to die
> And I really don't know why.
> But look in my eye
> When I tell you good-bye.
> I think I'm going to die.

QUESTIONS ON MEANING

1. Which appears to be the dominant PURPOSE of Trillin's essay: to report a death, to tell why it happened, or to tell a revealing story?
2. How would you characterize Leo and JoAnn Cooper?
3. Of all the people who talk about FaNee and her problems, who seems to understand her best?
4. In paragraph 18, Trillin hints that Leo Cooper might have felt threatened had Charlie Stevens won acquittal. What, exactly, is the threat?
5. What do the samples of FaNee's writing that appear in Trillin's essay (paragraphs 2, 4, 5, 11, 21) contribute to your understanding of her behavior?

QUESTIONS ON WRITING STRATEGY

1. In paragraph 5, Trillin talks about the Jocks in a Knox County high school. What makes this material more than mere digression?
2. What do the direct quotations — from Leo and JoAnn Cooper; the friend called Marcia; the counselor, Jim Griffin; FaNee herself; Charlie Stevens; Cooper's lawyer — contribute to Trillin's narrative, other than local color?
3. Does Trillin seem to be biased against or in favor of anyone in his narrative? Or does he conceal all bias? Muster EVIDENCE for your answer.
4. In his final paragraph, Trillin asks a series of questions. Do they provide a satisfactory CONCLUSION to his narrative? Discuss.
5. In his introduction to *Killings*, Trillin recalls that local newspaper reporters he met while working on the story of FaNee Cooper did not understand his interest in the case. "They couldn't imagine why I had come all the way from New York to write about a death that probably hadn't even made their front page. Only one person had died, and she had not been an important person." How might the AUDIENCE of *The New Yorker*, a nationally circulated magazine of fiction, poetry, humor, and general commentary, read about a killing with expectations different from those of readers of a local newspaper?

QUESTIONS ON LANGUAGE

1. Consult your dictionary if you need help defining the following: introspective, errant, magnanimous, gentility (paragraph 1); affliction (2); decrepit (10); incorrigibles (11); deposition, indicted (16); construed, vindictive (18).
2. What do the Jocks mean when they "talk about having a real good Christian witness" (paragraph 5)?
3. What do you infer about the author's feelings toward Leo Cooper when he describes Cooper as having "a manner that may come from years of trying to leave errant junior-high-school students with the impression that a responsible adult is magnanimous, even humble, about invariably being in the right" (paragraph 1)?

SUGGESTIONS FOR WRITING

1. Suppose that Mr. Cooper had been able to stop Charlie Stevens's car before FaNee was killed — and that you, as the reporter, beginning after paragraph 13 in "It's Just Too Late," have to tell what

happened next. Imagine and write a new, briefer ending for Trillin's narrative.

2. As objectively as you can, narrate the experience of a high-school acquaintance who committed a rebellious act that had dire (but not necessarily fatal) consequences.

Calvin Trillin on Writing

In a conversation on his writing practices, Calvin Trillin was asked, "To what extent is the research — the details — important in the finished story?"

He replied: "If the story is a murder story, that has within it its own narrative line — its own beginning, middle, and end, and its own details — then what I try to do when I write is to get out of the way and just let the story tell itself. I try to get as many of the details as cleanly as possible into the story and try to get all the marks of writing off. Sometimes I think of it as trying to change clothes inside a tiny closet.

"But if it's a story about the search for barbecued mutton in western Kentucky, for instance, which is really just based on my notions of eating thrown together with some experiences — there's no beginning, no middle or end — something different than gathering as many facts as possible is called for.

"And then . . . sometimes a story changes along the way, causing the balance between straight reporting and my personal reactions to the reporting to change with it. But usually, except in extreme cases, like western Kentucky's barbecued mutton, it's not easy to tell how a story will turn out when I begin to write. So I still have to do all the reporting and gather as many facts as I can."

The interviewer persisted. "What do you usually end up with, then, after you finish reporting and are ready to start writing and what do you do with it?"

"What I have when I get home," said Trillin, "is a notebook full of handwritten notes, and sometimes, if I've been conscientious, some notes which I've typed up either late at night or early in the morning as a way of sharpening my notes a bit. As I type out notes, I remember things that were said or fill out sentences that aren't really carefully done. Also, I find out what I don't know — that there are questions that I will have to ask the next day. In addition to that, I usually have a lot of xeroxes of newspaper clippings, and sometimes I even have copies of court transcripts, brochures, etc. Whatever I have, it is often a fairly sizeable pile. Then, the day after I get home, I do a kind of pre-draft — what I call a 'vomit-out.' I don't even look at my notes to write it. It . . . starts out, at least, in the form of a story. But it degenerates fairly quickly, and by page four or five sometimes the sentences aren't complete. I write almost the length of the story in this way. The whole operation takes no more than an hour at the typewriter, but it sometimes takes me all day to do it because I'm tired and I've put it off a bit. Sometimes I don't even look at the vomit-out for the rest of the week and I have an absolute terror of anybody seeing it. It's a very embarrassing document. I tear it up at the end of the week.

"I don't write a predraft for fiction or for humor, but I can't seem to do without one for nonfiction. I've tried to figure out why I need it, what purpose it serves. I think it gives me an inventory of what I want to say and an opportunity to see which way the tone of the story is going to go, which is very important. Also, this is about the time that I begin to see technical problems that will come up — for example, that one part of the story doesn't lead into the next, or that I should write the story in the first person, or start it in a different way." ("A Writer's Process: A Conversation with Calvin Trillin," by Alice Trillin, *Journal of Basic Writing*, Fall/Winter 1981, pp. 5–18.)

FOR DISCUSSION

1. What, according to Trillin, are the advantages of writing a "vomit-out"?
2. In what ways does "It's Just Too Late" reflect Trillin's method of telling a murder story: trying "to get out of the way and just let the story tell itself"? To what extent does the writer himself remain invisible? Does he succeed in making you forget that the story required notetaking, legwork, extensive conversations with people?

· Ernest Hemingway ·

ERNEST HEMINGWAY (1889–1961), whose crisp, close-lipped style had a profound effect on other American writers and whose work and colorful personality made him an international celebrity, was born in Oak Park, Illinois. Instead of going to college, he became a cub reporter for the *Kansas City Star*. At eighteen, a volunteer ambulance driver in Italy during World War I, he was wounded by Austrian fire. In his first novel, *The Sun Also Rises* (1926), Hemingway spoke for a "lost generation" of disillusioned young Americans who, after the war, drifted about Europe aimlessly. More best-selling novels followed: *A Farewell to Arms* (1929), about a wartime love affair, and *For Whom the Bell Tolls* (1940), set in Spain during civil war. A short parable-novel, *The Old Man and the Sea* (1952), won a Pulitzer Prize; in 1954 Hemingway received a Nobel Prize for literature. In *Death in the Afternoon* (1932) and *The Dangerous Summer* (1985), he wrote knowledgeably of bullfighting. In matadors, soldiers, and prizefighters, he found values to admire: endurance, respect for skill, a sense of honor. Hemingway died as his father had died; suffering from incurable illness, he shot himself. He left much work in manuscript, notably *A Moveable Feast* (1964), a memoir of days as a young writer in Paris, and *The Garden of Eden* (1986), an unfinished novel given some editorial shaping. For decades, Hemingway lived strenuously in the public spotlight, surviving plane crashes, shooting lions in Africa, machine gunning sharks at Key West, hunting Nazi submarines off the coast of Cuba (his home for twenty years), entering Paris in 1944 with the liberating American army. But behind his image of a machismo adventurer, which he did not disclaim, dwelt a perceptive moralist and a subtle observer of humanity.

Hills Like White Elephants

Hemingway's finest short stories have had an enduring popularity. "Hills Like White Elephants," the last story he wrote for his collection *Men Without Women* (1927), is one of them. It exhibits the author's reluctance to discuss the feelings of his characters; instead, he lets us intuit these feelings from what the characters say. Much of the story is therefore told in dialogue — a means of narration often found in fiction, less often in essays. Novelist Ford Maddox Ford once tried to sum up the celebrated Hemingway style: "Hemingway's words strike you, each one, as if they were pebbles fetched fresh from a brook. They live and shine, each in its place." This style is evident especially in descriptive passages, such as the opening paragraph of this story.

The hills across the valley of the Ebro were long and white.   1
On this side there was no shade and no trees and the station was between two lines of rails in the sun. Close against the side of the station there was the warm shadow of the building and a curtain, made of strings of bamboo beads, hung across the open door into the bar, to keep out flies. The American and the girl with him sat at a table in the shade, outside the building. It was very hot and the express from Barcelona would come in forty minutes. It stopped at this junction for two minutes and went on to Madrid.

"What should we drink?" the girl asked. She had taken off her hat and put it on the table.

"It's pretty hot," the man said.

"Let's drink beer."

"Dos cervezas," the man said into the curtain.   5

"Big ones?" a woman asked from the doorway.

"Yes. Two big ones."

The woman brought two glasses of beer and two felt pads. She put the felt pads and the beer glasses on the table and looked at the man and the girl. The girl was looking off at the line of hills. They were white in the sun and the country was brown and dry.

"They look like elephants," she said.

"I've never seen one," the man drank his beer.   10

"No, you wouldn't have."

"I might have," the man said. "Just because you say I wouldn't have doesn't prove anything."

The girl looked at the bead curtain. "They've painted something on it," she said. "What does it say?"

"Anis del Toro. It's a drink."

"Could we try it?"   15

The man called "Listen" through the curtain. The woman came out from the bar.

"Four reales."

"We want two Anis del Toro."

"With water?"

"Do you want it with water?"   20

"I don't know," the girl said. "Is it good with water?"

"It's all right."

"You want them with water?" asked the woman.

"Yes, with water."

"It tastes like licorice," the girl said and put the glass down.   25

"That's the way with everything."

"Yes," said the girl. "Everything tastes of licorice. Especially all the things you've waited so long for, like absinthe."

"Oh, cut it out."

"You started it," the girl said. "I was being amused. I was having a fine time."

"Well, let's try and have a fine time."   30

"All right. I was trying. I said the mountains looked like white elephants. Wasn't that bright?"

"That was bright."

"I wanted to try this new drink. That's all we do, isn't it — look at things and try new drinks?"

"I guess so."

The girl looked across at the hills.   35

"They're lovely hills," she said. "They don't really look like white elephants. I just meant the coloring of their skin through the trees."

"Should we have another drink?"

"All right."

The warm wind blew the bead curtain against the table.

"The beer's nice and cool," the man said.   40

"It's lovely," the girl said.

"It's really an awfully simple operation, Jig," the man said. "It's not really an operation at all."

The girl looked at the ground the table legs rested on.

"I know you wouldn't mind it, Jig. It's really not anything. It's just to let the air in."

The girl did not say anything.   45

"I'll go with you and I'll stay with you all the time. They just let the air in and then it's all perfectly natural."

"Then what will we do afterward?"

"We'll be fine afterward. Just like we were before."

"What makes you think so?"

"That's the only thing that bothers us. It's the only thing   50
that's made us unhappy."

The girl looked at the bead curtain, put her hand out and took hold of two of the strings of beads.

"And you think then we'll be all right and be happy."

"I know we will. You don't have to be afraid. I've known lots of people that have done it."

"So have I," said the girl. "And afterward they were all so happy."

"Well," the man said, "if you don't want to you don't have   55
to. I wouldn't have you do it if you didn't want to. But I know it's perfectly simple."

"And you really want to?"

"I think it's the best thing to do. But I don't want you to do it if you don't really want to."

"And if I do it you'll be happy and things will be like they were and you'll love me?"

"I love you now. You know I love you."

"I know. But if I do it, then it will be nice again if I say things   60
are like white elephants, and you'll like it?"

"I'll love it. I love it now but I just can't think about it. You know how I get when I worry."

"If I do it you won't ever worry?"

"I won't worry about that because it's perfectly simple."

"Then I'll do it. Because I don't care about me."

"What do you mean?"   65

"I don't care about me."

"Well, I care about you."

"Oh, yes. But I don't care about me. And I'll do it and then everything will be fine."

"I don't want you to do it if you feel that way."

The girl stood up and walked to the end of the station. 70 Across, on the other side, were fields of grain and trees along the banks of the Ebro. Far away, beyond the river, were mountains. The shadow of a cloud moved across the field of grain and she saw the river through the trees.

"And we could have all this," she said. "And we could have everything and every day we make it more impossible."

"What did you say?"

"I said we could have everything."

"We can have everything."

"No, we can't." 75

"We can have the whole world."

"No, we can't."

"We can go everywhere."

"No, we can't. It isn't ours any more."

"It's ours." 80

"No, it isn't. And once they take it away, you never get it back."

"But they haven't taken it away."

"We'll wait and see."

"Come on back in the shade," he said. "You mustn't feel that way."

"I don't feel any way," the girl said. "I just know things." 85

"I don't want you to do anything that you don't want to do —— "

"Nor that isn't good for me," she said. "I know. Could we have another beer?"

"All right. But you've got to realize —— "

"I realize," the girl said. "Can't we maybe stop talking?"

They sat down at the table and the girl looked across at the 90 hills on the dry side of the valley and the man looked at her and at the table.

"You've got to realize," he said, "that I don't want you to do it if you don't want to. I'm perfectly willing to go through with it if it means anything to you."

"Doesn't it mean anything to you? We could get along."

"Of course it does. But I don't want anybody but you. I don't want anyone else. And I know it's perfectly simple."

"Yes, you know it's perfectly simple."

"It's all right for you to say that, but I do know it."   95

"Would you do something for me now?"

"I'd do anything for you."

"Would you please please please please please please please stop talking?"

He did not say anything but looked at the bags against the wall of the station. There were labels on them from all the hotels where they had spent nights.

"But I don't want you to," he said, "I don't care anything   100
about it."

"I'll scream," the girl said.

The woman came out through the curtains with two glasses of beer and put them down on the damp felt pads. "The train comes in five minutes," she said.

"What did she say?" asked the girl.

"That the train is coming in five minutes."

The girl smiled brightly at the woman, to thank her.   105

"I'd better take the bags over to the other side of the station," the man said. She smiled at him.

"All right. Then come back and we'll finish the beer."

He picked up the two heavy bags and carried them around the station to the other tracks. He looked up the tracks but could not see the train. Coming back, he walked through the barroom, where people waiting for the train were drinking. He drank an Anis at the bar and looked at the people. They were all waiting reasonably for the train. He went out through the bead curtain. She was sitting at the table and smiled at him.

"Do you feel better?" he asked.

"I feel fine," she said. "There's nothing wrong with me. I feel 110
fine."

QUESTIONS ON MEANING

1. What problem has arisen in this love affair? How does the woman's attitude toward it differ from or conflict with the man's?
2. In what speeches does either character seem to contradict herself or himself, to lie, or to try to gloss over unpleasant facts? Comment, for a start, on the man's remarks in paragraph 91 ("You've got to realize . . .").
3. Why, in paragraph 101, does the girl say, "I'll scream"?
4. Does the author remain completely aloof from this story? Do you have any sense, when you finish reading, that he sides with one character more than the other? Discuss.
5. How would you answer a reader who complained, "Nothing happens! There's no CONCLUSION! You call this a story?"

QUESTIONS ON WRITING STRATEGY

1. Comment on the effectiveness of Hemingway's setting this story in a hot, shadeless railroad station swarming with flies. Would the story have been improved if he had set it in a cool café surrounded by pleasant fountains?
2. From what POINT OF VIEW does Hemingway tell this story? Does he ever take us inside the minds of the characters, or does he remain outside, like an impartial observer or disinterested eavesdropper? Point to passages in the story itself to defend your answer.
3. Why is this point of view an effective means of storytelling? (Suggestion: Imagine the story told from a different POINT OF VIEW. Imagine it told, say, by the man, in the first person. Why would that radical change make for a poorer story?)
4. Much of the dialogue seems small talk about the weather, the refreshments, the surroundings. But what speeches seem full of suggestions? Consider, for instance, paragraph 27: "Everything tastes of licorice." What do you understand by this offhand remark?
5. Explain why the last line of the story — "I feel fine" — displays IRONY.

QUESTIONS ON LANGUAGE

1. What generalizations about Hemingway's STYLE and DICTION can you make from "Hills Like White Elephants"? Give examples.

2. How does the title of this story seem appropriate? What is a "white elephant"? What else in this story might seem a white elephant besides the hills?

SUGGESTIONS FOR WRITING

1. Hemingway has been charged with an inability to portray a convincing woman character, with an unsympathetic, machismo attitude toward women. In light of this charge, attack or defend "Hills Like White Elephants." How convincing is Jig in this story? How sympathetic is Hemingway's portrait of her?
2. Hemingway's way of telling a story has been called "cinematic." In two or three paragraphs, demonstrate why "Hills Like White Elephants" would be easy to translate to the screen.

Ernest Hemingway on Writing

"A country, finally, erodes and the dust blows away," Hemingway observed in *The Green Hills of Africa.* "The people all die and none of them were of any importance permanently, except those who practiced the arts." For him, good writing was the most vital art, and the most vital thing in the world.

But writing for Hemingway was hard work. A day's toil, according to his biographer Carlos Baker, would customarily leave him exhausted, after having produced no more than 500 or 600 words. "A writer's problem does not change," he once remarked. "He himself changes, but his problem remains the same. It is always how to write truly and, having found what is true, to project it in such a way that it becomes a part of the experience of the person who reads it." (Speech to the American Writer's Congress, New York, 1937.)

Hemingway rarely discussed his writing in public. "The book you talk about," he told a visitor, "is the one you don't write." But he gave many interviews and entertained many visitors; many of his ideas about writing are on record, and are quotable.

"I rewrite so much that the first chapter of a book may be rewritten forty or fifty times. . . . It's this way, see — when a writer first starts out, he gets a big kick from the stuff he does, and the reader doesn't get any; then, after a while, the writer gets a little kick and the reader gets a little kick; and, finally, if the writer's any good, he doesn't get any kick at all and the reader gets everything." (Conversation reported in *The New Yorker*, January 4, 1947.)

"When I am working on a book or a story I write every morning as soon after first light as possible. There is no one to disturb you and it is cool or cold and you come to your work and warm as you write. You read what you have written and, as you always stop when you know what is going to happen next, you go on from there. You write until you come to a place where you still have your juice and know what will happen next and you stop and try to live through until the next day when you hit it again. You have started at six in the morning, say, and may go on until noon or be through before that. When you stop you are as empty, and at the same time never empty but filling, as when you have made love to someone you love. Nothing can hurt you, nothing can happen, nothing means anything until the next day when you do it again. It is the wait until the next day that is hard to get through." (Interview with George Plimpton in *The Paris Review*, 1958.)

"The best way is always to stop when you are going good. If you do that you'll never be stuck. And don't think or worry about it until you start to write again the next day. That way your subconscious will be working on it all the time, but if you worry about it, your brain will get tired before you start again. But work every day. No matter what has happened the day or night before, get up and bite on the nail.

"When you walk into a room and you get a certain feeling or emotion, remember back until you see exactly what it was that gave you the emotion. Remember what the noises and smells were, and what was said. Then write it down, making it clear so the reader will see it too and have the same feeling you had.

And watch people, observe, try to put yourself in somebody else's head. If two men argue, don't just think who is right and who is wrong. Think what both their sides are. . . . You know who is right and who is wrong; you have to judge. As a writer, you should not judge, you should understand." (Quoted by Edward Stafford in "An Afternoon with Hemingway," *Writer's Digest*, 1964.)

FOR DISCUSSION

1. What drives Hemingway to rewrite the first chapter of a book as many as forty or fifty times?
2. Which seems more important to Hemingway's writing, the conscious mind or the unconscious? Give reasons for your answer.

· ADDITIONAL WRITING TOPICS ·
NARRATION

1. Write a narrative with one of the following as your subject. It may be (as your instructor may advise) either a first-person memoir, or a story written in the third person, observing the experience of someone else. Decide before you begin whether you are writing (1) an anecdote; (2) an essay consisting mainly of a single narrative; or (3) an essay that includes more than one story.

   A memorable experience from your early life
   A lesson you learned the hard way
   A trip into unfamiliar territory
   An embarrassing moment that taught you something
   A brush with death
   A monumental misunderstanding
   An accident
   An unexpected encounter
   A story about a famous person, or someone close to you
   A conflict or contest
   An assassination attempt
   A historic event of significance

2. Tell a true story of your early or recent school days, either humorous or serious, showing what a struggle school or college has been for you. (For comparable stories, see Thurber's "University Days" or, in Chapter 10, Richard Rodriguez's "Aria.")

2

DESCRIPTION

Writing with Your Senses

THE METHOD

Like narration, description is a familiar method of expression, already a working part of you. In any talk-fest with friends, you probably do your share of describing. You depict in words someone you've met by describing her clothes, the look on her face, the way she walks. You describe somewhere you've been, something you admire, something you just can't abide. In a diary or in a letter to a friend, you describe your college (cast concrete buildings, crowded walks, pigeons rattling their wings); or perhaps you describe your brand-new secondhand car, from the snakelike glitter of its hubcaps to the odd antiques in its trunk, bequeathed by its previous owner. You hardly can live a day without describing (or hearing described) some person, place, or thing. Small wonder that, in written discourse, description is almost as indispensable as paper.

Description reports the testimony of your senses. It invites your readers to imagine that they too not only see, but perhaps also hear, taste, smell, and touch the subject you describe. Usually, you write a description for either of two purposes: (1) to convey information without bias or emotion; or (2) to convey it with feeling.

In writing with the first purpose in mind, you write an *objective* (or *impartial, public,* or *functional*) description. You describe your subject so clearly and exactly that your reader will understand it or recognize it, and you leave your emotions out. Technical or scientific descriptive writing is usually objective: a manual detailing the parts of an internal combustion engine, a biologist's report of a previously unknown species of frog. You write this kind of description in sending a friend directions for finding your house ("Look for the green shutters on the windows and a new garbage can at the front door"). Although in a personal letter describing your house you might very well become emotionally involved with it (and call it, perhaps, a "fleabag"), in writing an objective description your purpose is not to convey your feelings. You are trying to make the house easily recognized.

The other type of descriptive writing is *subjective* (or *emotional, personal,* or *impressionistic*) description. This is the kind included in a magazine advertisement for a new car. It's what you write in your letter to a friend setting forth what your college is like — whether you are pleased or displeased with it. In this kind of description, you may use biases and personal feelings — in fact, they are essential. Let us consider a splendid example: a subjective description of a storm at sea. Charles Dickens, in his memoir *American Notes,* conveys his passenger's-eye view of an Atlantic steamship on a morning when the ocean is wild:

> Imagine the ship herself, with every pulse and artery of her huge body swollen and bursting . . . sworn to go on or die. Imagine the wind howling, the sea roaring, the rain beating; all in furious array against her. Picture the sky both dark

and wild, and the clouds in fearful sympathy with the waves, making another ocean in the air. Add to all this the clattering on deck and down below; the tread of hurried feet; the loud hoarse shouts of seamen; the gurgling in and out of water through the scuppers; with every now and then the striking of a heavy sea upon the planks above, with the deep, dead, heavy sound of thunder heard within a vault; and there is the head wind of that January morning.

    I say nothing of what may be called the domestic noises of the ship; such as the breaking of glass and crockery, the tumbling down of stewards, the gambols, overhead, of loose casks and truant dozens of bottled porter, and the very remarkable and far from exhilarating sounds raised in their various staterooms by the seventy passengers who were too ill to get up to breakfast.

Notice how many *sounds* are included in this primarily ear-minded description. We can infer how Dickens feels about the storm. It is a terrifying event that reduces the interior of the vessel to chaos; and yet the writer (in hearing the loose barrels and beer bottles merrily *gambol,* in finding humor in the seasick passengers' plight) apparently delights in it. Writing subjectively, he intrudes his feelings. Think of what a starkly different description of the very same storm the captain might set down — *objectively* — in the ship's log: "At 0600 hours, watch reported a wind from due north of 70 knots. Whitecaps were noticed, in height two ells above the bow. Below deck, much gear was reported adrift, and ten casks of ale were broken and their staves strewn about. Mr. Liam Jones, chief steward, suffered a compound fracture of the left leg. . . . " But Dickens, not content simply to record information, strives to ensure that the mind's eye is dazzled and the mind's ear regaled.

    Description is usually found in the company of other methods of writing. Often, for instance, it will enliven narration and make the people in the story and the setting unmistakably clear. Writing an argument in his essay "Why Don't We Complain?", William F. Buckley begins with a description of eighty suffering commuters perspiring in an overheated train; the description makes the argument more powerful. Description will help a writer in examining the effects of a flood, or in comparing and contrasting two towns. Keep the method of description in mind when you come to try expository and argumentative writing.

THE PROCESS

Understand, first of all, your purpose in writing a description. Are you going to write a subjective description, expressing your personal feelings? Or, instead, do you want to write an objective description, trying only to see and report, leaving out your emotions and biases?

Give a little thought to your audience. What do your readers need to be told, if they are to share the feelings you would have them share, if they are clearly to behold what you want them to? If, let's say, you are describing a downtown street on a Saturday night for an audience of fellow students who live in the same city and know it well, then you need not dwell on the street's familiar geography. What must you tell? Only those details that make the place different on a Saturday night. But if you are remembering your home city, and writing for readers who don't know it, you'll need to establish a few central landmarks to sketch (in their minds) an unfamiliar street on a Saturday night.

Before you begin to write a description, go look at your subject. If that is not possible, your next best course is to spend a few minutes imagining the subject until, in your mind's eye, you can see every flyspeck on it.

Then, having fixed your subject in mind, ask yourself which of its features you'll need to report to your particular audience, for your particular purpose. If you plan to write a subjective description of an old house, laying weight on its spooky atmosphere for readers you wish to make shiver, then you might mention its squeaking bats and its shadowy halls, leaving out any reference to its busy swimming pool and the stomping disco music that billows from its interior. If, however, you are describing the house in a classified ad, for an audience of possible buyers, you might focus instead on its eat-in kitchen, working fireplace, and proximity to public transportation. Details have to be carefully selected. Too many will blur the effect and only confuse your reader.

Let your description, as a whole, convey one dominant impression. (The swimming pool and the disco music might be details useful in a description meant to convey that the house is full of merriment.) Perhaps many details will be worth noticing; if so, you will want to arrange them so that your reader will see which matter most. In his description of the storm at sea — a subjective description — Charles Dickens sorts out the pandemonium for us. He groups the various sounds into two classes: those of sea and sailors, and the "domestic noises" of the ship's passengers — their smashing dishes, their rolling bottles, the crashing of stewards who wait on them. Like many effective descriptions, this one clearly reveals a principle of organization.

In organizing your description, you may find it helpful to be aware of your *point of view* — the physical angle from which you're perceiving and describing. In the previous chapter, on narration, we spoke of point of view: how essential it is for a story to have a narrator — one who, from a certain position, reports what takes place. A description, too, needs a consistent point of view: that of an observer who stays put and observes steadily. For instance, when describing a landscape as seen from the air, do not swoop suddenly to earth.

You can organize a description in several ways. Some writers, as they describe something, make a carefully planned inspection tour of its details, moving spatially (from left to right, from near to far, from top to bottom, from center to periphery), or perhaps moving from prominent objects to tiny ones, from dull to bright, from commonplace to extraordinary — or vice versa. The plan you choose is the one that best fulfills your purpose. If you were to describe, for instance, a chapel in the middle of a desert, you might begin with the details of the lonely terrain. Then, as if approaching the chapel with the aid of a zoom lens, you might detail its exterior and then go on inside. That might be a workable method to write a description *if* your purpose were to emphasize the sense that the chapel is an island of beauty and warmth in the midst of desolation. Say, however, that your purpose was quite different: to emphasize the interior

design of the chapel. You might then begin your description inside the structure, perhaps with its most prominent feature, the
stained glass windows. You might mention the surrounding desert later in your description, but only incidentally. An effective
description makes a definite impression. The writer arranges details so that the reader is firmly left with the feeling the writer intends to convey.

Whatever method you follow in arranging details, stick with
it all the way through. Don't start out describing a group of cats
by going from old cats to kittens, then switch in the middle of
your description and line up the cats according to color. If your
arrangement would cause any difficulty for the reader, you need
to rearrange your details. If a writer, in describing a pet shop,
should skip about wildly from clerks to cats to customers to cat
food to customers to cat food to clerks, the reader may quickly
be lost. Instead, the writer might group clerks together with customers, and cats together with cat food (or in some other clear
order). But suppose (the writer might protest) it's a wildly confused pet shop I'm trying to describe? No matter — the writer
nevertheless has to write in an orderly manner, if the reader is to
understand. Dickens describes a scene of shipboard chaos, yet
his prose is orderly.

Feel no grim duty to include every perceptible detail. To do
so would only invite chaos — or perhaps, for the reader, mere
tedium. Pick out the features that matter most. One revealing,
hard-to-forget detail (such as Dickens's truant porter bottles) is,
like a single masterly brush stroke, worth a whole coat of dull
paint. In selecting or discarding details, ask, What am I out to
accomplish? What main impression of my subject am I trying to
give?

Luckily, to write a memorable description, you don't need a
storm at sea or any other awe-inspiring subject. As E. B. White
demonstrates in his essay in this chapter, "Once More to the
Lake," you can write about a summer cabin on a lake as effectively as you can write about a tornado. Here is humorist S. J.
Perelman using metaphor to convey the garish brightness of a
certain low-rent, furnished house. Notice how he makes clear
the spirit of the place: "After a few days, I could have sworn that

our faces began to take on the hue of Kodachromes, and even the dog, an animal used to bizarre surroundings, developed a strange, off-register look, as if he were badly printed in overlapping colors."[1]

When you, too, write an effective description, you'll convey your sensory experience as exactly as possible. Find vigorous, specific words, and you will enable your reader to behold with the mind's eye — and to feel with the mind's fingertips.

DESCRIPTION IN A PARAGRAPH: TWO ILLUSTRATIONS

1. Using Description to Write about Television

At 2:59 this Monday afternoon, a thick hush settles like cigarette smoke inside the sweat-scented TV room of Harris Hall. First to arrive, freshman Lee Ann squashes down into the catbird seat in front of the screen. Soon she is flanked by roommates Lisa and Kate, silent, their mouths straight lines, their upturned faces lit by the nervous flicker of a detergent ad. To the left and right of the couch, Pete and Anse crouch on the floor, leaning forward like runners awaiting a starting gun. Behind them, stiff standees line up at attention. Farther back still, English majors and jocks compete for an unobstructed view. Fresh from class, shirttail flapping, arm crooking a bundle of books, Dave barges into the room demanding, "Has it started? Has it started yet?" He is shushed. Somebody shushes a popped-open can of Dr. Pepper whose fizz is distractingly loud. What do these students so intently look forward to — the announcement of World War III? A chord of music climbs and the screen dissolves to a title: "General Hospital."

COMMENT. Although in the end the anticipated mindblower turns out to be merely an installment of a gripping soap opera, the purpose of this description is to build one definite impression: that something vital is about to arrive. Details are

---

[1]"The Marx Brothers," in *The Last Laugh* (New York: Simon and Schuster, 1981), p. 152.

selected accordingly: *thick hush, nervous flicker,* people jostling one another for a better view. The watchers are portrayed as tense and expectant, their mouths straight lines, their faces up-turned, the men on the floor crouching forward. The chief appeal is to our visual imaginations, but a few details address our auditory imaginations (the fizz of a can of soda, people saying *Shhh-h-h!*) and our olfactory imaginations (*sweat-scented*).

In organizing this description, the writer's scrutiny moves outward from the television screen: first to the students immediately in front of it, then to those on either side, next to the second row, then to the third, and finally to the last anxious arrival. By this arrangement, the writer presents the details to the reader in a natural order. The main impression is enforced, since the TV screen is the center for all eyes.

2. Using Description in an Academic Discipline

While working on *The Battle of Anghiari,* Leonardo painted his most famous portrait, the *Mona Lisa.* The delicate *sfumato* already noted in the *Madonna of the Rocks* is here so perfected that it seemed miraculous to the artist's contemporaries. The forms are built from layers of glazes so gossamer-thin that the entire panel seems to glow with a gentle light from within. But the fame of the *Mona Lisa* comes not from this pictorial subtlety alone; even more intriguing is the psychological fascination of the sitter's personality. Why, among all the smiling faces ever painted, has this particular one been singled out as "mysterious"? Perhaps the reason is that, as a portrait, the picture does not fit our expectations. The features are too individual for Leonardo to have simply depicted an ideal type, yet the element of idealization is so strong that it blurs the sitter's character. Once again the artist has brought two opposites into harmonious balance. The smile, too, may be read in two ways: as the echo of a momentary mood, and as a timeless, symbolic expression (somewhat like the "Archaic smile" of the Greeks . . .). Clearly, the *Mona Lisa* embodies a quality of maternal tenderness which was to Leonardo the essence of womanhood. Even the landscape in the background, composed mainly of rocks and water, suggests elemental generative forces.

COMMENT. Taken from page 421 of H. W. Janson's *History of Art: A Survey of the Major Visual Arts from the Dawn of History to the Present Day* (New York: Harry N. Abrams, Inc., Publishers, 2nd Edition, 1979), this paragraph describes the world's most famous portrait in oils, the *Mona Lisa*. In a section of the book dealing with the achievement of Leonardo da Vinci, the author makes clear that this painting amply demonstrates the artist's genius. He does so by describing both the picture's subject and some of the painting techniques that bring it alive — the layering of glazes, the tension the viewer can discern between Mona Lisa the individual and Mona Lisa the ideal type. Note the words and phrases he uses that appeal to the senses: "delicate," "gossamer-thin," "glow with a gentle light." By directing the readers' attention to the painting's details, Janson has used description as a teaching tool of tremendous usefulness.

· Annie Dillard ·

ANNIE DILLARD is accomplished as a prose writer, poet, and literary critic. Born in 1945, she earned a B.A. (1967) and an M.A. (1968) from Hollins College in Virginia. She is now a contributing editor for *Harper's* and Adjunct Professor at Wesleyan University in Middletown, Connecticut. The author of six books of poetry and prose, she won a general nonfiction Pulitzer Prize for *Pilgrim at Tinker Creek* (1974), a work alive with close, intense, and poetic descriptions of the natural world. *Teaching a Stone to Talk* (1982), a collection of essays; *Encounters with Chinese Writers* (1984), narrative nonfiction; and *An American Childhood* (1987), an autobiographical memoir, are her most recent books.

Singing with the Fundamentalists

Early in life, Annie Dillard began training her powers of description. "When I worked as a detective in Pittsburgh," she recalls in *An American Childhood*, "(strictly freelance, because I was only ten years old), I drew suspects' faces from memory." These powers are evident in all her writing, including this remarkable essay, first published in 1985 in a literary and scholarly magazine, the *Yale Review*. In her fresh and unsimplified view of the college students she describes, Dillard, although not a Fundamentalist herself, writes with surprising empathy.

It is early spring. I have a temporary office at a state university on the West Coast. The office is on the third floor. It looks down on the Square, the enormous open courtyard at the center of the campus. From my desk I see hundreds of people moving between classes. There is a large circular fountain in the Square's center.

Early one morning, on the first day of spring quarter, I hear singing. A pack of students has gathered at the fountain. They are singing something which, at this distance, and through the heavy window, sounds good.

I know who these singing students are: they are the Funda- 3
mentalists. This campus has a lot of them. Mornings they sing on the Square; it is their only perceptible activity. What are they singing? Whatever it is, I want to join them, for I like to sing; whatever it is, I want to take my stand with them, for I am drawn to their very absurdity, their innocent indifference to what people think. My colleagues and students here, and my friends everywhere, dislike and fear Christian fundamentalists. You may never have met such people, but you've heard what they do: they pile up money, vote in blocs, and elect right-wing crazies; they censor books; they carry handguns; they fight fluoride in the drinking water and evolution in the schools; probably they would lynch people if they could get away with it. I'm not sure my friends are correct. I close my pen and join the singers on the Square.

There is a clapping song in progress. I have to concentrate to 4
follow it:

> Come on, rejoice,
> And let your heart sing,
> Come on, rejoice,
> Give praise to the king.
> Singing alleluia —
> He is the king of kings;
> Singing alleluia —
> He is the king of kings.

Two song leaders are standing on the broad rim of the fountain; the water is splashing just behind them. The boy is short, hard-faced, with a moustache. He bangs his guitar with the backs of his fingers. The blonde girl, who leads the clapping, is bouncy; she wears a bit of makeup. Both are wearing blue jeans.

The students beside me are wearing blue jeans too — and 5
athletic jerseys, parkas, football jackets, turtlenecks, and hiking shoes or jogging shoes. They all have canvas or nylon book bags. They look like any random batch of seventy or eighty students at this university. They are grubby or scrubbed, mostly scrubbed; they are tall, fair, or red-headed in large proportions.

Their parents are white-collar workers, blue-collar workers, farmers, loggers, orchardists, merchants, fishermen; their names are, I'll bet, Olsen, Jensen, Seversen, Hansen, Klokker, Sigurdsen.

Despite the vigor of the clapping song, no one seems to be giving it much effort. And no one looks at anyone else; there are no sentimental glances and smiles, no glances even of recognition. These kids don't seem to know each other. We stand at the fountain's side, out on the broad, bricked Square in front of the science building, and sing the clapping song through three times.

It is quarter to nine in the morning. Hundreds of people are crossing the Square. These passersby — faculty, staff, students — pay very little attention to us; this morning singing has gone on for years. Most of them look at us directly, then ignore us, for there is nothing to see; no animal sacrifices, no lynchings, no collection plate for Jesse Helms, no seizures, snake handling, healing, or glossolalia. There is barely anything to hear. I suspect the people glance at us to learn if we are really singing: How could so many people make so little sound? My fellow singers, who ignore each other, certainly ignore passersby as well. Within a week, most of them will have their eyes closed anyway.

We move directly to another song, a slower one.

> He is my peace
> Who has broken down every wall;
> He is my peace,
> He is my peace.
>
> Cast all your cares on him,
> For he careth for you — oo — oo
> He is my peace,
> He is my peace.

I am paying strict attention to the song leaders, for I am singing at the top of my lungs and I've never heard any of these songs before. They are not the old American low-church Protestant hymns; they are not the old European high-church Protestant hymns. These hymns seem to have been written just yesterday, apparently by the same people who put out lyrical Christian greeting cards and bookmarks.

"Where do these songs come from?" I ask a girl standing   10
next to me. She seems appalled to be addressed at all, and startled by the question. "They're from the praise albums!" she explains, and moves away.

The songs' melodies run dominant, subdominant, domi-   11
nant, tonic, dominant. The pace is slow, about the pace of "Tell
Laura I Love Her," and with that song's quavering, long notes.
The lyrics are simple and repetitive; there are very few of them
to which a devout Jew or Mohammedan could not give whole-
hearted assent. These songs are similar to the things Catholics
sing in church these days. I don't know if any studies have been
done to correlate the introduction of contemporary songs into
Catholic churches with those churches' decline in membership,
or with the phenomenon of Catholic converts' applying to enter
cloistered monasteries directly, without passing through parish
churches.

> I'm set free to worship,
> I'm set free to praise him,
> I'm set free to dance before the Lord . . .

At nine o'clock sharp we quit and scatter. I hear a few quiet   12
"see you"s. Mostly the students leave quickly, as if they didn't
want to be seen. The Square empties.

The next day we show up again, at twenty to nine. The   13
same two leaders stand on the fountain's rim; the fountain is
pouring down behind them.

After the first song, the boy with the moustache hollers,   14
"Move on up! Some of you guys aren't paying attention back
there! You're talking to each other. I want you to concentrate!"
The students laugh, embarrassed for him. He sounds like a
teacher. No one moves. The girl breaks into the next song,
which we join at once:

> In my life, Lord,
> Be glorified, be glorified, be glorified;
> In my life, Lord,
> Be glorified, be glorified, today.

At the end of this singularly monotonous verse, which is straining my tolerance for singing virtually anything, the boy with the
moustache startles me by shouting, "Classes!"

At once, without skipping a beat, we sing, "In my classes,   15
Lord, be glorified, be glorified . . . " I give fleet thought to the
class I'm teaching this afternoon. We're reading a little "Talk of
the Town" piece called "Eggbag," about a cat in a magic store on
Eighth Avenue. "Relationships!" the boy calls. The students
seem to sing "In my relationships, Lord," more easily than they
sang "classes." They seemed embarrassed by "classes." In fact, to
my fascination, they seemed embarrassed by almost everything.
Why are they here? I will sing with the Fundamentalists every
weekday morning all spring; I will decide, tentatively, that they
come pretty much for the same reasons I do: Each has a private
relationship with "the Lord" and will put up with a lot of junk
for it.

I have taught some Fundamentalist students here, and know   16
a bit of what they think. They are college students above all,
worried about their love lives, their grades, and finding jobs.
Some support moderate Democrats; some support moderate Republicans. Like their classmates, most support nuclear freeze,
ERA, and an end to the draft. I believe they are divided on
abortion and busing. They are not particularly political. They
read *Christianity Today* and *Campus Life* and *Eternity* — moderate, sensible magazines, I think; they read a lot of C. S. Lewis.
(One such student, who seemed perfectly tolerant of me and my
shoddy Christianity, introduced me to C. S. Lewis's critical
book on Charles Williams.) They read the Bible. I think they all
"believe in" organic evolution. The main thing about them is
this: There isn't any "them." Their views vary. They don't know
each other.

Their common Christianity puts them, if anywhere, to the   17
left of their classmates. I believe they also tend to be more able
than their classmates to think well in the abstract, and also to
recognize the complexity of moral issues. But I may be wrong.

In 1980, the media were certainly wrong about television   18
evangelists. Printed estimates of Jerry Falwell's television audi-

ence ranged from 18 million to 30 million people. In fact, according to Arbitron's actual counts, fewer than 1.5 million people were watching Falwell. And, according to an Emory University study, those who did watch television evangelists didn't necessarily vote with them. Emory University sociologist G. Melton Mobley reports, "When that message turns political, they cut it off." Analysis of the 1982 off-year election turned up no Fundamentalist bloc voting. The media were wrong, but no one printed retractions.

The media were wrong, too, in a tendency to identify all   19 fundamentalist Christians with Falwell and his ilk, and to attribute to them, across the board, conservative views.

Someone has sent me two recent issues of *Eternity: The Evan-*   20 *gelical Monthly*. One lead article criticizes a television preacher for saying that the United States had never used military might to take land from another nation. The same article censures Newspeak, saying that government rhetoric would have us believe in a "clean bomb," would have us believe that we "defend" America by invading foreign soil, and would have us believe that the dictatorships we support are "democracies." "When the President of the United States says that one reason to support defense spending is because it creates jobs," this lead article says, "a little bit of *1984*[1] begins to surface." Another article criticizes a "heavy-handed" opinion of Jerry Falwell Ministries — in this case a broadside attack on artificial insemination, surrogate motherhood, and lesbian motherhood. Browsing through *Eternity*, I find a double crosstic.[2] I find an intelligent, analytical, and enthusiastic review of the new London Philharmonic recording of Mahler's second symphony — a review which stresses the "glorious truth" of the Jewish composer's magnificent work, and cites its recent performance in Jerusalem to celebrate the recapture of the Western Wall following the Six Day War. Surely, the evangelical Christians who read this magazine are not book-burners. If by chance they vote with the magazine's editors, then

---

[1]George Orwell's novel depicting a totalitarian state whose economy depends on war. — EDS.

[2]A difficult and demanding form of crossword puzzle. — EDS.

it looks to me as if they vote with the American Civil Liberties Union and Americans for Democratic Action.

Every few years some bold and sincere Christian student at this university disagrees with a professor in class — usually about the professor's out-of-hand dismissal of Christianity. Members of the faculty, outraged, repeat the stories of these rare and uneven encounters for years on end, as if to prove that the crazies are everywhere, and gaining ground. The notion is, apparently, that these kids can't think for themselves. Or they wouldn't disagree.

Now again the moustached leader asks us to move up. There is no harangue, so we move up. (This will be a theme all spring. The leaders want us closer together. Our instinct is to stand alone.) From behind the tall fountain comes a wind; on several gusts we get sprayed. No one seems to notice.

We have time for one more song. The leader, perhaps sensing that no one likes him, blunders on. "I want you to pray this one through," he says. "We have a lot of people here from a lot of different fellowships, but we're all one body. Amen?" They don't like it. He gets a few polite Amens. We sing:

> Bind us together, Lord,
> With a bond that can't be broken;
> Bind us together, Lord,
> With love.

Everyone seems to be in a remarkably foul mood today. We don't like this song. There is no one here under seventeen, and, I think, no one here who believes that love is a bond that can't be broken. We sing the song through three times; then it is time to go.

The leader calls after our retreating backs, "Hey, have a good day! Praise Him all day!" The kids around me roll up their eyes privately. Some groan; all flee.

The next morning is very cold. I am here early. Two girls are talking on the fountain's rim; one is part Indian. She says, "I've got the Old Testament, but I can't get the New. I screw up the New." She takes a breath and rattles off a long list, ending with

"Jonah, Micah, Nahum, Habakkuk, Zephaniah, Haggai, Zechariah, Malachi." The other girl produces a slow, sarcastic applause. I ask one of the girls to help me with the words to a song. She is agreeable, but says, "I'm sorry, I can't. I just became a Christian this year, so I don't know all the words yet."

The others are coming; we stand and separate. The boy with 26 the moustache is gone, replaced by a big, serious fellow in a green down jacket. The bouncy girl is back with her guitar; she's wearing a skirt and wool knee socks. We begin, without any preamble, by singing a song that has so few words that we actually stretch one syllable over eleven separate notes. Then we sing a song in which the men sing one phrase and the women echo it. Everyone seems to know just what to do. In the context of our vapid songs, the lyrics of this one are extraordinary:

> I was nothing before you found me.
> Heartache! Broken people! Ruined lives
> Is why you died on Calvary.

The last line rises in a regular series of half-notes. Now at last some people are actually singing; they throw some breath into the business. There is a seriousness and urgency to it: "Heartache! Broken people! Ruined lives . . . I was nothing."

We don't look like nothing. We look like a bunch of stu- 27 dents of every stripe, ill-shaven or well-shaven, dressed up or down, but dressed warmly against the cold: jeans and parkas, jeans and heavy sweaters, jeans and scarves and blow-dried hair. We look ordinary. But I think, quite on my own, that we are here because we know this business of nothingness, brokenness, and ruination. We sing this song over and over.

Something catches my eye. Behind us, up in the science 28 building, professors are standing alone at opened windows.

The long brick science building has three upper floors of fac- 29 ulty offices, thirty-two windows. At one window stands a bearded man, about forty; his opening his window is what caught my eye. He stands full in the open window, his hands on his hips, his head cocked down toward the fountain. He is drawn to look, as I was drawn to come. Up on the building's top floor, at the far right window, there is another: An Asian-American professor, wearing a white shirt, is sitting with one hip on his desk, looking out and down. In the middle of the row of windows, another one, an old professor in a checked shirt, stands sideways to the open window, stands stock-still, his long, old ear to the air. Now another window cranks open, another professor—or maybe a graduate student — leans out, his hands on the sill.

We are all singing, and I am watching these five still men,   30
my colleagues, whose office doors are surely shut — for that is the custom here: five of them alone in their offices in the science building who have opened their windows on this very cold morning, who motionless hear the Fundamentalists sing, utterly unknown to each other.

We sing another four songs, including the clapping song,   31
and one which repeats, "This is the day which the Lord hath made; rejoice and be glad in it." All the professors but one stay by their opened windows, figures in a frieze. When after ten minutes we break off and scatter, each cranks his window shut. Maybe they have nine o'clock classes too.

I miss a few sessions. One morning of the following week, I   32
rejoin the Fundamentalists on the Square. The wind is blowing from the north; it is sunny and cold. There are several new developments.

Someone has blown up rubber gloves and floated them in   33
the fountain. I saw them yesterday afternoon from my high office window, and couldn't quite make them out: I seemed to see hands in the fountain waving from side to side, like those hands wagging on springs which people stick in the back windows of their cars. I saw these many years ago in Quito and Guayaquil, where they were a great fad long before they showed up here. The cardboard hands said, on their palms, HOLA GENTE, hello people. Some of them just said HOLA, hello, with a little wave to the universe at large, in case anybody happened to be looking. It is like sending radio signals to planets in other galaxies: HOLA, if anyone is listening. Jolly folk, these Ecuadorians, I thought.

Now, waiting by the fountain for the singing, I see that these   34
particular hands are long surgical gloves, yellow and white, ten of them tied off at the cuff. They float upright and they wave,

hola, hola, hola; they mill around like a crowd, bobbing under the fountain's spray and back again to the pool's rim, *hola.* It is a good prank. It is far too cold for the university's maintenance crew to retrieve them without turning off the fountain and putting on rubber boots.

From all around the Square, people are gathering for the singing. There is no way I can guess which kids, from among the masses crossing the Square, will veer off to the fountain. When they get here, I never recognize anybody except the leaders.   35

The singing begins without ado as usual, but there is something different about it. The students are growing prayerful, and they show it this morning with a peculiar gesture. I'm glad they weren't like this when I first joined them, or I never would have stayed.   36

Last night there was an educational television special, part of "Middletown." It was a segment called "Community of Praise," and I watched it because it was about Fundamentalists. It showed a Jesus-loving family in the Midwest; the treatment was good and complex. This family attended the prayer meetings, healing sessions, and church services of an unnamed sect — a very low-church sect, whose doctrine and culture were much more low-church than those of the kids I sing with. When the members of this sect prayed, they held their arms over their heads and raised their palms, as if to feel or receive a blessing or energy from above.   37

Now today on the Square there is a new serious mood. The leaders are singing with their eyes shut. I am impressed that they can bang their guitars, keep their balance, and not fall into the pool. It is the same bouncy girl and earnest boy. Their eyeballs are rolled back a bit. I look around and see that almost everyone in this crowd of eighty or so has his eyes shut and is apparently praying the words of this song or praying some other prayer.   38

Now as the chorus rises, as it gets louder and higher and simpler in melody —   39

> I exalt thee,
> I exalt thee,
> I exalt thee,
> Thou art the Lord —

then, at this moment, hands start rising. All around me, hands are going up — that tall girl, that blond boy with his head back, the red-headed boy up front, the girl with the MacDonald's jacket. Their arms rise as if pulled on strings. Some few of them have raised their arms very high over their heads and are tilting back their palms. Many, many more of them, as inconspicuously as possible, have raised their hands to the level of their chins.

What is going on? Why are these students today raising   40
their palms in this gesture, when nobody did it last week? Is it because the leaders have set a prayerful tone this morning? Is it because this gesture always accompanies this song, just as clapping accompanies other songs? Or is it, as I suspect, that these kids watched the widely publicized documentary last night just as I did, and are adopting, or trying out, the gesture?

It is a sunny morning, and the sun is rising behind the lead-   41
ers and the fountain, so those students have their heads tilted, eyes closed, and palms upraised toward the sun. I glance up at the science building and think my own prayer: Thank God no one is watching this.

The leaders cannot move around much on the fountain's   42
rim. The girl has her eyes shut; the boy opens his eyes from time to time, glances at the neck of his guitar, and closes his eyes again.

When the song is over, the hands go down, and there is   43
some desultory chatting in the crowd, as usual: Can I borrow your library card? And, as usual, nobody looks at anybody.

All our songs today are serious. There is a feudal theme to   44
them, or a feudal analogue:

> I will eat from abundance of your household.
> I will dream beside your streams of righteousness.
>
> You are my king.
>
> Enter his gates
> with thanksgiving in your heart;
> come before his courts with praise.
>
> He is the king of kings.
>
> Thou art the Lord.

All around me, eyes are closed and hands are raised. There   45
is no social pressure to do this, or anything else. I've never
known any group to be less cohesive, imposing fewer controls.
Since no one looks at anyone, and since passersby no longer
look, everyone out here is inconspicuous and free. Perhaps the
palm-raising has begun because the kids realize by now that they
are not on display; they're praying in their closets, right out here
on the Square. Over the course of the next weeks, I will learn
that the palm-raising is here to stay.

The sun is rising higher. We are singing our last song. We   46
are praying. We are alone together.

> He is my peace
> Who has broken down every wall . . .

When the song is over, the hands go down. The heads   47
lower, the eyes open and blink. We stay still a second before we
break up. We have been standing in a broad current; now we
have stepped aside. We have dismantled the radar cups; we have
closed the telescope's vault. Students gather their book bags and
go. The two leaders step down from the fountain's rim and pack
away their guitars. Everyone scatters. I am in no hurry, so I stay
after everyone is gone. It is after nine o'clock, and the Square is
deserted. The fountain is playing to an empty house. In the pool
the cheerful hands are waving over the water, bobbing under
the fountain's veil and out again in the current, *hola*.

QUESTIONS ON MEANING

1. What reasons does Dillard give for her decision to join the Fundamentalist students in their singing sessions?
2. What qualities does the author emphasize in her description of the
   students?
3. What is Dillard's main point in paragraph 11? How does paragraph 26 develop the point?
4. Explain the Fundamentalist students' reactions to their moustached leader.
5. To what extent is Dillard's essay more than simple description? See
   especially paragraphs 3 and 16–21.

QUESTIONS ON WRITING STRATEGY

1. What is the basic organization of Dillard's essay? Where does the author vary this organization?
2. Is the essay written mainly from an observer's or a participant's POINT OF VIEW? Give EVIDENCE for your answer.
3. Where in her account does the author include touches of humor?
4. How much knowledge of Christian Fundamentalists does Dillard expect of her readers? How much did Dillard herself need to write "Singing with the Fundamentalists"?

QUESTIONS ON LANGUAGE

1. If necessary, look up the following words in your dictionary: perceptible (paragraph 3); seizures, glossolalia (7); appalled (10); dominant, subdominant, tonic, cloistered (11); tentatively (15); shoddy (16); complexity (17); ilk (19); censures, rhetoric, analytical, evangelical (20); harangue (22); preamble, vapid (26); frieze (31); inconspicuously (39); desultory (43); feudal, analogue (44).
2. What exactly *is* a Fundamentalist?
3. In paragraph 16, Dillard puts quotation marks around the phrase "believe in." Would the sentence have been better or worse without them? Explain.
4. What, in paragraph 20, does the author mean by "Newspeak"?

SUGGESTIONS FOR WRITING

1. Like Dillard, write an essay correcting the false impression you believe most people have concerning a group you know something about. Suggestions to start you thinking: members of the army, navy, or marines; single-parent families; adolescent moviegoers; housewives or househusbands; ballet dancers; motorcyclists; fraternity or sorority members.
2. Go somewhere — the student union, a bus terminal, a dining hall, a park, to name a few possibilities — where you can observe your fellow human beings. While you watch, write a paragraph or two describing what the people around you have in common.

Annie Dillard on Writing

"Description's not too hard," according to Annie Dillard, "if you mind your active verbs, keep ticking off as many sense impressions as you can, and omit feelings." In descriptive writing, apparently, she believes in paying attention first of all to the world outside herself.

Writing for *The Bedford Reader*, Dillard has testified to her work habits. Rarely satisfied with an essay until it has gone through many drafts, she sometimes goes on correcting and improving it even after it has been published. "I always have to condense or toss openings," she affirms; "I suspect most writers do. When you begin something, you're so grateful to have begun you'll write down anything, just to prolong the sensation. Later, when you've learned what the writing is really about, you go back and throw away the beginning and start over."

Often she replaces a phrase or sentence with a shorter one. In one essay, to tell how a drop of pond water began to evaporate on a microscope slide, she first wrote, "Its contours pulled together." But that sentence seemed to suffer from "tortured abstraction." She made the sentence read instead, "Its edges shrank." Dillard observes, "I like short sentences. They're forceful, and they can get you out of big trouble."

FOR DISCUSSION

1. Why, according to Dillard, is it usually necessary for writers to revise the opening paragraphs of what they write?
2. Dillard says that short sentences "can get you out of big trouble." What kinds of "big trouble" do you suppose she means?

· E. B. White ·

ELWYN BROOKS WHITE (1899–1985) for half a century was a regular contributor to *The New Yorker*, and his essays, editorials, anonymous features for "The Talk of the Town," and fillers helped build the magazine a reputation for wit and good writing. If as a child you read *Charlotte's Web* (1952), you have met E. B. White before. The book reflects some of his own life on a farm in North Brooklin, Maine. His *Letters* were collected in 1976, his *Essays* in 1977, and his *Poems and Sketches* in 1981. On July 4, 1963, President Kennedy named White in the first group of Americans to receive the Presidential Medal of Freedom, with a citation that called him "an essayist whose concise comment on men and places has revealed to yet another age the vigor of the English sentence."

Once More to the Lake

"The essayist," says White in a foreword to his *Essays*, "is a self-liberated man, sustained by the childish belief that everything he thinks about, everything that happens to him, is of general interest." In White's case this belief is soundly justified. Perhaps if a duller writer had written "Once More to the Lake," or an essay by that title, we wouldn't much care about it, for at first its subject seems as personal, flat, and ordinary as a letter home. White's loving and exact description, however, brings this lakeside camp to life for us. In the end, the writer arrives at an awareness that shocks him — shocks us, too, by a familiar sensory detail in the last line.

August 1941

One summer, along about 1904, my father rented a camp on a lake in Maine and took us all there for the month of August. We all got ringworm from some kittens and had to rub Pond's Extract on our arms and legs night and morning, and my father rolled over in a canoe with all his clothes on; but outside of that the vacation was a success and from then on none of us ever thought there was any place in the world like that lake in Maine. We returned summer after summer — always on August 1 for one month. I have since become a salt-water man, but sometimes in summer there are days when the restlessness of the tides and the fearful cold of the sea water and the incessant wind that blows across the afternoon and into the evening make me wish for the placidity of a lake in the woods. A few weeks ago this feeling got so strong I bought myself a couple of bass hooks and a spinner and returned to the lake where we used to go, for a week's fishing and to revisit old haunts.

I took along my son, who had never had any fresh water up 2 his nose and who had seen lily pads only from train windows. On the journey over to the lake I began to wonder what it would be like. I wondered how time would have marred this unique, this holy spot — the coves and streams, the hills that the sun set behind, the camps and the paths behind the camps. I was sure that the tarred road would have found it out, and I wondered in what other ways it would be desolated. It is strange how much you can remember about places like that once you allow your mind to return into the grooves that lead back. You remember one thing, and that suddenly reminds you of another thing. I guess I remembered clearest of all the early mornings, when the lake was cool and motionless, remembered how the bedroom smelled of the lumber it was made of and of the wet woods whose scent entered through the screen. The partitions in the camp were thin and did not extend clear to the top of the rooms, and as I was always the first up I would dress softly so as not to wake the others, and sneak out into the sweet outdoors and start out in the canoe, keeping close along the shore in the long shadows of the pines. I remembered being very careful never to rub my paddle against the gunwale for fear of disturbing the stillness of the cathedral.

The lake had never been what you would call a wild lake. 3 There were cottages sprinkled around the shores, and it was in farming country although the shores of the lake were quite heavily wooded. Some of the cottages were owned by nearby farmers, and you would live at the shore and eat your meals at the farmhouse. That's what our family did. But although it wasn't wild, it was a fairly large and undisturbed lake and there were places in it that, to a child at least, seemed infinitely remote and primeval.

I was right about the tar: it led to within half a mile of the shore. But when I got back there, with my boy, and we settled into a camp near a farmhouse and into the kind of summertime I had known, I could tell that it was going to be pretty much the same as it had been before — I knew it, lying in bed the first morning smelling the bedroom and hearing the boy sneak quietly out and go off along the shore in a boat. I began to sustain the illusion that he was I, and therefore, by simple transposition, that I was my father. This sensation persisted, kept cropping up all the time we were there. It was not an entirely new feeling, but in this setting it grew much stronger. I seemed to be living a dual existence. I would be in the middle of some simple act, I would be picking up a bait box or laying down a table fork, or I would be saying something and suddenly it would be not I but my father who was saying the words or making the gesture. It gave me a creepy sensation.

We went fishing the first morning. I felt the same damp moss covering the worms in the bait can, and saw the dragonfly alight on the tip of my rod as it hovered a few inches from the surface of the water. It was the arrival of this fly that convinced me beyond any doubt that everything was as it always had been, that the years were a mirage and that there had been no years. The small waves were the same, chucking the rowboat under the chin as we fished at anchor, and the boat was the same boat, the same color green and the ribs broken in the same places, and under the floorboards the same fresh water leavings and débris — the dead hellgrammite, the wisps of moss, the rusty discarded fishhook, the dried blood from yesterday's catch. We stared silently at the tips of our rods, at the dragonflies that came and went. I lowered the tip of mine into the water, tentatively, pensively dislodging the fly, which darted two feet away, poised, darted two feet back, and came to rest again a little farther up the rod. There had been no years between the ducking of this dragonfly and the other one — the one that was part of memory. I looked at the boy, who was silently watching his fly, and it was my hands that held his rod, my eyes watching. I felt dizzy and didn't know which rod I was at the end of.

We caught two bass, hauling them in briskly as though they were mackerel, pulling them over the side of the boat in a businesslike manner without any landing net, and stunning them with a blow on the back of the head. When we got back for a swim before lunch, the lake was exactly where we had left it, the same number of inches from the dock, and there was only the merest suggestion of a breeze. This seemed an utterly enchanted sea, this lake you could leave to its own devices for a few hours and come back to, and find that it had not stirred, this constant and trustworthy body of water. In the shallows, the dark, water-soaked sticks and twigs, smooth and old, were undulating in clusters on the bottom against the clean ribbed sand, and the track of the mussel was plain. A school of minnows swam by, each minnow with its small individual shadow, doubling the attendance, so clear and sharp in the sunlight. Some of the other campers were in swimming, along the shore, one of them with a cake of soap, and the water felt thin and clear and unsubstantial. Over the years there had been this person with the cake of soap, this cultist, and here he was. There had been no years.

Up to the farmhouse to dinner through the teeming dusty field, the road under our sneakers was only a two-track road. The middle track was missing, the one with the marks of the hooves and the splotches of dried, flaky manure. There had always been three tracks to choose from in choosing which track to walk in; now the choice was narrowed down to two. For a moment I missed terribly the middle alternative. But the way led past the tennis court, and something about the way it lay there in the sun reassured me; the tape had loosened along the backline, the alleys were green with plantains and other weeds, and the net (installed in June and removed in September) sagged in the dry noon, and the whole place steamed with midday heat and hunger and emptiness. There was a choice of pie for dessert, and one was blueberry and one was apple, and the waitresses were the same country girls, there having been no passage of time, only the illusion of it as in a dropped curtain — the waitresses were still fifteen; their hair had been washed, that was the only difference — they had been to the movies and seen the pretty girls with the clean hair.

Summertime, oh, summertime, pattern of life indelible with fade-proof lake, the wood unshatterable, the pasture with the sweetfern and the juniper forever and ever, summer without end; this was the background, and the life along the shore was the design, the cottages with their innocent and tranquil design, their tiny docks with the flagpole and the American flag floating against the white clouds in the blue sky, the little paths over the roots of the trees leading from camp to camp and the paths leading back to the outhouses and the can of lime for sprinkling, and at the souvenir counters at the store the miniature birchbark canoes and the postcards that showed things looking a little better than they looked. This was the American family at play, escaping the city heat, wondering whether the newcomers in the camp at the head of the cove were "common" or "nice," wondering whether it was true that the people who drove up for Sunday dinner at the farmhouse were turned away because there wasn't enough chicken.

It seemed to me, as I kept remembering all this, that those times and those summers had been infinitely precious and worth saving. There had been jollity and peace and goodness. The arriving (at the beginning of August) had been so big a business in itself, at the railway station the farm wagon drawn up, the first smell of the pine-laden air, the first glimpse of the smiling farmer, and the great importance of the trunks and your father's enormous authority in such matters, and the feel of the wagon under you for the long ten-mile haul, and at the top of the last long hill catching the first view of the lake after eleven months of not seeing this cherished body of water. The shouts and cries of the other campers when they saw you, and the trunks to be unpacked, to give up their rich burden. (Arriving was less exciting nowadays, when you sneaked up in your car and parked it under a tree near the camp and took out the bags and in five minutes it was all over, no fuss, no loud wonderful fuss about trunks.)

Peace and goodness and jollity. The only thing that was wrong now, really, was the sound of the place, an unfamiliar nervous sound of the outboard motors. This was the note that jarred, the one thing that would sometimes break the illusion and set the years moving. In those other summertimes all motors were inboard; and when they were at a little distance, the noise they made was a sedative, an ingredient of summer sleep. They were one-cylinder and two-cylinder engines, and some were make-and-break and some were jump-spark, but they all made a sleepy sound across the lake. The one-lungers throbbed and fluttered, and the twin-cylinder ones purred and purred, and that was a quiet sound, too. But now the campers all had outboards. In the daytime, in the hot mornings, these motors made a petulant, irritable sound; at night in the still evening when the afterglow lit the water, they whined about one's ears like mosquitoes. My boy loved our rented outboard, and his great desire was to achieve single-handed mastery over it, and authority, and he soon learned the trick of choking it a little (but not too much), and the adjustment of the needle valve. Watching him I would remember the things you could do with the old one-cylinder engine with the heavy flywheel, how you could have it eating out of your hand if you got really close to it spiritually. Motorboats in those days didn't have clutches, and you would make a landing by shutting off the motor at the proper time and coasting in with a dead rudder. But there was a way of reversing them, if you learned the trick, by cutting the switch and putting it on again exactly on the final dying revolution of the flywheel, so that it would kick back against compression and begin reversing. Approaching a dock in a strong following breeze, it was difficult to slow up sufficiently by the ordinary coasting method, and if a boy felt he had complete mastery over his motor, he was tempted to keep it running beyond its time and then reverse it a few feet from the dock. It took a cool nerve, because if you threw the switch a twentieth of a second too soon you would catch the flywheel when it still had speed enough to go up past center, and the boat would leap ahead, charging bull-fashion at the dock.

We had a good week at the camp. The bass were biting well and the sun shone endlessly, day after day. We would be tired at night and lie down in the accumulated heat of the little bed-

11

rooms after the long hot day and the breeze would stir almost imperceptibly outside and the smell of the swamp drift in through the rusty screens. Sleep would come easily and in the morning the red squirrel would be on the roof, tapping out his gay routine. I kept remembering everything, lying in bed in the mornings — the small steamboat that had a long rounded stern like the lip of a Ubangi, and how quietly she ran on the moonlight sails, when the older boys played their mandolins and the girls sang and we ate doughnuts dipped in sugar, and how sweet the music was on the water in the shining night, and what it had felt like to think about girls then. After breakfast we would go up to the store and the things were in the same place — the minnows in a bottle, the plugs and spinners disarranged and pawed over by the youngsters from the boys' camp, the Fig Newtons and the Beeman's gum. Outside, the road was tarred and cars stood in front of the store. Inside, all was just as it had always been, except there was more Coca-Cola and not so much Moxie and root beer and birch beer and sarsaparilla. We would walk out with the bottle of pop apiece and sometimes the pop would backfire up our noses and hurt. We explored the streams, quietly, where the turtles slid off the sunny logs and dug their way into the soft bottom; and we lay on the town wharf and fed worms to the tame bass. Everywhere we went I had trouble making out which was I, the one walking at my side, the one walking in my pants.

One afternoon while we were at that lake a thunderstorm came up. It was like the revival of an old melodrama that I had seen long ago with childish awe. The second-act climax of the drama of the electrical disturbance over a lake in America had not changed in any important respect. This was the big scene, still the big scene. The whole thing was so familiar, the first feeling of oppression and heat and a general air around camp of not wanting to go very far away. In midafternoon (it was all the same) a curious darkening of the sky, and a lull in everything that had made life tick; and then the way the boats suddenly swung the other way at their moorings with the coming of a breeze out of the new quarter, and the premonitory rumble. Then the kettle drum, then the snare, then the bass drum and cymbals, then crackling light against the dark, and the gods grinning and licking their chops in the hills. Afterward the calm, the rain steadily rustling in the calm lake, the return of light and hope and spirits, and the campers running out in joy and relief to go swimming in the rain, their bright cries perpetuating the deathless joke about how they were getting simply drenched, and the children screaming with delight at the new sensation of bathing in the rain, and the joke about getting drenched linking the generations in a strong indestructible chain. And the comedian who waded in carrying an umbrella.

When the others went swimming my son said he was going in, too. He pulled his dripping trunks from the line where they had hung all through the shower and wrung them out. Languidly, and with no thought of going in, I watched him, his hard little body, skinny and bare, saw him wince slightly as he pulled up around his vitals the small, soggy, icy garment. As he buckled the swollen belt, suddenly my groin felt the chill of death.   13

QUESTIONS ON MEANING

1. When E. B. White takes his son to the summer place he himself had loved as a child, what changes does he find there? What things have stayed the same?
2. How do you account for the distortions that creep into the author's sense of time?
3. What does the discussion of inboard and outboard motors (paragraph 10) have to do with the author's divided sense of time?
4. What do you take to be White's main PURPOSE in this essay? At what point do you become aware of it?

QUESTIONS ON WRITING STRATEGY

1. To what degree does White make us aware of the impression that this trip to the lake makes on his son?
2. In paragraph 4, the author first introduces his confused feeling that he has gone back in time to his own childhood, an idea that he repeats and expands throughout his account. What is the function of these repetitions?

3. Try to describe the impact of the essay's final paragraph. By what means is it achieved?
4. To what extent is this essay written to appeal to any but middle-aged readers? Is it comprehensible to anyone whose vacations were never spent at a Maine summer cottage?
5. What is the TONE of White's essay?

QUESTIONS ON LANGUAGE

1. Be sure you know the meanings of the following words: incessant, placidity (paragraph 1); gunwale (2); primeval (3); transposition (4); hellgrammite (5); undulating, cultist (6); indelible, tranquil (8); petulant (10); imperceptibly (11); premonitory (12); languidly (13).
2. Comment on White's DICTION in his reference to the lake as "this unique, this holy spot" (paragraph 2).
3. Explain what White is describing in the sentence that begins, "Then the kettle drum . . . " (paragraph 12). Where else does the author use METAPHORS?
4. Where in his essay does White use IMAGES effectively?

SUGGESTIONS FOR WRITING

1. In a descriptive paragraph, try to appeal to each of your reader's five senses.
2. Describe in a brief essay a place you loved as a child. Or, if you have ever returned to a favorite old haunt, describe the experience. Was it pleasant or painful — or both? What, exactly, made it so?

E. B. White on Writing

"You asked me about writing — how I did it," E. B. White replied to a seventeen-year-old who had written to him, wanting to become a professional writer but feeling discouraged. "There is no trick to it. If you like to write and want to write, you write, no matter where you are or what else you are doing or whether anyone pays any heed. I must have written half a million words (mostly in my journal) before I had anything published, save for a couple of short items in *St. Nicholas*.[1] If you want to write about feelings, about the end of the summer, about growing, write about it. A great deal of writing is not 'plotted' — most of my essays have no plot structure, they are a ramble in the woods, or a ramble in the basement of my mind. You ask, 'Who cares?' Everybody cares. You say, 'It's been written before.' Everything has been written before. . . . Henry Thoreau, who wrote *Walden*, said, 'I learned this at least by my experiment: that if one advances confidently in the direction of his dreams and endeavors to live the life which he has imagined, he will meet with a success unexpected in common hours.' The sentence, after more than a hundred years, is still alive. So, advance confidently." (*Letters of E. B. White* [New York: Harper & Row, 1976], pp. 649–650.)

In trying to characterize his own writing, White was modest in his claims. To his brother Stanley Hart White, he once remarked, "I discovered a long time ago that writing of the small things of the day, the trivial matters of the heart, the inconsequential but near things of this living, was the only kind of creative work which I could accomplish with any sincerity or grace. As a reporter, I was a flop, because I always came back laden not with facts about the case, but with a mind full of the little difficulties and amusements I had encountered in my travels. Not till *The New Yorker* came along did I ever find any means of expressing those impertinences and irrelevancies. Thus yesterday,

[1] A magazine for children, popular early in the century. — Eds.

setting out to get a story on how police horses are trained, I ended by writing a story entitled "How Police Horses Are Trained" which never even mentions a police horse, but has to do entirely with my own absurd adventures at police headquarters. The rewards of such endeavor are not that I have acquired an audience or a following, as you suggest (fame of any kind being a Pyrrhic victory), but that sometimes in writing of myself — which is the only subject anyone knows intimately — I have occasionally had the exquisite thrill of putting my finger on a little capsule of truth, and heard it give the faint squeak of mortality under my pressure, an antic sound." (*Letters*, pp. 84–85.)

FOR DISCUSSION

1. Sometimes young writers are counseled to study the market and then try to write something that will sell. How would you expect E. B. White to have reacted to such advice?
2. What, exactly, does White mean when he says, "Everything has been written before"? How might an aspiring writer take this remark as encouragement?
3. What interesting distinction does White make between reporting and essay writing?

· Flannery O'Connor ·

FLANNERY O'CONNOR (1925–1964) was born in Milledgeville, Georgia, attended college in her hometown, and later studied at the University of Iowa's School for Writers. Stricken with a fatal disease, lupus erythematosus, she returned home in 1951 to live out her short life in Milledgeville with her mother and to write. She is remembered for her short stories and for two novels, *Wise Blood* (1952) and *The Violent Bear It Away* (1960). *The Complete Stories of Flannery O'Connor* (1971) received a posthumous National Book Award. Famed for its Christian themes and its stark and at times humorous portrayals of country people who encounter the irrational, the grotesque, and the absurd, O'Connor's fiction has attracted steadily increasing notice from readers and critics alike. Her remarkable letters have been edited by Sally Fitzgerald in *The Habit of Being* (1979).

The King of the Birds

Flannery O'Connor had a wealth of detailed knowledge of peacocks: She raised the colorful birds on her mother's farm in Milledgeville and won prizes for them. This famous essay first appeared in *Holiday* (September 1961), a popular magazine of travel and leisure, under the title "Living with a Peacock." When Sally and Robert Fitzgerald collected it in O'Connor's posthumous *Mystery and Manners: Occasional Prose* (1969), they restored the title she had originally given it.

When I was five, I had an experience that marked me for life. Pathé News sent a photographer from New York to Savannah to take a picture of a chicken of mine. This chicken, a buff Cochin Bantam, had the distinction of being able to walk either forward or backward. Her fame had spread through the press, and by the time she reached the attention of Pathé News, I suppose there was nowhere left for her to go — forward or backward. Shortly after that she died, as now seems fitting.

If I put this information in the beginning of an article on peacocks, it is because I am always being asked why I raise them, and I have no short or reasonable answer. 2

From that day with the Pathé man I began to collect chickens. What had been only a mild interest became a passion, a quest. I had to have more and more chickens. I favored those with one green eye and one orange or with overlong necks and crooked combs. I wanted one with three legs or three wings but nothing in that line turned up. I pondered over the picture in Robert Ripley's book, *Believe It or Not,* of a rooster that had survived for thirty days without his head; but I did not have a scientific temperament. I could sew in a fashion and I began to make clothes for chickens. A gray bantam named Colonel Eggbert wore a white piqué coat with a lace collar and two buttons in the back. Apparently Pathé News never heard of any of these other chickens of mine; it never sent another photographer. 3

My quest, whatever it was actually for, ended with peacocks. Instinct, not knowledge, led me to them. I had never seen or heard one. Although I had a pen of pheasants and a pen of quail, a flock of turkeys, seventeen geese, a tribe of mallard ducks, three Japanese silky bantams, two Polish Crested ones, and several chickens of a cross between these last and the Rhode Island Red, I felt a lack. I knew that the peacock had been the bird of Hera, the wife of Zeus, but since that time it had probably come down in the world — the Florida *Market Bulletin* advertised three-year-old peafowl at sixty-five dollars a pair. I had been quietly reading these ads for some years when one day, seized, I circled an ad in the *Bulletin* and passed it to my mother. The ad was for a peacock and hen with four seven-week-old peabiddies. "I'm going to order me those," I said. 4

My mother read the ad. "Don't those things eat flowers?" she asked. 5

"They'll eat Startena like the rest of them," I said. 6

The peafowl arrived by Railway Express from Eustis, Florida, on a mild day in October. When my mother and I arrived at the station, the crate was on the platform and from one end of it protruded a long, royal-blue neck and crested head. A white line above and below each eye gave the investigating head an expression of alert composure. I wondered if this bird, accustomed 7 to parade about in a Florida orange grove, would readily adjust himself to a Georgia dairy farm. I jumped out of the car and bounded forward. The head withdrew.

At home we uncrated the party in a pen with a top on it. The man who sold me the birds had written that I should keep them penned up for a week or ten days and then let them out at dusk at the spot where I wanted them to roost; thereafter, they would return every night to the same roosting place. He had also warned me that the cock would not have his full complement of tail feathers when he arrived; the peacock sheds his tail in late summer and does not regain it fully until after Christmas.

As soon as the birds were out of the crate, I sat down on it and began to look at them. I have been looking at them ever since, from one station or another, and always with the same awe as on that first occasion; though I have always, I feel, been able to keep a balanced view and an impartial attitude. The peacock I had bought had nothing whatsoever in the way of a tail, but he carried himself as if he not only had a train behind him but a retinue to attend it. On that first occasion, my problem was so greatly what to look at first that my gaze moved constantly from the cock to the hen to the four young peachickens, while they, except that they gave me as wide a berth as possible, did nothing to indicate they knew I was in the pen.

Over the years their attitude toward me has not grown more generous. If I appear with food, they condescend, when no other way can be found, to eat it from my hand; if I appear without food, I am just another object. If I refer to them as "my" peafowl, the pronoun is legal, nothing more. I am the menial, at the beck and squawk of any feathered worthy who wants service. When I first uncrated these birds, in my frenzy I said, "I want so many of them that every time I go out the door, I'll run into one." Now every time I go out the door, four or five run into me — and give me only the faintest recognition. Nine years have passed since my first peafowl arrived. I have forty beaks to feed. Necessity is the mother of several other things besides invention.

For a chicken that grows up to have such exceptional good looks, the peacock starts life with an inauspicious appearance. The peabiddy is the color of those large objectionable moths

that flutter about light bulbs on summer nights. Its only distinguished features are its eyes, a luminous gray, and a brown crest
which begins to sprout from the back of its head when it is ten
days old. This looks at first like a bug's antennae and later like
the head feathers of an Indian. In six weeks green flecks appear
in its neck, and in a few more weeks a cock can be distinguished
from a hen by the speckles on his back. The hen's back gradually fades to an even gray and her appearance becomes shortly
what it will always be. I have never thought the peahen unat-
tractive, even though she lacks a long tail and any significant
decoration. I have even once or twice thought her more attractive than the cock, more subtle and refined; but these moments
of boldness pass.

The cock's plumage requires two years to attain its pattern,   12
and for the rest of his life this chicken will act as though he designed it himself. For his first two years he might have been put
together out of a rag bag by an unimaginative hand. During his
first year he has a buff breast, a speckled back, a green neck like
his mother's, and a short gray tail. During his second year he
has a black breast, his sire's blue neck, a back which is slowly
turning the green and gold it will remain; but still no long tail.
In his third year he reaches his majority and acquires his tail.
For the rest of his life — and a peachicken may live to be thirty-
five — he will have nothing better to do than manicure it, furl it
and unfurl it, dance forward *and backward* with it spread, scream
when it is stepped upon, and arch it carefully when he steps
through a puddle.

Not every part of the peacock is striking to look at, even   13
when he is full-grown. His upper wing feathers are a striated
black and white and might have been borrowed from a Barred
Rock fryer; his end wing feathers are the color of clay; his legs
are long, thin, and iron-colored; his feet are big; and he appears
to be wearing the short pants now so much in favor with play-
boys in the summer. These extend downward, buff-colored and
sleek, from what might be a blue-black waistcoat. One would
not be disturbed to find a watch chain hanging from this, but
none does. Analyzing the appearance of the peacock as he
stands with his tail folded, I find the parts incommensurate with
the whole. The fact is that with his tail folded, nothing but his

bearing saves this bird from being a laughingstock. With his tail spread, he inspires a range of emotions, but I have yet to hear laughter.

The usual reaction is silence, at least for a time. The cock 14 opens his tail by shaking himself violently until it is gradually lifted in an arch around him. Then, before anyone has had a chance to see it, he swings around so that his back faces the spectator. This has been taken by some to be insult and by others to be whimsey. I suggest it means only that the peacock is equally well satisfied with either view of himself. Since I have been keeping peafowl, I have been visited at least once a year by first-grade schoolchildren, who learn by living. I am used to hearing this group chorus as the peacock swings around, "Oh, look at his underwear!" This "underwear" is a stiff gray tail, raised to support the larger one, and beneath it a puff of black feathers that would be suitable for some really regal woman — a Cleopatra or a Clytemnestra — to use to powder her nose.

When the peacock has presented his back, the spectator will 15 usually begin to walk around him to get a front view; but the peacock will continue to turn so that no front view is possible. The thing to do then is to stand still and wait until it pleases him to turn. When it suits him, the peacock will face you. Then you will see in a green-bronze arch around him a galaxy of gazing, haloed suns. This is the moment when most people are silent.

"Amen! Amen!" an old Negro woman once cried when this 16 happened, and I have heard many similar remarks at this moment that show the inadequacy of human speech. Some people whistle; a few, for once, are silent. A truck driver who was driving up with a load of hay and found a peacock turning before him in the middle of the road shouted, "Get a load of that bastard!" and braked his truck to a shattering halt. I have never known a strutting peacock to budge a fraction of an inch for truck or tractor or automobile. It is up to the vehicle to get out of the way. No peafowl of mine has ever been run over, though one year one of them lost a foot in the mowing machine.

Many people, I have found, are congenitally unable to ap- 17 preciate the sight of a peacock. Once or twice I have been asked what the peacock is "good for" — a question which gets no answer from me because it deserves none. The telephone company sent a lineman out one day to repair our telephone. After the job was finished, the man, a large fellow with a suspicious expression half hidden by a yellow helmet, continued to idle about, trying to coax a cock that had been watching him to strut. He wished to add this experience to a large number of others he had apparently had. "Come on now, bud," he said, "get the show on the road, upsy-daisy, come on now, snap it up, snap it up."

The peacock, of course, paid no attention to this.   18

"What ails him?" the man asked.   19

"Nothing ails him," I said. "He'll put it up terreckly. All you   20
have to do is wait."

The man trailed about after the cock for another fifteen   21
minutes or so; then, in disgust, he got back in his truck and started off. The bird shook himself and his tail rose around him.

"He's doing it!" I screamed. "Hey, wait! He's doing it!"   22

The man swerved the truck back around again just as the   23
cock turned and faced him with the spread tail. The display was perfect. The bird turned slightly to the right and the little planets above him hung in bronze, then he turned slightly to the left and they were hung in green. I went up to the truck to see how the man was affected by the sight.

He was staring at the peacock with rigid concentration, as if   24
he were trying to read fine print at a distance. In a second the cock lowered his tail and stalked off.

"Well, what did you think of that?" I asked.   25

"Never saw such long ugly legs," the man said. "I bet that   26
rascal could outrun a bus."

Some people are genuinely affected by the sight of a pea-   27
cock, even with his tail lowered, but do not care to admit it; others appear to be incensed by it. Perhaps they have the suspicion that the bird has formed some unfavorable opinion of them. The peacock himself is a careful and dignified investigator. Visitors to our place, instead of being barked at by dogs rushing from under the porch, are squalled at by peacocks whose blue necks and crested heads pop up from behind tufts of grass, peer out of bushes, and crane downward from the roof of the house, where the bird has flown, perhaps for the view. One of mine

stepped from under the shrubbery one day and came forward to inspect a carful of people who had driven up to buy a calf. An old man and five or six white-haired, barefooted children were piling out of the back of the automobile as the bird approached. Catching sight of him they stopped in their tracks and stared, plainly hacked to find this superior figure blocking their path. There was silence as the bird regarded them, his head drawn back at its most majestic angle, his folded train glittering behind him in the sunlight.

"Whut is thet thang?" one of the small boys asked finally in a sullen voice. 28

The old man had got out of the car and was gazing at the peacock with an astounded look of recognition. "I ain't seen one of them since my grandaddy's day," he said, respectfully removing his hat. "Folks used to have 'em, but they don't no more." 29

"Whut is it?" the child asked again in the same tone he had used before. 30

"Churren," the old man said, "that's the king of the birds!" 31

The children received this information in silence. After a minute they climbed back into the car and continued from there to stare at the peacock, their expressions annoyed, as if they disliked catching the old man in truth. 32

The peacock does most of his serious strutting in the spring and summer when he has a full tail to do it with. Usually he begins shortly after breakfast, struts for several hours, desists in the heat of the day, and begins again in the late afternoon. Each cock has a favorite station where he performs every day in the hope of attracting some passing hen; but if I have found anyone indifferent to the peacock's display, besides the telephone lineman, it is the peahen. She seldom casts an eye at it. The cock, his tail raised in a shimmering arch around him, will turn this way and that, and with his clay-colored wing feathers touching the ground, will dance forward and backward, his neck curved, his beak parted, his eyes glittering. Meanwhile the hen goes about her business, diligently searching the ground as if any bug in the grass were of more importance that the unfurled map of the universe which floats nearby. 33

Some people have the notion that only the peacock spreads 34 his tail and that he does it only when the hen is present. This is not so. A peafowl only a few hours hatched will raise what tail he has — it will be about the size of a thumbnail — and will strut and turn and back and bow exactly as if he were three years old and had some reason to be doing it. The hens will raise their tails when they see an object on the ground which alarms them, or sometimes when they have nothing better to do and the air is brisk. Brisk air goes at once to the peafowl's head and inclines him to be sportive. A group of birds will dance together, or four or five will chase one another around a bush or tree. Sometimes one will chase himself, end his frenzy with a spirited leap into the air, and then stalk off as if he had never been involved in the spectacle.

Frequently the cock combines the lifting of his tail with the raising of his voice. He appears to receive through his feet some shock from the center of the earth, which travels upward through him and is released: *Eee-ooo-ii! Eee-ooo-ii!* To the melancholy this sound is melancholy and to the hysterical it is hysterical. To me it has always sounded like a cheer for an invisible parade. 35

The hen is not given to these outbursts. She makes a noise like a mule's bray — *heehaw, heehaw, aa-aawww* — and makes it only when necessary. In the fall and winter, peafowl are usually silent unless some racket disturbs them; but in the spring and summer, at short intervals during the day and night, the cock, lowering his neck and throwing back his head, will give out with seven or eight screams in succession as if this message were the one on earth which needed most urgently to be heard. 36

At night these calls take on a minor key and the air for miles around is charged with them. It has been a long time since I let my first peafowl out at dusk to roost in the cedar trees behind the house. Now fifteen or twenty still roost there; but the original old cock from Eustis, Florida, stations himself on top of the barn, the bird who lost his foot in the mowing machine sits on a flat shed near the horse stall, there are others in the trees by the pond, several in the oaks at the side of the house, and one that cannot be dissuaded from roosting on the water tower. From all these stations calls and answers echo through the 37 night. The peacock perhaps has violent dreams. Often he wakes and screams "Help! Help!" and then from the pond and the barn and the trees around the house a chorus of adjuration begins:

> Lee-yon lee-yon,
> Mee-yon mee-yon!
> Eee-e-yoy eee-e-yoy!
> Eee-e-yoy eee-e yoy!

The restless sleeper may wonder if he wakes or dreams.					38

It is hard to tell the truth about this bird. The habits of any peachicken left to himself would hardly be noticeable, but multiplied by forty, they become a situation. I was correct that my peachickens would all eat Startena; they also eat everything else. Particularly they eat flowers. My mother's fears were all borne out. Peacocks not only eat flowers, they eat them systematically, beginning at the head of a row and going down it. If they are not hungry, they will pick the flower anyway, if it is attractive, and let it drop. For general eating they prefer chrysanthemums and roses. When they are not eating flowers, they enjoy sitting on top of them, and where the peacock sits he will eventually fashion a dusting hole. Any chicken's dusting hole is out of place in a flower bed, but the peafowl's hole, being the size of a small crater, is more so. When he dusts he all but obliterates the sight of himself with sand. Usually when someone arrives at full gallop with the leveled broom, he can see nothing through the cloud of dirt and flying flowers but a few green feathers and a beady, pleasure-taking eye.					39

From the beginning, relations between these birds and my mother were strained. She was forced, at first, to get up early in the morning and go out with her clippers to reach the Lady Bankshire and the Herbert Hoover roses before some peafowl had breakfasted upon them; now she has halfway solved her problem by erecting hundreds of feet of twenty-four-inch-high wire to fence the flower beds. She contends that peachickens do not have enough sense to jump over a low fence. "If it were a high wire," she says, "they would jump onto it and over, but they don't have sense enough to jump over a low wire."					40

It is useless to argue with her on this matter. "It's not a chal-   41
lenge," I say to her; but she has made up her mind.

In addition to eating flowers, peafowl also eat fruit, a habit   42
which has created a lack of cordiality toward them on the part
of my uncle, who had the fig trees planted about the place because he has an appetite for figs himself. "Get that scoundrel out
of that fig bush!" he will roar, rising from his chair at the sound
of a limb breaking, and someone will have to be dispatched with
a broom to the fig trees.

Peafowl also enjoy flying into barn lofts and eating peanuts   43
off peanut hay; this has not endeared them to our dairyman.
And as they have a taste for fresh garden vegetables, they have
often run afoul of the dairyman's wife.

The peacock likes to sit on gates or fence posts and allow his   44
tail to hang down. A peacock on a fence post is a superb sight.
Six or seven peacocks on a gate are beyond description; but it is
not very good for the gate. Our fence posts tend to lean in one
direction or another and all our gates open diagonally.

In short, I am the only person on the place who is willing to   45
underwrite, with something more than tolerance, the presence
of peafowl. In return, I am blessed with their rapid multiplica-
tion. The population figure I give out is forty, but for some time
now I have not felt it wise to take a census. I had been told before I bought my birds that peafowl are difficult to raise. It is not
so, alas. In May the peahen finds a nest in some fence corner
and lays five or six large buff-colored eggs. Once a day, thereafter, she gives an abrupt *hee-haa-awww!* and shoots like a rocket
from her nest. Then for half an hour, her neck ruffled and
stretched forward, she parades around the premises, announcing what she is about. I listen with mixed emotions.

In twenty-eight days the hen comes off with five or six   46
mothlike, murmuring peachicks. The cock ignores these unless
one gets under his feet (then he pecks it over the head until it
gets elsewhere), but the hen is a watchful mother and every year
a good many of the young survive. Those that withstand ill-
nesses and predators (the hawk, the fox, and the opossum) over
the winter seem impossible to destroy, except by violence.

A man selling fence posts tarried at our place one day and   47
told me that he had once had eighty peafowl on his farm. He

cast a nervous eye at two of mine standing nearby. "In the spring, we couldn't hear ourselves think," he said. "As soon as you lifted your voice, they lifted their'n, if not before. All our fence posts wobbled. In the summer they ate all the tomatoes off the vines. Scuppernongs went the same way. My wife said she raised her flowers for herself and she was not going to have them eat up by a chicken no matter how long his tail was. And in the fall they shed them feathers all over the place anyway and it was a job to clean up. My old grandmother was living with us then and she was eighty-five. She said, 'Either they go, or I go.'"

"Who went?" I asked. 48

"We still got twenty of them in the freezer," he said. 49

"And how," I asked, looking significantly at the two standing nearby, "did they taste?" 50

"No better than any other chicken," he said, "but I'd a heap rather eat them than hear them." 51

I have tried imagining that the single peacock I see before me is the only one I have, but then one comes to join him; another flies off the roof, four or five crash out of the crêpe-myrtle hedge; from the pond one screams and from the barn I hear the dairyman denouncing another that has got into the cowfeed. My kin are given to such phrases as, "Let's face it." 52

I do not like to let my thoughts linger in morbid channels, but there are times when such facts as the price of wire fencing and the price of Startena and the yearly gain in peafowl all run uncontrolled through my head. Lately I have had a recurrent dream: I am five years old and a peacock. A photographer has been sent from New York and a long table is laid in celebration. The meal is to be an exceptional one: myself. I scream, "Help! Help!" and awaken. Then from the pond and the barn and the trees around the house, I hear that chorus of jubilation begin: 53

> *Lee-yon lee-yon,*
> *Mee-yon mee-yon!*
> *Eee-e-yoy eee-e-yoy!*
> *Eee-e-yoy eee-e-yoy!*

I intend to stand firm and let the peacocks multiply, for I am sure that, in the end, the last word will be theirs. 54

QUESTIONS ON MEANING

1. How would you reply to the student who said, "This essay is not earthshaking, to put it mildly. I can't imagine why O'Connor wrote it, or why I should read it"?
2. O'Connor makes clear that there are disadvantages to raising peacocks. What are they?
3. Where in her essay does the author reveal how she feels about peacocks? Which of their characteristics strike her with special force?
4. What is the attitude of O'Connor's mother toward the peacocks? How does the author account for this attitude?

QUESTIONS ON WRITING STRATEGY

1. How does O'Connor justify starting an essay about peacocks with an anecdote about a chicken? By what means does she tie the two subjects together?
2. To what extent does the author use NARRATION in this descriptive essay to make a point? Does its use strengthen or weaken her writing?
3. Does O'Connor describe anything other than peacocks in her essay? If so, what?
4. What is the TONE of "The King of the Birds"? In which passages does O'Connor vary it?
5. To which of the reader's five senses does O'Connor's essay chiefly appeal? Find examples that support your answer.

QUESTIONS ON LANGUAGE

1. Examine O'Connor's DICTION. Where do you find examples of NONSTANDARD ENGLISH? Of COLLOQUIAL EXPRESSIONS? Of dialect? What do these examples contribute to the essay? How would you translate *terreckly* (paragraph 20) and *churren* (31) into standard English?
2. Make sure the following words are part of your vocabulary: piqué (paragraph 3); composure (7); retinue, berth (9); inauspicious (11); striated, incommensurate (13); whimsey (14); inadequacy (16); congenitally (17); incensed (27); desists (33); adjuration (37); obliterates (39); underwrite (45); scuppernongs (47).
3. Where in her essay does the author use SIMILES or other FIGURES OF SPEECH effectively?

SUGGESTIONS FOR WRITING

1. In a paragraph or two, describe one of the following: a pair of cardinals, a mother cat, a crow, a butterfly, a tank full of goldfish, a sunrise or sunset, or any other manifestation of the natural world. Load your description with closely observed details.
2. Have you ever had a hobby, a collection, an interest that got out of hand because you couldn't control your enthusiasm for it? If so, write a brief essay in which you convey your perhaps misplaced enthusiasm to your readers.

Flannery O'Connor on Writing

Storywriting, Flannery O'Connor insisted, was the only kind of writing she knew anything about. In examining her own stories and those of others, she was a critic hard to please. Talking to students at a writing conference, she complained that, among the characters in the student stories she read, there seemed a dearth of distinctive personalities. "In most good stories," she explained, "it is the character's personality that creates the action of the story. In most of these stories, I feel that the writer has thought of some action and then scrounged up a character to perform it. You will usually be more successful if you start the other way around. If you start with a real personality, a real character, then something is bound to happen." ("Writing Short Stories," *Mystery and Manners* [New York, Farrar, Straus & Giroux, 1961], pp. 105–106.)

Although she offered no specific advice on writing a description, O'Connor was clearly aware that, in her own writing, concrete description was essential. "Fiction operates through the senses," she maintained, "and I think one reason that people find it so difficult to write stories is that they forget how much time and patience is required to convince through the senses. No reader who doesn't actually experience, who isn't made to feel, the story is going to believe anything the fiction writer merely tells him. The first and most obvious characteristic of fiction is that it deals with reality through what can be seen, heard, smelt, tasted, and touched.

"Now this is something that can't be learned only in the head; it has to learned in the habits. It has to become a way that you habitually look at things. The fiction writer has to realize that he can't create compassion with compassion, or emotion with emotion, or thought with thought. He has to provide all these things with a body; he has to create a world with weight and extension." ("Writing Short Stories," *Mystery and Manners*, pp. 91–92.)

FOR DISCUSSION

1. What is it that makes O'Connor's advice about writing fiction applicable to writing description? What do these two kinds of writing have in common?
2. Are there any kinds of writing that *don't* need to "convince through the senses"? If so, what are they?

· Todd Alexander Senturia ·

TODD SENTURIA, born in Boston in 1965, wrote this essay while a college undergraduate. As a freshman, he played on Harvard's NCAA championship squash team; he attained national ranking among the top twenty junior squash players of his age. A summer job teaching sports to teenage refugees from Laos and Cambodia helped him decide to major in East Asian Studies. He has worked in refugee communities, serving as deputy director of Boston's Asian Newcomer Youth Program. Senturia was graduated in 1985 and is currently business manager for Micromet Instruments, an electronics firm in Cambridge, Mass. Chindaree, the subject of his student essay, has since become his wife.

At Home in America

How a Cambodian family survives and flourishes in new and radically different surroundings, a low-rent neighborhood in East Boston, is vividly shown in this outstanding piece of student writing. Chindaree, an "eighteen-year-old Cambodian woman-child," is clearly the center of Senturia's description, but other members of her family, her neighborhood, and a Cambodian meal are also described with attention to detail. Senturia wrote "At Home in America" in 1982 to fulfill an assignment for his freshman composition course: to produce a descriptive essay. Subsequently entered in a nationwide contest, the paper won a 1983 Bedford Prize in Student Writing and was published in *Student Writers at Work: The Bedford Prizes*, edited by Nancy Sommers and Donald McQuade (1984). May it suggest how well you too can write, even for an assignment, when you find a subject you know, closely observe, and deeply care about.

Chindaree's delicate oval face is framed by thick black hair which flows in shifting waves down across her shoulders and back. As she leans forward, a wrinkle of concern shades her forehead for the tendril of hair which curls across one eye. She brushes the lock away with her forearm. The pan on the burner fills the small kitchen with smells recognizable to my American senses only as delicious. The aromas somehow match the brightly colored flower patterns of the cotton sarong wrapped tightly around the girl's waist.

Something in the pan displeases her, and she crosses the   2 tiny space in search of additional spices. In one fluid motion, she slips from a standing position into a squat which would look ugly and awkward on an American but graces the full figure of this eighteen-year-old Cambodian woman-child. She rummages briefly in the cabinet and rises triumphant, holding a bottle whose label boasts no English, only the decorative scripts of the Khmer and Thai languages. She adds a certain amount from this new bottle, the tendons in her wrist standing out as she stirs the liquid in with a spoon. She smiles lightly as the results meet with her approval, then winces as a drop of fat pops, spattering her arm. A single bead of sweat gathers on her nose, glinting in the light.

Exotic and familiar sounds crowd the small apartment in a   3 clashing of cultures. Occasionally the popping from the stove punctuates the rhythmic melodies of the *romvong*, Cambodian dance music which accompanies Chindaree's efforts on a cassette recorder. Much of her family sits in the next room. Their conversation, of which I can understand only a few words — *maa*, mother; *ñam baay*, eat rice; *tiv salaa*, go to school — contends with the babble of the television set. Chindaree's baby niece cries in no particular language at all. Outside, of course, the sounds of an East Boston neighborhood preside: cars honking, dogs barking, and residents hanging out of windows shouting the latest gossip back and forth.

One of Chindaree's sisters, Pharee, lured by the aroma of   4 lunch, slips past where I stand and into the kitchen. Pharee is only fifteen, thin and lithe, not as fully figured as her older sister but with the same oval face and rich black hair. She carries herself as regally here at home in blue jeans and sneakers as when she performs the ancient Khmer classical dances up on stage in front of hundreds of people. She leans over her sister and asks a question in the jarring syllables of their language. As the two talk, Pharee slips her arm around her sister's waist and rests her head upon Chindaree's shoulder.

The telephone shatters the moment, as Pharee picks it up with a cautious "Allo . . . ?" She listens briefly, then puts the phone down on the table, calling, "Nee, mao nih, Theavy . . . " Phanee, the youngest girl, bounds in, all smiles. Only thirteen, boyish and energetic, her hair pulled back from her face in a pony tail, Phanee nonetheless unmistakably resembles her sisters. The oval features which in Chindaree's face are subdued and unassuming, and in Pharee's regal and almost haughty, come out in Phanee as impishly angelic. The glint in her dark eyes and the slight smile playing around the corners of her mouth hint at some secret joke which she might tell you, and then again might not.

Later, Chindaree and I eat at the table. A bowl of white rice sits at each place, along with fork, spoon, and chopsticks, as the different plates of food vie for attention. A beef and vegetable dish seasoned heavily with ginger proves itself magnificent. A cold, spicy cucumber salad which looks somewhat dubious conquers me as well, and I eat nearly the whole bowl. Another plate, filled with strips of cooked pork and beef, sits next to a small saucer holding an innocuous-looking red sauce. Chindaree takes a strip of meat from the platter with her chopsticks, dips it into the sauce, and brings it directly to her mouth. I copy her example, but as I'm about to open my mouth, she warns, "Kdav nah" — very spicy. It is, but equally delicious, and she and I share a companionable time of alternating bites. Chindaree eats as gracefully as she does everything else, a slight frown of concentration between her arched eyebrows as she manipulates her chopsticks or spoons up the last bit of rice from her bowl.

As we sit at the table, the other members of the household drift in and out, serving themselves food and then going to sit either outside on the porch, which looks out over clotheslines and backyard lots, or back into the room with the TV. Pharee, Phanee, and a girl from downstairs, fresh-faced and bright, troop in, take their food, and settle on the porch for a playful meal full of shrieks and laughter.

Vuthy and Chindee, the two older boys in the family, come

in to take their share. Vuthy, seventeen years old, tall and well proportioned, wears just shorts, and the hairless skin of his chest and arms gleams slightly with sweat. He carries a hand exerciser and a pair of nunchuks. His regal bearing recalls Pharee, and, indeed, Vuthy often dances the male lead opposite his sister. Chindee, twenty years old, is darkly handsome, with a flash of white smile. His button-down shirt, open at the neck, shows a densely muscled chest, and as he spoons rice from the stove into a bowl, his biceps bulge. His left eye doesn't focus very well, though, as he's not yet fully recovered from the beating he took at the hands of six East Boston kids. His broken nose has healed, but his tentative, gloomy, smileless air contrasts sadly with his previous cheerful spirit.

The door to the porch bounds open, and in struts the   9
youngest family member. Pausing for a moment in the doorway, he poses in his Superman T-shirt, flexing an imagined bicep. Finding the beat in the *romvong,* he dances wildly across the small floor to the stove. His name is Chearee, and at twelve years old he already speaks more English than anyone in the family except Chindaree. He departs as dramatically as he entered, holding his bowl aloft as if it were an offering to Buddha. He disappears into the TV room, and soon his accented voice rises in song, accompanying the commercials — "What a great place, it's a great place to start."

As my hostess washes the dishes, humming to herself in   10
Khmer, she glows with life and color against the stark, dingy kitchen. Her bright green sarong, wrapped around her waist, fits snugly about her hips and falls in folds nearly to the floor. Her sandals peek out from beneath the swaying fabric as she moves back and forth. A cockroach scurries out from beneath the sink, and Chindaree casually stamps on it with her sandal, briefly exposing an ankle and lower calf. Her hair, held away from her face now by a pair of enameled combs, cascades down her back, almost to her waist, starkly black against the greens of her shirt and sarong. Her breasts stretch the fabric of the shirt, lengthening the slight V-neck to expose the smooth white skin of her neck and collarbone. Droplets of water cling to the down of her arms, darkening it slightly. The steam from the sink colors

Chindaree's cheeks and dampens the stray strands of hair on her forehead. That same bead of sweat forms at the tip of her nose. Her long eyelashes highlight the color of her eyes against the fairness of her skin, which is especially light for a Khmer.

She turns her head suddenly and catches me watching her. 11 She smiles at me briefly from the depths of her dark eyes, then turns back away from me, a slight blush heightening the color in her cheeks and even tinting her throat. She begins to hum again. Among the chaotic sounds of laughing, crying, music playing, and dogs barking, she appears calm and composed. Against the backdrop of bare pipes and peeling paint, she sparkles with an innocent beauty. Even her name, Chindaree, suits the image of this delicate, exotic Cambodian flower flourishing here in the poverty and dirt of East Boston's slums.

QUESTIONS ON MEANING

1. What clues does Senturia's essay provide about the economic status of Chindaree and her family?
2. To what degree do these Cambodians seem integrated into their new way of life? Cite EVIDENCE for your answer.
3. From Senturia's essay, what do you learn about Cambodian culture? What does the writer tell you about the East Boston neighborhood in which Chindaree and her family live?

QUESTIONS ON WRITING STRATEGY

1. To what extent does Senturia's writing contain sensory detail? Give two or three examples in which the writer appeals to the reader's sense of sight. Of hearing. Of smell. Of taste. Of touch. What do these details contribute to Senturia's essay?
2. Point to passages in the essay where the writer singles out the incongruities he perceives between the family members and their new surroundings.
3. From what POINT OF VIEW is this essay written?
4. By what means does the writer make sure his readers will be able to distinguish each member of Chindaree's family from the others?

5. How does Senturia feel about Chindaree and her family? How does he reveal his feelings?

QUESTIONS ON LANGUAGE

1. Be sure you know how to define the following: tendril, sarong (paragraph 1); innocuous (6); tentative (8); starkly (10); chaotic (11).
2. Is the title "At Home in America" an accurate reference to the essay's contents, an ironic comment on the essay, or both? Explain.
3. List five of the words Senturia uses in his essay that seem to you heavy with CONNOTATION. In each sentence where they appear, substitute a synonym for the word you have listed. In each case, how does the substitution affect the sentence?

SUGGESTIONS FOR WRITING

1. Write an essay describing a group of people who interest you. Concentrate on their physical characteristics and their surroundings.
2. On the basis of your knowledge of immigration and immigrants, write a paragraph in which you set forth what seems to you the most formidable challenge facing anyone from a foreign country who decides to settle in the United States.

Todd Alexander Senturia on Writing

Soon after his essay won a Bedford prize, Senturia wrote the following comments on his writing. "The easiest part of any paper for me," he explained, "has always been the production of a first draft. I have always been able to sit down and write a decent paper the first time through. My professors today, however, continue to point out that my greatest weakness stems from this ability: I find it very difficult to rework my essays from a new perspective, and as a result my papers occasionally end up 'one small step away from excellent.'

"I read all my papers aloud to myself. By repeating aloud the phrases and ideas I wanted to remember, I found that I could develop a language free, for the most part, from verbal pomposities and pedantic earsores, so common in written prose. In this way I am writing by instinct, for if I can't read a phrase aloud fluently, then I change it until it sounds right. I think that a lot of writers can benefit from this practice. It results in easily readable prose, and it is much easier to catch grammatical mistakes and verbal malapropisms with the help of the ear than to try to pick them up from the flat page."

FOR DISCUSSION

1. What do you think of Senturia's method of going over his writing? Besides the benefits he mentions, what other likely benefits might follow from reading your work out loud?
2. Read some of your own writing aloud to yourself, listening to it critically. Then report: What did this experiment indicate to you?

· D. H. Lawrence ·

David Herbert Lawrence (1885–1930), son of a coal miner, was born in a drab hamlet in Nottinghamshire, England. *The White Peacock* (1911) launched his career as a professional writer; other acclaimed novels followed, among them *Sons and Lovers*, *The Rainbow*, and *Women in Love*. Censors once banned Lawrence's sexually explicit novel *Lady Chatterley's Lover* (1923) in Britain and America; today, it seems tame and innocuous. In search of a healthful climate, Lawrence, a tuberculosis sufferer, and his wife, Frieda von Richthofen, roamed the Mediterranean, France, Australia, and the American Southwest. Besides fiction, Lawrence produced a substantial *Collected Poems*, much lively criticism including *Studies in Classic American Literature* (1922), and some memorable travel books, among them *Mornings in Mexico* (1922). Throughout his writing, Lawrence is an impassioned spokesman for the unconscious, intuitive side of humankind, which (in his view) educated English-speaking people of this century have neglected. "My great religion," he said in 1912, "is a belief in the blood, the flesh, as being wiser than the intellect. We can go wrong in our minds. But what the blood feels, and believes, and says, is always true."

Snake

One morning while living in Taormina, Sicily, during the years 1920–1921, Lawrence watched a poisonous snake drink from his water trough. The sight prompted him to write "Snake," among the most famous of his poems. First published in a literary magazine, *The Dial*, in 1921, the poem became part of Lawrence's collection *Birds, Beasts and Flowers* (1923). As you will discover, the poet makes the physical snake vivid and real; at the same time, he relates this small and ordinary creature to larger and stranger things.

A snake came to my water-trough
On a hot, hot day, and I in pajamas for the heat,
To drink there.

In the deep, strange-scented shade of the great dark carob-tree

I came down the steps with my pitcher   5
And must wait, must stand and wait, for there he was at the
    trough before me.

He reached down from a fissure in the earth-wall in the gloom
And trailed his yellow-brown slackness soft-bellied down, over
    the edge of the stone trough
And rested his throat upon the stone bottom,
And where the water had dripped from the tap, in a small clear-
    ness,   10
He sipped with his straight mouth,
Softly drank through his straight gums, into his slack long body,
Silently.

Someone was before me at my water-trough,
And I, like a second comer, waiting.   15

He lifted his head from his drinking, as cattle do.
And looked at me vaguely, as drinking cattle do,
And flickered his two-forked tongue from his lips, and mused a

And stooped and drank a little more,
Being earth-brown, earth-golden from the burning bowels of the
    earth   20
On the day of Sicilian July, with Etna smoking.

The voice of my education said to me
He must be killed,
For in Sicily the black, black snakes are innocent, the gold are
    venomous.

And voices in me said, If you were a man   25
You would take a stick and break him now, and finish him off.

But must I confess how I liked him,
How glad I was he had come like a guest in quiet, to drink at my
    water-trough
And depart peaceful, pacified, and thankless,
Into the burning bowels of this earth?   30

Was it cowardice, that I dared not kill him?
Was it perversity, that I longed to talk to him?

Was it humility, to feel so honored?
I felt so honored.

And yet those voices: 35
If you were not afraid, you would kill him!

And truly I was afraid, I was most afraid,
But even so, honored still more
That he should seek my hospitality
From out the dark door of the secret earth.   40

He drank enough
And lifted his head, dreamily, as one who has drunken,
And flickered his tongue like a forked night on the air, so black;
Seeming to lick his lips,
And looked around like a god, unseeing, into the air,   45
And slowly turned his head,
And slowly, very slowly, as if thrice adream,
Proceeded to draw his slow length curving round
And climb again the broken bank of my wall-face.

And as he put his head into that dreadful hole,   50
And as he slowly drew up, snake-easing his shoulders, and en-
     tered farther,
A sort of horror, a sort of protest against his withdrawing into
     that horrid black hole,
Deliberately going into the blackness, and slowly drawing him-
     self after,
Overcame me now his back was turned.

I looked round, I put down my pitcher,   55
I picked up a clumsy log
And threw it at the water-trough with a clatter.

I think it did not hit him,
But suddenly that part of him that was left behind convulsed in
     undignified haste,
Writhed like lightning, and was gone   60
Into the black hole, the earth-lipped fissure in the wall-front,
At which, in the intense still noon, I stared with fascination.

And immediately I regretted it.
I thought how paltry, how vulgar, what a mean act!

I despised myself and the voices of my accursed human educa-
tion.   65

And I thought of the albatross,

For he seemed to me again like a king,
Like a king in exile, uncrowned in the underworld,
Now due to be crowned again.   70

And so, I missed my chance with one of the lords
Of life.
And I have something to expiate;
A pettiness.

QUESTIONS ON MEANING

1. "I despised myself and the voices of my accursed human education" (line 65). How do you account for the speaker's repugnance,
   his change of heart?
2. What do you understand Lawrence to mean in line 66: "And I
   thought of the albatross"? What does he mean by calling the snake
   "a king in exile, uncrowned in the underworld,/Now due to be
   crowned again" (69–70)? Explain these ALLUSIONS.
3. Discuss this criticism of the poem: "Lawrence is a silly kook: He
   makes a common garden variety of snake into a god. After all, this
   is only a snake that came out of a wall."

QUESTIONS ON WRITING STRATEGY

1. What details in Lawrence's description place this snake clearly and
   memorably in your mind's eye?
2. How does the poet make his subject seem likable?

QUESTIONS ON LANGUAGE

1. In what respects does Lawrence make the snake almost human?
   Superhuman? Like some other animal? Point to FIGURES OF SPEECH
   that make striking comparisons.

2. Read line 8 aloud, or sound it in your mind: "And trailed his yel-low-brown slackness soft-bellied down, over the edge of the stone trough." Notice the rimes (*brown, down, stone*), the near-rime of *soft* and *trough*; notice the EFFECT of the several *s*-sounds and *l*-sounds. Find other lines in which the poet's words contain especially mem-orable music.

SUGGESTIONS FOR WRITING

1. In a paragraph rich in concrete particulars, describe a snake, or other creature you have met, that you vividly remember.
2. In a descriptive poem of your own, recall some natural phenome-non (animal, bird, river, forest, thunderstorm or whatever) that you have personally seen or experienced, and that stirred your feelings. Your poem, like Lawrence's, may be written in free verse and need not contain rime or fixed rhythm; its lines may be of var-ious lengths. As Lawrence does, describe your subject in detail, and appeal to your reader's senses. Be prepared to read your work aloud in class.

D. H. Lawrence on Writing

When he wrote fiction, D. H. Lawrence did not agonize long over his words. He seldom crossed out and revised. If dis-satisfied with a finished work, he preferred to write the whole thing over again. For this reason, multiple versions of entire novels exist — for example, *Lady Chatterley's Lover*. But in writ-ing poetry, he appears to have worked differently. As his manu-scripts reveal, Lawrence often revised, sometimes working on a recalcitrant poem for years.

"Some of the earliest poems," Lawrence explained in a pref-ace to his *Collected Poems* of 1928, "are a good deal rewritten. They were struggling to say something which it takes a man twenty years to be able to say. . . . A young man is afraid of his demon and puts his hand over the demon's mouth sometimes and speaks for him. And the things the young man says are very rarely poetry. So I have tried to let the demon say his say, and to remove the passages where the young man intruded." Many of Lawrence's later poems, however, were revised very little, or not at all. "The demon," said the poet, "when he's really there, makes his own form willy-nilly, and is unchangeable."

FOR DISCUSSION

1. How would you define "demon" as the author uses it here?
2. According to Lawrence, how does the young poet's work differ from that of the older poet?

· Emily Dickinson ·

For most of her life, EMILY DICKINSON (1830–1886) kept to the shadowy privacy of her family mansion in Amherst, Massachusetts, farming village and site of Amherst College. Her father, an eminent lawyer, was for a time a United States congressman. One brief trip to Philadelphia and Washington, two semesters at New England Female Seminary (ending with Emily's refusal to declare herself a Christian despite pressure on her), and a few months with nieces in Cambridge, Massachusetts, while having her eyes treated, were all the poet's travels away from home. Her work on her brilliantly original poems intensified in the years 1858–1862. In later years, Emily Dickinson withdrew more and more from the life of the town into her private thoughts, correspondence with friends, and the society of only her closest family. After her death, her poems were discovered in manuscript (stitched into little booklets), and a first selection was published in 1890. Since then, her personal legend and the devotion of readers have grown vastly and steadily.

A narrow Fellow
in the Grass

In her lifetime, Emily Dickinson published only seven of her more than a thousand poems. "A narrow Fellow in the Grass," one of this handful, was first printed anonymously in 1866 in a newspaper, the *Springfield Republican*. There, without the poet's consent, it was titled "The Snake" and rearranged into eight-line stanzas. Such high-handed treatment seems to have confirmed Dickinson in her dread of publication. For the rest of her life, she preferred to store her poems in the attic. In shape, this poem and most of her others owe much to hymn tunes she had heard in church as a girl. Like "A narrow Fellow in the Grass," about half her poems fall into "common meter": stanzas of four lines, alternating eight syllables and six syllables, the shorter lines rhyming either exactly or roughly. Notice the lively verbs in this poem, its images, its sense of the physical world. On first reading it, Samuel Bowles, the poem's first editor, admiringly wondered aloud: "How did that girl ever know that a boggy field wasn't good for corn?"

A narrow Fellow in the Grass
Occasionally rides–
You may have met Him–did you not
His notice sudden is–

The Grass divides as with a Comb–   5
A spotted shaft is seen–
And then it closes at your feet
And opens further on–

He likes a Boggy Acre
A Floor too cool for Corn–   10
Yet when a Boy, and Barefoot–
I more than once at Noon

Have passed, I thought, a Whip lash
Unbraiding in the Sun
When stooping to secure it   15
It wrinkled, and was gone–

Several of Nature's People
I know, and they know me–
I feel for them a transport
Of cordiality–   20

But never met this Fellow
Attended, or alone
Without a tighter breathing
And Zero at the Bone–

QUESTIONS ON MEANING

1. How would you sum up the poet's attitude toward this Fellow? Is she playful, serious, or both? Point to lines in the poem to support your view.
2. Recast in your own words the thought in Dickinson's lines 17–24.

QUESTIONS ON WRITING STRATEGY

1. By what details does the poet make the snake seem elusive and mysterious?
2. What does the poem gain from the speaker's claim to have once been a barefoot boy? By her PERSONIFICATION of the snake as a Fellow, one of Nature's People?

QUESTIONS ON LANGUAGE

1. Besides PERSONIFICATION, what other FIGURES OF SPEECH enrich this poem?
2. Which pairs of riming words chime exactly? Which rimes seem rough or far out? Dickinson's early editors tried to regularize her inexact rimes. But how might these rimes be defended?
3. Can you see any justification for the poet's personal, homemade system of punctuation — the half-dashes?

SUGGESTION FOR WRITING

1. In a paragraph or two, compare Dickinson's poem with Lawrence's "Snake." Consider especially the poets' attitudes toward their subjects. In making your comparison, the idea of TONE may come in handy.

Emily Dickinson on Writing

Though Emily Dickinson never spelled out in detail her methods of writing, her practices are clear to us from the work of scholars who have studied her manuscripts. Evidently she liked to rewrite extensively both poetry and prose, with the result that many poems and some letters exist in multiple versions. Usually, a poem proceeded through three stages: a first, worksheet draft; a semifinal draft; and final copy. Occasionally, in later years, she would return to a poem, tinkering, striving for improvements. (In a few cases, she reduced a previously finished poem to a permanent confusion.)

Her admiration for the work of writer and lecturer Thomas Wentworth Higginson began after he published his "Letter to a Young Contributor" in the *Atlantic Monthly* in 1862. In it, he advised novice writers, "Charge your style with life." Echoing Higginson's remark with approval, Dickinson sent him some of her poems and asked, "Are you too deeply occupied to say if my Verse is alive?" Writers might attain liveliness, Higginson had maintained, by choosing plain words, as few of them as possible. We might expect this advice to find favor with Emily Dickinson, who once wrote:

> A word is dead
> When it is said,
> Some say.
> I say it just
> Begins to live
> That day.

FOR DISCUSSION

1. In what sense might a word "begin to live" when it's said?
2. If *you* had been advised to "charge your style with life," how would you go about it?

1. This is an in-class writing experiment. Describe another person in the room so clearly and unmistakably that when you read your description aloud, your subject will be recognized. (Be objective. No insulting descriptions, please!)

2. Write three paragraphs describing one subject from *each* of the following categories. It will be up to you to make the general subject refer to a particular person, place, or thing. Write at least one paragraph as an *objective* description and at least one as a *subjective* description. (Identify your method in each case, so that your instructor can see how well you carry it out.)

Person

A friend or roommate
A typical high-school student
One of your parents
An elderly person you know
A prominent politician
A historic figure

Place

A classroom
A college campus
A vacation spot
A hospital emergency room
A forest
A waiting room

Thing

A dentist's drill
A painting or photograph
A foggy day
A season of the year
A musical instrument
A train

3. In a brief essay, describe your ideal place: an apartment, a bookstore, a dorm room, a vacation spot, a classroom, a restaurant, a

gym, a supermarket or convenience store, a garden, a golf course. With concrete details, try to make the ideal seem actual.

NARRATION AND DESCRIPTION

4. Use a combination of narration and description to develop any one of the following topics:

My first day on the job
My first day at college
Returning to an old neighborhood
Getting lost
A brush with a celebrity
Delivering bad (or good) news

3

EXAMPLE

Pointing to Instances

THE METHOD

"There are many women runners of distinction," a writer begins, and quickly goes on, "among them Joan Benoit, Mary Decker, Grete Waitz. . . ."

You have just seen examples at work. An example (from the Latin *exemplum*: "one thing selected from among many") is an instance that reveals a whole type. By selecting an example, a writer shows the nature or character of the group from which it is taken. In a written essay, an example will often serve to illustrate a general statement. For example, here is film critic Pauline Kael, making a point about the work of a veteran actor, Cary Grant:

> The romantic male stars aren't necessarily sexually aggressive. Henry Fonda wasn't; neither was James Stewart, or,

later, Marcello Mastroianni. The foursquare Clark Gable, with his bold, open challenge to women, was more the exception than the rule, and Gable wasn't romantic, like Grant. Gable got down to brass tacks; his advances were basic, his unspoken question was "Well, sister, what do you say?" If she said no, she was failing what might almost be nature's test. She'd become overcivilized, afraid of her instincts — afraid of being a woman. There was a violent, primal appeal in Gable's sex scenes; it was all out front — in the way he looked at her, man to woman. Cary Grant doesn't challenge a woman that way. (When he tried, as the frontiersman in *The Howards of Virginia*, he looked thick and stupid.)[1]

Kael might have allowed the opening sentence of her paragraph — the topic sentence — to remain a vague generalization. Instead, she follows it immediately with the names of three male movie stars who gently charm rather than sexually challenge their women audiences. Then, to show the style of acting she *doesn't* mean, she gives the example of Clark Gable. Her main purpose (in her paragraph, and in fact, in her whole essay) is to set forth the style of Cary Grant. That is why she adds an example of a film in which, when Grant tried to play a sexually aggressive character, he failed miserably. By all of these examples, Kael not only explains and supports her generalization, she lends life to it.

The method of giving examples — of illustrating what you're saying with a "for instance" — is not merely helpful to practically all kinds of writing, it is indispensable. Bad writers — those who bore us, or lose us completely — often have an ample supply of ideas; their trouble is that they never pull their ideas down out of the clouds. A dull writer, for instance, might declare, "The true romantic film star is a man of gentle style"; but, instead of giving examples, the writer might go on, "Romantic film stars thus strike nonaggressive blows for the dignity of womankind," or something — adding still another large, unillustrated idea. Specific examples are *needed* elements in good prose. Not only do they make ideas understandable, but they also keep

[1]"The Man from Dream City," in *When the Lights Go Down* (New York: Holt, Rinehart and Winston, 1980), p. 4.

Example **157**

readers awake. (The previous paragraphs have tried — by giving examples from Pauline Kael and from "a dull writer" — to illustrate this point.)

THE PROCESS

Where do you find examples? In anything you know — or care to learn. Start close to home. Seek examples in your own immediate knowledge and experience. When assigned an elephant-sized subject that you think you know nothing about — ethical dilemmas, for instance — rummage your memory and you may discover that you know more than you thought. In what ethical dilemmas have you ever found yourself? Deciding whether or not to date your best friend's fiancé (or fiancée) when your best friend is out of town? Being tempted to pilfer from the jelly jar of a small boy's Kool-Aid stand when you need a quarter for a bus? No doubt you can supply your own examples. It is the method — exemplifying — that matters. To bring some huge and ethereal concept down to earth may just set your expository faculties galloping over the plains of your own life to the sound of "hi-yo, Silver!" For different examples, you can explore your conversations with others, your studies, and the storehouse of information you have gathered from books, newspapers, magazines, radio and TV, and from popular hearsay: proverbs and sayings, bits of wisdom you've heard voiced in your family, folklore, popular song.

Now and again, you may feel an irresistible temptation to make up an example out of thin air. This procedure is risky, but can work wonderfully — if, that is, you have a wonder-working imagination. When Henry David Thoreau, in *Walden*, attacks Americans' smug pride in the achievements of nineteenth-century science and industry, he wants to illustrate that kind of invention or discovery "which distracts our attention from serious things." And so he makes up the examples — farfetched, but pointed — of a transatlantic speaking tube and what it might convey: "We are eager to tunnel under the Atlantic and bring the Old World some weeks nearer to the New; but perchance the first news that will leak through into the broad, flapping

American ear will be that the Princess Adelaide has the whooping cough."

These examples (and the sarcastic phrase about the American ear) bespeak genius; but, of course, not every writer can be a Thoreau — or needs to be. A hypothetical example may well be better than no example at all; yet, as a rule, an example from fact or experience is likely to carry more weight. Suppose you have to write about the benefits — any benefits — that recent science has conferred upon the nation. You might imagine one such benefit: the prospect of one day being able to vacation in outer space and drift about in free-fall like a soap bubble. That imagined benefit would be all right, but it is obviously a conjecture that you dreamed up without going to the library. Do a little digging in recent books and magazines (for the latter, with the aid of the *Readers' Guide to Periodical Literature*). Your reader will feel better informed to be told that science — specifically, the NASA space program — has produced useful inventions. You add:

> Among these are the smoke detector, originally developed as Skylab equipment; the inflatable air bag to protect drivers and pilots, designed to cushion astronauts in splashdowns; a walking chair that enables paraplegics to mount stairs and travel over uneven ground, derived from the moonwalkers' surface buggy; the technique of cryosurgery, the removal of cancerous tissue by fast freezing.

By using specific examples like these, you render the idea of "benefits to society" more concrete and more definite. Such examples are not prettifications of your essay; they are necessary if you are to hold your readers' attention and convince them that you are worth listening to.

When giving examples, you'll find the methods of *narration* (Chapter 1) and *description* (Chapter 2) particularly useful. Sometimes an example takes the form of a narrative: a brief story, an anecdote, or a case history. Sometimes it embodies a vivid description of a person, place, or thing. Still another method, *analogy*, dealt with in Chapter 7, is sometimes invaluable. It uses a familiar, simple example to make an unfamiliar or complicated thing clear.

Example 159

Lazy writers think, "Oh well, I can't come up with any example here — I'll just leave it to the reader to find one." The flaw in this assumption is that the reader may be as lazy as the writer. As a result, a perfectly good idea may be left suspended in the stratosphere. S. I. Hayakawa tells the story of a professor who, in teaching a philosophy course, spent a whole semester on the theory of beauty. When students asked him for a few examples of beautiful paintings, symphonies, or works of nature, he refused, saying, "We are interested in principles, not in particulars." The professor himself may well have been interested in principles, but it is a safe bet that his classroom resounded with snores. In written exposition, it is undoubtedly the particulars — the pertinent examples — that keep a reader awake and having a good time, and taking in the principles besides.

EXAMPLE IN A PARAGRAPH:
TWO ILLUSTRATIONS

1. Using Example to Write about Television

To simulate reality must be among television's main concerns, for the airwaves glow with programs that create a smooth and enjoyable imitation of life. Take, for example, wrestling. Stripped to their essentials (and to their gaudy tights), the heroes and villains of TV wrestling matches parade before us like walking abstractions: the Sly Braggart, the Well-Barbered Athlete, the Evil Russian. Larger than life, wrestlers are also louder. They seldom speak; they bellow instead. Part of our enjoyment comes from recognizing the phoniness of it all: When blows fail to land, the intended recipients groan anyway. On Saturday mornings we can even enjoy a simulation of a simulation: a cartoon version of the living sport, "Hulk Hogan's Rock 'n' Wrestling!" Some simulations are less obvious: for instance, the long-running "People's Court." "What you're about to see is real," a voice-over tells us. In fact, the litigants are not professional actors but people who have filed to appear in a small claims court. Enticed to drop their complaints and instead appear on "People's Court" before the admirably fair Judge Wapner, they play themselves and are rewarded with instant fame and a paycheck. We enjoy the illusion that a genuine legal dispute can be as dramatic as a soap opera. And happily, it can always be settled in exactly ten minutes, between commercials.[2]

COMMENT.   To explain the general notion that television often gives us a glossy imitation of life, this paragraph uses three chief examples: wrestling, a cartoon show, and "People's Court." Inside his brief discussion of wrestling, the writer exemplifies still further: He mentions and invents names for familiar types of wrestling champions (The Sly Braggart and others). The result is that, in only a few lines, the intangible idea of simulating life becomes clear and unmistakable. So does the still more abstract idea of simulating a simulation — thanks to the example of the Hulk Hogan animated cartoon. Fun to read, these examples also pack weight: They convince us that the writer knows what he's talking about.

2. Using Example in an Academic Discipline

The primary function of the market is to bring together suppliers and demanders so that they can trade with one another. Buyers and sellers do not necessarily have to be in face-to-face contact; they can signal their desires and intentions through various intermediaries. For example, the demand for green beans in California is not expressed directly by the green bean consumers to the green bean growers. People who want green beans buy them at the grocery store; the store orders them from a vegetable wholesaler; the wholesaler buys them from a bean cooperative, whose manager tells local farmers of the size of the current demand for green beans. The demanders of green beans are able to signal their demand schedule to the original suppliers, the farmers who raise the beans, without any personal communication between the two parties.

COMMENT.   Taken from the third edition of *Microeconomics*, a textbook written by Lewis C. Solmon (Reading, Massachusetts: Addison-Wesley Publishing Company, 1980, p. 198), this

---

[2]The examples in this paragraph have been drawn from Michael Sorkin's article "Faking It" in *Watching Television*, Todd Gitlin, ed. (New York: Pantheon Books, 1986).

Example **161**

paragraph uses a simple example to demonstrate the primary function of the market. By showing step-by-step how green bean growers are brought together with green bean buyers, the author can make clear in a single paragraph a concept that would take much longer to explain in abstract terms — thus doing his audience a favor. Most readers can more easily grasp a concept when they are shown rather than merely told how it works. In this case, by personalizing the four intermediaries between the buyers and sellers of green beans, the author lends life and vigor as well as clarity to his explanation.

ROGER ROSENBLATT, born in 1940, received his Ph.D. from Harvard and served from 1970 to 1973 as director of the expository writing program there. Deciding to leave the academic world, he moved to Washington, D.C., where he became literary editor of *The New Republic* and a columnist and member of the editorial board of the Washington *Post*. Now a senior writer for *Time* magazine, he has written one book of literary criticism, *Black Fiction* (1974), *Children of War* (1984), a survey of the effects of political violence on children around the world, and *Witness: The World Since Hiroshima* (1985), a summing-up of the profound changes in our lives due to the atomic bomb.

Oops! How's That Again?

For the past few years *Time* has been printing a weekly essay on a large and significant general subject. "Oops! How's That Again?", a contribution to this series, appeared in 1981. Rosenblatt, despite the space limit imposed on him, manages to enrich his discussion with memorable examples; and although, as befits its subject, the tone of his essay is humorous, Rosenblatt is concerned with the psychological causes of bloopers. The essay is funny, but it is also much more.

> "That is not what I meant at all. That is not it, at all."
> — T. S. Eliot, "The Love Song of J. Alfred Prufrock"

At a royal luncheon in Glasgow last month, Businessman Peter Balfour turned to the just-engaged Prince Charles and wished him long life and conjugal happiness with Lady Jane. The effect of the sentiment was compromised both by the fact that the Prince's betrothed is Lady Diana (Spencer) and that Lady Jane (Wellesley) is one of his former flames. "I feel a perfect fool," said Balfour, who was unnecessarily contrite. Slips of the tongue

1

occur all the time. In Chicago recently, Governor James Thompson was introduced as "the mayor of Illinois," which was a step down from the time he was introduced as "the Governor of the United States." Not all such fluffs are so easy to take, however. During the primaries, Nancy Reagan telephoned her husband as her audience listened in, to say how delighted she was to be looking at all "the beautiful white people." And France's Prime Minister Raymond Barre, who has a reputation for putting his *pied* in his *bouche*, described last October's bombing of a Paris synagogue as "this odious attack that was aimed at Jews and that struck at innocent Frenchmen" — a crack that not only implied Jews were neither innocent nor French but also suggested that the attack would have been less odious had it been more limited.

One hesitates to call Barre sinister, but the fact is that verbal errors can have a devastating effect on those who hear them and on those who make them as well. Jimmy Carter never fully recovered from his reference to Polish lusts for the future in a mistranslated speech in 1977, nor was Chicago's Mayor Daley ever quite the same after assuring the public that "the policeman isn't there to create disorder, the policeman is there to preserve disorder." Dwight Eisenhower, John Kennedy, Spiro Agnew, Gerald Ford, all made terrible gaffes, with Ford perhaps making the most unusual ("Whenever I can I always watch the Detroit Tigers on radio"). Yet this is no modern phenomenon. The term *faux pas* goes back at least as far as the seventeenth century, having originally referred to a woman's lapse from virtue. Not that women lapse more than men in this regard. Even Marie Antoinette's fatal remark about cake and the public, if true, was due to poor translation.

In fact, mistranslation accounts for a great share of verbal errors. The slogan "Come Alive with Pepsi" failed understandably in German when it was translated: "Come Alive out of the Grave with Pepsi." Elsewhere it was translated with more precision: "Pepsi Brings Your Ancestors Back from the Grave." In 1965, prior to a reception for Queen Elizabeth II outside Bonn, Germany's President Heinrich Lübke, attempting an English translation of *"Gleich geht es los"* (It will soon begin), told the Queen: "Equal goes it loose." The Queen took the news well, but no better than the President of India, who was greeted at an airport in 1962 by Lübke, who, intending to ask, "How are you?" instead said: "Who are you?" To which his guest answered responsibly: "I am the President of India."

The most prodigious collector of modern slips was Kermit   4 Schafer, whose "blooper" records of mistakes made on radio and television consisted largely of toilet jokes, but were nonetheless a great hit in the 1950s. Schafer was an avid self-promoter and something of a blooper himself, but he did have an ear for such things as the introduction by Radio Announcer Harry von Zell of President "Hoobert Heever," as well as the interesting message: "This portion of *Women on the Run* is brought to you by Phillips' Milk of Magnesia." Bloopers are the lowlife of verbal error, but spoonerisms are a different fettle of kitsch. In the early 1900s the Rev. William Archibald Spooner caused a stir at New College, Oxford, with his famous spoonerisms, most of which were either deliberate or apocryphal. But a real one — his giving out a hymn in chapel as "Kinquering Kongs Their Titles Take" — is said to have brought down the house of worship, and to have kicked off the genre. After that, spoonerisms got quite elaborate. Spooner once reportedly chided a student: "You have hissed all my mystery lectures. In fact, you have tasted the whole worm, and must leave by the first town drain."

Such missteps, while often howlingly funny to ignorami like   5 us, are deadly serious concerns to psychologists and linguists. Victoria Fromkin of the linguistics department at U.C.L.A. regards slips of the tongue as clues to how the brain stores and articulates language. She believes that thought is placed by the brain into a grammatical framework before it is expressed — this in spite of the fact that she works with college students. A grammatical framework was part of Walter Annenberg's trouble when, as the newly appointed U.S. Ambassador to Britain, he was asked by the Queen how he was settling in to his London residence. Annenberg admitted to "some discomfiture as a result of a need for elements of refurbishing." Either he was overwhelmed by the circumstance or he was losing his mind.

When you get to that sort of error, you are nearing a psy-   6 chological abyss. It was Freud who first removed the element of accident from language with his explanation of "slips," but lately others have extended his theories. Psychiatrist Richard Yazmajian, for example, suggests that there are some incorrect words that exist in associative chains with the correct ones for which they are substituted, implying a kind of "dream pair" of elements in the speaker's psyche. The nun who poured tea for the Irish bishop and asked, "How many lords, my lump?" might therefore have been asking a profound theological question.

On another front, Psychoanalyst Ludwig Eidelberg made 7 Freud's work seem childishly simple when he suggested that a slip of the tongue involves the entire network of id, ego, and superego. He offers the case of the young man who entered a restaurant with his girlfriend and ordered a room instead of a table. You probably think that you understand that error. But just listen to Eidelberg: "All the wishes connected with the word 'room' represented a countercathexis mobilized as a defense. The word 'table' had to be omitted, because it would have been used for infantile gratification of a repressed oral, aggressive, and scopophilic wish connected with identification with the preoedipal mother." Clearly, this is no laughing matter.

Why then do we hoot at these mistakes? For one thing, it 8 may be that we simply find conventional discourse so predictable and boring that any deviation comes as a delightful relief. In his deeply unfunny *Essay on Laughter* the philosopher Henri Bergson theorized that the act of laughter is caused by any interruption of normal human fluidity or momentum (a pie in the face, a mask, a pun). Slips of the tongue, therefore, are like slips on banana peels; we crave their occurrence if only to break the monotonies. The monotonies run to substance. When that announcer introduced Hoobert Heever, he may also have been saying that the nation had had enough of Herbert Hoover.

Then too there is the element of pure meanness in such 9 laughter, both the meanness of enjoyment in watching an embarrassed misspeaker's eyes roll upward as if in prayer — his hue turn magenta, his hands like homing larks fluttering to his mouth — and the mean joy of discovering his hidden base motives and critical intent. At the 1980 Democratic National Convention, Jimmy Carter took a lot of heat for referring to Hubert Humphrey as Hubert Horatio Hornblower because it was instantly recognized that Carter thought Humphrey a windbag. David Hartman of *Good Morning America* left little doubt about his feelings for a sponsor when he announced: "We'll be right back after this word from General Fools." At a conference in Berlin in 1954, France's Foreign Minister Georges Bidault was hailed as "that fine little French tiger, Georges Bidet," thus belittling the tiger by the tail. When we laugh at such stuff, it is the harsh and bitter laugh, the laugh at the disclosure of inner condemning truth.

Yet there is also a more kindly laugh that occurs when a blunderer does not reveal his worst inner thoughts, but his most charitable or optimistic. Gerald Ford's famous error in the 1976 presidential debate, in which he said that Poland was not under Soviet domination, for instance. In a way, that turned out to contain a grain of truth, thanks to Lech Walesa and the strikes; in any case it was a nice thing to wish. As was U.N. Ambassador Warren Austin's suggestion in 1948 that Jews and Arabs resolve their differences "in a true Christian spirit." Similarly, Nebraska's former Senator Kenneth Wherry might have been thinking dreamily when, in an hour-long speech on a country in Southeast Asia, he referred throughout to "Indigo-China." One has to be in the mood for such a speech.

Of course, the most interesting laugh is the one elicited by the truly bizarre mistake, because such a mistake seems to disclose a whole new world of logic and possibility, a deranged double for the life that is. What Lewis Carroll displayed through the looking glass, verbal error also often displays by conjuring up ideas so supremely nutty that the laughter it evokes is sublime. The idea that Pepsi might actually bring one back from the grave encourages an entirely new view of experience. In such a view it is perfectly possible to lust after the Polish future, to watch the Tigers on the radio, to say "Equal goes it loose" with resounding clarity.

Still, beyond all this is another laugh entirely, that neither condemns, praises, ridicules nor conspires, but sees into the essential nature of a slip of the tongue and consequently sympathizes. After all, most human endeavor results in a slip of the something — the best-laid plans gone suddenly haywire by nat-

ural blunder: the chair, cake, or painting that turns out not exactly as one imagined; the kiss or party that falls flat; the life that
is not quite what one had in mind. Nothing is ever as dreamed.

So we laugh at each other, perfect fools all, flustered by the   13
mistake of our mortality.

QUESTIONS ON MEANING

1. In which paragraphs of Rosenblatt's essay do you find any of these
   PURPOSES: to illustrate different kinds of verbal errors, to probe
   why they happen, to explain why we laugh at them, or simply to
   entertain us? Which seems Rosenblatt's main purpose?
2. Quote the famous remark by Marie Antoinette to which Rosenblatt refers in paragraph 2.
3. What explanations does Rosenblatt advance for the human tendency to make verbal errors? Is the reader meant to regard all of
   the theories with equal seriousness?
4. What relationship does Rosenblatt discover between verbal errors
   and the work of Lewis Carroll?
5. What examples of verbal error (public blunders, memorable mis-
   translations, "bloopers," spoonerisms) have you heard or read
   about recently? When you cite one that seems particularly revealing, take a guess at its possible cause.

QUESTIONS ON WRITING STRATEGY

1. What is the TOPIC SENTENCE in paragraph 2? In illustrating this general statement, how many examples does Rosenblatt give? Where
   does he draw them from?
2. Into what groups has Rosenblatt organized his numerous examples
   of verbal missteps?
3. What EFFECT does the author achieve by using the first PERSON plural in his CONCLUSION?
4. Recall the fact that this essay first appeared in *Time*, a news magazine whose AUDIENCE largely consists of people in business and in
   the professions (medicine, law, teaching, media, technology). Why
   would you expect such readers to find verbal errors a subject of
   personal interest?

QUESTIONS ON LANGUAGE

1. Rosenblatt occasionally uses French words. Be sure you know the meanings of *pied, bouche* (paragraph 1), and *faux pas* (2); and you will more fully appreciate the humor in paragraph 9 if you know what a *bidet* is.
2. Look up *bar sinister* in the dictionary. Then explain Rosenblatt's play on words when he says, "One hesitates to call Barre sinister. . . . " (paragraph 2).
3. From examples that the author gives in paragraph 4, explain what a *spoonerism* is. What is *kitsch*?

SUGGESTIONS FOR WRITING

1. If you have ever had the experience of putting your *pied* in your *bouche*, recount it and its consequences. You might, as an alternative, tell how this fate befell someone else.
2. Examine some other variety of verbal behavior for which you can collect enough examples. (Some possibilities: nicknames, sportswriters' colorful figures of speech, coined words, slang, the invented names of fast foods, the special vocabulary of a subculture such as runners or poker players, dialect and regional speech.) Like Rosenblatt, give examples and then try to account for the phenomenon they exemplify.

Roger Rosenblatt on Writing

In an account of the genesis of "Oops! How's That Again?" supplied especially for *The Bedford Reader*, Roger Rosenblatt confided that when he began writing he had no idea how his essay would turn out. Beginning with "a slip of the tongue concerning Prince Charles," he went on to search for other verbal slips. Once he had decided which ones to use, he put them in his early paragraphs. "When dealing with a humorous subject," he remarked, "there are two advantages in spreading out one's examples as early as possible. For one thing, the examples warm up the audience; even before knowing what the essay is going to be about, people will feel kindly toward it. (Readers are impatient animals, and as a general rule I find that it helps to win their interest or affection within the first couple of sentences.) Second, by spilling most of my beans in the beginning I was able to tell the readers in effect: Let's lap up this material, but let's also put it behind us, since we may be getting to more serious business later on. In other words, if the readers get most of the horse laughs out of their systems at the outset, they may sooner, on their own, arrive at the question, 'What am I laughing at?' which is also the central question of the essay."

As he wrote, Rosenblatt paid serious attention to the tone of his essay, and, he said, "I'm still not sure that I got it right. What I sought was a voice that was at once superior to the people making the verbal errors (since laughter usually derives from feelings of superiority) and, at the same time, sympathetic. Perhaps subconsciously I was anticipating the essay's final point, long before it actually occurred to me, by creating a tone that would be consistent with it. Why I punned so often, I cannot explain. Punning cools a tone, and I may have wanted to avoid any hint of warmth in the piece until the very end.

"The 'lecture' or substance of the essay," he went on to say, "occurs in the final six paragraphs, where five discrete explanations are offered for why we laugh at slips of the tongue. By the time I got to this point in the writing, I had begun to brood on the subject and was able to come up with some definite reasons for the phenomenon. The process of this sort of thinking is always mysterious to me; you hit upon idea after idea, all of which stay fairly close to the subject. Then suddenly something strikes you that is much wider and deeper than the matter at hand, but is nonetheless connected to it. Technically one calls this a generalization, but it seems much more. In a way it is a leap of faith, a taking-off from a small particular into everything that is most wonderful and terrible about our lives.

"Whenever this happens, I wonder if the thought was always there in the first place, lying hidden, waiting for some event to spring it free. No discussion of process will explain such things satisfactorily."

FOR DISCUSSION

1. How much of what Rosenblatt says about writing a humorous essay seems to you to apply equally well to other kinds of writing?
2. What is it that Rosenblatt finds "mysterious" about the process of writing?

· Brent Staples ·

BRENT STAPLES is first assistant metropolitan editor of the *New York Times*. Born in 1951 in Chester, Pennsylvania, Staples has a B.A. in behavioral science from Widener University in Chester, Pennsylvania, and a Ph.D. in psychology from the University of Chicago. Before joining the *New York Times* in 1985, he worked for the *Chicago Sun-Times* and several weekly magazines and newspapers in Chicago.

Black Men and Public Space

"Black Men and Public Space" appeared in the December 1987 issue of *Harper's* magazine. It was originally published, in a slightly different version, in *Ms.* magazine (September 1986), under the title "Just Walk on By." This essay, part of Staples's unpublished autobiography, relates incidents he has experienced "as a night walker in the urban landscape."

My first victim was a woman — white, well dressed, proba- 1
bly in her late twenties. I came upon her late one evening on a deserted street in Hyde Park, a relatively affluent neighborhood in an otherwise mean, impoverished section of Chicago. As I swung onto the avenue behind her, there seemed to be a discreet, uninflammatory distance between us. Not so. She cast back a worried glance. To her, the youngish black man — a broad six feet two inches with a beard and billowing hair, both hands shoved into the pockets of a bulky military jacket — seemed menacingly close. After a few more quick glimpses, she picked up her pace and was soon running in earnest. Within seconds she disappeared into a cross street.

That was more than a decade ago. I was twenty-two years 2
old, a graduate student newly arrived at the University of Chicago. It was in the echo of that terrified woman's footfalls that I first began to know the unwieldy inheritance I'd come into —

the ability to alter public space in ugly ways. It was clear that she thought herself the quarry of a mugger, a rapist, or worse. Suffering a bout of insomnia, however, I was stalking sleep, not defenseless wayfarers. As a softy who is scarcely able to take a knife to a raw chicken — let alone hold one to a person's throat — I was surprised, embarrassed, and dismayed all at once. Her flight made me feel like an accomplice in tyranny. It also made it clear that I was indistinguishable from the muggers who occasionally seeped into the area from the surrounding ghetto. That first encounter, and those that followed, signified that a vast, unnerving gulf lay between nighttime pedestrians — particularly women — and me. And I soon gathered that being perceived as dangerous is a hazard in itself. I only needed to turn a corner into a dicey situation, or crowd some frightened, armed person in a foyer somewhere, or make an errant move after being pulled over by a policeman. Where fear and weapons meet — and they often do in urban America — there is always the possibility of death.

    In that first year, my first away from my hometown, I was to 3 become thoroughly familiar with the language of fear. At dark, shadowy intersections, I could cross in front of a car stopped at a traffic light and elicit the *thunk, thunk, thunk, thunk* of the driver — black, white, male, or female — hammering down the door locks. On less traveled streets after dark, I grew accustomed to but never comfortable with people crossing to the other side of the street rather than pass me. Then there were the standard unpleasantries with policemen, doormen, bouncers, cabdrivers, and others whose business it is to screen out troublesome individuals *before* there is any nastiness.

    I moved to New York nearly two years ago and I have re- 4 mained an avid night walker. In central Manhattan, the near-constant crowd cover minimizes tense one-on-one street encounters. Elsewhere — in SoHo, for example, where sidewalks are narrow and tightly spaced buildings shut out the sky — things can get very taut indeed.

    After dark, on the warrenlike streets of Brooklyn where I 5 live, I often see women who fear the worst from me. They seem to have set their faces on neutral, and with their purse straps strung across their chests bandolier-style, they forge ahead as though bracing themselves against being tackled. I understand, of course, that the danger they perceive is not a hallucination. Women are particularly vulnerable to street violence, and young black males are drastically overrepresented among the perpetrators of that violence. Yet these truths are no solace against the kind of alienation that comes of being ever the suspect, a fearsome entity with whom pedestrians avoid making eye contact.

It is not altogether clear to me how I reached the ripe old age of twenty-two without being conscious of the lethality nighttime pedestrians attributed to me. Perhaps it was because in Chester, Pennsylvania, the small, angry industrial town where I came of age in the 1960s, I was scarcely noticeable against a backdrop of gang warfare, street knifings, and murders. I grew up one of the good boys, had perhaps a half-dozen fistfights. In retrospect, my shyness of combat has clear sources. 6

As a boy, I saw countless tough guys locked away; I have since buried several, too. They were babies, really — a teenage cousin, a brother of twenty-two, a childhood friend in his mid-twenties — all gone down in episodes of bravado played out in the streets. I came to doubt the virtues of intimidation early on. I chose, perhaps unconsciously, to remain a shadow — timid, but a survivor. 7

The fearsomeness mistakenly attributed to me in public places often has a perilous flavor. The most frightening of these confusions occured in the late 1970s and early 1980s, when I worked as a journalist in Chicago. One day, rushing into the office of a magazine I was writing for with a deadline story in hand, I was mistaken for a burglar. The office manager called security and, with an ad hoc posse, pursued me through the labyrinthine halls, nearly to my editor's door. I had no way of proving who I was. I could only move briskly toward the company of someone who knew me. 8

Another time I was on assignment for a local paper and killing time before an interview. I entered a jewelry store on the city's affluent Near North Side. The proprietor excused herself and returned with an enormous red Doberman pinscher straining at the end of a leash. She stood, the dog extended toward 9 me, silent to my questions, her eyes bulging nearly out of her head. I took a cursory look around, nodded, and bade her good night.

Relatively speaking, however, I never fared as badly as an-   10
other black male journalist. He went to nearby Waukegan, Illinois, a couple of summers ago to work on a story about a murderer who was born there. Mistaking the reporter for the killer,
police officers hauled him from his car at gunpoint and but for
his press credentials would probably have tried to book him.
Such episodes are not uncommon. Black men trade tales like
this all the time.

Over the years, I learned to smother the rage I felt at so of-   11
ten being taken for a criminal. Not to do so would surely have
led to madness. I now take precautions to make myself less
threatening. I move about with care, particularly late in the evening. I give a wide berth to nervous people on subway platforms
during the wee hours, particularly when I have exchanged business clothes for jeans. If I happen to be entering a building behind some people who appear skittish, I may walk by, letting
them clear the lobby before I return, so as not to seem to be following them. I have been calm and extremely congenial on
those rare occasions when I've been pulled over by the police.

And on late-evening constitutionals I employ what has   12
proved to be an excellent tension-reducing measure: I whistle
melodies from Beethoven and Vivaldi and the more popular
classical composers. Even steely New Yorkers hunching toward
nighttime destinations seem to relax, and occasionally they even
join in the tune. Virtually everybody seems to sense that a mugger wouldn't be warbling bright, sunny selections from Vivaldi's
Four Seasons. It is my equivalent of the cowbell that hikers wear
when they know they are in bear country.

QUESTIONS ON MEANING

1. What is the PURPOSE of this essay? Do you think Staples believes
   that he (or other black men) will cease "to alter public space in
   ugly ways" in the near future? Does he suggest any long-term solu-

tion for "the kind of alienation that comes of being ever the suspect" (paragraph 5)?

2. In paragraph 5, Staples says he understands that the danger women fear when they see him "is not a hallucination." Do you take this to mean that Staples perceives himself to be dangerous? Explain.

3. Staples says, "I chose, perhaps unconsciously, to remain a shadow — timid, but a survivor" (7). What are the usual CONNOTATIONS of the word "survivor"? Is "timid" one of them? How can you explain this apparent discrepancy?

QUESTIONS ON WRITING STRATEGY

1. Staples opens his essay with an anecdote, rather than with EXPOSITION; that is, he starts out with an example before announcing the idea he plans to illustrate. Why is this strategy so effective?

2. The concept of altering public space is relatively abstract. How does Staples convince you that this phenomenon really takes place?

3. The author employs a large number of examples in a fairly small space. He cites three specific instances that involved him, several general situations, and one incident involving another black male journalist. How does Staples avoid having the piece sound like one long list? How does he establish coherence among all these examples?

QUESTIONS ON LANGUAGE

1. What does the author accomplish by using the word "victim" in the essay's first paragraph? Is the word used literally? What TONE does it set for the essay?

2. Be sure you know how to define the following words, as used in this essay: affluent, uninflammatory (paragraph 1); unwieldy, tyranny, pedestrians (2); intimidation (7); congenial (11); constitutionals (12).

3. The word "dicey" (2) is British slang and so will not appear in most of your dictionaries. If you don't know what it means, can you figure it out from the context in which it appears?

SUGGESTIONS FOR WRITING

1. Write an essay explaining what it means to alter public space. Isn't there a certain amount of power implicit in this ability? It seems clear that Staples would rather not have this power, but would

such power always be undesirable? Can you imagine an instance in which the ability to alter public space might be a *good* thing? Whatever your response, be sure to illustrate your answer with specific examples.

2. Are you aware of any incident in which *you* altered public space? That is, where your entry into a situation, or simply your presence, brought about changes in peoples' attitudes or behavior? Write a narrative essay describing this experience. Or write an essay about witnessing someone else altering public space, whether in a negative or positive way. What changes did you observe in the behavior of the people around you? Was your behavior similarly affected? In retrospect, do you feel your reactions were justified?

· Banesh Hoffmann ·

Born in Richmond, England, in 1906, BANESH HOFFMANN has pursued a distinguished career as mathematician and physicist, author and teacher. After taking his B.A. from Oxford, he crossed the Atlantic to study at Princeton, where he completed his Ph.D. Later, as a member of Princeton's Institute for Advanced Study, he became a colleague of Albert Einstein. For more than forty years (1937–1977), Hoffmann was a professor of mathematics at Queens College in Flushing, New York. Among his several books are *The Strange Story of the Quantum* (1959), *The Tyranny of Testing* (1978), and in collaboration with Helen Dukas, Einstein's personal secretary, two highly praised studies: *Albert Einstein: Creator and Rebel* (1973), a biography that centers on Einstein the theoretical physicist, and *Albert Einstein: The Human Side* (1979). Hoffmann also has written for magazines as diverse as the *American Scholar* and the *Baker Street Journal* (for fans of Sherlock Holmes).

My Friend, Albert Einstein

Most of us know Einstein as the brilliant mathematician and scientist who propounded the theory of relativity and the quantum theory of light. To Banesh Hoffmann, the great thinker was also a friend. He writes about Einstein with respect and affection, and some of what the author says about Einstein may surprise you. The essay appeared first in *Reader's Digest* and was reprinted later in *Unforgettable Characters* (1980), a volume compiled by the magazine's editors.

He was one of the greatest scientists the world has ever known, yet if I had to convey the essence of Albert Einstein in a single word, I would choose *simplicity*. Perhaps an anecdote will help. Once, caught in a downpour, he took off his hat and held it under his coat. Asked why, he explained, with admirable logic, that the rain would damage the hat, but his hair would be none the worse for its wetting. This knack for going instinctively to the heart of a matter was the secret of his major scientific discoveries — this and his extraordinary feeling for beauty.

I first met Albert Einstein in 1935, at the famous Institute for Advanced Study in Princeton, N.J. He had been among the first to be invited to the Institute, and was offered *carte blanche* as to salary. To the director's dismay, Einstein asked for an impossible sum: It was far too *small*. The director had to plead with him to accept a larger salary.

I was in awe of Einstein, and hesitated before approaching him about some ideas I had been working on. When I finally knocked on his door, a gentle voice said, "Come" — with a rising inflection that made the single word both a welcome and a question. I entered his office and found him seated at a table, calculating and smoking his pipe. Dressed in ill-fitting clothes, his hair characteristically awry, he smiled a warm welcome. His utter naturalness at once set me at ease.

As I began to explain my ideas, he asked me to write the equations on the blackboard so he could see how they developed. Then came the staggering — and altogether endearing — request: "Please go slowly. I do not understand things quickly." This from Einstein! He said it gently, and I laughed. From then on, all vestiges of fear were gone.

Einstein was born in 1879 in the German city of Ulm. He had been no infant prodigy; indeed, he was so late in learning to speak that his parents feared he was a dullard. In school, though his teachers saw no special talent in him, the signs were already there. He taught himself calculus, for example, and his teachers seemed a little afraid of him because he asked questions they could not answer. At the age of 16, he asked himself whether a light wave would seem stationary if one ran abreast of it. From that innocent question would arise, ten years later, his theory of relativity.

Einstein failed his entrance examinations at the Swiss Federal Polytechnic School, in Zurich, but was admitted a year later. There he went beyond his regular work to study the masterworks of physics on his own. Rejected when he applied for academic positions, he ultimately found work, in 1902, as a patent examiner in Berne, and there in 1905 his genius burst into fabulous flower.

Among the extraordinary things he produced in that memorable year were his theory of relativity, with its famous offshoot, $E = mc^2$ (energy equals mass times the speed of light squared), and his quantum theory of light. These two theories were not only revolutionary, but seemingly contradictory: The former was intimately linked to the theory that light consists of waves, while the latter said it consists somehow of particles. Yet this unknown young man boldly proposed both at once — and he was right in both cases, though how he could have been is far too complex a story to tell here.

Collaborating with Einstein was an unforgettable experience. In 1937, the Polish physicist Leopold Infeld and I asked if we could work with him. He was pleased with the proposal, since he had an idea about gravitation waiting to be worked out in detail. Thus we got to know not merely the man and the friend, but also the professional.

The intensity and depth of his concentration were fantastic. When battling a recalcitrant problem, he worried it as an animal worries its prey. Often, when we found ourselves up against a seemingly insuperable difficulty, he would stand up, put his pipe on the table, and say in his quaint English, "I will a little tink" (he could not pronounce "th"). Then he would pace up and down, twirling a lock of his long, graying hair around his forefinger.

A dreamy, faraway and yet inward look would come over his face. There was no appearance of concentration, no furrowing of the brow — only a placid inner communion. The minutes would pass, and then suddenly Einstein would stop pacing as his face relaxed into a gentle smile. He had found the solution to the problem. Sometimes it was so simple that Infeld and I could have kicked ourselves for not having thought of it. But the magic had been performed invisibly in the depths of Einstein's mind, by a process we could not fathom.

When his wife died he was deeply shaken, but insisted that now more than ever was the time to be working hard. I remember going to his house to work with him during that sad time.

His face was haggard and grief-lined, but he put forth a great effort to concentrate. To help him, I steered the discussion away from routine matters into more difficult theoretical problems, and Einstein gradually became absorbed in the discussion. We kept at it for some two hours, and at the end his eyes were no longer sad. As I left, he thanked me with moving sincerity. "It was a fun," he said. He had had a moment of surcease from grief, and then groping words expressed a deep emotion.

Although Einstein felt no need for religious ritual and be-   12
longed to no formal religious group, he was the most deeply religious man I have known. He once said to me, "Ideas come from God," and one could hear the capital "G" in the reverence with which he pronounced the word. On the marble fireplace in the mathematics building at Princeton University is carved, in the original German, what one might call his scientific credo: "God is subtle, but he is not malicious." By this Einstein meant that scientists could expect to find their task difficult, but not hopeless: The Universe was a Universe of law, and God was not confusing us with deliberate paradoxes and contradictions.

Einstein was an accomplished amateur musician. We used to   13
play duets, he on the violin, I at the piano. One day he surprised me by saying Mozart was the greatest composer of all. Beethoven "created" his music, but the music of Mozart was of such purity and beauty one felt he had merely "found" it — that it had always existed as part of the inner beauty of the Universe, waiting to be revealed.

It was this very Mozartean simplicity that most character-   14
ized Einstein's methods. His 1905 theory of relativity, for example, was built on just two simple assumptions. One is the so-called principle of relativity, which means, roughly speaking, that we cannot tell whether we are at rest or moving smoothly. The other assumption is that the speed of light is the same no matter what the speed of the object that produces it. You can see how reasonable this is if you think of agitating a stick in a lake to create waves. Whether you wiggle the stick from a stationary pier, or from a rushing speedboat, the waves, once generated, are on their own, and their speed has nothing to do with that of the stick.

Each of these assumptions, by itself, was so plausible as to 15
seem primitively obvious. But together they were in such violent
conflict that a lesser man would have dropped one or the other
and fled in panic. Einstein daringly kept both — and by so doing he revolutionized physics. For he demonstrated they could,
after all, exist peacefully side by side, provided we gave up cherished beliefs about the nature of time.

Science is like a house of cards, with concepts like time and 16
space at the lowest level. Tampering with time brought most of
the house tumbling down, and it was this that made Einstein's
work so important — and controversial. At a conference in
Princeton in honor of his 70th birthday, one of the speakers, a
Nobel Prize winner, tried to convey the magical quality of Einstein's achievement. Words failed him, and with a shrug of helplessness he pointed to his wristwatch, and said in tones of awed
amazement, "It all came from this." His very ineloquence made
this the most eloquent tribute I have heard to Einstein's genius.

Although fame had little effect on Einstein as a person, he 17
could not escape it; he was, of course, instantly recognizable.
One autumn Saturday, I was walking with him in Princeton discussing some technical matters. Parents and alumni were
streaming excitedly toward the stadium, their minds on the
coming football game. As they approached us, they paused in
sudden recognition, and a momentary air of solemnity came
over them as if they had been reminded of a different world. Yet
Einstein seemed totally unaware of this effect and went on with
the discussion as though they were not there.

We think of Einstein as one concerned only with the deep- 18
est aspects of science. But he saw scientific principles in everyday
things to which most of us would give barely a second thought.
He once asked me if I had ever wondered why a man's feet will
sink into either dry or completely submerged sand, while sand
that is merely damp provides a firm surface. When I could not
answer, he offered a simple explanation.

It depends, he pointed out, on *surface tension*, the elastic-skin 19
effect of a liquid surface. This is what holds a drop together, or
causes two small raindrops on a windowpane to pull into one big
drop the moment their surfaces touch.

When sand is damp, Einstein explained, there are tiny   20
amounts of water between grains. The surface tensions of these
tiny amounts of water pull all the grains together, and friction
then makes them hard to budge. When the sand is dry, there is
obviously no water between grains. If the sand is fully immersed,
there is water between grains, but no water *surface* to pull them
together.

This is not as important as relativity; yet there is no telling   21
what seeming trifle will lead an Einstein to a major discovery.
And the puzzle of the sand does give us an inkling of the power
and elegance of his mind.

Einstein's work, performed quietly with pencil and paper,   22
seemed remote from the turmoil of everyday life: But his ideas
were so revolutionary they caused violent controversy and irrational anger. Indeed, in order to be able to award him a belated
Nobel Prize, the selection committee had to avoid mentioning
relativity, and pretend the prize was awarded primarily for his
work on the quantum theory.

Political events upset the serenity of his life even more.   23
When the Nazis came to power in Germany, his theories were
officially declared false because they had been formulated by a
Jew. His property was confiscated, and it is said a price was put
on his head.

When scientists in the United States, fearful that the Nazis   24
might develop an atomic bomb, sought to alert American authorities to the danger, they were scarcely heeded. In desperation, they drafted a letter which Einstein signed and sent directly to President Roosevelt. It was this act that led to the
fateful decision to go all-out on the production of an atomic
bomb — an endeavor in which Einstein took no active part.
When he heard of the agony and destruction that his $E = mc^2$
had wrought, he was dismayed beyond measure, and from then
on there was a look of ineffable sadness in his eyes.

There was something elusively whimsical about Einstein. It   25
is illustrated by my favorite anecdote about him. In his first year
in Princeton, on Christmas Eve, so the story goes, some children
sang carols outside his house. Having finished, they knocked on

his door and explained they were collecting money to buy Christmas presents. Einstein listened, then said, "Wait a moment." He put on his scarf and overcoat, and took his violin from its case. Then, joining the children as they went from door to door, he accompanied their singing of "Silent Night" on his violin.

How shall I sum up what it meant to have known Einstein   26
and his works? Like the Nobel Prize winner who pointed helplessly at his watch, I can find no adequate words. It was akin to the revelation of great art that lets one see what was formerly hidden. And when, for example, I walk on the sand of a lonely beach, I am reminded of his ceaseless search for cosmic simplicity — and the scene takes on a deeper, sadder beauty.

QUESTIONS ON MEANING

1. Which of the following do you find Hoffmann doing: writing a biography, reminiscing, entertaining his readers, explaining relativity, illustrating some point about Einstein? Which PURPOSE seems to predominate?
2. What qualities did Einstein possess that gave him a permanent place in the author's affections?
3. From his essay, what are you able to learn about the author himself?
4. What connections between Einstein the scientist and Einstein the man does Hoffmann's essay reveal to us?

QUESTIONS ON WRITING STRATEGY

1. If Hoffmann were to rewrite "My Friend, Albert Einstein," addressing himself only to an AUDIENCE of scientists, what changes in his essay might result?
2. What is Hoffmann's THESIS? Where does he state it?
3. Study three or four of the examples Hoffmann includes in his essay. What is the function of each?
4. How do paragraphs 5–7 and 14–15 differ from most of the others in Hoffmann's essay? Does the material in these paragraphs contribute something of value to the essay? If so, what?

5. Where in his essay does Hoffmann use physical DESCRIPTION? Where does he include a brief ANALOGY?

QUESTIONS ON LANGUAGE

1. Look up the following words if you do not know what they mean: essence (paragraph 1); *carte blanche* (2); inflection, awry (3); vestiges (4); prodigy (5); recalcitrant, insuperable (9); placid (10); surcease (11); paradoxes (12); ineffable (24); elusively, whimsical (25).
2. In his essay, the author more than once uses the word *anecdote*. Is an anecdote the same as an example? Explain.

SUGGESTIONS FOR WRITING

1. Write a reply to the student who said, "If Einstein had never lived, the world would be a better place because the atomic bomb would never have been invented."
2. Write an essay about someone whose behavior you can illustrate with vivid examples. Your subject need not be a famous person, merely someone you know fairly well: a relative, teacher, or friend; a colorful town character; a leader, or a zealous follower. If possible, choose examples that will highlight the one or two traits that seem to you most worth noticing.

· Alice Walker ·

ALICE WALKER is best known for her novel *The Color Purple* (1982), which won both a Pulitzer Prize and an American Book Award. Born into a sharecropping family in Eatonton, Georgia, in 1944, Walker is the youngest of eight children. She spent two years at Spelman College in Atlanta before transferring to Sarah Lawrence College, where she studied with the poet Muriel Rukeyser. Upon graduation, Walker became active in the civil rights movement, helping to register voters in Georgia by day and pursuing her writing by night. She won her first writing fellowship in 1966 and went on to earn many others, among them fellowships from the Radcliffe Institute, the Guggenheim Foundation, and the National Endowment for the Arts. In addition to *The Color Purple*, Walker's books include *Meridian* (1976) and *The Third Life of Grange Copeland* (1970), both novels; three volumes of poetry; two short story collections; a biography of Langston Hughes; an anthology of the work of Zora Neale Hurston; and *In Search of Our Mothers' Gardens: Womanist Prose* (1983). Walker served as a Contributing Editor for *Ms.* magazine for thirteen years and has taught at numerous colleges and universities, including Wellesley, Yale, Brandeis, and the University of California at Berkeley. She lives in San Francisco, where she has recently started her own publishing company, Wild Trees Press.

In Search of
Our Mothers' Gardens

"In Search of Our Mothers' Gardens," the title essay in Alice Walker's book of the same name, was originally published in *Ms.* magazine in 1974. The essay is based on her childhood belief "that there was nothing, literally nothing, [her] mother couldn't do." Walker explores how that belief shaped her own writing, and as you will discover, gives us much more than an exercise in autobiography. Notice how she moves beyond her own personal experience to state a truth about other black woman artists, perhaps all other black women as well.

185

I described her own nature and temperament. Told how they
needed a larger life for their expression. . . . I pointed out that
in lieu of proper channels, her emotions had overflowed into
paths that dissipated them. I talked, beautifully I thought,
about an art that would be born, an art that would open the
way for women the likes of her. I asked her to hope, and build
up an inner life against the coming of that day. . . . I sang,
with a strange quiver in my voice, a promise song.
                              — "Avey," Jean Toomer, *Cane*
                              The poet speaking to a prostitute who
                              falls asleep while he's talking.

When the poet Jean Toomer walked through the South in   1
the early twenties, he discovered a curious thing: black women
whose spirituality was so intense, so deep, so *unconscious*, they
were themselves unaware of the richness they held. They stumbled blindly through their lives: creatures so abused and mutilated in body, so dimmed and confused by pain, that they considered themselves unworthy even of hope. In the selfless
abstractions their bodies became to the men who used them,
they became more than "sexual objects," more even than mere
women: They became "Saints." Instead of being perceived as
whole persons, their bodies became shrines: What was thought
to be their minds became temples suitable for worship. These
crazy Saints stared out at the world, wildly, like lunatics — or
quietly, like suicides; and the "God" that was in their gaze was
as mute as a great stone.

Who were these Saints? These crazy, loony, pitiful women?   2

Some of them, without a doubt, were our mothers and   3
grandmothers.

In the still heat of the post-Reconstruction South, this is   4
how they seemed to Jean Toomer: exquisite butterflies trapped
in an evil honey, toiling away their lives in an era, a century,
that did not acknowledge them, except as "the *mule* of the
world." They dreamed dreams that no one knew — not even
themselves, in any coherent fashion — and saw visions no one
could understand. They wandered or sat about the countryside
crooning lullabies to ghosts, and drawing the mother of Christ
in charcoal on courthouse walls.

They forced their minds to desert their bodies and their   5
striving spirits sought to rise, like frail whirlwinds from the hard
red clay. And when those frail whirlwinds fell, in scattered particles, upon the ground, no one mourned. Instead, men lit candles
to celebrate the emptiness that remained, as people do who enter a beautiful but vacant space to resurrect a God.

Our mothers and grandmothers, some of them: moving to   6
music not yet written. And they waited.

They waited for a day when the unknown thing that was in   7
them would be made known; but guessed, somehow in their
darkness, that on the day of their revelation they would be long
dead. Therefore to Toomer they walked, and even ran, in slow
motion. For they were going nowhere immediate, and the future
was not yet within their grasp. And men took our mothers and
grandmothers, "but got no pleasure from it." So complex was
their passion and their calm.

To Toomer, they lay vacant and fallow as autumn fields,   8
with harvest time never in sight: and he saw them enter loveless
marriages, without joy; and become prostitutes, without resistance; and become mothers of children, without fulfillment.

For these grandmothers and mothers of ours were not   9
Saints, but Artists; driven to a numb and bleeding madness by
the springs of creativity in them for which there was no release.
They were Creators, who lived lives of spiritual waste, because
they were so rich in spirituality — which is the basis of Art —
that the strain of enduring their unused and unwanted talent
drove them insane. Throwing away this spirituality was their pathetic attempt to lighten the soul to a weight their work-worn,
sexually abused bodies could bear.

What did it mean for a black woman to be an artist in our   10
grandmothers' time? In our great-grandmothers' day? It is a
question with an answer cruel enough to stop the blood.

Did you have a genius of a great-great-grandmother who   11
died under some ignorant and depraved white overseer's lash?
Or was she required to bake biscuits for a lazy backwater tramp,
when she cried out in her soul to paint watercolors of sunsets, or
the rain falling on the green and peaceful pasturelands? Or was
her body broken and forced to bear children (who were more of-

ten than not sold away from her) — eight, ten, fifteen, twenty children — when her one joy was the thought of modeling heroic figures of rebellion, in stone or clay?

How was the creativity of the black woman kept alive, year 12 after year and century after century, when for most of the years black people have been in America, it was a punishable crime for a black person to read or write? And the freedom to paint, to sculpt, to expand the mind with action did not exist. Consider, if you can bear to imagine it, what might have been the result if singing, too, had been forbidden by law. Listen to the voices of Bessie Smith, Billie Holiday, Nina Simone, Roberta Flack, and Aretha Franklin, among others, and imagine those voices muzzled for life. Then you may begin to comprehend the lives of our "crazy," "Sainted" mothers and grandmothers. The agony of the lives of women who might have been Poets, Novelists, Essayists, and Short-Story Writers (over a period of centuries), who died with their real gifts stifled within them.

And, if this were the end of the story, we would have cause 13 to cry out in my paraphrase of Okot p'Bitek's great poem:

> O, my clanswomen
> Let us all cry together!
> Come,
> Let us mourn the death of our mother,
> The death of a Queen
> The ash that was produced
> By a great fire!
> O, this homestead is utterly dead
> Close the gates
> With *lacari* thorns,
> For our mother
> The creator of the Stool is lost!
> And all the young men
> Have perished in the wilderness!

But this is not the end of the story, for all the young women 14 — our mothers and grandmothers, *ourselves* — have not perished in the wilderness. And if we ask ourselves why, and search for and find the answer, we will know beyond all efforts to erase

it from our minds, just exactly who, and of what, we black
American women are.

One example, perhaps the most pathetic, most misunder-   15
stood one, can provide a backdrop for our mothers' work: Phillis
Wheatley, a slave in the 1700s.

Virginia Woolf, in her book *A Room of One's Own*, wrote   16
that in order for a woman to write fiction she must have two
things, certainly: a room of her own (with key and lock) and
enough money to support herself.

What then are we to make of Phillis Wheatley, a slave, who   17
owned not even herself? This sickly, frail black girl who required
a servant of her own at times — her health was so precarious —
and who, had she been white, would have been easily considered the intellectual superior of all the women and most of the
men in the society of her day.

Virginia Woolf wrote further, speaking of course not of our   18
Phillis, that "any woman born with a great gift in the sixteenth
century [insert "eighteenth century," insert "black woman," insert "born or made a slave"] would certainly have gone crazed,
shot herself, or ended her days in some lonely cottage outside
the village, half witch, half wizard [insert "Saint"], feared and
mocked at. For it needs little skill and psychology to be sure that
a highly gifted girl who had tried to use her gift of poetry would
have been so thwarted and hindered by contrary instincts [add
"chains, guns, the lash, the ownership of one's body by someone
else, submission to an alien religion"], that she must have lost
her health and sanity to a certainty."

The key words, as they relate to Phillis, are "contrary in-   19
stincts." For when we read the poetry of Phillis Wheatley — as
when we read the novels of Nella Larsen or the oddly false-
sounding autobiography of that freest of all black women writers, Zora Hurston — evidence of "contrary instincts" is everywhere. Her loyalties were completely divided, as was, without
question, her mind.

But how could this be otherwise? Captured at seven, a slave   20
of wealthy, doting whites who instilled in her the "savagery" of
the Africa they "rescued" her from . . . one wonders if she was

even able to remember her homeland as she had known it, or as it really was.

Yet, because she did try to use her gift for poetry in a world   21
that made her a slave, she was "so thwarted and hindered by . . . contrary instincts, that she . . . lost her health. . . . " In the last years of her brief life, burdened not only with the need to express her gift but also with a penniless, friendless "freedom" and several small children for whom she was forced to do strenuous work to feed, she lost her health, certainly. Suffering from malnutrition and neglect and who knows what mental agonies, Phillis Wheatley died.

So torn by "contrary instincts" was black, kidnapped, enslaved Phillis that her description of "the Goddess" — as she poetically called the Liberty she did not have — is ironically, cruelly humorous. And, in fact, has held Phillis up to ridicule for more than a century. It is usually read prior to hanging Phillis's memory as that of a fool. She wrote:

> The Goddess comes, she moves divinely fair,
> Olive and laurel binds her *golden* hair.
> Wherever shines this native of the skies,
> Unnumber'd charms and recent graces rise. [My italics]

It is obvious that Phillis, the slave, combed the "Goddess's"   23
hair every morning; prior, perhaps, to bringing in the milk, or fixing her mistress's lunch. She took her imagery from the one thing she saw elevated above all others.

With the benefit of hindsight we ask, "How could she?"   24

But at last, Phillis, we understand. No more snickering   25
when your stiff, struggling, ambivalent lines are forced on us. We know now that you were not an idiot or a traitor; only a sickly little black girl, snatched from your home and country and made a slave; a woman who still struggled to sing the song that was your gift, although in a land of barbarians who praised you for your bewildered tongue. It is not so much what you sang, as that you kept alive, in so many of our ancestors, *the notion of song.*

Black women are called, in the folklore that so aptly identi-   26
fied one's status in society, "the *mule* of the world," because we

have been handed the burdens that everyone else — *everyone else* — refused to carry. We have also been called "Matriarchs," "Superwomen," and "Mean and Evil Bitches." Not to mention "Castraters" and "Sapphire's Mama." When we have pleaded for understanding, our character has been distorted; when we have asked for simple caring, we have been handed empty inspirational appellations, then stuck in the farthest corner. When we have asked for love, we have been given children. In short, even our plainer gifts, our labors of fidelity and love, have been knocked down our throats. To be an artist and a black woman, even today, lowers our status in many respects, rather than raises it: And yet, artists we will be.

Therefore we must fearlessly pull out of ourselves and look   27
at and identify with our lives the living creativity some of our great-grandmothers were not allowed to know. I stress *some* of them because it is well known that the majority of our great-grandmothers knew, even without "knowing" it, the reality of their spirituality, even if they didn't recognize it beyond what happened in the singing at church — and they never had any intention of giving it up.

How they did it — those millions of black women who were   28
not Phillis Wheatley, or Lucy Terry or Frances Harper or Zora Hurston or Nella Larsen or Bessie Smith; or Elizabeth Catlett, or Katherine Dunham, either — brings me to the title of this essay, "In Search of Our Mothers' Gardens," which is a personal account that is yet shared, in its theme and its meaning, by all of us. I found, while thinking about the far-reaching world of the creative black woman, that often the truest answer to a question that really matters can be found very close.

In the late 1920s my mother ran away from home to marry   29
my father. Marriage, if not running away, was expected of seventeen-year-old girls. By the time she was twenty, she had two children and was pregnant with a third. Five children later, I was born. And this is how I came to know my mother: She seemed a large, soft, loving-eyed woman who was rarely impatient in our home. Her quick, violent temper was on view only a

few times a year, when she battled with the white landlord who
had the misfortune to suggest to her that her children did not
need to go to school.

She made all the clothes we wore, even my brothers' over-   30
alls. She made all the towels and sheets we used. She spent the
summers canning vegetables and fruits. She spent the winter
evenings making quilts enough to cover our beds.

During the "working" day, she labored beside — not be-   31
hind — my father in the fields. Her day began before sunup, and
did not end until late at night. There was never a moment for
her to sit down, undisturbed, to unravel her own private
thoughts; never a time free from interruption — by work or the
noisy inquiries of her many children. And yet, it is to my
mother — and all our mothers who were not famous — that I
went in search of the secret of what has fed that muzzled and often mutilated, but vibrant, creative spirit that the black woman
has inherited, and that pops out in wild and unlikely places to
this day.

But when, you will ask, did my overworked mother have   32
time to know or care about feeding the creative spirit?

The answer is so simple that many of us have spent years   33
discovering it. We have constantly looked high, when we should
have looked high — and low.

For example: In the Smithsonian Institution in Washington,   34
D.C., there hangs a quilt unlike any other in the world. In fanciful, inspired, and yet simple and identifiable figures, it portrays
the story of the Crucifixion. It is considered rare, beyond price.
Though it follows no known pattern of quilt-making, and
though it is made of bits and pieces of worthless rags, it is obviously the work of a person of powerful imagination and deep
spiritual feeling. Below this quilt I saw a note that says it was
made by "an anonymous Black woman in Alabama, a hundred
years ago."

If we could locate this "anonymous" black woman from Ala-   35
bama, she would turn out to be one of our grandmothers — an
artist who left her mark in the only materials she could afford,
and in the only medium her position in society allowed her to
use.

As Virginia Woolf wrote further, in *A Room of One's Own*:   36

> Yet genius of a sort must have existed among women as it must have existed among the working class. [Change this to "slaves" and "the wives and daughters of sharecroppers."] Now and again an Emily Brontë or a Robert Burns [change this to "a Zora Hurston or a Richard Wright"] blazes out and proves its presence. But certainly it never got itself on to paper. When, however, one reads of a witch being ducked, of a woman possessed by devils [or "Sainthood"], of a wise woman selling herbs [our root workers], or even a very remarkable man who had a mother, then I think we are on the track of a lost novelist, a suppressed poet, or some mute and inglorious Jane Austen. . . . Indeed, I would venture to guess that Anon, who wrote so many poems without signing them, was often a woman. . . .

And so our mothers and grandmothers have, more often   37 than not anonymously, handed on the creative spark, the seed of the flower they themselves never hoped to see: or like a sealed letter they could not plainly read.

And so it is, certainly, with my own mother. Unlike "Ma"   38 Rainey's songs, which retained their creator's name even while blasting forth from Bessie Smith's mouth, no song or poem will bear my mother's name. Yet so many of the stories that I write, that we all write, are my mother's stories. Only recently did I fully realize this: That through years of listening to my mother's stories of her life, I have absorbed not only the stories themselves, but something of the manner in which she spoke, something of the urgency that involves the knowledge that her stories — like her life — must be recorded. It is probably for this reason that so much of what I have written is about characters whose counterparts in real life are so much older than I am.

But the telling of these stories, which came from my moth-   39 er's lips as naturally as breathing, was not the only way my mother showed herself as an artist. For stories, too, were subject to being distracted, to dying without conclusion. Dinners must be started, and cotton must be gathered before the big rains. The artist that was and is my mother showed itself to me only after many years. This is what I finally noticed:

Like Mem, a character in *The Third Life of Grange Copeland*,   40
my mother adorned with flowers whatever shabby house we
were forced to live in. And not just your typical straggly country
stand of zinnias, either. She planted ambitious gardens — and
still does — with over fifty different varieties of plants that
bloom profusely from early March until late November. Before
she left home for the fields, she watered her flowers, chopped up
the grass, and laid out new beds. When she returned from the
fields, she might divide clumps of bulbs, dig a cold pit, uproot
and replant roses, or prune branches from her taller bushes or
trees — until night came and it was too dark to see.

Whatever she planted grew as if by magic, and her fame as a   41
grower of flowers spread over three counties. Because of her creativity with her flowers, even my memories of poverty are seen
through a screen of blooms — sunflowers, petunias, roses, dahl-
ias, forsythia, spirea, delphiniums, verbena . . . and on and on.

And I remember people coming to my mother's yard to be   42
given cuttings from her flowers; I hear again the praise showered
on her because whatever rocky soil she landed on, she turned
into a garden. A garden so brilliant with colors, so original in its
design, so magnificent with life and creativity, that to this day
people drive by our house in Georgia — perfect strangers and
imperfect strangers — and ask to stand or walk among my
mother's art.

I notice that it is only when my mother is working in her   43
flowers that she is radiant, almost to the point of being invisible
— except as Creator: hand and eye. She is involved in work her
soul must have. Ordering the universe in the image of her personal conception of Beauty.

Her face, as she prepares the Art that is her gift, is a legacy   44
of respect she leaves to me, for all that illuminates and cherishes
life. She has handed down respect for the possibilities — and the
will to grasp them.

For her, so hindered and intruded upon in so many ways,   45
being an artist has still been a daily part of her life. This ability
to hold on, even in very simple ways, is work black women have
done for a very long time.

This poem is not enough, but it is something, for the woman   46
who literally covered the holes in our walls with sunflowers:

> They were women then
> My mama's generation
> Husky of voice — Stout of
> Step
> With fists as well as
> Hands
> How they battered down
> Doors
> And ironed
> Starched white
> Shirts
> How they led
> Armies
> Headragged Generals
> Across mined
> Fields
> Booby-trapped
> Kitchens
> To discover books
> Desks
> A place for us
> How they knew what we
> *Must* know
> Without knowing a page
> Of it
> Themselves

Guided by my heritage of a love of beauty and a respect for   47
strength — in search of my mother's garden, I found my own.

And perhaps in Africa over two hundred years ago, there   48
was just such a mother; perhaps she painted vivid and daring
decorations in oranges and yellows and greens on the walls of
her hut; perhaps she sang — in a voice like Roberta Flack's —
sweetly over the compounds of her village; perhaps she wove the
most stunning mats or told the most ingenious stories of all the
village storytellers. Perhaps she was herself a poet — though
only her daughter's name is signed to the poems that we know.

Perhaps Phillis Wheatley's mother was also an artist.   49

Perhaps in more than Phillis Wheatley's biological life is her   50
mother's signature made clear.

QUESTIONS ON MEANING

1. What does the essay's title mean? Is the phrase "our mothers' gardens" to be taken literally? What other meanings might it suggest?
2. Why does Walker label early twentieth-century black women "Saints"? How does she define "saint"? What is the connection between saints and artists?
3. What is the point of the story about Phillis Wheatley? What does Walker mean by "contrary instincts"? If Wheatley's loyalties and mind were divided, what is it that divided them? Why does Walker feel Phillis Wheatley is not to blame for the fact that she depicts "liberty" as a *white* "goddess" in her poem? Why, according to Walker, does Wheatley deserve praise?
4. When *did* Alice Walker's mother have time "to know or care about feeding the creative spirit"? (See paragraph 32.) Walker claims the answer is "simple." What does she apparently think that answer is?

QUESTIONS ON WRITING STRATEGY

1. Review the examples in this essay and consider the order in which they appear. The author begins with a general discussion of the southern black woman's plight in the early 1920s, and then moves to a discussion of one such woman, Phillis Wheatley. Then Walker turns to another specific illustration: her mother. How effective is the order in which the author presents her examples?
2. To illustrate the main ideas of her essay, Walker uses two extended examples — Phillis Wheatley and Walker's mother. What do these women have in common, and how do they differ? What kind of knowledge does Walker have about her mother? Compared to that knowledge, how would you characterize Walker's knowledge of Phillis Wheatley? How are these two examples different from the examples given (in the form of a list of singers) in paragraph 12?
3. How do the Jean Toomer and Virginia Woolf quotations strengthen this essay?

4. The author makes parenthetical additions to Woolf's statements. Are these additions fair? That is, do they follow Woolf's general meaning, or do they take her words out of context?

QUESTIONS ON LANGUAGE

1. Look at the simile in paragraph 5: "They forced their minds to desert their bodies and their striving spirits sought to rise, like frail whirlwinds from the hard red clay." Find other FIGURES OF SPEECH in the essay, especially those involving images of the land and nature. How do these images connect with each other, and with the essay's title?
2. Where does the author use CONCRETE language? Where is the language more ABSTRACT? What relationship do you sense between the kind of language being used and the kind of example being presented?
3. Consult your dictionary if you need help defining the following words or phrases: in lieu of, dissipated (epigraph); abstractions (paragraph 1); fallow (8); ambivalent (25); matriarchs, appellations (26); inglorious (quotation in 36); profusely (40); legacy (44); ingenious (48).

SUGGESTIONS FOR WRITING

1. In paragraph 14, Walker writes that " . . . all the young women . . . have not perished in the wilderness. And if we ask ourselves why . . . we will know . . . just exactly who, and of what, we black American women are." Using examples, write an essay explaining, according to this essayist, who and what black American women are. Keep in mind the author's concepts of saints, spirituality, creativity, and art.
2. Consider some routine and daily chore (such as brushing your teeth, washing the dishes, doing the laundry, mowing the lawn) or an uninteresting, even oppressive job you may have held (working the counter at a fast-food restaurant, typing or filing, handing out leaflets on a crowded street corner). Try to imagine this activity as an art rather than an unpleasant task. Imagining yourself as a skilled artist, write an essay describing yourself at work. If you prefer, you may cast this essay in the third person, imagining someone else at work.

Alice Walker on Writing

In an interview with David Bradley, Alice Walker has described her method of writing as waiting for friendly spirits to visit her. Usually, she doesn't outline or devote much time to preliminary organization. She plunges in with a passion, and she sees a definite purpose in most of her work: to correct injustices. "I was brought up to try to see what was wrong, and right it. Since I am a writer, writing is how I right it. I was brought up to look at things that are out of joint, out of balance, and to try to bring them into balance. And as a writer that's what I do."

An articulate feminist, Walker has written in support of greater rights for women, including blacks. If most of her works are short — stories, essays, and poems — there is a reason: She sees thick, long-winded volumes as alien to a female sensibility. "The books women write can be more like us — much thinner, much leaner, much cleaner."

Much of Alice Walker's writing has emerged from painful experience: She has written of her impoverished early days on a Georgia sharecropper's farm, a childhood accident with a BB gun that cost her the sight of one eye, a traumatic abortion, years as a civil rights worker in Mississippi. "I think," she says, "writing really helps you heal yourself. I think if you write long enough, you will be a healthy person. That is, if you write what you need to write, as opposed to what will make money or what will make fame." (Quoted in "Telling the Black Woman's Story," *New York Times Magazine*, January 8, 1984, pp. 24–37.)

FOR DISCUSSION

1. What does the author mean when she speaks of the importance of writing "what you need to write"?
2. What writers can you think of whose work has helped to right the world's wrongs?
3. Can you cite any exceptions to Walker's generalization that long books are alien to women's sensibilities?

1. Select one of the following general statements, or set forth a general statement of your own that one of these inspires. Making it your central idea (or THESIS), maintain it in an essay full of examples. Draw your examples from your reading, your studies, your conversation, or your own experience.

   People one comes to admire don't always at first seem likable.
   Fashions this year are loonier than ever before.
   Bad habits are necessary to the nation's economy.
   Each family has its distinctive life-style.
   Certain song lyrics, closely inspected, will prove obscene.
   Comic books are going to the dogs.
   At some point in life, most people triumph over crushing difficulties.
   Churchgoers aren't perfect.
   TV commercials suggest: Buy this product and your love life will improve like crazy.
   Home cooking can't win over fast food.
   Ordinary lives sometimes give rise to legends.
   Some people I know are born winners (or losers).
   Books can change our lives.
   Certain machines *do* have personalities.
   Some road signs lead drivers astray.

2. In a brief essay, make some GENERALIZATION about either the terrors or the joys that ethnic minorities seem to share. To illustrate your generalization, draw examples from personal experience, from outside reading, or from two or three of the following *Bedford Reader* essays: Maya Angelou's "Champion of the World" in Chapter 1; Todd Alexander Senturia's "At Home in America" in Chapter 2; Brent Staples's "Black Men and Public Space" and Alice Walker's "In Search of Our Mothers' Gardens" in Chapter 3; A. M. Rosenthal's "No News from Auschwitz" in Chapter 4; Richard Rodriguez's "Aria" and Martin Luther King, Jr.'s "I Have a Dream" in Chapter 10; Joan Didion's "Miami: The Cuban Presence" in For Further Reading.

4

COMPARISON AND CONTRAST

Setting Things Side by Side

THE METHOD

Should we pass laws to regulate pornography, or just let pornography run wild? Which team do you place your money on, the Dolphins or the Colts? To go to school full-time or part-time: What are the rewards and drawbacks of each way of life? How do the Republican and the Democratic platforms stack up against each other? How is the work of Picasso like or unlike that of Matisse? These are questions that may be addressed by the dual method of *comparison and contrast*. In comparing, you point to similarities; in contrasting, to differences. Together, the two strategies use one subject to explain or clarify another by setting both subjects side by side.

With the aid of this method, you can show why you prefer one thing to another, one course of action to another, one idea to another. In an argument in which you support one of two possible choices, a careful and detailed comparison and contrast of the choices may be extremely convincing. In an expository essay, it can demonstrate that you understand your subjects thoroughly. That is why, on exams that call for essay answers, often you will be asked to compare and contrast. Sometimes the examiner will come right out and say, "Compare and contrast nineteenth-century methods of treating drug addiction with those of the present day." Sometimes, however, comparison and contrast won't even be mentioned by name; instead, the examiner will ask, "What resemblances and differences do you find between John Updike's short story 'A & P' and the Grimm fairy tale 'Godfather Death'?" Or, "Evaluate the relative desirability of holding a franchise as against going into business as an independent proprietor." But those — as you realize when you begin to plan your reply — are just other ways of asking you to compare and contrast.

In practice, the two methods are usually inseparable. A little reflection will show you why you need both. Say you intend to write a portrait-in-words of two people. No two people are in every respect exactly the same, or entirely dissimilar. Simply to compare them, or to contrast them, would not be true to life. To set them side by side and portray them accurately, you must consider both similarities and differences.

A good essay in comparing and contrasting serves a purpose. Most of the time, the writer of such an essay has one of two purposes in mind:

1. *The purpose of showing each of two subjects distinctly by considering both side by side.* Writing with such a purpose, the writer doesn't necessarily find one of the subjects better than the other. In "The Black and White Truth about Basketball" in this chapter, Jeff Greenfield details two styles of playing the game; and his conclusion is not that either black or white basketball is the more beautiful, but that the two styles can complement each other on the same court.

2. *The purpose of evaluating, or judging between two things.* In daily life, we often compare and contrast two possibilities to choose between them: which college course to elect, which

movie to see, which luncheon special to take — chipped beef over green noodles or fried smelt on a bun? Our thinking on a matter such as the last is quick and informal: "Hmmmm, the smelt *looks* better. Red beef, green noodles — ugh, what a sight! Smelt has bones, but the beef is rubbery. Still, I don't like the smell of that smelt. I'll go for the beef (or maybe just grab a hamburger after class)." In essays, too, a writer, by comparing points, decides which of two things is more admirable: "Organic Gardening, Yes; Gardening with Chemical Fertilizers, No!" — or "Skydiving versus the Safe, Sane Life." In writing, as in thinking, you need to consider the main features of both subjects, the positive features and the negative, and to choose the subject whose positive features more clearly predominate.

THE PROCESS

The first step in comparing and contrasting is to select subjects that will display a clear basis for comparison. In other words, you have to pick two subjects that have enough in common to be worth placing side by side. You'll have the best luck if you choose two of a kind: two California wines, two mystery writers, two schools of political thought. You can't readily compare and contrast, say, bowling in America with teacher training in Sweden, because the basis for comparison isn't apparent. You'll need to show your reader a valid reason for bringing the two together. From the title of his essay "Grant and Lee," Bruce Catton leads us to expect insights into the characters of the two Civil War generals. But in an essay called "General Grant and Mick Jagger," you would be hard-pressed to find any real basis for comparison. Although the writer might wax ingenious and claim, "Like Grant, Jagger has posed a definite threat to Nashville," the ingenuity would wear thin and soon the yoking together of general and rock star would fall apart.

The basis for comparison has to be carefully limited. You would be overly ambitious to try to compare and contrast the Soviet way of life with the American way of life in 500 words; you probably couldn't include all the important similarities and differences. In a brief paper, you would be wise to select a single point: to show, for instance, how day care centers in Russia and the United States are both alike and dissimilar.

Students occasionally groan when asked to compare and contrast things; but, in fact, this method isn't difficult. You have only to plan your paper carefully, make an outline (in your head or on paper), and then follow it. Here are two common ways to compare and contrast:

1. *Subject by subject.* Set forth all your facts about Subject A, then do the same for Subject B. Next, sum up their similarities and differences. In your conclusion, state what you think you have shown. This procedure works for a paper of a couple of paragraphs, but for a longer one, it has a built-in disadvantage. Readers need to remember all the facts about Subject A while they read about Subject B. If the essay is long and lists many facts, this procedure may burden the reader.

2. *Point by point.* Usually more workable in writing a long paper than the first method, a different method is to compare and contrast as you go. You consider one point at a time, taking up your two subjects alternately. In this way, you continually bring the subjects together, perhaps in every paragraph. Your outline might look like this:

TITLE: "Jed and Jake: Two Bluegrass Banjo-pickers"

PURPOSE: To show the distinct identities of the two musicians

INTRODUCTION: Who are Jed and Jake?

1. *Training*

   Jed: studied under Scruggs
   Jake: studied under Segovia

2. *Choice of material*

   Jed: traditional
   Jake: innovative

3. *Technical dexterity*

   Jed: highly skilled
   Jake: highly skilled

4. *Playing style*

> Jed: likes to show off
> Jake: keeps work simple

5. *On-stage manner*

> Jed: theatrical
> Jake: cool and reserved

CONCLUSION

And your conclusion might be: Although similar in degree of skill, the two differ greatly in aims and in personalities. Jed is better suited to the Grand Ol' Opry; Jake, to a concert hall. Now, this is a more extensive outline than you would need for a brief (say, 250-word) essay; but it might be fine for an essay of seven substantial paragraphs. (If you were writing only 250 words, you might not need any formal outline at all. You might just say your say about Jed, then do the same for Jake, briefly sum up the differences and similarities between the two, and then conclude.) Another way to organize a longer paper would be to group together all the similarities, then group together all the differences. No matter how you group your points, they have to balance; you can't discuss Jed's on-stage manner without discussing Jake's too. If you have nothing to say about Jake's on-stage manner, then you might as well omit the point.

As you write, an outline will help you see the shape of your paper and keep your procedure in mind. A sure-fire loser is the paper that proposes to compare and contrast two subjects but then proceeds to discuss quite different elements in each: Jed's playing style and Jake's choice of material, Jed's fondness for smelt on a bun and Jake's hobby of antique car collecting. The writer of such a paper doesn't compare and contrast the two musicians at all, but provides two quite separate discussions.

By the way, comparison and contrast works most efficiently for a *pair* of subjects. If you want to write about *three* banjo-pickers, you might first consider Jed and Jake, then Jake and Josh, then Josh and Jed — but it would probably be easiest to compare and contrast all three point by point.

In writing an essay of this variety, you may find an outline your firmest friend, but don't be the simple tool of your outline. Few essays are more boring to read than the long comparison-and-contrast written mechanically. The reader comes to feel like a weary tennis spectator, whose head has to swivel from side to side: now Jed, now back to Jake; now Jed again, now back to Jake again. No law decrees that an outline has to be followed in lock step order, nor that a list of similarities and a list of differences must be of the same length, nor that if you spend fifty words discussing Jed's banjo-picking skill, you are obliged to give Jake his fifty, too. Your essay, remember, doesn't need to be as symmetrical as a pair of salt and pepper shakers. What is your outline but a simple means to organize your account of a complicated reality? As you write, keep casting your thoughts upon a living, particular world — not twisting and squeezing that world into a rigid scheme, but moving through it with open senses, being patient and faithful and exact in your telling of it.

COMPARISON AND CONTRAST
IN A PARAGRAPH: TWO ILLUSTRATIONS

1. Using Comparison and Contrast
to Write about Television

Seen on aged 16-millimeter film, the original production of Paddy Chayevsky's "Marty" makes clear the differences between television drama of 1953 and that of today. Today there's no weekly Goodyear Playhouse to showcase original one-hour plays; most scriptwriters write serials about familiar characters. "Marty" features no car chases, no bodice ripping, no "Dallas" mansion. Instead, it simply shows the awakening of love between a heavyset butcher and a mousy high-school teacher: both single, lonely, and shy, never twice dating the same person. Unlike the writer of today, Chayevsky couldn't set scenes outdoors or on location. In one small studio, in slow lingering takes (some five minutes long — not eight to twelve seconds, as we now expect), the camera probes the faces of two seated characters as Marty and his pal Angie plan Saturday night ("What do you want to do?" — "I dunno, what do *you*?"). Oddly, the effect is spellbinding. To bring such scenes to life, the actors must project with vigor; and like the finer actors of today, Rod Steiger as Marty exploits each moment. In 1953, plays were telecast live. Today, well-edited videotape may eliminate blown lines, but a chill slickness prevails. Technically, "Marty" is primitive, yet it probes souls. Most televised drama today displays a physically larger world — only to nail a box around it.

COMMENT. The writer of this closely knit paragraph compares and contrasts televised drama of today with drama of television's so-called Golden Age — in particular, "Marty," an outstanding example. Most of his paragraph is taken up with differences. That both eras of television have actors who make the most of their time on screen is the one similarity he notices. In building his paragraph, the writer followed this outline:

1. *Today*: mostly serials
   Then: Goodyear Playhouse, weekly series of new plays
2. *Today*: violence, sex, luxury
   Then: simplicity
3. *Today*: scenes outdoors, on location
   Then: one small studio
4. *Today*: brief takes
   Then: long, slow takes
5. *Today*: good acting
   Then: good acting
6. *Today*: plays videotaped
   Then: plays telecast live
7. *Conclusion*: TV drama today shows a more limited world.

In fulfilling this outline, the writer didn't proceed in a rigid, mechanical alternation of *Today* and *Then*, but took each point in whatever order came naturally. This is a long outline, as a paragraph so full and meaty required, and it might have sufficed for a whole essay had the writer wanted to develop his comparison at greater length with the aid of other examples.

2. Using Comparison and Contrast in an Academic Discipline

The difference between adaptation and adaptability relates to another important distinction among species: the difference between *specialized* and *generalized* species. A special-

ized species depends heavily on adaptation for survival; a
generalized species depends more heavily on adaptability. The
difference may be clarified by an illustration. Koala bears are
mammals, sharing in many respects the extraordinary adaptability which characterizes mammals as a class. In the fundamental respect of subsistence, however, koala bears are specialized: They eat the leaves of only one species of eucalyptus
trees. Disease could wipe out the species of eucalyptus trees
and, as a result, the koala bears as well. *Homo sapiens* is a good
illustration of a generalized species; we are able to thrive almost anywhere. Our strong dependence upon culture for survival constitutes a unique form of specialized adaptation.

COMMENT.   Taken from the third edition of *Physical Anthropology* by A. J. Kelso and Wenda Trevathan (Englewood Cliffs,
New Jersey: Prentice-Hall, Inc., 1984, p. 71), this paragraph
makes clear what both generalized and specialized species are by
contrasting the two. Notice how the paragraph is organized.
The authors start by introducing their topic. Then they state
the major difference between specialized and generalized species:
The first depends upon adaptation, the second upon adaptability for survival. In the rest of the paragraph, the authors make
clear the difference by giving an example of each — the koala
and *homo sapiens* — to help readers grasp the general statement.
Why does this paragraph spend more time dealing with differences than with similarities between the koala and *homo sapiens*?
We can answer that question with another: What is the paragraph's purpose?

· Jeff Greenfield ·

JEFF GREENFIELD, born in 1943, was graduated from Yale University School of Law. He became a sportswriter, humorist, and media commentator for CBS-TV, and at present he is a political and media analyst for ABC News and a syndicated columnist. Earlier in his career, he served as a staff aide and writer of speeches for both John V. Lindsay, former mayor of New York City, and the late attorney general Robert F. Kennedy. His books include *A Populist Manifesto* (1972), *Where Have You Gone, Joe DiMaggio?* (1973), *The World's Greatest Team* (a history of the Boston Celtics, 1976), *Television: The First 50 Years* (1977), *Playing to Win: An Insider's Guide to Politics* (1980), and *The Real Campaign* (1982).

The Black and White Truth about Basketball

When Jeff Greenfield's survey of "black" and "white" basketball, subtitled "A Skin-Deep Theory of Style," was first published in *Esquire* magazine in 1975, it provoked immediate interest and controversy. For this edition of *The Bedford Reader*, Greenfield again revised his essay and brought it up to date. (His thesis in this 1988 version is essentially unchanged.)

The dominance of black athletes over professional basketball is beyond dispute. Two-thirds of the players are black, and the number would be greater were it not for the continuing practice of picking white bench warmers for the sake of balance. Over the last two decades, no more than three white players have been among the ten starting players on the National Basketball Association's All-Star team, and in the last quarter century, only two white players — Dave Cowens and Larry Bird of the Boston Celtics — have ever been chosen as the NBA's Most Valuable Player.

And at a time when a baseball executive could lose his job for asserting that blacks lacked "the necessities" to become pro

209

sports executives and when the National Football League still has not hired a single black head coach, the NBA stands as a pro sports league that hired its first black head coach in 1968 (Bill Russell) and its first black general manager in the early 1970s (Wayne Embry of the Milwaukee Bucks). What discrimination remains — lack of equal opportunity for speaking engagements and product endorsements — has more to do with society than with basketball.

This dominance reflects a natural inheritance: Basketball is   3
a pastime of the urban poor. The current generation of black athletes are heirs to a tradition more than half a century old. In a neighborhood without the money for bats, gloves, hockey sticks and ice skates, or shoulder pads, basketball is an eminently accessible sport. "Once it was the game of the Irish and Italian Catholics in Rockaway and the Jews on Fordham Road in the Bronx," writes David Wolf in his brilliant book, *Foul!* "It was recreation, status, and a way out." But now the ethnic names have been changed: Instead of the Red Holzmans, Red Auerbachs, and the McGuire brothers, there are Julius Ervings and Michael Jordans, Ralph Sampsons and Kareem Abdul-Jabbars. And professional basketball is a sport with national television exposure and million-dollar salaries.

But the mark on basketball of today's players can be mea-   4
sured by more than money or visibility. It is a question of style. For there is a clear difference between "black" and "white" styles of play that is as clear as the difference between 155th Street at Eighth Avenue and Crystal City, Missouri. Most simply (remembering we are talking about culture, not chromosomes), "black" basketball is the use of superb athletic skill to adapt to the limits of space imposed by the game. "White" ball is the pulverization of that space by sheer intensity.[1]

---

[1]This distinction has nothing to do with the question of whether whites can play as "well" as blacks. In 1987, the Detroit Pistons' Isaiah Thomas quipped that the Celtics' Larry Bird was "a pretty good player," but would be much less celebrated and wealthy if he were black. As Thomas later said, Bird is one of the greatest pro players in history. Nor is this distinction about "smart," although the Los Angeles Lakers' Magic Johnson is right in saying that too many journalists ascribe brilliant strategy by black players to be solely due to "innate" ability.

It takes a conscious effort to realize how constricted the space is on a basketball court. Place a regulation court (ninety-four by fifty feet) on a football field, and it will reach from the back of the end zone to the twenty-one-yard line; its width will cover less than a third of the field. On a baseball diamond, a basketball court will reach from home plate to first base. Compared to its principal indoor rival, ice hockey, basketball covers about one-fourth the playing area. Moreover, during the normal flow of the game, most of the action takes place on the third of the court nearest the basket. It is in this dollhouse space that ten men, each of them half a foot taller than the average man, come together to battle each other.

There is, thus, no room; basketball is a struggle for the edge: the half step with which to cut around the defender for a lay-up, the half second of freedom with which to release a jump shot, the instant a head turns allowing a pass to a teammate breaking for the basket. It is an arena for the subtlest of skills: the head fake, the shoulder fake, the shift of body weight to the right and the sudden cut to the left. Deception is crucial to success; and to young men who have learned early and painfully that life is a battle for survival, basketball is one of the few pursuits in which the weapon of deception is a legitimate tactic rather than the source of trouble.

If there is, then, the need to compete in a crowd, to battle for the edge, then the surest strategy is to develop the *unexpected*: to develop a shot that is simply and fundamentally different from the usual methods of putting the ball in the basket. Drive to the hoop, but go under it and come up the other side; hold the ball at waist level and shoot from there instead of bringing the ball up to eye level; leap into the air, but fall away from the basket instead of toward it. All these tactics, which a fan can see embodied in the astonishing play of the Chicago Bulls' Michael Jordan, take maximum advantage of the crowding on the court. They also stamp uniqueness on young men who may feel it nowhere else.

"For many young men in the slums," David Wolf writes, "the school yard is the only place they can feel true pride in what they do, where they can move free of inhibitions and where they can, by being spectacular, rise for the moment against the drabness and anonymity of their lives. Thus, when a player develops extraordinary 'school yard' moves and shots . . . [they] become his measure as a man."

So the moves that begin as tactics for scoring soon become   9
calling cards. You don't just lay the ball in for an uncontested basket; you take the ball in both hands, leap as high as you can, and slam the ball through the hoop. When you jump in the air, fake a shot, bring the ball back to your body, and throw up a shot, all without coming back down, you have proven your worth in uncontestable fashion.

This liquid grace is an integral part of "black" ball, almost   10
exclusively the province of the playground player. Some white stars like Bob Cousy, Billy Cunningham, and Doug Collins had it, and the Celtics' Kevin McHale has it now: the body control, the moves to the basket, the free-ranging mobility. Most of them also possessed the surface ease that is integral to the "black" style; an incorporation of the ethic of mean streets — to "make it" is not just to have wealth but to have it without strain. Whatever the muscles and organs are doing, the face of the "black" star almost never shows it. Magic Johnson of the Lakers can bring the ball down court with two men on him, whip a pass through an invisible opening, cut to the basket, take a return pass, and hit the shot all with no more emotion than a quick smile. So stoic was San Antonio Spurs' great George Gervin that he earned the nickname "Ice Man." (Interestingly, a black coach like Boston's K. C. Jones exhibits far less emotion on the bench than a white counterpart like Dick Motta or Jack Ramsey.)

If there is a single trait that characterizes "black" ball it is   11
leaping ability. Bob Cousy, ex-Celtic great and former pro coach, says that "when coaches get together, one is sure to say, 'I've got the one black kid in the country who can't jump.' When coaches see a white boy who can jump or who moves with extraordinary quickness, they say, 'He should have been born black, he's that good.' "

Don Nelson, now a top executive with the Golden State   12
Warriors, recalls that back in 1970, Dave Cowens, then a relatively unknown graduate of Florida State, prepared for his rookie pro season by playing in the Rucker League, an outdoor competition in Harlem playgrounds that pits pros against college

kids and playground stars. So ferocious was Cowens' leaping ability, Nelson says, that "when the summer was over, everyone wanted to know who the white son of a bitch was who could jump so high." That's another way to overcome a crowd around the basket — just go over it.

Speed, mobility, quickness, acceleration, "the moves" — all of these are catch-phrases that surround the "black" playground athlete, the style of play. So does the most racially tinged of attributes, "rhythm." Yet rhythm is what the black stars themselves talk about: feeling the flow of the game, finding the tempo of the dribble, the step, the shot. It is an instinctive quality (although it stems from hundreds of hours of practice), and it is one that has led to difficulty between system-oriented coaches and free-form players. 13

"Cats from the street have their own rhythm when they play," said college dropout Bill Spivey, onetime New York high school star. "It's not a matter of somebody setting you up and you shooting. You *feel* the shot. When a coach holds you back, you lose the feel and it isn't fun anymore." 14

When legendary Brooklyn playground star Connie Hawkins was winding up his NBA career under Laker coach Bill Sharman, he chafed under the methodical style of play. "He's systematic to the point where it begins to be a little too much. It's such an action-reaction type of game that when you have to do everything the same way, I think you lose something." 15

There is another kind of basketball that has grown up in America. It is not played on asphalt playgrounds with a crowd of kids competing for the court; it is played on macadam driveways by one boy with a ball and a backboard nailed over the garage; it is played in gyms in the frigid winter of the rural Midwest and on Southern dirt courts. It is a mechanical, precise development of skills (when Don Nelson was an Iowa farm boy, his incentive to make his shots was that an errant rebound would land in the middle of chicken droppings). It is a game without frills, without flow, but with effectiveness. It is "white" basketball: jagged, sweaty, stumbling, intense. Where a "black" player overcomes an obstacle with finesse and body control, a "white" player reacts by outrunning or overpowering the obstacle. 16

By this definition, the Boston Celtics are a classically 17

"white" team. They rarely suit up a player with dazzling moves; indeed such a player would probably make Red Auerbach swallow his cigar. Instead, the Celtics wear you down with execution, with constant running, with the same play run again and again and again. The rebound by Robert Parrish triggers the fast break, as everyone races downcourt; the ball goes to Larry Bird, who pulls up and takes the shot or who drives and then finds Danny Ainge or Kevin McHale free for an easy basket.

Perhaps the most definitively "white" position is that of the quick forward, one without great moves to the basket, without highly developed shots, without the height and mobility for rebounding effectiveness. So what does he do?   18

He runs. He runs from the opening jump to the final buzzer. He runs up and down the court, from base line to base line, back and forth under the basket, looking for the opening, the pass, the chance to take a quick step, the high percentage shot. To watch San Antonio's Mark Olberding or Detroit's Bill Lambeer, players without speed or obvious moves, is to wonder what they are doing in the NBA — until you see them swing free and throw up a shot that, without demanding any apparent skill, somehow goes in the basket more frequently than the shots of many of their more skilled teammates. And to have watched the New York Knicks' (now U.S. Senator) Bill Bradley, or the Celtics' John Havlicek, is to have watched "white" ball at its best.   19

Havlicek or Lambeer, or the Lakers' Kurt Rambis, stand in dramatic contrast to Michael Jordan or to the Philadelphia 76ers' legend, Julius Erving. Erving had the capacity to make legends come true, leaping from the foul line and slam-dunking the ball on his way down; going up for a lay-up, pulling the ball to his body, and driving under and up the other side of the rim, defying gravity and probability with impossible moves and jumps. Michael Jordan of the Chicago Bulls has been seen by thousands spinning a full 360 degrees in midair before slamming the ball through the hoop.   20

When John Havlicek played, by contrast, he was the living embodiment of his small-town Ohio background. He would bring the ball downcourt, weaving left, then right, looking for a path. He would swing the ball to a teammate, cut behind the pick, take the pass, and release the shot in a flicker of time. It   21 looked plain, unvarnished. But it was a blend of skills that not more than half a dozen other players in the league possessed.

To former pro Jim McMillian, a black who played quick forward with "white" attributes, "it's a matter of environment. Julius Erving grew up in a different environment from Havlicek. John came from a very small town in Ohio. There everything was done the easy way, the shortest distance between two points. It's nothing fancy; very few times will he go one-on-one. He hits the lay-up, hits the jump shot, makes the free throw, and after the game you look up and say, 'How did he hurt us that much?' "

"White" ball, then, is the basketball of patience, method and sometimes brute strength. "Black" ball is the basketball of electric self-expression. One player has all the time in the world to perfect his skills, the other a need to prove himself. These are slippery categories, because a poor boy who is black can play "white" and a white boy of middle-class parents can play "black." Bill Cartwright of the New York Knicks and Steve Alford of the Dallas Mavericks are athletes who seem to defy these categories.

And what makes basketball the most intriguing of sports is how these styles do not necessarily clash; how the punishing intensity of "white" players and the dazzling moves of the "blacks" can fit together, a fusion of cultures that seems more and more difficult in the world beyond the out-of-bounds line.

QUESTIONS ON MEANING

1. According to Greenfield, how did black athletes come to dominate professional basketball?
2. What differences does the author discern between "black" and "white" styles of play? How do exponents of the two styles differ in showing emotion?
3. How does Greenfield account for these differences? Sum up in your own words the author's point about school yards (paragraph 8) and his point about macadam driveways, gyms, and dirt courts (paragraph 16). Explain "the ethic of mean streets" (paragraph 10).
4. Does Greenfield stereotype black and white players? Where in his

essay does he admit there are players who don't fit neatly into his
two categories?

5. Do you agree with the author's observations about playing style?
Can you think of any EVIDENCE to the contrary?

QUESTIONS ON WRITING STRATEGY

1. How much do we have to know about professional basketball to
appreciate Greenfield's essay? Is it written only for basketball fans,
or for a general AUDIENCE?

2. In what passage in his essay does Greenfield begin comparing and
contrasting? What has been the function of the paragraphs that
have come before this passage?

3. In paragraph 5 the author compares a basketball court to a football field, a baseball diamond, and an ice hockey arena. What is
the basis for his comparison?

4. Where in his essay does Greenfield concentrate on "black" basketball? Where does he explain what "white" basketball is? To which
of the two styles does he devote more space? Where does he illustrate both together?

QUESTIONS ON LANGUAGE

1. Consult the dictionary if you need help in defining the following
words: ethnic (3); constricted (5); inhibitions, anonymity (8); uncontestable (9); finesse (16); execution (17); embodiment (21).

2. Talk to someone who knows basketball if you need help in understanding the head fake, the shoulder fake (paragraph 6); fast break
(17); high-percentage shot (19); jump shot (22). What kind of DIC-
TION do you find in these instances?

3. When Greenfield says, "We are talking about culture, not chromosomes" (paragraph 4), how would you expect him to define these
terms?

4. Explain the author's reference to the word *rhythm* as "the most racially tinged of attributes" (paragraph 13).

SUGGESTIONS FOR WRITING

1. In a paragraph or two, discuss how well you think Greenfield has
surmounted the difficulties facing any writer who makes GENERAL-
IZATIONS about people.

2. Compare and contrast college basketball and professional basketball (or, for a narrower subject, a college team and a pro team).

3. Write a brief essay in which you compare and contrast the styles of any two athletes who play the same game.
4. Compare and contrast the styles of two people in the same line of work, showing how their work is affected by their different personalities. You might take, for instance, two singers, two taxidrivers, two bank tellers, two evangelists, two teachers, or two symphony orchestra conductors.

Jeff Greenfield on Writing

For *The Bedford Reader*, Jeff Greenfield told how he gathered his information for "The Black and White Truth about Basketball" from basketball professionals, and how he tried to contrast the two styles of play with humor and goodwill. "In the early 1970s," he commented, "I was spending a good deal of time playing hookey from my work as a political consultant writing books and magazine articles; and no writing was more enjoyable than sports reporting. . . . Coming from the world of politics where everything was debatable — who would win, whose position was right, who was engaging in 'desperation smear tactics' — I relished the world of sports, where winners and losers were clearly identifiable. . . .

"It was while writing about various star basketball players of the time — men like the New York Knicks' Willis Reed, the Boston Celtics' Dave Cowens — that I first began noticing how often offhand, utterly unmalicious racial references were being thrown about. A white player in practice would miss a rebound, and a black teammate would joke, 'Come on, man, jump like a brother.' A black player would lose a footrace for a ball, and someone would quip, 'Looks black, plays white.' It slowly became clear to me that many of those in the basketball world freely acknowledged that there were different styles of play that broke down, roughly speaking, into black and white characteristics.

"At first, it did not even occur to me that this would make a publishable magazine piece. For one thing, I came from a typical post-war liberal family, repulsed by the racial stereotypes which still dominated 'respectable' conversation. In a time when black Americans were heavily portrayed as happy-go-lucky, shiftless, childlike adults, consigned to success as athletes and tap-dancers, the idea that there was anything like a 'black' or 'white' way to play basketball would have seemed something out of a segregationist manifesto.

"For another, I have always been an enthusiastic follower of the sports pages and had never seen any such analysis in the many newspapers I read. Apparently, most sportswriters felt equally uncomfortable with a foray into race; it had, after all, taken baseball more than a half a century to admit blacks into its ranks. Indeed, one of the more common assertions of bigots in the 1930s and 1940s was that blacks could not be great athletes because 'they couldn't take the pressure.' It is easy to understand why race was not a comfortable basis on which to analyze athletic grace.

"In the end, I decided to write about 'black' and 'white' basketball because it made the game more enjoyable to me. Clearly, there *were* different ways to play the game; clearly the kind of self-assertion represented by the spectacular moves of black schoolyard ball was a reflection of how important the game was to an inner-city kid, for whom the asphalt court was the cheapest — maybe the only — release from a nasty, sometimes brutish, existence. And books such as Pete Axthelm's *The City Game* and David Wolf's *Foul!* had brilliantly explored the significance of basketball in the urban black world of modern America.

"I talked with players and sportswriters alike when I wrote the article; without exception, they approached the subject as I did: with humor, unself-consciously. Perhaps it is a measure of the progress we have made in racial matters that no one — black or white — thought it insulting or offensive to remark on the different styles of play, to note that the gravity-defying slam-dunks of a Julius Erving and the carefully-calibrated shots of a Kevin McHale are two facets of the same game."

FOR DISCUSSION

1. What gave Greenfield the idea for his essay?
2. What aspects of his topic made Greenfield hesitant to write about it? What persuaded him to go ahead?

· Suzanne Britt ·

SUZANNE BRITT was born in Winston-Salem, North Carolina, and studied at Salem College and Washington University. She is a regular columnist for the *Dickens Dispatch*, a national newsletter for Charles Dickens disciples, and for the Research Triangle Park *Leader*, which serves Chapel Hill, Durham, and Raleigh, North Carolina. In addition, Britt frequently contributes to *Books & Religion*, a newspaper of social and theological comment, published by Duke University. She has also written for the Des Moines *Register* and *Tribune*, the Baltimore *Sun*, *Newsday*, and the *New York Times*; and she has had five essays published in the "My Turn" column of *Newsweek* magazine. Her books include *Show and Tell* (1983) and *Skinny People are Dull and Crunchy Like Carrots* (1982).

Neat People vs. Sloppy People

"Neat People vs. Sloppy People" appears in Britt's collection of informal essays, *Show and Tell* (Raleigh, North Carolina, 1983). Mingling humor with seriousness (as she often does), Britt has called the book a report on her journey into "the awful cave of self: You shout your name and voices come back in exultant response, telling you their names." In this essay about certain inescapable personality traits, you may recognize some aspects of your *own* self, awful or otherwise.

I've finally figured out the difference between neat people and sloppy people. The distinction is, as always, moral. Neat people are lazier and meaner than sloppy people.

Sloppy people, you see, are not really sloppy. Their sloppiness is merely the unfortunate consequence of their extreme moral rectitude. Sloppy people carry in their mind's eye a heavenly vision, a precise plan, that is so stupendous, so perfect, it can't be achieved in this world or the next.

Sloppy people live in Never-Never Land. Someday is their métier. Someday they are planning to alphabetize all their books

219

and set up home catalogues. Someday they will go through their wardrobes and mark certain items for tentative mending and certain items for passing on to relatives of similar shape and size. Someday sloppy people will make family scrapbooks into which they will put newspaper clippings, postcards, locks of hair, and the dried corsage from their senior prom. Someday they will file everything on the surface of their desks, including the cash receipts from coffee purchases at the snack shop. Someday they will sit down and read all the back issues of *The New Yorker*.

For all these noble reasons and more, sloppy people never   4
get neat. They aim too high and wide. They save everything, planning someday to file, order, and straighten out the world. But while these ambitious plans take clearer and clearer shape in their heads, the books spill from the shelves onto the floor, the clothes pile up in the hamper and closet, the family mementos accumulate in every drawer, the surface of the desk is buried under mounds of paper and the unread magazines threaten to reach the ceiling.

Sloppy people can't bear to part with anything. They give   5
loving attention to every detail. When sloppy people say they're going to tackle the surface of the desk, they really mean it. Not a paper will go unturned; not a rubber band will go unboxed. Four hours or two weeks into the excavation, the desk looks exactly the same, primarily because the sloppy person is meticulously creating new piles of papers with new headings and scrupulously stopping to read all the old book catalogs before he throws them away. A neat person would just bulldoze the desk.

Neat people are bums and clods at heart. They have cavalier   6
attitudes toward possessions, including family heirlooms. Everything is just another dust-catcher to them. If anything collects dust, it's got to go and that's that. Neat people will toy with the idea of throwing the children out of the house just to cut down on the clutter.

Neat people don't care about process. They like results.   7
What they want to do is get the whole thing over with so they can sit down and watch the rasslin' on TV. Neat people operate on two unvarying principles: Never handle any item twice, and throw everything away.

The only thing messy in a neat person's house is the trash 8
can. The minute something comes to a neat person's hand, he
will look at it, try to decide if it has immediate use and, finding
none, throw it in the trash.

Neat people are especially vicious with mail. They never go 9
through their mail unless they are standing directly over a trash
can. If the trash can is beside the mailbox, even better. All ads,
catalogs, pleas for charitable contributions, church bulletins and
money-saving coupons go straight into the trash can without being opened. All letters from home, postcards from Europe, bills
and paychecks are opened, immediately responded to, then
dropped in the trash can. Neat people keep their receipts only
for tax purposes. That's it. No sentimental salvaging of birthday
cards or the last letter a dying relative ever wrote. Into the trash
it goes.

Neat people place neatness above everything, even eco- 10
nomics. They are incredibly wasteful. Neat people throw away
several toys every time they walk through the den. I knew a neat
person once who threw away a perfectly good dish drainer because it had mold on it. The drainer was too much trouble to
wash. And neat people sell their furniture when they move.
They will sell a La-Z-Boy recliner while you are reclining in it.

Neat people are no good to borrow from. Neat people buy 11
everything in expensive little single portions. They get their
flour and sugar in two-pound bags. They wouldn't consider clipping a coupon, saving a leftover, reusing plastic non-dairy
whipped cream containers or rinsing off tin foil and draping
it over the unmoldy dish drainer. You can never borrow a
neat person's newspaper to see what's playing at the movies.
Neat people have the paper all wadded up and in the trash by
7:05 A.M.

Neat people cut a clean swath through the organic as well as 12
the inorganic world. People, animals, and things are all one to
them. They are so insensitive. After they've finished with the
pantry, the medicine cabinet, and the attic, they will throw out
the red geranium (too many leaves), sell the dog (too many
fleas), and send the children off to boarding school (too many
scuffmarks on the hardwood floors).

QUESTIONS ON MEANING

1. "Suzanne Britt believes that neat people are lazy, mean, petty, callous, wasteful, and insensitive." How would you respond to this statement?
2. Is the author's main PURPOSE to make fun of neat people, to assess the habits of neat and sloppy people, to help neat and sloppy people get along better, to amuse and entertain, or to prove that neat people are morally inferior to sloppy people? Discuss.
3. What is meant by "as always" in the sentence "The distinction is, as always, moral" (paragraph 1)? Does the author seem to be suggesting that any and all distinctions between people are moral?

QUESTIONS ON WRITING STRATEGY

1. What is the general TONE of this essay? What words and phrases help you determine that tone?
2. Consider the following GENERALIZATIONS: "For all these noble reasons and more, sloppy people never get neat" (paragraph 4) and "The only thing messy in a neat person's house is the trash can" (paragraph 8). How can you tell that these statements are generalizations? Look for other generalizations in the essay. What is the EFFECT of using so many?
3. What similarities does Britt see between neat and sloppy people? If a good essay in comparing and contrasting examines both similarities and differences, does that mean this is not a good essay? Why might a writer deliberately focus on differences and give very little time to similarities?

QUESTIONS ON LANGUAGE

1. Consult your dictionary for definitions of these words: rectitude (paragraph 2); métier, tentative (3); accumulate (4); excavation, meticulously, scrupulously (5); salvaging (9).
2. How do you understand the use of the word *noble* in the first sentence of paragraph 4? Is it meant literally? Are there other words in the essay that appear to be written in a similar tone?

SUGGESTIONS FOR WRITING

1. Write an essay in which you compare and contrast two apparently dissimilar groups of people: for example, blue-collar workers and

white-collar workers, people who write letters and people who don't write letters, runners and football players, readers and TV watchers, or any other variation you choose. Your approach may be either lighthearted or serious, but make sure you come to some conclusion about your subjects. Which group do you favor? Why?

2. Analyze the similarities and differences between two characters in your favorite novel, story, film, or television show. Which aspects of their personalities make them work well together, within the context in which they appear? Which characteristics work against each other, and therefore provide the necessary conflict to hold the readers' or viewers' attention?

Suzanne Britt on Writing

Asked to tell how she writes, Suzanne Britt contributed the following comment to *The Bedford Reader.*

"The question 'How do you write?' gets a snappy, snappish response from me. The first commandment is 'Live!' And the second is like unto it: 'Pay attention!' I don't mean that you have to live high or fast or deep or wise or broad. And I certainly don't mean you have to live true and upright. I just mean that you have to suck out all the marrow of whatever you do, whether it's picking the lint off the navy-blue suit you'll be wearing to Cousin Ione's funeral or popping an Aunt Jemimah frozen waffle into the toaster oven or lying between sand dunes, watching the way the sea oats slice the azure sky. The ominous question put to me by students on all occasions of possible accountability is 'Will this count?' My answer is rock bottom and hard: 'Everything counts,' I say, and silence falls like prayers across the room.

"The same is true of writing. Everything counts. Despair is good. Numbness can be excellent. Misery is fine. Ecstasy will work — or pain or sorrow or passion. The only thing that won't work is indifference. A writer refuses to be shocked and appalled by anything going or coming, rising or falling, singing or soundless. The only thing that shocks me, truth to tell, is indifference. How dare you not fight for the right to the crispy end piece on the standing-rib roast? How dare you let the fragrance of Joy go by without taking a whiff of it? How dare you not see the old woman in the snap-front housedress and the rolled-down socks, carrying her Polident and Charmin in a canvas tote that says, simply, elegantly, Le Bag?

"After you have lived, paid attention, seen connections, felt the harmony, writhed under the dissonance, fixed a Diet Coke, popped a big stick of Juicy Fruit in your mouth, gathered your life around you as a mother hen gathers her brood, as a queen settles the folds in her purple robes, you are ready to write. And what you will write about, even if you have one of those teachers who makes you write about, say, Guatemala, will be something very exclusive and intimate — something just between you and Guatemala. All you have to find out is what that small intimacy might be. It is there. And having found it, you have to make it count.

"There is no rest for a writer. But there is no boredom either. A Sunday morning with a bottle of extra-strength aspirin within easy reach and an ice bag on your head can serve you very well in writing. So can a fly buzzing at your ear or a heart-stopping siren in the night or an interminable afternoon in a biology lab in front of a frog's innards.

"All you need, really, is the audacity to believe, with your whole being, that if you tell it right, tell it truly, tell it so we can all see it, the 'it' will play in Peoria, Poughkeepsie, Pompeii, or Podunk. In the South we call that conviction, that audacity, an act of faith. But you can call it writing."

FOR DISCUSSION

1. What advice does Britt offer a student assigned to write a paper about, say, Guatemala? If you were that student, how would you go about taking her advice?
2. Where in her comment does the author use colorful and effective FIGURES OF SPEECH?
3. What is the TONE of Britt's remarks? Sum up her attitude toward her subject, writing.

· Bruce Catton ·

BRUCE CATTON (1899–1978) became America's best-known historian of the Civil War. As a boy in Benzonia, Michigan, Catton acted out historical battles on local playing fields. In his memoir *Waiting for the Morning Train* (1972), he recalls how he would listen by the hour to the memories of Union Army veterans. His studies at Oberlin College interrupted by service in World War I, Catton never finished his bachelor's degree. Instead, he worked as a reporter, columnist, and editorial writer for the Cleveland *Plain Dealer* and other newspapers, then became a speechwriter and information director for government agencies. Of Catton's eighteen books, seventeen were written after his fiftieth year. *A Stillness at Appomattox* (1953) won him both a Pulitzer Prize for history and a National Book Award; other notable works include *This Hallowed Ground* (1956) and *Gettysburg: The Final Fury* (1974). From 1954 until his death, Catton edited *American Heritage*, a magazine of history. President Gerald Ford awarded him a Medal of Freedom for his life's accomplishment.

Grant and Lee:
A Study in Contrasts

"Grant and Lee: A Study in Contrasts" first appeared in *The American Story*, a book of essays written by eminent historians. In his discussion of the two great Civil War generals, Catton contrasts not only two very different men, but the conflicting traditions they represented. Catton's essay builds toward the conclusion that, in one outstanding way, the two leaders were more than a little alike.

When Ulysses S. Grant and Robert E. Lee met in the parlor of a modest house at Appomattox Court House, Virginia, on April 9, 1865, to work out the terms for the surrender of Lee's Army of Northern Virginia, a great chapter in American life came to a close, and a great new chapter began.

These men were bringing the Civil War to its virtual finish.   2
To be sure, other armies had yet to surrender, and for a few days
the fugitive Confederate government would struggle desperately
and vainly, trying to find some way to go on living now that its
chief support was gone. But in effect it was all over when Grant
and Lee signed the papers. And the little room where they wrote
out the terms was the scene of one of the poignant, dramatic
contrasts in American history.

They were two strong men, these oddly different generals,   3
and they represented the strengths of two conflicting currents
that, through them, had come into final collision.

Back of Robert E. Lee was the notion that the old aristo-   4
cratic concept might somehow survive and be dominant in
American life.

Lee was tidewater Virginia, and in his background were   5
family, culture, and tradition . . . the age of chivalry trans-
planted to a New World which was making its own legends and
its own myths. He embodied a way of life that had come down
through the age of knighthood and the English country squire.
America was a land that was beginning all over again, dedicated
to nothing much more complicated than the rather hazy belief
that all men had equal rights, and should have an equal chance
in the world. In such a land Lee stood for the feeling that it was
somehow of advantage to human society to have a pronounced
inequality in the social structure. There should be a leisure class,
backed by ownership of land; in turn, society itself should be
keyed to the land as the chief source of wealth and influence. It
would bring forth (according to this ideal) a class of men with a
strong sense of obligation to the community; men who lived not
to gain advantage for themselves, but to meet the solemn obliga-
tions which had been laid on them by the very fact that they
were privileged. From them the country would get its leadership;
to them it could look for the higher values — of thought, of conduct, of personal deportment — to give it strength and virtue.

Lee embodied the noblest elements of this aristocratic ideal.   6
Through him, the landed nobility justified itself. For four years,
the Southern states had fought a desperate war to uphold the
ideals for which Lee stood. In the end, it almost seemed as if the

Confederacy fought for Lee; as if he himself was the Confederacy . . . the best thing that the way of life for which the Confederacy stood could ever have to offer. He had passed into legend before Appomattox. Thousands of tired, underfed, poorly clothed Confederate soldiers, long-since past the simple enthusiasm of the early days of the struggle, somehow considered Lee the symbol of everything for which they had been willing to die. But they could not quite put this feeling into words. If the Lost Cause, sanctified by so much heroism and so many deaths, had a living justification, its justification was General Lee.

Grant, the son of a tanner on the Western frontier, was everything Lee was not. He had come up the hard way, and embodied nothing in particular except the eternal toughness and sinewy fiber of the men who grew up beyond the mountains. He was one of a body of men who owed reverence and obeisance to no one, who were self-reliant to a fault, who cared hardly anything for the past but who had a sharp eye for the future. 7

These frontier men were the precise opposites of the tidewater aristocrats. Back of them, in the great surge that had taken people over the Alleghenies and into the opening Western country, there was a deep, implicit dissatisfaction with a past that had settled into grooves. They stood for democracy, not from any reasoned conclusion about the proper ordering of human society, but simply because they had grown up in the middle of democracy and knew how it worked. Their society might have privileges, but they would be privileges each man had won for himself. Forms and patterns meant nothing. No man was born to anything, except perhaps to a chance to show how far he could rise. Life was competition. 8

Yet along with this feeling had come a deep sense of belonging to a national community. The Westerner who developed a farm, opened a shop, or set up in business as a trader could hope to prosper only as his own community prospered — and his community ran from the Atlantic to the Pacific and from Canada down to Mexico. If the land was settled, with towns and highways and accessible markets, he could better himself. He saw his fate in terms of the nation's own destiny. As its horizons expanded, so did his. He had, in other words, an acute dollars- 9 and-cents stake in the continued growth and development of his country.

And that, perhaps, is where the contrast between Grant   10
and Lee becomes most striking. The Virginia aristocrat, inevitably, saw himself in relation to his own region. He lived in a static society which could endure almost anything except change. Instinctively, his first loyalty would go to the locality in which that society existed. He would fight to the limit of endurance to defend it, because in defending it he was defending everything that gave his own life its deepest meaning.

The Westerner, on the other hand, would fight with an   11
equal tenacity for the broader concept of society. He fought so because everything he lived by was tied to growth, expansion, and a constantly widening horizon. What he lived by would survive or fall with the nation itself. He could not possibly stand by unmoved in the face of an attempt to destroy the Union. He would combat it with everything he had, because he could only see it as an effort to cut the ground out from under his feet.

So Grant and Lee were in complete contrast, representing   12
two diametrically opposed elements in American life. Grant was the modern man emerging; beyond him, ready to come on the stage, was the great age of steel and machinery, of crowded cities and a restless, burgeoning vitality. Lee might have ridden down from the old age of chivalry, lance in hand, silken banner fluttering over his head. Each man was the perfect champion of his cause, drawing both his strengths and his weaknesses from the people he led.

Yet it was not all contrast, after all. Different as they were —   13
in background, in personality, in underlying aspiration — these two great soldiers had much in common. Under everything else, they were marvelous fighters. Furthermore, their fighting qualities were really very much alike.

Each man had, to begin with, the great virtue of utter tenac-   14
ity and fidelity. Grant fought his way down the Mississippi Valley in spite of acute personal discouragement and profound military handicaps. Lee hung on in the trenches at Petersburg after hope itself had died. In each man there was an indomitable quality . . . the born fighter's refusal to give up as long as he can still remain on his feet and lift his two fists.

Daring and resourcefulness they had, too; the ability to 15
think faster and move faster than the enemy. These were the
qualities which gave Lee the dazzling campaigns of Second
Manassas and Chancellorsville and won Vicksburg for Grant.

Lastly, and perhaps greatest of all, there was the ability, at 16
the end, to turn quickly from war to peace once the fighting was
over. Out of the way these two men behaved at Appomattox
came the possibility of a peace of reconciliation. It was a possibility not wholly realized, in the years to come, but which did, in
the end, help the two sections to become one nation again . . .
after a war whose bitterness might have seemed to make such a
reunion wholly impossible. No part of either man's life became
him more than the part he played in their brief meeting in the
McLean house at Appomattox. Their behavior there put all succeeding generations of Americans in their debt. Two great
Americans, Grant and Lee — very different, yet under everything very much alike. Their encounter at Appomattox was one
of the great moments of American history.

QUESTIONS ON MEANING

1. What is Bruce Catton's PURPOSE in writing: to describe the meeting
   of two generals at a famous moment in history; to explain how the
   two men stood for opposing social forces in America; or to show
   how the two differed in personality?
2. Summarize the background and the way of life that produced Robert E. Lee; then do the same for Ulysses S. Grant. According to
   Catton, what ideals did each man represent?
3. In the historian's view, what essential traits did the two men have
   in common? Which trait does Catton think most important of all?
   For what reason?
4. How does this essay help you understand why Grant and Lee were
   such determined fighters?
5. Although slavery, along with other issues, helped precipitate the
   Civil War, Catton in this particular essay does not deal with it. If
   he had recalled the facts of slavery, would he have destroyed his
   thesis that Lee had a "strong sense of obligation to the community"? (*What* community?)

QUESTIONS ON WRITING STRATEGY

1. From the content of this essay, and from knowing where it first appeared, what can you infer about Catton's original AUDIENCE? At what places in his essay does the writer expect of his readers a great familiarity with United States history?
2. What effect does the writer achieve by setting both his INTRODUCTION and his CONCLUSION in Appomattox?
3. For what reasons does Catton contrast the two generals *before* he compares them? Suppose he had reversed his outline, and had dealt first with Grant and Lee's mutual resemblances. Why would his essay have been less effective?
4. Pencil in hand, draw a single line down the margin of every paragraph in which you find the method of contrast. Then draw a *double* line next to every paragraph in which you find the method of comparison. How much space does Catton devote to each method? Why didn't he give comparison and contrast equal time?
5. Closely read the first sentence of every paragraph and underline each word or phrase in it that serves as a TRANSITION. Then review your underlinings. How much COHERENCE has Catton given his essay?
6. What is the TONE of this essay — that is, what is the writer's attitude toward his two subjects? Is Catton poking fun at Lee by imagining the Confederate general as a knight of the Middle Ages, "lance in hand, silken banner fluttering over his head" (paragraph 12)?
7. Does Catton's treatment of the two generals as SYMBOLS obscure the reader's sense of them as individuals? (Lee, at least, is called a symbol in paragraph 6.) Discuss this question, keeping in mind what you decided to be Catton's purpose in writing his essay.

QUESTIONS ON LANGUAGE

1. In his opening paragraph, Catton uses a METAPHOR: American life is a book containing chapters. Find other FIGURES OF SPEECH in his essay. What do they contribute?
2. Look up *poignant* in the dictionary. Why is it such a fitting word in paragraph 2? Why wouldn't *touching*, *sad*, or *teary* have been as good?
3. What information do you glean from the sentence, "Lee was tidewater Virginia" (paragraph 5)?
4. Define *aristocratic* as Catton uses it in paragraphs 4 and 6.
5. Define obeisance (paragraph 7); indomitable (14).

SUGGESTIONS FOR WRITING

1. Compare and contrast two other figures of American history with whom you are familiar: Franklin D. Roosevelt and John F. Kennedy, Lincoln and Douglas, or Susan B. Anthony and Elizabeth Cady Stanton — to suggest only a few.
2. In a brief essay full of specific examples, discuss: Do the "two diametrically opposed elements in American life" (as Catton calls them) still exist in the country today? Are there still any "landed nobility"?
3. In your thinking and your attitudes, whom do you more closely resemble — Grant or Lee? Compare and contrast your outlook with that of one famous American or the other. (A serious tone for this topic isn't required.)

Bruce Catton on Writing

Most of Bruce Catton's comments on writing, those that have been preserved, refer to the work of others. As editor of *American Heritage*, he was known for his blunt, succinct comments on unsuccessful manuscripts: "This article can't be repaired and wouldn't be much good if it were." Or: "The highwater mark of this piece comes at the bottom of page one, where the naked Indian nymph offers the hero strawberries. Unfortunately, this level is not maintained."

In a memoir, Catton's associate Oliver Jensen has marveled that, besides editing *American Heritage* for twenty-four years (and contributing to nearly every issue), Catton managed to produce so many substantial books. "Concentration was no doubt the secret, that and getting an early start. For many years Catton was always the first person in the office, so early that most of the staff never knew when he did arrive. On his desk the little piles of yellow sheets grew slowly, with much larger piles in the wastebasket. A neat and orderly man, he preferred to type a new page than correct very much in pencil." (Introduction to *Bruce Catton's America* [New York: American Heritage, 1979], pp. 9–10.)

His whole purpose as a writer, Catton once said, was "to re-examine [our] debt to the past."

FOR DISCUSSION

1. To which of Catton's traits does Oliver Jensen attribute the historian's impressive output?
2. Which characteristics of Catton the editor would you expect to have served him well as a writer?

· A. M. Rosenthal ·

ABRAHAM MICHAEL ROSENTHAL, born in 1922 in Ontario, Canada, came to the United States when he was four. His long association with the *New York Times* began in 1944: Since then, he has served the newspaper as correspondent at the United Nations and in India, Poland, Switzerland, and Japan; as managing editor; as executive editor; and currently, as a regular columnist. The author of *38 Witnesses* (1964), Rosenthal also has written articles for the *New York Times Magazine*, *Saturday Evening Post*, and *Foreign Affairs*. In 1960 his reporting of international news won him a Pulitzer Prize.

No News from Auschwitz

"No News from Auschwitz" was first published in the *New York Times* on August 31, 1958, when Rosenthal was a correspondent assigned to Warsaw, Poland. At the time, mention of the holocaust had practically disappeared from American newspapers and periodicals — as though Hitler's murder of six million Jews and countless other victims seemed too horrendous to recall. Rosenthal's article served in 1958 as a powerful reminder. It still does.

BRZEZINKA, POLAND — The most terrible thing of all, somehow, was that at Brzezinka the sun was bright and warm, the rows of graceful poplars were lovely to look upon and on the grass near the gates children played. 1

It all seemed frighteningly wrong, as in a nightmare, that at Brzezinka the sun should ever shine or that there should be light and greenness and the sound of young laughter. It would be fitting if at Brzezinka the sun never shone and the grass withered, because this is a place of unutterable terror. 2

And yet, every day, from all over the world, people come to Brzezinka, quite possibly the most grisly tourist center on earth. They come for a variety of reasons — to see if it could really have been true, to remind themselves not to forget, to pay hom- 3

233

age to the dead by the simple act of looking upon their place of suffering.

Brzezinka is a couple of miles from the better-known south- 4 ern Polish town of Oswiecim. Oswiecim has about 12,000 inhab- itants, is situated about 171 miles from Warsaw and lies in a damp, marshy area at the eastern end of the pass called the Mo- ravian Gate. Brzezinka and Oswiecim together formed part of that minutely organized factory of torture and death that the Nazis called Konzentrationslager Auschwitz.

By now, fourteen years after the last batch of prisoners was 5 herded naked into the gas chambers by dogs and guards, the story of Auschwitz has been told a great many times. Some of the inmates have written of those memories of which sane men cannot conceive. Rudolf Franz Ferdinand Hoess, the superin- tendent of the camp, before he was executed wrote his detailed memoirs of mass exterminations and the experiments on living bodies. Four million people died here, the Poles say.

And so there is no news to report about Auschwitz. There is 6 merely the compulsion to write something about it, a compul- sion that grows out of a restless feeling that to have visited Auschwitz and then turned away without having said or written anything would somehow be a most grievous act of discourtesy to those who died here.

Brzezinka and Oswiecim are very quiet places now; the 7 screams can no longer be heard. The tourist walks silently, quickly at first to get it over with and then, as his mind peoples the barracks and the chambers and the dungeons and flogging posts, he walks draggingly. The guide does not say much either, because there is nothing much for him to say after he has pointed.

For every visitor, there is one particular bit of horror that he 8 knows he will never forget. For some it is seeing the rebuilt gas chamber at Oswiecim and being told that this is the "small one." For others it is the fact that at Brzezinka, in the ruins of the gas chambers and the crematoria the Germans blew up when they retreated, there are daisies growing.

There are visitors who gaze blankly at the gas chambers and 9 the furnaces because their minds simply cannot encompass them, but stand shivering before the great mounds of human hair behind the plate-glass window or the piles of babies' shoes or the brick cells where men sentenced to death by suffocation were walled up.

One visitor opened his mouth in a silent scream simply at   10
the sight of boxes — great stretches of three-tiered wooden boxes in the women's barracks. They were about six feet wide, about three feet high, and into them from five to ten prisoners were shoved for the night. The guide walks quickly through the barracks. Nothing more to see here.

A brick building where sterilization experiments were car-   11
ried out on women prisoners. The guide tries the door — it's locked. The visitor is grateful that he does not have to go in, and then flushes with shame.

A long corridor where rows of faces stare from the walls.   12
Thousands of pictures, the photographs of prisoners. They are all dead now, the men and women who stood before the cameras, and they all knew they were to die.

They all stare blank-faced, but one picture, in the middle of   13
a row, seizes the eye and wrenches the mind. A girl, 22 years old, plumply pretty, blond. She is smiling gently, as at a sweet, treasured thought. What was the thought that passed through her young mind and is now her memorial on the wall of the dead at Auschwitz?

Into the suffocation dungeons the visitor is taken for a mo-   14
ment and feels himself strangling. Another visitor goes in, stumbles out and crosses herself. There is no place to pray at Auschwitz.

The visitors look pleadingly at each other and say to the   15
guide, "Enough."

There is nothing new to report about Auschwitz. It was a   16
sunny day and the trees were green and at the gates the children played.

QUESTIONS ON MEANING

1. What reason does Rosenthal give for having written this essay?
2. What do the responses of his fellow tourists contribute to your understanding of the author's own reactions?

3. If Rosenthal had gone into greater detail about each of the horrors his pilgrimage revealed, do you think his essay would have been stronger or weaker? Explain.

QUESTIONS ON WRITING STRATEGY

1. Comment on the IRONY implicit in Rosenthal's choice of a title.
2. In paragraph 6, the author writes, "And so there is no news to report about Auschwitz"; and he begins paragraph 16 by declaring, "There is nothing new to report about Auschwitz." What do these two echoes of the title lend to the essay's impact?
3. On what aspect of the contrast between past and present does Rosenthal focus his attention? By what means does he lay EMPHASIS on the contrast?

QUESTIONS ON LANGUAGE

1. Comment on Rosenthal's choice of words in his assertion that sunshine, light, greenness, and young laughter seem "wrong." With what justification can daisies growing in the ruins be called "horrible"?
2. Explain the author's use of the word *shame* in paragraph 11.

SUGGESTIONS FOR WRITING

1. In a brief essay convey your personal responses to some historic site you have visited or to a moving historic event you have read about. To help the reader share your reactions, include precise, carefully chosen details in your writing rather than merely venting your feelings in a general way. Show what you felt through your description of what you saw or read.
2. Choose an old building in your town, a park, a ghost town, a converted schoolhouse, or any other place with a past. Write an essay in which you compare and contrast the place as it is now and as it once was.

A. M. Rosenthal on Writing

In a memoir of his forty years as a newspaper reporter and editor, A. M. Rosenthal has recalled a lesson he learned at the start of his career. "The very first day I was on the job as a reporter — a real reporter, with a press card in my pocket and a light in my heart — I learned all about the First Amendment. It was a Saturday and I was sitting in the *Times*'s newsroom when an assistant editor walked over, told me that there had been a murder or a suicide at the Mayflower Hotel in midtown, and why didn't I go over and see what it was all about. Yes, sir! I rushed out, jumped on a bus, got to the hotel, asked an elevator operator where the trouble was. Ninth floor, he told me, and up I went. A push of the buzzer and the door opened. Standing there was a police detective. He was twelve and half feet tall. I started to walk in and he put his hand into my face. That hand was just a bit larger than a basketball.

" 'Where are you going, kid?' he said.

" 'I'm a reporter,' I said. '*Times*. I want to see the body.'

"He looked at me, up and down, slowly. 'Beat it,' he proposed.

"Beat it? I hadn't realized anybody talked to *Times* reporters that way. I knew there had to be some misunderstanding. So I smiled, pulled out my press card, and showed it to him. He took it, read it carefully front and back, handed it back, and said: 'Shove it in your ear.'

"Shove it in my ear? I could not comprehend what was taking place. 'But I'm from the *Times*,' I explained. 'A reporter from the *New York Times*. Don't you want me to get the story right?'

" 'Listen, Four Eyes,' he said, 'I don't care if you drop dead.' Then he slammed the door in my face and there I stood, staring at that door. I slunk off to a pay phone in the lobby and called the special reporters' number that had been confided to me — LAckawanna 4-1090, I've never forgotten it — and confessed to the clerk on the city desk that I had not only been unable to crack the case but had never even seen the corpse.

" 'Don't worry about it kid,' he said. 'We got it already from the A.P.[1] They called the police headquarters and got the story. Come on in.'

"Right there at the Mayflower I learned my first lesson about the First Amendment. The First Amendment means I have the right to ask anybody any question I wish. And anybody has the right to tell me to shove it in my ear. I have been involved in First Amendment cases for more than twenty years, but when I began as a reporter I was not answering any call to protect and defend the Constitution of the United States. I was not even thinking about the Constitution of the United States. All I was thinking about was the pleasure and joy of newspapering, of the wonderful zest of being able to run around, see things, find out what was going on, write about it. . . . That was what the newspaper business meant to me then and mostly still does — the delight of discovery, the exhilaration of writing a story and the quick gratification of seeing it in the paper; ink, ink, ink, even if it does rub off on your fingers just a tiny bit.

"We newspaper people are given to talking and writing about journalistic philosophy and I certainly have done my share. . . . But newspapering is not a philosophy, it is a way of spending a lifetime, and most of us in it know that if you really don't love it, love the whole mixture of searching, finding, and telling, love the strange daily rhythm where you have to climb higher and higher during the day instead of slackening off as the day goes on as normal people do, if you don't have a sensation of apprehension when you set out to find a story and a swagger when you sit down to write it, you are in the wrong business. You can make more money as a dentist and cops won't tell you to shove it in your ear." ("Learning on the Job," *New York Times Magazine*, December 14, 1986, pp. 44–45.)

[1]Associated Press. — EDS.

FOR DISCUSSION

1. What is the First Amendment to the Constitution and exactly what did Rosenthal learn about it?

2. What aspects of being a reporter have the greatest appeal for Rosenthal?
3. As Rosenthal recounts the joys of a reporter's life, he also reveals, directly or indirectly, some of the disadvantages. What are they?

· ADDITIONAL WRITING TOPICS ·

COMPARISON AND CONTRAST

1. In an essay replete with examples, compare and contrast the two
   subjects in any one of the following pairs:

   Women and men as consumers
   The styles of two runners
   Alexander Hamilton and Thomas Jefferson: their opposing views
     of central government
   How city dwellers and country dwellers spend their leisure time
   The presentation styles of two television news commentators

2. Approach a comparison and contrast essay on one of the following general subjects by explaining why you prefer one thing to the
   other:

   Two football teams
   German-made cars and Detroit-made cars
   Two horror movies
   Television when you were a child and television today
   City life and small-town or rural life
   Malls and main streets
   Two neighborhoods
   Two sports

3. Write an essay in which you compare a reality with an ideal,
   such as:

   The house you live in and the house of your dreams
   A real vacation and an ideal one
   The job you have and the job you dream of
   The car you own and the car you'd love to own
   Some present ability and some ideal ability
   Your study habits and those you wish you had

5

PROCESS ANALYSIS

Explaining Step by Step

THE METHOD

A chemist working for a soft-drink firm is handed a six-pack of a competitor's product: Orange Quench. "Find out what this bellywash is," he is told. First, perhaps, he smells the stuff and tastes it. Then he boils a sample, examines the powdery residue, and tests for sugar and acid. At last, he draws up a list of the mysterious drink's ingredients: water, corn syrup, citric acid, sodium benzoate, coloring. Methodically, the chemist has performed an analysis. The nature of Orange Quench stands revealed.

Analysis, also called *division,* is the separation of something into its parts, the better to understand it. An action, or a series of actions, may be analyzed, too. Writing a report to his boss, the soft-drink chemist might tell how he went about learning the ingredients of Orange Quench. Perhaps, if the company wanted to imitate the competitor's product, he might provide instructions for making something just like Orange Quench out of the same ingredients. Writing with either of those purposes, the chemist would be using the method of *process analysis*: explaining step by step how something is done or how to do something.

Like any type of analysis, process analysis divides a subject into its components. It divides a continuous action into stages. Processes much larger and more involved than the making of Orange Quench also may be analyzed. When a news commentator reports the overthrow of a government by armed rebels — a process that may have taken years — she may point out how the fighting began and how it spread, how the capital city was surrounded, how the national television station was seized, how the former president was taken prisoner, and how a general was proclaimed the new president. Exactly what does the commentator do? She takes a complicated event and divides it into parts. She explains what happened first, second, third, and finally. Others, to be sure, may analyze the event differently, but the commentator gives us one interpretation of what took place, and of how it came about.

Because it is useful in explaining what is complicated, process analysis is a favorite method of news commentators — and of scientists who explain how atoms behave when split, or how to go about splitting them. The method, however, may be useful to anybody. Two kinds of process analysis are very familiar to you. The first (or *directive*) kind tells a reader how to do something or make something. You meet it when you read a set of instructions for assembling newly purchased stereo components, or follow the directions to a stereo store ("Turn right at the blinker and follow Patriot Boulevard for 2.4 miles. . . . "). The second (or *informative*) kind of process analysis tells us how something is done, or how it takes place. This is the kind we often read out of curiosity. Such an essay may tell of events beyond our control: how the Grand Canyon was formed, how lions hunt, how a fertilized egg develops into a child. In this chapter, you will find examples of both kinds of process analysis — both the "how to" and the "how." In a practical directive, Peter Elbow tells you how to write when a deadline looms and you absolutely have to produce. Jessica Mitford, in a spellbinding informative essay, explains how corpses are embalmed; but, clearly, she doesn't expect you to rush down to your basement and give her instructions a try.

Sometimes the method is used very imaginatively. Foreseeing that the sun eventually will cool, the earth shrink, the oceans freeze, and all life perish, an astronomer who cannot possibly behold the end of the world nevertheless can write a process analysis of it. An exercise in learned guesswork, such an essay divides a vast and almost inconceivable event into stages that, taken one at a time, become clearer and more readily imaginable.

Whether it is useful or useless (but fun to imagine), an effective essay in process analysis holds a certain fascination. Leaf through a current issue of a newsstand magazine, and you will find that process analysis abounds in it. You may meet, for instance, articles telling you how to tenderize cuts of meat, sew homemade designer jeans, lose fat, cut hair, play the money markets, arouse a bored mate, and program a computer. Less practical, but not necessarily less interesting, are the informative articles: how brain surgeons work, how diamonds are formed, how cities fight crime. Readers, it seems, have an unslakable thirst for process analysis. In one recent issue of the *New York Times Book Review*, we find lists of best-selling books, some designated "Advice, How-to and Miscellaneous." Among the most popular are books that explain processes: diet books such as Robert E. Kowalski's *The 8-Week Cholesterol Cure*, which tells how to lower the level of your blood cholesterol, and Jean Perry's *The 35-Plus Diet for Women*, which advises a woman of 36 or more years how to eat to stay slim and vigorous. From Robin Norwood's *Women Who Love Too Much* a reader can learn how to break off an unhappy affair, while from Margaret Kent's *How To Marry the Man of Your Choice* she can learn how to start a new one. Evidently, if anything will still make an American crack a book, it is a step-by-step explanation of how he or she, too, can be a success — at anything from lovemaking to weight-losing.

THE PROCESS

Here are suggestions for writing an effective process analysis of your own. (In fact, what you are about to read is itself a process analysis.)

1. Understand clearly the process you are about to analyze. Think it through. This preliminary survey will make the task of writing far easier for you.

2. If you are giving a set of detailed instructions, ask yourself: Are there any preparatory steps a reader ought to take? If there are, list them. (These might include: "Remove the packing from the components," or, "First, lay out three eggs, one pound of Sheboygan bratwurst. . . . ")

3. List the steps or stages in the process. Try setting them down in chronological order, one at a time — if this is possible. Some processes, however, do not happen in an orderly sequence, but occur all at once. If, for instance, you are writing an account of a typical earthquake, what do you mention first? The shifting of underground rock strata? Cracks in the earth? Falling houses? Bursting water mains? Toppling trees? Mangled cars? Casualties? (Here is a subject for which the method of *classification*, to be discussed in Chapter 6, may come to your aid. You might sort out apparently simultaneous events into categories: injury to people; damage to homes, to land, to public property.)

4. Now glance back over your list, making sure you haven't omitted anything or instructed your reader to take the steps in the wrong order. Sometimes a stage of a process may contain a number of smaller stages. Make sure none has been left out. If any seems particularly tricky or complicated, underline it on your list to remind yourself when you write your essay to slow down and detail it with extra care.

5. Ask yourself: Will I use any specialized or technical terms? If you will, be sure to define them. You'll sympathize with your reader if you have ever tried to work a Hong Kong–made short-wave radio that comes with an instruction booklet written in

translatorese, full of unexplained technical jargon; or if you have ever tried to assemble a plastic tricycle according to a directive that reads, "Position sleeve casing on wheel center in fork with shaft in tong groove, and gently but forcibly tap in medium pal nut head. . . . "

6. Use time-markers. That is, indicate *when* one stage of a process stops and the next begins. By doing so, you will greatly aid your reader in following you. Here, for example, is a paragraph of plain medical prose that makes good use of helpful time-markers. (In this passage, the time-markers are the words in *italics*.)

> In the human, *thirty-six hours after* the egg is fertilized, a two-cell egg appears. A twelve-cell development takes place *in seventy-two hours*. The egg is still round and has increased little in diameter. In this respect it is like a real estate development. *At first* a road bisects the whole area; *then* a cross road divides it into quarters, and *later* other roads divide it into eighths and twelfths. This happens without the taking of any more land, simply by subdivision of the original tract. *On the third or fourth day*, the egg passes from the Fallopian tube into the uterus. *By the fifth day* the original single large cell has subdivided into sixty small cells and floats about the slitlike uterine cavity *a day or two longer*, *then* adheres to the cavity's inner lining. *By the twelfth day* the human egg is already firmly implanted. Impregnation is *now* completed, *as yet* unbeknown to the woman. *At present*, she has not even had time to miss her first menstrual period, and other symptoms of pregnancy are *still several days distant*.[1]

Brief as these time-markers are, they define each stage of the human egg's journey. Note how the writer, after declaring in the second sentence that the egg forms twelve cells, backtracks for a moment and retraces the process by which the egg has subdivided, comparing it (by a brief analogy) to a piece of real estate. (For more examples of *analogy*, see Chapter 7.) By showing your reader how one event follows another, time-markers serve as transitions. Vary them so that they won't seem mechanical. If

---

[1]Adapted from *Pregnancy and Birth* by Alan F. Guttmacher, M.D. (New York: New American Library, 1970).

you can, avoid the monotonous repetition of a fixed phrase (*In the fourteenth stage . . . , In the fifteenth stage . . .*). Even boring time-markers, though, are better than none at all. As in any chronological narrative, words and phrases such as *in the beginning, first, second, next, after that, three seconds later, at the same time,* and *finally* can help a process to move smoothly in the telling and lodge firmly in the reader's mind.

7. When you begin writing a first draft, state your analysis in generous detail, even at the risk of being wordy. When you revise, it will be easier to delete than to amplify.

8. Finally, when your essay is finished, reread it carefully. If it is a simple *directive* ("How to Eat an Ice Cream Cone without Dribbling"), ask a friend to try it out. See if somebody else can follow your instructions without difficulty. If you have written an *informative* process analysis ("How a New Word Enters the Dictionary"), however, ask others to read your essay and tell you whether the process unfolds as clearly in their minds as it does in yours.

PROCESS ANALYSIS IN A PARAGRAPH: TWO ILLUSTRATIONS

1. Using Process Analysis to Write about Television

Almost anyone can rise to television stardom: witness Vanna White, flipper of letter-cards on "Wheel of Fortune." But in the case of Max Headroom, the starmaking process did not end up with a human being. Seeking a character for a series of music videos, British producer Peter Wagg hit upon the idea of a talking head. Together with a writer and two computer graphic animators, Wagg created Max: supposedly, the psyche of a reporter, Edison Carter, that has been captured on software; in reality, actor Matt Frewer in a latex mask, his image altered electronically, a synthesized st-st-stutter in his voice. An instant hit on London television, Max's show soon reached cable TV in twenty countries. Wagg's next step was to authorize T-shirts, male cosmetics, and a book, *Max Headroom's Guide to Life*. The following year, Cinemax cable service brought Max to America, where his wisecracking talk show quickly won a following. Then Coca-Cola, looking for a way to ingratiate its new Coke with teenagers, hired him for commercials. In April 1987, ABC began featuring Max in a drama series set in an absurd, nightmarish near-future world whose TV sets lack OFF buttons. Perhaps the next big television star will need no human elements at all.

COMMENT. In this meaty paragraph of about 200 words, the writer sums up stages in the process through which Peter Wagg and his associates created Max Headroom and made the computer-enhanced head into a star. The stages are indicated with time-markers (*soon, the following year, then, in April 1987*) and other transitions (*next step, at last*). In the fourth sentence, we get a smaller, subsidiary process analysis: in the brief account of how the illusion of the talking head is obtained, "his image altered electronically, a synthesized st-st-stutter in his voice." In revising this paragraph, the writer discarded many ideas, such as the story that Max and his fictional Network 23 were named after the legend MAX. HEADROOM 2.3m, the last thing Edison Carter saw before crashing his motorcycle through the gate of a parking lot and blacking out. Though interesting, such a point did not advance the purpose of the paragraph: to analyze how the nonhuman star was born. Irrelevant, too, is a fact that might have been mentioned: that ABC's Max series proved short-lived. This paragraph illustrates the kind of writing you often do in a research paper: condensing evidence you have read or collected.

2. Using Process Analysis in an Academic Discipline

The generation of rain by the coalescence process depends on the occurrence of oversize water droplets that are larger than twenty micrometers in radius. An oversize droplet falls just a bit faster than the typical droplet, and it grows by colliding with and sweeping up smaller droplets in its path. Rising currents of air carry the swelling droplets upward faster than they can fall out of the cloud, allowing them more time to grow. A droplet requires about half an hour to grow to raindrop size by coalescence, and the rain cloud must be at least 2.5 km (1.6 miles) thick to contain the growing drops long enough for them to become raindrops. Thinner clouds limit the growth of drops by coalescence, resulting in *drizzle*, a form of precipitation that consists of very tiny drops that "float" rather than fall to the surface. Pavements made wet by drizzle can be very hazardous for motorists, but drizzle never produces signficant quantities of precipitation.

COMMENT. This paragraph, from the third edition of *Physical Geography Today: A Portrait of a Planet* by Robert A. Muller and Theodore M. Oberlander (New York: Random House, 1984, p. 114), clearly illustrates the method of informative process analysis. In it, the authors detail one of the ways in which miniscule water droplets coalesce to form raindrops large enough to fall to earth. The most interesting detail, perhaps, is that the droplets have to travel upward and collide and combine with other droplets before they have enough weight to fall down. In organizing their analysis, the authors proceed step by step, making the point as they move through the process that conditions have to be right: The clouds have to be thick enough. If they aren't, the end result will be drizzle rather than rain.

· Jessica Mitford ·

Born in Batsford Mansion, England, in 1917, the daughter of Lord and Lady Redesdale, JESSICA MITFORD devoted much of her early life to defying her aristocratic upbringing. In her autobiography *Daughters and Rebels* (1960), she tells how she received a genteel schooling at home, then as a young woman moved to Loyalist Spain durng the violent Spanish Civil War. Later, she emigrated to America, where for a time she worked in Miami as a bartender. She has since become one of her adopted country's most noted reporters: *Time* called her "Queen of the Muckrakers." Exposing with her typewriter what she regards as corruption, abuse, and absurdity, Mitford has written *The American Way of Death* (1963), *Kind and Unusual Punishment: The Prison Business* (1973), and *Poison Penmanship* (1979), a collection of articles from *The Atlantic*, *Harper's*, and other magazines. *A Fine Old Conflict* (1976) is the second volume of Mitford's autobiography; the recent *Faces of Philip* (1984) contains her memoirs of a friend and fellow writer, the English novelist Philip Toynbee.

Behind the Formaldehyde Curtain

The most famous (or notorious) thing Jessica Mitford has written is *The American Way of Death*. The following essay is a self-contained selection from it. In the book, Mitford criticizes the mortuary profession; and when her work landed on bestseller lists, the author was the subject of bitter attacks from funeral directors all over North America. To finish reading the essay, you will need a stable stomach as well as an awareness of Mitford's outrageous sense of humor. "Behind the Formaldehyde Curtain" is a clear, painstaking process analysis, written with masterly style.

The drama begins to unfold with the arrival of the corpse at the mortuary. 1

249

Alas, poor Yorick! How surprised he would be to see how   2
his counterpart of today is whisked off to a funeral parlor and is
in short order sprayed, sliced, pierced, pickled, trussed,
trimmed, creamed, waxed, painted, rouged, and neatly dressed
— transformed from a common corpse into a Beautiful Memory
Picture. This process is known in the trade as embalming and restorative art, and is so universally employed in the United States
and Canada that the funeral director does it routinely, without
consulting corpse or kin. He regards as eccentric those few who
are hardy enough to suggest that it might be dispensed with. Yet
no law requires embalming, no religious doctrine commends it,
nor is it dictated by considerations of health, sanitation, or even
of personal daintiness. In no part of the world but in Northern
America is it widely used. The purpose of embalming is to make
the corpse presentable for viewing in a suitably costly container;
and here too the funeral director routinely, without first consulting the family, prepares the body for public display.

Is all this legal? The processes to which a dead body may be   3
subjected are after all to some extent circumscribed by law. In
most states, for instance, the signature of next of kin must be obtained before an autopsy may be performed, before the deceased
may be cremated, before the body may be turned over to a medical school for research purposes; or such provision must be
made in the decedent's will. In the case of embalming, no such
permission is required nor is it ever sought. A textbook, *The
Principles and Practices of Embalming*, comments on this: "There
is some question regarding the legality of much that is done
within the preparation room." The author points out that it
would be most unusual for a responsible member of a bereaved
family to instruct the mortician, in so many words, to "*embalm*"
the body of a deceased relative. The very term "embalming" is
so seldom used that the mortician must rely upon custom in the
matter. The author concludes that unless the family specifies
otherwise, the act of entrusting the body to the care of a funeral
establishment carries with it an implied permission to go ahead
and embalm.

Embalming is indeed a most extraordinary procedure, and   4
one must wonder at the docility of Americans who each year

pay hundreds of millions of dollars for its perpetuation, blissfully ignorant of what it is all about, what is done, how it is done. Not one in ten thousand has any idea of what actually takes place. Books on the subject are extremely hard to come by. They are not to be found in most libraries or bookshops.

In an era when huge television audiences watch surgical operations in the comfort of their living rooms, when, thanks to the animated cartoon, the geography of the digestive system has become familiar territory even to the nursery school set, in a land where the satisfaction of curiosity about almost all matters is a national pastime, the secrecy surrounding embalming can, surely, hardly be attributed to the inherent gruesomeness of the subject. Custom in this regard has within this century suffered a complete reversal. In the early days of American embalming, when it was performed in the home of the deceased, it was almost mandatory for some relative to stay by the embalmer's side and witness the procedure. Today, family members who might wish to be in attendance would certainly be dissuaded by the funeral director. All others, except apprentices, are excluded by law from the preparation room.

A close look at what does actually take place may explain in large measure the undertaker's intractable reticence concerning a procedure that has become his major *raison d'être*. Is it possible he fears that public information about embalming might lead patrons to wonder if they really want this service? If the funeral men are loath to discuss the subject outside the trade, the reader may, understandably, be equally loath to go on reading at this point. For those who have the stomach for it, let us part the formaldehyde curtain. . . .

The body is first laid out in the undertaker's morgue — or rather, Mr. Jones is reposing in the preparation room — to be readied to bid the world farewell.

The preparation room in any of the better funeral establishments has the tiled and sterile look of a surgery, and indeed the embalmer-restorative artist who does his chores there is beginning to adopt the term "dermasurgeon" (appropriately corrupted by some mortician-writers as "demi-surgeon") to describe his calling. His equipment, consisting of scalpels, scissors, augers, forceps, clamps, needles, pumps, tubes, bowls, and basins, is crudely imitative of the surgeon's, as is his technique, acquired in a nine- or twelve-month post-high-school course in an embalming school. He is supplied by an advanced chemical industry with a bewildering array of fluids, sprays, pastes, oils, powders, creams, to fix or soften tissue, shrink or distend it as needed, dry it here, restore the moisture there. There are cosmetics, waxes, and paints to fill and cover features, even plaster of Paris to replace entire limbs. There are ingenious aids to prop and stabilize the cadaver: a Vari-Pose Head Rest, the Edwards Arm and Hand Positioner, the Repose Block (to support the shoulders during the embalming), and the Throop Foot Positioner, which resembles an old-fashioned stocks.

Mr. John H. Eckels, president of the Eckels College of Mortuary Science, thus describes the first part of the embalming procedure: "In the hands of a skilled practitioner, this work may be done in a comparatively short time and without mutilating the body other than by slight incision — so slight that it scarcely would cause serious inconvenience if made upon a living person. It is necessary to remove the blood, and doing this not only helps in the disinfecting, but removes the principal cause of disfigurements due to discoloration."

Another textbook discusses the all-important time element: "The earlier this is done, the better, for every hour that elapses between death and embalming will add to the problems and complications encountered. . . . " Just how soon should one get going on the embalming? The author tells us, "On the basis of such scanty information made available to this profession through its rudimentary and haphazard system of technical research, we must conclude that the best results are to be obtained if the subject is embalmed before life is completely extinct — that is, before cellular death has occurred. In the average case, this would mean within an hour after somatic death." For those who feel that there is something a little rudimentary, not to say haphazard, about this advice, a comforting thought is offered by another writer. Speaking of fears entertained in early days of premature burial, he points out, "One of the effects of embalming by chemical injection, however, has been to dispel fears of live burial." How true; once the blood is removed, chances of live burial are indeed remote.

To return to Mr. Jones, the blood is drained out through   11
the veins and replaced by embalming fluid pumped in through the arteries. As noted in *The Principles and Practices of Embalming*, "every operator has a favorite injection and drainage point — a fact which becomes a handicap only if he fails or refuses to forsake his favorites when conditions demand it." Typical favorites are the carotid artery, femoral artery, jugular vein, subclavian vein. There are various choices of embalming fluid. If Flextone is used, it will produce a "mild, flexible rigidity. The skin retains a velvety softness, the tissues are rubbery and pliable. Ideal for women and children." It may be blended with B. and G. Products Company's Lyf-Lyk tint, which is guaranteed to reproduce "nature's own skin texture . . . the velvety appearance of living tissue." Suntone comes in three separate tints: Suntan; Special Cosmetic Tint, a pink shade "especially indicated for female subjects"; and Regular Cosmetic Tint, moderately pink.

About three to six gallons of a dyed and perfumed solution   12
of formaldehyde, glycerin, borax, phenol, alcohol, and water is soon circulating through Mr. Jones, whose mouth has been sewn together with a "needle directed upward between the upper lip and gum and brought out through the left nostril," with the corners raised slightly "for a more pleasant expression." If he should be bucktoothed, his teeth are cleaned with Bon Ami and coated with colorless nail polish. His eyes, meanwhile, are closed with flesh-tinted eye caps and eye cement.

The next step is to have at Mr. Jones with a thing called a   13
trocar. This is a long, hollow needle attached to a tube. It is jabbed into the abdomen, poked around the entrails and chest cavity, the contents of which are pumped out and replaced with "cavity fluid." This done, and the hole in the abdomen sewn up, Mr. Jones's face is heavily creamed (to protect the skin from burns which may be caused by leakage of the chemicals), and he is covered with a sheet and left unmolested for a while. But not for long — there is more, much more, in store for him. He has

been embalmed, but not yet restored, and the best time to start
the restorative work is eight to ten hours after embalming, when
the tissues have become firm and dry.

The object of all this attention to the corpse, it must be re-   14
membered, is to make it presentable for viewing in an attitude of
healthy repose. "Our customs require the presentation of our
dead in the semblance of normality . . . unmarred by the rav-
ages of illness, disease, or mutilation," says Mr. J. Sheridan
Mayer in his *Restorative Art.* This is rather a large order since few
people die in the full bloom of health, unravaged by illness and
unmarked by some disfigurement. The funeral industry is equal
to the challenge: "In some cases the gruesome appearance of a
mutilated or disease-ridden subject may be quite discouraging.
The task of restoration may seem impossible and shake the confidence of the embalmer. This is the time for intestinal fortitude
and determination. Once the formative work is begun and affected tissues are cleaned or removed, all doubts of success van-
ish. It is surprising and gratifying to discover the results which
may be obtained."

The embalmer, having allowed an appropriate interval to   15
elapse, returns to the attack, but now he brings into play the
skill and equipment of sculptor and cosmetician. Is a hand missing? Casting one in plaster of Paris is a simple matter. "For replacement purposes, only a cast of the back of the hand is necessary; this is within the ability of the average operator and is
quite adequate." If a lip or two, a nose, or an ear should be missing, the embalmer has at hand a variety of restorative waxes
with which to model replacements. Pores and skin texture are
simulated by stippling with a little brush, and over this cosmetics are laid on. Head off? Decapitation cases are rather routinely
handled. Ragged edges are trimmed, and head joined to torso
with a series of splints, wires, and sutures. It is a good idea to
have a little something at the neck — a scarf or a high collar —
when time for viewing comes. Swollen mouth? Cut out tissue as
needed from inside the lips. If too much is removed, the surface
contour can easily be restored by padding with cotton. Swollen
necks and cheeks are reduced by removing tissue through vertical incisions made down each side of the neck. "When the de-

ceased is casketed, the pillow will hide the suture incisions . . . as an extra precaution against leakage, the suture may be painted with liquid sealer."

The opposite condition is more likely to present itself — that of emaciation. His hypodermic syringe now loaded with massage cream, the embalmer seeks out and fills the hollowed and sunken areas by injection. In this procedure the backs of the hands and fingers and the under-chin area should not be neglected. [16]

Positioning the lips is a problem that recurrently challenges the ingenuity of the embalmer. Closed too tightly, they tend to give a stern, even disapproving expression. Ideally, embalmers feel, the lips should give the impression of being ever so slightly parted, the upper lip protruding slightly for a more youthful appearance. This takes some engineering, however, as the lips tend to drift apart. Lip drift can sometimes be remedied by pushing one or two straight pins through the inner margin of the lower lip and then inserting them between the two front upper teeth. If Mr. Jones happens to have no teeth, the pins can just as easily be anchored in his Armstrong Face Former and Denture Replacer. Another method to maintain lip closure is to dislocate the lower jaw, which is then held in its new position by a wire run through holes which have been drilled through the upper and lower jaws at the midline. As the French are fond of saying, *il faut souffrir pour être belle.*[1] [17]

If Mr. Jones has died of jaundice, the embalming fluid will very likely turn him green. Does this deter the embalmer? Not if he has intestinal fortitude. Masking pastes and cosmetics are heavily laid on, burial garments and casket interiors are color-correlated with particular care, and Jones is displayed beneath rose-colored lights. Friends will say "How *well* he looks." Death by carbon monoxide, on the other hand, can be rather a good thing from the embalmer's viewpoint: "One advantage is the fact that this type of discoloration is an exaggerated form of a natural pink coloration." This is nice because the healthy glow is already present and needs but little attention. [18]

---

[1]You have to suffer to be beautiful. — EDS.

The patching and filling completed, Mr. Jones is now   19
shaved, washed, and dressed. Cream-based cosmetic, available in
pink, flesh, suntan, brunette, and blond, is applied to his hands
and face, his hair is shampooed and combed (and, in the case of
Mrs. Jones, set), his hands manicured. For the horny-handed
son of toil special care must be taken; cream should be applied to
remove ingrained grime, and the nails cleaned. "If he were not
in the habit of having them manicured in life, trimming and
shaping is advised for better appearance — never questioned by
kin."

Jones is now ready for casketing (this is the present participle   20
of the verb "to casket"). In this operation his right shoulder
should be depressed slightly "to turn the body a bit to the right
and soften the appearance of lying flat on the back." Positioning
the hands is a matter of importance, and special rubber positioning blocks may be used. The hands should be cupped slightly for
a more lifelike, relaxed appearance. Proper placement of the
body requires a delicate sense of balance. It should lie as high as
possible in the casket, yet not so high that the lid, when lowered, will hit the nose. On the other hand, we are cautioned,
placing the body too low "creates the impression that the body
is in a box."

Jones is next wheeled into the appointed slumber room   21
where a few last touches may be added — his favorite pipe
placed in his hand or, if he was a great reader, a book propped
into position. (In the case of little Master Jones a Teddy bear
may be clutched.) Here he will hold open house for a few days,
visiting hours 10 A.M. to 9 P.M.

All now being in readiness, the funeral director calls a staff   22
conference to make sure that each assistant knows his precise
duties. Mr. Wilber Kriege writes: "This makes your staff feel that
they are a part of the team, with a definite assignment that must
be properly carried out if the whole plan is to succeed. You
never heard of a football coach who failed to talk to his entire
team before they go on the field. They have drilled on the plays
they are to execute for hours and days, and yet the successful
coach knows the importance of making even the bench-warm-
ing third-string substitute feel that he is important if the game is

to be won." The winning of *this* game is predicated upon glass-smooth handling of the logistics. The funeral director has notified the pallbearers whose names were furnished by the family, has arranged for the presence of clergyman, organist, and soloist, has provided transportation for everybody, has organized and listed the flowers sent by friends. In *Psychology of Funeral Service* Mr. Edward A. Martin points out: "He may not always do as much as the family thinks he is doing, but it is his helpful guidance that they appreciate in knowing they are proceeding as they should. . . . The important thing is how well his services can be used to make the family believe they are giving unlimited expression to their own sentiment."

The religious service may be held in a church or in the   23
chapel of the funeral home; the funeral director vastly prefers the latter arrangement, for not only is it more convenient for him but it affords him the opportunity to show off his beautiful facilities to the gathered mourners. After the clergyman has had his say, the mourners queue up to file past the casket for a last look at the deceased. The family is *never* asked whether they want an open-casket ceremony; in the absence of their instruction to the contrary, this is taken for granted. Consequently well over 90 per cent of all American funerals feature the open casket — a custom unknown in other parts of the world. Foreigners are astonished by it. An English woman living in San Francisco described her reaction in a letter to the writer:

> I myself have attended only one funeral here — that of an elderly fellow worker of mine. After the service I could not understand why everyone was walking towards the coffin (sorry, I mean casket), but thought I had better follow the crowd. It shook me rigid to get there and find the casket open and poor old Oscar lying there in his brown tweed suit, wearing a suntan makeup and just the wrong shade of lipstick. If I had not been extremely fond of the old boy, I have a horrible feeling that I might have giggled. Then and there I decided that I could never face another American funeral — even dead.

The casket (which has been resting throughout the service   24
on a Classic Beauty Ultra Metal Casket Bier) is now transferred by a hydraulically operated device called Porto-Lift to a balloon-

tired, Glide Easy casket carriage which will wheel it to yet another conveyance, the Cadillac Funeral Coach. This may be
lavender, cream, light green — anything but black. Interiors, of
course, are color-correlated, "for the man who cannot stop short
of perfection."

At graveside, the casket is lowered into the earth. This of-   25
fice, once the prerogative of friends of the deceased, is now performed by a patented mechanical lowering device. A "Lifetime
Green" artificial grass mat is at the ready to conceal the sere
earth, and overhead, to conceal the sky, is a portable Steril
Chapel Tent ("resists the intense heat and humidity of summer
and the terrific storms of winter . . . available in Silver Grey,
Rose, or Evergreen"). Now is the time for the ritual scattering of
earth over the coffin, as the solemn words "earth to earth, ashes
to ashes, dust to dust" are pronounced by the officiating cleric.
This can today be accomplished "with a mere flick of the wrist
with the Gordon Leak-Proof Earth Dispenser. No grasping of a
handful of dirt, no soiled fingers. Simple, dignified, beautiful,
reverent! The modern way!" The Gordon Earth Dispenser (at
$5) is of nickel-plated brass construction. It is not only "attrac-
tive to the eye and long wearing"; it is also "one of the 'tools' for
building better public relations" if presented as "an appropriate
non-commercial gift" to the clergyman. It is shaped something
like a saltshaker.

Untouched by human hand, the coffin and the earth are   26
now united.

It is in the function of directing the participants through this   27
maze of gadgetry that the funeral director has assigned to himself his relatively new role of "grief therapist." He has relieved
the family of every detail, he has revamped the corpse to look
like a living doll, he has arranged for it to nap for a few days in a
slumber room, he has put on a well-oiled performance in which
the concept of *death* has played no part whatsoever — unless it
was inconsiderately mentioned by the clergyman who conducted the religious service. He has done everything in his
power to make the funeral a real pleasure for everybody concerned. He and his team have given their all to score an upset
victory over death.

QUESTIONS ON MEANING

1. What was your emotional response to this essay? Can you analyze your feelings?
2. To what does the author attribute the secrecy that surrounds the process of embalming?
3. What, according to Mitford, is the mortician's intent? What common obstacles to fulfilling it must be surmounted?
4. What do you understand from Mitford's remark in paragraph 10, on dispelling fears of live burial: "How true; once the blood is removed, chances of live burial are indeed remote"?
5. Do you find any implied PURPOSE in this essay? Does Mitford seem primarily out to rake muck, or does she offer any positive suggestions to Americans?

QUESTIONS ON WRITING STRATEGY

1. What is Mitford's TONE? In her opening two paragraphs, exactly what shows her attitude toward her subject?
2. Why do you think Mitford goes into so much grisly detail? How does it serve her purpose?
3. What is the EFFECT of calling the body Mr. Jones (or Master Jones)?
4. Paragraph by paragraph, what time-markers does the author employ? (If you need a refresher on this point, see the discussion of time-markers on page 245.)
5. Into what stages has the author divided the embalming process?
6. To whom does Mitford address her process analysis? How do you know she isn't writing for an AUDIENCE of professional morticians?
7. Consider one of the quotations from the journals and textbooks of professionals and explain how it serves the author's general purpose.
8. Of what value to the essay is the letter from the English woman in San Francisco (paragraph 23)?

QUESTIONS ON LANGUAGE

1. Explain the ALLUSION to Yorick in paragraph 2.
2. What IRONY do you find in Mitford's statement in paragraph 7, "The body is first laid out in the undertaker's morgue — or rather, Mr. Jones is reposing in the preparation room"? Pick out any other

words or phrases in the essay that seem ironic. Comment especially on those you find in the essay's last two sentences.

3. Why is it useful to Mitford's purpose that she cites the brand names of morticians' equipment and supplies (the Edwards Arm and Hand Positioner, Lyf-Lyk tint)? List all the brand names in the essay that are memorable.

4. Define counterpart (paragraph 2); circumscribed, autopsy, cremated, decedent, bereaved (3); docility, perpetuation (4); inherent, mandatory (5); intractable, reticence, *raison d'être*, formaldehyde (6); "dermasurgeon," augers, forceps, distend, stocks (8); somatic (10); carotid artery, femoral artery, jugular vein, subclavian vein, pliable (11); glycerin, borax, phenol, bucktoothed (12); trocar, entrails (13); stippling, sutures (15); emaciation (16); jaundice (18); predicated (22); queue (23); hydraulically (24); cleric (25); therapist (27).

SUGGESTIONS FOR WRITING

1. Defend the ritual of the American funeral, or of the mortician's profession, against Mitford's sarcastic attack.

2. Compare and contrast the custom of embalming the corpse for display, as described by Mitford, with a possible alternative way of dealing with the dead.

3. With the aid of the *Readers' Guide to Periodical Literature*, find information about the recent phenomenon of quick-freezing the dead. Set forth this process, including its hoped-for result of reviving the corpses in the far future.

4. Analyze some other process whose operations may not be familiar to everyone. (Have you ever held a job, or helped out in a family business, that has taken you behind the scenes? How is fast food prepared? How are cars serviced? How is a baby sat? How is a house constructed?) Detail it step by step in an essay that includes time-markers.

Jessica Mitford on Writing

"Choice of subject is of cardinal importance," declares Jessica Mitford in *Poison Penmanship*. "One does by far one's best work when besotted by and absorbed in the matter at hand." After *The American Way of Death* was published, Mitford received hundreds of letters suggesting alleged rackets that ought to be exposed, and to her surprise, an overwhelming majority of these letters complained about defective and overpriced hearing aids. But Mitford never wrote a book blasting the hearing aid industry. "Somehow, although there may well be need for such an exposé, I could not warm up to hearing aids as a subject for the kind of thorough, intensive, long-range research that would be needed to do an effective job." She once taught a course at Yale in muckraking, with each student choosing a subject to investigate. "Those who tackled hot issues on campus, such as violations of academic freedom or failure to implement affirmative-action hiring policies, turned in some excellent work; but the lad who decided to investigate 'waste in the Yale dining halls' was predictably unable to make much of this trivial topic." (The editors interject: We aren't sure that the topic is necessarily trivial, but obviously not everyone would burn to write about it!)

The hardest problem Mitford faced in writing *The American Way of Death*, she recalls, was doing her factual, step-by-step account of the embalming process. She felt "determined to describe it in all its revolting details, but how to make this subject palatable to the reader?" Her solution was to cast the whole process analysis in the official jargon of the mortuary industry, drawing on lists of taboo words and their euphemisms (or acceptable synonyms), as published in the trade journal *Casket & Sunnyside*: "Mr., Mrs., Miss Blank, not corpse or body; preparation room, not morgue; reposing room, not laying-out room. . . ." The story of Mr. Jones thus took shape; and Mitford's use of jargon, she found, added macabre humor to the proceedings.

FOR DISCUSSION

1. What seem to be Mitford's criteria for an effective essay or book?
2. What is muckraking? Why do you suppose anyone would want to do it?

· Peter Elbow ·

PETER ELBOW is well known as a director of writing programs for community groups and for college students. Born in 1935, he received his education at Williams College and at Brandeis, Harvard, and Oxford. He has taught at Wesleyan University, M.I.T., Franconia College, and the Harvard Graduate School of Education, as well as at Evergreen State College in Olympia, Washington. Recently he started the highly acclaimed "Workshop in Language and Thinking" at Bard College, and served as director of the Writing Program at the State University of New York, Stony Brook. He is the author of many articles and of the influential *Writing without Teachers* (1973), *Writing with Power* (1981), and *Embracing Contraries: Explorations in Learning and Teaching* (1986). Currently, he teaches at the University of Massachusetts, Amherst.

Desperation Writing

What do you do when you have a paper due but can't think of a word to say about the assigned subject? This is a problem faced by most college students at one time or another. But take heart. Peter Elbow has come up with a solution. What's more, if you try to follow his advice, you will find it much less painful than you expected. "Desperation Writing" has offered solace and help to thousands since it first appeared in *Writing without Teachers*.

I know I am not alone in my recurring twinges of panic that   1
I won't be able to write something when I need to, I won't be able to produce coherent speech or thought. And that lingering doubt is a great hindrance to writing. It's a constant fog or static that clouds the mind. I never got out of its clutches till I discovered that it was possible to write something — not something great or pleasing but at least something usable, workable — when my mind is out of commission. The trick is that you have

to do all your cooking out on the table: Your mind is incapable of doing any inside. It means using symbols and pieces of paper not as a crutch but as a wheel chair.

The first thing is to admit your condition: Because of some 2 mood or event or whatever, your mind is incapable of anything that could be called thought. It can put out a babbling kind of speech utterance, it can put a simple feeling, perception, or sort-of-thought into understandable (though terrible) words. But it is incapable of considering anything in relation to anything else. The moment you try to hold that thought or feeling up against some other to see the relationship, you simply lose the picture — you get nothing but buzzing lines or waving colors.

So admit this. Avoid anything more than one feeling, per- 3 ception, or thought. Simply write as much as possible. Try sim- ply to steer your mind in the direction or general vicinity of the thing you are trying to write about and start writing and keep writing.

Just write and keep writing. (Probably best to write on only 4 one side of the paper in case you should want to cut parts out with scissors — but you probably won't.) Just write and keep writing. It will probably come in waves. After a flurry, stop and take a brief rest. But don't stop too long. Don't think about what you are writing or what you have written or else you will overload the circuit again. Keep writing as though you are drugged or drunk. Keep doing this till you feel you have a lot of material that might be useful; or, if necessary, till you can't stand it any more — even if you doubt that there's anything use- ful there.

Then take a pad of little pieces of paper — or perhaps 3×5 5 cards — and simply start at the beginning of what you were writing, and as you read over what you wrote, every time you come to any thought, feeling, perception, or image that could be gathered up into one sentence or one assertion, do so and write it by itself on a little sheet of paper. In short, you are trying to turn, say, ten or twenty pages of wandering mush into twenty or thirty hard little crab apples. Sometimes there won't be many on a page. But if it seems to you that there are none on a page, you are making a serious error — the same serious error that put you in this comatose state to start with. You are mistaking lousy, stupid, second-rate, wrong, childish, foolish, worthless ideas for no ideas at all. Your job is not to pick out *good* ideas but to pick out ideas. As long as you were conscious, your words will be full of things that could be called feelings, utterances, ideas — things that can be squeezed into one simple sentence. This is your job. Don't ask for too much.

After you have done this, take those little slips or cards, read through them a number of times — not struggling with them, simply wandering and mulling through them; perhaps shifting them around and looking through them in various sequences. In a sense these are cards you are playing solitaire with, and the rules of this particular game permit shuffling the unused pile. 6

The goal of this procedure with the cards is to get them to distribute themselves in two or three or ten or fifteen different piles on your desk. You can get them to do this almost by themselves if you simply keep reading through them in different orders; certain cards will begin to feel like they go with other cards. I emphasize this passive, thoughtless mode because I want to talk about desperation writing in its pure state. In practice, almost invariably at some point in the procedure, your sanity begins to return. It is often at this point. You actually are moved to have thoughts or — and the difference between active and passive is crucial here — to *exert* thought; to hold two cards together and *build* or *assert* a relationship. It is a matter of bringing energy to bear. 7

So you may start to be able to do something active with these cards, and begin actually to think. But if not, just allow the cards to find their own piles with each other by feel, by drift, by intuition, by mindlessness. 8

You have now engaged in the two main activities that will permit you to get something cooked out on the table rather than in your brain: writing out into messy words, summing up into single assertions, and even sensing relationships between assertions. You can simply continue to deploy these two activities. 9

If, for example, after that first round of writing, assertion-making, and pile-making, your piles feel as though they are use- 10

ful and satisfactory for what you are writing — paragraphs or
sections or trains of thought — then you can carry on from
there. See if you can gather each pile up into a single assertion.
When you can, then put the subsidiary assertions of that pile
into their best order to fit with that single unifying one. If you
can't get the pile into one assertion, then take the pile as the basis for doing some more writing out into words. In the course of
this writing, you may produce for yourself the single unifying assertion you were looking for; or you may have to go through the
cycle of turning the writing into assertions and piles and so
forth. Perhaps more than once. The pile may turn out to want
to be two or more piles itself; or it may want to become part of a
pile you already have. This is natural. This kind of meshing into
one configuration, then coming apart, then coming together
and meshing into a different configuration — this is growing
and cooking. It makes a terrible mess, but if you can't do it in
your head, you have to put up with a cluttered desk and a lot of
confusion.

 If, on the other hand, all that writing _didn't_ have useful ma- 11
terial in it, it means that your writing wasn't loose, drifting,
quirky, jerky, associative enough. This time try especially to let
things simply remind you of things that are seemingly crazy or
unrelated. Follow these odd associations. Make as many metaphors as you can — be as nutty as possible — and explore the
metaphors themselves — open them out. You may have all your
energy tied up in some area of your experience that you are leaving out. Don't refrain from writing about whatever else is on
your mind: how you feel at the moment, what you are losing
your mind over, randomness that intrudes itself on your consciousness, the pattern on the wallpaper, what those people you
see out the window have on their minds — though keep coming
back to the whateveritis you are supposed to be writing about.
Treat it, in short, like ten-minute writing exercises. Your best
perceptions and thoughts are always going to be tied up in whatever is really occupying you, and that is also where your energy
is. You may end up writing a love poem — or a hate poem — in
one of those little piles while the other piles will finally turn into

a lab report on data processing or whatever you have to write about. But you couldn't, in your present state of having your head shot off, have written that report without also writing the poem. And the report will have some of the juice of the poem in it and vice versa.

QUESTIONS ON MEANING

1. On what assumptions does Elbow base his advice?
2. Where in his essay does the author reveal his PURPOSE?
3. What value does Elbow discern in "lousy, stupid, second-rate, wrong, childish, foolish, worthless ideas" (paragraph 5)?
4. In your own words, describe the role of the unconscious in the process Elbow analyzes. Where in the process does the conscious mind have to do its part?
5. How does the author justify writing a poem when the assignment is to write a lab report?

QUESTIONS ON WRITING STRATEGY

1. What EFFECT does the author achieve by opening his essay in the first PERSON?
2. At what AUDIENCE does Elbow direct his advice?
3. Into how many steps does the author break down the process he analyzes? What are they?
4. Point to effective samples of time-markers in this essay. (Time-markers are discussed on page 245.)
5. Point to phrases or sentences in the essay that seem to you designed to offer encouragement and comfort.

QUESTIONS ON LANGUAGE

1. Where in his essay does the author make good use of FIGURES OF SPEECH?
2. Using a dictionary if necessary, define the following words: coherent, hindrance (paragraph 1); assertion, comatose (5); configuration (10).

SUGGESTIONS FOR WRITING

1. Approach a writing assignment for any one of your classes by following Peter Elbow's advice. Write steadily in the manner prescribed for at least ten minutes; then sort out any ideas you may have brought forth. If you have no class assignment that involves writing, work instead on a journal entry about some recent event, book, idea, or experience that impressed you. When your exercise has been completed, write a paragraph in which you evaluate how well Elbow's method succeeded for you. Did it lead to any good results? Any surprises?

2. In a brief essay, explain how to tackle any job you're not in the mood for: researching a paper, preparing a speech, performing a lab experiment, studying for a test, cleaning your house, washing your car, getting up in the morning. The process should involve at least three steps.

Peter Elbow on Writing

Peter Elbow's best known work is devoted, like "Desperation Writing," to encouraging people to write. Much of his advice comes from his writing experience. His own life is the source for one of his latest articles, "Closing My Eyes as I Speak: An Argument for Ignoring Audience" (*College English*, January 1987).

That it often helps writers to be aware of their readers is an article of faith for many college writing instructors; it is an assumption we make in *The Bedford Reader*. Without denying that a sense of audience is sometimes valuable, Elbow makes a persuasive case for sometimes trying to forget that an audience is there. "When I am talking to a person or a group," he begins, "and struggling to find words or thoughts, I often find myself involuntarily closing my eyes as I speak. I realize now that this behavior is an instinctive attempt to blot out awareness of audience when I need all my concentration for just trying to figure out or express what I want to say. Because the audience is so imperiously *present* in a speaking situation, my instinct reacts with this active attempt to avoid audience awareness. This behavior — in a sense impolite or antisocial — is not so uncommon. Even when we write, alone in a room to an absent audience, there are occasions when we are struggling to figure something out and need to push aside awareness of those absent readers."

Some audiences — like a readership of close friends — are helpful to keep in mind. "When we think about them from the start, we think of more and better things to say." But other audiences are powerfully inhibiting, and keeping them in mind as we write may put up writer's blocks. "For example, when we have to write to someone we find intimidating (and of course students often perceive teachers as intimidating), we often start thinking wholly defensively. As we write down each thought or sentence, our mind fills with thoughts of how the intended reader will criticize or object to it. So we try to qualify or soften what we've just written — or write out some answer to a possible objection. Our writing becomes tangled. Sometimes we get so tied in knots that we cannot even figure out what we think."

The solution? "We can ignore that audience altogether during the *early* stages of writing and direct our words only to ourselves or to no one in particular — or even to the 'wrong' audience, that is, to an *inviting* audience of trusted friends or allies. . . . Putting audience out of mind is of course a traditional practice: Serious writers have long used private journals for early explorations of feeling, thinking, or language." In contrast, inferior newspaper or business writing often reminds us of "the ineffective actor whose consciousness of self distracts us: He makes us too aware of his own awareness of us. When we read such prose, we wish the writer would stop thinking about us — would stop trying to adjust or fit what he is saying to our frame of reference. 'Damn it, put all your attention on what you are saying,' we want to say, 'and forget about us and how we are reacting.'

"When we examine really good student or professional writing, we can often see that its goodness comes from the writer's having gotten sufficiently wrapped up in her meaning and her language as to forget all about audience needs: The writer manages to 'break through.'"

To overcome the problem of being painfully conscious of readers, if it is a problem you've met, Elbow advises writing more than one draft of everything. "*After* we have figured out our thinking in copious exploratory or draft writing — perhaps finding the right voice or stance as well — *then* we can follow the traditional rhetorical advice: Think about readers and revise carefully to adjust our words and thoughts to our intended audience."

FOR DISCUSSION

1. How faithfully do Peter Elbow's observations reflect your own writing experience? Do you ever worry so hard about what your reader will think that you become pen-tied? Or do you usually close your eyes to your audience, and just write?
2. What is wrong with the following attempt to state Elbow's thesis: "A writer should simply forget about audience"?
3. If you feel uncomfortable when you write, too keenly aware of the reader "looking over your shoulder," what advice of Elbow's might you follow? Can you suggest any other advice to relieve a writer's self-consciousness?

· David Quammen ·

Novelist and essayist DAVID QUAMMEN was born in Cincinnati in 1948. After taking a B.A. in English from Yale, he attended Oxford University as a Rhodes Scholar, receiving his master's degree in literature. Most often, despite his literary training, Quammen writes about science and natural history, subjects he treats with a rare blend of insight, wit, and reverence. His books include *To Walk the Line* (1970) and *The Zolla Configuration* (1983), both novels; and *Natural Acts: A Sidelong View of Science and Nature* (1985), a collection of essays. His most recent novel is *The Soul of Viktor Tronko* (1987). Besides contributing the column "Natural Acts" to *Outside* magazine, Quammen has written for *Audubon, Esquire, Smithsonian,* the *New York Times Book Review, Montana Outdoors,* and *Rolling Stone.*

Is Sex Necessary?
Virgin Birth and Opportunism
in the Garden

The title refers to a classic work of comedy: James Thurber and E. B. White's *Is Sex Necessary?* (1929). Although the earlier book is a spoof on self-help manuals (and you don't need to have read it to understand Quammen's essay), Quammen is mostly serious in his investigation of the mysteries of parthenogenesis. Yet you'll find humor here, too — as in his tongue-in-cheek suggestion that "biology has great potential as vulgar entertainment." Originally published in *Outside* for October 1982, Quammen's essay was collected in his book *Natural Acts.*

Birds do it, bees do it, goes the tune. But the songsters, as   1
usual, would mislead us with drastic oversimplifications. The full truth happens to be more eccentrically nonlibidinous: Sometimes they *don't* do it, those very creatures, and get the

same results anyway. Bees of all species, for instance, are notable to geneticists precisely for their ability to produce offspring while doing *without*. Likewise at least one variety of bird — the Beltsville Small White turkey, a domestic dinner-table model out of Beltsville, Maryland — has achieved scientific renown for a similar feat. What we are talking about here is celibate motherhood, procreation without copulation, a phenomenon that goes by the technical name *parthenogenesis*. Translated from the Greek roots: virgin birth.

And you don't have to be Catholic to believe in this one.   2

Miraculous as it may seem, parthenogenesis is actually   3
rather common throughout nature, practiced regularly or intermittently by at least some species within almost every group of animals except (for reasons still unknown) dragonflies and mammals. Reproduction by virgin females has been discovered among reptiles, birds, fishes, amphibians, crustaceans, mollusks, ticks, the jellyfish clan, flatworms, roundworms, segmented worms; and among insects (notwithstanding those unrelentingly sexy dragonflies) it is especially favored. The order Hymenoptera, including all bees and wasps, is uniformly parthenogenetic in the manner by which males are produced: Every male honeybee is born without any genetic contribution from a father. Among the beetles, there are thirty-five different forms of parthenogenetic weevil. The African weaver ant employs parthenogenesis, as do twenty-three species of fruit fly and at least one kind of roach. The gall midge *Miastor* is notorious for the exceptionally bizarre and grisly scenario that allows its fatherless young to see daylight: *Miastor* daughters cannibalize the mother from inside, with ruthless impatience, until her hollowed-out skin splits open like the door of an overcrowded nursery. But the foremost practitioners of virgin birth — their elaborate and versatile proficiency unmatched in the animal kingdom — are undoubtedly the aphids.

Now no sensible reader of even this book can be expected, I   4
realize, to care faintly about aphid biology *qua* aphid biology. That's just asking too much. But there's a larger rationale for dragging you aphid-ward. The life cycle of these little nebbishy sap-sucking insects, the very same that infest rose bushes and

house plants, not only exemplifies *how* parthenogenetic reproduction is done; it also very clearly shows *why*.

First the biographical facts. A typical aphid, which feeds entirely on plant juices tapped off from the vascular system of young leaves, spends winter dormant and protected, as an egg. The egg is attached near a bud site on the new growth of a poplar tree. In March, when the tree sap has begun to rise and the buds have begun to burgeon, an aphid hatchling appears, plugging its sharp snout (like a mosquito's) into the tree's tenderest plumbing. This solitary individual aphid will be, necessarily, a wingless female. If she is lucky, she will become sole founder of a vast aphid population. Having sucked enough poplar sap to reach maturity, she produces — by *live birth* now, and without benefit of a mate — daughters identical to herself. These wingless daughters also plug into the tree's flow of sap, and they also produce further wingless daughters, until sometime in late May, when that particular branch of that particular tree can support no more thirsty aphids. Suddenly there is a change: The next generation of daughters are born with wings. They fly off in search of a better situation.

One such aviatrix lands on an herbaceous plant — say a young climbing bean in some human's garden — and the pattern repeats. She plugs into the sap ducts on the underside of a new leaf, commences feasting destructively, and delivers by parthenogenesis a great brood of wingless daughters. The daughters beget more daughters, those daughters beget still more, and so on, until the poor bean plant is encrusted with a solid mob of these fat little elbowing greedy sisters. Then again, neatly triggered by the crowded conditions, a generation of daughters are born with wings. Away they fly, looking for prospects, and one of them lights on, say, a sugar beet. (The switch from bean to beet is fine, because our species of typical aphid is not inordinately choosy.) The sugar beet before long is covered, sucked upon mercilessly, victimized by a horde of mothers and nieces and granddaughters. Still not a single male aphid has appeared anywhere in the chain.

The lurching from one plant to another continues; the alternation between wingless and winged daughters continues. But in September, with fresh tender plant growth increasingly hard to find, there is another change.

Flying daughters are born who have a different destiny: 8 They wing back to the poplar tree, where they give birth to a crop of wingless females that are unlike any so far. These latest girls know the meaning of sex! Meanwhile, at long last, the starving survivors back on that final bedraggled sugar beet have brought forth a generation of males. The males have wings. They take to the air in quest of poplar trees and first love. *Et voilà*. The mated females lay eggs that will wait out the winter near bud sites on that poplar tree, and the circle is thus completed. One single aphid hatchling — call her the *fundatrix* — in this way can give rise in the course of a year, from her own ovaries exclusively, to roughly a zillion aphids.

Well and good, you say. A zillion aphids. But what is the 9 point of it?

The point, for aphids as for most other parthenogenetic ani- 10 mals, is (1) exceptionally fast reproduction that allows (2) maximal exploitation of temporary resource abundance and unstable environmental conditions, while (3) facilitating the successful colonization of unfamiliar habitats. In other words the aphid, like the gall midge and the weaver ant and the rest of their fellow parthenogens, is by its evolved character a galloping opportunist.

This is a term of science, not of abuse. Population ecologists 11 make an illuminating distinction between what they label *equilibrium* and *opportunistic* species. According to William Birky and John Gilbert, from a paper in the journal *American Zoologist:* "Equilibrium species, exemplified by many vertebrates, maintain relatively constant population sizes, in part by being adapted to reproduce, at least slowly, in most of the environmental conditions which they meet. Opportunistic species, on the other hand, show extreme population fluctuations; they are adapted to reproduce only in a relatively narrow range of conditions, but make up for this by reproducing extremely rapidly in favorable circumstances. At least in some cases, opportunistic organisms can also be categorized as colonizing organisms." Birky and Gilbert also emphasize that "The potential for rapid reproduction is the essential evolutionary ticket for entry into the opportunistic life style."

And parthenogenesis, in turn, is the greatest time-saving gimmick in the history of animal reproduction. No hours or days are wasted while a female looks for a mate; no minutes lost to the act of mating itself. The female aphid attains sexual maturity and, bang, she becomes automatically pregnant. No waiting, no courtship, no fooling around. She delivers her brood of daughters, they grow to puberty and, zap, another generation immediately. If humans worked as fast, Jane Fonda today would be a great-grandmother. The time saved to parthenogenetic species may seem trivial, but it is not. It adds up dizzyingly: In the same time taken by a sexually reproducing insect to complete three generations for a total of 1,200 offspring, an aphid (assuming the *same* time required for each female to mature, and the *same* number of progeny in each litter), squandering no time on courtship or sex, will progress through six generations for an extended family of 318,000,000.

Even this isn't speedy enough for some restless opportunists. That matricidal gall midge *Miastor*, whose larvae feed on fleeting eruptions of fungus under the bark of trees, has developed a startling way to cut further time from the cycle of procreation. Far from waiting for a mate, *Miastor* does not even wait for maturity. When food is abundant, it is the *larva*, not the adult female fly, who is eaten alive from inside by her own daughters. And as those voracious daughters burst free of the husk that was their mother, each of them already contains further larval daughters taking shape ominously within its own ovaries. While the food lasts, while opportunity endures, no *Miastor* female can live to adulthood without dying of motherhood.

The implicit principle behind all this nonsexual reproduction, all this hurry, is simple: Don't argue with success. Don't tamper with a genetic blueprint that works. Unmated female aphids, and gall midges, pass on their own gene patterns virtually unaltered (except for the occasional mutation) to their daughters. Sexual reproduction, on the other hand, constitutes, by its essence, genetic tampering. The whole purpose of joining sperm with egg is to shuffle the genes of both parents and come up with a new combination that might perhaps be more advantageous. Give the kid something neither Mom nor Pop ever had. Parthenogenetic species, during their hurried phases at least, dispense with this genetic shuffle. They stick stubbornly to the gene pattern that seems to be working. They produce (with certain complicated exceptions) natural clones of themselves.

But what they gain thereby in reproductive rate, in great explosions of population, they give up in flexibility. They minimize their genetic options. They lessen their chances of adapting to unforeseen changes of circumstance.   15

Which is why more than one biologist has drawn the same conclusion as M. J. D. White: "Parthenogenetic forms seem to be frequently successful in the particular ecological niche which they occupy, but sooner or later the inherent disadvantages of their genetic system must be expected to lead to a lack of adaptability, followed by eventual extinction, or perhaps in some cases by a return to sexuality."   16

So it *is* necessary, at least intermittently (once a year, for the aphids, whether they need it or not), this thing called sex. As of course you and I knew it must be. Otherwise surely, by now, we mammals and dragonflies would have come up with something more dignified.   17

QUESTIONS ON MEANING

1. How would you state, in your own words, the THESIS of this essay?
2. What does the title tell you about the subject of this essay? What does the subtitle tell you? How well would the title work without the subtitle, and vice versa? What does Quammen gain, in this case, by choosing a title that two humorists had already used?
3. At the end of paragraph 4, the author states that "the life cycle of these . . . insects . . . not only exemplifies *how* parthenogenetic reproduction is done; it also very clearly shows *why*." What is your understanding of why this type of reproduction takes place?
4. In the process described in this essay, at what point are female aphids born with wings? At what point are males born? According to Quammen, what triggers each of these events?

QUESTIONS ON WRITING STRATEGY

1. What is the TONE of the statements "no waiting, no courtship, no fooling around" and "squandering no time on courtship or sex" (paragraph 12)? Do you think Quammen feels that courtship and sex are an unfortunate waste of time for mammals and other creatures that reproduce in this way?
2. For what AUDIENCE is Quammen writing? Where does he specifically state this? If he were writing this essay for a scientific magazine, what might he do differently?
3. What process is analyzed in this essay? Where in the essay does the analysis of this process begin? What time-markers does Quammen use to help his readers follow the process?
4. Consider the phrase "the poor bean plant is encrusted with a solid mob of these fat little elbowing greedy sisters" (paragraph 6). Find other FIGURES OF SPEECH that vividly illustrate Quammen's exposition. How do they help you understand the complex natural process of parthenogenesis?

QUESTIONS ON LANGUAGE

1. Explain the ALLUSION to Catholicism in paragraph 2.
2. In labeling aphids "opportunists" (see paragraph 10), Quammen writes: "This is a term of science, not abuse" (paragraph 11). What meaning of the word "opportunist" are you familiar with, and how does that differ from the definition provided in paragraphs 10 and 11?
3. What does the phrase "aphid biology *qua* aphid biology" in paragraph 4 mean?
4. Define eccentrically, nonlibidinous, celibate, procreation (paragraph 1); intermittently, cannibalize, practitioners, proficiency (3); dormant, burgeon (5); inordinately (6); exploitation, facilitating (10); exemplified, fluctuations (11); matricidal (13); implicit (14); ecological, niche (16).

SUGGESTIONS FOR WRITING

1. Drawing on written information or your observations, write an essay in which you tell how any creature gives birth to or hatches its young.
2. Write an essay in which you analyze an activity with which you are familiar, but which you should assume your readers have never

tried. Be sure to define any technical terms your readers may not know. At the same time remember that your readers are intelligent, and avoid condescending to them. Make sure you explain the purpose of every step, so your readers understand its importance. Possible topics include developing photographs in your own darkroom, giving your car a tune-up, making a complicated dish or sauce in the kitchen, setting up an aquarium, hunting for fossils, listening to a symphony.

David Quammen on Writing

"Lively writing about science and nature," says David Quammen, "depends less on the offering of good answers, I think, than on the offering of good questions. My own taste runs toward questions such as *What are the redeeming merits, if any, of the mosquito? Or Why is the act of sex invariably fatal for some species of salmon? Or Are crows too intelligent for their station in life? Why do certain bamboo species wait 120 years before bursting into bloom?*"

Quammen is the first to point out that, unlike Lewis Thomas, Stephen Jay Gould, Alan Lightman, and other popular writers on scientific subjects, he is not a scientist. "What I am is a dilettante and a haunter of libraries and a snoop. The sort of person who has his nose in the way constantly during other people's field trips, asking too many foolish questions and occasionally scribbling notes. My own formal scientific training has been minuscule (and confined largely to the ecology of rivers). Gould and Thomas and Lightman actually do science, in addition to writing about it. I merely follow science. In my other set of pajamas I'm not a biologist but a novelist." (Introduction to *Natural Acts* [New York: Nick Lyons Books, 1985], pp. xi, xiv.)

FOR DISCUSSION

1. Quammen points out that he is not a scientist. Can you see any significant differences between his writing on scientific subjects

and that of the scientists (Lewis Thomas, Stephen Jay Gould, Carl Sagan) whose essays are included in *The Bedford Reader*?
2. What advantages are there to approaching a writing project armed with "good questions"?

· Linnea Saukko ·

LINNEA SAUKKO was born in Warren, Ohio, in 1956. After receiving a degree in environmental quality control from Muskingum Area Technical College, she spent three years as an environmental technician, developing hazardous waste programs and acting as advisor on chemical safety at a large corporation. Concerned about the lack of safe methods for disposing of hazardous waste, Saukko went back to school to earn a B.A. in geology (Ohio State University, 1985) so she could help address this issue. She currently lives in Columbus, where she evaluates landfills, investigates leaking dumps, and handles citizens' complaints about their water for the Ohio Environmental Protection Agency. Saukko recently completed a Groundwater Monitoring Guidance Document, which outlines the proper procedure for an investigation, for the Environmental Protection Agency.

How to Poison the Earth

"How to Poison the Earth" was written in response to an assignment given in a freshman composition class and was awarded a 1983 Bedford Prize in Student Writing. It was one of thirty-one winners chosen from over 1,100 essays submitted to this nationwide contest and was subsequently published in *Student Writers at Work: The Bedford Prizes*, edited by Nancy Sommers and Donald McQuade (1984). In this satirical essay, Saukko shares with readers some of what she has learned on the job, and suggests one way we can guarantee the fate of the earth.

Poisoning the earth can be difficult because the earth is always trying to cleanse and renew itself. Keeping this in mind, we should generate as much waste as possible from substances such as uranium-238, which has a half-life (the time it takes for half of the substance to decay) of one million years, or plutonium, which has a half-life of only 0.5 million years but is so toxic that if distributed evenly, ten pounds of it could kill every person on the earth. Because the United States generates about eighteen tons of plutonium per year, it is about the best substance for long-term poisoning of the earth. It would help if we would build more nuclear power plants because each one generates only 500 pounds of plutonium each year. Of course, we must include persistent toxic chemicals such as polychlorinated biphenyl (PCB) and dichlorodiphenyl trichloroethane (DDT) to make sure we have enough toxins to poison the earth from the core to the outer atmosphere. First, we must develop many different ways of putting the waste from these nuclear and chemical substances in, on, and around the earth.

Putting these substances in the earth is a most important step in the poisoning process. With deep-well injection we can ensure that the earth is poisoned all the way to the core. Deep-well injection involves drilling a hole that is a few thousand feet deep and injecting toxic substances at extremely high pressures so they will penetrate deep into the earth. According to the Environmental Protection Agency (EPA), there are about 360 such deep injection wells in the United States. We cannot forget the groundwater aquifers that are closer to the surface. These must also be contaminated. This is easily done by shallow-well injection, which operates on the same principle as deep-well injection, only closer to the surface. The groundwater that has been injected with toxins will spread the contamination beneath the earth. The EPA estimates that there are approximately 500,000 shallow injection wells in the United States.

Burying the toxins in the earth is the next best method. The toxins from landfills, dumps, and lagoons slowly seep into the earth, guaranteeing that contamination will last a long time. Because the EPA estimates there are only about 50,000 of these dumps in the United States, they should be located in areas where they will leak to the surrounding ground and surface water.

Applying pesticides and other poisons on the earth is another part of the poisoning process. This is good for coating the earth's surface so that the poisons will be absorbed by plants, will seep into the ground, and will run off into surface water.

Surface water is very important to contaminate because it will transport the poisons to places that cannot be contaminated directly. Lakes are good for long-term storage of pollutants while they release some of their contamination to rivers. The only trouble with rivers is that they act as a natural cleansing system for the earth. No matter how much poison is dumped into them, they will try to transport it away to reach the ocean eventually.

The ocean is very hard to contaminate because it has such a large volume and a natural buffering capacity that tends to neutralize some of the contamination. So in addition to the pollution from rivers, we must use the ocean as a dumping place for as many toxins as possible. The ocean currents will help transport the pollution to places that cannot otherwise be reached.   6

Now make sure that the air around the earth is very polluted. Combustion and evaporation are major mechanisms for doing this. We must continuously pollute because the wind will disperse the toxins while rain washes them from the air. But this is good because a few lakes are stripped of all living animals each year from acid rain. Because the lower atmosphere can cleanse itself fairly easily, we must explode nuclear test bombs that shoot radioactive particles high into the upper atmosphere where they will circle the earth for years. Gravity must pull some of the particles to earth, so we must continue exploding these bombs.   7

So it is that easy. Just be sure to generate as many poisonous substances as possible and be sure they are distributed in, on, and around the entire earth at a greater rate than it can cleanse itself. By following these easy steps we can guarantee the poisoning of the earth.   8

QUESTIONS ON MEANING

1. Is the author's main PURPOSE to amuse and entertain, to inform readers of ways they can make better use of natural resources, to warn readers about threats to the future of our planet, or to make fun of scientists? Support your answer with EVIDENCE from the essay.

2. Describe at least three of the earth's mechanisms for cleansing its land, water, and atmosphere, as presented in this essay.

3. According to Saukko, many of our actions are detrimental, if not outright destructive, to our environment. Identify these practices and discuss them. If these activities are harmful to the earth, why are they permitted? Do they serve some other important goal or purpose? If so, what? Are there other ways that these goals might be reached?

QUESTIONS ON WRITING STRATEGY

1. How is Saukko's essay organized? Follow the process carefully to determine whether it happens chronologically, with each step depending on the one before it, or whether it follows another order. How effective is this method of organization and presentation?
2. For what AUDIENCE is this essay intended? How can you tell?
3. What is the TONE of this essay? Consider especially the title and the last paragraph. Provide examples from the essay to support your answer.
4. How detailed and specific are Saukko's instructions for poisoning the earth? Which steps in this process would you be able to carry out, once you finished reading the essay? In what instances might an author choose *not* to provide concrete, comprehensive instructions for a procedure? Relate your answer to the tone and purpose of this essay.

QUESTIONS ON LANGUAGE

1. How do the phrases "next best method" (paragraph 3), "another part of the poisoning process" (4), and "lakes are good for long-term storage of pollutants" (5) signal the tone of this essay? Should they be read literally, ironically, metaphorically, or some other way?
2. Be sure you know how to define the following words: generate, nuclear, toxins (paragraph 1); lagoons, contamination (3); buffering, neutralize (6); combustion (7).

SUGGESTIONS FOR WRITING

1. Write a satirical essay in which you propose the solution to a problem or the means to an end. Make sure your tone signals your satiric intent. Describe your solution in detail, using time-markers to indicate the order of steps or events.

2. Write an essay defending and justifying the use of nuclear power plants, pesticides, or other pollutants Saukko mentions. This essay will require some research because you will need to argue that the benefits of these methods outweigh their hazardous and destructive effects. Be sure to support your claims with factual information and statistics. Or, approach the issue from the same point of view that Saukko did, and argue against the use of nuclear power plants and pesticides. Substantiate your argument with data and facts, and make sure to propose alternative sources of power and alternative methods of insect control.

Linnea Saukko on Writing

"After I have chosen a topic," says Linnea Saukko, "the easiest thing for me to do is to write about how I really feel about it. The goal of 'How To Poison the Earth' was to inform people, or more specifically, to open their eyes.

"As soon as I decided on my topic, I made a list of all the types of pollution and I sat down and basically wrote the paper in less than two hours. The information seemed to pour from me onto the page. Of course I did a lot of editing afterward, but I never changed the idea and the tone that I started with."

FOR DISCUSSION

1. When have you had the experience of writing on a subject that compelled your words to pour forth with little effort? What was the subject? What did you learn from this experience?

1. Write a *directive* process analysis (a "how to" essay) in which, drawing on your own knowledge, you instruct someone in doing or making something. Divide the process into steps and be sure to detail each step thoroughly. Some possible subjects (any of which may be modified or narrowed with the approval of your instructor):

How to enlist people's confidence
How to bake bread
How to meditate
How to teach a child to swim
How to select a science fiction novel
How to select a rental video tape
How to drive a car
How to prepare yourself to take an intelligence test
How to compose a photograph
How to judge cattle
How to buy a used motorcycle
How to enjoy an opera
How to organize your own rock group
How to eat an artichoke
How to groom a horse
How to bellydance
How to make a movie
How to build (or fly) kites
How to start lifting weights
How to aid a person who is choking
How to behave on a first date
How to get your own way
How to kick a habit
How to lose weight
How to win at poker
How to make an effective protest or complaint

Or, if you don't like any of those topics, what else do you know that others might care to learn from you?

2. Step by step, working in chronological order, write a careful *informative* analysis of any one of the following processes. (This is not to be a "how to" essay, but an essay that explains how something happens.) Make use of description wherever necessary, and be sure to include frequent time-markers. If one of these topics should give you a better idea for a paper, discuss your choice of subject with your instructor.

How a student is processed during orientation or registration
How a professional umpire (or an insurance underwriter, or some other professional) does his or her job
How an amplifier works
How a political candidate runs for office
How birds teach their young (or some other process in the natural world: how sharks feed, how a snake swallows an egg)
How the Appalachian Trail was blazed
How a Rubik's cube functions (or how it drives people crazy)
How police control crowds
How people usually make up their minds when shopping for new cars (or new clothes)
How an idea has come to be accepted

3. Write a directive process analysis in which you use a light tone. Although you do not take your subject in deadly earnest, your humor will probably be effective only if you take the method of process analysis seriously. Make clear each stage of the process and explain it in sufficient detail.

How to get through the month of November (or March)
How to flunk out of college swiftly and efficiently
How to outwit a pinball machine
How to choose a mate
How to go broke
How to sell something that nobody wants

DIVISION AND CLASSIFICATION

Slicing into Parts, Sorting into Kinds

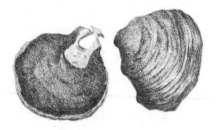

THE METHOD

If you have read the last chapter, you'll recall that *division* (also called *analysis*) is the act of separating a thing into its parts. By this method, a chemist breaks down an unfamiliar substance into its components. In writing a process analysis, a writer divides a process into its stages: telling us step by step how a fertilized human egg grows, or how to build a hang glider.

Think of the method of division, then, as an instrument ready to use and gleaming in your hand. With its aid, you can slice a large and complicated subject into smaller parts that you can deal with more easily — and that your reader can grasp more readily. At this point, kindly underline the following two sentences, because they're essential. You can apply the method of division not only to processes, but also to other subjects. In so doing, you take a thing and — much as you do with a process — separate it into its component parts. If, for example, your subject were fried chicken, you could divide it into breast, thighs, wings, drumsticks, and the part that goes over the fence last; and you could write an essay discussing each part and its respective merits. In their guidebook *New York on $20 a Day*, Joan Hamburg and Norma Ketay divide the city into sections: Midtown East, Midtown West, Pennsylvania Station and Chelsea, Little Italy, and so on. In reality, New York is not a distinctly different place from one street to the next; but by dividing New York into neighborhoods, the writers have organized their book in a way that will help the reader-tourist more easily take in the city's complicated geography.

Useful for tangible things like chicken and cities, the method of division also suits more abstract subjects. That is why writers of college textbooks do a lot of dividing. An economics book divides a labor union into its elements, a psychology book divides the psychoanalytical movement into separate schools of thought. In "I Want a Wife," an essay in this chapter, Judy Syfers divides the role of a wife into its various functions or services. In an essay called "Teacher," Robert Francis divides the knowledge of poetry he imparted to his class into six pie sections. The first slice is what he told his students that they knew already.

> The second slice is what I told them that they could have found out just as well or better from books. What, for instance, is a sestina?
> The third slice is what I told them that they refused to accept. I could see it on their faces, and later I saw the evidence in their writing.
> The fourth slice is what I told them that they were willing to accept and may have thought they accepted but couldn't accept since they couldn't fully understand. This also I saw in their faces and in their work. Here, no doubt, I was mostly to blame.
> The fifth slice is what I told them that they discounted as whimsy or something simply to fill up time. After all, I was being paid to talk.

> The sixth slice is what I didn't tell them, for I didn't try to tell them all I knew. Deliberately I kept back something — a few professional secrets, a magic formula or two.[1]

There are always multiple ways to divide a subject, just as there are many ways to slice a pie. Francis could have divided his knowledge of poetry into knowledge of English poetry, knowledge of American poetry, and so forth; or the writers of the New York guidebook could have divided the city into historic landmarks, centers of entertainment, shopping districts, and so on. (Incidentally, Francis's account of slicing his pie is also an *analogy*, a method of illustrating a difficult idea by comparing it to something familiar. See Chapter 7 for more examples.)

Half-brother to division is the method of *classification*, the sorting out of things into categories. The method of classification is familiar to us from everyday life. Preparing to can peaches, we might begin by classifying the peaches on hand into three groups: firm, soft, and rotten. To classify is a way to make sense of the world. Zoologists classify animals, botanists classify plants — and their classifications help us to understand a vast and complex subject: life on earth. To help us find books in a library, librarians classify books into categories: fiction, biography, history, psychology, and so forth. For the convenience of readers, newspapers run classified advertising, grouping many small ads into categories such as HELP WANTED and CARS FOR SALE.

When you classify, your subject is always a *number* of things. Say, for instance, you're going to write an essay explaining that people differ widely in their sleep habits. Your subject is people as sleepers, and you might classify them into late sleepers, midmorning sleepers, early risers, and insomniacs.

Like division, classification is done for a purpose. In the case of peaches, we might sort them to decide which to can at once, which to set aside for canning later, and which to eat immediately. Writers, too, classify things for reasons. In their New York City guidebook, Hamburg and Ketay cast their discussion of low-priced hotels into categories: Rooms for Singles and Stu-

---

[1]*Pot Shots at Poetry* (Ann Arbor: University of Michigan Press, 1980).

dents, Rooms for Families, Rooms for Servicemen, and Rooms for General Occupancy. Their purpose is to match up the visitor with a suitable kind of room. Their subject, remember, is multiple: hundreds of hotels.

Just as you can divide a pie in many ways, you can classify a subject according to many principles. A different New York guidebook might classify hotels according to price: grand luxury class, luxury class, commercial class, budget class, fleabag, and flophouse. The purpose of this classification would be to match visitors to hotels fitting their pocketbooks. The principle you use in classifying things depends on your purpose. A linguist might write an essay classifying the languages of the world according to their origins (Romance languages, Germanic languages, Coptic languages . . .), but a student battling with a college language requirement might write a humorous essay classifying them into three groups: hard to learn, harder to learn, and unlearnable. (Either way of sorting languages would be classification and not division, because the subject would be many languages, not one language. You could, of course, write an essay *dividing* the English language into British English, North American English, Australian English, and so on — *if* your purpose were to show regional varieties of English around the world.)

The simplest method of classification is *binary* (or *two-part*) *classification*, in which you sort things out into (1) those with a certain distinguishing feature and (2) those without it. You might classify a number of persons, let's say, into smokers and nonsmokers, blind people and sighted people, runners and nonrunners, believers and nonbelievers. Binary classification is most useful when your subject is easily divisible into positive and negative categories.

Classification is a method particularly favored by writers who evaluate things. In a survey of current movies, a newspaper critic might classify the films into categories: "Don't Miss," "Worth Seeing," "So-So," and "Never Mind." This kind of classifying is the method of the magazine *Consumer Reports* in its comments on different brands of stereo speakers or canned tuna. Products are sorted into groups (excellent, good, fair, poor, and not acceptable), and the merits of each are discussed by the method of description. (Of a frozen pot pie: "Bottom crust gummy, meat spongy when chewed, with nondescript old-poultry and stale-flour flavor.")

As Jonathan Swift reminds us,

> So, naturalists observe, a flea
> Hath smaller fleas that on him prey,
> And these have smaller yet to bite 'em,
> And so proceed *ad infinitum*.

In being faithful to reality, you will sometimes find that you have to slice parts into smaller parts, or sort out the members of categories into subcategories. Writing about the varieties of English spoken around the world, a writer could subclassify them into regional dialects: breaking North American English into British Columbian English, Southern Appalachian English, and so on. To be more exact, a guidebook to New York might subdivide Midtown West into the Bryant Park area, Times Square, and the West Side.

To tell the two methods apart, remember that when you divide, your subject is always a single thing: one pie, one city, one government. When you classify, your subject is two or more: the different types of pies, cities, or governments. If you divide a peach, you take the knife and separate your subject into skin, a pit, and two halves. You might even write an essay about that peach by the method of division and possibly interest a botanist, a farmer, or a cannery owner. Writing another essay, also dividing, you might split a hotel into its component parts: lobby, rooms, coffee shop, restaurant, bar, ballroom, kitchen, laundry, parking garage, and offices. But when you classify, you start not with one thing but with many. You might sort a quart of marbles according to a common quality, say, color: all the red ones into one group, blue ones into another, green ones into a third. You form groups from a variety of things. Similarly, in writing a classification essay, you might categorize a dozen senators by their political persuasions ("liberals, conservatives, middle-of-the-roaders . . . "), or a dozen theories of the origin of the universe according to complexity. Division proceeds from a whole to its parts; classification, from many pigeons to few pigeon-holes.

Which method you choose, division or classification, depends on whether you view your subject as one or as many. Take "the college student populace," slice this throng into smokers and nonsmokers, and you are dividing. But start with individuals, sort them into smokers and nonsmokers ("Tom smokes, Dick doesn't. . . ."), and you are classifying, even though you go on sorting till you have labeled every student alive.

As readers, we all enjoy watching a clever writer sort things into categories, or break things into elements. We like to meet classifications or divisions that strike us as true and familiar. This pleasure may account for the appeal of popular magazine articles that classify things ("The Seven Common Garden Vari-eties of Moocher," "Five Embarrassing Types of Social Blun-der") or divide whole subjects ("Success in Life: What Are Its El-ements?", "The Nine Components of a Kiss").

Simple as division and classification are, and readily as they may lend themselves to playful thinking, both methods can help us make sense of complex realities. Both separate a subject into units smaller and more easily comprehensible. For the writer as well as for the reader, both methods make large ideas easier to grasp.

THE PROCESS

In writing by either division or classification, having an out-line at your elbow is a help. When dividing a subject into parts, you'll want to make sure you don't omit any. When classifying the members of a group into various pigeonholes, you'll proba-bly need to glance at your outline from time to time, to keep your pigeonholes straight.

In writing her brief essay "I Want a Wife," Judy Syfers must have needed an outline to work out carefully the different activi-ties of a wife before she began, so that she clearly knew where to draw her distinctions between them. Making a valid division is chiefly a matter of giving your subject thought, but for the division to seem useful and convincing to your reader, it will have to refer to the world of the senses. The method requires not only cogitation, but open eyes and a willingness to provide examples and evidence.

In a workable classification, make sure that the categories you choose don't overlap. If you were writing a survey of popular magazines for adults and you were sorting your subject into categories that included women's magazines and sports magazines, you might soon run into trouble. Into which category would you place *Women's Sports?* The trouble is that both categories take in the same item. To avoid this problem, you'll need to reorganize your classification on a different principle. You might sort out the magazines by their audiences: magazines for women, magazines for men, magazines for women and men. Or you might group them according to subject matter: sports magazines, literary magazines, astrology magazines, fashion magazines, TV fan magazines, trade journals, and so on. *Women's Sports* would fit into either of those classification schemes.

Things may be classified into categories that reveal truth, or into categories that don't tell us a thing. To sort out ten U.S. cities according to their relative freedom from air pollution, or their cost of living, or the degree of progress they have made in civil rights might prove highly informative and useful. Such a classification might even tell us where we'd want to live. But to sort out the cities according to a superficial feature such as the relative size of their cat and dog populations wouldn't interest anyone, probably, except a veterinarian looking for a job. Let your reader in on the basis for classification that you choose, and explain why you have chosen it.

When you draw up a scheme of classification, be sure you include all essential categories. Omitting an important category can weaken the effect of your essay, no matter how well-written it is. It would be a major oversight, for example, if you were to classify the residents of a dormitory according to their religious affiliations and not include a category for the numerous nonaffiliated. Your reader might wonder if your sloppiness in forgetting a category extended to your thinking about the topic as well.

For both division and classification, show your reader *why* you went to all the work of dividing or classifying, anyway, and what you have learned by it. In making your division or classification did you come to any conclusion? If so, state it. ("After dividing San Francisco into neighborhoods, and then classifying the neighborhoods, I feel sure that Minneapolis is the place for me after all.")

DIVISION AND CLASSIFICATION
IN PARAGRAPHS: FOUR ILLUSTRATIONS

1. Using Division
to Write about Television

A canned laugh, whatever its style, is made up of three elements. The first is intensity, for a laugh machine can deliver a product of any desired volume, whether mild, medium, or ear splitting. Duration is the second ingredient, for a laugh may be short, medium, or long. By jiggling keys, the machine operator supplies a third ingredient: a fixed number of laughers. Any number is on tap, from a handful of titterers to a roaring throng. Even though situation comedies like "The Cosby Show" and "Cheers" are taped in front of studio audiences, the producer is under a strong temptation to add an element of canned laughter. If a live audience should fail to react to jokes they have heard run through two or three times before, a longer or louder laugh is always available. At the dubbing session, furiously working keys and tromping pedals, the operator of the laugh machine blends these ingredients like a maestro weaving a symphony out of brass, woodwinds, percussion, and strings.

COMMENT. The laugh machine, as you may have gathered, is used to fill a moment of silence in the soundtrack of a comedy program. Most televised comedies, even some that boast they have live audiences, rely on it. According to rumor (for its exact workings are a secret), the machine contains a bank of thirty-two tapes, which the operator turns on singly or in combination. In this paragraph, the writer proceeds by the method of division, taking a single subject — one machine-made laugh — and breaking it into its components: intensity, duration, and the size (and composition) of the laughing audience desired.

2. Using Classification
to Write about Television

Though the laugh machine will supply thirty-two differ-ent styles of laughter, most laughs fall into one of five reliable types. There is the *titter*, a light vocal laugh with which an imaginary audience responds to a comedian's least wriggle or grimace. Some producers rely heavily on the *chuckle*, a deeper, more chesty response. Most profound of all, the *belly laugh* is summoned to acclaim broader jokes and sexual innuendos. When provided at full level of sound and in longest duration, the belly laugh becomes the Big Boffola. There is also the *wild howl* or *screamer*, an extreme response used not more than three times per show, lest it seem fake. These are crowd laughs, and yet the machine also offers the *freaky laugh*, the piercing, eccentric screech of a solitary kook. With it, a pro-ducer affirms that even a canned audience may include one thorny individualist.

COMMENT. Continuing to explain the workings of television comedy's useful laugh machine, the writer classifies mechani-cally produced laughs into five types. Like anything else written by the method of classification, you'll notice, this paragraph takes as its subject a *number* of things, which it then sorts out. The writer has troubled to find clear labels for the five categories of canned laughter: from the *titter* to the *freaky laugh*. Simple but memorable, these labels help each category to register (and stay distinct) in the reader's mind.

3. Using Division
in an Academic Discipline

For convenience in studying and talking about the brain, neuroanatomists have divided each of the hemispheres (left and right halves) of the brain into four separate areas, called *lobes*. They are the *frontal* (which contains the prefrontal, the premotor, and the motor cortices), the *temporal*, the *parietal*, and the *occipital* lobes. The most forward part of the cerebral cortex, that portion just behind the eyes and forehead, is the *prefrontal cortex*, a region involved in planning, forethought, and judgment. Just behind this is the *premotor cortex*, which programs complex movement. Behind the premotor cortex is the *motor cortex*, which controls movements of the various body parts. The *temporal lobes* play a major role in auditory perception and in some learning and memory functions. The *parietal lobes* play a major role in spatial perception, tactile perception, and body image. At the very back of the brain is the *occipital lobe*, an area primarily concerned with vision. While recent research points to some specialization within these lobes, each one is involved with a variety of different functions.

COMMENT.   Occasionally writers are called upon not to divide a subject themselves, but to explain a division that researchers before them have made and that has become accepted knowledge in their field. Such is the case in this paragraph from page 53 of *Psychology* by Diane E. Papalia and Sally Wendkos Olds (New York: McGraw-Hill Book Co., 1985). The authors have not themselves divided the brain into parts and labeled them. Their aim, rather, is to make the discoveries of earlier brain researchers available to the college students who use *Psychology* as a text. The result here is a paragraph that not only imparts information, but clearly and succinctly demonstrates the method of division.

4. Using Classification
in an Academic Discipline

Sheldon described three types of physical physique: the *endomorph*, who is overweight, with poorly developed bones and muscles; the *mesomorph*, muscular, strong, and athletic; and the thin, fragile *ectomorph*. He then came up with three clusters of personality traits: *viscerotonia* (comfort-loving, food-oriented, sociable, relaxed); *somatotonia* (aggressive, adventure-loving, risk-taking); and *cerebrotonia* (restrained, self-conscious, introverted). When Sheldon rated men according to where they stood with regard to both body types and personality traits, he found high correlations. Extremely endomorphic men were likely to be viscerotonic, mesomorphs tended to be somatotonic, and ectomorphs were cerebrotonic.

COMMENT. The Papalia and Olds psychology text also yields this clear-cut illustration of classification. As in the division example, the authors here set out to explain the research of someone else, in this case a medical doctor and scholar named William H. Sheldon. It was Sheldon who classified people's body types as endomorphic, mesomorphic, and ectomorphic, and their personalities as viscerotonic, somatotonic, and cerebrotonic. He also found the correlations described between body types and personalities. Papalia and Olds go on in a subsequent paragraph to say that later researchers found fewer correlations between body type and personality than Sheldon did; but his classification contains enough of the truth, apparently, to be still worth mentioning. Like all classifiers, Sheldon takes *many* things — in this case physical and personality traits — and sorts them into categories. Papalia and Olds set forth his results.

· Judy Syfers ·

JUDY SYFERS, born in 1937 in San Francisco, where she now lives, earned a B.F.A. in painting from the University of Iowa in 1962. Drawn into political action by her work in the feminist movement, she went to Cuba in 1973, where she studied class relationships as a way of understanding change in a society. "I am not a 'writer,' " Syfers declares, "but really am a disenfranchised (and fired) housewife, now secretary. I have published other articles in various types of publications (one on abortion, one on union organizing, for instance) and have written for, edited, and produced a newsletter for school paraprofessionals in San Francisco."

I Want a Wife

"I Want a Wife" first appeared in the December 1971 issue of *Ms.* magazine. It has since become one of the best-known manifestos in popular feminist writing, and it has been reprinted widely. In her essay, Syfers trenchantly divides the work of a wife into five parts, explains each part, and comes to an inescapable conclusion.

I belong to that classification of people known as wives. I am A Wife. And, not altogether incidentally, I am a mother. 1

Not too long ago a male friend of mine appeared on the scene fresh from a recent divorce. He had one child, who is, of course, with his ex-wife. He is looking for another wife. As I thought about him while I was ironing one evening, it suddenly occurred to me that I, too, would like to have a wife. Why do I want a wife? 2

I would like to go back to school so that I can become economically independent, support myself, and, if need be, support those dependent upon me. I want a wife who will work and send me to school. And while I am going to school I want a wife to take care of my children. I want a wife to keep track of the children's doctor and dentist appointments. And to keep track of 3 mine, too. I want a wife to make sure my children eat properly and are kept clean. I want a wife who will wash the children's clothes and keep them mended. I want a wife who is a good nurturant attendant to my children, who arranges for their schooling, makes sure that they have an adequate social life with their peers, takes them to the park, the zoo, etc. I want a wife who takes care of the children when they are sick, a wife who arranges to be around when the children need special care, because, of course, I cannot miss classes at school. My wife must arrange to lose time at work and not lose the job. It may mean a small cut in my wife's income from time to time, but I guess I can tolerate that. Needless to say, my wife will arrange and pay for the care of the children while my wife is working.

I want a wife who will take care of *my* physical needs. I want   4
a wife who will keep my house clean. A wife who will pick up after my children, a wife who will pick up after me. I want a wife who will keep my clothes clean, ironed, mended, replaced when need be, and who will see to it that my personal things are kept in their proper place so that I can find what I need the minute I need it. I want a wife who cooks the meals, a wife who is a *good* cook. I want a wife who will plan the menus, do the necessary grocery shopping, prepare the meals, serve them pleasantly, and then do the cleaning up while I do my studying. I want a wife who will care for me when I am sick and sympathize with my pain and loss of time from school. I want a wife to go along when our family takes a vacation so that someone can continue to care for me and my children when I need a rest and change of scene.

I want a wife who will not bother me with rambling com-   5
plaints about a wife's duties. But I want a wife who will listen to me when I feel the need to explain a rather difficult point I have come across in my course of studies. And I want a wife who will type my papers for me when I have written them.

I want a wife who will take care of the details of my social   6
life. When my wife and I are invited out by my friends, I want a wife who will take care of the babysitting arrangements. When I meet people at school that I like and want to entertain, I want a wife who will have the house clean, will prepare a special meal, serve it to me and my friends, and not interrupt when I talk

about things that interest me and my friends. I want a wife who will have arranged that the children are fed and ready for bed before my guests arrive so that the children do not bother us. I want a wife who takes care of the needs of my guests so that they feel comfortable, who makes sure that they have an ashtray, that they are passed the hors d'oeuvres, that they are offered a second helping of the food, that their wine glasses are replenished when necessary, that their coffee is served to them as they like it. And I want a wife who knows that sometimes I need a night out by myself.

I want a wife who is sensitive to my sexual needs, a wife who makes love passionately and eagerly when I feel like it, a wife who makes sure that I am satisfied. And, of course, I want a wife who will not demand sexual attention when I am not in the mood for it. I want a wife who assumes the complete responsibility for birth control, because I do not want more children. I want a wife who will remain sexually faithful to me so that I do not have to clutter up my intellectual life with jealousies. And I want a wife who understands that *my* sexual needs may entail more than strict adherence to monogamy. I must, after all, be able to relate to people as fully as possible.

If, by chance, I find another person more suitable as a wife than the wife I already have, I want the liberty to replace my present wife with another one. Naturally, I will expect a fresh, new life; my wife will take the children and be solely responsible for them so that I am left free.

When I am through with school and have a job, I want my wife to quit working and remain at home so that my wife can more fully and completely take care of a wife's duties.

My God, who *wouldn't* want a wife?

QUESTIONS ON MEANING

1. Sum up the duties of a wife as Syfers sees them.
2. To what inequities in the roles traditionally assigned to men and to women does "I Want a Wife" call attention?

3. What is the THESIS of this essay? Is it stated or implied?
4. Is Syfers unfair to men?

QUESTIONS ON WRITING STRATEGY

1. What EFFECT does Syfers obtain with the title "I Want a Wife"?
2. What do the first two paragraphs accomplish?
3. What is the TONE of this essay?
4. How do you explain the fact that Syfers never uses the pronoun *she* to refer to a wife? Does this make her prose unnecessarily awkward?
5. In what order or sequence does the author arrange her paragraphs? (To see it, try rearranging them.)
6. Knowing that this essay was first published in *Ms.* magazine in 1971, what can you guess about its intended readers? Does "I Want a Wife" strike a college AUDIENCE today as revolutionary?
7. In her first sentence, Syfers says she belongs "to that classification of people known as wives"; but she develops her essay by division. In what way would the essay be different if the author had used classification?

QUESTIONS ON LANGUAGE

1. What is achieved by the author's frequent repetition of the phrase *I want a wife?*
2. Be sure you know how to define the following words as Syfers uses them: nurturant (paragraph 3); replenished (6); adherence, monogamy (7).
3. In general, how would you describe the DICTION of this essay? How well does it suit the essay's intended audience?

SUGGESTIONS FOR WRITING

1. Write a brief essay entitled "I Want a Husband" in which, using examples as Syfers does, you enumerate the stereotyped roles traditionally assigned to men in our society.
2. Classify types of husbands, or types of wives.
3. Imagining that you want to employ someone to do a specific job, divide the task into two or three parts. Then, guided by your divisions, write an accurate job description in essay form.

· Robertson Davies ·

ROBERTSON DAVIES, born in Ontario in 1913, is a novelist, playwright, and scholar. One of Canada's foremost men of letters, he is the author of more than two dozen books. Davies attended Upper Canada College in Toronto and Queens College in Ontario; and he earned his degree in literature from Balliol College in Oxford, England. Although best known for his novels, plays, and essays, he has made his mark as an actor, journalist, and critic as well. After studying acting for two years with the Old Vic Company in London, Davies became the editor, and later the publisher, of Ontario's *Peterborough Examiner*. From 1963–1981 he was a professor of English and Master of Massey College, University of Toronto, where he is now Master Emeritus. While teaching, Davies wrote the critically acclaimed Deptford trilogy, consisting of the novels *Fifth Business* (1970), *The Manticore* (1972), and *World of Wonders* (1975). His most recent books are *What's Bred in the Bone* (1985), a novel, and *The Papers of Samuel Marchbanks* (1986), a collection of newspaper articles originally published under a pseudonym.

A Few Kind Words
for Superstition

"A Few Kind Words for Superstition" originally appeared in *Newsweek* magazine (November 20, 1978). Looking closely at why some people believe in magic and chance, Davies divides superstition into categories for the purpose of analyzing this complex topic. The four divisions he presents are certainly familiar to most of us, though few of us have taken the time to label them. In taking a rational approach to what many people consider to be an irrational subject, Davies offers some fascinating observations about human nature.

In grave discussions of "the renaissance of the irrational" in   1
our time, superstition does not figure largely as a serious chal-

lenge to reason or science. Parapsychology, UFOs, miracle cures, transcendental meditation, and all the paths to instant enlightenment are condemned, but superstition is merely deplored. Is it because it has an unacknowledged hold on so many of us?

Few people will admit to being superstitious; it implies naiveté or ignorance. But I live in the middle of a large university, and I see superstition in its four manifestations, alive and flourishing among people who are indisputably rational and learned.

You did not know that superstition takes four forms? Theologians assure us that it does. First is what they call Vain Observances, such as not walking under a ladder, and that kind of thing. Yet I saw a deeply learned professor of anthropology, who had spilled some salt, throwing a pinch of it over his left shoulder; when I asked him why, he replied, with a wink, that it was "to hit the Devil in the eye." I did not question him further about his belief in the Devil: But I noticed that he did not smile until I asked him what he was doing.

The second form is Divination, or consulting oracles. Another learned professor I know, who would scorn to settle a problem by tossing a coin (which is a humble appeal to Fate to declare itself), told me quite seriously that he has resolved a matter related to university affairs by consulting the *I Ching.*[1] And why not? There are thousands of people on this continent who appeal to the *I Ching*, and their general level of education seems to absolve them of superstition. Almost, but not quite. The *I Ching*, to the embarrassment of rationalists, often gives excellent advice.

The third form is Idolatry, and universities can show plenty of that. If you have ever supervised a large examination room, you know how many jujus, lucky coins, and other bringers of luck are placed on the desks of the candidates. Modest idolatry, but what else can you call it?

The fourth form is Improper Worship of the True God. A while ago, I learned that every day, for several days, a $2 bill (in Canada we have $2 bills, regarded by some people as unlucky)

---

[1]Classic Chinese book that offers slightly ambiguous advice on how to act. — EDS.

had been tucked under a candlestick on the altar of a college chapel. Investigation revealed that an engineering student, worried about a girl, thought that bribery of the Deity might help. When I talked with him, he did not think he was pricing God cheap because he could afford no more. A reasonable argument, but perhaps God was proud that week, for the scientific oracle went against him.

Superstition seems to run, a submerged river of crude religion, below the surface of human consciousness. It has done so for as long as we have any chronicle of human behavior, and although I cannot prove it, I doubt if it is more prevalent today than it has always been. Superstition, the theologians tell us, comes from the Latin *supersisto*, meaning to stand in terror of the Deity. Most people keep their terror within bounds, but they cannot root it out, nor do they seem to want to do so.   7

The more the teaching of formal religion declines, or takes a sociological form, the less God appears to great numbers of people as a God of Love, resuming his older form of a watchful, minatory power, to be placated and cajoled. Superstition makes its appearance, apparently unbidden, very early in life, when children fear that stepping on cracks in the sidewalk will bring ill fortune. It may persist even among the greatly learned and devout, as in the case of Dr. Samuel Johnson, who felt it necessary to touch posts that he passed in the street. The psychoanalysts have their explanation, but calling a superstition a compulsion neurosis does not banish it.   8

Many superstitions are so widespread and so old that they must have risen from a depth of the human mind that is indifferent to race or creed. Orthodox Jews place a charm on their doorposts; so do (or did) the Chinese. Some peoples of Middle Europe believe that when a man sneezes, his soul, for that moment, is absent from his body, and they hasten to bless him, lest the soul be seized by the Devil. How did the Melanesians come by the same idea? Superstition seems to have a link with some body of belief that far antedates the religions we know — religions which have no place for such comforting little ceremonies and charities.   9

People who like disagreeable historical ceremonies recall that when Rome was in decline, superstition proliferated wildly,   10 and that something of the same sort is happening in our Western world today. They point to the popularity of astrology, and it is true that sober newspapers that would scorn to deal in love philters carry astrology columns and the fashion magazines count them among their most popular features. But when has astrology not been popular? No use saying science discredits it. When has the heart of man given a damn for science?

Superstition in general is linked to man's yearning to know   11
his fate, and to have some hand in deciding it. When my mother was a child, she innocently joined her Roman Catholic friends in killing spiders on July 11, until she learned that this was done to ensure heavy rain the day following, the anniversary of the Battle of Boyne, when the Orangemen would hold their parade.[2] I knew an Italian, a good scientist, who watched every morning before leaving his house, so that the first person he met would not be a priest or a nun, as this would certainly bring bad luck.

I am not one to stand aloof from the rest of humanity in this   12
matter, for when I was a university student, a gypsy woman with a child in her arms used to appear every year at examination time, and ask a shilling of anyone who touched the Lucky Baby; that swarthy infant cost me four shillings altogether, and I never failed an examination. Of course, I did it merely for the joke — or so I thought then. Now, I am humbler.

QUESTIONS ON MEANING

1. Is the main PURPOSE of this essay to establish that superstition is foolish; to explain that superstition and religion are one and the same; to take a closer look at how superstitions arise, and at our attitudes toward them; or to assert that most highly educated people are superstitious? Discuss.
2. What is your understanding of Davies's statement, in paragraph 4,

---

[2]The Orangemen, or Protestants from Northern Ireland, celebrated the battle of 1690, in which the forces of William of Orange defeated exiled Catholic King James II and placed Ireland under British Protestant rule. — EDS.

that "their general level of education seems to absolve them of superstition"? What relationship is Davies suggesting between education and superstition?

3. According to Davies, why and how do superstitions arise? And
   what does superstition have to do with the decline of the teaching
   of formal religion?
4. Does Davies seem to consider himself superstitious? Does he see superstition as good or bad? Provide EVIDENCE for your answer.

QUESTIONS ON WRITING STRATEGY

1. Davies makes it clear that he lives "in the middle of a large university" (paragraph 2), and that he has seen "learned" professors behave in the most superstitious fashion. What is the EFFECT of his
   using this setting and these examples?
2. Do Davies's four types of superstitions make sense to you, or do
   they seem arbitrary? How do they help you understand the essay's
   subject, superstition?
3. What is the TONE of the sixth paragraph? Does Davies seem to
   think the engineering student was unlucky in love because he
   priced "God cheap," and that he might have been luckier had he
   left more money?

QUESTIONS ON LANGUAGE

1. In his first paragraph, Davies asserts that transcendental meditation and other paths to "instant enlightenment are condemned,
   but superstition is merely deplored." What distinction is Davies
   making between *condemned* and *deplored*?
2. What do you make of the metaphor labeling superstition "a submerged river of crude religion" (paragraph 7)? Does Davies seem to
   equate superstition and religion? What do you take this phrase to
   mean?
3. Consult your dictionary if you need help in defining the following
   words: manifestations (paragraph 2); theologians (3); absolve (4);
   jujus (5); prevalent (7); minatory, placated, cajoled (8); proliferated, philter (10).

SUGGESTIONS FOR WRITING

1. Write an essay in which you take the position that superstitions
   are irrational and silly, with no bearing on anything that happens
   in real life. Or, insist that acting on superstitions does, in fact,

serve some purpose (which may or may not be the avoidance of bad luck). In either case, be sure to back your argument with strong EVIDENCE. Perhaps you might defend your own favorite superstitions.

2. Consider the four categories into which Davies divides superstition. Are these categories all-encompassing, or has he left out any types of superstition you would add? Do you see the categories he names as distinct, or do any overlap? In an essay in which you respond to these questions, combine and redefine any categories you think should be changed. Make sure you have evidence, in the form of examples of your own, to justify the changes.

Robertson Davies on Writing

Robertson Davies, in a speech to students at York University in Ontario, once summed up his writing experience. "I combine writing with other sorts of work," he said. "For twenty-eight years I have been a journalist — not just a writer, but an editor, an employer, a man who had to make sure that his newspaper did not lose money, who had to worry about new machinery, new buildings, new contracts with unions, and continually to be concerned with an obligation to a community. When I had spent the day doing this I went home and wrote. . . . I have always been grateful for my journalistic experience, which amounts to millions of words of writing, because it kept my technique in good muscular shape. I can write now without that humming and hawing and staring at the ceiling which plagues so many writers who have trouble getting started.

"I have of late become a university professor and head of a college, and these tasks can hardly be regarded as a rest-cure. . . . I have also had the ordinary family experiences. I am married and have three children, now all grown up, and I have spent countless happy hours in domestic pursuits. . . . I have sat on committees, and boards; I have made a great many speeches, and I have listened to what seem, in recollection, to be millions of speeches.

"All of this I consider necessary to my life as a writer. It has kept me from too great a degree of that fruitless self-preoccupation which is one of the worst diseases of the literary life. It has provided me with the raw material for what I write. The raw material, you observe; before it becomes the finished product it must undergo a process of distillation and elimination. . . . I do not write in my spare time, I write all the time; whatever I may be doing, the literary aspect of my mind is fully at work: It is not only the hours at the desk or the typewriter, but the hours spent in other kinds of work and in many kinds of diversion when I am busily observing, shaping, rejecting, and undergoing a wide variety of feelings that are the essential material of writing. Notice that I said feeling — not thoughts, but feelings." (Remarks condensed from "The Conscience of the Writer" in *One Half of Robertson Davies* [New York: Viking Press, 1977], pp. 130–132.)

FOR DISCUSSION

1. Sum up the main point of Davies's remarks. In your own life, what work and experiences have especially nourished your writing?

· Gail Sheehy ·

GAIL SHEEHY was born in 1937. She earned her B.S. degree from the University of Vermont in 1958 and was a fellow in Columbia University's Journalism School in 1970. A contributor to the *New York Times Magazine, Esquire, McCall's, Ms., Cosmopolitan, Rolling Stone,* and other magazines, she has also written a novel, *Lovesounds* (1970), and several popular studies of contemporary life: *Speed Is of the Essence* (1971), *Panthermania* (1971), *Hustling* (1973), *Passages* (1976), and *Pathfinders* (1981). In *The Spirit of Survival* (1986), Sheehy has written a recent history of strife and deprivation in Cambodia. The book includes a narrative told from the point of view of Mohm, a twelve-year-old Cambodian child adopted by Sheehy and her husband, Clay Felker, a New York editor.

Predictable Crises
of Adulthood

"Predictable Crises of Adulthood" is adapted from the second chapter of *Passages*. In the essay, Sheehy identifies six stages that most of us experience between the ages of eighteen and fifty. The author, as she herself makes clear, is not a theorist or a scholar, but an artful reporter of recent findings in a new social science, adult development. In the *Washington Post*, reviewer Roderick MacLeish called *Passages* "a work of revelation for the layman as he tries to understand the inevitable movement of his life . . . a stunning accomplishment." Not everyone goes through the stages Sheehy traces at exactly the same time, but see whether any of the following crises sound familiar to you.

We are not unlike a particularly hardy crustacean. The lob- 1
ster grows by developing and shedding a series of hard, protective shells. Each time it expands from within, the confining shell

must be sloughed off. It is left exposed and vulnerable until, in time, a new covering grows to replace the old.

With each passage from one stage of human growth to the   2
next we, too, must shed a protective structure. We are left exposed and vulnerable — but also yeasty and embryonic again, capable of stretching in ways we hadn't known before. These sheddings may take several years or more. Coming out of each passage, though, we enter a longer and more stable period in which we can expect relative tranquility and a sense of equilibrium regained. . . .

As we shall see, each person engages the steps of develop-   3
ment in his or her own characteristic *step-style*. Some people never complete the whole sequence. And none of us "solves" with one step — by jumping out of the parental home into a job or marriage, for example — the problems in separating from the caregivers of childhood. Nor do we "achieve" autonomy once and for all by converting our dreams into concrete goals, even when we attain those goals. The central issues or tasks of one period are never fully completed, tied up, and cast aside. But when they lose their primacy and the current life structure has served its purpose, we are ready to move on to the next period.

Can one catch up? What might look to others like listless-   4
ness, contrariness, a maddening refusal to face up to an obvious task may be a person's own unique detour that will bring him out later on the other side. Developmental gains won can later be lost — and rewon. It's plausible, though it can't be proven, that the mastery of one set of tasks fortifies us for the next period and the next set of challenges. But it's important not to think too mechanistically. Machines work by units. The bureaucracy (supposedly) works step by step. Human beings, thank God, have an individual inner dynamic that can never be precisely coded.

Although I have indicated the ages when Americans are   5
likely to go through each stage, and the differences between men and women where they are striking, do not take the ages too seriously. The stages are the thing, and most particularly the sequence.

Here is the briefest outline of the developmental ladder.   6

Pulling Up Roots

Before 18, the motto is loud and clear: "I have to get away 7 from my parents." But the words are seldom connected to action. Generally still safely part of our families, even if away at school, we feel our autonomy to be subject to erosion from moment to moment.

After 18, we begin Pulling Up Roots in earnest. College, mil- 8 itary service, and short-term travels are all customary vehicles our society provides for the first round trips between family and a base of one's own. In the attempt to separate our view of the world from our family's view, despite vigorous protestations to the contrary — "I know exactly what I want!" — we cast about for any beliefs we can call our own. And in the process of testing those beliefs we are often drawn to fads, preferably those most mysterious and inaccessible to our parents.

Whatever tentative memberships we try out in the world, 9 the fear haunts us that we are really kids who cannot take care of ourselves. We cover that fear with acts of defiance and mimicked confidence. For allies to replace our parents, we turn to our contemporaries. They become conspirators. So long as their perspective meshes with our own, they are able to substitute for the sanctuary of the family. But that doesn't last very long. And the instant they diverge from the shaky ideals of "our group," they are seen as betrayers. Rebounds to the family are common between the ages of 18 and 22.

The tasks of this passage are to locate ourselves in a peer 10 group role, a sex role, an anticipated occupation, an ideology or world view. As a result, we gather the impetus to leave home physically and the identity to *begin* leaving home emotionally.

Even as one part of us seeks to be an individual, another 11 part longs to restore the safety and comfort of merging with another. Thus one of the most popular myths of this passage is: We can piggyback our development by attaching to a Stronger One. But people who marry during this time often prolong financial and emotional ties to the family and relatives that impede them from becoming self-sufficient.

A stormy passage through the Pulling Up Roots years will 12

probably facilitate the normal progression of the adult life cycle. If one doesn't have an identity crisis at this point, it will erupt during a later transition, when the penalties may be harder to bear.

The Trying Twenties

The Trying Twenties confront us with the question of how to take hold in the adult world. Our focus shifts from the interior turmoils of late adolescence — "Who am I?" "What is truth?" — and we become almost totally preoccupied with working out the externals. "How do I put my aspirations into effect?" "What is the best way to start?" "Where do I go?" "Who can help me?" "How did *you* do it?"

In this period, which is longer and more stable compared with the passage that leads to it, the tasks are as enormous as they are exhilarating: To shape a Dream, that vision of ourselves which will generate energy, aliveness, and hope. To prepare for a lifework. To find a mentor if possible. And to form the capacity for intimacy, without losing in the process whatever consistency of self we have thus far mustered. The first test structure must be erected around the life we choose to try.

Doing what we "should" is the most pervasive theme of the twenties. The "shoulds" are largely defined by family models, the press of the culture, or the prejudices of our peers. If the prevailing cultural instructions are that one should get married and settle down behind one's own door, a nuclear family is born. If instead the peers insist that one should do one's own thing, the 25-year-old is likely to harness himself onto a Harley-Davidson and burn up Route 66 in the commitment to have no commitments.

One of the terrifying aspects of the twenties is the inner conviction that the choices we make are irrevocable. It is largely a false fear. Change is quite possible, and some alteration of our original choices is probably inevitable.

Two impulses, as always, are at work. One is to build a firm, safe structure for the future by making strong commitments, to "be set." Yet people who slip into a ready-made form without much self-examination are likely to find themselves *locked in*.

The other urge is to explore and experiment, keeping any 18
structure tentative and therefore easily reversible. Taken to the
extreme, these are people who skip from one trial job and one
limited personal encounter to another, spending their twenties
in the *transient* state.

Although the choices of our twenties are not irrevocable, 19
they do set in motion a Life Pattern. Some of us follow the lock-
in pattern, others the transient pattern, the wunderkind pattern, the caregiver pattern, and there are a number of others.
Such patterns strongly influence the particular questions raised
for each person during each passage. . . .

Buoyed by powerful illusions and belief in the power of the 20
will, we commonly insist in our twenties that what we have chosen to do is the one true course in life. Our backs go up at the
merest hint that we are like our parents, that two decades of parental training might be reflected in our current actions and attitudes.

"Not me," is the motto, "I'm different." 21

Catch-30

Impatient with devoting ourselves to the "shoulds," a new 22
vitality springs from within as we approach 30. Men and women
alike speak of feeling too narrow and restricted. They blame all
sorts of things, but what the restrictions boil down to are the
outgrowth of career and personal choices of the twenties. They
may have been choices perfectly suited to that stage. But now
the fit feels different. Some inner aspect that was left out is striving to be taken into account. Important new choices must be
made, and commitments altered or deepened. The work involves great change, turmoil, and often crisis — a simultaneous
feeling of rock bottom and the urge to bust out.

One common response is the tearing up of the life we spent 23
most of our twenties putting together. It may mean striking out
on a secondary road toward a new vision or converting a dream
of "running for president" into a more realistic goal. The single
person feels a push to find a partner. The woman who was previously content at home with children chafes to venture into the
world. The childless couple reconsiders children. And almost

everyone who is married, especially those married for seven years, feels a discontent.

If the discontent doesn't lead to a divorce, it will, or should, 24 call for a serious review of the marriage and of each partner's aspirations in their Catch-30 condition. The gist of that condition was expressed by a 29-year-old associate with a Wall Street law firm:

"I'm considering leaving the firm. I've been there four years 25 now; I'm getting good feedback, but I have no clients of my own. I feel weak. If I wait much longer, it will be too late, too close to that fateful time of decision on whether or not to become a partner. I'm success-oriented. But the concept of being 55 years old and stuck in a monotonous job drives me wild. It drives me crazy now, just a little bit. I'd say that 85 percent of the time I thoroughly enjoy my work. But when I get a screwball case, I come away from court saying, 'What am I doing here?' It's a *visceral* reaction that I'm wasting my time. I'm trying to find some way to make a social contribution or a slot in city government. I keep saying, 'There's something more.' "

Besides the push to broaden himself professionally, there is a 26 wish to expand his personal life. He wants two or three more children. "The concept of a home has become very meaningful to me, a place to get away from troubles and relax. I love my son in a way I could not have anticipated. I never could live alone."

Consumed with the work of making his own critical life- 27 steering decisions, he demonstrates the essential shift at this age: an absolute requirement to be more self-concerned. The self has new value now that his competency has been proved.

His wife is struggling with her own age-30 priorities. She 28 wants to go to law school, but he wants more children. If she is going to stay home, she wants him to make more time for the family instead of taking on even wider professional commitments. His view of the bind, of what he would most like from his wife, is this:

"I'd like not to be bothered. It sounds cruel, but I'd like not 29 to have to worry about what she's going to do next week. Which is why I've told her several times that I think she should do something. Go back to school and get a degree in social work or geography or whatever. Hopefully that would fulfill her, and then I wouldn't have to worry about her line of problems. I want her to be decisive about herself."

The trouble with his advice to his wife is that it comes out of 30 concern with *his* convenience, rather than with *her* development. She quickly picks up on this lack of goodwill: He is trying to dispose of her. At the same time, he refuses her the same latitude to be "selfish" in making an independent decision to broaden her horizons. Both perceive a lack of mutuality. And that is what Catch-30 is all about for the couple.

Rooting and Extending

Life becomes less provisional, more rational and orderly in 31 the early thirties. We begin to settle down in the full sense. Most of us begin putting down roots and sending out new shoots. People buy houses and become very earnest about climbing career ladders. Men in particular concern themselves with "making it." Satisfaction with marriage generally goes downhill in the thirties (for those who have remained together) compared with the highly valued, vision-supporting marriage of the twenties. This coincides with the couple's reduced social life outside the family and the in-turned focus on raising their children.

The Deadline Decade

In the middle of the thirties we come upon a crossroads. We 32 have reached the halfway mark. Yet even as we are reaching our prime, we begin to see there is a place where it finishes. Time starts to squeeze.

The loss of youth, the faltering of physical powers we have 33 always taken for granted, the fading purpose of stereotyped roles by which we have thus far identified ourselves, the spiritual dilemma of having no absolute answers — any or all of these shocks can give this passage the character of crisis. Such thoughts usher in a decade between 35 and 45 that can be called the Deadline Decade. It is a time of both danger and opportunity. All of us have the chance to rework the narrow identity by which we defined ourselves in the first half of life. And those of us who make the most of the opportunity will have a full-out authenticity crisis.

To come through this authenticity crisis, we must reexam-   34
ine our purposes and reevaluate how to spend our resources from now on. "Why am I doing all this? What do I really believe in?" No matter what we have been doing, there will be parts of ourselves that have been suppressed and now need to find expression. "Bad" feelings will demand acknowledgment along with the good.

It is frightening to step off onto the treacherous footbridge   35
leading to the second half of life. We can't take everything with us on this journey through uncertainty. Along the way, we discover that we are alone. We no longer have to ask permission because we are the providers of our own safety. We must learn to give ourselves permission. We stumble upon feminine or masculine aspects of our natures that up to this time have usually been masked. There is grieving to be done because an old self is dying. By taking in our suppressed and even our unwanted parts, we prepare at the gut level for the reintegration of an identity that is ours and ours alone — not some artificial form put together to please the culture or our mates. It is a dark passage at the beginning. But by disassembling ourselves, we can glimpse the light and gather our parts into a renewal.

Women sense this inner crossroads earlier than men do.   36
The time pinch often prompts a woman to stop and take an all-points survey at age 35. Whatever options she has already played out, she feels a "my last chance" urgency to review those options she has set aside and those that aging and biology will close off in the *now foreseeable* future. For all her qualms and confusion about where to start looking for a new future, she usually enjoys an exhilaration of release. Assertiveness begins rising. There are so many firsts ahead.

Men, too, feel the time push in the mid-thirties. Most men   37
respond by pressing down harder on the career accelerator. It's "my last chance" to pull away from the pack. It is no longer enough to be the loyal junior executive, the promising young novelist, the lawyer who does a little *pro bono* work on the side.

He wants now to become part of top management, to be recognized as an established writer, or an active politician with his own legislative program. With some chagrin, he discovers that he has been too anxious to please and too vulnerable to criticism. He wants to put together his own ship.

During this period of intense concentration on external advancement, it is common for men to be unaware of the more difficult, gut issues that are propelling them forward. The survey that was neglected at 35 becomes a crucible at 40. Whatever rung of achievement he has reached, the man of 40 usually feels stale, restless, burdened, and unappreciated. He worries about his health. He wonders, "Is this all there is?" He may make a series of departures from well-established lifelong base lines, including marriage. More and more men are seeking second careers in midlife. Some become self-destructive. And many men in their forties experience a major shift of emphasis away from pouring all their energies into their own advancement. A more tender, feeling side comes into play. They become interested in developing an ethical self.

38

Renewal or Resignation

Somewhere in the mid-forties, equilibrium is regained. A new stability is achieved, which may be more or less satisfying.

39

If one has refused to budge through the midlife transition, the sense of staleness will calcify into resignation. One by one, the safety and supports will be withdrawn from the person who is standing still. Parents will become children; children will become strangers; a mate will grow away or go away; the career will become just a job — and each of these events will be felt as an abandonment. The crisis will probably emerge again around 50. And although its wallop will be greater, the jolt may be just what is needed to prod the resigned middle-ager toward seeking revitalization.

40

On the other hand . . .

41

If we have confronted ourselves in the middle passage and found a renewal of purpose around which we are eager to build a more authentic life structure, these may well be the best years.

42

Personal happiness takes a sharp turn upward for partners who can now accept the fact: "I cannot expect *anyone* to fully understand me." Parents can be forgiven for the burdens of our childhood. Children can be let go without leaving us in collapsed silence. At 50, there is a new warmth and mellowing. Friends become more important than ever, but so does privacy. Since it is so often proclaimed by people past midlife, the motto of this stage might be "No more bullshit."

QUESTIONS ON MEANING

1. In your own words, describe each of Sheehy's six predictable stages of adult life.
2. According to the author, what happens to people who fail to experience a given stage of growth at the usual time?
3. How would you characterize Sheehy's attitude toward growth and change in adult life?
4. For what PURPOSE does Sheehy employ the method of division? How does it serve her readers, too?

QUESTIONS ON WRITING STRATEGY

1. How apt, do you think, is the opening METAPHOR: the comparison between a lobster periodically shedding its shell and a person entering each new phase of growth?
2. What, if anything, does the author gain by writing her essay in the first PERSON plural?
3. What difficulties go along with making GENERALIZATIONS about human beings? To what extent does Sheehy surmount these difficulties?
4. How much knowledge of psychology does Sheehy expect of her AUDIENCE?

QUESTIONS ON LANGUAGE

1. Consult your dictionary if you need help in defining the following words: crustacean (paragraph 1); embryonic, tranquility, equilibrium (2); autonomy, primacy (3); plausible (4); inaccessible (8);

sanctuary (9); impetus (10); exhilarating, mentor (14); pervasive (15); irrevocable (16); tentative (18); wunderkind (19); visceral (25); mutuality (30); dilemma (33); *pro bono*, chagrin, vulnerable (37); crucible (38); calcify (40).

2. What is a *nuclear family* (paragraph 15)?
3. The author coins a few phrases of her own. Refer to the context in which they appear to help you define the following: *step-style* (paragraph 3); Stronger One (11); *locked in* (17); Catch-30 (24); authenticity crisis (33).

SUGGESTIONS FOR WRITING

1. From your experience, observation, or reading, test the accuracy of one of Sheehy's accounts of a typical period of crisis.
2. Inspired by Sheehy's division of life after eighteen into phases, look back on your own earlier life or that of a younger person you know, and detail a series of phases in it. Invent names for the phases.

· Paul Fussell ·

PAUL FUSSELL (the last name rhymes with *muscle*), literary critic and cultural historian, was born in 1924 in Pasadena, California. After taking his Ph.D. at Harvard, he taught English at Connecticut College, then at Rutgers for twenty-eight years. Earlier in his career, Fussell won high repute for his *Poetic Meter and Poetic Form* (1965, revised in 1979) and for his studies in the British eighteenth century. In 1975, with *The Great War and Modern Memory*, a study of World War I and its literature, his work reached a wider audience and gained him a National Book Award, an award from the National Book Critics Circle, and the Ralph Waldo Emerson Award of Phi Beta Kappa. Some of Fussell's knowledge of war was personal: As an infantry officer in World War II, he had received the Bronze Star and twice had been wounded in combat. He now serves as contributing editor for *Harper's* and *The New Republic*, and as Donald T. Regan Professor of English at the University of Pennsylvania. Among his recent books are *Abroad: British Literary Traveling between the Wars* (1980), *Class: A Guide through the American Status System* (1983), and an anthology, *The Norton Book of Travel* (1987). Fussell, now writing a book about World War II, has declared, "I think I'd like at some point to write a biography of somebody I admire. The problem is to find that person."

Notes on Class

This lively, debatable partitioning of American society first appeared in 1980 in *The New Republic*, a serious but not solemn magazine of comment on the nation and the world. Later, Fussell reprinted it in a varied gathering of his essays from American and British magazines, *The Boy Scout Handbook and Other Observations* (1982). "Notes on Class" contains premises and scaffolding on which Fussell was to build later in *Class*. More amply in that whole book, he sets forth his analysis, devoting chapters to indicators such as personal appearance and clothing, houses and cars, consumption (drinking, eating out, traveling, catalog shopping), education and reading (if any), and choice of words. He also makes sharp remarks about both social climbing and social sinking; if these short "Notes" intrigue you, don't miss the book.

The task of dividing American society into levels is clearly formidable. Class isn't a subject that most Americans talk about much; one great value of Fussell's essay may be to help us face matters that often worry us more than we admit.

If the dirty little secret used to be sex, now it is the facts 1
about social class. No subject today is more likely to offend. Over thirty years ago Dr. Kinsey generated considerable alarm by disclosing that despite appearances one-quarter of the male population had enjoyed at least one homosexual orgasm. A similar alarm can be occasioned today by asserting that despite the much-discussed mechanism of "social mobility" and the constant redistribution of income in this country, it is virtually impossible to break out of the social class in which one has been nurtured. Bad news for the ambitious as well as the bogus, but there it is.

Defining class is difficult, as sociologists and anthropologists 2
have learned. The more data we feed into the machines, the less likely it is that significant formulations will emerge. What follows here is based not on interviews, questionnaires, or any kind of quantitative technique but on perhaps a more trustworthy method — perception. Theory may inform us that there are three classes in America, high, middle, and low. Perception will tell us that there are at least nine, which I would designate and arrange like this:

> Top Out-of-Sight
> Upper
> Upper Middle
> _____
> Middle
> High-Proletarian
> Mid-Proletarian
> Low-Proletarian
> _____
> Destitute
> Bottom Out-of-Sight

In addition, there is a floating class with no permanent location in this hierarchy. We can call it Class X. It consists of well-to-do hippies, "artists," "writers" (who write nothing), floating bohemians, politicians out of office, disgraced athletic coaches, residers abroad, rock stars, "celebrities," and the shrewder sort of spies.

The quasi-official division of the population into three economic classes called high-, middle-, and low-income groups rather misses the point, because as a class indicator the amount of money is not as important as the source. Important distinctions at both the top and bottom of the class scale arise less from degree of affluence than from the people or institutions to whom one is beholden for support. For example, the main thing distinguishing the top three classes from each other is the amount of money inherited in relation to the amount currently earned. The Top Out-of-Sight Class (Rockefellers, du Ponts, Mellons, Fords, Whitneys) lives on inherited capital entirely. Its money is like the hats of the Boston ladies who, asked where they got them, answer, "Oh, we *have* our hats." No one whose money, no matter how ample, comes from his own work, like film stars, can be a member of the Top Out-of-Sights, even if the size of his income and the extravagance of his expenditure permit him temporary social access to it.

Since we expect extremes to meet, we are not surprised to find the very lowest class, Bottom Out-of-Sight, similar to the highest in one crucial respect: It is given its money and kept sort of afloat not by its own efforts but by the welfare machinery or the prison system. Members of the Top Out-of-Sight Class sometimes earn some money, as directors or board members of philanthropic or even profitable enterprises, but the amount earned is laughable in relation to the amount already possessed. Membership in the Top Out-of-Sight Class depends on the ability to flourish without working at all, and it is this that suggests a curious brotherhood between those at the top and the bottom of the scale.

It is this also that distinguishes the Upper Class from its betters. It lives on both inherited money and a salary from attractive, if usually slight, work, without which, even if it could survive and even flourish, it would feel bored and a little ashamed. The next class down, the Upper Middle, may possess virtually as much as the two above it. The difference is that it has earned most of it, in law, medicine, oil, real-estate, or even the more honorific forms of trade. The Upper Middles are afflicted with a bourgeois sense of shame, a conviction that to live on the earnings of others, even forebears, is not entirely nice.

The Out-of-Sight Classes at top and bottom have something else in common: They are literally all but invisible (hence their name). The façades of Top Out-of-Sight houses are never seen from the street, and such residences (like Rockefeller's upstate New York premises) are often hidden away deep in the hills, safe from envy and its ultimate attendants, confiscatory taxation and finally expropriation. The Bottom Out-of-Sight Class is equally invisible. When not hidden away in institutions or claustrated in monasteries, lamaseries, or communes, it is hiding from creditors, deceived bail-bondsmen, and merchants intent on repossessing cars and furniture. (This class is visible briefly in one place, in the spring on the streets of New York City, but after this ritual yearly show of itself it disappears again.) When you pass a house with a would-be impressive façade addressing the street, you know it is occupied by a mere member of the Upper or Upper Middle Class. The White House is an example. Its residents, even on those occasions when they are Kennedys, can never be classified as Top Out-of-Sight but only Upper Class. The house is simply too conspicuous, and temporary residence there usually constitutes a come-down for most of its occupants. It is a hopelessly Upper- or Upper-Middle-Class place.

Another feature of both Top and Bottom Out-of-Sight Classes is their anxiety to keep their names out of the papers, and this too suggests that socially the President is always rather vulgar. All the classes in between Top and Bottom Out-of-Sight slaver for personal publicity (monograms on shirts, inscribing one's name on lawn-mowers and power tools, etc.), and it is this lust to be known almost as much as income that distinguishes them from their Top and Bottom neighbors. The High- and Mid-Prole Classes can be recognized immediately by their pride in advertising their physical presence, a way of saying, "Look! We pay our bills and have a known place in the community, and you can find us there any time." Thus hypertrophied house-

6

7

numbers on the front, or house numbers written "Two Hundred Five" ("Two Hundred and Five" is worse) instead of 205, or flamboyant house or family names blazoned on façades, like "The Willows" or "The Polnickis."

(If you go behind the façade into the house itself, you will find a fairly trustworthy class indicator in the kind of wood visible there. The top three classes invariably go in for hardwoods for doors and panelling; the Middle and High-Prole Classes, pine, either plain or "knotty." The knotty-pine "den" is an absolute stigma of the Middle Class, one never to be overcome or disguised by temporarily affected higher usages. Below knotty pine there is plywood.)   8

Façade study is a badly neglected anthropological field. As we work down from the (largely white-painted) bank-like façades of the Upper and Upper Middle Classes, we encounter such Middle and Prole conventions as these, which I rank in order of social status: 9

Middle	1.	A potted tree on either side of the front door, and the more pointy and symmetrical the better.
	2.	A large rectangular picture-window in a split-level "ranch" house, displaying a table-lamp between two side curtains. The cellophane on the lampshade must be visibly inviolate.
	3.	Two chairs, usually metal with pipe arms, disposed on the front porch as a "conversation group," in stubborn defiance of the traffic thundering past.
High-Prole	4.	Religious shrines in the garden, which if small and understated, are slightly higher class than
Mid-Prole	5.	Plaster gnomes and flamingos, and blue or lavender shiny spheres supported by fluted cast-concrete pedestals.
Low-Prole	6.	Defunct truck tires painted white and enclosing flower beds. (Auto tires are a grade higher.)
	7.	Flower-bed designs worked in dead light bulbs or the butts of disused beer bottles.

The Destitute have no façades to decorate, and of course the Bottom Out-of-Sights, being invisible, have none either, although both these classes can occasionally help others decorate theirs — painting tires white on an hourly basis, for example, or even watering and fertilizing the potted trees of the Middle Class. Class X also does not decorate its façades, hoping to stay loose and unidentifiable, ready to re-locate and shape-change the moment it sees that its cover has been penetrated.

In this list of façade conventions an important principle emerges. Organic materials have higher status than metal or plastic. We should take warning from Sophie Portnoy's[1] aluminum venetian blinds, which are also lower than wood because the slats are curved, as if "improved," instead of classically flat. The same principle applies, as *The Preppy Handbook*[2] has shown so effectively, to clothing fabrics, which must be cotton or wool, never Dacron or anything of that prole kind. In the same way, yachts with wood hulls, because they must be repaired or re-placed (at high cost) more often, are classier than yachts with fi-berglass hulls, no matter how shrewdly merchandised. Plastic hulls are cheaper and more practical, which is precisely why they lack class.

As we move down the scale, income of course decreases, but income is less important to class than other seldom-invoked measurements: for example, the degree to which one's work is supervised by an omnipresent immediate superior. The more free from supervision, the higher the class, which is why a den-tist ranks higher than a mechanic working under a foreman in a large auto shop, even if he makes considerably more money than the dentist. The two trades may be thought equally dirty: It is the dentist's freedom from supervision that helps confer class upon him. Likewise, a high-school teacher obliged to file weekly "lesson plans" with a principal or "curriculum co-ordina-tor" thereby occupies a class position lower than a tenured pro-fessor, who reports to no one, even though the high-school teacher may be richer, smarter, and nicer. (Supervisors and In-spectors are titles that go with public schools, post offices, and

[1]Mother of the central character in *Portnoy's Complaint* (1969), a comic novel by Philip Roth. — EDS.

[2]Popular humor book (1980), purportedly a guide to the looks, dress, tastes, and habits of students and ex-students of private preparatory schools. — EDS.

10

11

police departments: The student of class will need to know no more.) It is largely because they must report that even the highest members of the naval and military services lack social status: They all have designated supervisors — even the Chairman of the Joint Chiefs of Staff has to report to the President.

Class is thus defined less by bare income than by constraints and insecurities. It is defined also by habits and attitudes. Take television watching. The Top Out-of-Sight Class doesn't watch at all. It owns the companies and pays others to monitor the thing. It is also entirely devoid of intellectual or even emotional curiosity: It *has* its ideas the way it has its money. The Upper Class does look at television but it prefers Camp[3] offerings, like the films of Jean Harlow or Jon Hall. The Upper Middle Class regards TV as vulgar except for the highminded emissions of National Educational Television, which it watches avidly, especially when, like the Shakespeare series, they are the most incompetently directed and boring. Upper Middles make a point of forbidding children to watch more than an hour a day and worry a lot about violence in society and sugar in cereal. The Middle Class watches, preferring the more "beautiful" kinds of non-body-contact sports like tennis or gymnastics or figure-skating (the music is a redeeming feature here). With High-, Mid-, and Low-Proles we find heavy viewing of the soaps in the daytime and rugged body-contact sports (football, hockey, boxing) in the evening. The lower one is located in the Prole classes the more likely one is to watch "Bowling for Dollars" and "Wonder Woman" and "The Hulk" and when choosing a game show to prefer "Joker's Wild" to "The Family Feud," whose jokes are sometimes incomprehensible. Destitutes and Bottom Out-of-Sights have in common a problem involving choice. Destitutes usually "own" about three color sets, and the problem is which three programs to run at once. Bottom Out-of-Sights exercise no choice at all, the decisions being made for them by correctional or institutional personnel.

───

[3]This term may be applied to anything cutesy, banal, inappropriate, artificial but not artistic, and in spectacularly bad taste: plastic statues of the Venus de Milo, for example, with alarm clocks where their navels ought to be. — EDS.

The time when the evening meal is consumed defines class 13 better than, say, the presence or absence on the table of ketchup bottles and ashtrays shaped like little toilets enjoining the diners to "Put Your Butts Here." Destitutes and Bottom Out-of-Sights eat dinner at 5:30, for the Prole staff on which they depend must clean up and be out roller-skating or bowling early in the evening. Thus Proles eat at 6:00 or 6:30. The Middles eat at 7:00, the Upper Middles at 7:30 or, if very ambitious, at 8:00. The Uppers and Top Out-of-Sights dine at 8:30 or 9:00 or even later, after nightly protracted "cocktail" sessions lasting usually around two hours. Sometimes they forget to eat at all.

Similarly, the physical appearance of the various classes de- 14 fines them fairly accurately. Among the top four classes thin is good, and the bottom two classes appear to ape this usage, although down there thin is seldom a matter of choice. It is the three Prole classes that tend to fat, partly as a result of their use of convenience foods and plenty of beer. These are the classes too where anxiety about slipping down a rung causes nervous overeating, resulting in fat that can be rationalized as advertising the security of steady wages and the ability to "eat out" often. Even "Going Out for Breakfast" is not unthinkable for Proles, if we are to believe that they respond to the McDonald's TV ads as they're supposed to. A recent magazine ad for a diet book aimed at Proles stigmatizes a number of erroneous assumptions about body weight, proclaiming with some inelegance that "They're all a crock." Among such vulgar errors is the proposition that "All Social Classes Are Equally Overweight." This the ad rejects by noting quite accurately:

> Your weight is an advertisement of your social standing. A century ago, corpulence was a sign of success. But no more. Today it is the badge of the lower-middle-class, where obesity is *four times* more prevalent than it is among the upper-middle and middle classes.

It is not just four times more prevalent. It is at least four times more visible, as any observer can testify who has witnessed Prole women perambulating shopping malls in their bright, very tight jersey trousers. Not just obesity but the flaunting of obesity is the Prole sign, as if the object were to give maximum aesthetic offense to the higher classes and thus achieve a form of revenge.

Another physical feature with powerful class meaning is the   15
wearing of plaster casts on legs and ankles by members of the top three classes. These casts, a sort of white badge of honor, betoken stylish mishaps with frivolous but costly toys like horses, skis, snowmobiles, and mopeds. They signify a high level of conspicuous waste in a social world where questions of unpayable medical bills or missed working days do not apply. But in the matter of clothes, the Top Out-of-Sight is different from both Upper and Upper Middle Classes. It prefers to appear in new clothes, whereas the class just below it prefers old clothes. Likewise, all three Prole classes make much of new garments, with the highest possible polyester content. The question does not arise in the same form with Destitutes and Bottom Out-of-Sights. They wear used clothes, the thrift shop and prison supply room serving as their Bonwit's and Korvette's.

This American class system is very hard for foreigners to   16
master, partly because most foreigners imagine that since America was founded by the British it must retain something of British institutions. But our class system is more subtle than the British, more a matter of gradations than of blunt divisions, like the binary distinction between a gentleman and a cad. This seems to lack plausibility here. One seldom encounters in the United States the sort of absolute prohibitions which (half-comically, to be sure) one is asked to believe define the gentleman in England. Like these:

> A gentleman never wears brown shoes in the city, or
> A gentleman never wears a green suit, or
> A gentleman never has soup at lunch, or
> A gentleman never uses a comb, or
> A gentleman never smells of anything but tar, or
> "No gentleman can fail to admire Bellini." — W. H. Auden[4]

---

[4]Vincenzo Bellini (1801–1835) was the Italian composer of *Norma* and other operas; Auden (1903–1973), an English-born American poet, critic, and translator of opera librettos. — EDS.

In America it seems to matter much less the way you present yourself — green, brown, neat, sloppy, scented — than what your backing is — that is, where your money comes from. What the upper orders display here is no special uniform but the kind of psychological security they derive from knowing that others recognize their freedom from petty anxieties and trivial prohibitions.

"Language most shows a man," Ben Jonson used to say. 17
"Speak, that I may see thee." As all acute conservatives like Jonson know, dictional behavior is a powerful signal of a firm class line. Nancy Mitford so indicated in her hilarious essay of 1955, "The English Aristocracy," based in part on Professor Alan S. C. Ross's more sober study "Linguistic Class-Indicators in Present-Day English." Both Mitford and Ross were interested in only one class demarcation, the one dividing the English Upper Class ("U," in their shorthand) from all below it ("non-U"). Their main finding was that euphemism and genteelism are vulgar. People who are socially secure risk nothing by calling a spade a spade, and indicate their top-dog status by doing so as frequently as possible. Thus the U-word is *rich*, the non-U *wealthy*. What U-speakers call *false teeth* non-U's call *dentures*. The same with *wigs* and *hairpieces*, *dying* and *passing away* (or *over*).

For Mitford, linguistic assaults from below are sometimes so 18
shocking that the only kind reaction of a U-person is silence. It is "the only possible U-response," she notes, "to many embarrassing modern situations: the ejaculation of 'cheers' before drinking, for example, or 'It was so nice seeing you' after saying goodbye. In silence, too, one must endure the use of the Christian name by comparative strangers. . . ." In America, although there are more classes distinguishable here, a linguistic polarity is as visible as in England. Here U-speech (or our equivalent of it) characterizes some Top Out-of-Sights, Uppers, Upper Middles, and Class X's. All below is a waste land of genteelism and jargon and pretentious mispronunciation, pathetic evidence of the upward social scramble and its hazards. Down below, the ear is bad and no one has been trained to listen. Culture words especially are the downfall of the aspiring. Sometimes it is diph-

thongs that invite disgrace, as in *be-yóu-ti-ful*. Sometimes the as-pirant rushes full-face into disaster by flourishing those secret class indicators, the words *exquisite* and *despicable*, which, like another secret sign, *patina*, he (and of course she as often) stresses on the middle syllable instead of the first. High-class names from cultural history are a frequent cause of betrayal, es-pecially if they are British, like Henry Purcell.[5] In America non-U speakers are fond of usages like "Between he and I." Recalling vaguely that mentioning oneself last, as in "He and I were there," is thought gentlemanly, they apply that principle uni-formly, to the entire destruction of the objective case. There's also a problem with *like*. They remember something about the dangers of illiteracy its use invites, and hope to stay out of trou-ble by always using *as* instead, finally saying things like "He looks as his father." These contortions are common among young (usually insurance or computer) trainees, raised on Leon Uris,[6] and *Playboy*, most of them Mid- or High-Proles pounding on the firmly shut door of the Middle Class. They are the care-ful, dark-suited first-generation aspirants to American respecta-bility and (hopefully, as they would put it) power. Together with their deployment of the anomalous nominative case on all occa-sions goes their preference for jargon (you can hear them going at it on airplanes) like *parameters* and *guidelines* and *bottom lines* and *funding, dialogue, interface,* and *lifestyles.* Their world of lan-guage is one containing little more than smokescreens and knowing innovations. "Do we gift the Johnsons, dear?" the cor-porate wife will ask the corporate husband at Christmas time.

Just below these people, down among the Mid- and Low- 19 Proles, the complex sentence gives trouble. It is here that we get sentences beginning with elaborate pseudo-genteel participles like "Being that it was a cold day, the furnace was on." All classes below those peopled by U-speakers find the gerund out of reach and are thus forced to multiply words and say, "The peo-

[5]English composer and organist (1659–1695), whose name the English pronounce like *purse'll* in "Your purse'll be stolen if you don't watch it" (not "pur-*sell*"). — Eds.

[6]American novelist of war and strife, author of *Battle Cry* (1953), *Exodus* (1957), *Trinity* (1976), and other best-sellers. — Eds.

ple in front of him at the theater got mad due to the fact that he talked so much" instead of "His talking at the theater annoyed the people in front." (But *people* is not really right: *individuals* is the preferred term with non-U speakers. Grander, somehow.) It is also in the domain of the Mid- and Low-Prole that the double negative comes into its own as well as the superstitious avoidance of *lying* because it may be taken to imply telling untruths. People are thus depicted as always *laying* on the beach, the bed, the grass, the sidewalk, and without the slightest suggestion of their performing sexual exhibitions. A similar unconscious inhibition determines that *set* replace *sit* on all occasions, lest low excremental implications be inferred. The ease with which *sit* can be interchanged with the impolite word is suggested in a Second World War anecdote told by General Matthew Ridgway. Coming upon an unidentifiable head and shoulders peeping out of a ditch near the German border, he shouted, "Put up your hands, you son of a bitch!", to be answered, so he reports, "Aaah, go sit in your hat."

All this is evidence of a sad fact. A deep class gulf opens between two current generations: the older one that had some Latin at school or college and was taught rigorous skeptical "English," complete with the diagramming of sentences; and the younger one taught to read by the optimistic look-say method and encouraged to express itself — as the saying goes — so that its sincerity and well of ideas suffer no violation. This new generation is unable to perceive the number of syllables in a word and cannot spell and is baffled by all questions of etymology (it thinks *chauvinism* has something to do with gender aggressions). It cannot write either, for it has never been subjected to tuition in the sort of English sentence structure which resembles the sonata in being not natural but artificial, not innate but mastered. Because of its misspent, victimized youth, this generation is already destined to fill permanently the middle-to-low slots in the corporate society without ever quite understanding what devilish mechanism has prevented it from ascending. The disappearance of Latin as an adjunct to the mastery of English can be measured by the rapid replacement of words like *continuing* by solecisms like *ongoing*. A serious moment in cultural history oc-

20

curred a few years ago when gasoline trucks changed the warning word on the rear from *Inflammable* to *Flammable*. Public education had apparently produced a population which no longer knew *In-* as an intensifier. That this happened at about the moment when every city was rapidly running up a "Cultural Center" might make us laugh, if we don't cry first. In another few generations Latinate words will be found only in learned writing, and the spoken language will have returned to the state it was in before the revival of learning. Words like *intellect* and *curiosity* and *devotion* and *study* will have withered away together with the things they denote.

There's another linguistic class-line, dividing those who persist in honoring the nineteenth-century convention that advertising, if not commerce itself, is reprehensible and not at all to be cooperated with, and those proud to think of themselves not as skeptics but as happy consumers, fulfilled when they can image themselves as functioning members of a system by responding to advertisements. For U-persons a word's succeeding in an ad is a compelling reason never to use it. But possessing no other source of idiom and no extra-local means of criticizing it, the subordinate classes are pleased to appropriate the language of advertising for personal use, dropping brand names all the time and saying things like "They have some lovely fashions in that store." In the same way they embrace all sub-professional euphemisms gladly and employ them proudly, adverting without irony to hair stylists, sanitary engineers, and funeral directors in complicity with the consumer world which cynically casts them as its main victims. They see nothing funny in paying a high price for an article and then, after a solemn pause, receiving part of it back in the form of a "rebate." Trapped in a world wholly defined by the language of consumption and the hype, they harbor restively, defending themselves against actuality by calling habitual drunkards *people with alcohol problems*, madness *mental illness*, drug use *drug abuse*, building lots *homesites*, houses *homes* ("They live in a lovely $250,000 home"), and drinks *beverages*.

Those delighted to employ the vacuous commercial "Have a nice day" and those who wouldn't think of saying it belong manifestly to different classes, no matter how we define them, and it is unthinkable that those classes will ever meld. Calvin Coolidge said that the business of America is business. Now apparently the business of America is having a nice day. Tragedy? Don't need it. Irony? Take it away. Have a nice day. Have a nice day. A visiting Englishman of my acquaintance, a U-speaker if there ever was one, has devised the perfect U-response to "Have a nice day": "Thank you," he says, "but I have other plans." The same ultimate divide separates the two classes who say respectively when introduced, "How do you do?" and "Pleased to meet you." There may be comity between those who think *prestigious* a classy word and those who don't, but it won't survive much strain, like relations between those who think *momentarily* means in a moment (airline captain over loudspeaker: "We'll be taking off momentarily, folks") and those who know it means for a moment. Members of these two classes can sit in adjoining seats on the plane and get along fine (although there's a further division between those who talk to their neighbors in planes and elevators and those who don't), but once the plane has emptied, they will proceed toward different destinations. It's the same with those who conceive that *type* is an adjective ("He's a very classy type person") and those who know it's only a noun or verb.

The pretense that either person can feel at ease in the presence of the other is an essential element of the presiding American fiction. Despite the lowness of the metaphor, the idea of the melting pot is high-minded and noble enough, but empirically it will be found increasingly unconvincing. It is our different language habits as much as anything that make us, as the title of Richard Polenberg's book puts it, *One Nation Divisible*.   23

Some people invite constant class trouble because they believe the official American publicity about these matters. The official theory, which experience is constantly disproving, is that one can earn one's way out of his original class. Richard Nixon's behavior indicates dramatically that this is not so. The sign of the Upper Class to which he aspired is total psychological security, expressed in loose carriage, saying what one likes, and imperviousness to what others think. Nixon's vast income from law and politics — his San Clemente property aped the style of   24 the Upper but not the Top Out-of-Sight Class, for everyone knew where it was, and he wanted them to know — could not alleviate his original awkwardness and meanness of soul or his nervousness about the impression he was making, an affliction allied to his instinct for cunning and duplicity. Hammacher Schlemmer might have had him specifically in mind as the consumer of their recently advertised "Champagne Recork": "This unusual stopper keeps 'bubbly' sprightly, sparkling after uncorking ceremony is over. Gold electro-plated." I suspect that it is some of these same characteristics that make Edward Kennedy often seem so inauthentic a member of the Upper Class. (He's not Top Out-of-Sight because he chooses to augment his inheritance by attractive work.)

What, then, marks the higher classes? Primarily a desire for   25
privacy, if not invisibility, and a powerful if eccentric desire for freedom. It is this instinct for freedom that may persuade us that inquiring into the American class system this way is an enterprise not entirely facetious. Perhaps after all the whole thing has something, just something, to do with ethics and aesthetics. Perhaps a term like *gentleman* still retains some meanings which are not just sartorial and mannerly. Freedom and grace and independence: It would be nice to believe those words still mean something, and it would be interesting if the reality of the class system — and everyone, after all, hopes to rise — should turn out to be a way we pay those notions a due if unwitting respect.

QUESTIONS ON MEANING

1. What is Fussell's main PURPOSE in "Notes on Class"?
2. Why does he reject the usual division of Americans into high-, middle-, and low-income groups? In his own nine-part division, what several factors determine class?
3. What interesting similarities does Fussell discover between people at the very top of his class ladder and those at the very bottom?
4. What do you have to do to belong to Class X?

5. In Fussell's CONCLUSION (paragraph 25), what does he see the "higher classes" trying to achieve? Explain his remark, "Perhaps a term like *gentleman* still retains some meanings which are not just sartorial and mannerly."

QUESTIONS ON WRITING STRATEGY

1. Do Fussell's sympathies appear to lie with any particular class or classes? Does he scorn anyone? What is the general TONE of his essay? Does he seem to be kidding, or serious?
2. How heavily does Fussell use examples? Where did he obtain his EVIDENCE?
3. In paragraph 3, how does he distinguish the three top classes from one another?
4. For readers of what class or classes did Fussell originally write? What evidence of his awareness of his AUDIENCE do you find in his essay?

QUESTIONS ON LANGUAGE

1. According to Fussell, how important is language in placing a person in the class structure? Where do you place if you say "between he and I"? Explain Fussell's remark about the younger generation in paragraph 20: "Because of its misspent, victimized youth, this generation is already destined to fill permanently the middle-to-low slots in the corporate society without ever quite understanding what devilish mechanism has prevented it from ascending." Discuss.
2. Look up in your dictionary the preferred pronunciations of "those secret class indicators" that Fussell cites in paragraph 18: *exquisite, despicable,* and *patina.* (What, by the way, is a patina?) How would you guess Fussell expects a non-upper-class speaker to mispronounce these words? What is wrong with the statement, "We'll be taking off *momentarily,* folks" (22)?
3. Note Fussell's discussion of JARGON (at the end of paragraph 18). How do you define this term? What other people use jargon besides air travelers in business suits? What other gems of jargon have you seen or heard lately?
4. How extensive is Fussell's own vocabulary? Define proletarian, bohemians (paragraph 2); façades, confiscatory, expropriation, claustrated (6); hypertrophied (7); stigmatizes (14); dictional behavior, euphemism, genteelism (17); a linguistic polarity, diphthongs,

anomalous (18); chauvinism (20); idiom, adverting, complicity (21); vacuous, comity (22); imperviousness (24); sartorial (25).

SUGGESTIONS FOR WRITING

1. Pointing to specifics in "Notes on Class," attack or defend this proposition: "Paul Fussell is a snob."
2. In paragraph 9 Fussell classifies particular examples of home-decoration into categories ("Middle," "high prole," etc.). Write a similar list classifying things according to some other principle: the cars people drive, the movies or the snack foods they favor, attitudes toward women's liberation. If you need more information about the classes and their preferences, do some digging first: talk with friends, take a walk through different neighborhoods with your senses open. Be prepared to read your list aloud and to justify your classifications.
3. Analyze an issue of one of these magazines: *The New Yorker, Vogue, Town & Country, The Atlantic, Gourmet, National Enquirer* (in appearance, a tabloid newspaper), *Good Housekeeping, Hustler,* or some other periodical suggested by your instructor. Try to determine the Fussellian class or classes of its audience. (You can usually tell who reads a magazine by closely inspecting its advertisements.) In an essay of 500–700 words, report your findings, giving evidence and illustrating your paper with a few clippings from the magazine (or, if it's the library's, photocopies).
4. Write a two- or three-paragraph essay under one of these titles (which you can modify to suit yourself):

   Don't Dump on Us Top Out-of-Sighters
   A Defense of My Own Good Old Middle Class
   I'm a Prole and Proud of It — Want to Fight?

Paul Fussell on Writing

According to an account written for *The Bedford Reader*, Paul Fussell found inspiration for "Notes on Class" in an old party game called "Categories." "To play my game of 'Class,' " he explained, "I made a large chart out of cardboard, listing across the top the nine classes as I'd distinguished them and, along the left side, entering a series of social class indicators like clothes, house fronts, food, drink, dining hours, body weight, TV habits, language, reading, and the like. Then I filled in the squares, and in writing the essay I proceeded down and across. I would hope that the method and atmosphere of *game* would suggest to the reader that the essay belongs more to the world of *play* than to the world of *responsible study*."

As he worked on his essay, Fussell paid careful attention not only to his categories but to his tone. "In 'Notes on Class,' " he said, "part of the fun for me was managing language so as to generate an ironic tone of mock-pedantry. (The pompous phrase *façade study* is an example.) By this tone I hoped to signal that my approach to the topic — although in part serious, as in the last paragraph — was at bottom satiric and comic. By invoking a "high" word like *enjoining* close to a "low" word like *butts*, one sets in motion a comedy of conscious inappropriateness. That method of straight-faced surprise, and sometimes shock, is what the essay depends on. Sometimes the surprise results from the speaker's mock-aristocratic, breezy, totally self-assured tone, as when he stigmatizes all occupants of the White House as rather common because of their visibility, or indicates that he conceives dentistry to be quite dirty work because it involves sticking your fingers in other people's mouths."

At the end of his comments about writing his essay, Fussell comes back to the matter of tone. "The big problem in writing 'Notes on Class' was to keep my annoyance — at the sight of ugly fat people or the sound of pretentious euphemisms — under control, to prevent its perverting the comedy into solemnity or anger. I'm not sure I've succeeded in sustaining the perfect balance between the ludicrous and the serious that satire requires."

FOR DISCUSSION

1. What were some of the devices Fussell used to give "Notes on Class" a comic, satiric tone?
2. Fussell hopes that his essay "belongs more to the world of *play* than to the world of *responsible study*." To what extent does his essay reflect this attitude?

1. Write an essay by the method of division, in which you analyze one of the following subjects. In breaking your subject into its component parts, explain or describe each part in some detail; try to indicate how each part functions, or how it contributes to the whole. If you have to subdivide any parts into smaller ones, go ahead, but clearly indicate to your reader what you are doing.

An event to remember
A year in the life of a student
A paycheck at your disposal
Your favorite sonnet
A short story, a play, or a dramatic film that made you think
The government of your community
The most popular bookstore (or other place of business) in town
The Bible
A band or orchestra
A famous painting or statue

2. Write an essay by the method of classification, in which you sort out the following subjects into categories. Make clear your purpose in classifying things, and the basis of your classification. This essay shouldn't turn out to be a disconnected list, but should break down the subject into groups. You may find it helpful to make up a name for each group, or otherwise clearly identify it. One way to approach this assignment would be to build qualifiers into your introduction. Let your audience know that of all the types there are, you plan to write, say, about those that are "among the best" or "among the worst"; "the outstanding" or "the most ridiculous."

The records you own	Comic strips
Families	Movie monsters
Stand-up comedians	Sports announcers
Present-day styles of marriage	Inconsiderate people
Vacations	Radio stations
College students today	Mall millers (people who mill
Paperback novels	around malls)
Waiters you'd never tip	

· 7 ·

ANALOGY

Drawing a Parallel

THE METHOD

The photography instructor is perspiring. He is trying to explain the workings of a typical camera to people who barely know how to pop a film cartridge into an Instamatic. "Let me give you an analogy," he offers — and from that moment, the faces of his class start coming alive. They understand him. What helps is his *analogy*: a point-by-point comparison that explains something unknown in terms of something familiar.

"Like the pupil in the human eye," the instructor begins, "the aperture of a camera — that's the opening in front — is adjustable. It contracts or it widens, letting in a lesser or a greater amount of light. The film in the camera is like the retina at the back of the eye — it receives an image. . . ." And the instructor continues, taking up one point at a time, working out the similarities between camera and eye.

To make clear his explanation, the instructor uses an analogy often found in basic manuals of photography. The inner workings of a Konica FS-1 may be mysterious to a beginning student of photography, but the parts of the eye are familiar to anyone who has looked in a mirror, or has had to draw and label the parts of the eye in sixth grade. Not every time you write an essay, but once in a while, analogy will be a wonderfully useful method. With its help you can explain a subject that is complicated, unfamiliar, or intangible. You can put it into terms as concrete and understandable as nuts and nutcrackers.

Like comparison and contrast, analogy is a method of explanation that sets things side by side. But the former is a way to explain two obviously similar things, to consider both their differences and their similarities. You might show, in writing a comparison and contrast, how San Francisco is quite unlike Boston in history, climate, and predominant life-styles, but like it in being a seaport and a city proud of its own (and neighboring) colleges. That isn't the way an analogy works. In an analogy you yoke together two apparently unlike things (eye and camera, the task of navigating a spacecraft and the task of sinking a putt), and all you care about is their major similarities.

If the photography instructor had said, "The human eye is a kind of camera," he would have stated a *metaphor*. As you may recall from having read any poetry, a metaphor is a figure of speech that declares one thing to be another — even though it isn't, in a strictly literal sense — for the purpose of making us aware of similarity. "Hope," says the poet Emily Dickinson, "is the thing with feathers / That perches in the soul" — thus pointing to the similarity between a feeling and a bird (also between the human soul and a tree that birds light in). By its very nature, an analogy is a kind of extended metaphor: *extended*, because usually it goes on longer than a line of poetry and it touches on a number of similarities. Here is an example. In August 1981, after *Voyager 2* transmitted to Earth its spectacular pictures of Saturn, NASA scientists held a news briefing. They wanted to explain to the public the difficulty of what they had achieved. They realized, however, that most people have no clear idea of the distance from Earth to Saturn, nor of the complexities of space navigation; and so they used an analogy. To bring *Voyager 2* within close range of Saturn, they explained, was analogous to sinking a putt from 500 miles away. Extending the metaphor, one scientist added, "Of course, you should allow the golfer to run alongside the ball and make trajectory corrections by blowing on it."[1] A listener can immediately grasp the point: Such a feat is colossally hard.

Scientists explaining their work to nonscientists are particularly fond of such analogies because they deal with matters that an audience without technical training may find difficult. But the method is a favorite, too, of preachers and philosophers, because it can serve to make things beyond the experience of our senses vivid and graspable. We see this happening in one of the most famous passages in medieval literature. It is an analogy given by the eighth-century English historian Bede, who tells how in the year 627 King Edwin of Northumbria summoned a council to decide whether to accept the strange new religion of Christianity. Said one counselor:

> Your Majesty, when we compare the present life of man on earth with that time of which we have no knowledge, it seems to me like the swift flight of a single sparrow through the banqueting-hall where you are sitting at dinner on a winter's day with your thanes and counselors. In the midst there is a comforting fire to warm the hall; outside, the storms of winter rain or snow are raging. This sparrow flies swiftly in through one door of the hall, and out through another. While he is inside, he is safe from the winter storms; but after a few moments of comfort, he vanishes from sight into the wintry world from which he came. Even so, man appears on earth for a little while; but of what went before this life or of what follows, we know nothing. Therefore, if this new teaching has brought any more certain knowledge, it seems only right that we should follow it.[2]

Why, after twelve centuries, has this analogy remained un-

---

[1]Quoted by Robert Cooke in a news story, "Voyager Sends a Surprise Package," Boston *Globe*, August 27, 1981.

[2]*A History of the English Church and People*, trans. Leo Sherley-Price, rev. R. E. Latham (Baltimore: Penguin Books, 1968), p. 127.

forgotten? Our minds cannot grasp infinite time, and we hardly can comprehend humankind's relation to it. But we can readily visualize a winter's snow and rain and a sparrow's flight through a banquet hall.

Like a poet, who also discovers metaphors, the writer who draws an analogy gives pleasure by making a comparison that offers a reader a little surprise. In setting forth vigorous, concrete, and familiar examples, an analogy strikes us with poemlike force. For this reason, it is sometimes used by a writer who wishes to sway and arouse an audience, to engrave a message in memory. In his celebrated speech, "I Have a Dream," Martin Luther King, Jr., draws a remarkable analogy to express the anger and disappointment of American blacks that, one hundred years after Lincoln's Emancipation Proclamation, their full freedom has yet to be achieved. "It is obvious today," declares Dr. King, "that America has defaulted on this promissory note"; and he compares the founding fathers' written guarantee — of the rights of life, liberty, and the pursuit of happiness — to a bad check returned for insufficient funds. Yet his speech ends on a different note, and with a different analogy. He prays that the "jangling discords of our nation" will become in time a "symphony of brotherhood." This last is an example of a *short analogy*, one contained in a few words. For another example, see Gail Sheehy's opening paragraphs (page 309), comparing a human being and a lobster. (For the entire "I Have a Dream" speech, see Chapter 10.)

Dr. King does not pretend to set forth a logical argument. There may be logic in his poetic words, but his purpose is to rouse his listeners and inspire them to fight on. Sometimes, however, you find the method of analogy used in an argument that pretends to be carefully reasoned, but really isn't logical at all. (For more about this misuse of analogy, see *Argument from Analogy* in the list of logical fallacies on page 508.)

THE PROCESS

When you set forth a subject that you believe will be unfamiliar to your readers, then analogy may come to your aid. In explaining some special knowledge, the method is most likely to be valuable. Did you ever play some unusual sport? Are you expert in a particular skill, or knowledgeable in some hobby? Did you ever travel to some place your readers may not have visited? Have you ever learned the workings of some specialized machine (a mechanical potato peeler, say, or an automatic pinsetter)? Have you had any experience that most people haven't? Is your family background, perhaps, unusual? You may then have a subject that will be made clearer by the method of analogy.

With subject in hand, consider: Exactly what will your analogy be? A bright idea has to dawn on you. If none *does* dawn, then it's far better to write your essay by some other method than to contrive a laborious, forced analogy. "Death is a dollar bill," one writer began — but the analogy that followed seemed a counterfeit. Remember: An effective analogy points to real similarities, not manufactured ones. (The author of the dollar bill essay went on: "Death is a cold condition, like cold, hard cash. . . ." — inflating an already weak currency.)

An analogy likens its subject to something more familiar than itself — as space navigation is likened to a game of golf. Your subject may be an abstraction or a feeling, but in analogy you can't use another abstraction or feeling to explain it. Were a scientist, for instance, to liken the steering of *Voyager 2* to the charting of a person's spiritual course through life, the result might be a fascinating essay, but it wouldn't explain the steering of the spacecraft. (If the scientist's main *subject* were the charting of a spiritual course, and if he were writing for an audience of technicians to whom the steering of *Voyager 2* was familiar, then indeed, he could write an analogy.)

There's one more preliminary test of your idea. Like all good metaphors, an analogy sets forth a writer's fresh discovery. The reader ought to think, "Look at that! Those two things are a lot alike! Who would have thought so?" (You, the writer — that's who.) That is why the analogy of a camera to the human eye (if you haven't heard it before) is striking; and why Bede's comparison of a life to the flight of a sparrow through a warm room is effective. You could write an essay likening toothpaste to bar soap, and remark that both make suds and float dirt away; but the result would probably put the reader to sleep, and anyhow, it wouldn't be an analogy. Both things would be simple and fa-

miliar, and too similar. You wouldn't be using one to explain
the other. Dissimilarity, as well as similarity, has to be present to
make an analogy. And so, before you write, make sure that
your subject and what you explain it with are noticeably *unlike*
each other.

   You now have your bright idea. Next you make a brief outline, listing your subject, what you'll use to explain it, and their
similarities. Most analogies begin by likening the two, then go
on to work through the similarities one point at a time. Never
mind the differences. If your analogy is to form only a part of
your essay, then later, perhaps, you will want to mention the
differences — but wait until you have completed your analogy.

   At last, with your outline before you, you are ready to write.
As you work, visualize your subject (*if* it can be visualized —
Bede's subject, the brevity of life, can't). Be sure to hold in your
mind's eye the thing with which you explain your subject. Try
for the most exact, concrete words you can find. An effective
analogy is definite. It makes something swing wide, as a key un-
locks a door.

ANALOGY IN A PARAGRAPH: TWO ILLUSTRATIONS

1. Using Analogy to Write about Television

   Public television is hugely more popular in Japan than in
America. In fact, Japanese viewers spend more time in watching the programs of NHK than in watching those of the
ninety-nine commercial-carrying stations put together. NHK
has a high and ambitious goal: not merely to entertain, but to
educate and inspire. Independently run, under no government authority, the network dedicates itself to preserving national culture and "furthering world peace and the good of
humankind." In this regard, the Japanese public broadcasting
system resembles not an American TV network but an American college. Although its programming, like a college curriculum, includes sports — wrestling and baseball are covered
faithfully — the network's central concern is the life of the
mind. NHK's schedule reads almost like the course listings in
a college catalog. Seventy-five percent of its programming is

spent on news and video lessons (brush calligraphy; musical instruction; courses in natural history, English, and sociology), while NHK's second channel is wholly devoted to education: programs for public schools, serious music, classic drama — both Kabuki plays and Shakespeare's. Like the campus Mardi Gras or barbecue, fun has its minor place on NHK. Comedy is popular, and there is even a fifteen-minute commercial-free soap opera ("Oshin"), about a farmer's daughter turned grocery magnate. Finally, like an American college, NHK demands tuition: a voluntary fee, which practically all Japanese viewers pay willingly.

COMMENT. In its four opening sentences, this paragraph is devoted to the nature of Japanese television — specifically, NHK, the unfamiliar subject to be explained. Then the writer helps us understand the public broadcasting system's "high and ambitious goal" by an analogy — likening NHK to a college. She does so by selecting four areas in which North American college life resembles NHK's programming: in sports, coursework, just-for-fun activities, and tuition fees. What the writer makes clear, without coming out and hitting us over the head with her point, is that watching Japanese television is a little like going to school. This may be an unfamiliar notion to us, but as the analogy makes clear, NHK apparently satisfies its highly literate audience.

2. Using Analogy in an Academic Discipline

You may have experienced the first postulate while sitting on a train in a station. You suddenly notice that the train on the next track has begun to creep out of the station. However, after several moments you realize that it is your own train that is moving and that the other is still motionless on its tracks. Consider another example. Suppose you are floating in a spaceship in interstellar space and another spaceship comes coasting by. You might conclude that it is moving and you are not, but someone in the other ship might be equally sure that you are moving and they are not. The principle of relativity says that there is no experiment you could perform to decide which ship is moving and which is not. This means there is no such thing as absolute rest — all motion is relative.

COMMENT. As we have seen, analogy is especially useful for explaining a complicated idea in a way that readers will grasp easily. In this paragraph, adapted from the 1986 edition of *Fundamentals of Astronomy* by Michael A. Seeds (Belmont, Calif.: Wadsworth Publishing Co., p. 138), the author sets out to clarify for his student readers the first postulate of the theory of relativity: "Observers can never detect their *uniform* motion except relative to other objects." To do so, the author calls up an experience familiar to most readers — that of sitting on a moving train and thinking that it stands still. Then, substituting spaceships for trains, he amplifies the first example with one less familiar but still comprehensible to his audience. By placing two concrete experiences before his readers, by supplying vivid mental pictures they can easily comprehend, he makes clear in a few words a difficult concept that might have taken many paragraphs to explain in abstract language.

· Paul and Anne Ehrlich ·

PAUL and ANNE EHRLICH are well known for their impressive body of work on the subjects of global ecology, population control, and environmental concerns. The Ehrlichs have conducted field work on six continents, and have coauthored numerous books, including *Population, Resources, Environment: Issues in Human Ecology* (1970), *The End of Affluence: A Blueprint for Your Future* (1974), *Extinction: The Causes and Consequences of the Disappearance of Species* (1981), and *Earth* (1988).

Born in Philadelphia in 1932, Paul Ehrlich received his M.A. and Ph.D. from the University of Kansas. Anne Ehrlich, born in 1933 in Des Moines, Iowa, also attended the University of Kansas. The Ehrlichs married, then moved to Stanford University in 1958, where Paul began teaching and Anne became a research assistant and scientific illustrator. In 1980 Anne Ehrlich served as a consultant for the White House Council on Environmental Qualities Global 200 report, and since 1981 she has taught a course in environmental policy at Stanford. She has also contributed to the *New York Times Magazine*, *Saturday Review*, and *American Naturalist*. Paul Ehrlich has written or cowritten many other books, including *The Population Bomb* (1968), *Global Ecology: Readings toward a Rational Strategy for Man* (1971), *The Race Bomb: Skin Color, Prejudice, and Intelligence* (1977), and several textbooks.

The Rivet Poppers

Some ideas, if tremendously complex and vast in scale, are hard to hold clearly in mind. One such idea is the ecology of the earth on which we live: its elaborate, delicately balanced, and profoundly interrelated natural systems. The beauty of "The Rivet Poppers" is that the authors make this idea vivid and urgent to us by means of an analogy. Their self-contained essay appears as the preface to the Ehrlichs' book *Extinction* (1981), and opens the way to the authors' thesis: that with each species of life that disappears, humankind is threatened as well.

As you walk from the terminal toward your airliner, you no- 1
tice a man on a ladder busily prying rivets out of its wing. Somewhat concerned, you saunter over to the rivet popper and ask
him just what the hell he's doing.

"I work for the airline — Growthmania Intercontinental," 2
the man informs you, "and the airline has discovered that it can
sell these rivets for two dollars apiece."

"But how do you know you won't fatally weaken the wing 3
doing that?" you inquire.

"Don't worry," he assures you. "I'm certain the manufac- 4
turer made this plane much stronger than it needs to be, so no
harm's done. Besides, I've taken lots of rivets from this wing and
it hasn't fallen off yet. Growthmania Airlines needs the money;
if we didn't pop the rivets, Growthmania wouldn't be able to
continue expanding. And I need the commission they pay me —
fifty cents a rivet!"

"You must be out of your mind!" 5

"I told you not to worry; I know what I'm doing. As a mat- 6
ter of fact, I'm going to fly on this flight also, so you can see
there's absolutely nothing to be concerned about."

Any sane person would, of course, go back into the termi- 7
nal, report the gibbering idiot and Growthmania Airlines to the
FAA, and make reservations on another carrier. You never *have*
to fly on an airliner. But unfortunately all of us are passengers
on a very large spacecraft — one on which we have no option
but to fly. And, frighteningly, it is swarming with rivet poppers
behaving in ways analogous to that just described.

The rivet poppers on Spaceship Earth include such people 8
as the President of the United States, the Chairman of the Soviet Communist Party, and most other politicians and decision
makers; many big businessmen and small businessmen; and, inadvertently, most other people on the planet, including you and
us. Philip Handler, the president of the United States National
Academy of Sciences, is an important rivet popper, and so are
industrialist Daniel Ludwig (who is energetically chopping down
the Amazon rainforest), Senator Howard Baker, enemy of the
Snail Darter, and Vice President George Bush, friend of nuclear

war. Others prominent on the rivet-popper roster include Japanese whalers and woodchippers, many utility executives, the auto moguls of Detroit, the folks who run the AMAX corporation, almost all economists, the Brazilian government, Secretary of the Interior James Watt, the editors of *Science, Scientific American*, and the *Wall Street Journal*, the bosses of the pesticide industry, some of the top bureaucrats of the U.S. Department of Agriculture and some of those in the Department of the Interior, the officers of the Entomological Society of America, the faculties of every engineering school in the world, the Army Corps of Engineers, and the hierarchy of the Roman Catholic Church.

Now all of these people (and especially you and we) are certainly not crazy or malign. Most of them are in fact simply uninformed — which is one reason for writing a book on the processes and consequences of rivet-popping. 9

Rivet-popping on Spaceship Earth consists of aiding and abetting the extermination of species and populations of nonhuman organisms. The European Lion, the Passenger Pigeon, the Carolina Parakeet, and the Sthenele Brown Butterfly are some of the numerous rivets that are now irretrievably gone; the Chimpanzee, Mountain Gorilla, Siberian Tiger, Right Whale, and California Condor are prominent among the many rivets that are already loosened. The rest of the perhaps ten million species and billions of distinct populations still more or less hold firm. Some of these species supply or could supply important direct benefits to humanity, and all of them are involved in providing free public services without which society could not persist. 10

The natural ecological systems of Earth, which supply these vital services, are analogous to the parts of an airplane that make it a suitable vehicle for human beings. But ecosystems are much more complex than wings or engines. Ecosystems, like well-made airplanes, tend to have redundant subsystems and other "design" features that permit them to continue functioning after absorbing a certain amount of abuse. A dozen rivets, or a dozen species, might never be missed. On the other hand, a 11 thirteenth rivet popped from a wing flap, or the extinction of a key species involved in the cycling of nitrogen, could lead to a serious accident.

In most cases an ecologist can no more predict the conse-   12
quences of the extinction of a given species than an airline pas-
senger can assess the loss of a single rivet. But both can easily foresee the long-term results of continually forcing species to extinction or of removing rivet after rivet. No sensible airline pas-
senger today would accept a continuous loss of rivets from jet transports. Before much more time has passed, attitudes must be changed so that no sane passenger on Spaceship Earth will accept a continuous loss of populations or species of nonhuman organisms.

Over most of the several billion years during which life has   13
flourished on this planet, its ecological systems have been under what would be described by the airline industry as "progressive maintenance." Rivets have dropped out or gradually worn out, but they were continuously being replaced; in fact, over much of the time our spacecraft was being strengthened by the insertion of more rivets than were being lost. Only since about ten thousand years ago has there been any sign that that process might be more or less permanently reversed. That was when a single species, *Homo sapiens*, began its meteoric rise to planetary domi-
nance. And only in about the last half-century has it become clear that humanity has been forcing species and populations to extinction at a rate greatly exceeding that of natural attrition and far beyond the rate at which natural processes can replace them. In the last twenty-five years or so, the disparity between the rate of loss and the rate of replacement has become alarming; in the next twenty-five years, unless something is done, it promises to become catastrophic for humanity.

The form of the catastrophe is, unfortunately, difficult to   14
predict. Perhaps the most likely event will be an end of civilization in T. S. Eliot's whimper. As nature is progressively impov-
erished, its ability to provide a moderate climate, cleanse air and water, recycle wastes, protect crops from pests, replenish soils, and so on will be increasingly degraded. The human population

will be growing as the capacity of Earth to support people is shrinking. Rising death rates and a falling quality of life will lead to a crumbling of post-industrial civilization. The end may come so gradually that the hour of its arrival may not be recognizable, but the familiar world of today will disappear within the life span of many people now alive.

Of course, the "bang" is always possible. For example, it is likely that destruction of the rich complex of species in the Amazon basin could trigger rapid changes in global climate patterns. Agriculture remains heavily dependent on stable climate, and human beings remain heavily dependent on food. By the end of the century the extinction of perhaps a million species in the Amazon basin could have entrained famines in which a billion human beings perished. And if our species is very unlucky, the famines could lead to a thermonuclear war, which could extinguish civilization.

Fortunately, the accelerating rate of extinctions can be arrested. It will not be easy; it will require both the education of, and concerted action by, hundreds of millions of people. But no tasks are more important, because extinctions of other organisms must be stopped before the living structure of our spacecraft is so weakened that at a moment of stress it fails and civilization is destroyed.

QUESTIONS ON MEANING

1. What cause do the authors support? What belief about the future of our planet do they hold?
2. What do you take to be the central PURPOSE of this essay? Do the Ehrlichs want to educate and inform, make us skeptical about airline safety, amuse and entertain, or frighten us into action? Discuss.
3. In your own words, define the essay's key term, "rivet poppers." What people are included in the name?
4. According to the authors, what is it that interrupted the "progressive maintenance" of the earth's ecological systems? How?

QUESTIONS ON WRITING STRATEGY

1. An expository essay on this subject might have begun with the statement "The future of our planet is in danger." How would the effect of such an essay probably differ from the effect of the essay you have just read?
2. What is the essay's central analogy? What is likened to what? Which element is familiar or easy to grasp, and which is unfamiliar?
3. For what AUDIENCE is this essay written? In what ways would the essay be different if it had been intended for the scientific community?
4. What is the EFFECT of the second person pronoun ("you") in the opening anecdote (paragraphs 1–6) of this essay?

QUESTIONS ON LANGUAGE

1. Explain the phrase "free public services" in paragraph 10. What services do the authors assume that all of "perhaps ten million species" have to offer?
2. Make sure the following words are part of your vocabulary: rivets (paragraph 1); analogous (7); bureaucrat, hierarchy (8); malign (9); ecosystems (11); meteoric, attrition (13).

SUGGESTIONS FOR WRITING

1. By what other comparison, besides likening the earth to an airplane, might a writer make clear our dependence on our planet? Discover a *different* analogy to explain a relationship between the earth and people. Set it forth in a paragraph or more. (To start you discovering, here is an illustration of another such analogy. Novelist William Faulkner once likened the human race to the fleas on a dog's back. His point was that we had better not annoy our host, or else we might be shaken off. But think of your own analogy.)
2. With the words *whimper* and *bang* (paragraphs 14–15), the Ehrlichs refer to T. S. Eliot's poem "The Hollow Men," the last two lines of which read:

> *This is the way the world ends*
> *Not with a bang but a whimper.*

If you are not familiar with the poem, look it up in Eliot's *Collected Poems 1909–1962* and see how it connects with the essay. What visions do Eliot and the Ehrlichs seem to share? Write a paragraph explaining whatever sense you make of this pointed ALLUSION.

3. Write an essay in which you discuss the effects on the environment of some human activity: for instance, manufacturing; the disposal of chemical wastes; the production of nuclear energy; the commercial taking of seals, whales, or other wild animals. Decide whether to take an OBJECTIVE or a SUBJECTIVE attitude toward your material. If possible, choose some situation that you know from reading or personal experience.

· Henry David Thoreau ·

HENRY DAVID THOREAU (1817–1862) was born in Concord, Massachusetts, where, except for short excursions, he remained for the whole of his life. After his graduation from Harvard College, he taught school briefly, worked irregularly as surveyor and house painter, and for a time worked in his father's pencil factory (and greatly improved the product). The small sales of his first, self-published book, *A Week on the Concord and Merrimac Rivers* (1849), led him to remark, "I have now a library of nearly nine hundred volumes, over seven hundred of which I wrote myself."

The philosopher Ralph Waldo Emerson befriended his neighbor Thoreau; but although the two agreed that a unity exists between man and nature, they did not always see eye to eye on matters of politics. Unlike Emerson, Thoreau was an activist. He helped escaped slaves flee to Canada; he went to jail rather than pay his poll tax to a government that made war against Mexico. He recounts this brush with the law in his essay "Civil Disobedience" (1849), in which later readers (including Mahatma Gandhi of India and Martin Luther King, Jr.) have found encouragement for their own nonviolent resistance. One other book appeared in Thoreau's lifetime: *Walden* (1854), a searching account of his life in (and around, and beyond) the one-room cabin he built for himself at Walden Pond near Concord. When Thoreau lay dying, an aunt asked whether he had made his peace with God. "I did not know we had quarreled," he replied.

The Battle of the Ants

At Walden Pond, Thoreau mercilessly simplified his needs. Making himself almost self-sustaining, he proved to his own satisfaction that he could write, read Plato, grow beans, and observe in minute detail the natural world. In the following famous section of *Walden*, Thoreau reports a war he happened to observe while going to fetch wood. It is artful reporting, for Thoreau wrote with care: like a craftsman lovingly joining wood to make a cabinet. To revise *Walden*, a relatively short book, took him seven years. Thoreau's is a style marked by a New England Yankee tightness of lip — indeed, there are no useless words — and by an evident delight in setting forth an analogy.

One day when I went out to my wood-pile, or rather my pile of stumps, I observed two large ants, the one red, the other much larger, nearly half an inch long, and black, fiercely contending with one another. Having once got hold they never let go, but struggled and wrestled and rolled on the chips incessantly. Looking farther, I was surprised to find that the chips were covered with such combatants, that it was not a *duellum*, but a *bellum*,[1] a war between two races of ants, the red always pitted against the black, and frequently two red ones to one black. The legions of these Myrmidons[2] covered all the hills and vales in my wood-yard, and the ground was already strewn with the dead and dying, both red and black. It was the only battle which I have ever witnessed, the only battle-field I ever trod while the battle was raging; internecine war; the red republicans on the one hand, and the black imperialists on the other. On every side they were engaged in deadly combat, yet without any noise that I could hear, and human soldiers never fought so resolutely. I watched a couple that were fast locked in each other's embraces, in a little sunny valley amid the chips, now at noonday prepared to fight till the sun went down, or life went out. The smaller red champion had fastened himself like a vice to his adversary's front, and through all the tumblings on that field never for an instant ceased to gnaw at one of his feelers near the root, having already caused the other to go by the board; while the stronger black one dashed him from side to side, and, as I saw on looking nearer, had already divested him of several of his members. They fought with more pertinacity than bulldogs. Neither manifested the least disposition to retreat. It was evi-

[1]Not a hand-to-hand combat, but a whole war.— Eds.
[2]Fierce warriors, originally not men but a tribe of ants. In Homer's *Iliad* the god Zeus, transforming them, sends them to help fight the war against Troy.— Eds.

dent that their battle-cry was "Conquer or die." In the meanwhile there came along a single red ant on the hillside of this valley, evidently full of excitement, who either had dispatched his
foe, or had not yet taken part in the battle; probably the latter,
for he had lost none of his limbs; whose mother had charged
him to return with his shield or upon it. Or perchance he was
some Achilles, who had nourished his wrath apart, and had
now come to avenge or rescue his Patroclus.[3] He saw this unequal combat from afar — for the blacks were nearly twice the
size of the red — he drew near with rapid pace till he stood on
his guard within half an inch of the combatants; then, watching
his opportunity, he sprang upon the black warrior, and com-
menced his operations near the root of his right foreleg, leaving
the foe to select among his own members; and so there were
three united for life, as if a new kind of attraction had been invented which put all other locks and cements to shame. I should
not have wondered by this time to find that they had their respective musical bands stationed on some eminent chip, and
playing their national airs the while, to excite the slow and cheer
the dying combatants. I was myself excited somewhat even as if
they had been men. The more you think of it, the less the difference. And certainly there is not the fight recorded in Concord
history, at least, if in the history of America, that will bear a moment's comparison with this, whether for the numbers engaged
in it, or for the patriotism and heroism displayed. For numbers
and for carnage it was an Austerlitz or Dresden.[4] Concord
Fight! Two killed on the patriots' side, and Luther Blanchard
wounded! Why here every ant was a Buttrick — "Fire! for God's
sake fire!" — and thousands shared the fate of Davis and Hos-
mer.[5] There was not one hireling there. I have no doubt that it
was a principle they fought for, as much as our ancestors, and
not to avoid a three-penny tax on their tea; and the results of

[3]In the *Iliad* again, the Greek hero Achilles and his slain comrade-in-
arms.— Eds.
[4]Battles that Napoleon waged with great loss of life.— Eds.
[5]Minutemen who fought the British redcoats in the Battle of Concord
Bridge, 1775.— Eds.

this battle will be as important and memorable to those whom it concerns as those of the battle of Bunker Hill, at least.

I took up the chip on which the three I have particularly described were struggling, carried it into my house, and placed it under a tumbler on my window-sill, in order to see the issue. Holding a microscope to the first-mentioned red ant, I saw that, though he was assiduously gnawing at the near foreleg of his enemy, having severed his remaining feeler, his own breast was all torn away, exposing what vitals he had there to the jaws of the black warrior, whose breastplate was apparently too thick for him to pierce; and the dark carbuncles of the sufferer's eyes shone with ferocity such as war only could excite. They struggled half an hour longer under the tumbler, and when I looked again the black soldier had severed the heads of his foes from their bodies, and the still living heads were hanging on either side of him like ghastly trophies at his saddle-bow, still apparently as firmly fastened as ever, and he was endeavoring with feeble struggles, being without feelers, and with only the remnant of a leg, and I know not how many other wounds, to divest himself of them, which at length, after half an hour more, he accomplished. I raised the glass, and he went off over the window-sill in that crippled state. Whether he finally survived that combat, and spent the remainder of his days in some Hôtel des Invalides,[6] I do not know; but I thought that his industry would not be worth much thereafter. I never learned which party was victorious, nor the cause of the war, but I felt for the rest of that day as if I had my feelings excited and harrowed by witnessing the struggle, the ferocity and carnage, of a human battle before my door.

Kirby and Spence tell us that the battles of ants have long been celebrated and the date of them recorded, though they say that Huber[7] is the only modern author who appears to have witnessed them. "Aeneas Sylvius," say they, "after giving a very circumstantial account of one contested with great obstinacy by a

---

[6]In Paris, a home for old soldiers.— EDS.

[7]Three leading entomologists (or zoologists specializing in insects) of Thoreau's day: Kirby and Spence in America, Huber in Switzerland.— EDS.

great and small species on the trunk of a pear tree," adds that "'this action was fought in the pontificate of Eugenius the Fourth, in the presence of Nicholas Pistoriensis, an eminent lawyer, who related the whole history of the battle with the greatest fidelity.' A similar engagement between great and small ants is recorded by Olaus Magnus, in which the small ones, being victorious, are said to have buried the bodies of their own soldiers, but left those of their giant enemies a prey to the birds. This event happened previous to the expulsion of the tyrant Christian the Second from Sweden." The battle which I witnessed took place in the Presidency of Polk, five years before the passage of Webster's Fugitive-Slave Bill.

QUESTIONS ON MEANING

1. In finding the Battle of Concord Bridge a minor skirmish when compared to the battle of the ants, in crediting the ant soldiers with greater heroism (paragraph 1), is Thoreau putting down patriotism? Does he hint that the American Revolution didn't matter? What is his point?
2. For what PURPOSE (or purposes) does Thoreau seem to write such a detailed account of so trifling a war?

QUESTIONS ON WRITING STRATEGY

1. "Human soldiers," says Thoreau in paragraph 1, "never fought so resolutely." With what specific examples and observations does he support his GENERALIZATION? Point to memorable details that make us see the ant soldiers' inhuman determination.
2. In drawing his analogy, does Thoreau seek to explain the behavior of ants by comparing it to human war, or to explain human war by comparing it to the behavior of ants? (Which of the two kinds of warfare — ant or human — does Thoreau appear to regard as strange and unfamiliar, and therefore in greater need of explaining?)
3. What is the TONE of this essay? In his attitude toward the ant war (and human war), does Thoreau seem grim, amused, appalled, disgusted, mocking, or what? How can you tell?

4. Do Thoreau's ALLUSIONS to history and to Greek literature seem decorations meant to show off his knowledge? What do they add to the essay? Look closely at one or two of them.
5. In many anthologies, you will find this selection with paragraph 3 shaved off. Why is Thoreau's CONCLUSION so effective? If it is omitted, what is lost?

QUESTIONS ON LANGUAGE

1. What is an *internecine war* (paragraph 1)?
2. Define any of these other words you may have doubts about: perchance, eminent (paragraph 1); assiduously, carbuncles, saddlebow, carnage (2); circumstantial, obstinacy (3).
3. In noting that the black ant has a *breastplate* (paragraph 2), Thoreau sees the ant soldier as wearing armor like a man. What other examples of PERSONIFICATION do you find?
4. Is this essay written in the technical vocabulary of a professional entomologist? Glance again at Thoreau's microscopic description of the ants (paragraph 2): How specialized are its words?

SUGGESTIONS FOR WRITING

1. In a paragraph, draw an analogy between some *typical* person, whose general sort you've observed, and some animal, bird, or insect. You might consider someone bursting with energy; someone who takes until eleven o'clock in the morning to wake up; a belligerent sort; a talkative scold; a ravenous eater; or — what kind of person interests you?
2. Describe some phenomenon or some creature in the natural world that has fascinated you. If, as you write, an analogy occurs to you, put it in; but don't force one if it doesn't come naturally.
3. Like Thoreau, the ancient Greek writer Aesop was fond of likening animals to persons. Some of his *Fables* may be familiar to you: the one about the hare and the tortoise (with the slow, persistent plodder winning the race), the tale of the fox and the grapes (about the fox who, when he couldn't reach the tempting fruit, decided that it must be sour anyway), and that of the mice who wanted to bell the cat (but who couldn't get one of their number to volunteer). An Aesop fable usually sums up the point of a story in a closing moral ("Slow and steady is sure to win," "There is comfort in pretending that the unattainable is not worth having," "It is easier to plan than to fulfill"). Read or reread a few of Aesop's fables, then try writing one of your own.

Henry David Thoreau on Writing

"Keep a journal," Emerson had urged Thoreau, and in 1837 the younger writer began making entries. For the rest of his life, he continued to be a faithful journal keeper. Into this intimate volume, kept only for his own eyes, Thoreau poured ideas, opinions, impressions, poems, meditations, passages from his reading that he wished to remember. Much of this raw material found its way into *Walden* and other published works. From Thoreau's *Journal*, here is a provocative sampling of his thoughts about writing. (To help identify each, we have given them subject headings.)

Physical Exercise. How vain it is to sit down to write when you have not stood up to live! Methinks that the moment my legs begin to move, my thoughts begin to flow, as if I had given vent to the stream at the lower end and consequently new fountains flowed into it at the upper. A thousand rills which have their rise in the sources of thought burst forth and fertilize my brain. . . . The writing which consists with habitual sitting is mechanical, wooden, dull to read. (August 19, 1851)

Not Saying Everything. It is the fault of some excellent writers — De Quincey's first impressions on seeing London suggest it to me — that they express themselves with too great fullness and detail. They give the most faithful, natural, and lifelike account of their sensations, mental and physical, but they lack moderation and sententiousness. They do not affect us by an intellectual earnestness and a reserve of meaning, like a stutterer; they say all they mean. Their sentences are not concentrated and nutty. Sentences which suggest far more than they say, which have an atmosphere about them, which do not merely report an old, but make a new impression; sentences which suggest as many things and are as durable as a Roman aqueduct: to frame these, that is the *art* of writing. Sentences which are expensive, towards which so many volumes, so much life, went; which lie like boulders on the page, up and down or across; which contain the seed of other sentences, not mere repetition, but creation: which a man might sell his grounds and castles to build. (August 22, 1851)

Writing with Body and Senses. We cannot write well or truly but what we write with gusto. The body, the senses, must conspire with the mind. Expression is the act of the whole man, that our speech may be vascular. The intellect is powerless to express thought without the aid of the heart and liver and of every member. Often I feel that my head stands out too dry, when it should be immersed. A writer, a man writing, is the scribe of all nature; he is the corn and the grass and the atmosphere of writing. It is always essential that we love what we are doing, do it with a heart. (September 2, 1851)

Drawing Analogies. Be greedy of occasions to express your thought. Improve the opportunity to draw analogies. (September 4, 1851)

Thought and Style. Shall I not have words as fresh as my thoughts? Shall I use any other man's word? A genuine thought or feeling can find expression for itself, if it have to invent hieroglyphics. It has the universe for type-metal. It is for want of original thought that one man's style is like another's. (September 8, 1851)

Revision. In correcting my manuscripts, which I do with sufficient phlegm, I find that I invariably turn out much that is good along with the bad, which it is then impossible for me to distinguish — so much for keeping bad company; but after the lapse of time, having purified the main body and thus created a distinct standard for comparison, I can review the rejected sentences and easily detect those which deserve to be readmitted. (March 1, 1854)

The Value of Lapsed Time. Often I can give the truest and most interesting account of any adventure I have had after years have elapsed, for then I am not confused, only the most significant facts surviving in my memory. Indeed, all that continues to interest me after such a lapse of time is sure to be pertinent, and I may safely record all that I remember. (March 28, 1857)

Self-Inspiration. The writer must to some extent inspire himself. Most of his sentences may at first lie dead in his essay, but when all are arranged, some life and color will be reflected on them from the mature and successful lines; they will appear to pulsate with fresh life, and he will be enabled to eke out their slumbering sense, and make them worthy of their neighborhood. . . . Most that is first written on any subject is a mere groping after it, mere rubble-stone and foundation. (February 3, 1859)

Thought Breeds Thought. The Scripture rule, "Unto him that hath shall be given," is true of composition. The more you have thought and written on a given theme, the more you can still write. Thought breeds thought. It grows under your hands. (February 13, 1860)

FOR DISCUSSION

1. What connection does Thoreau find between life and art?
2. What are the author's views about revision?
3. What does Thoreau recommend for writers who "express themselves with too great fullness and detail"?

· Lewis Thomas ·

LEWIS THOMAS, a prominent and longstanding member of the medical and scientific communities, has held teaching, research, and administrative positions at numerous medical schools and hospitals, including Johns Hopkins, Cornell, Harvard, and Massachusetts General, among others. In addition, Thomas has served as dean of the School of Medicine at both Yale and New York universities, and as president of the Sloan-Kettering Cancer Center in New York City. Born in 1913 in Flushing, New York, Thomas attended Princeton University and Harvard Medical School, and most of his early writings were technical papers on his specialty, pathology. He did write poetry too and, as a medical student, published some of it in *The Atlantic* and other magazines. Still, it wasn't until 1971, when he began to write a monthly column for the *New England Journal of Medicine*, that Thomas came to the attention of the general public. His column, "Notes of a Biology Watcher," allowed him to pursue his own meditations on science, and to explore the less technical, more humanitarian and philosophical issues science sometimes raises. Many of these columns appear in his first book, *Lives of a Cell* (1974), which won a National Book Award — in part because Thomas writes with a unique candor, humor, grace, and style. Other books include *The Medusa and the Snail* (1979) and *Late Night Thoughts on Listening to Mahler's Ninth Symphony* (1983), both essay collections; and *The Youngest Science* (1983), a memoir about becoming a doctor. Thomas, a member of the National Academy of Sciences, has also contributed to *Nature*, *Science*, *Daedalus*, the *Saturday Review of Science*, and many medical journals.

The Attic of the Brain

"The Attic of the Brain" originally appeared in *Discover* magazine, and is included in Thomas's most recent collection of essays, *Late Night Thoughts on Listening to Mahler's Ninth Symphony*. Though Thomas is a scientist, no special knowledge is needed to understand this essay, for his approach to his subject is not technical, and the metaphor he extends is as famil-

iar to most of us as the street on which we grew up. With the
help of an analogy, Thomas is able to discuss one of the most
complex entities in the world: the human brain.

My parents' house had an attic, the darkest and strangest   1
part of the building, reachable only by placing a stepladder beneath the trapdoor and filled with unidentifiable articles too important to be thrown out with the trash but no longer suitable
to have at hand. This mysterious space was the memory of the
place. After many years all the things deposited in it became,
one by one, lost to consciousness. But they were still there, we
knew, safely and comfortably stored in the tissues of the house.

These days most of us live in smaller, more modern houses   2
or in apartments, and attics have vanished. Even the deep
closets in which we used to pile things up for temporary forgetting are rarely designed into new homes.

Everything now is out in the open, openly acknowledged   3
and displayed, and whenever we grow tired of a memory, an old
chair, a trunkful of old letters, they are carted off to the dump
for burning.

This has seemed a healthier way to live, except maybe for   4
the smoke — everything out to be looked at, nothing strange
hidden under the roof, nothing forgotten because of no place
left in impenetrable darkness to forget. Openness is the new life-
style, no undisclosed belongings, no private secrets. Candor is
the rule in architecture. The house is a machine for living, and
what kind of a machine would hide away its worn-out, obsolescent parts?

But it is in our nature as human beings to clutter, and we   5
hanker for places set aside, reserved for storage. We tend to accumulate and outgrow possessions at the same time, and it is an
endlessly discomforting mental task to keep sorting out the ones
to get rid of. We might, we think, remember them later and find
a use for them, and if they are gone for good, off to the dump,
this is a source of nervousness. I think it may be one of the reasons we drum our fingers so much these days.

We might take a lesson here from what has been learned 6
about our brains in this century. We thought we discovered,
first off, the attic, although its existence has been mentioned
from time to time by all the people we used to call great writers.
What we really found was the trapdoor and a stepladder, and off
we clambered, shining flashlights into the corners, vacuuming
the dust out of bureau drawers, puzzling over the names of objects, tossing them down to the floor below, and finally paying
around fifty dollars an hour to have them carted off for burning.

After several generations of this new way of doing things we 7
took up openness and candor with the febrile intensity of a new
religion, everything laid out in full view, and as in the design of
our new houses it seemed a healthier way to live, except maybe
again for smoke.

And now, I think, we have a new kind of worry. There is no 8
place for functionless, untidy, inexplicable notions, no dark
comfortable parts of the mind to hide away the things we'd like
to keep but at the same time forget. The attic is still there, but
with the trapdoor always open and the stepladder in place we
are always in and out of it, flashing lights around, naming everything, unmystified.

I have an earnest proposal for psychiatry, a novel set of ther- 9
apeutic rules, although I know it means waiting in line.

Bring back the old attic. Give new instructions to the pa- 10
tients who are made nervous by our times, including me, to
make a conscious effort to hide a reasonable proportion of
thought. It would have to be a gradual process, considering how
far we have come in the other direction talking, talking all the
way. Perhaps only one or two thoughts should be repressed each
day, at the outset. The easiest, gentlest way might be to start
with dreams, first by forbidding the patient to mention any
dream, much less to recount its details, then encouraging the
outright forgetting that there was a dream at all, remembering
nothing beyond the vague sense that during sleep there had
been the familiar sound of something shifting and sliding, up
under the roof.

We might, in this way, regain the kind of spontaneity and 11
zest for ideas, things popping into the mind, uncontrollable and

ungovernable thoughts, the feel that this notion is somehow connected unaccountably with that one. We could come again into possession of real memory, the kind of memory that can come from jumbled forgotten furniture, old photographs, fragments of music.

It has been one of the great errors of our time to think that   12
by thinking about thinking, and then talking about it, we could possibly straighten out and tidy up our minds. There is no delusion more damaging than to get the idea in your head that you understand the functioning of your own brain. Once you acquire such a notion, you run the danger of moving in to take charge, guiding your thoughts, shepherding your mind from place to place, *controlling* it, making lists of regulations. The human mind is not meant to be governed, certainly not by any book of rules yet written; it is supposed to run itself, and we are obliged to follow it along, trying to keep up with it as best we can. It is all very well to be aware of your awareness, even proud of it, but never try to operate it. You are not up to the job.

I leave it to the analysts to work out the techniques for do-   13
ing what now needs doing. They are presumably the professionals most familiar with the route, and all they have to do is turn back and go the other way, session by session, step by step. It takes a certain amount of hard swallowing and a lot of revised jargon, and I have great sympathy for their plight, but it is time to reverse course.

If after all, as seems to be true, we are endowed with uncon-   14
scious minds in our brains, these should be regarded as normal structures, installed wherever they are for a purpose. I am not sure what they are built to contain, but as a biologist, impressed by the usefulness of everything alive, I would take it for granted that they are useful, probably indispensable organs of thought. It cannot be a bad thing to own one, but I would no more think of meddling with it than trying to exorcise my liver, an equally mysterious apparatus. Until we know a lot more, it would be wise, as we have learned from other fields in medicine, to let them be, above all not to interfere. Maybe, even — and this is the notion I wish to suggest to my psychiatric friends — to stock them up, put more things into them, make *use* of them. Forget

whatever you feel like forgetting. From time to time, practice *not* being open, discover new things *not* to talk about, learn reserve, hold the tongue. But above all, develop the human talent for forgetting words, phrases, whole unwelcome sentences, all experiences involving wincing. If we should ever lose the loss of memory, we might lose as well that most attractive of signals ever flashed from the human face, the blush. If we should give away the capacity for embarrassment, the touch of fingertips might be the next to go, and then the suddenness of laughter, the unaccountable sure sense of something gone wrong, and, finally, the marvelous conviction that being human is the best thing to be.

Attempting to operate one's own mind, powered by such a 15 magical instrument as the human brain, strikes me as rather like using the world's biggest computer to add columns of figures, or towing a Rolls-Royce with a nylon rope.

I have tried to think of a name for the new professional ac- 16 tivity, but each time I think of a good one I forget it before I can get it written down. Psychorepression is the only one I've hung on to, but I can't guess at the fee schedule.

QUESTIONS ON MEANING

1. State, in your own words, the THESIS of this essay.
2. In paragraph 4, Thomas links the amount of space we live in to certain aspects of our life-styles. What relationship is he suggesting here? Do you think it's valid, or is he perhaps reaching a bit too far for the sake of his analogy? Support your answer with examples from your own experience as well as from the essay.
3. The author works from the premise that we need a place "for functionless, untidy, inexplicable notions" (paragraph 8). Why does he seem to think that such a place is necessary?
4. According to Thomas, why is it "time to reverse course" (paragraph 13)? What does he find wrong with the course we're on, and what will we gain by learning reserve, by not being open, by forgetting certain things?

QUESTIONS ON WRITING STRATEGY

1. What analogy does Thomas draw? Identify, as succinctly as possible, the two things he compares.
2. What is the TONE of the sentence, "Perhaps only one or two thoughts should be repressed each day, at the outset" (paragraph 10)?
3. What is the tone of the last paragraph, particularly the phrase "each time I think of a good one I forget it before I can get it written down"? Would you label this humor silly, ironic, gentle, or sarcastic? Is Thomas completely serious about the PURPOSE of the essay? If so, why do you think he introduces humor?
4. The author makes the assumption that the unconscious mind is a normal structure, and therefore useful. As a biologist, however, Thomas surely knows for a fact that some living things and structures — such as the vestigial appendix in the human body — aren't useful. Does it weaken his essay that he doesn't address this fact?

QUESTIONS ON LANGUAGE

1. Consult your dictionary if you need help in defining the following words: candor, obsolescent (paragraph 4); febrile (7); exorcise, apparatus (14).
2. Consider the last sentence in paragraph 6, which ends "and off we clambered . . . puzzling over the names of objects, tossing them down to the floor below, and finally paying around fifty dollars an hour to have them carted off for burning." Explain the reference to having the objects carted off for burning. Is the author suggesting we'd pay fifty dollars an hour to have someone do *that*? Discuss.
3. Be sure you understand the distinction Thomas makes between being "aware of your awareness" and trying "to operate it" (paragraph 12).

SUGGESTIONS FOR WRITING

1. Consider Thomas's statement, "it is in our nature as human beings to clutter" (paragraph 5). Do you agree that this is a fundamental part of human nature? Write an essay responding to this statement. Be sure to provide enough examples to make your case convincing; generalizing from one illustration is not an effective strategy.

2. Thomas approaches this essay with a healthy respect for the human mind and its ability to do what it's supposed to, even if we can't be sure exactly what that is. Write a brief essay in which you argue that the human mind *does* need to be governed, and that repressing or forgetting things is psychologically damaging. Or, if you prefer, argue in support of Thomas's thesis, taking care to provide enough fresh EVIDENCE that you are not merely repeating what Thomas has already said. Whichever topic you choose, see whether a new analogy might help you illustrate any point.

Lewis Thomas on Writing

Lewis Thomas has found little similarity between his popular essays and the scientific articles he has written for specialized journals. Some of the latter, he recalls with amusement, have been quoted to illustrate "how awful the prose is in scientific papers."

Still, he admits, his essays do in a way resemble scientific writing: They report experiments in thought. "Although I usually think I know what I'm going to be writing about, what I'm going to say, most of the time it doesn't happen that way at all. At some point I get misled down a garden path. I get surprised by an idea that I hadn't anticipated getting, which is a little bit like being in a laboratory. Including, in fact, that the outcome in writing essays, like the outcome in a laboratory, often enough turns out to be a dud." (Quoted by David Hellerstein, "The Muse of Medicine," *Esquire*, March 1984, p. 77.)

FOR DISCUSSION

1. Lewis Thomas the essayist has a reputation as a stylist. How do you account for some of his scientific articles having been held up as "how awful the prose is in scientific papers"? Who might have made such a judgment?
2. What important similarities does the author see between scientists in the laboratory and essayists? What new light does this comparison cast on the ordinary citizen's usual view of scientists?

1. Develop one of these topics by the method of analogy. (You might consider several of these topics, until one of them blooms into a bright idea for an analogy.)

The training of a professional writer
The body's circulatory system
The way a rumor spreads
Succeeding in whatever you do
The way a child learns to walk and talk
What it's like to get behind in your schoolwork
Becoming sure of yourself in a new situation
Trying to understand a difficult concept
Getting the job done through cooperation instead of competition
Teaching worthwhile values to a child
How violent crime intrudes on our lives
Competition between the sexes
Building character
A crushing failure
The brightest spot in your day
Learning a new skill
How your body fights germs
Being a nonconformist
Trying to get by without sufficient preparation
Going into debt
An allergic reaction
The experience of unexpected happiness

2. In one meaty paragraph, set forth an analogy between practicing some sport you know well (playing basketball, climbing a mountain, running, sailing) and some other activity familiar to most people. Your purpose is to explain the nature of the sport to a reader unfamiliar with it. You might show, for example, how trying to sink a basket on a crowded court is like trying to buy a gift on Christmas Eve in a busy department store, or how climbing a mountain is like climbing many flights of cluttered stairs. If you like, you might explain instead of a sport some physical task (taking a photograph, diapering a baby, getting up in the morning, driving a motorcycle).

· 8 ·

CAUSE AND EFFECT

Asking Why

THE METHOD

Press the button of a doorbell and, inside the house or apartment, chimes sound. Why? Because the touch of your finger on the button closed an electrical circuit. But why did you ring the doorbell? Because you were sent by your dispatcher: You are a bill collector calling on a customer whose payments are three months overdue.

The touch of your finger on the button is the *immediate cause* of the chimes: the event that precipitates another. That you were ordered by your dispatcher to go ring the doorbell is a *remote cause*: an underlying, more basic reason for the event, not apparent to an observer. Probably, ringing the doorbell will lead to some results: The door will open, and you may be given a check — or a kick in the teeth.

To divide the flow of events into reasons and results: This is the kind of analysis you make when you write by the method of *cause and effect*. You try to answer the question, Why did something happen? or the question, What were the consequences?

Seeking causes, you can ask, for example, Why did guerrilla warfare erupt in El Salvador? For what reason or reasons do birds migrate? What has caused sales of Detroit-made cars to pick up lately? Looking for effects, you can ask, What have been the effects of the birth-control pill on the typical American family? What impact has the personal computer had on the nursing profession? You can look to a possible future and ask, Of what use might a course in psychology be to me if I become an office manager? Suppose a new comet the size of Halley's were to strike Philadelphia — what would be the probable consequences? Essay exams in history and economics courses tend often to ask for either causes or effects: What were the principal causes of America's involvement in the war in Vietnam? What were the immediate effects on the world monetary system of Franklin D. Roosevelt's removing the United States from the gold standard?

Don't, by the way, confuse cause and effect with the method of process analysis. Some process analysis essays, too, deal with happenings; but they ask the question, *How* (not why) did something happen? If you were explaining the process by which the doorbell rings, you might break the happening into stages — (1) the finger presses the button; (2) the circuit closes; (3) the current travels the wire; (4) the chimes make music — and you'd set forth the process in detail. But why did the finger press the button? What happened because the doorbell rang? To answer those questions, you need cause and effect.

Sometimes one event will appear to trigger another, and it in turn will trigger yet another, and another still, in an order we call a *causal chain*. A classic example of such a chain is set forth in a Mother Goose rhyme:

> For want of a nail the shoe was lost,
> For want of a shoe the horse was lost,
> For want of a horse the rider was lost,
> For want of a rider the battle was lost,
> For want of a battle the kingdom was lost —
> And all for the want of a nail.

In reality, causes are seldom so easy to find as that missing nail: They tend to be many and complicated. A battle may be lost for more than one reason. Perhaps the losing general had fewer soldiers, and had a blinding hangover the morning he mapped out his battle strategy. Perhaps winter set in, expected reinforcements failed to arrive, and a Joan of Arc inspired the winning army. The downfall of a kingdom is not to be explained as though it were the toppling of the last domino in a file. Still, one event precedes another in time, and in discerning causes you don't ignore chronological order; you pay attention to it.

In trying to account for some public event (a strike, say, or the outcome of an election), in trying to explain a whole trend in today's society (toward nonsmoking, or late marriage), you can expect to find a whole array of causes — interconnected, perhaps, like the strands of a spiderweb. You'll want to do an honest job of unraveling. This may take time. For a jury to decide why an accused slayer acted as he did, weeks of testimony from witnesses, detectives, and psychiatrists may be required, then days of deliberation. It took a great historian, Jakob Burckhardt, most of his lifetime to set forth a few reasons for the dawn of the Italian Renaissance. To be sure, juries must take great care when a life hangs in the balance; and Burckhardt, after all, was writing an immense book. To produce a college essay, you don't have forty years; but before you start to write, you will need to devote extra time and thought to seeing which facts are the causes, and which matter most.

To answer the questions Why? and What followed as a result? may sometimes be hard, but it can be satisfying — even illuminating. Indeed, to seek causes and effects is one way for the mind to discover order in a reality that otherwise might seem (as life came to seem to Macbeth) a tale told by an idiot, full of sound and fury, signifying nothing.

THE PROCESS

In writing an essay that seeks causes or one that seeks effects, first make sure that your subject is manageable. Choose a subject you can get to the bottom of, given the time and information you have. For a 500-word essay due Thursday, the causes of teenage rebellion would be a topic less wieldy than why a certain thirteen-year-old you know ran away from home. Excellent papers may be written on large subjects, and yet they may be written on smaller, more personal subjects as well. You can ask yourself, for instance, why you behaved in a certain way at a certain moment. You can examine the reasons for your current beliefs and attitudes. Such a paper might be rewarding: You might happen upon a truth you hadn't realized before. In fact, both you and your reader may profit from an essay that seeks causes along the lines of these: "Why I Espouse Nudism," or "Why I Quit College and Why I Returned." Such a paper, of course, takes thought. It isn't easy to research your own motivations. A thoughtful, personal paper that discerns *effects* might follow from a topic such as "Where Nudism Led Me" or "What Happened When I Quit College."

When seeking remote causes, look only as far back as necessary. Explaining why a small town has fallen on hard times, you might confine yourself to the immediate cause of the hardship: the closing of a factory. You might explain what caused the shutdown: a dispute between union and management. You might even go back to the cause of the dispute (announced firings) and the cause of the firings (loss of sales to a Japanese competitor). For a short essay, that might be far enough back in time to go; but if you were writing a whole book (*Pottsville 1988: Its Glorious Past and Its Present Agony*), you might look to causes still more remote. You could trace the beginning of the decline of Pottsville back to the discovery, in Kyoto in 1845, of a better carrot grater. A manageable short paper showing *effect* might work in the other direction, moving from the factory closing to its impact on the town: unemployment, the closing of stores and the only movie house, people packing up and moving away.

When you can see a number of apparent causes, weigh them and assign each a relative importance. Which do you find matter most? Often, you will see that causes are more important or less so: *major* or *minor*. If Judd acquires a heavy drug habit and also takes up video game playing, and as a result finds himself penniless, it is probably safe to assume that the drug habit is the major cause of his going broke and his addiction to Frogger a minor one. If you were writing about his sad case, you'd probably emphasize the drug habit by giving it most of your space, perhaps touching on video games in a brief sentence.

You can plan out an essay by arranging events in chronological order (or in reverse order: from a recent event back to past events that cause it). If Judd drops out of college, the most immediate cause might be his inability to meet a tuition payment. But his lack of money might have a cause, too: his having earlier acquired a heavy drug habit. The cause of his addiction might be traced back further still: to a period of depression he suffered, and to an even earlier, more remote cause — the death of a friend in a car accident. In writing about him, you might begin with the accident, and then step by step work out its consequences; or you could begin with Judd's withdrawal from school, and trace a causal chain back to the accident.

In so doing beware of the logical fallacy "after this, therefore because of this" (in Latin, *post hoc, ergo propter hoc*) — that is, don't expect Event A to cause Event B just because A happened before B. This is the error of the superstitious man who decides that he lost his job because a black cat walked in front of him. Another error is to oversimplify the causal chain to two links (when it has many links and several connected lengths) — to claim, say, that violent crime is simply a result of "all those gangster shows on TV." Avoid such wrong turns in reasoning by patiently looking for evidence before you write, and by giving it careful thought. (For a fuller list of such *logical fallacies* or errors in reasoning, see pages 506–508.)

To understand the deep-down causes of a person's act takes thought. Before you write, you can ask yourself a few searching questions. These have been suggested by the work of literary critic Kenneth Burke. Burke asks (and answers) the questions in a complicated way, but for most practical purposes, before you write about the cause of a human act, ask yourself these five questions:

1. What act am I trying to explain?
2. What is the character, personality, or mental state of whoever acted?

3. In what scene or location did the act take place, and in what circumstances?
4. What instruments or means did the person use?
5. For what purpose did he or she act?

Burke calls these elements a *pentad* (or set of five): the *act*, the *actor*, the *scene*, the *agency*, and the *purpose*. If you are trying to explain, for instance, why a person burned down a liquor shop, it will be revealing to ask about his character and mental state. Was the act committed by the shop's worried, debt-ridden owner? A mentally disturbed antialcohol crusader? A drunk who had been denied a purchase? The scene of the burning, too, might tell you something. Was the shop near a church, a mental hospital, or a fireworks factory? And what was the agency (or means of the act): a flaming torch or a flipped-away cigarette butt? To learn the purpose might be illuminating, whether it was to collect insurance on the shop, to get revenge, or to work what the actor believed to be the will of the Lord.

You can further deepen your inquiry by seeing relationships between the terms of the pentad. Ask, for instance, what does the actor have to do with this scene? (Is he or she the preacher in the church across the street, who has been staring at the liquor shop resentfully for the past twenty years?) If you are interested and care to explore the possibilities of Burke's pentad, you can pair up its five terms in ten different ways.[1]

You can use Burke's pentad to help explain the acts of groups as well as those of individuals. Why, for instance, did the sophomore class revel degenerate into a brawl? Here are some possible answers:

1. *Act:* the brawl
2. *Actors:* the sophs were letting off steam after exams, and a mean, tense spirit prevailed
3. *Scene:* a keg-beer party outdoors in the quad at midnight on a sticky and hot May night

---

[1]Act to actor, actor to scene, actor to agency, actor to purpose, act to scene, act to agency, act to purpose, scene to agency, scene to purpose, agency to purpose. This approach can go profoundly deep; if you truly wish to explore it, we suggest you try writing ten questions (one for each pair) in the form, What does act have to do with actor? Ask them of some act you'd like to explain.

4. *Agencies:* fists and beer bottles
5. *Purpose:* the brawlers were seeking to punish whoever kicked over the keg

Don't worry if not all the questions apply, if not all the answers are immediately forthcoming. Bring the pentad to bear on the sad case of Judd, and probably only the question about his character and mental state would help you much. Even a single hint, though, can help you write. Burke's pentad isn't meant to be a grim rigmarole; it is a means of discovery, to generate a lot of possible material for you — insights, observations, hunches to pursue. It won't solve each and every human mystery, but sometimes it will helpfully deepen your thought.

In stating what you believe to be causes and effects, don't be afraid to voice a well-considered hunch. Your instructor doesn't expect you to write, in a short time, a *definitive* account of the causes of an event or a belief or a phenomenon — only to write a coherent and reasonable one. To discern all causes — including remote ones — and all effects is beyond the power of any one human mind. Still, admirable and well-informed writers on matters such as politics, economics, and world and national affairs are often canny guessers and brave drawers of inferences. At times, even the most cautious and responsible writer has to leap boldly over a void to strike firm ground on the far side. Consider your evidence. Think about it hard. Look well before leaping. Then take off.

CAUSE AND EFFECT IN A PARAGRAPH:
TWO ILLUSTRATIONS

1. Using Cause and Effect
to Write about Television

Why is it that, despite a growing interest in soccer among American athletes, and despite its ranking as the most popular sport in the world, commercial television ignores it? To see a televised North American Soccer League game, you have to tune at odd hours to public TV. Part of the reason stems from the basic nature of network television, which exists not to inform and entertain but to sell. During most major sporting events on television — football, baseball, basketball, boxing — producers can take advantage of natural interruptions in the action to broadcast sales pitches; or, if the natural breaks occur too infrequently, the producers can contrive time-outs for the sole purpose of airing lucrative commercials. But soccer is played in two solid halves of forty-five minutes each; not even injury to a player is cause for a time-out. How, then, to insert the requisite number of commercial breaks without resorting to false fouls or other questionable tactics? After CBS aired a soccer match, on May 27, 1967, players reported, according to Stanley Frank, that before the game the referee had instructed them "to stay down every nine minutes." The resulting hue and cry rose all the way to the House Communications Subcommittee. From that day to this, no one has been able to figure out how to screen advertising jingles during a televised soccer game. The result is that the commercial networks have to treat the North American Soccer League as if it didn't exist.

COMMENT. In this paragraph, the writer seeks a cause, and in her opening sentence poses the Why? question she will answer. The middle portion of the paragraph explains that soccer, unlike other sports, is difficult to adapt to commercial television. In mentioning the famous case reported by Frank, she shows what happened when, for a change, a soccer game was telecast, but was artificially orchestrated so as to allow blank moments for commercials. There is only one cause to be found, and it is stated (together with its effect) in the concluding two sentences. Note how the writer illustrates her generalizations with examples. The only unillustrated one is the statement that network TV exists for the purpose of selling things; and this seems an apparent truth we all know already.

2. Using Cause and Effect in an Academic Discipline

Many factors played a role in Johnson's fateful decision. But the most obvious explanation is that the new president faced many pressures to expand the American involvement and only a very few to limit it. As the untested successor to a revered and martyred president, he felt obliged to prove his worthiness for the office by continuing the policies of his predecessor. Aid to South Vietnam had been one of the most prominent of those policies. Johnson also felt it necessary to retain in his administration many of the important figures of the Kennedy years. In doing so, he surrounded himself with a group of foreign policy advisers — Secretary of State Dean Rusk, Secretary of Defense Robert McNamara, National Security Adviser McGeorge Bundy — who strongly believed not only that the United States had an important obligation to resist communism in Vietnam, but that it possessed the ability and resources to make that resistance successful. As a result, Johnson seldom had access to information making clear how difficult the new commitment might become. A compliant Congress raised little protest to, and indeed at one point openly endorsed, Johnson's use of executive powers to lead the nation into war. And for several years at least, public opinion remained firmly behind him — in part because Barry Goldwater's bellicose remarks about the war during the 1964 campaign made Johnson seem by comparison to be a moderate on the issue. Above all, intervention in South Vietnam was fully consistent with nearly twenty years of American foreign policy. An anticommunist ally was appealing to the United States for assistance; all the assumptions of the containment doctrine seemed to require the nation to oblige. Johnson seemed unconcerned that the government of South Vietnam existed only because the United States had put it there, and that the regime had never succeeded in acquiring the loyalty of its people. Vietnam, he believed, provided a test of American willingness to fight communist aggression, a test he was determined not to fail.

COMMENT. The ability both to probe causes and to discern effects is fundamental to the study of history, and both are apparent in this paragraph from the sixth edition of *American History: A Survey* by Richard N. Current, T. Harry Williams, Frank Freidel, and Alan Brinkley (New York: Alfred A. Knopf, 1983, p. 902). The authors examine a number of possible reasons for President Lyndon B. Johnson's having escalated our country's involvement in Vietnam into "a full-scale American war" during his first two years in the White House. The thesis sentence, coming right after the transitional sentence that introduces the paragraph, makes clear the authors' belief that not one but many causes resulted in this decision on the part of the president. Succinctly, they list and explain them.

· Gore Vidal ·

GORE VIDAL was born in 1925 at the U.S. Military Academy at West Point, where his father was an instructor. At the age of nineteen, he wrote his first novel, *Williwaw* (1946), while serving as a warrant officer aboard an army supply ship. Among the later (and more popular) of his twenty novels are *Duluth* (1983), *Lincoln* (1984), and *Empire* (1987). He has also written mysteries under the pen name Edgar Box. As a playwright, he is best known for *Visit to a Small Planet* (1957), which was made into a film. The grandson of Senator T. P. Gore, who represented Oklahoma for thirty years, Vidal himself entered politics in 1960 as a Democratic-Liberal candidate for the House of Representatives. In 1982 he ran again: as a candidate for the Senate in the California Democratic primary. A frequent contributor of brilliant, opinionated essays to *The New York Review of Books*, Vidal divides his time between Italy and America.

Drugs

Vidal, whom some critics have called America's finest living essayist, first published "Drugs" on the "op ed" page of the *New York Times* (the page opposite the editorial page, reserved for diverse opinions). Vidal included it in *Homage to Daniel Shays: Collected Essays 1952–1972*. In the essay, he suggests some generally unrecognized causes for the nation's problems with drug addiction, and proposes a radical solution. See if you think it might work.

It is possible to stop most drug addiction in the United 1 States within a very short time. Simply make all drugs available and sell them at cost. Label each drug with a precise description of what effect — good and bad — the drug will have on the taker. This will require heroic honesty. Don't say that marijuana is addictive or dangerous when it is neither, as millions of people know — unlike "speed," which kills most unpleasantly, or heroin, which is addictive and difficult to kick.

For the record, I have tried — once — almost every drug   2
and liked none, disproving the popular Fu Manchu theory that
a single whiff of opium will enslave the mind. Nevertheless many
drugs are bad for certain people to take and they should be told
why in a sensible way.

Along with exhortation and warning, it might be good for   3
our citizens to recall (or learn for the first time) that the United
States was the creation of men who believed that each man has
the right to do what he wants with his own life as long as he
does not interfere with his neighbor's pursuit of happiness.
(That his neighbor's idea of happiness is persecuting others does
confuse matters a bit.)

This is a startling notion to the current generation of Ameri-   4
cans. They reflect a system of public education which has made
the Bill of Rights, literally, unacceptable to a majority of high
school graduates (see the annual Purdue reports) who now form
the "silent majority" — a phrase which that underestimated wit
Richard Nixon took from Homer who used it to describe the
dead.

Now one can hear the warning rumble begin: If everyone is   5
allowed to take drugs everyone will and the GNP will decrease,
the Commies will stop us from making everyone free, and we
shall end up a race of zombies, passively murmuring "groovy" to
one another. Alarming thought. Yet it seems most unlikely that
any reasonably sane person will become a drug addict if he
knows in advance what addiction is going to be like.

Is everyone reasonably sane? No. Some people will always   6
become drug addicts just as some people will always become alcoholics, and it is just too bad. Every man, however, has the
power (and should have the legal right) to kill himself if he
chooses. But since most men don't, they won't be mainliners either. Nevertheless, forbidding people things they like or think
they might enjoy only makes them want those things all the
more. This psychological insight is, for some mysterious reason,
perennially denied our governors.

It is a lucky thing for the American moralist that our coun-   7
try has always existed in a kind of time-vacuum: We have no
public memory of anything that happened before last Tuesday.
No one in Washington today recalls what happened during the

years alcohol was forbidden to the people by a Congress that thought it had a divine mission to stamp out Demon Rum — launching, in the process, the greatest crime wave in the country's history, causing thousands of deaths from bad alcohol, and creating a general (and persisting) contempt among the citizenry for the laws of the United States.

The same thing is happening today. But the government has 8 learned nothing from past attempts at prohibition, not to mention repression.

Last year when the supply of Mexican marijuana was 9 slightly curtailed by the Feds, the pushers got the kids hooked on heroin and deaths increased dramatically, particularly in New York. Whose fault? Evil men like the Mafiosi? Permissive Dr. Spock? Wild-eyed Dr. Leary? No.

The Government of the United States was responsible for 10 those deaths. The bureaucratic machine has a vested interest in playing cops and robbers. Both the Bureau of Narcotics and the Mafia want strong laws against the sale and use of drugs because if drugs are sold at cost there would be no money in it for anyone.

If there was no money in it for the Mafia, there would be no 11 friendly playground pushers, and addicts would not commit crimes to pay for the next fix. Finally, if there was no money in it, the Bureau of Narcotics would wither away, something they are not about to do without a struggle.

Will anything sensible be done? Of course not. The Ameri- 12 can people are as devoted to the idea of sin and its punishment as they are to making money — and fighting drugs is nearly as big a business as pushing them. Since the combination of sin and money is irresistible (particularly to the professional politician), the situation will only grow worse.

QUESTIONS ON MEANING

1. How readily do you accept Vidal's implicit assumption that a person with easy access to drugs would be unlikely to "interfere with his neighbor's pursuit of happiness"?

2. Spend enough time in the library to learn more about the era of Prohibition in the United States. To what extent do the facts support Vidal's contention that Prohibition was a bad idea?
3. For what reasons, according to Vidal, is it unlikely that our drug laws will be eased? Can you suggest other possible reasons why the Bureau of Narcotics favors strict drug laws?
4. Vidal's essay was first published in 1970. Do you find the views expressed in it still timely, or hopelessly out of date?
5. What do you take to be Vidal's main PURPOSE in writing this essay? How well does he accomplish it?

QUESTIONS ON WRITING STRATEGY

1. How would you characterize Vidal's humor? Find some examples of it.
2. In paragraphs 3 and 4, Vidal summons our founding fathers and the Bill of Rights to his support. Is this tactic fair or unfair? Explain.
3. In paragraph 10, Vidal asserts that the government of the United States is the cause of heroin deaths among the young in New York. By what steps does he reach this judgment? Is the author guilty of oversimplification? (See the discussion of *oversimplification* on page 507.)
4. Where in the essay does Vidal appear to anticipate the response of his AUDIENCE? How can you tell?
5. What function do the essay's RHETORICAL QUESTIONS perform?

QUESTIONS ON LANGUAGE

1. Know the definitions of the following terms: exhortation (paragraph 3); GNP (5); mainliners, perennially (6); curtailed (9).
2. How do you interpret Vidal's use of the phrase *underestimated wit* to describe Richard Nixon?

SUGGESTIONS FOR WRITING

1. Write a paragraph in which you try to predict both the good and the ill effects you think might result from following Vidal's advice to "make all drugs available and sell them at cost."
2. In a short essay, evaluate Vidal's suggestion that every drug be labeled with a description of its probable effect on the taker. How

likely does it seem to you that the warnings printed on containers of addictive or dangerous drugs would be heeded?

Gore Vidal on Writing

"Do you find writing easy?" an interviewer asked Gore Vidal. "Do you enjoy it?"

"Oh, yes, of course I enjoy it," he shot back. "I wouldn't do it if I didn't. Whenever I get up in the morning, I write for about three hours. I write novels in longhand on yellow pads, exactly like the First Criminal Nixon. For some reason I write plays and essays on the typewriter. The first draft usually comes rather fast. One oddity: I never reread a text until I have finished the first draft. Otherwise it's too discouraging. Also, when you have the whole thing in front of you for the first time, you've forgotten most of it and see it fresh. Rewriting, however, is a slow, grinding business.

"When I first started writing, I used to plan everything in advance, not only chapter to chapter but page to page. Terribly constricting — like doing a film from someone else's meticulous treatment. About the time of *The Judgment of Paris* [a novel published in 1952] I started improvising. I began with a mood. A sentence. The first sentence is all-important. [My novel] *Washington, D.C.* began with a dream, a summer storm at night in a garden above the Potomac — that was Merrywood, where I grew up.

"The most interesting thing about writing is the way that it obliterates time. Three hours seem like three minutes. Then there is the business of surprise. I never know what is coming next. The phrase that sounds in the head changes when it appears on the page. Then I start probing it with a pen, finding new meanings. Sometimes I burst out laughing at what is happening as I twist and turn sentences. Strange business, all in all. One never gets to the end of it. That's why I go on, I suppose. To see what the next sentences I write will be." (Interview with

Gerald Clark in *Writers at Work: The Paris Review Interviews, Fifth Series,* edited by George Plimpton [New York: Viking, 1981], pp. 304–305, 311.)

FOR DISCUSSION

1. What is it that Vidal seems to enjoy most about writing?
2. What advantage does he find in not planning every page in advance?

· Marie Winn ·

MARIE WINN was born in Czechoslovakia in 1936. As a child she emigrated with her family to New York City, where she attended the public schools. She was graduated from Radcliffe College and went on to Columbia University for further study. A regular contributor to the *New York Times Magazine*, she is the author of eleven books for both adults and children, including *The Fireside Book of Fun and Game Songs* (1974). *The Plug-In Drug: Television, Children and the Family* (1977) attracted a great deal of attention when it was published; so did *Children without Childhood* (1983).

The End of Play

A few years ago "What Became of Childhood Innocence?" by Marie Winn appeared as a cover story in the *New York Times Magazine*. The article was the seed from which *Children without Childhood* grew. To put together her book, Winn interviewed hundreds of parents and children. The interviews revealed that since the 1960s American children have changed markedly, and so has society's attitude — not only toward children but toward the whole idea of childhood as a golden age of protected innocence. *Children without Childhood* documents those changes. "The End of Play," a chapter from the book, outlines one of them and examines some of its causes.

Of all the changes that have altered the topography of childhood, the most dramatic has been the disappearance of childhood play. Whereas a decade or two ago children were easily distinguished from the adult world by the very nature of their play, today children's occupations do not differ greatly from adult diversions.

Infants and toddlers, to be sure, continue to follow certain timeless patterns of manipulation and exploration; adolescents, too, have not changed their free-time habits so very much, turning as they ever have towards adult pastimes and amusements in their drive for autonomy, self-mastery, and sexual discovery. It is among the ranks of school-age children, those six-to-twelve-year-olds who once avidly filled their free moments with childhood play, that the greatest change is evident. In the place of traditional, sometimes ancient childhood games that were still popular a generation ago, in the place of fantasy and make-believe play — "You be the mommy and I'll be the daddy" — doll play or toy-soldier play, jump-rope play, ball-bouncing play, today's children have substituted television viewing and, most recently, video games.

Many parents have misgivings about the influence of television. They sense that a steady and time-consuming exposure to passive entertainment might damage the ability to play imaginatively and resourcefully, or prevent this ability from developing in the first place. A mother of two school-age children recalls: "When I was growing up, we used to go out into the vacant lots and make up week-long dramas and sagas. This was during third, fourth, fifth grades. But my own kids have never done that sort of thing, and somehow it bothers me. I wish we had cut down on the TV years ago, and maybe the kids would have learned how to play." 3

The testimony of parents who eliminate television for periods of time strengthens the connection between children's television watching and changed play patterns. Many parents discover that when their children don't have television to fill their free time, they resort to the old kinds of imaginative, traditional "children's play." Moreover, these parents often observe that under such circumstances "they begin to seem more like children" or "they act more childlike." Clearly, a part of the definition of childhood, in adults' minds, resides in the nature of children's play. 4

Children themselves sometimes recognize the link between play and their own special definition as children. In an interview about children's books with four ten-year-old girls, one of them said: "I read this story about a girl my age growing up twenty years ago — you know, in 1960 or so — and she seemed so much younger than me in her behavior. Like she might be playing 5 with dolls, or playing all sorts of children's games, or jump-roping or something." The other girls all agreed that they had noticed a similar discrepancy between themselves and fictional children in books of the past: Those children seemed more like children. "So what do *you* do in your spare time, if you don't play with dolls or play make-believe games or jump rope or do things kids did twenty years ago?" they were asked. They laughed and answered, "We watch TV."

But perhaps other societal factors have caused children to   6
give up play. Children's greater exposure to adult realities, their knowledge of adult sexuality, for instance, might make them more sophisticated, less likely to play like children. Evidence from the counterculture communes of the sixties and seventies adds weight to the argument that it is television above all that has eliminated children's play. Studies of children raised in a variety of such communes, all television-free, showed the little communards continuing to fill their time with those forms of play that have all but vanished from the lives of conventionally reared American children. And yet these counterculture kids were casually exposed to all sorts of adult matters — drug taking, sexual intercourse. Indeed, they sometimes incorporated these matters into their play: "We're mating," a pair of six-year-olds told a reporter to explain their curious bumps and grinds. Nevertheless, to all observers the commune children preserved a distinctly childlike and even innocent demeanor, an impression that was produced mainly by the fact that they spent most of their time playing. Their play defined them as belonging to a special world of childhood.

Not all children have lost the desire to engage in the old-   7
style childhood play. But so long as the most popular, most dominant members of the peer group, who are often the most socially precocious, are "beyond" playing, then a common desire to conform makes it harder for those children who still have the drive to play to go ahead and do so. Parents often report that their children seem ashamed of previously common forms of play and hide their involvement with such play from their peers. "My fifth-grader still plays with dolls," a mother tells, "but she keeps them hidden in the basement where nobody will see

them." This social check on the play instinct serves to hasten the end of childhood for even the least advanced children.

What seems to have replaced play in the lives of great num- 8 bers of preadolescents these days, starting as early as fourth grade, is a burgeoning interest in boy-girl interactions — "going out" or "going together." These activities do not necessarily involve going anywhere or doing anything sexual, but nevertheless are the first stage of a sexual process that used to commence at puberty or even later. Those more sophisticated children who are already involved in such manifestly unchildlike interests make plain their low opinion of their peers who still *play*. "Some of the kids in the class are real weird," a fifth-grade boy states. "They're not interested in going out, just in trucks and stuff, or games pretending they're monsters. Some of them don't even *try* to be cool."

Video Games versus Marbles

Is there really any great difference, one might ask, between 9 that gang of kids playing video games by the hour at their local candy store these days and those small fry who used to hang around together spending equal amounts of time playing marbles? It is easy to see a similarity between the two activities: Each requires a certain amount of manual dexterity, each is almost as much fun to watch as to play, each is simple and yet challenging enough for that middle-childhood age group for whom time can be so oppressive if unfilled.

One significant difference between the modern pre-teen fad 10 of video games and the once popular but now almost extinct pastime of marbles is economic: Playing video games costs twenty-five cents for approximately three minutes of play; playing marbles, after a small initial investment, is free. The children who frequent video-game machines require a considerable outlay of quarters to subsidize their fun; two, three, or four dollars is not an unusual expenditure for an eight- or nine-year-old spending an hour or two with his friends playing Asteroids or Pac-Man or Space Invaders. For most of the children the money comes from their weekly allowance. Some augment this amount by enterprising commercial ventures — trading and selling comic books, or doing chores around the house for extra money.

But what difference does it make *where* the money comes 11 from? Why should that make video games any less satisfactory as an amusement for children? In fact, having to pay for the entertainment, whatever the source of the money, and having its duration limited by one's financial resources changes the nature of the game, in a subtle way diminishing the satisfactions it offers. Money and time become intertwined, as they so often are in the adult world and as, in the past, they almost never were in the child's world. For the child playing marbles, meanwhile, time has a far more carefree quality, bounded only by the requirements to be home by suppertime or by dark.

But the video-game-playing child has an additional burden 12 — a burden of choice, of knowing that the money used for playing Pac-Man could have been saved for Christmas, could have been used to buy something tangible, perhaps something "worthwhile," as his parents might say, rather than being "wasted" on video games. There is a certain sense of adultness that spending money imparts, a feeling of being a consumer, which distinguishes a game with a price from its counterparts among the traditional childhood games children once played at no cost.

There are other differences as well. Unlike child-initiated 13 and child-organized games such as marbles, video games are adult-created mechanisms not entirely within the child's control, and thus less likely to impart a sense of mastery and fulfillment: The coin may get jammed, the machine may go haywire, the little blobs may stop eating the funny little dots. Then the child must go to the storekeeper to complain, to get his money back. He may be "ripped off" and simply lose his quarter, much as his parents are when they buy a faulty appliance. This possibility of disaster gives the child's play a certain weight that marbles never imposed on its light-hearted players.

Even if a child has a video game at home requiring no coin 14 outlay, the play it provides is less than optimal. The noise level of the machine is high — too high, usually, for the child to conduct a conversation easily with another child. And yet, according to its enthusiasts, this very noisiness is a part of the game's attraction. The loud whizzes, crashes, and whirrs of the video-game machine "blow the mind" and create an excitement that is quite apart from the excitement generated simply by trying to win a game. A traditional childhood game such as marbles, on the other hand, has little built-in stimulation; the excitement of playing is generated entirely by the players' own actions. And while the pace of a game of marbles is close to the child's natural physiological rhythms, the frenzied activities of video games serve to "rev up" the child in an artificial way, almost in the way a stimulant or an amphetamine might. Meanwhile the perceptual impact of a video game is similar to that of watching television — the action, after all, takes place on a television screen — causing the eye to defocus slightly and creating a certain alteration in the child's natural state of consciousness.

Parents' instinctive reaction to their children's involvement 15
with video games provides another clue to the difference between this contemporary form of play and the more traditional pastimes such as marbles. While parents, indeed most adults, derive open pleasure from watching children at play, most parents today are not delighted to watch their kids flicking away at the Pac-Man machine. This does not seem to them to be real play. As a mother of two school-age children anxiously explains, "We used to do real childhood sorts of things when I was a kid. We'd build forts and put on crazy plays and make up new languages, and just generally we *played*. But today my kids don't play that way at all. They like video games and of course they still go in for sports outdoors. They go roller skating and ice skating and skiing and all. But they don't seem to really *play*."

Some of this feeling may represent a certain nostalgia for the 16
past and the old generation's resistance to the different ways of the new. But it is more likely that most adults have an instinctive understanding of the importance of play in their own childhood. This feeling stokes their fears that their children are being deprived of something irreplaceable when they flip the levers on

the video machines to manipulate the electronic images rather than flick their fingers to send a marble shooting towards another marble.

Play Deprivation

In addition to television's influence, some parents and teachers ascribe children's diminished drive to play to recent changes in the school curriculum, especially in the early grades.   17

"Kindergarten, traditionally a playful port of entry into formal school, is becoming more academic, with children being taught specific skills, taking tests, and occasionally even having homework," begins a report on new directions in early childhood education. Since 1970, according to the United States census, the proportion of three- and four-year-olds enrolled in school has risen dramatically, from 20.5 percent to 36.7 percent in 1980, and these nursery schools have largely joined the push towards academic acceleration in the early grades. Moreover, middle-class nursery schools in recent years have introduced substantial doses of academic material into their daily programs, often using those particular devices originally intended to help culturally deprived preschoolers in compensatory programs such as Headstart to catch up with their middle-class peers. Indeed, some of the increased focus on academic skills in nursery schools and kindergartens is related to the widespread popularity among young children and their parents of *Sesame Street*, a program originally intended to help deprived children attain academic skills, but universally watched by middle-class toddlers as well.   18

Parents of the *Sesame Street* generation often demand a "serious," skill-centered program for their preschoolers in school, afraid that the old-fashioned, play-centered curriculum will bore their alphabet-spouting, number-chanting four- and five-year-olds. A few parents, especially those whose children have not attended television classes or nursery school, complain of the high-powered pace of kindergarten these days. A father whose five-year-old daughter attends a public kindergarten declares: "There's a lot more pressure put on little kids these days than when we were kids, that's for sure. My daughter never went to   19 nursery school and never watched *Sesame*, and she had a lot of trouble when she entered kindergarten this fall. By October, just a month and a half into the program, she was already flunking. The teacher told us our daughter couldn't keep up with the other kids. And believe me, she's a bright kid! All the other kids were getting gold stars and smiley faces for their work, and every day Emily would come home in tears because she didn't get a gold star. Remember when we were in kindergarten? We were *children* then. We were allowed just to play!"

A kindergarten teacher confirms the trend towards early academic pressure. "We're expected by the dictates of the school system to push a lot of curriculum," she explains. "Kids in our kindergarten can't sit around playing with blocks any more. We've just managed to squeeze in one hour of free play a week, on Fridays."   20

The diminished emphasis on fantasy and play and imaginative activities in early childhood education and the increased focus on early academic-skill acquisition have helped to change childhood from a play-centered time of life to one more closely resembling the style of adulthood: purposeful, success-centered, competitive. The likelihood is that these preschool "workers" will not metamorphose back into players when they move on to grade school. This decline in play is surely one of the reasons why so many teachers today comment that their third- or fourth-graders act like tired businessmen instead of like children.   21

What might be the consequences of this change in children's play? Children's propensity to engage in that extraordinary series of behaviors characterized as "play" is perhaps the single great dividing line between childhood and adulthood, and has probably been so throughout history. The make-believe games anthropologists have recorded of children in primitive societies around the world attest to the universality of play and to the uniqueness of this activity to the immature members of each society. But in those societies, and probably in Western society before the middle or late eighteenth century, there was always a certain similarity between children's play and adult work. The child's imaginative play took the form of imitation of various as-   22 pects of adult life, culminating in the gradual transformation of the child's play from make-believe work to *real* work. At this point, in primitive societies or in our own society of the past, the child took her or his place in the adult work world and the distinctions between adulthood and childhood virtually vanished. But in today's technologically advanced society there is no place for the child in the adult work world. There are not enough jobs, even of the most menial kind, to go around for adults, much less for children. The child must continue to be dependent on adults for many years while gaining the knowledge and skills necessary to become a working member of society.

This is not a new situation for children. For centuries children have endured a prolonged period of dependence long after the helplessness of early childhood is over. But until recent years children remained childlike and playful far longer than they do today. Kept isolated from the adult world as a result of deliberate secrecy and protectiveness, they continued to find pleasure in socially sanctioned childish activities until the imperatives of adolescence led them to strike out for independence and self-sufficiency.   23

Today, however, with children's inclusion in the adult world both through the instrument of television and as a result of a deliberately preparatory, integrative style of child rearing, the old forms of play no longer seem to provide children with enough excitement and stimulation. What then are these so-called children to do for fulfillment if their desire to play has been vitiated and yet their entry into the working world of adulthood must be delayed for many years? The answer is precisely to get involved in those areas that cause contemporary parents so much distress: addictive television viewing during the school years followed, in adolescence or even before, by a search for similar oblivion via alcohol and drugs; exploration of the world of sensuality and sexuality before achieving the emotional maturity necessary for altruistic relationships.   24

Psychiatrists have observed among children in recent years a marked increase in the occurrence of depression, a state long considered antithetical to the nature of childhood. Perhaps this phenomenon is at least somewhat connected with the current   25 sense of uselessness and alienation that children feel, a sense that play may once upon a time have kept in abeyance.

QUESTIONS ON MEANING

1. How many causes does the author find for the decline of play among children today? What are they?
2. What similarities exist, according to Winn, between playing marbles and playing video games? Sum up the important differences between the two activities.
3. Does Winn's essay seem to you to reveal any PURPOSE other than to inform? Give EVIDENCE for your answer.
4. For discussion: Are there factors in addition to those Winn mentions that divert today's children from spontaneous play? If so, what are they?

QUESTIONS ON WRITING STRATEGY

1. Winn opens her essay with a startling GENERALIZATION. What is the strongest evidence she includes in support of it? What is the weakest?
2. At the start of paragraph 6, Winn suggests and then dismisses one explanation for the decline of play. What reason does she give for dismissing this second explanation? Does its inclusion strengthen or weaken her THESIS?
3. What does the essay gain from direct quotation?
4. How might Winn's essay be different had she written it for an AUDIENCE of child development experts rather than for an audience of general readers?
5. Would you call Winn's writing OBJECTIVE or SUBJECTIVE?

QUESTIONS ON LANGUAGE

1. Consult your dictionary if you need to look up definitions for the following words: topography (paragraph 1); autonomy (2); discrepancy (5); societal, demeanor (6); precocious (7); burgeoning, puberty (8); augment (10); tangible (12); optimal, perceptual (14); nostalgia (16); compensatory (18); metamorphose (21); propensity, culminating (22); imperatives (23); vitiated, altruistic (24); antithetical, abeyance (25).

2. What seems to be the author's rationale for enclosing certain words and short phrases in quotation marks?
3. How well is Winn's DICTION tailored to the audience she aims to reach? To what extent, for instance, does she use occupational JARGON? Unfamiliar words?

SUGGESTIONS FOR WRITING

1. Write a paragraph in which you describe and evaluate the view of the world you think television imparts to children.
2. Write from the POINT OF VIEW of a child today, complaining either that you are being hurried to grow up, or that you are being held back from maturity.

Marie Winn on Writing

For Marie Winn, the most enjoyable part of writing is making improvements. "I love spending an hour or two with a dictionary and a thesaurus looking for a more nearly perfect word," she declares in an account of her working habits written for *The Bedford Reader*. "Or taking my pen and ruthlessly pruning all the unnecessary adjectives (a practice I can wholeheartedly recommend to you), or fooling around with the rhythm of a sentence or a paragraph by changing a verb into a participle, or making any number of little changes that a magazine editor I work with ruefully calls 'mouse milking.'"

But the proportion of time Winn spends at this "delightful occupation" is small. "For me, the pleasure and pain of writing go on simultaneously. Once I have finally forced myself to bite the bullet and get to work, as soon as the flow of writing stops — after a few sentences or paragraphs or, if I am extraordinarily lucky, a few pages — then, as a little reward for having actually written something and also as a procrastinating measure to delay the painful necessity of having to write something again, I play with the words and sentences on the page.

"That's the trouble, of course: There have to be words and sentences on the page before I can enjoy the pleasure of playing with them. Somehow I have to transform the vague and confused tangle of ideas in my head into an orderly and logical sequence on a blank piece of paper. That's the real hell of writing: the inescapable need to think clearly. . . . You have to figure it out, make it all hang together, consider the implications, the alternatives, eliminate the contradictions, the extraneous thoughts, the illogical conclusions. I *hate* that part of writing and I have a feeling you know perfectly well what I'm talking about.

"There's another phase of each writing project, however, that falls somewhere between the pain of actual writing and the pure pleasure of polishing: the time spent gathering together the material about which to write. For the chapter included here, 'The End of Play,' the research phase lasted almost a year. During that time I interviewed parents in three geographically diverse communities about the kinds of play they remembered from their own childhoods and how these resembled or differed from their children's play patterns today. I talked to teachers about their perceptions of change in children's play and about changes in school curricula that have affected play. I observed and talked to many children at their homes, at school, at playgrounds and video arcades, among other places. And I spent many hours in the library, reading books and scholarly papers about children's play in other cultures and at other historical times. All this may sound quite enjoyable — talking to people, reading books — and indeed it would be, if it weren't for the fact that one has to write about it afterwards. When interviewing parents or teachers or children, I cannot sit back and simply enjoy a conversation, listening and reacting, going back and forth the way one usually does. Though it is often difficult, I must suppress my own thoughts and reactions during an interview and focus entirely on what the other person is saying, and, especially, what she or he is *not* saying. I have to devise strategies at getting those crucial, unsaid thoughts out into the open, even when they are obviously painful or embarrassing. Since this goes against so many deeply ingrained social instincts, it takes away much of the enjoyment I might normally feel when talking to another person. But here is the most distressing thing of all: As I gather material for an article or book, as I interview people, as I read books or papers on my subject, I have to concentrate on what I am reading or hearing or seeing with all the intensity I can muster. In fact, I have to *think*."

FOR DISCUSSION

1. For Winn, what is the most difficult part of the writing process? What part does she most enjoy?
2. What does the author see as the role that thinking plays in writing?
3. What differences does Winn find between interviewing people and just conversing with them?

"The remarkable thing about Stephen Jay Gould," said John Tierney in a *Rolling Stone* interview, "is that he is a scientist who speaks intelligible English." A paleontologist and collector of snails, STEPHEN JAY GOULD was born in New York City in 1941, went to Antioch College, and took a doctorate from Columbia University. Since the age of twenty-five, Gould has taught biology, geology, and the history of science at Harvard, where his courses are among the most popular. Although he has written for specialists (*Ontogeny and Phylogeny*, 1977), Gould is best known for *The Mismeasure of Man* (1981), a book that deflates attempts to prove the biological superiority of white males, and for more than a hundred essays that explore science in prose a layperson can enjoy. These have proliferated because Gould writes a monthly column (called "This View of Life") for *Natural History* magazine. His essays have been collected in *Ever Since Darwin* (1977), *The Panda's Thumb* (1980), *Hens' Teeth and Horses' Toes* (1983), *The Flamingo's Smile* (1985), and *An Urchin in the Storm* (1987). *Time's Arrow, Time's Cycle* (1987) is a history of geologists' discovery of the age of the earth. In 1981, Gould received a National Book Award, an award from the National Book Critics Circle, and $200,000 (popularly called a "genius grant") from the MacArthur Foundation, which subsidizes the work of original artists and thinkers. Gould makes his home in Cambridge, Massachusetts, with his wife Deborah Lee, a teaching artist. He recently won a battle with cancer — because, he says, "I simply had to see my children grow up [and] it would be perverse to come this close to the millennium and then blow it."

Sex, Drugs, Disasters, and the Extinction of Dinosaurs

In this essay, Stephen Jay Gould tackles one of the greatest mysteries in the evolution of life on this planet: the extinction of dinosaurs. Working backward from this concrete "effect" (the fact that dinosaurs are extinct), Gould employs both scholarship and wit to analyze several possible causes of this event. "Sex, Drugs, Disasters, and the Extinction of Dinosaurs" originally appeared in *Discover* magazine in March 1984, and it is included in Gould's fourth collection of essays, *The Flamingo's Smile: Reflections in Natural History* (New York: Norton, 1985).

Science, in its most fundamental definition, is a fruitful   1
mode of inquiry, not a list of enticing conclusions. The conclusions are the consequence, not the essence.

My greatest unhappiness with most popular presentations of   2
science concerns their failure to separate fascinating claims from the methods that scientists use to establish the facts of nature. Journalists, and the public, thrive on controversial and stunning statements. But science is, basically, a way of knowing — in P. B. Medawar's apt words, "the art of the soluble." If the growing corps of popular science writers would focus on *how* scientists develop and defend those fascinating claims, they would make their greatest possible contribution to public understanding.

Consider three ideas, proposed in perfect seriousness to explain that greatest of all titillating puzzles — the extinction of dinosaurs. Since these three notions invoke the primally fascinating themes of our culture — sex, drugs, and violence — they surely reside in the category of fascinating claims. I want to show why two of them rank as silly speculation, while the other represents science at its grandest and most useful.

Science works with testable proposals. If, after much compilation and scrutiny of data, new information continues to affirm a hypothesis, we may accept it provisionally and gain confidence as further evidence mounts. We can never be completely sure that a hypothesis is right, though we may be able to show with confidence that it is wrong. The best scientific hypotheses are also generous and expansive: They suggest extensions and implications that enlighten related, and even far distant, subjects. Simply consider how the idea of evolution has influenced virtually every intellectual field.

Useless speculation, on the other hand, is restrictive. It gen-   5
erates no testable hypothesis, and offers no way to obtain poten-
tially refuting evidence. Please note that I am not speaking of
truth or falsity. The speculation may well be true; still, if it provides, in principle, no material for affirmation or rejection, we
can make nothing of it. It must simply stand forever as an
intriguing idea. Useless speculation turns in on itself and leads
nowhere; good science, containing both seeds for its potential
refutation and implications for more and different testable
knowledge, reaches out. But, enough preaching. Let's move on
to dinosaurs, and the three proposals for their extinction.

1. <u>Sex</u>. Testes function only in a narrow range of temperature
   (those of mammals hang externally in a scrotal sac because
   internal body temperatures are too high for their proper
   function). A worldwide rise in temperature at the close of the
   Cretaceous period caused the testes of dinosaurs to stop functioning and led to their extinction by sterilization of males.
2. <u>Drugs</u>. Angiosperms (flowering plants) first evolved toward
   the end of the dinosaurs' reign. Many of these plants contain
   psychoactive agents, avoided by mammals today as a result of
   their bitter taste. Dinosaurs had neither means to taste the
   bitterness nor livers effective enough to detoxify the substances. They died of massive overdoses.
3. <u>Disasters</u>. A large comet or asteroid struck the earth some 65
   million years ago, lofting a cloud of dust into the sky and
   blocking sunlight, thereby suppressing photosynthesis and so
   drastically lowering world temperatures that dinosaurs and
   hosts of other creatures became extinct.

Before analyzing these three tantalizing statements, we must establish a basic ground rule often violated in proposals for the dinosaurs' demise. *There is no separate problem of the extinction of di-*
nosaurs. Too often we divorce specific events from their wider
contexts and systems of cause and effect. The fundamental fact
of dinosaur extinction is its synchrony with the demise of so
many other groups across a wide range of habitats, from terrestrial to marine.

The history of life has been punctuated by brief episodes of   6
mass extinction. A recent analysis by University of Chicago pa-
leontologists Jack Sepkoski and Dave Raup, based on the best
and most exhaustive tabulation of data ever assembled, shows
clearly that five episodes of mass dying stand well above the
"background" extinctions of normal times (when we consider all
mass extinctions, large and small, they seem to fall in a regular
26-million-year cycle). The Cretaceous debacle, occurring 65
million years ago and separating the Mesozoic and Cenozoic
eras of our geological time scale, ranks prominently among the
five. Nearly all the marine plankton (single-celled floating creatures) died with geological suddenness; among marine inverte-
brates, nearly 15 percent of all families perished, including many
previously dominant groups, especially the ammonites (relatives
of squids in coiled shells). On land, the dinosaurs disappeared
after more than 100 million years of unchallenged domination.

In this context, speculations limited to dinosaurs alone ig-   7
nore the larger phenomenon. We need a coordinated explanation for a system of events that includes the extinction of dinosaurs as one component. Thus it makes little sense, though it
may fuel our desire to view mammals as inevitable inheritors of
the earth, to guess that dinosaurs died because small mammals
ate their eggs (a perennial favorite among untestable speculations). It seems most unlikely that some disaster peculiar to dinosaurs befell these massive beasts — and that the debacle happened to strike just when one of history's five great dyings had
enveloped the earth for completely different reasons.

The testicular theory, an old favorite from the 1940s, had its   8
root in an interesting and thoroughly respectable study of temperature tolerances in the American alligator, published in the
staid *Bulletin of the American Museum of Natural History* in 1946
by three experts on living and fossil reptiles — E. H. Colbert,
my own first teacher in paleontology; R. B. Cowles; and C. M.
Bogert.

The first sentence of their summary reveals a purpose be-   9
yond alligators: "This report describes an attempt to infer the reactions of extinct reptiles, especially the dinosaurs, to high temperatures as based upon reactions observed in the modern

alligator." They studied, by rectal thermometry, the body temperatures of alligators under changing conditions of heating and cooling. (Well, let's face it, you wouldn't want to try sticking a thermometer under a 'gator's tongue.) The predictions under test go way back to an old theory first stated by Galileo in the 1630s — the unequal scaling of surfaces and volumes. As an animal, or any object, grows (provided its shape doesn't change), surface areas must increase more slowly than volumes — since surfaces get larger as length squared, while volumes increase much more rapidly, as length cubed. Therefore, small animals have high ratios of surface to volume, while large animals cover themselves with relatively little surface.

Among cold-blooded animals lacking any physiological   10 mechanism for keeping their temperatures constant, small creatures have a hell of a time keeping warm — because they lose so much heat through their relatively large surfaces. On the other hand, large animals, with their relatively small surfaces, may lose heat so slowly that, once warm, they may maintain effectively constant temperatures against ordinary fluctuations of climate. (In fact, the resolution of the "hot-blooded dinosaur" controversy that burned so brightly a few years back may simply be that, while large dinosaurs possessed no physiological mechanism for constant temperature, and were not therefore warm-blooded in the technical sense, their large size and relatively small surface area kept them warm.)

Colbert, Cowles, and Bogert compared the warming rates of   11 small and large alligators. As predicted, the small fellows heated up (and cooled down) more quickly. When exposed to a warm sun, a tiny 50-gram (1.76-ounce) alligator heated up one degree Celsius every minute and a half, while a large alligator, 260 times bigger at 13,000 grams (28.7 pounds), took seven and a half minutes to gain a degree. Extrapolating up to an adult 10–ton dinosaur, they concluded that a one-degree rise in body temperature would take eighty-six hours. If large animals absorb heat so slowly (through their relatively small surfaces), they will also be unable to shed any excess heat gained when temperatures rise above a favorable level.

The authors then guessed that large dinosaurs lived at or   12 near their optimum temperatures; Cowles suggested that a rise in global temperatures just before the Cretaceous extinction caused the dinosaurs to heat up beyond their optimal tolerance — and, being so large, they couldn't shed the unwanted heat. (In a most unusual statement within a scientific paper, Colbert and Bogert then explicitly disavowed this speculative extension of their empirical work on alligators.) Cowles conceded that this excess heat probably wasn't enough to kill or even to enervate the great beasts, but since testes often function only within a narrow range of temperature, he proposed that this global rise might have sterilized all the males, causing extinction by natural contraception.

The overdose theory has recently been supported by UCLA   13
psychiatrist Ronald K. Siegel. Siegel has gathered, he claims, more than 2,000 records of animals who, when given access, administer various drugs to themselves — from a mere swig of alcohol to massive doses of the big H. Elephants will swill the equivalent of twenty beers at a time, but do not like alcohol in concentrations greater than 7 percent. In a silly bit of anthropocentric speculation, Siegel states that "elephants drink, perhaps, to forget . . . the anxiety produced by shrinking rangeland and the competition for food."

Since fertile imaginations can apply almost any hot idea to   14
the extinction of dinosaurs, Siegel found a way. Flowering plants did not evolve until late in the dinosaurs' reign. These plants also produced an array of aromatic, amino-acid-based alkaloids — the major group of psychoactive agents. Most mammals are "smart" enough to avoid these potential poisons. The alkaloids simply don't taste good (they are bitter); in any case, we mammals have livers happily supplied with the capacity to detoxify them. But, Siegel speculates, perhaps dinosaurs could neither taste the bitterness nor detoxify the substances once ingested. He recently told members of the American Psychological Association: "I'm not suggesting that all dinosaurs OD'd on plant drugs, but it certainly was a factor." He also argued that death by overdose may help explain why so many dinosaur fossils are found in contorted positions. (Do not go gentle into that good night.)

Extraterrestrial catastrophes have long pedigrees in the popular literature of extinction, but the subject exploded again in 1979, after a long lull, when the father-son, physicist-geologist team of Luis and Walter Alvarez proposed that an asteroid, some 10 km in diameter, struck the earth 65 million years ago (comets, rather than asteroids, have since gained favor. Good science is self-corrective).   15

The force of such a collision would be immense, greater by far than the megatonnage of all the world's nuclear weapons. In trying to reconstruct a scenario that would explain the simultaneous dying of dinosaurs on land and so many creatures in the sea, the Alvarezes proposed that a gigantic dust cloud, generated by particles blown aloft in the impact, would so darken the earth that photosynthesis would cease and temperatures drop precipitously. (Rage, rage against the dying of the light.) The single-celled photosynthetic oceanic plankton, with life cycles measured in weeks, would perish outright, but land plants might survive through the dormancy of their seeds (land plants were not much affected by the Cretaceous extinction, and any adequate theory must account for the curious pattern of differential survival). Dinosaurs would die by starvation and freezing; small, warm-blooded mammals, with more modest requirements for food and better regulation of body temperature, would squeak through. "Let the bastards freeze in the dark," as bumper stickers of our chauvinistic neighbors in sunbelt states proclaimed several years ago during the Northeast's winter oil crisis.   16

All three theories, testicular malfunction, psychoactive overdosing, and asteroidal zapping, grab our attention mightily. As pure phenomenology, they rank about equally high on any hit parade of primal fascination. Yet one represents expansive science, the others restrictive and untestable speculation. The proper criterion lies in evidence and methodology; we must probe behind the superficial fascination of particular claims.   17

How could we possibly decide whether the hypothesis of testicular frying is right or wrong? We would have to know things that the fossil record cannot provide. What temperatures were optimal for dinosaurs? Could they avoid the absorption of excess heat by staying in the shade, or in caves? At what tempera-   18 tures did their testicles cease to function? Were late Cretaceous climates ever warm enough to drive the internal temperatures of dinosaurs close to this ceiling? Testicles simply don't fossilize, and how could we infer their temperature tolerances even if they did? In short, Cowles's hypothesis is only an intriguing speculation leading nowhere. The most damning statement against it appeared right in the conclusion of Colbert, Cowles, and Bogert's paper, when they admitted: "It is difficult to advance any definite arguments against this hypothesis." My statement may seem paradoxical — isn't a hypothesis really good if you can't devise any arguments against it? Quite the contrary. It is simply untestable and unusable.

Siegel's overdosing has even less going for it. At least Cowles   19 extrapolated his conclusion from some good data on alligators. And he didn't completely violate the primary guideline of siting dinosaur extinction in the context of a general mass dying — for rise in temperature could be the root cause of a general catastrophe, zapping dinosaurs by testicular malfunction and different groups for other reasons. But Siegel's speculation cannot touch the extinction of ammonites or oceanic plankton (diatoms make their own food with good sweet sunlight; they don't OD on the chemicals of terrestrial plants). It is simply a gratuitous, attention-grabbing guess. It cannot be tested, for how can we know what dinosaurs tasted and what their livers could do? Livers don't fossilize any better than testicles.

The hypothesis doesn't even make any sense in its own con-   20 text. Angiosperms were in full flower ten million years before dinosaurs went the way of all flesh. Why did it take so long? As for the pains of a chemical death recorded in contortions of fossils, I regret to say (or rather I'm pleased to note for the dinosaurs' sake) that Siegel's knowledge of geology must be a bit deficient: Muscles contract after death and geological strata rise and fall with motions of the earth's crust after burial — more than enough reason to distort a fossil's pristine appearance.

The impact story, on the other hand, has a sound basis in   21 evidence. It can be tested, extended, refined and, if wrong, disproved. The Alvarezes did not just construct an arresting guess for public consumption. They proposed their hypothesis after laborious geochemical studies with Frank Asaro and Helen Michael had revealed a massive increase of iridium in rocks deposited right at the time of extinction. Iridium, a rare metal of the platinum group, is virtually absent from indigenous rocks of the earth's crust; most of our iridium arrives on extraterrestrial objects that strike the earth.

The Alvarez hypothesis bore immediate fruit. Based originally on evidence from two European localities, it led geochemists throughout the world to examine other sediments of the same age. They found abnormally high amounts of iridium everywhere — from continental rocks of the western United States to deep sea cores from the South Atlantic. 22

Cowles proposed his testicular hypothesis in the mid-1940s. Where has it gone since then? Absolutely nowhere, because scientists can do nothing with it. The hypothesis must stand as a curious appendage to a solid study of alligators. Siegel's overdose scenario will also win a few press notices and fade into oblivion. The Alvarezes' asteroid falls into a different category altogether, and much of the popular commentary has missed this essential distinction by focusing on the impact and its attendant results, and forgetting what really matters to a scientist — the iridium. If you talk just about asteroids, dust, and darkness, you tell stories no better and no more entertaining than fried testicles or terminal trips. It is the iridium — the source of testable evidence — that counts and forges the crucial distinction between speculation and science. 23

The proof, to twist a phrase, lies in the doing. Cowles's hypothesis has generated nothing in thirty-five years. Since its proposal in 1979, the Alvarez hypothesis has spawned hundreds of studies, a major conference, and attendant publications. Geologists are fired up. They are looking for iridium at all other extinction boundaries. Every week exposes a new wrinkle in the scientific press. Further evidence that the Cretaceous iridium represents extraterrestrial impact and not indigenous volcanism continues to accumulate. As I revise this essay in November 1984 (this paragraph will be out of date when [it] is published), new data include chemical "signatures" of other isotopes indicating unearthly provenance, glass spherules of a size and sort 24 produced by impact and not by volcanic eruptions, and high-pressure varieties of silica formed (so far as we know) only under the tremendous shock of impact.

My point is simply this: Whatever the eventual outcome (I   25
suspect it will be positive), the Alvarez hypothesis is exciting, fruitful science because it generates tests, provides us with things to do, and expands outward. We are having fun, battling back and forth, moving toward a resolution, and extending the hypothesis beyond its original scope.

As just one example of the unexpected, distant cross-fertil-   26
ization that good science engenders, the Alvarez hypothesis made a major contribution to a theme that has riveted public attention in the past few months — so-called nuclear winter. In a speech delivered in April 1982, Luis Alvarez calculated the energy that a ten-kilometer asteroid would release on impact. He compared such an explosion with a full nuclear exchange and implied that all-out atomic war might unleash similar consequences.

This theme of impact leading to massive dust clouds and   27
falling temperatures formed an important input to the decision of Carl Sagan and a group of colleagues to model the climatic consequences of nuclear holocaust. Full nuclear exchange would probably generate the same kind of dust cloud and darkening that may have wiped out the dinosaurs. Temperatures would drop precipitously and agriculture might become impossible. Avoidance of nuclear war is fundamentally an ethical and political imperative, but we must know the factual consequences to make firm judgments. I am heartened by a final link across disciplines and deep concerns — another criterion, by the way, of science at its best:[1] A recognition of the very phenomenon that made our evolution possible by exterminating the previously dominant dinosaurs and clearing a way for the evolution of large mammals, including us, might actually help to save us from joining those magnificent beasts in contorted poses among the strata of the earth.

[1]This quirky connection so tickles my fancy that I break my own strict rule about eliminating redundancies from [this essay]. . . . — Gould's note.

QUESTIONS ON MEANING

1. According to Gould, what constitutes a scientific hypothesis? What constitutes useless speculation? Where in the essay do you find his definitions of these terms?
2. State, in your own words, the THESIS of this essay.
3. What does Gould perceive to be the major flaws in the testicular malfunction and drug overdose theories about the extinction of dinosaurs? Cite his specific reasons for discrediting each theory.
4. What is the connection between nuclear holocaust and the extinction of dinosaurs? (See the essay's last paragraph.)

QUESTIONS ON WRITING STRATEGY

1. The rhetorical modes of example, comparison and contrast, process analysis, and analogy are all at work in this essay. Identify instances of each, and discuss the function each performs in the essay.
2. What is the TONE of the sentence in paragraph 14: "Since fertile imaginations can apply almost any hot idea to the extinction of dinosaurs, Siegel found a way"? What does the tone imply about the validity of Siegel's ideas?
3. How do you understand the phrases "hit parade of primal fascination" (paragraph 17) and "the hypothesis of testicular frying" (18)? Is the tone here somber, silly, whimsical, ironic, or what?
4. Paragraphs 14 and 16 both contain references to Dylan Thomas's poem, "Do Not Go Gentle into That Good Night." (The poem's title is used in paragraph 14; "Rage, rage against the dying of the light," one of the poem's refrains, appears in paragraph 16.) If you are not familiar with the poem, look it up. Is it necessary to know the poem to understand Gould's use of these lines? What is the effect of this ALLUSION?

QUESTIONS ON LANGUAGE

1. What do you take the sentence "There is no separate problem of the extinction of dinosaurs" (paragraph 5) to mean? Separate from what? According to Gould, then, what *is* the problem being discussed?

2. Be sure you can define the following words: enticing (paragraph 1); hypothesis (4); psychoactive, photosynthesis, synchrony (5); paleontology (8); extrapolating (11); empirical (12); gratuitous (19).

SUGGESTIONS FOR WRITING

1. Write a paragraph addressing either the causes or effects of a situation or circumstance in which you are directly involved. Possible situations might include working in the school cafeteria, taking a psychology class offered only on Wednesday evenings, or anything else that interests you. Make sure that you consider the remote cause as well as the immediate.

2. Read, if you haven't already, the essays by David Quammen and Lewis Thomas, both among the "growing corps of popular science writers" Gould mentions in his second paragraph. Consider whether either of these writers focuses on how scientists develop and defend their claims. If so, try to locate such instances. Choose one of these essays, and write a paragraph explaining how these instances work within the essay. Or, if you think either Quammen or Thomas does not focus on how scientists develop and defend their claims, write a paragraph addressing that issue. Why do you think the author chose a different focus? What is that essay's focus?

Stephen Jay Gould on Writing

Stephen Jay Gould sees himself as belonging to a long and respectable tradition of writers who communicate scientific ideas to a general audience. To popularize, he says, does not mean to trivialize, cheapen, or adulterate. "I follow one cardinal rule in writing these essays," he insists. "No compromises. I will make language accessible by defining or eliminating jargon; I will not simplify concepts. I can state all sorts of highfalutin, moral justifications for this approach (and I do believe in them), but the basic reason is simple and personal. I write these essays primarily to aid my own quest to learn and understand as much as possible about nature in the short time allotted."

In his own view, Gould is lucky: He is a writer carried along by a single, fascinating theme. "If my volumes work at all, they owe their reputation to coherence supplied by the common theme of evolutionary theory. I have a wonderful advantage among essayists because no other theme so beautifully encompasses both the particulars that fascinate and the generalities that instruct. . . . Each essay is both a single long argument and a welding together of particulars." (Prologue, *The Flamingo's Smile* [New York: Norton, 1985], pp. 13–14, 15, 16.)

FOR DISCUSSION

1. In Gould's view, what central theme informs his writing?
2. What differences would occur naturally between the work of a scientist writing for other scientists and Gould, who writes about science for a general AUDIENCE?
3. How does the author defend himself against the possible charge that, as a popularizer of science, he trivializes his subject?

· Carl Sagan ·

Known widely as an interpreter of science to common readers (and television viewers), CARL SAGAN is himself a noted astronomer. For his leading role in the *Mariner*, *Viking*, and *Voyager* expeditions to other planets, he has received medals from the National Aeronautics and Space Administration. His work was vital in establishing the surface temperatures of Venus and in understanding the seasonal changes on Mars, and he has been responsible for four messages addressed to intelligent extraterrestrials, carried into space by *Pioneer 10* and *11* and *Voyager 1* and *2*. Born in New York City in 1934, Sagan completed four degrees at the University of Chicago. He now directs the Laboratory for Planetary Studies and holds a professorship of astronomy and space sciences at Cornell. Active in the Union of Concerned Scientists, Sagan in 1983 co-authored a petition whose signers, forty leading scientists, called for an international treaty to ban all weapons from space. Among his books are several nonfiction best-sellers: *The Dragons of Eden* (1977), winner of the Pulitzer Prize for literature; *Broca's Brain: Reflections on the Romance of Science* (1979); and *Cosmos* (1980), based on Sagan's PBS television series of the same title, in which he appeared as narrator. Lately, Sagan has become a novelist: with *Contact* (1985), in which a radio astronomer deciphers a message from another world.

The Nuclear Winter

Sagan has written more than 400 articles for popular magazines and for professional journals. Of all of them, the following essay may be of most immediate concern. Citing scientific findings, it shows how a nuclear war might affect our earth and its people. Sagan first published the essay in the Sunday newspaper supplement *Parade* on October 30, 1983, perhaps in the hope of alerting and alarming that popular weekly's millions of readers. "The Nuclear Winter" happens to be a memorable study in cause and effect; but, more important, it states an urgent, even frightening thesis. This is one essay we urge you to read, reread, and remember.

Into the eternal darkness, into fire, into ice.
— Dante, *The Inferno*

Except for fools and madmen, everyone knows that nuclear 1
war would be an unprecedented human catastrophe. A more or
less typical strategic warhead has a yield of 2 megatons, the explosive equivalent of 2 million tons of TNT. But 2 million tons
of TNT is about the same as all the bombs exploded in World
War II — a single bomb with the explosive power of the entire
Second World War but compressed into a few seconds of time
and an area 30 or 40 miles across . . .

In a 2-megaton explosion over a fairly large city, buildings 2
would be vaporized, people reduced to atoms and shadows, out-
lying structures blown down like matchsticks and raging fires ig-
nited. And if the bomb were exploded on the ground, an enormous crater, like those that can be seen through a telescope on
the surface of the Moon, would be all that remained where midtown once had been. There are now more than 50,000 nuclear
weapons, more than 13,000 megatons of yield, deployed in the
arsenals of the United States and the Soviet Union — enough
to obliterate a million Hiroshimas.

But there are fewer than 3,000 cities on the Earth with popu- 3
lations of 100,000 or more. You cannot find anything like a million Hiroshimas to obliterate. Prime military and industrial targets that are far from cities are comparatively rare. Thus, there
are vastly more nuclear weapons than are needed for any plausible deterrence of a potential adversary.

Nobody knows, of course, how many megatons would be 4
exploded in a real nuclear war. There are some who think that a
nuclear war can be "contained," bottled up before it runs away
to involve many of the world's arsenals. But a number of detailed analyses, war games run by the U.S. Department of Defense and official Soviet pronouncements, all indicate that this
containment may be too much to hope for: Once the bombs begin exploding, communications failures, disorganization, fear,
the necessity of making in minutes decisions affecting the fates
of millions and the immense psychological burden of knowing
that your own loved ones may already have been destroyed are

likely to result in a nuclear paroxysm. Many investigations, including a number of studies for the U.S. government, envision the explosion of 5,000 to 10,000 megatons — the detonation of tens of thousands of nuclear weapons that now sit quietly, inconspicuously, in missile silos, submarines, and long-range bombers, faithful servants awaiting orders.

The World Health Organization, in a recent detailed study chaired by Sune K. Bergstrom (the 1982 Nobel laureate in physiology and medicine), concludes that 1.1 billion people would be killed outright in such a nuclear war, mainly in the United States, the Soviet Union, Europe, China, and Japan. An additional 1.1 billion people would suffer serious injuries and radiation sickness, for which medical help would be unavailable. It thus seems possible that more than 2 billion people — almost half of all the humans on Earth — would be destroyed in the immediate aftermath of a global thermonuclear war. This would represent by far the greatest disaster in the history of the human species and, with no other adverse effects, would probably be enough to reduce at least the Northern Hemisphere to a state of prolonged agony and barbarism. Unfortunately, the real situation would be much worse.

In technical studies of the consequences of nuclear weapons explosions, there has been a dangerous tendency to underestimate the results. This is partly due to a tradition of conservatism which generally works well in science but which is of more dubious applicability when the lives of billions of people are at stake. In the Bravo test of March 1, 1954, a 15-megaton thermonuclear bomb was exploded on Bikini Atoll. It had about double the yield expected, and there was an unanticipated last-minute shift in the wind direction. As a result, deadly radioactive fallout came down on Rongelap in the Marshall Islands, more than 200 kilometers away. Almost all the children on Rongelap subsequently developed thyroid nodules and lesions, and other long-term medical problems, due to the radioactive fallout.

Likewise, in 1973, it was discovered that high-yield airbursts will chemically burn the nitrogen in the upper air, converting it into oxides of nitrogen; these, in turn, combine with and destroy the protective ozone in the Earth's stratosphere. The surface of the Earth is shielded from deadly solar ultraviolet radiation by a layer of ozone so tenuous that, were it brought down to sea level, it would be only 3 millimeters thick. Partial destruction of this ozone layer can have serious consequences for the biology of the entire planet.

These discoveries, and others like them, were made by chance. They were largely unexpected. And now another consequence — by far the most dire — has been uncovered, again more or less by accident.

The U.S. Mariner 9 spacecraft, the first vehicle to orbit another planet, arrived at Mars in late 1971. The planet was enveloped in a global dust storm. As the fine particles slowly fell out, we were able to measure temperature changes in the atmosphere and on the surface. Soon it became clear what had happened:

The dust, lofted by high winds off the desert into the upper Martian atmosphere, had absorbed the incoming sunlight and prevented much of it from reaching the ground. Heated by the sunlight, the dust warmed the adjacent air. But the surface, enveloped in partial darkness, became much chillier than usual. Months later, after the dust fell out of the atmosphere, the upper air cooled and the surface warmed, both returning to their normal conditions. We were able to calculate accurately, from how much dust there was in the atmosphere, how cool the Martian surface ought to have been.

Afterwards, I and my colleagues, James B. Pollack and Brian Toon of NASA's Ames Research Center, were eager to apply these insights to the Earth. In a volcanic explosion, dust aerosols are lofted into the high atmosphere. We calculated by how much the Earth's global temperature should decline after a major volcanic explosion and found that our results (generally a fraction of a degree) were in good accord with actual measurements. Joining forces with Richard Turco, who has studied the effects of nuclear weapons for many years, we then began to turn our attention to the climatic effects of nuclear war. [The scientific paper, "Global Atmospheric Consequences of Nuclear

War," is written by R. P. Turco, O. B. Toon, T. P. Ackerman, J. B. Pollack, and Carl Sagan. From the last names of the authors, this work is generally referred to as "TTAPS."]

We knew that nuclear explosions, particularly ground- 12
bursts, would lift an enormous quantity of fine soil particles into the atmosphere (more than 100,000 tons of fine dust for every megaton exploded in a surface burst). Our work was further spurred by Paul Crutzen of the Max Planck Institute for Chemistry in Mainz, West Germany, and by John Birks of the University of Colorado, who pointed out that huge quantities of smoke would be generated in the burning of cities and forests following a nuclear war.

Groundbursts — at hardened missile silos, for example — 13
generate fine dust. Airbursts — over cities and unhardened military installations — make fires and therefore smoke. The amount of dust and soot generated depends on the conduct of the war, the yields of the weapons employed and the ratio of groundbursts to airbursts. So we ran computer models for several dozen different nuclear war scenarios. Our baseline case, as in many other studies, was a 5,000-megaton war with only a modest fraction of the yield (20 percent) expended on urban or industrial targets. Our job, for each case, was to follow the dust and smoke generated, see how much sunlight was absorbed and by how much the temperatures changed, figure out how the particles spread in longitude and latitude, and calculate how long before it all fell out of the air back onto the surface. Since the radioactivity would be attached to these same fine particles, our calculations also revealed the extent and timing of the subsequent radioactive fallout.

Some of what I am about to describe is horrifying. I know, 14
because it horrifies me. There is a tendency — psychiatrists call it "denial" — to put it out of our minds, not to think about it. But if we are to deal intelligently, wisely, with the nuclear arms race, then we must steel ourselves to contemplate the horrors of nuclear war.

The results of our calculations astonished us. In the baseline 15
case, the amount of sunlight at the ground was reduced to a few percent of normal — much darker, in daylight, than in a heavy

overcast and too dark for plants to make a living from photosynthesis. At least in the Northern Hemisphere, where the great preponderance of strategic targets lies, an unbroken and deadly gloom would persist for weeks.

Even more unexpected were the temperatures calculated. In the baseline case, land temperatures, except for narrow strips of coastline, dropped to minus 25° Celsius (minus 13° Fahrenheit) and stayed below freezing for months — even for a summer war. (Because the atmospheric structure becomes much more stable as the upper atmosphere is heated and the lower air is cooled, we may have severely *under*estimated how long the cold and the dark would last.) The oceans, a significant heat reservoir, would not freeze, however, and a major ice age would probably not be triggered. But because the temperatures would drop so catastrophically, virtually all crops and farm animals, at least in the Northern Hemisphere, would be destroyed, as would most varieties of uncultivated or undomesticated food supplies. Most of the human survivors would starve.

In addition, the amount of radioactive fallout is much more than expected. Many previous calculations simply ignored the intermediate time-scale fallout. That is, calculations were made for the prompt fallout — the plumes of radioactive debris blown downwind from each target — and for the long-term fallout, the fine radioactive particles lofted into the stratosphere that would descend about a year later, after most of the radioactivity had decayed. However, the radioactivity carried into the upper atmosphere (but not as high as the stratosphere) seems to have been largely forgotten. We found for the baseline case that roughly 30 percent of the land at northern midlatitudes could receive a radioactive dose greater than 250 rads, and that about 50 percent of northern midlatitudes could receive a dose greater than 100 rads. A 100-rad dose is the equivalent of about 1,000 medical X-rays. A 400-rad dose will, more likely than not, kill you.

The cold, the dark, and the intense radioactivity, together lasting for months, represent a severe assault on our civilization and our species. Civil and sanitary services would be wiped out. Medical facilities, drugs, the most rudimentary means for relieving the vast human suffering, would be unavailable. Any but the most elaborate shelters would be useless, quite apart from the question of what good it might be to emerge a few months later. Synthetics burned in the destruction of the cities would produce a wide variety of toxic gases, including carbon monoxide, cyanides, dioxins, and furans. After the dust and soot settled out, the solar ultraviolet flux would be much larger than its present value. Immunity to disease would decline. Epidemics and pandemics would be rampant, especially after the billion or so unburied bodies began to thaw. Moreover, the combined influence of these severe and simultaneous stresses on life are likely to produce even more adverse consequences — biologists call them synergisms — that we are not yet wise enough to foresee.

So far, we have talked only of the Northern Hemisphere.   19
But it now seems — unlike the case of a single nuclear weapons test — that in a real nuclear war, the heating of the vast quantities of atmospheric dust and soot in northern midlatitudes will transport these fine particles toward and across the Equator. We see just this happening in Martian dust storms. The Southern Hemisphere would experience effects that, while less severe than in the Northern Hemisphere, are nevertheless extremely ominous. The illusion with which some people in the Northern Hemisphere reassure themselves — catching an Air New Zealand flight in a time of serious international crisis, or the like — is now much less tenable, even on the narrow issue of personal survival for those with the price of a ticket.

But what if nuclear wars *can* be contained, and much less   20
than 5,000 megatons is detonated? Perhaps the greatest surprise in our work was that even small nuclear wars can have devastating climatic effects. We considered a war in which a mere 100 megatons were exploded, less than one percent of the world arsenals, and only in low-yield airbursts over cities. This scenario, we found, would ignite thousands of fires, and the smoke from these fires alone would be enough to generate an epoch of cold and dark almost as severe as in the 5,000-megaton case. The threshold for what Richard Turco has called the Nuclear Winter is very low.

Could we have overlooked some important effect? The car- 21
rying of dust and soot from the Northern to the Southern Hemisphere (as well as more local atmospheric circulation) will certainly thin the clouds out over the Northern Hemisphere. But,
in many cases, this thinning would be insufficient to render the
climatic consequences tolerable — and every time it got better in the Northern Hemisphere, it would get worse in the
Southern.

Our results have been carefully scrutinized by more than 22
100 scientists in the United States, Europe, and the Soviet Union. There are still arguments on points of detail. But the overall
conclusion seems to be agreed upon: There are severe and previously unanticipated global consequences of nuclear war — sub-
freezing temperatures in a twilit radioactive gloom lasting for
months or longer.

Scientists initially underestimated the effects of fallout, were 23
amazed that nuclear explosions in space disabled distant satel-
lites, had no idea that the fireballs from high-yield thermonuclear explosions could deplete the ozone layer, and missed altogether the possible climatic effects of nuclear dust and smoke.
What else have we overlooked?

Nuclear war is a problem that can be treated only theoreti- 24
cally. It is not amenable to experimentation. Conceivably, we
have left something important out of our analysis, and the effects are more modest than we calculate. On the other hand, it
is also possible — and, from previous experience, even likely —
that there are further adverse effects that no one has yet been
wise enough to recognize. With billions of lives at stake, where
does conservatism lie — in assuming that the results will be better than we calculate, or worse?

Many biologists, considering the nuclear winter that these 25
calculations describe, believe they carry somber implications for
life on Earth. Many species of plants and animals would become
extinct. Vast numbers of surviving humans would starve to
death. The delicate ecological relations that bind together organisms on Earth in a fabric of mutual dependency would be torn,

perhaps irreparably. There is little question that our global civilization would be destroyed. The human population would be reduced to prehistoric levels, or less. Life for any survivors would be extremely hard. And there seems to be a real possibility of the extinction of the human species.

It is now almost forty years since the invention of nuclear 26 weapons. We have not yet experienced a global thermonuclear war — although on more than one occasion we have come tremulously close. I do not think our luck can hold forever. Men and machines are fallible, as recent events remind us. Fools and madmen do exist, and sometimes rise to power. Concentrating always on the near future, we have ignored the long-term consequences of our actions. We have placed our civilization and our species in jeopardy.

Fortunately, it is not yet too late. We can safeguard the 27 planetary civilization and the human family if we so choose. There is no more important or more urgent issue.

QUESTIONS ON MEANING

1. Evaluate the reasons Sagan gives for his skepticism about the possibility of "contained nuclear war."
2. "Nuclear war is a problem that can be treated only theoretically" (paragraph 24). To what extent does this fact affect the author's credibility?
3. According to the author, what is the chief effect of a nuclear airburst?
4. What similarities exist between the effects of a volcanic eruption and those of a nuclear groundburst? What is the most important difference between the two?
5. From what sources does Sagan draw EVIDENCE for his conviction that a "nuclear winter" would follow a nuclear war? What difference would it make to the climate if the conflict were a "contained nuclear war"?
6. Where in the essay do you find support for the idea that Sagan has a PURPOSE other than merely to frighten his readers?

QUESTIONS ON WRITING STRATEGY

1. How does Sagan's capsule history of the Bravo test help support his essay's central THESIS?
2. In paragraphs 9 and 10, Sagan details the results of a dust storm on Mars. What connection does this material have with the main body of the essay? Does its inclusion impair the essay's UNITY?
3. Where in his essay does Sagan make effective use of RHETORICAL QUESTIONS?
4. What sentences or passages effectively serve as TRANSITIONS?
5. What constraints or limitations would an AUDIENCE of *Parade* magazine readers have placed on Sagan? How well has he triumphed over these limitations?

QUESTIONS ON LANGUAGE

1. Be sure you understand, from context or with the aid of your dictionary, what the following words mean: unprecedented (paragraph 1); obliterate (2); plausible, adversary (3); paroxysm (4); barbarism (5); applicability, nodules, lesions (6); oxides, tenuous (7); photosynthesis, preponderance (15); catastrophically (16); rudimentary, flux, pandemics, rampant (18); ominous, tenable (19); epoch (20); deplete (23); amenable (24); somber, irreparably (25); tremulously, fallible, jeopardy (26).
2. Where in his essay does the author lapse into scientific JARGON? Could he have substituted plainer words? To what extent does Sagan's use of jargon interfere with the average reader's understanding?
3. In paragraphs 2, 4, 7, and 25, Sagan uses vivid SIMILES, METAPHORS, and IMAGES. What do these FIGURES OF SPEECH contribute to the essay's impact?
4. Twice in his essay (in paragraphs 1 and 26) Sagan employs the phrase *fools and madmen*. In each case, how does the context affect the image conjured up by the phrase?

SUGGESTIONS FOR WRITING

1. In his final paragraph Sagan writes, "We can safeguard the planetary civilization and the human family if we so choose." Write a brief process analysis (see Chapter 5) in which you suggest how this might be accomplished.

2. Write an essay in which you detail some effects of the nuclear buildup other than possible all-out holocaust. How, for instance, has the buildup affected our national budget? What is its psychological effect on the populace? To what extent is the buildup a deterrent to war? What effect does government secrecy about nuclear warheads have on the American people? How does our stockpile of nuclear arms affect our image abroad? Be sure to back up your assertions with evidence.

Carl Sagan on Writing

Sometimes, the prolific Carl Sagan has written first for a nonprint medium, then rewritten his work for publication in book form. *The Dragons of Eden* grew from a lecture, six chapters in *Broca's Brain* were first written to be delivered as speeches, and the best-selling *Cosmos* was based on a television series. Turning television scripts into a book produced certain unexpected improvements, Sagan found. As he noted in his introduction to *Cosmos*, "There is much more freedom for the author in choosing the range and depth of topics for a chapter in a book than for the procrustean fifty-eight minutes, thirty seconds of a noncommercial television program. This book goes more deeply into many topics than does the television series."

As a writer, Sagan sees his audience to be the general public: anyone seeking a better understanding of science. Such writing, he believes, gives pleasure to both writer and reader: "If you make a person understand something, you make that person happy — you communicate joy." Accepting with pride the label of a "generalist," Sagan has written in many fields (besides brain research) in which he has no professional credentials. "But such insights as I've been able to achieve have been at the borders of the sciences, where different disciplines overlap. That's where the excitement is, and that's where I want to be." He distrusts the notion that scientists are "authorities." "Experts, yes, but not authorities. In science every idea must be challenged." (Interview by John F. Baker, *Publishers Weekly*, May 2, 1977, p. 8.)

FOR DISCUSSION

1. What does *procrustean* mean?
2. What subtle shade of difference does Sagan see between "authorities" and "experts"? What reason does he give for not wanting scientists to be regarded as authorities?

1. In a short essay, explain *either* the causes *or* the effects of a situation that concerns you. Narrow your topic enough to treat it in some detail, and provide more than a mere list of causes or effects. If seeking causes, you will have to decide carefully how far back to go in your search for remote causes. If stating effects, fill your essay with examples. Here are some topics to consider:

Friction between two roommates, or two friends

The pressure on students to get good grades

The fact that important sports events are often televised on holidays

Some quirk in your personality, or a friend's

The increasing need for more than one breadwinner per family

The temptation to do something dishonest to get ahead

The popularity of a particular television program, comic strip, rock group, or popular singer

The steady increase in college costs

The scarcity of people in training for employment as skilled workers: plumbers, tool and die makers, electricians, masons, carpenters, to name a few

A decision to enter the ministry or a religious order

The fact that cigarette advertising has been banned from television

The installation of seat belts in all new cars

The absence of a peacetime draft

The fact that more couples are choosing to have only one child, or none

The growing popularity of private elementary and high schools

The fact that most Americans can communicate in no language other than English

Being "born again"

The grim tone of recent novels for young people (such as Robert Cormier's *I Am the Cheese* and other best-selling juvenile fiction dealing with violence, madness, and terror)

The fact that women increasingly are training for jobs formerly regarded as men's only

The pressure on young people to conform to the standards of their peers

The emphasis on competitive sports in high school and college

Children's watching soft-core pornography on cable television

2. In *Blue Highways* (1982), an account of his rambles around America, William Least Heat Moon asserts why Americans, and not the British, settled the vast tract of northern land that lies between the Mississippi and the Rockies. He traces what he believes to be the major cause in this paragraph:

> Were it not for a web-footed rodent and a haberdashery fad in eighteenth-century Europe, Minnesota might be a Canadian province today. The beaver, almost as much as the horse, helped shape the course of early American history. Some *Mayflower* colonists paid their passage with beaver pelts; and a good fur could bring an Indian three steel knifes or a five-foot stack could bring a musket. But even more influential were the trappers and fur traders penetrating the great Northern wilderness between the Mississippi River and the Rocky Mountains, since it was their presence that helped hold the Near West against British expansion from the north; and it was their explorations that opened the heart of the nation to white settlement. These men, by making pelts the currency of the wilds, laid the base for a new economy that quickly overwhelmed the old. And all because European men of mode simply had to wear a beaver hat.

In a Least Heat Moon–like paragraph of your own, explain how a small cause produced a large effect. You might generate ideas by browsing in a history book — where you might find, for instance, that a cow belonging to Mrs. Patrick O'Leary is believed to have started the Great Chicago Fire of 1871 by kicking over a lighted lantern — or in a collection of *Ripley's Believe It or Not*. If some small event in your life has had large consequences, you might care to write instead from personal experience.

·9·

DEFINITION

Tracing a Boundary

THE METHOD

As a rule, when we hear the word *definition*, we immediately think of a dictionary. In that helpful storehouse — a writer's best friend — we find the literal and specific meaning (or meanings) of a word. The dictionary supplies this information concisely: in a sentence, in a phrase, or even in a synonym — a single word that means the same thing ("**narrative** [năr - ə - tǐv] *n.* **1:** story . . .").

To state such a definition is often an excellent way for the writer of an essay to begin. A short definition may clarify your subject to your reader, and perhaps help you to limit what you have to say. If, for instance, you are going to discuss a demolition derby, explaining such a spectacle to readers who may never have seen one, you might offer at the outset a short definition of *demolition derby*, your subject and your key term.

In constructing a short definition, the usual procedure is this: First, you state the general class to which your subject belongs; then you add any particular features that distinguish it. You could say: "A demolition derby is a contest" — that is its general class — "in which drivers ram old cars into one another until only one car is left running." Short definitions may also be useful at *any* moment in your essay. If you introduce a technical term, you'll want to define it briefly: "As the derby proceeds, there's many a broken manifold — that's the fitting that connects the openings of a car engine's exhaust."

In this chapter, however, we are mainly concerned with another sort of definition. It is *extended definition*, a kind of expository writing that relies on a variety of other methods. Suppose you wanted to write an essay to make clear what *poetry* means. You'd cite poems as examples. You might compare and contrast poetry with prose. You could analyze (or divide) poetry by specifying its elements: rhythm, metaphor and other figures of speech, imagery, and so on. You could distinguish it from prose by setting forth its effects on the reader. (Emily Dickinson, a poet herself, once stated the effect that reading a poem had on her: "I feel as if the top of my head were taken off.") In fact, extended definition, unlike other methods of writing discussed in this book, is perhaps less a method in itself than the application of a variety of methods to clarify a purpose. Like description, extended definition tries to *show* a reader its subject. It does so by establishing boundaries, for its writer tries to differentiate a subject from anything that might be confused with it. When Tom Wolfe, in his essay in this chapter, seeks to define a certain trend he has noticed in newspapers, books, and television, he describes exactly what he sees happening, so that we, too, will understand what he calls "the pornography of violence." In an extended definition, a writer studies the nature of a subject, carefully sums up its chief characteristics, and strives to answer the question, What is this? — or, What makes this what it is, not something else?

An extended definition can *define* (from the Latin, "to set bounds to") a word, or it can define a thing (a laser beam), a concept (male chauvinism), or a general phenomenon (the popularity of the demolition derby). Unlike a sentence definition, or any you would find in a standard dictionary, an extended definition takes room: at least a paragraph, perhaps an entire volume. The subject may be as large as the concepts of *superstition* and *vulgarity*.

Outside an English course, how is this method of writing used? In a newspaper feature, a sports writer defines what makes a "great team" great. In a journal article, a physician defines the nature of a previously unknown syndrome or disease. In a written opinion, a judge defines not only a word but a concept, *obscenity*. In a book review, a critic defines a newly prevalent kind of poem. In a letter to a younger brother or sister contemplating college, a student might define a *gut course* and how to recognize one.

Unlike a definition in a dictionary that sets forth the literal meaning of a word in an unimpassioned manner, some definitions imply biases. In defining *patron* to the earl of Chesterfield, who had tried to befriend him after ignoring his petitions for aid during his years of grinding poverty, Samuel Johnson wrote scornfully: "Is not a Patron, my Lord, one who looks with unconcern on a man struggling for life in the water, and, when he has reached the ground, encumbers him with help?" Irony, metaphor, and short definition have rarely been wielded with such crushing power. (*Encumbers*, by the way, is a wonderfully physical word in its context: It means "to burden with dead weight.") In his extended definition of *pornoviolence*, Tom Wolfe is biased, even jaundiced, in his view of American media. In having many methods of writing at their disposal, writers of extended definitions have ample freedom and wide latitude.

THE PROCESS

Writing an extended definition, you'll want to employ whatever method or methods of writing can best answer the question, What is the nature of this subject? You will probably find yourself making use of much that you have learned earlier from this book. If your subject is the phenomenon of the demolition derby, you might wish to begin by giving a short definition, like the definition of *demolition derby* on page 430. Feel no duty, however, to place a dictionaryish definition in the introduction of every essay you write. In explaining a demolition derby, you might decide that your readers already have at least a vague idea of the meaning of the term and that they need no short, formal definition of it. You might open your extended definition with the aid of *narration*. You could relate the events at a typical demolition derby, starting with the lineup of old, beat-up vehicles. Following the method of *description*, you might begin:

> One hundred worthless cars — everything from a 1940 Cadillac to a Dodge Dart to a recently wrecked Thunderbird, their glass removed, their radiators leaking — assemble on a racetrack or an open field. Their drivers, wearing crash helmets, buckle themselves into their seats, some pulling at beer cans to soften the blows to come.

You might proceed by *example*, listing demolition derbies you have known ("The great destruction of 184 vehicles took place at the Orleans County Fair in Barton, Vermont, in the summer of '81. . . ."). If you have enough examples, you might wish to *classify* them; or perhaps you might *divide* a demolition derby into its components — cars, drivers, judges, first-aid squad, and spectators — discussing each. You could *compare and contrast* a demolition derby with that amusement park ride known as Bumper Cars or Dodge-'ems, in which small cars with rubber bumpers bash one another head-on, but (unlike cars in the derby) harmlessly. A *process analysis* of a demolition derby might help your readers understand the nature of the spectacle: how in round after round cars are eliminated until one remains. You might ask: What causes the owners of old cars to want to smash them? Or perhaps: What causes people to watch the destruction? Or: What are the consequences? To answer such questions in an essay, you would apply the method of *cause and effect*. Perhaps an *analogy* might occur to you, one that would explain the demolition derby to someone unfamiliar with it: "It is like a birthday party in which every kid strives to have the last un-popped balloon."

Say you're preparing to write an extended definition of any-thing living or in motion (a basketball superstar, for instance, or a desert, or a comet). To discover points about your subject worth noticing, you may find it useful to ask yourself a series of questions. These questions may be applied both to individual subjects, such as the superstar, and to collective subjects — insti-tutions (like the American family, a typical savings bank, a uni-versity, the Church of Jesus Christ of Latter-Day Saints) and or-ganizations (IBM, the Mafia, a punk rock group, a Little League baseball team). To illustrate how the questions might work, at least in one instance, let's say you plan to write a paper defining a male chauvinist.[1]

1. *Is this subject unique, or are there others of its kind? If it re-sembles others, in what ways? How is it different?* As you can see, these last two questions invite you to compare and contrast. Ap-plied to the concept of male chauvinism, these questions might remind you that male chauvinists come in different varieties: middle-aged and college-aged, for instance, and you might care to compare and contrast the two kinds.

2. *In what different forms does it occur, while keeping its own identity?* Specific examples might occur to you: your Uncle George, who won't hire any "damned females" in his auto repair shop; some college-age male acquaintance who regards women as nothing but *Penthouse* centerfolds. Each form — Uncle George and the would-be stud — might rate a description.

3. *When and where do we find it? Under what circumstances and in what situations?* Well, where have you been lately? At any

---

[1]The six questions that follow are freely adapted from those first stated by Richard E. Young, Alton L. Becker, and Kenneth L. Pike, who have applied insights from psychology and linguistics to the writing process. Their proce-dure for generating ideas and discovering information is called *tagmemics*. To investigate subjects in greater depth, their own six questions may be used in nine possible combinations, as they explain in detail in *Rhetoric: Discovery and Change* (New York: Harcourt Brace Jovanovich, 1970).

parties where male chauvinism reared its ugly head? In any class-room discussions? Consider other areas of your experience: Did you meet any such male pigs while holding a part-time or summer job?

4. *What is it at the present moment?* Perhaps you might make the point that a few years ago male chauvinists used to be blatant tyrants and harsh critics of women. Today, wary of being recognized, they appear as ordinary citizens who now and then slip in a little tyranny, or make a nasty remark. You might care to draw examples from life.

5. *What does it do? What are its functions and activities?* Male chauvinists try to keep women in what they imagine to be women's place. These questions might even invite you to reply with a process analysis. You might show how some male chauvinist you know goes about implementing his views: how a personnel director you met, who determines pay scales, systematically eliminates women from better-paying jobs. How the *Penthouse* reader plots a seduction.

6. *How is it put together? What parts make it up? What holds these parts together?* You could apply analysis to the various beliefs and assumptions that, all together, make up a male chauvinist's attitude. This question might work well in writing about some organization: the personnel director's company, for instance, with its unfair hiring policies.

Not all these questions will fit every subject under the sun, and some may lead nowhere, but you will usually find them well worth asking. They can make you aware of points to notice, remind you of facts you already know. They can also suggest interesting points you need to find out more about.

In defining something, you need not try to forge a definition so absolute that it will stand till the mountains turn to plains. Like a mapmaker, the writer of an extended definition draws approximate boundaries, takes in only some of what lies within them, and ignores what lies outside. The boundaries, of course, may be wide; and for this reason, the writing of an extended definition sometimes tempts a writer to sweep across a continent airily and to soar off into abstract clouds. Like any other method of expository writing, though, definition will work only for the writer who remembers the world of the senses and supports every generalization with concrete evidence.

There may be no finer illustration of the perils of definition than the scene, in Charles Dickens's novel *Hard Times*, of the grim schoolroom of a teacher named Gradgrind, who insists on facts but who completely ignores living realities. When a girl whose father is a horse trainer is unable to define a horse, Gradgrind blames her for not knowing what a horse is; and he praises the definition of a horse supplied by a pet pupil: "Quadruped. Graminivorous. Forty teeth, namely twenty-four grinders, four eye-teeth, and twelve incisive. Sheds coat in the spring; in marshy countries, sheds hoofs, too. Hoofs hard, but requiring to be shod with iron. Age known by marks in mouth." To anyone who didn't already know what a horse is, this enumeration of statistics would prove of little help. In writing an extended definition, never lose sight of the reality you are attempting to bound, even if its frontiers are as inclusive as those of *psychological burnout* or *human rights*. Give your reader examples, tell an illustrative story, use an analogy, bring in specific description — in whatever method you use, keep coming down to earth. Without your eyes on the world, you will define no reality. You might define *animal husbandry* till the cows come home, and never make clear what it means.

DEFINITION IN A PARAGRAPH: TWO ILLUSTRATIONS

1. Using Definition to Write about Television

What is the nature of an ideal cop in "Miami Vice"? Contrary to what we might expect, he isn't one who upholds the letter of the law. Crockett and Tubbs, heroes of the series, continually break department rules and ride roughshod over civil liberties. When they set a trap for a drug dealer, using real heroin for bait, or when they kidnap some thug and slap him around a little, they don't fret about not going by the book. Time and again they defy petty bureaucrats who would hamper them. They ignore mayor, district attorney, and police commissioner, and sometimes even their sympathetic, frozen-faced boss, Lieutenant Castillo. As they move through the twilight world of big-time narcotics, Crockett and Tubbs, to do their jobs, need to break the law constantly. Despite their puny paychecks (which in real life would be about $459 a week), they live in high style, like the crooks they pursue. Glamorized figures in trendy clothes, they jet away to New York or Bogotá on fat expense accounts, enjoying the sports cars and fancy mansions lent to them for disguise. Society, it seems, is so corrupt and its police force so riddled with corruption that Crockett and Tubbs must take the law into their own hands and become outlaws themselves. An ideal cop, each of them listens not to printed statutes but to some higher code engraved upon his heart.

COMMENT. In setting forth a definition in a paragraph, this writer confines himself to a narrow subject: the idea of the ideal cop as shown in a single TV series. This seems enough matter for one paragraph. The main point of the definition, you'll notice, is that the ideal cop is himself a law-breaker. This point is made at the start of the paragraph and — to reinforce it and sum up — again at the end. But the writer suggests too that on "Miami Vice," the ideal cop is idealized in other ways: Crockett and Tubbs are "glamorized figures in trendy clothes" who drive borrowed sports cars. What makes the paragraph vivid and clear is that the writer keeps supplying examples. No sooner are we told that the two cops break the law than we learn that they set traps with real drugs. Do they violate civil liberties? An example follows: They rough up a criminal. When the writer says "bureaucrats," he mentions three kinds, and he names one individual, Lieutenant Castillo. Giving examples, as this paragraph shows, is one of the more effective ways to define.

2. Using Definition in an Academic Discipline

When the character traits found in any two species owe their resemblance to a common ancestry, taxonomists say the states are *homologous*, or are *homologues* of each other. *Homology* is defined as correspondence between two structures due to inheritance from a common ancestor. Homologous structures can be identical in appearance and can even be based on identical genes. However, such structures can diverge until they become very different in both appearance and function. Nevertheless, homologous structures usually retain certain basic features that betray a common ancestry. Consider the forelimbs of vertebrates. It is easy to make a detailed, bone-by-bone, muscle-by-muscle comparison of the forearm of a person and a monkey and to conclude that the forearms, as well as the various parts of the forearm, are homologous. The forelimb of a dog, however, shows marked differences from those of primates in both structure and function. The forelimb is used for locomotion by dogs but for grasping and manipulation by people and monkeys. Even so, all of the bones can still be matched. The wing of a bird and the flipper of a seal are even more different from each other or from the human forearm, yet they too are constructed around bones that can be matched on a nearly perfect one-to-one basis.

COMMENT. This textbook paragraph neatly illustrates how extended definition makes use of other rhetorical methods: in this case, example. From *Life: The Science of Biology*, by William K. Purves and Gordon H. Orians (Sunderland, Mass.: Sinauer Associates, Inc., Publishers, 1983, p. 805), the paragraph sets out to define *homology* and also to show how the two related forms of the word, *homologous* and *homologues*, are used. Students need to know the meanings of all three to study biology.

The authors begin with a brief definition, then emphasize that not all homologues closely resemble one another on the surface. To show the differences that species can display, as well as what they must have in common to be homologues, Purves and Orians amplify their definition with examples: The forearms of humans closely resemble those of monkeys, and the two are homologous. The forelimbs of dogs, the wings of birds, and the flippers of seals, however, are homologous with those of people even though they appear in many ways different. The examples are valuable here because they help to define the concepts.

· Joyce Carol Oates ·

Born in Lockport, New York, in 1938, JOYCE CAROL OATES published her first short story in *Mademoiselle* while she was still an undergraduate at Syracuse University. After earning her M.A. in literature from the University of Wisconsin, Oates went on to teach at the University of Detroit and the University of Windsor (Ontario). While she is best known for her fiction, which has earned her an O. Henry award and a National Book Award (for the novel *them*, in 1970), Oates is also a respected poet, literary critic, essayist, and dramatist. All told, Oates has written more than forty books — an average of more than a book a year since her first publication in 1959. Much of Oates's work is characterized by violence and the presence of evil because, she has said, "serious writers . . . take for their subjects the complexity of the world, its evils as well as its goods." Some of her recent publications include *A Bloodsmoor Romance* (1982); *The Profane Art: Essays and Reviews* (1983); *Last Days: Stories* (1984); *Solstice* (1985); *Marya: A Life* (1986); and *You Must Remember This* (1987). Oates now lives in Princeton, New Jersey, where she teaches and, together with her husband Raymond Smith, runs The Ontario Review Press and the literary magazine *The Ontario Review*.

On Boxing

The lore of boxing has long fascinated Joyce Carol Oates; in fact, the newest of her eighteen novels, *You Must Remember This* (1987), has a boxer for a major character. This essay was first published in 1985 in the *New York Times Magazine*. The author subsequently enlarged and published it as a book, *On Boxing* (1987), with photographs by John Renard. Here, Oates examines what distinguishes boxing from other sports and explores her own attraction to prizefighting and the ring.

They are young welterweight boxers so evenly matched they   1
might be twins — though one has a redhead's pallor and the
other is a dusky-skinned Hispanic. Circling each other in the

ring, they try jabs, tentative left hooks, right crosses that dissolve in midair or turn into harmless slaps. The Madison Square Garden crowd is derisive, impatient. "Those two! What'd they do, wake up this morning and decide they were boxers?" a man behind me says contemptuously. (He's dark, nattily dressed, with a neatly trimmed mustache and tinted glasses. A sophisticated fight fan. Two hours later he will be crying, "Tommy! Tommy! Tommy!" over and over in a paroxysm of grief as, on the giant closed-circuit television screen, middleweight champion Marvelous Marvin Hagler batters his challenger, Thomas Hearns, into insensibility.)

The young boxers must be conscious of the jeers and boos in 2 this great cavernous space reaching up into the $20 seats in the balconies amid the constant milling of people in the aisles, the smells of hotdogs, beer, cigarette and cigar smoke, hair oil. But they are locked desperately together, circling, jabbing, slapping, clinching, now a flurry of light blows, clumsy footwork, another sweaty stumbling despairing clinch into the ropes that provokes a fresh wave of derision. Why are they here in the Garden of all places, each fighting what looks like his first professional fight? What are they doing? Neither is angry at the other. When the bell sounds at the end of the sixth and final round, the crowd boos a little louder. The Hispanic boy, silky yellow shorts, damp, frizzy, floating hair, strides about his corner of the ring with his gloved hand aloft — not in defiance of the boos, which increase in response to his gesture, or even in acknowledgment of them. It's just something he has seen older boxers do. He seems to be saying "I'm here, I made it, I did it." When the decision is announced as a draw, the crowd's derision increases in volume. "Get out of the ring!" "Go home!" Contemptuous male laughter follows the boys in their robes, towels about their heads, sweating, breathless. Why had they thought they were boxers?

How can you enjoy so brutal a sport, people ask. Or don't 3 ask.

And it's too complicated to answer. In any case, I don't "enjoy" boxing, and never have; it isn't invariably "brutal"; I don't 4 think of it as a sport.

Nor do I think of it in writerly terms as a metaphor for   5
something else. (For *what* else?) No one whose interest in boxing
began in childhood — as mine did as an offshoot of my father's
interest — is likely to suppose it is a symbol of something beyond itself, though I can entertain the proposition that life is a
metaphor for boxing — for one of those bouts that go on and
on, round following round, small victories, small defeats, nothing determined, again the bell and again the bell and you and
your opponent so evenly matched it's clear your opponent *is*
you and why are the two of you jabbing and punching at each
other on an elevated platform enclosed by ropes as in a pen beneath hot crude all-exposing lights in the presence of an indifferent crowd: that sort of writerly metaphor. But if you have seen
five hundred boxing matches, you have seen five hundred boxing matches, and their common denominator, which surely exists, is not of primary interest to you. "If the Host is only a symbol," the Catholic writer Flannery O'Connor said, "I'd say the
hell with it."

Each boxing match is a story, a highly condensed, highly   6
dramatic story — even when nothing much happens: Then failure is the story. There are two principal characters in the story,
overseen by a shadowy third. When the bell rings no one knows
what will happen. Much is speculated, nothing known. The
boxers bring to the fight everything that is themselves, and everything will be exposed: including secrets about themselves
they never knew. There are boxers possessed of such remarkable
intuition, such prescience, one would think they had fought this
particular fight before. There are boxers who perform brilliantly, but mechanically, who cannot improvise in midfight;
there are boxers performing at the height of their skill who cannot quite comprehend that it won't be enough; to my knowledge there was only one boxer who possessed an extraordinary
and disquieting awareness, not only of his opponent's every
move or anticipated move, but of the audience's keenest shifts in
mood as well — Muhammad Ali, of course.
    In the ring, death is always a possibility, which is why I pre-   7
fer to see films or tapes of fights already past — already crystal-

lized into art. In fact, death is a statistically rare possibility of which no one likes to think — like your possible death tomorrow morning in an automobile crash, or in next month's airplane crash, or in a freak accident involving a fall on the stairs — a skull fracture, subarachnoid hemorrhage.

A boxing match is a play without words, which doesn't mean that it has no text or no language, only that the text is improvised in action, the language a dialogue between the boxers in a joint response to the mysterious will of the crowd, which is always that the fight be a worthy one so that the crude paraphernalia of the setting — the ring, the lights, the onlookers themselves — be obliterated. To go from an ordinary preliminary match to a "Fight of the Century" — like those between Joe Louis and Billy Conn, Muhammad Ali and Joe Frazier, most recently Marvin Hagler and Thomas Hearns — is to go from listening or half-listening to a guitar being idly plucked to hearing Bach's "Well-Tempered Clavier" being perfectly played, and that too is part of the story. So much is happening so swiftly and so subtly you cannot absorb it except to know that something memorable is happening and it is happening in a place beyond words.   8

The fighters in the ring are time-bound — is anything so excruciatingly long as a fiercely contested three-minute round? — but the fight itself is timeless. By way of films and tapes, it has become history, art. If boxing is a sport, it is the most tragic of all sports because, more than any human activity, it consumes the very excellence it displays: Its very drama is this consumption. To expend oneself in fighting the greatest fight of one's life is to begin immediately the downward turn that next time may be a plunge, a sudden incomprehensible fall. *I am the greatest*, Muhammad Ali says. *I am the greatest*, Marvin Hagler says. You always think you're going to win, Jack Dempsey wryly observed in his old age, otherwise you can't fight at all. The punishment — to the body, the brain, the spirit — a man must endure to become a great boxer is inconceivable to most of us whose idea of personal risk is largely ego related or emotional. But the punishment, as it begins to show in even a young and vigorous boxer, is closely assessed by his rivals. After junior-welterweight cham-   9 pion Aaron Pryor won a lackluster fight on points a few months ago, a younger boxer in his weight division, interviewed at ringside, said: "My mouth is watering."

So the experience of seeing great fighters of the past — and   10
great sporting events are always *past* — is radically different from having seen them when they were reigning champions. Jack Johnson, Jack Dempsey, Joe Louis, Sugar Ray Robinson, Willie Pep, Rocky Marciano, Muhammad Ali — as spectators we know not only how a fight ends but how a career ends. Boxing is always particulars, second by incalculable second, but in the abstract it suggests these haunting lines by Yeats:

> Everything that man esteems
> Endures a moment or a day.
> Love's pleasure drives his love away,
> The painter's brush consumes his dreams;
> The herald's cry, the soldier's tread
> Exhaust his glory and his might:
> Whatever flames upon the night
> Man's own resinous heart has fed.
> — from "The Resurrection"

The referee, the third character in the story, usually appears to be a mere observer, even an intruder, a near-ghostly presence as fluid in motion and quick-footed as the boxers themselves (he is frequently a former boxer). But so central to the drama of boxing is the referee that the spectacle of two men fighting each other unsupervised in an elevated ring would appear hellish, obscene — life rather than art. The referee is our intermediary in the fight. He is our moral conscience, extracted from us as spectators so that, for the duration of the fight, "conscience" is not a factor in our experience; nor is it a factor in the boxers' behavior.

Though the referee's role is a highly demanding one, and it   11
has been estimated that there are perhaps no more than a dozen really skilled referees in the world, it seems to be necessary in the intense dramatic action of the fight that the referee have no dramatic identity. Referees' names are quickly forgotten, even as they are announced over the microphone preceding a fight. Yet, paradoxically, the referee's position is one of crucial significance.

The referee cannot control what happens in the ring, but he can frequently control, to a degree, *that* it happens: He is responsible for the fight, if not for the individual fighter's performance. It is the referee solely who holds the power of life and death at certain times; whose decision to terminate a fight, or to allow it to continue, determines a man's fate. (One should recall that a well-aimed punch with a boxer's full weight behind it can have an astonishing impact — a blow that must be absorbed by the brain in its jelly sac.)

In a recent heavyweight fight in Buffalo, 220-pound Tim 12
Witherspoon repeatedly struck his 260-pound opponent, James Broad, caught in the ropes, while the referee looked on without acting — though a number of spectators called for the fight to be stopped. In the infamous Benny Paret–Emile Griffith fight of March 24, 1962, the referee Ruby Goldstein was said to have stood paralyzed as Paret, trapped in the ropes, suffered as many as eighteen powerful blows to the head before he fell. (He died ten days later.) Boxers are trained not to quit; if they are knocked down they will try to get up to continue the fight, even if they can hardly defend themselves. The primary rule of the ring — to defend oneself at all times — is both a parody and a distillation of life.

Boxing is a purely masculine world. (Though there are fe- 13
male boxers — the most famous is the black champion Lady Tyger Trimiar with her shaved head and tiger-striped attire — women's role in the sport is extremely marginal.) The vocabulary of boxing is attuned to a quintessentially masculine sensibility in which the role of patriarch/protector can only be assured if there is physical strength underlying it. First comes this strength — "primitive," perhaps; then comes civilization. It should be kept in mind that "boxing" and "fighting," though always combined in the greatest of boxers, can be entirely different and even unrelated activities. If boxing can be, in the lighter weights especially, a highly complex and refined skill belonging solely to civilization, fighting seems to belong to something predating civilization, the instinct not merely to defend oneself — for when has the masculine ego ever been assuaged by so mini-

mal a gesture? — but to attack another and to force him into absolute submission. Hence the electrifying effect upon a typical fight crowd when fighting emerges suddenly out of boxing — the excitement when a boxer's face begins to bleed. The flash of red is the visible sign of the fight's authenticity in the eyes of many spectators, and boxers are right to be proud — if they are — of their facial scars.

To the untrained eye, boxers in the ring usually appear to be angry. But, of course, this is "work" to them; emotion has no part in it, or should not. Yet in an important sense — in a symbolic sense — the boxers *are* angry, and boxing is fundamentally about anger. It is the only sport in which anger is accommodated, ennobled. Why are boxers angry? Because, for the most part, they belong to the disenfranchised of our society, to impoverished ghetto neighborhoods in which anger is an appropriate response. ("It's hard being black. You ever been black? I was black once — when I was poor," Larry Holmes has said.) Today, when most boxers — most good boxers — are black or Hispanic, white men begin to look anemic in the ring. Yet after decades of remarkable black boxers — from Jack Johnson to Joe Louis to Muhammad Ali — heavyweight champion Larry Holmes was the object of racist slurs and insults when he defended his title against the over-promoted white challenger Gerry Cooney a few years ago.

Liberals who have no personal or class reason to feel anger tend to disparage, if not condemn, such anger in others. Liberalism is also unfairly harsh in its criticism of all that predates civilization — or "liberalism" itself — without comprehending that civilization is a concept, an idea, perhaps at times hardly more than a fiction, attendant upon, and always subordinate to, physical strength: missiles, nuclear warheads. The terrible and tragic silence dramatized in the boxing ring is the silence of nature before language, when the physical *was* language, a means of communication swift and unmistakable.

The phrase "killer instinct" is said to have been coined in reference to Jack Dempsey in his famous early fights against Jess Willard, Georges Carpentier, Luis Firpo ("The Wild Bull of the Pampas"), and any number of other boxers, less renowned, whom he savagely beat. The ninth of eleven children born to an impoverished Mormon sharecropper and itinerant railroad worker, Dempsey seems to have been, as a young boxer in his prime, the very embodiment of angry hunger; and if he remains the most spectacular heavyweight champion in history, it is partly because he fought when rules governing boxing were somewhat casual by present-day standards. Where aggression must be learned, even cultivated, in some champion boxers (Tunney, Louis, Marciano, Patterson, for example), Dempsey's aggression was direct and natural: Once in the ring he seems to have wanted to kill his opponent.

Dempsey's first title fight in 1919, against the aging champion Jess Willard, was called "pugilistic murder" by some sportswriters and is said to have been one of boxing's all-time blood baths. Today, this famous fight — which brought the nearly unknown twenty-four-year-old Dempsey to national prominence — would certainly have been stopped in the first minute of the first round. Badly out of condition, heavier than Dempsey by almost sixty pounds, the thirty-seven-year-old Willard had virtually no defense against the challenger. By the end of the fight, Willard's jaw was broken, his cheekbone split, nose smashed, six teeth broken off at the gum, an eye was battered shut, much further damage was done to his body. Both boxers were covered in Willard's blood. Years later Dempsey's estranged manager Kearns confessed — perhaps falsely — that he had "loaded" Dempsey's gloves — treated his hand tape with a talcum substance that turned concrete-hard when wet. 17

For the most part, boxing matches today are scrupulously monitored by referees and ring physicians. The devastating knockout blow is frequently the one never thrown. In a recent televised junior-middleweight bout between Don Curry and James Green, the referee stopped the fight because Green seemed momentarily disabled: His logic was that Green had dropped his gloves and was therefore in a position to be hurt. (Green and his furious trainer protested the decision but the referee's word is final: No fight, stopped, can be resumed.) The drama of the ring begins to shift subtly as more and more frequently one sees a referee intervene to embrace a weakened or 18 defenseless man in a gesture of paternal solicitude that in itself carries much theatrical power — a gesture not so dramatic as the killing blow but one that suggests that the ethics of the ring are moving toward those that prevail beyond it. As if fighter-brothers whose mysterious animosity has somehow brought them to battle are saved by their father. . . .

In the final moment of the Hagler-Hearns fight, the dazed Hearns — on his feet but clearly not fully conscious, gamely prepared to take Hagler's next assault — was saved by the referee from what might well have been serious injury, if not death, considering the ferocity of Hagler's fighting and the personal anger he seems to have brought to it that night. This eight-minute fight, generally believed to be one of the great fights in boxing history, ends with Hearns in the referee's protective embrace — an image that is haunting, in itself profoundly mysterious, as if an indefinable human drama had been spontaneously created for us, brilliantly improvised, performed one time and one time only, yet permanently ingrained upon our consciousness.   19

Years ago in the early 1950s, when my father first took me to a Golden Gloves boxing tournament in Buffalo, I asked him why the boys wanted to fight one another, why they were willing to get hurt. My father said, "Boxers don't feel pain quite the way we do."   20

Gene Tunney's single defeat in an eleven-year career was to a flamboyant and dangerous fighter named Harry Greb ("The Human Windmill"), who seems to have been, judging from boxing literature, the dirtiest fighter in history. Low blows, butting, fouls, holding and hitting, using his laces on an opponent's eyes — Greb was famous for his lack of interest in the rules. He was world middleweight champion for three years but a presence in the boxing world for a long time. After the first of his several fights with Greb, the twenty-four-year-old Tunney had to spend a week in bed, he was so badly hurt; he'd lost two quarts of blood during the fifteen-round fight. But as Tunney said years afterward: "Greb gave me a terrible whipping. He broke my nose, maybe with a butt. He cut my eyes and ears, perhaps with his laces. . . . My jaw was swollen from the right temple down   21 the cheek, along under the chin and part way up the other side. The referee, the ring itself, was full of blood. . . . But it was in that first fight, in which I lost my American light-heavyweight title, that I knew I had found a way to beat Harry eventually. I was fortunate, really. If boxing in those days had been afflicted with the commission doctors we have today — who are always poking their noses into the ring and examining superficial wounds — the first fight with Greb would have been stopped before I learned how to beat him. It's possible, even probable, that if this had happened I would never have been heard of again."

Tommy Loughran, the light-heavyweight champion from 1927 to 1929, was a master boxer greatly admired by other boxers. He approached boxing literally as a science — as Tunney did — studying his opponents' styles and mapping out ring strategy for each fight. He rigged up mirrors in his basement so that he could see himself as he worked out — for, as Loughran realized, no boxer ever sees himself quite as he appears to his opponent. But the secret of Loughran's career was that he had a right hand that broke so easily he could use it only once in each fight: It had to be the knockout punch or nothing. "I'd get one shot, then the agony of the thing would hurt me if the guy got up. Anybody I ever hit with a left hook, I knocked flat on his face, but I would never take a chance for fear if my left hand goes, I'm done for." 22

Both Tunney and Loughran, it is instructive to note, retired from boxing before they were forced to retire. Tunney was a highly successful businessman and Loughran a successful sugar broker on the Wall Street commodities market — just to suggest that boxers are not invariably illiterate, stupid, or punch-drunk. 23

One of the perhaps not entirely acknowledged reasons for the attraction of serious writers to boxing (from Swift, Pope, Johnson to Hazlitt, Lord Byron, Hemingway, and our own Norman Mailer, George Plimpton, Wilfrid Sheed, Daniel Halpern, et al.) is the sport's systematic cultivation of pain in the interests of a project, a life-goal: the willed transposing of the sensation called "pain" (whether physical or psychological) into its opposite. If this is masochism — and I doubt that it is, or that it is 24 simply — it is also intelligence, cunning, strategy. It is the active welcoming of that which most living beings try to avoid and to flee. It is the active subsuming of the present moment in terms of the future. Pain now but control (and therefore pleasure) later.

Still, it is the rigorous training period leading up to the pub-   25 lic appearance that demands the most discipline. In this, too, the writer senses some kinship, however oblique and one-sided, with the professional boxer. The brief public spectacle of the boxing match (which could last as little as sixty seconds), like the publication of the writer's book, is but the final, visible stage in a long, arduous, fanatic, and sometimes quixotic, subordination of the self. It was Rocky Marciano who seems to have trained with the most monastic devotion, secluding himself from his wife and family for as long as three months before a fight. Quite apart from the grueling physical training of this period and the constant preoccupation with diet and weight, Marciano concentrated on only the upcoming fight, the opening bell, his opponent. Every minute of the boxer's life was planned for one purpose. In the training camp the name of the opponent was never mentioned and Marciano's associates were careful about conversation in his presence: They talked very little about boxing.

In the final month, Marciano would not write a letter. The   26 last ten days before a fight he saw no mail, took no telephone calls, met no new acquaintances. The week before the fight he would not shake hands with anyone. Or go for a ride in a car. No new foods! No envisioning the morning after the fight! All that was not *the fight* was taboo: When Marciano worked out punching the bag he saw his opponent before him, when he jogged early in the morning he saw his opponent close beside him. What could be a more powerful image of discipline — madness? — than this absolute subordination of the self, this celibacy of the fighter-in-training? Instead of focusing his energies and fantasies upon Woman, the boxer focuses them upon the Opponent.

No sport is more physical, more direct, than boxing. No   27 sport appears more powerfully homoerotic: the confrontation in the ring — the disrobing — the sweaty, heated combat that is part dance, courtship, coupling — the frequent urgent pursuit by one boxer of the other in the fight's natural and violent movement toward the "knockout." Surely boxing derives much of its appeal from this mimicry of a species of erotic love in which one man overcomes the other in an exhibition of superior strength.

Most fights, however fought, lead to an embrace between   28
the boxers after the final bell — a gesture of mutual respect and apparent affection that appears to the onlooker to be more than perfunctory. Rocky Graziano, often derided for being a slugger rather than a "classic" boxer, sometimes kissed his opponents out of gratitude for the fight. Does the boxing match, one almost wonders, lead irresistibly to this moment: the public embrace of two men who otherwise, in public or in private, could not approach each other with such passion. Are men privileged to embrace with love only after having fought? A woman is struck by the tenderness men will express for boxers who have been hurt, even if it is only by way of commentary on photographs: the startling picture of Ray (Boom Boom) Mancini after his second losing fight with Livingstone Bramble, for instance, when Mancini's face was hideously battered (photographs in *Sports Illustrated* and elsewhere were gory, near-pornographic); the much-reprinted photograph of the defeated Thomas Hearns being carried to his corner in the arms of an enormous black man in formal attire — the "Hit Man" from Detroit now helpless, only semiconscious, looking precisely like a black Christ taken from the cross. These are powerful, haunting, unsettling images, cruelly beautiful, very much bound up with the primitive appeal of the sport.

Yet to suggest that men might love one another directly   29
without the violent ritual of combat is to misread man's greatest passion — for war, not peace. Love, if there is to be love, comes second.

Boxing is, after all, about lying. It is about cultivating a dou-   30
ble personality. As José Torres, the ex-light-heavyweight champion who is now the New York State Boxing Commissioner, says: "We fighters understand lies. What's a feint? What's a left

hook off the jab? What's an opening? What's thinking one thing and doing another . . . ?"

There is nothing fundamentally playful about boxing, noth-   31
ing that seems to belong to daylight, to pleasure. At its moments of greatest intensity it seems to contain so complete and so powerful an image of life — life's beauty, vulnerability, despair, incalculable and often reckless courage — that boxing *is* life, and hardly a mere game. During a superior boxing match we are deeply moved by the body's communion with itself by way of another's flesh. The body's dialogue with its shadow-self — or Death. Baseball, football, basketball — these quintessentially American pastimes are recognizably sports because they involve play: They are games. One *plays* football; one doesn't *play* boxing.

Observing team sports, teams of adult men, one sees how   32
men are children in the most felicitous sense of the word. But boxing in its elemental ferocity cannot be assimilated into childhood — though very young men box, even professionally, and numerous world champions began boxing when they were hardly more than children. Spectators at public games derive much of their pleasure from reliving the communal emotions of childhood, but spectators at boxing matches relive the murderous infancy of the race. Hence the notorious cruelty of boxing crowds and the excitement when a man begins to bleed. ("When I see blood," says Marvin Hagler, "I become a bull." He means his own.)

The boxing ring comes to seem an altar of sorts, one of those   33
legendary magical spaces where the laws of a nation are suspended: Inside the ropes, during an officially regulated three-minute round, a man may be killed at his opponent's hands but he cannot be legally murdered. Boxing inhabits a sacred space predating civilization; or, to use D. H. Lawrence's phrase, before God was love. If it suggests a savage ceremony or a rite of atonement, it also suggests the futility of such rites. For what atonement is the fight waged, if it must shortly be waged again . . . ?

All this is to speak of the paradox of boxing — its obsessive   34
appeal for many who find in it not only a spectacle involving sensational feats of physical skill but an emotional experience impossible to convey in words; an art form, as I have suggested,

with no natural analogue in the arts. And of course this accounts, too, for the extreme revulsion it arouses in many people. ("Brutal," "disgusting," "barbaric," "inhuman," "a terrible, terrible sport" — typical comments on the subject.)

In December 1984, the American Medical Association 35 passed a resolution calling for the abolition of boxing on the principle that it is the only sport in which the *objective* is to cause injury. This is not surprising. Humanitarians have always wanted to reform boxing — or abolish it altogether. The 1896 heavyweight title match between Ruby Robert Fitzsimmons and Peter Maher was outlawed in many parts of the United States, so canny promoters staged it across the Mexican border four hundred miles from El Paso. (Some three hundred people made the arduous journey to see what must have been one of the most disappointing bouts in boxing history — Fitzsimmons knocked out his opponent in a mere ninety-five seconds.)

During the prime of Jack Dempsey's career in the 1920s, 36 boxing was illegal in many states, like alcohol, and like alcohol, seems to have aroused a hysterical public enthusiasm. Photographs of jammed outdoor arenas taken in the 1920s with boxing rings like postage-sized altars at their centers, the boxers themselves scarcely visible, testify to the extraordinary emotional appeal boxing had at that time, even as reform movements were lobbying against it. When Jack Johnson won the heavyweight title in 1908 (he had to pursue the white champion Tommy Burns all the way to Australia to confront him), the special "danger" of boxing was also that it might expose and humiliate white men in the ring. After Johnson's victory over the "White Hope" contender Jim Jeffries, there were race riots and lynchings throughout the United States; even films of some of Johnson's fights were outlawed in many states. And because boxing has become a sport in which black and Hispanic men have lately excelled, it is particularly vulnerable to attack by white middle-class reformers, who seem uninterested in lobbying against equally dangerous but "establishment" sports like football, auto racing, and thoroughbred horse racing.

There is something peculiarly American in the fact that, 37 while boxing is our most controversial sport, it is also the sport that pays its top athletes the most money. In spite of the controversy, boxing has never been healthier financially. The three highest paid athletes in the world in both 1983 and 1984 were boxers; a boxer with a long career like heavyweight champion Larry Holmes — forty-eight fights in thirteen years as a professional — can expect to earn somewhere beyond $50 million. (Holmes said that after retirement what he would miss most about boxing is his million-dollar checks.) Dempsey, who said that a man fights for one thing only — money — made somewhere beyond $3,500,000 in the ring in his long and varied career. Now $1.5 million is a fairly common figure for a single fight. Thomas Hearns made at least $7 million in his fight with Hagler while Hagler made at least $7.5 million. For the first of his highly publicized matches with Roberto Duran in 1980 — which he lost on a decision — the popular black welterweight champion Sugar Ray Leonard received a staggering $10 million to Duran's $1.3 million. And none of these figures takes into account various subsidiary earnings (from television commercials, for instance) which in Leonard's case are probably as high as his income from boxing.

Money has drawn any number of retired boxers back into   38
the ring, very often with tragic results. The most notorious example is perhaps Joe Louis, who, owing huge sums in back taxes, continued boxing well beyond the point at which he could perform capably. After a career of seventeen years he was stopped by Rocky Marciano — who was said to have felt as upset by his victory as Louis by the defeat. (Louis then went on to a degrading second career as a professional wrestler. This, too, ended abruptly when 300-pound Rocky Lee stepped on the forty-two-year-old Louis's chest and damaged his heart.) Ezzard Charles, Jersey Joe Walcott, Joe Frazier, Muhammad Ali — each continued fighting when he was no longer in condition to defend himself against young heavyweight boxers on the way up. Of all heavyweight champions, only Rocky Marciano, to whom fame and money were not of paramount significance, was prudent enough to retire before he was defeated. In any case, the prodigious sums of money a few boxers earn do not account for the sums the public is willing to pay them.

Though boxing has long been popular in many countries   39
and under many forms of government, its popularity in the
United States since the days of John L. Sullivan has a good deal
to do with what is felt as the spirit of the individual — his "physical" spirit — in conflict with the constrictions of the state. The
rise of boxing in the 1920s in particular might well be seen as a
consequence of the diminution of the individual vis-à-vis society; the gradual attrition of personal freedom, will, and strength
— whether "masculine" or otherwise. In the Eastern bloc of nations, totalitarianism is a function of the state; in the Western
bloc it has come to seem a function of technology, or history —
"fate." The individual exists in his physical supremacy, but does
the individual matter?

In the magical space of the boxing ring so disquieting a ques-   40
tion has no claim. There, as in no other public arena, the individual as a unique physical being asserts himself; there, for a dramatic if fleeting period of time, the great world with its moral
and political complexities, its terrifying impersonality, simply
ceases to exist. Men fighting one another with only their fists
and their cunning are all contemporaries, all brothers, belonging to no historical time. "He can run, but he can't hide" — so
said Joe Louis before his famous fight with young Billy Conn in
1941. In the brightly lighted ring, man is *in extremis*, performing
an atavistic rite or agon for the mysterious solace of those who
can participate only vicariously in such drama: the drama of life
in the flesh. Boxing has become America's tragic theater.

QUESTIONS ON MEANING

1. Does the author's main PURPOSE seem to be to inform and educate,
   to provide an impartial definition of boxing, or to advocate the institution of reforms in current boxing rules?
2. According to Oates, what is the distinction between fighting and
   boxing?
3. In paragraph 8, Oates writes, "A boxing match is a play without
   words." Find extensions of this METAPHOR elsewhere in the essay.

What is being compared to what? What purpose does this metaphor serve?

4. How do you understand the author's statements, in paragraph 4, that she doesn't "enjoy" boxing and that she doesn't "think of it as a sport"? In your own words, explain what she *does* think of it.

QUESTIONS ON WRITING STRATEGY

1. The author uses the methods of example, description, and analogy to build her definition. Locate at least one illustration of each, and explain how each works within the essay.

2. What do you think Oates means when she says that boxing happens "in a place beyond words" (paragraph 8)?

3. How do you think Oates came to the conclusion that man's greatest passion is "for war, not peace" (paragraph 29)? Is there EVIDENCE supporting this CLAIM in her essay? Does Oates provide any backing for this claim? Is the claim an integral part of this essay? Why or why not?

QUESTIONS ON LANGUAGE

1. Consult your dictionary if you need help defining these words: prescience (paragraph 6); paradoxically (11); quintessentially (13); pugilistic (17); quixotic, monastic (25); prodigious (38); atavistic, agon, vicariously (40).

2. What do you take the phrase "when the physical *was* language" (paragraph 15) to mean? What does Oates seem to be saying about the nature of boxing in the last sentence of this paragraph? If you had to sum up the description provided in this sentence in one word, what word would you choose?

SUGGESTIONS FOR WRITING

1. Has Oates convinced you that boxing is intrinsically different from every other sport? If so, write an essay explaining why, in your own words, this is so. Concentrate on defining other sports to show how they are similar to each other, but different from boxing. Or, write an essay defining another sport that you believe is, in some important way, distinct from all others. Establish, through definition, why this sport is fundamentally different.

2. In paragraph 6, Oates writes that "each boxing match is a story." But in paragraph 5, she says she does not think of boxing "as a met-

aphor for something else." Do you think these statements contradict each other, or can you reconcile them? Write a paragraph in which you explain your understanding of what Oates means by the phrase "each boxing match is a story."

Joyce Carol Oates on Writing

"I began writing in high school," Joyce Carol Oates told an interviewer, "consciously training myself by writing novel after novel and always throwing them out when I completed them." As an undergraduate at Syracuse University, she reportedly would finish a novel, turn over the resulting heap of paper, begin writing another novel on the reverse, and, when both sides were covered, throw all those practice sheets away.

Asked what kind of work schedule she follows today, she replied, "I haven't any formal schedule, but I love to write in the morning, before breakfast. Sometimes the writing goes so smoothly that I don't take a break for many hours — and consequently have breakfast at two or three in the afternoon on good days. On school days, days that·I teach, I usually write for an hour or forty-five minutes in the morning, before my first class. But I don't have any formal schedule, and at the moment I am feeling rather melancholy, or derailed, or simply lost, because I completed a novel some weeks ago and haven't begun another.

"My reputation for writing quickly and effortlessly notwithstanding, I am strongly in favor of intelligent, even fastidious revision, which is, or certainly should be, an art in itself. . . . There are pages in recent novels that I've rewritten as many as seventeen times, and a story, 'The Widows,' which I revised both before and after publication in *The Hudson Review*, and then revised slightly again before I included it in my next collection of stories — a fastidiousness that could go on into infinity."

Can she begin to write easily, no matter what mood she may be in? "In a sense," she said, "the writing will create the mood.

If art is, as I believe it to be, a genuinely transcendental function — a means by which we rise out of limited, parochial states of mind — then it should not matter very much what states of mind or emotion we are in. Generally, I've found this to be true: I have forced myself to begin writing when I've been utterly exhausted, when I've felt my soul as thin as a playing card, when nothing has seemed worth enduring for another five minutes . . . and somehow the activity of writing changes everything." (Interview with Robert Phillips in *Writers at Work: The Paris Review Interviews, Fifth Series,* edited by George Plimpton [New York: Viking, 1981], pp. 364–366, 377–378.)

FOR DISCUSSION

1. What would Oates be likely to reply to novice writers who believe they can't write unless or until inspiration strikes?
2. Do any of Oates's remarks surprise you? If so, which of your ideas about writers and writing does the author challenge?

· Tom Wolfe ·

TOM WOLFE, author, journalist, and cartoonist, was born in 1931 in Richmond, Virginia, and went to Washington and Lee University. After taking a Ph.D. in American Studies at Yale, he decided against an academic career and instead worked as a reporter for the Springfield (Massachusetts) *Union*, then as a correspondent for the Washington *Post* in Latin America. Early in the 1960s, Wolfe began writing his electrifying, satiric articles on the American scene (with special, mocking attention to subcultures and trend-setters), which have enlivened *New York*, *Esquire*, *Rolling Stone*, *Harper's*, and other sophisticated magazines. Among his books are *The Electric Kool-Aid Acid Test*, a memoir of LSD-spaced-out hippies (1965); *The Kandy-Kolored Tangerine-Flake Streamline Baby*, glimpses of popular follies and foibles, and *The Pump House Gang*, a study of California surfers (both 1968); *Radical Chic and Mau-Mauing the Flak Catchers*, an unflattering view of New York artists and literati (1970); *From Bauhaus to Our House* (1981), a complaint against modern architecture; a retrospective selection of essays, *The Purple Decades* (1983); and a novel, *The Bonfire of the Vanities* (1987). Recently, *The Right Stuff* (1979), a chronicle of America's first astronauts, became a movie.

Pornoviolence

This essay, from a collection raking over the 1970s, *Mauve Gloves & Madmen, Clutter & Vine* (1976), is vintage Tom Wolfe. He played a large part in the invention of "the new journalism" (a brand of reporting that tells the truth excitedly, as if it were fiction), and his essay is marked by certain breathless features of style: long sentences full of parenthetical asides, ellipses (. . .), generous use of italics. (For a sampling of lively reporting by Wolfe and others, see the anthology Wolfe edited with E. W. Johnson, *The New Journalism*, 1973.) In the following essay Wolfe coins a term to fit the blend of pornography and pandering to bloodlust that he finds creeping into the media. His remarks have dated little since they first appeared.

"*Keeps His Mom-in-law in Chains,* meet *Kills Son and Feeds*   1
Corpse to Pigs."

"Pleased to meet you."   2

"*Teenager Twists Off Corpse's Head . . . to Get Gold Teeth,*   3
meet *Strangles Girl Friend, Then Chops Her to Pieces.*"

"How you doing?"   4

"*Nurse's Aide Sees Fingers Chopped Off in Meat Grinder,* meet   5
I Left My Babies in the Deep Freeze."

"It's a pleasure."   6

It's a pleasure! No doubt about that! In all these years of   7
journalism I have covered more conventions than I care to remember. Podiatrists, theosophists, Professional Budget Finance
dentists, oyster farmers, mathematicians, truckers, dry cleaners,
stamp collectors, Esperantists, nudists, and newspaper editors —
I have seen them all, together, in vast assemblies, sloughing
through the wall-to-wall of a thousand hotel lobbies (the nudists
excepted) in their shimmering gray-metal suits and pajama-stripe
shirts with white Plasti-Coat name cards on their chests, and I
have sat through their speeches and seminars (the nudists included) and attentively endured ear baths such as you wouldn't
believe. And yet none has ever been quite like the convention of
the stringers for *The National Enquirer.*

The Enquirer is a weekly newspaper that is probably known   8
by sight to millions more than know it by name. No one who
ever came face-to-face with *The Enquirer* on a newsstand in its
wildest days is likely to have forgotten the sight: a tabloid with
great inky shocks of type all over the front page saying something on the order of *Gouges Out Wife's Eyes to Make Her Ugly,*
Dad Hurls Hot Grease in Daughter's Face, Wife Commits Suicide
after 2 Years of Poisoning Fails to Kill Husband . . .

The stories themselves were supplied largely by stringers,   9
i.e., correspondents, from all over the country, the world, for
that matter, mostly copy editors and reporters on local newspapers. Every so often they would come upon a story, usually via
the police beat, that was so grotesque the local sheet would dis-
card it or run it in a highly glossed form rather than offend or
perplex its readers. The stringers would preserve them for *The*
Enquirer, which always rewarded them well and respectfully.

One year *The Enquirer* convened and feted them at a hotel in Manhattan. This convention was a success in every way. The only awkward moment was at the outset when the stringers all pulled in. None of them knew each other. Their hosts got around the problem by introducing them by the stories they had supplied. The introductions went like this:

"Harry, I want you to meet Frank here. Frank did that story, you remember that story, *Midget Murderer Throws Girl Off Cliff after She Refuses to Dance with Him.*"

"Pleased to meet you. That was some story."

"And Harry did the one about *I Spent Three Days Trapped at Bottom of Forty-Foot-Deep Mine Shaft and Was Saved by a Swarm of Flies.*"

"Likewise, I'm sure."

And *Midget Murderer Throws Girl Off Cliff* shakes hands with *I Spent Three Days Trapped at Bottom of Forty-Foot-Deep Mine Shaft*, and *Buries Her Baby Alive* shakes hands with *Boy, Twelve, Strangles Two-Year-Old Girl*, and *Kills Son and Feeds Corpse to Pigs* shakes hands with *He Strangles Old Woman and Smears Corpse with Syrup, Ketchup, and Oatmeal* . . . and . . .

. . . There was a great deal of esprit about the whole thing. These men were, in fact, the avant-garde of a new genre that since then has become institutionalized throughout the nation without anyone knowing its proper name. I speak of the new pornography, the pornography of violence.

Pornography comes from the Greek word "*porne*," meaning harlot, and pornography is literally the depiction of the acts of harlots. In the new pornography, the theme is not sex. The new pornography depicts practitioners acting out another, murkier drive: people staving teeth in, ripping guts open, blowing brains out, and getting even with all those bastards . . .

The success of *The Enquirer* prompted many imitators to enter the field, *Midnight, The Star Chronicle, The National Insider, Inside News, The National Close-up, The National Tattler, The National Examiner.* A truly competitive free press evolved, and soon a reader could go to the newspaper of his choice for *Kill the Retarded! (Won't You Join My Movement?)* and *Unfaithful Wife? Burn Her Bed!, Harem Master's Mistress Chops Him with Machete,*

Babe Bites Off Boy's Tongue, and *Cuts Buddy's Face to Pieces for Stealing His Business and Fiancée.*

And yet the last time I surveyed the Violence press, I no- 19
ticed a curious thing. These pioneering journals seem to have
pulled back. They seem to be regressing to what is by now the
Redi-Mix staple of literate Americans, mere sex. *Ecstasy and Me
(by Hedy Lamarr),*[1] says *The National Enquirer. I Run a Sex Art
Gallery,* says *The National Insider.* What has happened, I think,
is something that has happened to avant-gardes in many fields,
from William Morris and the Craftsmen to the Bauhaus group.[2]
Namely, their discoveries have been preempted by the Establishment and so thoroughly dissolved into the mainstream they no
longer look original.

Robert Harrison, the former publisher of *Confidential,* and 20
later publisher of the aforementioned *Inside News,* was perhaps
the first person to see it coming. I was interviewing Harrison
early in January 1964 for a story in *Esquire* about six weeks after
the assassination of President Kennedy, and we were in a cab in
the West Fifties in Manhattan, at a stoplight, by a newsstand,
and Harrison suddenly pointed at the newsstand and said,
"Look at that. They're doing the same thing *The Enquirer* does."

There on the stand was a row of slick-paper, magazine-size 21
publications, known in the trade as one-shots, with titles like
*Four Days That Shook the World, Death of a President, An Ameri-
can Tragedy,* or just *John Fitzgerald Kennedy (1921–1963).* "You
want to know why people buy those things?" said Harrison.
"People buy those things to see a man get his head blown off."

And, of course, he was right. Only now the publishers were 22
in many cases the pillars of the American press. Invariably,

[1]*Ecstasy,* an early, European-made Hedy Lamarr film, was notorious for
its scenes of soft-core lovemaking. Later, paired with Charles ("Come with me
to the Casbah") Boyer, Lamarr rose to Hollywood stardom in *Algiers* (1938).
— Eds.

[2]Morris (1834–1896), English artist, poet, printer, and socialist, founded a
company of craftspeople to bring tasteful design to furniture (the Morris chair)
and other implements of everyday life. The Bauhaus, an influential art school
in Germany (1919–1933), taught crafts and brought new ideas of design to architecture and to goods produced in factories. — Eds.

these "special coverages" of the assassination bore introductions piously commemorating the fallen President, exhorting the American people to strength and unity in a time of crisis, urging greater vigilance and safeguards for the new President, and even raising the nice metaphysical question of collective guilt in "an age of violence."

In the years since then, of course, there has been an incessant replay, with every recoverable clinical detail, of those less than five seconds in which a man got his head blown off. And throughout this deluge of words, pictures, and film frames, I have been intrigued with one thing: The point of view, the vantage point, is almost never that of the victim, riding in the Presidential Lincoln Continental. What you get is . . . the view from Oswald's rifle. You can step right up here and look point-blank right through the very hairline cross in Lee Harvey Oswald's Optics Ordnance in weaponry four-power Japanese telescope sight and watch, frame by frame by frame by frame, as that man there's head comes apart. Just a little History there before your very eyes.

The television networks have schooled us in the view from Oswald's rifle and made it seem a normal pastime. The TV viewpoint is nearly always that of the man who is going to strike. The last time I watched *Gunsmoke*, which was not known as a very violent Western in TV terms, the action went like this: The Wellington agents and the stagecoach driver pull guns on the badlands gang leader's daughter and Kitty, the heart-of-gold saloonkeeper, and kidnap them. Then the badlands gang shoots two Wellington agents. Then they tie up five more and talk about shooting them. Then they desist because they might not be able to get a hotel room in the next town if the word got around. Then one badlands gang gunslinger attempts to rape Kitty while the gang leader's younger daughter looks on. Then Kitty resists, so he slugs her one in the jaw. Then the gang leader slugs him. Then the gang leader slugs Kitty. Then Kitty throws hot stew in a gang member's face and hits him over the back of the head with a revolver. Then he knocks her down with a rock. Then the gang sticks up a bank. Here comes the marshal, Matt Dillon. He shoots a gang member and breaks it up. Then the

23

24

gang leader shoots the guy who was guarding his daughter and the woman. Then the marshal shoots the gang leader. The final exploding bullet signals The End.

It is not the accumulated slayings and bone crushings that make this pornoviolence, however. What makes it pornoviolence is that in almost every case the camera angle, therefore the viewer, is with the gun, the fist, the rock. The pornography of violence has no point of view in the old sense that novels do. You do not live the action through the hero's eyes. You live with the aggressor, whoever he may be. One moment you are the hero. The next you are the villain. No matter whose side you may be on consciously, you are in fact with the muscle, and it is you who disintegrate all comers, villains, lawmen, women, anybody. On the rare occasions in which the gun is emptied into the camera — i.e., into your face — the effect is so startling that the pornography of violence all but loses its fantasy charm. There are not nearly so many masochists as sadists among those little devils whispering into one's ears.

In fact, sex — "sadomasochism" — is only a part of the pornography of violence. Violence is much more wrapped up, simply, with status. Violence is the simple, ultimate solution for problems of status competition, just as gambling is the simple, ultimate solution for economic competition. The old pornography was the fantasy of easy sexual delights in a world where sex was kept unavailable. The new pornography is the fantasy of easy triumph in a world where status competition has become so complicated and frustrating.

Already the old pornography is losing its kick because of overexposure. In the late thirties, Nathanael West published his last and best-regarded novel, *The Day of the Locust*, and it was a terrible flop commercially, and his publisher said if he ever published another book about Hollywood it would "have to be *My Thirty-nine Ways of Making Love by Hedy Lamarr*." He thought he was saying something that was funny because it was beyond the realm of possibility. Less than thirty years later, however, Hedy Lamarr's *Ecstasy and Me* was published. Whether she mentions thirty-nine ways, I'm not sure, but she gets off to a flying start: "The men in my life have ranged from a classic case history of impotence, to a whip-brandishing sadist who enjoyed sex only after he tied my arms behind me with the sash of his robe. There was another man who took his pleasure with a girl in my own bed, while he thought I was asleep in it."

Yet she was too late. The book very nearly sank without a 28 trace. The sin itself is wearing out. Pornography cannot exist without certified taboo to violate. And today Lust, like the rest of the Seven Deadly Sins — Pride, Sloth, Envy, Greed, Anger, and Gluttony — is becoming a rather minor vice. The Seven Deadly Sins, after all, are only sins against the self. Theologically, the idea of Lust — well, the idea is that if you seduce some poor girl from Akron, it is not a sin because you are ruining her, but because you are wasting your time and your energies and damaging your own spirit. This goes back to the old work ethic, when the idea was to keep every able-bodied man's shoulder to the wheel. In an age of riches for all, the ethic becomes more nearly: Let him do anything he pleases, as long as he doesn't get in my way. And if he does get in my way, or even if he doesn't . . . well . . . we have *new* fantasies for that. *Put hair on the walls.*

"Hair on the walls" is the invisible subtitle of Truman Ca- 29 pote's book *In Cold Blood.* The book is neither a who-done-it nor a will-they-be-caught, since the answers to both questions are known from the outset. It does ask why-did-they-do-it, but the answer is soon as clear as it is going to be. Instead, the book's suspense is based largely on a totally new idea in detective stories: the promise of gory details, and the withholding of them until the end. Early in the game one of the two murderers, Dick, starts promising to put "plenty of hair on them-those walls" with a shotgun. So read on, gentle readers, and on and on; you are led up to the moment before the crime on page 60 — yet the specifics, what happened, the gory details, are kept out of sight, in grisly dangle, until page 244.

But Dick and Perry, Capote's killers, are only a couple of 30 Low Rent bums. With James Bond the new pornography reached a dead center, the bureaucratic middle class. The appeal of Bond has been explained as the appeal of the lone man who can solve enormously complicated, even world problems through his own bravery and initiative. But Bond is not a lone man at all, of course. He is not the Lone Ranger. He is much easier to identify than that. He is a salaried functionary in a bureaucracy. He is a sport, but a believable one; not a millionaire, but a bureaucrat on an expense account. He is not even a high-level bureaucrat. He is an operative. This point is carefully and repeatedly made by having his superiors dress him down for violations of standard operating procedure. Bond, like the Lone Ranger, solves problems with guns and fists. When it is over, however, the Lone Ranger leaves a silver bullet. Bond, like the rest of us, fills out a report in triplicate.

Marshall McLuhan[3] says we are in a period in which it will become harder and harder to stimulate lust through words and pictures — i.e., the old pornography. In the latest round of pornographic movies the producers have found it necessary to introduce violence, bondage, torture, and aggressive physical destruction to an extraordinary degree. The same sort of bloody escalation may very well happen in the pure pornography of violence. Even such able craftsmen as Truman Capote, Ian Fleming, NBC, and CBS may not suffice. Fortunately, there are historical models to rescue us from this frustration. In the latter days of the Roman Empire, the Emperor Commodus became jealous of the celebrity of the great gladiators. He took to the arena himself, with his sword, and began dispatching suitably screened cripples and hobbled fighters. Audience participation became so popular that soon various *illuminati* of the Commodus set, various boys and girls of the year, were out there, suited up, gaily cutting a sequence of dwarfs and feebles down to short ribs. Ah, swinging generations, what new delights await?

[3]Canadian English professor (1911–1980); author of *The Medium Is the Message* (1967), *War and Peace in the Global Village* (1968), and other books, McLuhan analyzed the effects on world society of television and other electronic media. — EDS.

QUESTIONS ON MEANING

1. Which of these statements comes closest to summing up Tom Wolfe's main PURPOSE in writing "Pornoviolence"?
   Wolfe writes to define a word.

Wolfe writes to define a trend in society.

Wolfe writes to define a trend in the media that reflects a trend in society.

Wolfe writes to explain how John F. Kennedy was assassinated.

Wolfe writes to entertain us by mocking Americans' latest foolishness.

(If you don't find any of these statements adequate, compose your own.)

2. If you have ever read *The National Enquirer* or any of its imitators, test the accuracy of Wolfe's reporting. What is the purpose of a featured article in the *Enquirer*?

3. According to Wolfe, what POINT OF VIEW does the writer or producer of pornoviolence always take? What other examples of this point of view (in violent incidents on films or TV shows) can you supply? (Did you ever see a replay on TV news of Jack Ruby's shooting of Oswald, for instance?)

4. "Violence is the simple, ultimate solution for problems of status competition" (paragraph 26). What does Wolfe mean? (If you have read Paul Fussell's "Notes on Class" in Chapter 6, recall what Fussell has to say about status and competition for it.)

5. Wolfe does not explicitly pass judgment on Truman Capote's book *In Cold Blood*. But what is his opinion of it? How can you tell?

6. "No advocate of change for the sake of change, Tom Wolfe writes as a conservative moralist who, like Jonathan Swift, rankles with savage indignation." Does this critical remark fit this particular essay? What, in Wolfe's view, appears to be happening to America and Americans?

QUESTIONS ON WRITING STRATEGY

1. On first reading, what did you make of Wolfe's opening sentence, "*Keeps His Mom-in-Law in Chains*, meet *Kills Son and Feeds Corpse to Pigs*"? At what point did you first tumble to what the writer was doing? What IRONY do you find in the convention hosts' introducing people by the headlines of their gory stories? What advantage is it to Wolfe's essay that his INTRODUCTION (with its odd introductions) keeps you guessing for a while?

2. What is Wolfe's point in listing (in paragraph 7) some of the other conventions he has reported — gatherings of nudists, oyster farmers, and others?

3. At what moment does Wolfe give us his short definition of *pornoviolence*, or the new pornography? Do you think he would have

done better to introduce his short definition of the word in para-graph 1? Why or why not?
4. What rhetorical method does Wolfe employ in paragraph 30 to set James Bond and the Lone Ranger side by side?
5. What is the TONE or attitude of Wolfe's CONCLUSION (paragraph 31)? Note in particular the closing line.

QUESTIONS ON LANGUAGE

1. What help to the reader does Wolfe provide by noting the source of the word *pornography* (paragraph 17)?
2. "The television networks have schooled us in the view from Os-wald's rifle" (paragraph 24). What CONNOTATIONS enlarge the meaning of *schooled*?
3. Define *masochist* and *sadist* (paragraph 25). What kind of DICTION do you find in these terms? In "plenty of hair on them-those walls" (29)?
4. How much use does Wolfe make of COLLOQUIAL EXPRESSIONS? Point to examples.
5. What does Wolfe mean in noting that the fighters slain by the Em-peror Commodus were *hobbled* and the cripples were *suitably screened* (paragraph 31)? What unflattering connotations does this emperor's very name contain? (If you don't get this, look up *com-mode* in your desk dictionary.)

SUGGESTIONS FOR WRITING

1. In a paragraph, narrate or describe some recent example of porno-violence you have seen in the movies or on television or one that you have observed. In a second paragraph, comment on it.
2. Write an essay defining some current trend you've noticed in films or TV, popular music, sports, consumer buying, or some other large arena of life. Like Wolfe, invent a name for it. Use plenty of examples to make your definition clear.

Tom Wolfe on Writing

"What about your writing techniques and habits?" Tom Wolfe was asked. "The actual writing I do very fast," he said. "I make a very tight outline of everything I write before I write it. And often, as in the case of *The Electric Kool-Aid Acid Test*, the research, the reporting, is going to take me much longer than the writing. By writing an outline you really are writing in a way, because you're creating the structure of what you're going to do. Once I really know what I'm going to write, I don't find the actual writing takes all that long.

"*The Electric Kool-Aid Acid Test* in manuscript form was about 1,100 pages, triple-spaced, typewritten. That means about 200 words a page, and, you know, some of that was thrown out or cut eventually; but I wrote all of that in three and a half months. I had never written a full-length book before, and at first I decided I would treat each chapter as if it were a magazine article — because I *had* done that before. So I would set an artificial deadline, and I'd make myself meet it. And I did that for three chapters.

"But after I had done this three times and then I looked ahead and I saw that there were *twenty-five* more times I was going to have to do this, I couldn't face it anymore. I said, 'I cannot do this, even one more time, because there's no end to it.' So I completely changed my system, and I set up a quota for myself — of ten typewritten pages a day. At 200 words a page that's 2,000 words, which is not, you know, an overwhelming amount. It's a good clip, but it's not overwhelming. And I found this worked much better. I had my outline done, and sometimes ten pages would get me hardly an eighth-of-an-inch along the outline. It didn't bother me. Just like working in a factory — end of ten pages, I'd close my lunch pail. . . ." ("Sitting up with Tom Wolfe," interview by Joe David Bellamy in *Writer's Digest*, November 1974, pp. 22–23.)

FOR DISCUSSION

1. What is the nature of the preparation that Wolfe does when he's at work on a book?
2. What strategy did the author finally settle on to get himself through the toil of his first book? What made this strategy superior to the one he had used earlier?

· Gretel Ehrlich ·

GRETEL EHRLICH, who was born in Santa Barbara in 1946, attended Bennington College and the UCLA film school. She has been writing full-time since 1979, and her efforts have earned her awards from the American Academy of Arts and Letters, the Wyoming Council on the Arts, and the National Endowment for the Arts. Ehrlich's work has appeared in *Harper's*, the *Atlantic*, the *New York Times*, *Antaeus*, the *Boston Globe*, and many other publications. Her essays were collected in *The Solace of Open Spaces* (1985); other books include *Wyoming Stories* (a collection of short stories), and two volumes of poetry, *To Touch the Water* and *Geode, Rock Body*. Her first novel, *Heart Mountain*, and a new book of essays entitled *Islands, The Universe, Home* were both published in 1988. Ehrlich lives and works on a ranch in Wyoming, where, prior to embarking on her writing career, she worked as a documentary filmmaker.

About Men

"About Men," an essay defining the cowboy, appears in Gretel Ehrlich's collection of essays, *The Solace of Open Spaces*. Ehrlich can speak with authority about what a cowboy does, for she has done much of it herself and has seen the rest of it firsthand. A ranch owner who raises grain, hay, and beef cattle, Ehrlich has also spent time branding, herding sheep, and assisting at the births of lambs and calves. In this essay, she paints a picture of a cowboy very different from the one we're used to seeing in the movies.

When I'm in New York but feeling lonely for Wyoming I look for the Marlboro ads in the subway. What I'm aching to see is horseflesh, the glint of a spur, a line of distant mountains, brimming creeks, and a reminder of the ranchers and cowboys I've ridden with for the last eight years. But the men I see in

those posters with their stern, humorless looks remind me of no
one I know here. In our hellbent earnestness to romanticize the
cowboy we've ironically disesteemed his true character. If he's
"strong and silent" it's because there's probably no one to talk
to. If he "rides away into the sunset" it's because he's been on
horseback since four in the morning moving cattle and he's trying, fifteen hours later, to get home to his family. If he's "a rugged individualist" he's also part of a team: Ranch work is teamwork and even the glorified open-range cowboys of the 1880s
rode up and down the Chisholm Trail in the company of twenty
or thirty other riders. Instead of the macho, trigger-happy man
our culture has perversely wanted him to be, the cowboy is more
apt to be convivial, quirky, and softhearted. To be "tough" on a
ranch has nothing to do with conquests and displays of power.
More often than not, circumstances — like the colt he's riding
or an unexpected blizzard — are overpowering him. It's not
toughness but "toughing it out" that counts. In other words,
this macho, cultural artifact the cowboy has become is simply a
man who possesses resilience, patience, and an instinct for survival. "Cowboys are just like a pile of rocks — everything happens to them. They get climbed on, kicked, rained and snowed
on, scuffed up by wind. Their job is 'just to take it,'" one old-
timer told me.

A cowboy is someone who loves his work. Since the hours   2
are long — ten to fifteen hours a day — and the pay is $30 he
has to. What's required of him is an odd mixture of physical
vigor and maternalism. His part of the beef-raising industry is to
birth and nurture calves and take care of their mothers. For the
most part his work is done on horseback and in a lifetime he sees
and comes to know more animals than people. The iconic myth
surrounding him is built on American notions of heroism: the
index of a man's value as measured in physical courage. Such
ideas have perverted manliness into a self-absorbed race for
cheap thrills. In a rancher's world, courage has less to do with
facing danger than with acting spontaneously — usually on behalf of an animal or another rider. If a cow is stuck in a boghole
he throws a loop around her neck, takes his dally (a half hitch

around the saddle horn), and pulls her out with horsepower. If a calf is born sick, he may take her home, warm her in front of the kitchen fire, and massage her legs until dawn. One friend, whose favorite horse was trying to swim a lake with hobbles on, dove under water and cut her legs loose with a knife, then swam her to shore, his arm around her neck lifeguard-style, and saved her from drowning. Because these incidents are usually linked to someone or something outside himself, the westerner's courage is selfless, a form of compassion.

The physical punishment that goes with cowboying is   3
greatly underplayed. Once fear is dispensed with, the threshold of pain rises to meet the demands of the job. When Jane Fonda asked Robert Redford (in the film *Electric Horseman*) if he was sick as he struggled to his feet one morning, he replied, "No, just bent." For once the movies had it right. The cowboys I was sitting with laughed in agreement. Cowboys are rarely complainers; they show their stoicism by laughing at themselves.

If a rancher or cowboy has been thought of as a "man's   4
man" — laconic, hard-drinking, inscrutable — there's almost no place in which the balancing act between male and female, manliness and femininity, can be more natural. If he's gruff, handsome, and physically fit on the outside, he's androgynous at the core. Ranchers are midwives, hunters, nurturers, providers, and conservationists all at once. What we've interpreted as toughness — weathered skin, calloused hands, a squint in the eye and a growl in the voice — only masks the tenderness inside. "Now don't go telling me these lambs are cute," one rancher warned me the first day I walked into the football-field-sized lambing sheds. The next thing I knew he was holding a black lamb. "Ain't this little rat good-lookin'?"

So many of the men who came to the West were southern-   5
ers — men looking for work and a new life after the Civil War — that chivalrousness and strict codes of honor were soon thought of as western traits. There were very few women in Wyoming during territorial days, so when they did arrive (some as mail-order brides from places like Philadelphia) there was a standoffishness between the sexes and a formality that persists now.

Ranchers still tip their hats and say, "Howdy, ma'am" instead of shaking hands with me.

Even young cowboys are often evasive with women. It's not 6
that they're Jekyll and Hyde creatures — gentle with animals and rough on women — but rather, that they don't know how to bring their tenderness into the house and lack the vocabulary to express the complexity of what they feel. Dancing wildly all night becomes a metaphor for the explosive emotions pent up inside, and when these are, on occasion, released, they're so battery-charged and potent that one caress of the face or one "I love you" will peal for a long while.

The geographical vastness and the social isolation here 7
make emotional evolution seem impossible. Those contradictions of the heart between respectability, logic, and convention on the one hand, and impulse, passion, and intuition on the other, played out wordlessly against the paradisical beauty of the West, give cowboys a wide-eyed but drawn look. Their lips pucker up, not with kisses but with immutability. They may want to break out, staying up all night with a lover just to talk, but they don't know how and can't imagine what the consequences will be. Those rare occasions when they do bare themselves result in confusion. "I feel as if I'd sprained my heart," one friend told me a month after such a meeting.

My friend Ted Hoagland wrote, "No one is as fragile as a 8
woman but no one is as fragile as a man." For all the women here who use "fragileness" to avoid work or as a sexual ploy, there are men who try to hide theirs, all the while clinging to an adolescent dependency on women to cook their meals, wash their clothes, and keep the ranch house warm in winter. But there is true vulnerability in evidence here. Because these men work with animals, not machines or numbers, because they live outside in landscapes of torrential beauty, because they are confined to a place and a routine embellished with awesome variables, because calves die in the arms that pulled others into life, because they go to the mountains as if on a pilgrimage to find out what makes a herd of elk tick, their strength is also a softness, their toughness, a rare delicacy.

QUESTIONS ON MEANING

1. What, in your own words, is the THESIS of this essay?
2. How does Ehrlich define the American idea of heroism, and what does she think is wrong with it?
3. According to Ehrlich, why are so many cowboys formal and gruff in manner? Where in the essay does the author account for this behavior?

QUESTIONS ON WRITING STRATEGY

1. Do you think Ehrlich believes the "mixture of physical vigor and maternalism" (paragraph 2) is a strange one? Why or why not?
2. What is the overall TONE of this essay? Present EVIDENCE to support your answer.

QUESTIONS ON LANGUAGE

1. Explain the distinction the author makes, in the first paragraph, between "toughness" and "toughing it out."
2. In paragraph 7, how do you understand the phrase "emotional evolution"?
3. Look up the following words in the dictionary if you don't know what they mean: disesteemed, convivial (paragraph 1); iconic (2); laconic, inscrutable, androgynous (4); immutability (7).

SUGGESTIONS FOR WRITING

1. Consider the images of cowboys to which you've been exposed over the years. (Avoid the Marlboro Man and Robert Redford's character in *The Electric Horseman*, which Ehrlich discusses.) Write an essay in which you analyze a few of these images. Investigate whether each image perpetuates or works against the stereotype of cowboy as "strong, silent, rugged individualist."
2. Choose a group of people, or a type of person, about whom you believe the general public is ignorant or misinformed. Possible topics might include women who choose to remain home with their children rather than taking an outside job; or students your own

age who were born, and still live, in the U.S.S.R. Write a definition of this group, exploring (and perhaps destroying) common myths as you explain what these people are really like.

Gretel Ehrlich on Writing

"I wrote," says Gretel Ehrlich of her essay, "to see if I could break through the myth of the western man." Especially for *The Bedford Reader*, she has contributed an account of her experience in writing "About Men."

"Whenever I write an essay," she explains, "I go first to my journals. I write in 9" × 6" spiral notebooks, nothing fancy, and though they're not an exact daily record of everything I think, I do note down thoughts worth keeping as well as dreams, snatches of conversation, events that somehow feel larger than they look; i.e., that which seems to have a metaphorical value. This entry sparked something off:

> — to find what is female inside men, or male inside women. Where does the crossover take place, how is it registered in the body, when and why?
> — watching Stan massage the legs of a retarded calf. He spends hours with her. I wonder if he's that patient with his wife?

"But to start the essay off — because it's not very long — I dove right into the macho myth and tried to show the cowboy as a family man, a lonely and therefore vulnerable man, a social person, not a misfit, and someone who might be 'convivial, quirky, and softhearted.' I came right out and told the reader who a typical cowboy is and why our versions of *macho* are all wrong. Why be subtle, I thought as I wrote — the subject matter of the essay dictated the tone, which was to be forthright, to the point, and snappy.

"To write the second paragraph, I did some research on the American notions of heroism: I read Joseph Campbell[1] and Zane Grey,[2] Melville and Hemingway, and the things written about those men, then tried to understand what it is in a human being that evokes a sense of heroic awe in me. I came to that answer quickly. It's watching a cowboy massage a calf's legs, carrying it home in a snowstorm and warming it in the kitchen, or pulling a drowning horse or cow from a bog hole — in other words, saving lives with little concern for one's own comfort or convenience.

"It occurred to me then that another important element of heroism is humor, so I pulled an anecdote from memory to illustrate that point.

"The next paragraph contains material that might have been expanded into a whole book, so complex is it. But since I had set out to make this 'a quick study,' I pared it down to a skeleton and condensed it — perhaps too much. The Jungian questions of male and female principles, of tenderheartedness and warriorship, of social convention versus impulse, of emotional cowardice and courage, of passivity and passion. . . . these thoughts all rumbled through my mind as I wrote, though I knew what I didn't address in this essay would be undertaken in others — for years to come. I wasn't prepared to write about all those things at the time and knew they would keep.

"The last paragraph of 'About Men' addresses the question *why*. Why are men here softhearted, why behind their tough, gruff exteriors do I find tenderness? Once again I perused my journals. I knew my answer, but I wanted to back it up with fresh glimpses. Then I came on the essayist Edward Hoagland's line, 'No one is as fragile as a woman, but no one is as fragile as a

---

[1]American writer and educator (1904–1987), author of *The Hero with a Thousand Faces* (1949), *The Masks of God* (1959–67), and other studies of mythmaking. — Eds.

[2]American writer of Western stories (1875–1939), including *Riders of the Purple Sage* (1912) and other novels with idealized cowboy heroes. Grey was an Ohio-born dentist. — Eds.

man,' which I had jotted down some years before. In that one sentence, he did what I had taken an essay to do: He presented a stereotype, then revised it with a seeming contradiction. That quote was a window into which I could look at a man and see what was actually there, see the relentless need for men to express their frailty and the cultural obstacles put in the way of that expression. But I did see it. Every time I saw men working with animals the tenderness and humor and humility came out; I saw how true strength is actual tenderness. And that's what I wrote, that's how I finished the essay.

"I've written a novel and many essays since 'About Men,' and there are many different approaches. Unlike some, where I don't really know what I'm writing about until half or a third of the way through, I started 'About Men' with a specific idea and simply followed my mind as I wrote, moving swiftly from one idea to the next with little ado. This kind of essay is easy to write; it's the thinking about it that takes a long time."

FOR DISCUSSION

1. What do you suppose Ehrlich's reading (described in her second paragraph) contributed to the writing of her essay?
2. Compare Gretel Ehrlich's notebook-keeping habits with those of Joan Didion as set forth in her essay on page 654.

· Joseph Epstein ·

JOSEPH EPSTEIN, author, critic, and editor of *The American Scholar*, teaches writing and literature at Northwestern University. He was born in Chicago in 1937. A graduate of the University of Chicago, he served in the army from 1958 to 1960. His lively and incisive essays have appeared from time to time in such places as the *New York Times Book Review*, *Commentary*, *The New Criterion*, the *New York Times Magazine*, and *Harper's*. He is the author of *Divorce in America* (1975); *Familiar Territory* (1980); *Ambition* (1981); *The Middle of My Tether* (1983); *Plausible Prejudices* (1985); and *Once More Around the Block* (1987).

What Is Vulgar?

Epstein wrote "What Is Vulgar?" for *The American Scholar*, the magazine published by Phi Beta Kappa (the oldest American honor society for college students). Later he included it in *The Middle of My Tether*. In the essay Epstein seems to have a rollicking good time deciding what vulgarity is. He examines the history of both word and concept. He speculates about what vulgarity is *not*. He relishes colorful examples. Some aspects of his definition may surprise you; others may give you a jolt. We're sure they won't bore you.

What's vulgar? Some people might say that the contraction 1 of the words *what* and *is* itself is vulgar. On the other hand, I remember being called a stuffed shirt by a reviewer of a book of mine because I used almost no contractions. I have forgotten the reviewer's name but I have remembered the criticism. Not being of that category of writers who never forget a compliment, I also remember being called a racist by another reviewer for observing that failure to insist on table manners in children was to risk dining with Apaches. The larger criticisms I forget, but, oddly, these goofy little criticisms stick in the teeth like sesame seeds.

Yet that last trope — is it, too, vulgar? Ought I really to be picking my teeth in public, even metaphorically?

What, to return to the question in uncontractioned form, is   2
vulgar? Illustrations, obviously, are wanted. Consider a relative of mine, long deceased, my father's Uncle Jake and hence my grand-uncle. I don't wish to brag about bloodlines, but my Uncle Jake was a bootlegger during Prohibition who afterward went into the scrap-iron — that is to say, the junk — business. Think of the archetypal sensitive Jewish intellectual faces: of Spinoza, of Freud, of Einstein, of Oppenheimer.[1] In my uncle's face you would not have found the least trace of any of them. He was completely bald, weighed in at around two hundred fifty pounds, and had a complexion of clear vermilion. I loved him, yet even as a child I knew there was about him something a bit — how shall I put it? — outsized, and I refer not merely to his personal tonnage. When he visited our home he generally greeted me by pressing a ten- or twenty-dollar bill into my hand — an amount of money quite impossible, of course, for a boy of nine or ten, when what was wanted was a quarter or fifty-cent piece. A widower, he would usually bring a lady-friend along; here his tastes ran to Hungarian women in their fifties with operatic bosoms. These women wore large diamond rings, possibly the same rings, which my uncle may have passed from woman to woman. A big spender and a high roller, my uncle was an immigrant version of the sport, a kind of Diamond Chaim Brodsky.

But to see Uncle Jake in action you had to see him at table.   3
He drank whiskey with his meal, the bottle before him on the table along with another of seltzer water, both of which he supplied himself. He ate and drank like a character out of Rabelais.[2] My mother served him his soup course, not in a regular bowl,

---

[1]Benedict (or Baruch) Spinoza (1632–1677) was a Dutch philosopher; Sigmund Freud (1856–1939), the Austrian founder of psychoanalysis; J. Robert Oppenheimer (1904–1967), an American physicist who opposed the government's decision to develop the hydrogen bomb. For more about Albert Einstein (1879–1955), see the essay by Banesh Hoffmann in Chapter 3. — EDS.
[2]François Rabelais (1494?–1553?), French humorist who in *Gargantua and Pantagruel* (1532–1534) depicts two giants with tremendous appetites. — EDS.

but in a vessel more on the order of a tureen. He would eat hot soup and drink whiskey and sweat — my Uncle Jake did not, decidedly, do anything so delicate as perspire — and sometimes it seemed that the sweat rolled from his face right into his soup dish, so that, toward the end, he may well have been engaged in an act of liquid auto-cannibalism, consuming his own body fluids with a whiskey chaser.

He was crude, certainly, my Uncle Jake; he was coarse, of course; gross, it goes without saying; uncouth, beyond question. But was he vulgar? I don't think he was. For one thing, he was good-hearted, and it somehow seems wrong to call anyone vulgar who is good-hearted. But more to the point, I don't think that if you had accused him of being vulgar, he would have known what the devil you were talking about. To be vulgar requires at least a modicum of pretension, and this Uncle Jake sorely lacked. "Wulgar," he might have responded to the accusation that he was vulgar, "so vat's dis wulgar?" 4

To go from persons to things, and from lack of pretension to a mountain of it, let me tell you about a house I passed one night, in a neighborhood not far from my own, that so filled me with disbelief that I took a hard right turn at the next corner and drove round the block to make certain I had actually seen what I thought I had. I had, but it was no house — it was a bloody edifice! 5

The edifice in question totally fills its rather modest lot, leaving no backyard at all. It is constructed of a white stone, sanded and perhaps even painted, with so much gray-colored mortar that, even though it may be real, the stone looks fake. The roof is red. It has two chimneys, neither of which, I would wager, functions. My confidence here derives from the fact that nothing much else in the structure of the house seems to function. There is, for example, a balcony over a portico — a portico held up by columns — onto which the only possible mode of entry is by pole vault. There is, similarly, over the attached garage, a sun deck whose only access appears to be through a bathroom window. The house seems to have been built on the aesthetic formula of functionlessness follows formlessness. 6

But it is in its details that the true spirit of the house 7 emerges. These details are not minuscule, and neither are they subtle. For starters, outside the house under the portico, there is a chandelier. There are also two torch-shaped lamps on either side of the front door, which is carved in a scallop pattern, giving it the effect of seeming the back door to a much larger house. Along the short walk leading up to this front door stand, on short pillars, two plaster of paris lions — gilded. On each pillar, in gold and black, appears the owner's name. A white chain fence, strung along poles whose tops are painted gold, spans the front of the property; it is the kind of fence that would be more appropriate around, say, the tomb of Lenin. At the curb are two large cars, sheets of plastic covering their grills; there is also a trailer; and, in the summer months, a boat sits in the short driveway leading up to the garage. The lawn disappoints by being not Astro-Turf but, alas, real grass. However, closer inspection reveals two animals, a skunk and a rabbit, both of plastic, in petrified play upon the lawn — a nice, you might almost say a finishing, touch. Sometimes, on long drives or when unable to sleep at night, I have pondered upon the possible decor of this extraordinary house's den and upon the ways of man, which are various beyond imagining.

You want vulgar, I am inclined to exclaim, I'll show you vulgar: The house I have just described is vulgar, patently, palpably, pluperfectly vulgar. Forced to live in it for more than three hours, certain figures of refined sensibility — Edith Wharton or Harold Acton or Wallace Stevens[3] — might have ended as suicides. Yet as I described that house, I noted two contradictory feelings in myself: how pleasant it is to point out someone else's vulgarity, and yet the fear that calling someone else vulgar may itself be slightly vulgar. After all, the family that lives in this house no doubt loves it; most probably they feel that they have a real showplace. Their house, I assume, gives them a large measure of happiness. Yet why does my calling their home vulgar

8

[3]Edith Wharton (1862–1937), American novelist, who frequently wrote of well-to-do society; Harold Acton (1904–), British art critic, historian, and student of Chinese culture, author of *Memoirs of an Aesthete* (1948) and other works; Wallace Stevens (1879–1955), American poet and insurance company executive, who wrote with a philosopher's sensibility. — EDS.

also give me such a measure of happiness? I suppose it is because vulgarity can be so amusing — other people's vulgarity, that is.

Here I must insert that I have invariably thought that the people who have called me vulgar were themselves rather vulgar. So far as I know I have been called vulgar three times, once directly, once behind my back, and once by association. In each instance the charge was intellectual vulgarity: On one occasion a contributor to a collection of essays on contemporary writing that I once reviewed called me vulgar because I didn't find anything good to say about this book of some six hundred pages; once an old friend, an editor with whom I had had a falling out over politics, told another friend of mine that an article I had written seemed to him vulgar; and, finally, having patched things up with this friend and having begun to write for his magazine again, yet a third friend asked me why I allowed my writing to appear in that particular magazine, when it was so patently — you guessed her, Chester — vulgar. 9

None of these accusations stung in the least. In intellectual and academic life, vulgar is something one calls people with whom one disagrees. Like having one's ideas called reductionist, it is nothing to get worked up about — certainly nothing to take personally. What would wound me, though, is if word got back to me that someone had said that my manners at table were so vulgar that it sickened him to eat with me, or that my clothes were laughable, or that taste in general wasn't exactly my strong point. In a novel whose author or title I can no longer remember, I recall a female character who was described as having vulgar thumbs. I am not sure I have a clear picture of vulgar thumbs, but if it is all the same, I would just as soon not have them. 10

I prefer not to be thought vulgar in any wise. When not long ago a salesman offered to show me a winter coat that, as he put it, "has been very popular," I told him to stow it — if it has been popular, it is not for me. I comb my speech, as best I am able, of popular phrases: You will not hear an unfundamental "basically" or a flying "whatever" from these chaste lips. I do not utter "bottom line"; I do not mutter "trade-off." I am keen to cut myself out from the herd, at least when I can. In recent years 11 this has not been difficult. Distinction has lain in plain speech, plain dress, clean cheeks. The simple has become rococo, the rococo simple. But now I see that television anchormen, hairdressers, and other leaders in our society have adopted this plainer look. This is discomfiting news. Vulgar is, after all, as vulgar does.

Which returns us yet again to the question: What is vulgar? 12 *The Oxford English Dictionary*, which provides more than two pages on the word, is rather better at telling us what vulgar was than what it is. Its definitions run from "1. The common or usual language of a country; the vernacular. *Obs.*" to "13. Having a common and offensively mean character; coarsely commonplace; lacking in refinement or good taste; uncultured, ill-bred." Historically, the word vulgar was used in fairly neutral description up to the last quarter of the seventeenth century to mean and describe the common people. Vulgar was common but not yet contemned. I noted such a neutral usage as late as a William Hazlitt essay of 1818, "On the Ignorance of the Learned," in which Hazlitt writes: "The vulgar are in the right when they judge for themselves; they are wrong when they trust to their blind guides." Yet, according to the *OED*, in 1797 the *Monthly Magazine* remarked: "So the word *vulgar* now implies something base and groveling in actions."

From the early nineteenth century on, then, vulgar has 13 been purely pejorative, a key term in the lexicon of insult and invective. Its currency as a term of abuse rose with the rise of the middle class; its spread was tied to the spread of capitalism and democracy. Until the rise of the middle class, until the spread of capitalism and democracy, people perhaps hadn't the occasion or the need to call one another vulgar. The rise of the middle class, the spread of capitalism and democracy, opened all sorts of social doors; social classes commingled as never before; plutocracy made possible almost daily strides from stratum to stratum. Still, some people had to be placed outside the pale, some doors had to be locked — and the cry of vulgarity, properly intoned, became a most effective Close Sesame.

Such seems to me roughly the social history of the word vul- 14 gar. But the history of vulgarity, the thing itself even before it

had a name, is much longer. According to the French art historian Albert Dasnoy, aesthetic vulgarity taints Greek art of the
fourth and third centuries B.C. "An exhibition of Roman por-
traits," Dasnoy writes, "shows that, between the Etruscan style
of the earliest and the Byzantine style of the latest, vulgarity
made its first full-blooded appearance in the academic realism of
imperial Rome." Vulgarity, in Dasnoy's view, comes of the
shock of philosophic rationalism, when humankind divests itself
of belief in the sacred. "Vulgarity seems to be the price of man's
liberation," he writes, "one might even say, of his evolution. It is
unquestionably the price of the freeing of the individual personality." Certainly it is true that one would never think to call a
savage vulgar; a respectable level of civilization has to have been
reached to qualify for the dubious distinction of being called
vulgar.

"You have surely noticed the curious fact," writes Valéry,[4] 15
"that a certain *word*, which is perfectly clear when you hear or
use it in *everyday* speech, and which presents no difficulty when
caught up in the rapidity of an ordinary sentence, becomes mys-
teriously cumbersome, offers a strange resistance, defeats all efforts at definition, the moment you withdraw it from circulation
for separate study and try to find its meaning after taking away
its temporary function." Vulgar presents special difficulties,
though: While vulgarity has been often enough on display —
may even be a part of the human soul that only the fortunate
and the saintly are able to root out — every age has its own notion of what constitutes the vulgar. Riding a bicycle at Oxford in
the 1890s, Max Beerbohm reports, "was the earmark of vulgarity." Working further backward, we find that Matthew Arnold
frequently links the word vulgar with the word hideous and
hopes that culture "saves the future, as one may hope, from being vulgarized, even if it cannot save the present." "In Jane Aus-
ten's novels," Lionel Trilling writes, "vulgarity has these elements: smallness of mind, insufficiency of awareness, assertive
self-esteem, the wish to devalue, especially to devalue the human
worth of other people." Hazlitt found vulgarity in false feeling

---

[4]Paul Valéry (1871–1945), French poet and literary critic. — EDS.

among "the herd of pretenders to what they do not feel and to what is not natural to them, whether in high or low life."

Vulgarity, it begins to appear, is often in the eye of the beholder. What is more, it comes in so many forms. It is so multiple and so complex — so multiplex. There are vulgarities of taste, of manner, of mind, of spirit. There are whole vulgar ages — the Gilded Age in the United States, for one, at least to hear Mark Twain and Henry Adams tell it. (Is our own age another?) To compound the complication there is even likeable vulgarity. This is vulgarity of the kind that Cyril Connolly must have had in mind when he wrote, "Vulgarity is the garlic in the salad of life." In the realm of winning vulgarity are the novels of Balzac, the paintings of Frans Hals, some of the music of Tchaikovsky (excluding the cannon fire in the 1812 Overture, which is vulgarity of the unwinning kind). 16

Rightly used, profanity, normally deemed the epitome of vulgar manners, can be charming. I recently moved to a new apartment, and the person I dealt with at the moving company we employed, a woman whose voice had an almost strident matter-of-factness, instructed me to call back with an inventory of our furniture. When I did, our conversation, starting with my inventory of our living room, began: 17

"One couch." 18

"One couch." 19

"Two lamp tables, a coffee table, a small gateleg table." 20

"Four tables." 21

"Two wing chairs and an occasional chair." 22

"Three chairs." 23

"One box of bric-a-brac." 24

"One box of shit." 25

Heavy garlic of course is not to every taste; but then again some people do not much care for endive. I attended city schools, where garlic was never in short supply and where profanity, in proper hands, could be a useful craft turned up to the power of fine art. I have since met people so well-mannered, so icily, elegantly correct, that with a mere glance across the table or a word to a waiter they could put a chill on the wine and indeed on the entire evening. Some people have more, some less, 26 in the way of polish, but polish doesn't necessarily cover vulgarity. As there can be diamonds in the rough, so can there be sludge in the smooth.

It would be helpful in drawing a definitional bead on the 27 word vulgar if one could determine its antonym. But I am not sure that it has an antonym. Refined? I think not. Sophisticated? Not really. Elegant? Nope. Charming? Close, but I can think of charming vulgarians — M. Rabelais, please come forth and take a bow. Besides, charm is nearly as difficult to define as vulgarity. Perhaps the only safe thing to be said about charm is that if you think you have it, you can be fairly certain that you don't.

If vulgarity cannot be defined by its antonym, from the rear 28 so to say, examples may be more to the point. I once heard a friend describe a woman thus: "Next to Sam Jensen's prose, she's the vulgarest thing in New York." From this description, I had a fairly firm sense of what the woman was like. Sam Jensen is a writer for one of the newsmagazines; each week on schedule he makes a fresh cultural discovery, writing as if every sentence will be his last, every little movie or play he reviews will change our lives — an exhibitionist with not a great deal to exhibit. Sam Jensen is a fictitious name — made up to protect the guilty — but here are a few sentences that he, not I, made up:

> The great Victorian William Morris combined a practical socialism with a love for the spirit of the King Arthur legends. What these films show is the paradox democracy has forgotten — that the dream of Camelot is the ultimate dream of freedom and order in a difficult but necessary balance.

> The screenplay by Michael Wilson and Richard Maibaum is not from an Ian Fleming novel; it's really a cookbook that throws Roger Moore as Bond into these action recipes like a cucumber tossed into an Osterizer. Osterization is becoming more and more necessary for Moore; he's beginning to look a bit puckered, as if he's been bottled in Bond.

From these sentences — with their false paradoxes, muffed metaphors, obvious puns, and general bloat — I think I can extrapolate the woman who, next to this prose, is the vulgarest thing in New York. I see teeth, I see elaborate hairdo, much jewelry, flamboyant dress, a woman requiring a great deal of attention, who sucks up most of the mental oxygen in any room she is in — a woman, in sum, vastly overdone.

Coming at things from a different angle, I imagine myself in   29
session with a psychologist, playing the word association game. "Vulgar," he says, "quick, name ten items you associate with the word vulgar." "Okay," I say, "here goes:

   1. Publicity
   2. The Oscar awards
   3. The Aspen Institute for Humanistic Studies
   4. Talk shows
   5. Pulitzer Prizes
   6. Barbara Walters
   7. Interviews with writers
   8. Lauren Bacall
   9. Dialogue as an ideal
  10. Psychology."

This would not, I suspect, be everyone's list. Looking it over, I see that, of the ten items, several are linked with one another. But let me inquire into what made me choose the items I did.

Ladies first. Barbara Walters seems to me vulgar because for   30
a great many years now she has been paid to ask all the vulgar questions, and she seems to do it with such cheerfulness, such competence, such amiable insincerity. "What did you think when you first heard your husband had been killed?" she will ask, just the right hush in her voice. "What went on in your mind when you learned that you had cancer, now for the third time?" The questions that people with imagination do not need to ask, the questions that people with good hearts know they have no right to ask, these questions and others Barbara Walters can be depended upon to ask. "Tell me, Holy Father, have you never regretted not having children of your own?"

Lauren Bacall has only recently graduated to vulgarity, or at   31
least she has only in the past few years revealed herself vulgar. Hers is a double vulgarity: the vulgarity of false candor — the woman who, presumably, tells it straight — and the vulgarity provided by someone who has decided to cash in her chips. In

her autobiography, Miss Bacall has supposedly told all her secrets; when interviewed on television — by, for example, Barbara Walters — the tack she takes is that of the ringwise babe
over whose eyes no one, kiddo, is going to pull the cashmere.
Yet turn the channel or page, and there is Miss Bacall in a commercial or advertisement doing her best to pull the cashmere
over ours. Vulgar stuff.

Talk shows are vulgar for the same reason that Pulitzer   32
Prizes and the Aspen Institute for Humanistic Studies are vulgar. All three fail to live up to their pretensions, which are ex-
travagant: talk shows to being serious, Pulitzer Prizes to rewarding true merit, the Aspen Institute to promoting "dialogue" (see
item 9), "the bridging of cultures," "the interdisciplinary approach," and nearly every other phony shibboleth that has
cropped up in American intellectual life over the past three decades.

Publicity is vulgar because those who seek it — and even   33
those who are sought by it — tend almost without exception to
be divested of their dignity. You have to sell yourself, the sales
manuals used to advise, in order to sell your product. With publicity, though, one is selling only oneself, which is different.
Which is a bit vulgar, really.

The Oscar awards ceremony is the single item on my list   34
least in need of explanation, for it seems vulgar prima facie. It is
the air of self-congratulation — of, a step beyond, self-adulation
— that is so splendidly vulgar about the Oscar awards ceremony. Self-congratulation, even on good grounds, is best con-
cealed; on no grounds whatever, it is embarrassing. But then,
for vulgarity, there's no business like show business.

Unless it be literary business. The only thing worse than   35
false modesty is no modesty at all, and no modesty at all is what
interviews with writers generally bring out. "That most vulgar of
all crowds the literary," wrote Keats presciently — that is, before
the incontestable evidence came in with the advent and subsequent popularity of what is by now that staple of the book review and little magazine and talk show, the interview with the
great author. What these interviews generally come down to is
an invitation to writers to pontificate upon things for which it is

either unseemly for them to speak (the quality of their own work) or upon which they are unfit to judge (the state of the cosmos). Roughly a decade ago I watched Isaac Bashevis Singer,[5] when asked on a television talk show what he thought of the Vietnam War, answer, "I am a writer, and that doesn't mean I have to have an opinion on everything. I'd rather discuss literature." Still, how tempting it is, with an interviewer chirping away at your feet, handing you your own horn and your own drum, to blow it and beat it. As someone who has been interviewed a time or two, I can attest that never have I shifted spiritual gears so quickly from self-importance to self-loathing as during and after an interview. What I felt was, well, vulgar.

Psychology seems to me vulgar because it is too often overbearing in its confidence. Instead of saying, "I don't know," it readily says, "unresolved Oedipus complex" or "manic-depressive syndrome" or "identity crisis." As with other intellectual discoveries before (Marxism) and since (structuralism), psychology acts as if it is holding all the theoretical keys, but then in practice reveals that it doesn't even know where the doors are. As an old *Punch* cartoon once put it, "It's worse than wicked, my dear, it's vulgar." 36

Reviewing my list and attempting to account for the reasons why I have chosen the items on it, I feel I have a firmer sense of what I think vulgar. Exhibitionism, obviousness, pretentiousness, self-congratulation, self-importance, hypocrisy, overconfidence — these seem to me qualities at the heart of vulgarity in our day. It does, though, leave out common sense, a quality which, like clarity, one might have thought one could never have in overabundance. (On the philosophy table in my local bookstore, a book appeared with the title *Clarity Is Not Enough*; I could never pass it without thinking, "Ah, but it's a start.") Yet too great reliance on common sense can narrow the mind, make meager the imagination. Strict common sense abhors mystery, seldom allows for the attraction of tradition, is intolerant of questions that haven't any answers. The problem that common 37

[5]Singer (born in 1904), Polish-born American writer of fiction in Yiddish, received the Nobel Prize for Literature in 1978. — Eds.

sense presents is knowing the limits of common sense. The too commonsensical man or woman grows angry at anything that falls outside his or her common sense, and this anger seems to me vulgar.

Vulgarity is not necessarily stupid but it is always insensitive. Its insensitivity invariably extends to itself: The vulgar person seldom knows that he is vulgar, as in the old joke about the young woman whose fiancé reports to her that his parents found her vulgar, and who, enraged, responds, "What's this vulgar crap?" Such obvious vulgarity can be comical, like a nouveau riche man bringing opera glasses to a porno film, or the Chicago politician who, while escorting the then ruling British monarch through City Hall, supposedly introduced him to the assembled aldermen by saying, "King, meet the boys." But such things are contretemps merely, not vulgarity of the insidious kind. 38

In our age vulgarity does not consist in failing to recognize the fish knife or to know the wine list but in the inability to make distinctions. Not long ago I heard a lecture by a Harvard philosophy professor on a Howard Hawks movie, and thought, as one high reference after another was made in connection with this low subject, "Oh, Santayana,[6] 'tis better you are not alive to see this." A vulgar performance, clearly, yet few people in the audience of professors and graduate students seemed to notice. 39

A great many people did notice, however, when, in an act of singular moral vulgarity, a publisher, an editor, and a novelist recently sponsored a convicted murderer for parole, and the man, not long after being paroled, murdered again. The reason for these men speaking out on behalf of the convict's parole, they said, was his ability as a writer: His work appeared in the editor's journal; he was to have a book published by the publisher's firm; the novelist had encouraged him from the outset. Distinctions — crucial distinctions — were not made: first, that the man was not a very good writer, but a crudely Marxist one, whose work was filled with hatreds and half-truths; second, and more important, that, having killed before, he might kill again 40

[6]George Santayana (1863–1952) was a Spanish-born American poet and philosopher. — EDS.

— might just be a pathological killer. Not to have made these distinctions is vulgarity at its most vile. But to adopt a distinction new to our day, the publisher, the editor, and the novelist took responsibility for what they had done — responsibility but no real blame.

Can an entire culture grow vulgar? Matthew Arnold feared   41
such might happen in "the mechanical and material civilisation" of the England of his day. Vladimir Nabokov felt it already had happened in the Soviet Union, a country, as he described it, "of moral imbeciles, of smiling slaves and poker-faced bullies," without, as in the old days, "a Gogol, a Tolstoy, a Chekhov in quest of that simplicity of truth [who] easily distinguished the vulgar side of things as well as the trashy systems of pseudo-thought." Moral imbeciles, smiling slaves, poker-faced bullies — the curl of a sneer in those Nabokovian phrases is a sharp reminder of the force that the charge of "vulgar" can have as an insult — as well as a reminder of how deep and pervasive vulgarity can become.

But American vulgarity, if I may put it so, is rather more re-   42
fined. It is also more piecemeal than pervasive, and more insidious. Creeping vulgarity is how I think of it, the way Taft Republicans[7] used to think of creeping socialism. The insertion of a science fiction course in a major university curriculum, a television commercial by a once-serious actor for a cheap wine, an increased interest in gossip and trivia that is placed under the rubric Style in our most important newspapers: So the vulgar creeps along, while everywhere the third- and fourth-rate — in art, in literature, in intellectual life — is considered good enough, or at any rate highly interesting.

Yet being refined — or at least sophisticated — American   43
vulgarity is vulnerable to the charge of being called vulgar. "As long as war is regarded as wicked," said Oscar Wilde, "it will always have its fascination. When it is looked upon as vulgar, it will cease to be popular." There may be something to this, if not for war then at least for designer jeans, French literary criticism, and other fashions. The one thing the vulgar of our day do not like to be called is vulgar. So crook your little finger, purse your

[7]Robert A. Taft (1889–1953), U.S. senator from Ohio from 1939 to 1953, was a leading spokesperson for Republican conservatives. — Eds.

lips, distend your nostrils slightly as you lift your nose in the air the better to look down it, and repeat after me: *Vulgar! Vulgar! Vulgar!* The word might save us all.

QUESTIONS ON MEANING

1. On what basis does the author conclude that the house with the portico is vulgar and Uncle Jake is not?
2. To what events in history does Epstein attribute the growth of unfavorable CONNOTATIONS around the word *vulgar?*
3. What are the key words in Epstein's definition of vulgarity? Where does he list them? Which one seems at first glance the most surprising?
4. In which paragraph does the author most succinctly sum up his definition of vulgarity?
5. What points does Epstein make in paragraph 4 and in paragraph 38? Does he contradict himself? Explain.
6. Look up *vulgar* and *vulgarity* in your desk dictionary. In his essay, what liberties has Epstein taken with the dictionary definition? To what extent are these liberties justified? Do they hint at any PURPOSE besides definition?

QUESTIONS ON WRITING STRATEGY

1. Epstein uses the example of Uncle Jake to perform several functions in his essay. What are they?
2. What does Epstein's TONE contribute to his essay?
3. What proportion of Epstein's essay is devoted to illustrating what vulgarity is *not?* Of what value is this material to the essay as a whole?
4. What devices does Epstein use to give his long essay COHERENCE?
5. What segments of Epstein's AUDIENCE might be expected to enjoy his essay the most? Whom might it offend?

QUESTIONS ON LANGUAGE

1. Be sure you know what the following words mean as Epstein uses them: archetypal, vermilion, sport (paragraph 2); modicum, pretension (4); edifice (5); portico (6); minuscule (7); patently, palpa-

bly, pluperfectly, sensibility (8); reductionist (10); rococo, discomfiting (11); contemned (12); pejorative, lexicon, invective, commingled, plutocracy, stratum (13); aesthetic, rationalism, divests (14); epitome (17); extrapolate (28); shibboleth (32); prima facie (34); presciently, incontestable, advent, pontificate (35); theoretical (36); abhors (37); nouveau riche, contretemps, insidious (38); singular, pathological (40); pervasive (41); piecemeal, insidious (42).

2. What does the author mean by "operatic bosoms" (paragraph 2); "in petrified play" (7); "outside the pale" (13); "diamonds in the rough" (26); "drawing a definitional bead" (27)?

3. What ALLUSION do you find in the name "Diamond Chaim Brodsky" (paragraph 2)? In the phrases "functionlessness follows formlessness" (6); "Vulgar is . . . as vulgar does" (11); "Close Sesame" (13); and "pull the cashmere" (31)?

4. Where in the essay does Epstein use COLLOQUIAL EXPRESSIONS? Where does his word choice inject humor into the essay?

5. Identify the METAPHORS in paragraph 26. Do they have any function other than as word play? If so, what?

SUGGESTIONS FOR WRITING

1. Write your own definition of some quality other than vulgarity. Possible subjects might be refinement, prudishness, generosity, classiness, sensitivity, dishonesty, or snobbishness. One approach might be to tell what the quality is *not* as well as what it is. Load your essay with examples.

2. In paragraph 29, Epstein lists ten items he associates with the word *vulgar*. Paul Fussell, author of "Notes on Class" (Chapter 6), is another distinguished writer to ponder the subject of vulgarity. In his book *Class*, in a section of imaginary (and very funny) letters from his readers, he answers the request, "To settle a bet, would you indicate some things that are Vulgar?":

> I'd say these are vulgar, but in no particular order: Jerry Lewis's TV telethon; any "Cultural Center"; beef Wellington; cute words for drinks like *drinky-poos* or *nightcaps*; dinner napkins with high polyester content; colored wineglasses; oil paintings depicting members of the family; display of laminated diplomas.

(Old clothes and paper napkins, he adds, aren't vulgar; neither are fireworks on the Fourth of July.) In a paragraph, nominate a few other "vulgar" things and tell why you think each deserves its label.

Joseph Epstein on Writing

"As a professional writer, I have this in common with the student writer," says Joseph Epstein in a statement written for *The Bedford Reader*. "I cannot sit around and wait for inspiration to arrive."

Like most of what Epstein writes, "What Is Vulgar?" was written to a deadline. He planned for the essay, following a simple, workable system, which he recommends to students assigned to write a long paper. In a file folder, he notes everything he can think of that has any connection with the proposed subject of his essay: quotations, anecdotes, other books and articles on the subject to look into, stray ideas. On index cards and odd scraps of paper, he jots down any items that occur to him as the days pass; everything swells the folder. "Sometimes, while shopping or driving around, I will think up possible opening sentences for my essay. These, too, go into the folder. When I finally do sit down to the writing of my essay, I don't sit down empty-handed — or, perhaps more precisely, empty-minded. I have a store of material before me, which I find a very great aid to composition."

Epstein never uses an outline. "I am not opposed to outlines in logic or on principle but by temperament. I have never felt comfortable with them. I wonder if many serious essayists do use outlines. Aldous Huxley once described the method of the great French essayist Montaigne as 'free association artistically controlled.' I know something similar occurs in my own writing. We all free-associate easily enough; the trick is in the artistic control. But I know I have given up on outlines because I have discovered that there is no way I can know what will be in the second paragraph of something I write until I have written the first paragraph. My first paragraph may contain a phrase or end on a point I hadn't anticipated, and this phrase or point may send me off into an entirely unexpected direction in my second paragraph.

"When I set out to write the essay 'What Is Vulgar?' I had only a vague notion of what would go into it (apart from some of the scraps in that folder). Certainly, I was not yet clear about my thoughts on vulgarity. The chief point of the essay, for me, was to find out what I really did think about it. The essay itself, now that it is done, shows a writer in the act of thinking.

"Which is a roundabout way of saying that, for me, writing is foremost a mode of thinking and, when it works well, an act of discovery. I write to find out what I believe, what seems logical and sensible to me, what notions, ideas, and views I can live with. I don't mean to say that, when I begin an essay, I don't have some general view or feeling about my subject. I mean instead that, when I begin, I am never altogether sure how I am going to end. Robert Frost once said that whenever he knew how one of his poems was going to end, it almost invariably turned out to be a bad poem. I believe him. Writing for discovery, to find out what one truly thinks of things, may be a bit riskier than writing knowing one's conclusion in advance, but it figures to be much more interesting, more surprising, and, once one gets over one's early apprehension at the prospect of winging it, more fun."

FOR DISCUSSION

1. What makes Epstein skeptical of outlines?
2. Do you agree or disagree with Epstein's view of writing as a way of finding out what you believe? Can you think of any situations for which this approach would not work?

1. Write an essay in which you define an institution, a trend, a phenomenon, or an abstraction. Following are some suggestions designed to stimulate ideas. Before you begin, limit your subject as far as possible, and illustrate your essay with specific examples.

   Education
   Progress
   Advertising
   Happiness
   Overpopulation
   Personality
   Fads
   Women's liberation
   Marriage
   A fascist
   Sportsmanship
   Politics
   Leadership
   Leisure
   Originality
   Character
   Imagination
   Democracy
   A smile
   A classic (of music, literature, art, or film)
   Dieting
   Meditation
   A friend

2. In a brief essay, define one of the following. In each instance, you have a choice of something good or something bad to talk about.

   A good or bad boss
   A good or bad parent
   A good or bad host
   A good or bad TV newscaster
   A good or bad physician

A good or bad nurse
A good or bad minister, priest, or rabbi
A good or bad roommate
A good or bad driver
A good or bad disk jockey

3. In a paragraph, define one of the following for someone who has never heard the word: nerd, wimp, free spirit, preppie, "dog," "turkey," druggie, snob, freak, winner, loser, loner, freeloader, burnout, soul, mellowing out, quack, deadbeat, "bomb," pig-out, gross-out, winging it.

· 10 ·

ARGUMENT AND PERSUASION

Stating Opinions and Proposals

THE METHOD

Practically every day, we try to persuade ourselves, or some-one else. We usually attempt such persuasion without being aware that we follow any special method at all. (*Persuasion*, let's make clear, is the art of convincing people to change their minds — perhaps also to act.) Often, we'll state an opinion: We'll tell someone our own way of viewing things. We say to a friend, "I'm starting to like Senator Clark. Look at all she's done to help the handicapped. Look at her voting record on toxic waste. . . ." And, having stated these opinions, we might go on to propose some action to be taken. Addressing our friend, we might suggest, "Hey, Senator Clark is talking on campus at four-thirty. Want to come with me and listen to her?"

Sometimes you try to convince yourself that a certain way of interpreting things is right. You even set forth an opinion in writing — as in a letter to a friend who has asked, "Now that you're at Siwash College, how do you like the place?" You might write a letter of protest to a landlord who wants to raise your rent, pointing out that the bathroom hot water faucet doesn't work. As a concerned citizen, you may wish to speak your mind in an occasional letter to a newspaper or to your elected representative.

In truth, we live our lives under a steady rain of opinions and proposals. Campus organizations who work for a cause campaign with posters and place leaflets in our mailboxes. All hope that we will see things their way. Moreover, we are bombarded with proposals from people who wish us to act. Ministers, priests, and rabbis urge us to lead more virtuous lives. Advertisers urge us to rush right out and buy the large economy size.

If you should enter certain professions, you will be expected to persuade people in writing. Before arguing a case in court, a lawyer prepares briefs setting forth all the points in favor of his side. Business executives regularly put in writing their ideas for new products and ventures, for improvements in cost control and job efficiency. Researchers write proposals for grants to obtain money to support their work. Scientists write and publish papers to persuade the scientific community that their findings are valid, often stating hypotheses, or tentative opinions.

Small wonder, then, that persuasion — and how to resist persuasion — may be among the most useful skills a college student can acquire. Time and again, your instructors will ask you to state an opinion, either in class or in writing. You may be asked to state your view of anything from the electoral college to animal experimentation, the desirability or undesirability of compulsory testing for AIDS, or the revision of existing immigration laws. You may be asked to propose a solution to a problem. On an examination in, say, sociology, you might be asked, "Suggest three practical approaches to the most pressing needs of disadvantaged people in urban areas." Writing your answer, you will find, helps you make clear to yourself what you think. It also gives you the chance to share what you believe.

Unlike some television advertisers, college writers don't storm other people's minds. In writing a paper for a course, you persuade by gentler means: by sharing your view with a reader willing to consider it. You'll want to learn how to express your view clearly and vigorously. But to be fair and persuasive, it is important to understand your reader's view as well.

In stating your opinion, you present the truth as you see it: "I think Henry Moore is a great sculptor," or, "Henry Moore's art hits me as cold, dull, and full of holes." To persuade your readers that your view makes sense, you need not begin by proclaiming that, by Heaven, your view is absolutely right and should prevail. Instead, you might begin by trying to state what your reader probably thinks, as best you can infer it. You don't consider views that differ from your own merely to flatter your reader. You do so to correct your own view and make it more accurate. Regarded in this light, persuasive writing isn't a cynical way to pull other people's strings. Writer and reader become two sensible people trying to find a common ground. This view of persuasion will relieve you, whenever you have to state your opinions in writing, of the terrible obligation to be 100 percent right at all times.

In trying to win over a reader who doesn't share your view, you use *argument* — a useful means of persuading. In ordinary use, the word *argument* often means a fight (with words, or fists), as in the report, "After their cars crashed, the two drivers had a violent argument." But the knockdown, drag-out kind of argument isn't the kind we mean. Instead, we will be dealing with argument as a form of expression that, in ancient Greece, could be heard in speeches in a public forum. Today you find it in effective editorials, thoughtful articles, and other persuasive statements of a writer's view. In this sense, argument is reasoning: making statements that lead to a conclusion. (A fuller discussion of these methods is found in "A Note on Reasoning" later in this chapter.)

How do you write an argument? You assert whatever view or opinion you're going to defend. When stated in a sentence, it is sometimes called the *proposition* or *thesis* of your argument, or your *claim*. It is a statement of what you believe, and, if you are

writing a proposal, it is a statement of an action that you recommend. Sometimes, but not always, you make such a statement
at the beginning of your essay: "Welfare funds need to be
trimmed from our state budget," or, "To cut back welfare funds
now would be a mistake." To support your claim you need *evidence* — anything that demonstrates what you're trying to say.
Evidence may include facts, statistics (or facts expressed in numbers), expert opinions, illustrations and examples, reported experience.

Often, the writer of an effective argument will appeal both
to the readers' intelligence and to their feelings. In appealing to
reason, the writer tends to supply new facts and figures and
other evidence. In appealing to emotion, however, the writer
may simply restate what readers already know well. Editorials in
publications for special audiences (members of ethnic groups
and religious denominations, or people whose political views are
far to the left or right) tend to contain few factual surprises for
their subscribers, who presumably read to have their views rein-
forced. In spoken discourse, you can hear this kind of emotional
appeal in a commencement day speech or a Fourth of July ora-
tion. An impressive example of such emotional appeal is included in this chapter: the speech by Martin Luther King, Jr., "I
Have a Dream." Dr. King's speech did not tell its audience anything new to them, for the listeners were mostly blacks disap-
pointed in the American dream. The speaker appeals not primarily to reason, but to feelings — and to the willingness of his
listeners to be inspired.

Emotional argument, to be sure, can sometimes be cynical
manipulation. It can mean selling a sucker a bill of shoddy goods
by appealing to pride, or shame — "Don't you really want the
best for your children?" But emotional argument can also stir
readers to constructive action by fair means. It recognizes that
we are not intellectual robots, but creatures with feelings. Indeed, in any effective argument, a writer had better engage the
readers' feelings or they may reply, "True enough, but who
cares?" Argument, to succeed in persuading, makes us feel that a
writer's views are close to our own.

Yet another resource in argument is *ethical appeal*: impress-
ing your reader that you are a well-informed person of good will,

good sense, and good moral character — and, therefore, to be believed. You make such an appeal by reasoning carefully, writing well, and collecting ample evidence. You can also cite or quote respected authorities. If you don't know whether an authority is respected, you can ask a reference librarian for tips on finding out, or talk to an instructor who is a specialist in that field.

In arguing, you don't prove your assertion in the same irrefutable way in which a chemist demonstrates that hydrogen will burn. If you say, "Health insurance should be given top priority in Washington," that kind of claim isn't clearly either true or false. Argument takes place in areas that invite more than one opinion. In writing an argument, you help your reader see and understand just one open-eyed, open-minded view of reality.

A NOTE ON REASONING

When we argue (rationally, not with fists), we reason — that is, we make statements that lead to a conclusion. From the time of the Greek philosopher Aristotle down to our own day, distinctly different methods of proceeding from statements to conclusion have been devised. This section will tell you of a recent, informal method of reasoning and also of two traditional methods.

We include this information for those interested in it. If you aren't interested, or if your instructor encourages you to skip this part, turn to page 509 for The Process, a brief discussion of how to write opinions and proposals.

Data, Warrant, and Claim[1]

In recent years, a simple, practical method of reasoning has been devised by the British philosopher Stephen Toulmin. Helpfully, Toulmin has divided a typical argument into three parts:

1. *The data*, or evidence to prove something

[1]This discussion of data, warrant, and claim is taken from the authors' textbook, *The Bedford Guide for College Writers* (1987), pp. 227–229.

2. *The claim*, what you are proving with the data
3. *The warrant*, the thinking that leads from data to claim

Any clear, explicit argument has to have all three parts. Toulmin's own example of such an argument is this:

Harry was born in Bermuda ——⊤—— Harry is a British subject
(*Data*)   (*Claim*)

Since a man born in Bermuda
will be a British subject
(*Warrant*)

Of course, the data for a larger, more controversial claim will be more extensive. Here are some claims that would call for much more data, perhaps thousands of words.

Abortion should be forbidden by law.
Huckleberry Finn is the greatest American novel.
People who invest in South African mines are contemptible.

The warrant, that middle term, is often crucially important. It tells *why* the claim follows from the data. Often a writer won't bother to state a warrant because it is obvious: "In his bid for re-election, Mayor Perkins failed miserably. Out of 5,000 votes cast for both candidates, he received only 200." The warrant might be stated, "To make what I would consider a strong showing, he would have had to receive 2,000 votes or more," but it is clear that 200 out of 5,000 is a small minority, and no further explanation seems necessary.

A flaw in many arguments, though, is that the warrant is not clear. A clear warrant is essential. To be persuaded, a reader needs to understand your assumptions and the thinking that follows from them. If you were to argue, "In *Huckleberry Finn*, Mark Twain tells the story of how civilization spread westward and tamed the frontier. Therefore, *Huckleberry Finn* is the greatest American novel," then your reader might well be left wondering why the second statement follows from the first. But if you were to add, between the statements, "Because civilization's westward spread is the most important fact in American history, I believe that any American novel called 'greatest' ought to take it in," then you supply a warrant. You show why your claim follows from your data — from what you have observed in Mark Twain's book.

At times, though, your warrant may be perfectly clear without your even stating it. Say you are writing a paper about the recent problem of malicious people who uncap patent medicines in drugstores and slip in poison. If in giving your data you declare, "Packages of headache remedies sold in drug stores have sometimes been tampered with," and then right away go on to state your claim, "and so tamper-proof packaging is desirable," your warrant is already clear. You wouldn't even need to spell it out. If you did state it, it might be, "I assume that to let people introduce dangerous substances into medicines in drugstores is a bad idea." Most readers will need no such statement; they will have heard news reports of poisonings that resulted from such tampering, or they will readily imagine the bad results that tampering can produce.

Let's say, though, that you write a paper that starts by reporting the tampering and then states your claim, or opinion: "I find exercise the most admirable form of headache relief." To most readers, just how you went from that data to that claim might not be clear. You would need to make your warrant explicit. Perhaps it might be stated, "I think it's wise to avoid the risk of taking poisoned medicine by instead doing relaxation exercises whenever a headache strikes" (or you might state your warrant in any one of a dozen other ways).

Think of Toulmin's scheme and you will recognize when an argument is in trouble — either your own or another writer's. Then, apparently, the warrant needs to be expressed. To be sure, your readers may not accept your warrant. They may disagree about your definition of the most important fact in American history, or they may object that a great novel ought to do more than reflect history. But at least they will understand your reasoning.

In an assignment for her second-semester course in English composition, Maire Flynn was asked to set forth in three short paragraphs a condensed argument. The first paragraph was to set forth some data; the second, a claim; and the third, a warrant. The result became a kind of outline that the writer could then expand into a whole essay. Here is Flynn's argument.

DATA

Over the past five years in the state of Illinois, assistance in the form of food stamps has had the effect of increasing the number of people on welfare instead of reducing it. Despite this help, 95 percent of long-term recipients remain below the poverty line today.

CLAIM

I maintain that the present system of distributing food stamps is a dismal failure, a less effective way to help the needy than other possible ways.

WARRANT

No one is happy to receive charity. We need to encourage people to quit the welfare rolls; we need to make sure that government aid goes only to the deserving. More effective than giving out food might be to help untrained young people learn job skills; to help single mothers with small children to obtain child care, freeing them for the job market; and to enlarge and improve our state employment counseling and job-placement services. The problem of poverty will be helped only if more people will find jobs and become self-sufficient.

In her warrant paragraph, Flynn spells out her reasons for holding her opinion — the one she states in her claim. "The warrant," she found, "was the hardest part to write," but hers turned out to be clear. Like any good warrant, hers expresses those thoughts that her data set in motion. Another way of looking at the warrant: It is the thinking that led the writer on to the opinion she holds. In this statement of her warrant, Flynn makes clear her assumptions: that people who can support themselves don't deserve food stamps and that a person is better off (and happier) holding a job than receiving charity. By generating more ideas and evidence, she was easily able to expand both data paragraph and warrant paragraph, and the result was a coherent essay of 700 words.

How, by the way, would someone who didn't accept Flynn's warrant argue with her? What about old, infirm, or handicapped persons who cannot work? What quite different assumptions about poverty might be possible?

Deductive and Inductive Reasoning

Sometimes the writer of an argument will follow a traditional method of formal *logic*, the study of orderly thinking. We find such a method in a *syllogism*, a three-step form of reasoning practiced by Aristotle:

> All men are mortal.
> Socrates is a man.
> Therefore, Socrates is mortal.

The first statement is the *major premise*, the second the *minor premise*, and the third the *conclusion*. Few people today argue in this strict, three-part form; yet many writers argue by using the thinking behind the syllogism — *deductive reasoning*. Beginning with a statement of truth, this kind of logic moves to a statement of truth about an individual or particular. If you observe that conservative Republicans desire less government regulation of business and that William F. Buckley is a conservative Republican, and conclude that Buckley may be expected to desire less government regulation of business, then you employ deductive reasoning. If, on the other hand, you were to interview Buckley and a hundred other conservative Republicans, find that they were unanimous in their views, and then conclude that conservative Republicans favor less government regulation of business, you would be using the opposite method: *inductive reasoning*. Inductive reasoning is essential to the method of scientists, who collect many observations of individuals and then venture a general statement that applies to them all. In *Zen and the Art of Motorcycle Maintenance*, Robert M. Pirsig gives examples of deductive and inductive reasoning:

> If the cycle goes over a bump and the engine misfires, and
> then goes over another bump and the engine misfires, and

then goes over another bump and the engine misfires, and then goes over a long smooth stretch of road and there is no misfiring, and then goes over a fourth bump and the engine misfires again, one can logically conclude that the misfiring is caused by the bumps. That is induction: reasoning from particular experiences to general truths.

Deductive inferences do the reverse. They start with general knowledge and predict a specific observation. For example if, from reading the hierarchy of facts about the machine, the mechanic knows the horn of the cycle is powered exclusively by electricity from the battery, then he can logically infer that if the battery is dead the horn will not work. That is deduction.[2]

Either kind of reasoning, inductive or deductive, is only as accurate as the observations on which it is based. In 1633, Scipio Chiaramonti, professor of philosophy at the University of Pisa, came up with this untrustworthy syllogism: "Animals, which move, have limbs and muscles. The earth has no limbs and muscles. Hence, the earth does not move." This is bad deductive reasoning, and its flaw is to assume that all things need limbs and muscles to move — ignoring raindrops, rivers, and many other moving things.

Logical Fallacies

In arguments we read and hear, we often meet such *logical fallacies*: errors in reasoning that lead to wrong conclusions. From the time when you start thinking about your proposition or claim, and planning your paper, you'll need to watch out for them. To help you recognize logical fallacies when you see them or hear them, and so guard against them when you write, here is a list of the most common.

Non sequitur (from the Latin, "it does not follow"): stating a conclusion that doesn't follow from the first premise or premises. "I've lived in this town a long time — why, my grandfather

---

[2]*Zen and the Art of Motorcycle Maintenance* (New York: William Morrow, 1974), p. 107.

was the first mayor — so I'm against putting fluoride in the drinking water."

Oversimplification: supplying neat and easy explanations for large and complicated phenomena. "These scientists are always messing around with the moon and the planets; that's why the climate is changing nowadays." Oversimplified solutions are also popular: "All these teenage kids that get in trouble with the law — why, they ought to ship 'em over to Russia. That would straighten 'em out!"

Either/or reasoning: assuming that a reality may be divided into only two parts or extremes; assuming that a given problem has only one of two possible solutions. "What do we do about these sheiks who keep jacking up oil prices? Either we kowtow to 'em, or we bomb 'em off the face of the earth, right?" Obviously, either/or reasoning is another kind of extreme oversimplification.

Argument from doubtful or unidentified authority: "Certainly we ought to castrate all sex offenders; Uncle Oswald says we should." Or: "According to reliable sources, my opponent is lying."

Argumentation ad hominem (from the Latin, "argument to the man"): attacking a person's views by attacking his or her character. "Mayor Burns was seen with a prostitute on Taylor Street. How can we listen to his plea for a city nursing home?"

Begging the question: taking for granted from the start what you set out to demonstrate. When you reason in a *logical* way, you state that because something is true, then, as a result, some other truth follows. When you beg the question, however, you repeat that what is true is true. If you argue, for instance, that dogs are a menace to people because they are dangerous, you don't prove a thing, since the idea that dogs are dangerous is already assumed in the statement that they are a menace. Beggars of questions often just repeat what they already believe, only in different words. This fallacy sometimes takes the form of *arguing in a circle*, or demonstrating a premise by a conclusion and a conclusion by a premise: "I should go to college because that is the right thing to do. Going to college is the right thing to do because it is expected of me."

Post hoc, ergo propter hoc (from the Latin, "after this, therefore because of this"): confusing cause and effect. See page 377.

Argument from analogy: using an extended metaphor (discussed in Chapter 7) as though it offers evidence. Pierre Berton, a Canadian journalist, once wrote a clever article "Is There a Teacher in the House?" satirizing opponents of public health care. In it Berton writes in the voice of an after-dinner speaker alarmed by the idea of establishing a public school system — which of course, already exists:

> Under this foreign system each one of us would be forced by government edict, and under penalty of imprisonment, to send our children to school until each reaches the age of sixteen — whether we wish to or not. . . . Ask yourself, gentlemen, if it is economically sane to hand a free education, no strings attached, to everybody in the nation between the ages of six and sixteen!

Berton's speaker doesn't even mention free public health care, but he echoes accusations made familiar by its opponents. He calls the whole idea "foreign" and too costly; he complains that its advocates are "pie-in-the-sky idealists." We realize that we have heard these accusations before. Free clinics, Berton suggests, are just as practicable as free schools — a system we all take for granted. If Berton were writing a serious, reasoned argument, then an opponent might protest that clinics and schools aren't quite alike and that Berton omits their important differences. This is the central weakness in most arguments by analogy. Dwelling only on similarities, a writer doesn't consider *dissimilarities* — since to admit them might weaken the analogy.

In late years, the study of *logic*, or systematic reasoning, has seen exciting developments. If you care to venture more deeply into its fascinating territory, a good, lively (but challenging) introductory textbook is Albert E. Blumberg's *Logic* (New York: Knopf, 1976). Stephen Toulmin, in *The Uses of Argument* (Cambridge, Eng.: Cambridge University Press, 1969), sets forth his own system in detail. His views are further explained and applied by Douglas Ehninger and Wayne Brockriede in *Decision by*

Debate, 2nd ed. (New York: Harper & Row, 1978) and by Toulmin himself, with Richard Rieke and Allan Janik, in *An Introduction to Reasoning*, 2nd ed. (New York: Macmillan, 1984).

THE PROCESS

In stating an opinion, you set forth and support a claim — a truth you believe. You may find such a truth by thinking and feeling, by talking to your instructors or fellow students, by scanning a newspaper or reading books and magazines, by listening to a discussion of some problem or controversy.

In stating a proposal, you already have an opinion in mind, and from there, you go on to urge an action or a solution to a problem. Often these two statements will take place within the same piece of writing: First, a writer will set forth a view ("Compact disks are grossly overpriced"); and then, will go right on to a proposal ("Compact disk players should be in every college dorm room").

Whether your essay states only an opinion, only a proposal, or both, it is likely to contain similar ingredients. State clearly, if possible at the start of your essay, the proposition or claim you are going to defend. If you like, you can explain why you think it worth upholding — showing, perhaps, that it concerns your readers. If you plan to include both an opinion and proposal in your essay, you may wish to set forth your opinion first, saving your proposal for later — perhaps for your conclusion.

Your proposition stated, introduce your least important point first. Then build in a crescendo to the strongest point you have. This structure will lend emphasis to your essay, and perhaps make your chain of ideas more persuasive as the reader continues to follow it.

For every point, give evidence: facts, figures, or observations. If you introduce statistics, make sure that they are up to date and fairly represented. In an essay advocating a law against smoking, it would be unfair to declare that "in Pottsville, Illinois, last year, 50 percent of all deaths were caused by lung cancer," if only two people died in Pottsville last year — one of them struck by a car.

Provided you can face potential criticisms fairly, and give your critics due credit, you might want to recognize the objections you expect your assertion will meet. This is the strategy H. L. Mencken uses in "The Penalty of Death," and he introduces it in his essay near the beginning.

In your conclusion, briefly restate your claim, if possible in a fresh, pointed way. (For example, see the concluding sentence in the essay by William F. Buckley in this chapter.) In emotionally persuasive writing, you may want to end with a strong appeal. (See "I Have a Dream" by Martin Luther King, Jr.)

Finally, don't forget the power of humor in argument. You don't have to crack gratuitous jokes, but there is often an advantage in having a reader or listener who laughs on your side. When Abraham Lincoln debated Stephen Douglas, he triumphed in his reply to Douglas's snide remark that Lincoln had once been a bartender. "I have long since quit my side of the bar," Lincoln declared, "while Mr. Douglas clings to his as tenaciously as ever."

In arguing — doing everything you can to bring your reader around to your view — you can draw on any method of writing you have already learned. Arguing for or against welfare funding, you might give *examples* of wasteful spending, or of neighborhoods where welfare funds are needed. You might analyze the *causes* of social problems that might call for welfare funds, or foresee the likely *effects* of cutting welfare programs, or of keeping them. You might *compare and contrast* the idea of slashing welfare funds with the idea of increasing them. You could use *narration* to tell a pointed story; you could describe certain welfare recipients and their neighborhoods. If you wanted to, you could employ several of these methods in writing a single argument.

You will rarely find, when you begin to write a persuasive paper, that you have too much evidence to support your claim. But unless you're writing a term paper and have months to spend on it, you're limited in how much evidence you can gather. Begin by stating your claim. Make it narrow enough to support in the time you have available. For a paper due a week from now, the opinion that "Our city's downtown area has a serious litter problem" can probably be backed up in part by your own eyewitness reports. But to support the claim, "Litter is one of the worst environmental problems of North American cities," you would surely need to spend time in a library.

In rewriting, you may find yourself tempted to keep all the evidence you have collected with such effort. Of course, some of it may not support your claim; some may seem likely to persuade the reader only to go to sleep. If so, throw it out. A stronger argument will remain.

ARGUMENT AND PERSUASION
IN A PARAGRAPH: FOUR ILLUSTRATIONS

1. Stating an Opinion about Television

Television news has a serious failing: It's show business. Unlike a newspaper, its every word has to entertain the average beer drinker. To score high ratings and win advertisers, it must find drama, suspense, and human interest in each story, turning every kidnapping into a hostage crisis. A visual medium, it favors the spectacular: riots, tornados, air crashes. The fire that tore through six city blocks has more eye-appeal than ten fires prevented. Now that satellite transmission invites live coverage, newscasters go for the fast-breaking story at the expense of thoughtful analysis. "The more you can get data out instantly," says media critic Jeff Greenfield, "the more you rely on instant data to define the news." TV zooms in on people who make news, but, to avoid boredom, won't let them argue or explain. (How can they, in speeches limited to fifteen seconds?) On one infamous *Today* show, Senator Proxmire's ideas about nuclear attack were cut short so that viewers might see Seattle Slew waking up in his stall after his Kentucky Derby victory. On NBC late news for September 12, 1987, President Reagan blasted a plan to end war in Nicaragua. His address was clipped to sixty seconds, then an anchorwoman digested the opposition in one quick line: "Democrats tonight were critical of the President's remarks." Americans who rely on television for their news (64 percent, according to 1984 Roper polls) exist on a starvation diet.

COMMENT. The writer states his opinion in his opening line, then proceeds to back up his claim with evidence. He refers to

specific television shows and quotes Jeff Greenfield, a professional critic of the media. Some of his evidence — the bit about
President Reagan's condensed address — was obtained from
watching TV newscasts. In the last sentence, he restates his
opinion in a fresh way. Now he will take a further step and propose a cure.

2. Stating a Proposal about Television

To make television news more responsible to people who
depend on it for full and accurate information, I propose that
commercials be banned from local and network news programs. This ban would have the effect of freeing newscasters
from the obligation to score high ratings. Since 1963, when
NBC and CBS began the first thirty-minute evening newscasts, television news has dwindled in integrity. Back then, according to television historian Daniel C. Hallin, the news was
designed to earn prestige for the networks, not money. Today
the priorities have been reversed. We need a return to the
original situation. Eliminating commercials would hurt reve-
nues, it is true, but stations could make up their losses from
selling spots on prime-time shows clearly labeled "entertainment." No longer forced to highlight fires, storms, and other
violent scenes, no longer tempted to use live coverage (even
though the story covered may be trivial), news teams would
no longer strive to race with their rivals to break a story. At
last there would be time for more analysis, for the thoughtful
follow-up story. Television news would become less entertaining, no doubt, and fewer people would watch it. The reader
might object that, as a result, the mass of American viewers
would be even less well informed. But sheer entertainment
that passes for news is, I believe, more insidious than no news
at all.

COMMENT. Continuing the argument about television news
(begun in the paragraph stating an opinion), the writer makes a
radical proposal that he believes will greatly improve television
news. He gives us less evidence than in the opinion paragraph,
but then, less evidence seems necessary. He does, however, cite a
revealing comment from a television historian, and in a sentence ("Today the priorities have been reversed") contrasts
present and past. Showing an awareness for the skeptical reader,

the writer recognizes two possible objections to his proposal: (1) that stations would suffer losses; and (2) people would be less well informed. To each objection, he offers an answer and leaves us to ponder it.

3. Stating an Opinion in an Academic Discipline

We need wilderness, I believe, as an environment of humility. Civilization breeds arrogance. A modern human, armed with checkbook, television, and four-wheel drive, feels like a demigod. It is good to be reminded in wilderness of our true status as member — not master — of the natural world. It is good to rekindle the sense of restraint and limits that has been obscured by technological optimism. It is good to see natural powers and processes greater than our own. The lessons of such experiences are precisely what are needed if human-environment relations are to be harmonious and stable in the long run. Wilderness, then, is a profound educational resource, schooling overcivilized humans in what we once knew but unfortunately forgot.

COMMENT. *Living in the Environment,* by G. Tyler Miller, Jr. (Belmont, Calif.: Wadsworth Publishing Company, 2nd edition, 1979), is an unusual textbook because many of its chapters contain guest editorials written by respected experts. This paragraph by Roderick Nash, professor of history and environmental studies at the University of California, Santa Barbara, is taken from one of them. In his editorial, Nash states his opinion that wilderness areas are vitally important to all Americans for several reasons. One of those reasons is detailed in the paragraph cited here. Notice how briefly, concretely ("armed with checkbook, television, and four-wheel drive"), and effectively Nash sets it forth. He makes a convincing case for the usefulness of an "environment of humility."

4. Stating a Proposal in an Academic Discipline

Individual acts of consumption, litter, and so on, have contributed to the mess [in our environment]. When you are tempted to say this little bit won't hurt, multiply it by millions of others saying the same thing. Picking up a single beer can,

not turning on a light, using a car pool, writing on both sides
of a piece of paper, and not buying a grocery product with
more packages inside the outer package are all very significant
acts. Each small act reminds us of ecological thinking and
leads to other ecologically sound practices. Start now, with a
small concrete personal act and then expand your actions in
ever widening circles. Little acts can be used to expand our
awareness of the need for fundamental changes in our political, economic, and social systems over the next few decades.
These acts also help us to avoid psychological numbness when
we realize the magnitude of the job to be done.

COMMENT. From *Living in the Environment*, the same textbook from which we excerpted Roderick Nash's opinion, here is
another paragraph, one in which the author of the book, G.
Tyler Miller, Jr., makes a proposal. This paragraph in fact is labeled number seven in a whole list of proposals under the title
"What Can You Do?" The list is designed to convey a sense that
the world's environmental problems are not so overwhelming
that individual efforts can't contribute to solving them. "You
can do little things" is this paragraph's claim. Notice that almost
every sentence gives concrete suggestions for dealing in a small
but meaningful way with problems of great magnitude. The paragraph ends effectively, with the author supplying compelling
reasons for taking his advice.

· Ursula K. Le Guin ·

URSULA K. LE GUIN was born in 1929 in Berkeley, California, the daughter of two noted anthropologists, Alfred and Theodora Kroeber. After graduation from Radcliffe College in 1951, she took a master's degree in French and Italian from Columbia University. Ever since an older brother showed her how to hold a pencil, she has been writing stories. She produced an early novel while working as a secretary at Emory University; after her children were born, she wrote at night, and at thirty-two finally received a check for a story. Le Guin, who began by publishing in popular science fiction magazines, has been called the foremost woman in the science fiction field. But she once declared, "I write science fiction because that is what publishers call my books. Left to myself, I should call them novels." Indeed, Le Guin is a writer who eludes labels: She has written screenplays, a television script for her novel *The Lathe of Heaven*, two volumes of poetry, young adult fiction, and stories for general magazines such as *Redbook* and *The New Yorker*. *Always Coming Home* (1985) is her most recent novel. *The Left Hand of Darkness* (1969), an account of an alien people who can change sexes, won both Hugo and Nebula awards for best science fiction novel of its year; so did another novel, *The Dispossessed* (1974), in which Le Guin imagines an anarchist's utopia. Le Guin's prizes also include a Newbery honor medal for juvenile literature and a National Book Award. She lives in Portland, Oregon, in a house with a view of the shipyards along the Willamette

Why Are Americans Afraid of Dragons?

This essay was originally given as a talk to an assembly of librarians, the Pacific Northwest Library Association conference in Portland, Oregon; and was first published in the magazine *PNLA Quarterly* (Winter 1974). It appears in Le Guin's

collection of essays and literary criticism, *The Language of the
Night: Essays on Fantasy and Science Fiction* (New York: Putnam, 1979). In her essay, Le Guin has some surprising things
to say about the importance of fantasy, not only for children
but for adults. See whether you agree with the author's
thought-provoking opinion that Americans would be better
off if they lost their fear of dragons.

This was to be a talk about fantasy. But I have not been feel-   1
ing very fanciful lately, and could not decide what to say; so I
have been going about picking people's brains for ideas. "What
about fantasy? Tell me something about fantasy." And one
friend of mine said, "All right, I'll tell you something fantastic.
Ten years ago, I went to the children's room of the library of
such-and-such a city, and asked for *The Hobbit*; and the librarian told me, 'Oh, we keep that only in the adult collection; we
don't feel that escapism is good for children.'"

My friend and I had a good laugh and shudder over that,   2
and we agreed that things have changed a great deal in these
past ten years. That kind of moralistic censorship of works of
fantasy is very uncommon now, in the children's libraries. But
the fact that the children's libraries have become oases in the
desert doesn't mean that there isn't still a desert. The point of
view from which that librarian spoke still exists. She was merely
reflecting, in perfect good faith, something that goes very deep
in the American character: a moral disapproval of fantasy, a disapproval so intense, and often so aggressive, that I cannot help
but see it as arising, fundamentally, from fear.

So: Why are Americans afraid of dragons?   3

Before I try to answer my question, let me say that it isn't   4
only Americans who are afraid of dragons. I suspect that almost
all very highly technological peoples are more or less antifantasy. There are several national literatures which, like ours, have
had no tradition of adult fantasy for the past several hundred
years: the French, for instance. But then you have the Germans,
who have a good deal; and the English, who have it, and love it,
and do it better than anyone else. So this fear of dragons is not
merely a Western, or a technological, phenomenon. But I do

not want to get into these vast historical questions; I will speak of modern Americans, the only people I know well enough to talk about.

In wondering why Americans are afraid of dragons, I began 5 to realize that a great many Americans are not only antifantasy, but altogether antifiction. We tend, as a people, to look upon all works of the imagination either as suspect, or as contemptible.

"My wife reads novels. I haven't got the time." 6

"I used to read that science fiction stuff when I was a teen- 7 ager, but of course I don't now."

"Fairy stories are for kids. I live in the real world." 8

Who speaks so? Who is it that dismisses *War and Peace*, *The* 9 *Time Machine*, and *A Midsummer Night's Dream* with this perfect self-assurance? It is, I fear, the man in the street — the hard-working, over-thirty American male — the men who run this country.

Such a rejection of the entire art of fiction is related to sev- 10 eral American characteristics: our Puritanism, our work ethic, our profit-mindedness, and even our sexual mores.

To read *War and Peace* or *The Lord of the Rings* plainly is not 11 "work" — you do it for pleasure. And if it cannot be justified as "educational" or as "self-improvement," then, in the Puritan value system, it can only be self-indulgence or escapism. For pleasure is not a value, to the Puritan; on the contrary, it is a sin.

Equally, in the businessman's value system, if an act does 12 not bring in an immediate, tangible profit, it has no justification at all. Thus the only person who has an excuse to read Tolstoy or Tolkien is the English teacher, because he gets paid for it. But our businessman might allow himself to read a best-seller now and then: Not because it is a good book, but because it is a best-seller — it is a success, it has made money. To the strangely mystical mind of the money-changer, this justifies its existence; and by reading it he may participate, a little, in the power and mana of its success. If this is not magic, by the way, I don't know what is.

The last element, the sexual one, is more complex. I hope I 13 will not be understood as being sexist if I say that, within our culture, I believe that this antifiction attitude is basically a male one. The American boy and man is very commonly forced to define his maleness by rejecting certain traits, certain human gifts and potentialities, which our culture defines as "womanish" or "childish." And one of these traits or potentialities is, in cold sober fact, the absolutely essential human faculty of imagination.

Having got this far, I went quickly to the dictionary.   14

The *Shorter Oxford Dictionary* says: "Imagination. 1. The   15 action of imagining, or forming a mental concept of what is not actually present to the senses; 2. The mental consideration of actions or events not yet in existence."

Very well; I certainly can let "absolutely essential human   16 faculty" stand. But I must narrow the definition to fit our present subject. By "imagination," then, I personally mean the free play of the mind, both intellectual and sensory. By "play" I mean recreation, re-creation, the recombination of what is known into what is new. By "free" I mean that the action is done without an immediate object of profit — spontaneously. That does not mean, however, that there may not be a purpose behind the free play of the mind, a goal; and the goal may be a very serious object indeed. Children's imaginative play is clearly a practicing at the acts and emotions of adulthood; a child who did not play would not become mature. As for the free play of an adult mind, its result may be *War and Peace*, or the theory of relativity.

To be free, after all, is not to be undisciplined. I should say   17 that the discipline of the imagination may in fact be the essential method or technique of both art and science. It is our Puritanism, insisting that discipline means repression or punishment, which confuses the subject. To discipline something, in the proper sense of the word, does not mean to repress it, but to train it — to encourage it to grow, and act, and be fruitful, whether it is a peach tree or a human mind.

I think that a great many American men have been taught   18 just the opposite. They have learned to repress their imagination, to reject it as something childish or effeminate, unprofitable, and probably sinful.

They have learned to fear it. But they have never learned to   19 discipline it at all.

Now, I doubt that the imagination can be suppressed. If you 20
truly eradicated it in a child, he would grow up to be an egg-
plant. Like all our evil propensities, the imagination will out.
But if it is rejected and despised, it will grow into wild and weedy
shapes; it will be deformed. At its best, it will be mere ego-cen-
tered daydreaming; at its worst, it will be wishful thinking,
which is a very dangerous occupation when it is taken seriously.
Where literature is concerned, in the old, truly Puritan days, the
only permitted reading was the Bible. Nowadays, with our secular Puritanism, the man who refuses to read novels because it's
unmanly to do so, or because they aren't true, will most likely
end up watching bloody detective thrillers on the television, or
reading hack Westerns or sports stories, or going in for pornography, from *Playboy* on down. It is his starved imagination, crav-
ing nourishment, that forces him to do so. But he can rationalize such entertainment by saying that it is realistic — after all,
sex exists, and there are criminals, and there are baseball players, and there used to be cowboys — and also by saying that it is
virile, by which he means that it doesn't interest most women.

That all these genres are sterile, hopelessly sterile, is a re- 21
assurance to him, rather than a defect. If they were genuinely realistic, which is to say genuinely imagined and imaginative, he
would be afraid of them. Fake realism is the escapist literature of
our time. And probably the ultimate escapist reading is that
masterpiece of total unreality, the daily stock market report.

Now what about our man's wife? She probably wasn't re- 22
quired to squelch her private imagination in order to play her
expected role in life, but she hasn't been trained to discipline it,
either. She is allowed to read novels, and even fantasies. But,
lacking training and encouragement, her fancy is likely to glom
on to very sickly fodder, such things as soap operas, and "true
romances," and nursy novels, and historico-sentimental novels,
and all the rest of the baloney ground out to replace genuine
imaginative works by the artistic sweatshops of a society that is
profoundly distrustful of the uses of the imagination.

What, then, are the uses of the imagination? 23

You see, I think we have a terrible thing here: a hardwork- 24
ing, upright, responsible citizen, a full-grown, educated person,
who is afraid of dragons, and afraid of hobbits, and scared to

death of fairies. It's funny, but it's also terrible. Something has
gone very wrong. I don't know what to do about it but to try
and give an honest answer to that person's question, even
though he often asks it in an aggressive and contemptuous tone
of voice. "What's the good of it all?" he says. "Dragons and hobbits and little green men — what's the *use* of it?"

The truest answer, unfortunately, he won't even listen to.   25
He won't hear it. The truest answer is, "The use of it is to give
you pleasure and delight."

"I haven't got the time," he snaps, swallowing a Maalox pill   26
for his ulcer and rushing off to the golf course.

So we try the next-to-truest answer. It probably won't go   27
down much better, but it must be said: "The use of imaginative
fiction is to deepen your understanding of your world, and your
fellow men, and your own feelings, and your destiny."

To which I fear he will retort, "Look, I got a raise last year,   28
and I'm giving my family the best of everything, we've got two
cars and a color TV. I understand enough of the world!"

And he is right, unanswerably right, if that is what he   29
wants, and all he wants.

The kind of thing you learn from reading about the prob-   30
lems of a hobbit who is trying to drop a magic ring into an imaginary volcano has very little to do with your social status, or material success, or income. Indeed, if there is any relationship, it is
a negative one. There is an inverse correlation between fantasy
and money. That is a law, known to economists as Le Guin's
Law. If you want a striking example of Le Guin's Law, just give a
lift to one of those people along the roads who own nothing but
a backpack, a guitar, a fine head of hair, a smile, and a thumb.
Time and again, you will find that these waifs have read *The
Lord of the Rings* — some of them can practically recite it. But
now take Aristotle Onassis, or J. Paul Getty: Could you believe
that those men ever had anything to do, at any age, under any
circumstances, with a hobbit?

But, to carry my example a little further, and out of the   31
realm of economics, did you ever notice how very gloomy Mr.
Onassis and Mr. Getty and all those billionaires look in their
photographs? They have this strange, pinched look, as if they

were hungry. As if they were hungry for something, as if they had lost something and were trying to think where it could be, or perhaps what it could be, what it was they've lost.

Could it be their childhood? 32

So I arrive at my personal defense of the uses of the imagina- 33
tion, especially in fiction, and most especially in fairy tale, legend, fantasy, science fiction, and the rest of the lunatic fringe. I
believe that maturity is not an outgrowing, but a growing up:
that an adult is not a dead child, but a child who survived. I believe that all the best faculties of a mature human being exist in
the child, and that if these faculties are encouraged in youth
they will act well and wisely in the adult, but if they are repressed and denied in the child they will stunt and cripple the
adult personality. And finally, I believe that one of the most
deeply human, and humane, of these faculties is the power of
imagination: so that it is our pleasant duty, as librarians, or
teachers, or parents, or writers, or simply as grownups, to encourage that faculty of imagination in our children, to encourage it to grow freely, to flourish like the green bay tree, by giving
it the best, absolutely the best and purest, nourishment that it
can absorb. And never, under any circumstances, to squelch it,
or sneer at it, or imply that it is childish, or unmanly, or untrue.

For fantasy is true, of course. It isn't factual, but it is true. 34
Children know that. Adults know it too, and that is precisely
why many of them are afraid of fantasy. They know that its
truth challenges, even threatens, all that is false, all that is
phony, unnecessary, and trivial in the life they have let themselves be forced into living. They are afraid of dragons, because
they are afraid of freedom.

So I believe that we should trust our children. Normal chil- 35
dren do not confuse reality and fantasy — they confuse them
much less often than we adults do (as a certain great fantasist[1]
pointed out in a story called "The Emperor's New Clothes").
Children know perfectly well that unicorns aren't real, but they

---

[1]Hans Christian Andersen (1805–1875), a famous Danish author who wrote fairy tales, many of them intended for adult audiences. — Eds.

also know that books about unicorns, if they are good books, are true books. All too often, that's more than Mummy and Daddy know; for, in denying their childhood, the adults have denied half their knowledge, and are left with the sad, sterile little fact: "Unicorns aren't real." And that fact is one that never got anybody anywhere (except in the story "The Unicorn in the Garden," by another great fantasist,[2] in which it is shown that a devotion to the unreality of unicorns may get you straight into the loony bin). It is by such statements as, "Once upon a time there was a dragon," or "In a hole in the ground there lived a hobbit" — it is by such beautiful nonfacts that we fantastic human beings may arrive, in our peculiar fashion, at the truth.

QUESTIONS ON MEANING

1. In paragraph 10, Le Guin attributes the rejection of fiction to four American characteristics. What are they? To which of them does she allot the most attention?
2. According to the author, why do people fear fantasy?
3. How does Le Guin's idea of discipline differ from the idea of it she says we have derived from our Puritanism? What makes the distinction important?
4. Whose view is it that the imagination is one of "our evil propensities" (paragraph 20)?
5. What does Le Guin see as the duty of adults who deal with children?
6. Sum up Le Guin's defense of fantasy. Where in her essay does she state it most clearly? Do you agree or disagree with it?

QUESTIONS ON WRITING STRATEGY

1. What is the function of the first three paragraphs in Le Guin's essay? What reason does the author give for not pursuing the connections between technology and fantasy?

---

[2]James Thurber, American humorist (1894–1961). See his "University Days" in Chapter 1. — EDS.

2. What segment of Le Guin's AUDIENCE would you expect to enjoy this essay most?
3. Where in her essay does the author use NARRATION? DEFINITION? COMPARISON AND CONTRAST? any of the other methods of writing you have studied in *The Bedford Reader*?
4. In her first paragraph, the author makes clear that her essay started out as a talk. Where else in the essay do you find EVIDENCE that Le Guin originally addressed not readers but listeners?

QUESTIONS ON LANGUAGE

1. Be sure you know what Le Guin means by the following: escapism (paragraph 1); phenomenon (4); suspect, contemptible (5); tangible, mystical, mana (12); potentialities (13); effeminate (18); eradicated, propensities, secular, rationalize, virile (20); genres (21); contemptuous (24); inverse, waifs (30); faculties (33); fantasist (35).
2. In this essay Le Guin uses the word *dragons* both literally and as a SYMBOL. What do the dragons symbolize?
3. Put into your own words the distinction Le Guin makes in paragraph 34 between "factual" and "true."

SUGGESTIONS FOR WRITING

1. Notice the context in which Le Guin says, "Fake realism is the escapist literature of our time" (paragraph 21). Write a brief essay in which you agree or disagree with this view. Keep in mind that you will need EVIDENCE with which to support your opinion.
2. Is there a work of fiction — perhaps one you read (or had read to you) over and over again — that has nourished your own life and imagination? If so, write a paper in which you examine the effects the work had on you. This may take some thought. A book's effect upon a person's life is not necessarily obvious.

Ursula K. Le Guin on Writing

In an essay, "Talking about Writing," Ursula Le Guin has raised and tried to answer a familiar question.

"How do you become a writer? Answer: You write.

"It's amazing how much resentment and disgust and evasion this answer can arouse. Even among writers, believe me. It is one of those Horrible Truths one would rather not face.

"The most frequent evasive tactic for the would-be writer is to say, 'But before I have anything to say, I must get *experience*.' . . . But experience isn't something you go and *get* — it's a gift, and the only requisite for receiving it is that you be open to it. A closed soul can have the most immense adventures, go through a civil war or a trip to the moon, and have nothing to show for all that 'experience'; whereas the open soul can do wonders with nothing." For example, Le Guin recalls the sisters Emily and Charlotte Brontë, whose experience consisted of living in a remote vicarage in an English village, going to school for a year or two in Brussels ("surely the dullest city in all Europe"), and doing housework. Yet out of their lives and imaginations they distilled great novels: *Wuthering Heights* and *Jane Eyre*.

Learning to write, according to Le Guin, is like learning to play a tuba: "You sit down and you do it, and you do it, and you do it, until you have learned how to do it. Of course, there are differences. Writing makes no noise, except groans, and it can be done anywhere, and it is done alone. . . . I envy musicians very much, myself. They get to play together, their art is largely communal; and there are rules to it, an accepted body of axioms and techniques, which can be put into words and at least demonstrated, and so taught. Writing cannot be shared, nor can it be taught as a technique, except on the most superficial level. All a writer's real learning is done alone, thinking, reading other people's books, or writing — practicing. A really good writing class or workshop can give us some shadow of what musicians have all the time — the excitement of a group working together, so that each member outdoes himself — but what comes out of that is not a collaboration, a joint accomplishment, like a string quartet or a symphony performance, but a lot of totally separate, isolated works, expressions of individual souls. And therefore there are no rules, except those each individual makes up for himself.

"Put it this way: If you feel you need rules and want rules, and you find a rule that appeals to you or that works for you, then follow it. Use it. But if it doesn't appeal to you or doesn't work for you, then ignore it; in fact, if you want to and are able to, kick it in the teeth; break it; fold, staple, mutilate, and destroy it.

"See, the thing is, as a writer you are free. You are about the freest person that ever was. Your freedom is what you have bought with your solitude, your loneliness. . . . Absolute freedom is absolute responsibility. The writer's job, as I see it, is to tell the truth. The writer's truth — nobody else's. It is not an easy job. One of the biggest implied lies going around at present is the one that hides in phrases like 'self-expression' or 'telling it like it is' — as if that were easy, as if anybody could do it if they just let the words pour out and didn't get fancy. . . . Well, it just doesn't work that way. You know how hard it is to say to somebody, just somebody you know, how you *really* feel, what you *really* think — with complete honesty? You have to trust them; and you have to *know yourself*: before you can say anything anywhere near the truth. And it's hard. It takes a lot out of you.

"You multiply that by thousands; you remove the listener, the live flesh-and-blood friend you trust, and replace him with a faceless unknown audience of people who may possibly not even exist; and you try to write the truth to them, you try to draw them a map of your inmost mind and feelings, hiding nothing and trying to keep all the distances straight and the altitudes right and the emotions honest. And you never succeed. The map is never complete, or even accurate. You read it over and it may be beautiful but you realize that you have fudged here, and smeared there, and left this out, and put in some stuff that isn't really there at all, and so on — and there is nothing to do then but say OK, that's done; now I come back and start a new map and try to do it better, more truthfully. And all of this, every time, you do alone — absolutely alone. The only questions that really matter are the ones you ask yourself." (*The Language of the Night: Essays on Fantasy and Science Fiction* [New York: Perigee Books/Putnam's, 1979], pp. 197–200.)

FOR DISCUSSION

1. Why do you suppose people who want to be writers find themselves using "evasive tactics" like the one Le Guin describes?
2. Le Guin sees similarities between writers and musicians. In what ways do they differ? What are Le Guin's reasons for envying musicians?
3. According to Le Guin, what is wrong with the prevailing notion that writing is "self-expression" or "telling it like it is"?

· H. L. Mencken ·

HENRY LOUIS MENCKEN (1880–1956) was a native of Baltimore, where for four decades he worked as newspaper reporter, editor, and columnist. In the 1920s, his boisterous, cynical observations on American life, appearing regularly in *The Smart Set* and later in *The American Mercury* (which he founded and edited), made him probably the most widely quoted writer in the country. Mencken leveled blasts at pomp, hypocrisy, and the middle classes (whom he labeled "the booboisie"). As editor and literary critic, he championed Sinclair Lewis, Theodore Dreiser, and other realistic writers. In 1933, when Mencken's attempts to laugh off the Depression began to ring hollow, his magazine died. He then devoted himself to revising and supplementing *The American Language* (fourth edition, 1948), a learned and highly entertaining survey of a nation's speech habits and vocabulary. Two dozen of Mencken's books are now in print, including *A Mencken Chrestomathy* (1949), a representative selection of his best writings of various kinds; and *A Choice of Days* (1980), a selection from his memoirs.

The Penalty of Death

Above all, Mencken is a humorist whose thought has a serious core. He argues by first making the reader's jaw drop, then inducing a laugh, and finally causing the reader to ponder, "Hmmmm — what if he's right?" The following still-controversial essay, from *Prejudices, Fifth Series* (1926), shows Mencken the persuader in top form. His work is enjoying a revival of attention nowadays — not so much for his ideas as for his style. No writer is better at swinging from ornate and abstract words to salty and concrete ones, at tossing a metaphor that makes you smile even as it kicks in your teeth.

Of the arguments against capital punishment that issue from uplifters, two are commonly heard most often, to wit:

1. That hanging a man (or frying him or gassing him) is a dreadful

business, degrading to those who have to do it and revolting to those who have to witness it.

2. That it is useless, for it does not deter others from the same crime.

The first of these arguments, it seems to me, is plainly too weak to need serious refutation. All it says, in brief, is that the work of the hangman is unpleasant. Granted. But suppose it is? It may be quite necessary to society for all that. There are, indeed, many other jobs that are unpleasant, and yet no one thinks of abolishing them — that of the plumber, that of the soldier, that of the garbage-man, that of the priest hearing confessions, that of the sand-hog, and so on. Moreover, what evidence is there that any actual hangman complains of his work? I have heard none. On the contrary, I have known many who delighted in their ancient art, and practiced it proudly.

In the second argument of the abolitionists there is rather more force, but even here, I believe, the ground under them is shaky. Their fundamental error consists in assuming that the whole aim of punishing criminals is to deter other (potential) criminals — that we hang or electrocute A simply in order to so alarm B that he will not kill C. This, I believe, is an assumption which confuses a part with the whole. Deterrence, obviously, is *one* of the aims of punishment, but it is surely not the only one. On the contrary, there are at least a half dozen, and some are probably quite as important. At least one of them, practically considered, is *more* important. Commonly, it is described as revenge, but revenge is really not the word for it. I borrow a better term from the late Aristotle: *katharsis*. *Katharsis*, so used, means a salubrious discharge of emotions, a healthy letting off of steam. A school-boy, disliking his teacher, deposits a tack upon the pedagogical chair; the teacher jumps and the boy laughs. This is *katharsis*. What I contend is that one of the prime objects of all judicial punishments is to afford the same grateful relief (*a*) to the immediate victims of the criminal punished, and (*b*) to the general body of moral and timorous men.

These persons, and particularly the first group, are concerned only indirectly with deterring other criminals. The thing they crave primarily is the satisfaction of seeing the criminal actually before them suffer as he made them suffer. What they want is the peace of mind that goes with the feeling that accounts are squared. Until they get that satisfaction they are in a state of emotional tension, and hence unhappy. The instant they get it they are comfortable. I do not argue that this yearning is noble; I simply argue that it is almost universal among human beings. In the face of injuries that are unimportant and can be borne without damage it may yield to higher impulses; that is to say, it may yield to what is called Christian charity. But when the injury is serious Christianity is adjourned, and even saints reach for their sidearms. It is plainly asking too much of human nature to expect it to conquer so natural an impulse. A keeps a store and has a bookkeeper, B. B steals $700, employs it in playing at dice or bingo, and is cleaned out. What is A to do? Let B go? If he does so he will be unable to sleep at night. The sense of injury, of injustice, of frustration will haunt him like pruritus. So he turns B over to the police, and they hustle B to prison. Thereafter A can sleep. More, he has pleasant dreams. He pictures B chained to the wall of a dungeon a hundred feet underground, devoured by rats and scorpions. It is so agreeable that it makes him forget his $700. He has got his *katharsis*.

The same thing precisely takes place on a larger scale when there is a crime which destroys a whole community's sense of security. Every law-abiding citizen feels menaced and frustrated until the criminals have been struck down — until the communal capacity to get even with them, and more than even, has been dramatically demonstrated. Here, manifestly, the business of deterring others is no more than an afterthought. The main thing is to destroy the concrete scoundrels whose act has alarmed everyone, and thus made everyone unhappy. Until they are brought to book that unhappiness continues; when the law has been executed upon them there is a sigh of relief. In other words, there is *katharsis*.

I know of no public demand for the death penalty for ordinary crimes, even for ordinary homicides. Its infliction would shock all men of normal decency of feeling. But for crimes involving the deliberate and inexcusable taking of human life, by men openly defiant of all civilized order — for such crimes it seems, to nine men out of ten, a just and proper punishment. Any lesser penalty leaves them feeling that the criminal has got the better of society — that he is free to add insult to injury by laughing. That feeling can be dissipated only by a recourse to *katharsis*, the invention of the aforesaid Aristotle. It is more effectively and economically achieved, as human nature now is, by wafting the criminal to realms of bliss.

The real objection to capital punishment doesn't lie against   7
the actual extermination of the condemned, but against our brutal American habit of putting it off so long. After all, every one of us must die soon or late, and a murderer, it must be assumed, is one who makes that sad fact the cornerstone of his metaphysic. But it is one thing to die, and quite another thing to lie for long months and even years under the shadow of death. No sane man would choose such a finish. All of us, despite the Prayer Book, long for a swift and unexpected end. Unhappily, a murderer, under the irrational American system, is tortured for what, to him, must seem a whole series of eternities. For months on end he sits in prison while his lawyers carry on their idiotic buffoonery with writs, injunctions, mandamuses, and appeals. In order to get his money (or that of his friends) they have to feed him with hope. Now and then, by the imbecility of a judge or some trick of juridic science, they actually justify it. But let us say that, his money all gone, they finally throw up their hands. Their client is now ready for the rope or the chair. But he must still wait for months before it fetches him.

That wait, I believe, is horribly cruel. I have seen more than   8
one man sitting in the death-house, and I don't want to see any more. Worse, it is wholly useless. Why should he wait at all? Why not hang him the day after the last court dissipates his last hope? Why torture him as not even cannibals would torture their victims? The common answer is that he must have time to make his peace with God. But how long does that take? It may be accomplished, I believe, in two hours quite as comfortably as in two years. There are, indeed, no temporal limitations upon God. He could forgive a whole herd of murderers in a millionth of a second. More, it has been done.

QUESTIONS ON MEANING

1. Identify Mencken's main reason for his support of capital punishment. What is his THESIS?
2. In paragraph 3, Mencken asserts that there are at least half a dozen reasons for punishing offenders. In his essay, he mentions two, deterrence and revenge. What others can you supply?
3. For which class of offenders does Mencken advocate the death penalty?
4. What is Mencken's "real objection" to capital punishment?

QUESTIONS ON WRITING STRATEGY

1. How would you characterize Mencken's humor? Point to examples of it. In the light of his grim subject, do you find it funny?
2. In his first paragraph, Mencken pares his subject down to manageable size. What techniques does he employ for this purpose?
3. In paragraph 2, Mencken draws an analogy between the executioner's job and other jobs that are "unpleasant." How effective is this device? What flaw do you see in Mencken's argument by analogy? (For more on this fallacy, see p. 508.)
4. At the start of paragraph 7, Mencken shifts his stance from concern for the victims of crime to concern for prisoners awaiting execution. Does the shift help or weaken the effectiveness of his earlier justification for capital punishment?
5. Do you think the author expects his AUDIENCE to agree with him? At what points does he seem to recognize the fact that some readers may see things differently?

QUESTIONS ON LANGUAGE

1. Mencken opens his argument by referring to those who reject capital punishment as "uplifters." What CONNOTATIONS does this word have for you? Does the use of this "loaded" word strengthen or weaken Mencken's position? Explain.
2. Be sure you know the meanings of the following words: refutation, sand-hog (paragraph 2); salubrious, pedagogical, timorous (3); pruritus (4); wafting (6); mandamuses, juridic (7).

3. What emotional overtones can you detect in Mencken's reference to the hangman's job as an "ancient art" (paragraph 2)?
4. What does Mencken's argument gain from his substitution of the word *katharsis* for *revenge*?

SUGGESTIONS FOR WRITING

1. Write a paper in which you suggest one reform in current methods of apprehending, trying, and sentencing criminals. Supply EVIDENCE to persuade a reader that your idea would improve the system.
2. Write an essay in which you refute Mencken's case; or, take Mencken's side but use different arguments. Be sure to defend your stance, point by point.
3. Write several paragraphs in which you compare and contrast Mencken's views about capital punishment with those expressed by George Orwell in "A Hanging" (p. 39). Which of the two writers more nearly expresses your own view of the subject? Why do you believe as you do?

H. L. Mencken on Writing

"All my work," wrote H. L. Mencken, "hangs together, once the main ideas under it are discerned. Those ideas are chiefly of a skeptical character. I believe that nothing is unconditionally true, and hence I am opposed to every statement of positive truth and to every man who states it. Such men seem to me to be either idiots or scoundrels. To one category or the other belong all theologians, professors, editorial writers, right-thinkers, etc. . . . Whether [my work] appears to be burlesque, or serious criticism, or mere casual controversy, it is always directed against one thing: unwarranted pretension."

Mencken cheerfully acknowledged his debts to his teachers: chiefly writers he read as a young man and newspaper editors he worked under. "My style of writing is chiefly grounded upon an early enthusiasm for Huxley,[1] the greatest of all masters of orderly exposition. He taught me the importance of giving to every argument a simple structure. As for the fancy work on the surface, it comes chiefly from an anonymous editorial writer in the *New York Sun*, circa 1900. He taught me the value of apt phrases. My vocabulary is pretty large; it probably runs to 25,000 words. It represents much labor. I am constantly expanding it. I believe that a good phrase is better than a Great Truth — which is usually buncombe. I delight in argument, not because I want to convince, but because argument itself is an end." ("Addendum on Aims," in *H. L. Mencken: The American Scene*, edited by Huntington Cairns [New York: Random House, 1965], pp. 474–477.)

"What is in the head," Mencken wrote, "infallibly oozes out of the nub of the pen. If it is sparkling Burgundy the writing is full of life and charm. If it is mush the writing is mush too." He recalls the example of President Warren G. Harding, who once sent a message to Congress that was quite incomprehensible. "Why? Simply because Dr. Harding's thoughts, on the high and grave subjects he discussed, were so muddled that he couldn't understand them himself. But on matters within his range of customary meditation he was clear and even charming, as all of us are. . . . Style cannot go beyond the ideas which lie at the heart of it. If they are clear, it too will be clear. If they are held passionately, it will be eloquent." ("The Fringes of Lovely Letters," *Prejudices: Fifth Series* [New York: Knopf, 1926], pp. 196–202.)

FOR DISCUSSION

1. According to Mencken, what PURPOSE animates his writing?
2. What relationship does Mencken see between a writer's thought and his STYLE?
3. Where in his views on writing does Mencken use FIGURES OF SPEECH to advantage?

[1]Thomas Henry Huxley (1825–1895), English biologist and educator, who wrote many essays popularizing science. In Victorian England, Huxley was the leading exponent and defender of Charles Darwin's theory of evolution. — EDS.

· Barbara Ehrenreich ·

BARBARA EHRENREICH was born in 1941 in Butte, Montana.
After graduation from Reed College, she took her Ph.D. at
Rockefeller University, then taught at SUNY in Old West-
bury in the early 1970s. Since 1981 she has been a contribut-
ing editor for *Ms.* magazine, and since 1974 has edited *Seven
Days* magazine in Washington, D.C. As a writer, Ehrenreich
has been a hard-hitting investigative reporter, a popular histo-
rian, and an astute social commentator. Besides *The Hearts of
Men: American Dreams and the Flight from Commitment* (1983),
her books include *For Her Own Good: 150 Years of the Experts'
Advice to Women* (1978); (with Deirdre English) *The American
Health Empire* (1970) and *Complaints and Disorders: The Sexual
Politics of Sickness* (1973); (with her first husband, John
Ehrenreich) *Witches, Midwives, and Nurses: A History of
Women Healers* (1972); and (with Elizabeth Hess and Gloria
Jacobs) *Re-making Love: The Feminization of Sex* (1986).

Hope I Die before I Get Rich

Ehrenreich's essay first appeared in *Mother Jones*, a magazine
of social commentary with a liberal bias. ("Mother" Mary
Harris Jones was an early twentieth-century labor organizer.)
What Ehrenreich finds lamentably missing from life in the
1980s is a counterculture similar to those existing in recent
decades. In this lively essay, the author sets forth her opinion
that a new counterculture is needed now.

What America needs is a good strong counterculture, or at   1
least a few square blocks of bohemia for our youth to loiter in
before making the plunge into a career of investment banking or
futures trading. The '50s had the beats; the '60s had the hippies;
the '70s had subsistence farming in Vermont. But the '80s are
about as barren of countercultural impulse as Boston under
Cotton Mather's administration. Sure, there are still artists in

SoHo, but they're busy discussing tax shelters over their decaf cappuccino.

A true counterculture requires at least three things: (1) a distinctive mode of dress, which can include anything from recycled velvet to torn T-shirts, so long as no part of it can be purchased at Benetton; (2) some attempt at artistic or literary creativity, even if the only product is an occasional mimeographed disquisition on love, death, and other current issues; and (3) (this is indispensable) an absolute contempt for the bourgeoisie, which can be defined flexibly as the ruling class, any class that lets itself be ruled by it, or one's parents.

The key thing, underlying all of the above, is a massive, uncompromising indifference to money and all known methods of acquiring it, storing it, and displaying it. This is where members of today's artistic subculture fall down so grievously. Yes, they have a distinctive style of dress, generally modeled after Madonna with a hangover. And yes, they have artistic pretensions, and are mightily productive of items such as silk-screened renditions of Kraft grape jelly jars. But they love money, and this is why they thrive wherever art and real estate intersect in that special frenzy of speculation that defines New York's SoHo or San Francisco's SoMa.

The problem is that our educated young people have never heard of anyone — outside of certain monastic orders — subsisting voluntarily on less that $50,000 a year. The result is that middle-class youth have come to expect to leap directly from a college dorm to a condominium, eliminating that entire stage of the human life cycle known as "finding yourself." And that phase, now as in Jack Kerouac's day, is best conducted in a run-down sixth-floor walk-up apartment and on a diet of peanut butter and day-old bread.

You can't really blame today's young people for failing to invent their own counterculture. First, it's almost impossible these days to find low-rent sixth-floor walk-up apartments that are not subject to constant incendiary attacks by landlords bent on condominiumizing. Second, it's hard to find the personnel. All great countercultures arose from the intimate mixing of people of different classes and races (not to mention sexual orientations). But outside of Miller beer commercials, this doesn't happen much anymore.

Then there's the problem of coming up with something entirely new — post-Zen, post-LSD, post-punk, post-vegetarian, and (although the new art entrepreneurs don't know it yet) post-Warhol. I don't know what the shape of the next counterculture will be, or whether an aging ex-Ginsberg groupie like myself would feel comfortable in it. But I have confidence that the generation that invented Live Aid and constructed shantytowns on campus lawns to protest apartheid before even reaching the legal drinking age will figure something out.

6

QUESTIONS ON MEANING

1. Who was Cotton Mather (paragraph 1)?
2. What does Ehrenreich criticize about today's young people? What does she have to say in their favor?
3. What does the author reveal about herself when she confesses that she's "an aging ex-Ginsberg groupie" (paragraph 6)?
4. Where in her essay does Ehrenreich make clear her reasons for advocating "a good strong counterculture"?
5. According to the author, what are the ingredients needed for a counterculture? Of these, which one does she regard as most important?
6. What present-day trends besides the lack of a counterculture does Ehrenreich's humor target?

QUESTIONS ON WRITING STRATEGY

1. Is "Hope I Die before I Get Rich" a humorous essay, or does the author use humor to make a serious point? Explain.
2. Where in her essay does Ehrenreich make expert use of TRANSITIONS?

QUESTIONS ON LANGUAGE

1. Be sure you know what Ehrenreich means by the following: bohemia, subsistence, cappuccino (paragraph 1); disquisition (2); massive, subculture (3); incendiary (5); entrepreneurs (6).

2. Compare Ehrenreich's definition of *bourgeoisie* (paragraph 2) with the dictionary definition. How do you account for the differences?

SUGGESTIONS FOR WRITING

1. Write an essay in which you agree or disagree with Ehrenreich's apparent assumption that today's college students are all preparing to "plunge into a career of investment banking or futures trading." Be sure to back up your position with plenty of EVIDENCE.
2. If you had the power to invent a counterculture for your generation, of what ingredients would it consist? Write a paper in which you set forth those ingredients.

Barbara Ehrenreich on Writing

The printed word, in the view of Barbara Ehrenreich, should be a powerful instrument for reform. In a recent article, though, she complains about a tacit censorship in American magazines that has sometimes prevented her from fulfilling her purpose as a writer. Ehrenreich recalls the difficulties she had in trying to persuade the editor of a national magazine to assign her a story on the plight of Third World women refugees. "Sorry," said the editor, "Third World women have never done anything for me."

Ehrenreich infers that writers who write for such magazines must follow a rule: "You must learn not to stray from your assigned socio-demographic stereotype." She observes, "As a woman, I am generally asked to write on 'women's topics,' such as cooking, divorce, how to succeed in business, diet fads, and the return of the bustle. These are all fine topics and give great scope to my talents, but when I ask, in faltering tones, for an assignment on the arms race or on the trade deficit, I am likely to be told that *anyone* (Bill, Gerry, Bob) could cover that, whereas my 'voice' is *essential* for the aerobic toothbrushing story. This is not, strictly speaking, 'censorship' — just a division of labor in which white men cover politics, foreign policy, and the economy, and the rest of us cover what's left over, such as the bustle."

Over the years Ehrenreich has had many manuscripts rejected by editors who comment, "too angry," "too depressing," and "Where's the bright side?" She agrees with writer Herbert Gold, who once deduced that the American media want only "happy stories about happy people with happy problems." She concludes, "You can write about anything — death squads, AIDS, or the prospect for a Pat Robertson victory in '88 — so long as you make it 'upbeat.'" Despite such discouragements, Ehrenreich continues her battle to "disturb the stupor induced by six straight pages of Calvin Klein ads." ("Put on a Happy Face," article in *Mother Jones*, May 1987, p. 60.)

FOR DISCUSSION

1. Is Ehrenreich right about what she calls "a tacit censorship in American magazines"? Check some recent issue of a magazine that prints signed articles. How many of the articles *not* on "women's topics" are written by women? How many are written by men?
2. How many women can you name who write serious newspaper and magazine articles reporting on or arguing matters of general interest, as opposed to those meant to appeal chiefly to women?
3. To what extent do you agree with Ehrenreich — and with Herbert Gold — that the American media are interested only in "upbeat" stories?

· Richard Rodriguez ·

The son of Spanish-speaking Mexican-Americans, RICHARD
RODRIGUEZ was born in 1944 in San Francisco. After graduation from Stanford, he continued his studies at Columbia, the
Warburg Institute in London, and the University of California, Berkeley. Now a writer and journalist, Rodriguez has
been living recently in Mexico City, preparing a book about
Mexico and California. His essays have appeared in *The
American Scholar, Change, Saturday Review*, and other magazines; and he has published a widely discussed book of essays
in autobiography, *Hunger of Memory* (1982).

Aria: A Memoir of a Bilingual Childhood

"Aria: A Memoir of a Bilingual Childhood" is taken from
Hunger of Memory. First published in *The American Scholar* in
1981, it contains both poignant memoir and persuasive argument. Setting forth his views of bilingual education, the author measures the gains and losses that resulted when English
gradually replaced the Spanish spoken in his childhood
home. To the child Rodriguez, Spanish was a private language, English a public one. Would the boy have learned
faster and better if his teachers had allowed him the use of his
native language in school?

I remember, to start with, that day in Sacramento, in a Cali-   1
fornia now nearly thirty years past, when I first entered a classroom — able to understand about fifty stray English words. The
third of four children, I had been preceded by my older brother
and sister to a neighborhood Roman Catholic school. But neither of them had revealed very much about their classroom experiences. They left each morning and returned each afternoon,
always together, speaking Spanish as they climbed the five steps

to the porch. And their mysterious books, wrapped in brown shopping-bag paper, remained on the table next to the door, closed firmly behind them.

An accident of geography sent me to a school where all my   2
classmates were white and many were the children of doctors and lawyers and business executives. On that first day of school, my classmates must certainly have been uneasy to find themselves apart from their families, in the first institution of their lives. But I was astonished. I was fated to be the "problem student" in class.

The nun said, in a friendly but oddly impersonal voice: 3
"Boys and girls, this is Richard Rodriguez." (I heard her sound it out: *Rich-heard Road-ree-guess.*) It was the first time I had heard anyone say my name in English. "Richard," the nun repeated more slowly, writing my name down in her book. Quickly I turned to see my mother's face dissolve in a watery blur behind the pebbled-glass door.

Now, many years later, I hear of something called "bilingual   4
education" — a scheme proposed in the late 1960s by Hispanic-American social activists, later endorsed by a congressional vote. It is a program that seeks to permit non-English-speaking children (many from lower class homes) to use their "family language" as the language of school. Such, at least, is the aim its supporters announce. I hear them, and am forced to say no: It is not possible for a child, any child, ever to use his family's language in school. Not to understand this is to misunderstand the public uses of schooling and to trivialize the nature of intimate life.

Memory teaches me what I know of these matters. The boy   5
reminds the adult. I was a bilingual child, but of a certain kind: "socially disadvantaged," the son of working-class parents, both Mexican immigrants.

In the early years of my boyhood, my parents coped very   6
well in America. My father had steady work. My mother managed at home. They were nobody's victims. When we moved to a house many blocks from the Mexican-American section of town, they were not intimidated by those two or three neigh-

bors who initially tried to make us unwelcome. ("Keep your brats away from my sidewalk!") But despite all they achieved, or perhaps because they had so much to achieve, they lacked any deep feeling of ease, of belonging in public. They regarded the people at work or in crowds as being very distant from us. Those were the others, *los gringos*. That term was interchangeable in their speech with another, even more telling: *los americanos*.

I grew up in a house where the only regular guests were my relations. On a certain day, enormous families of relatives would visit us, and there would be so many people that the noise and the bodies would spill out to the backyard and onto the front porch. Then for weeks no one would come. (If the doorbell rang, it was usually a salesman.) Our house stood apart — gaudy yellow in a row of white bungalows. We were the people with the noisy dog, the people who raised chickens. We were the foreigners on the block. A few neighbors would smile and wave at us. We waved back. But until I was seven years old, I did not know the name of the old couple living next door or the names of the kids living across the street.

In public, my father and mother spoke a hesitant, accented, and not always grammatical English. And then they would have to strain, their bodies tense, to catch the sense of what was rapidly said by *los gringos*. At home, they returned to Spanish. The language of their Mexican past sounded in counterpoint to the English spoken in public. The words would come quickly, with ease. Conveyed through those sounds was the pleasing, soothing, consoling reminder that one was at home.

During those years when I was first learning to speak, my mother and father addressed me only in Spanish; in Spanish I learned to reply. By contrast, English (*inglés*) was the language I came to associate with gringos, rarely heard in the house. I learned my first words of English overhearing my parents speaking to strangers. At six years of age, I knew just enough words for my mother to trust me on errands to stores one block away — but no more.

I was then a listening child, careful to hear the very different sounds of Spanish and English. Wide-eyed with hearing, I'd listen to sounds more than to words. First, there were English (gringo) sounds. So many words still were unknown to me that when the butcher or the lady at the drugstore said something, exotic polysyllabic sounds would bloom in the midst of their sentences. Often the speech of people in public seemed to me very loud, booming with confidence. The man behind the counter would literally ask, "What can I do for you?" But by being so firm and clear, the sound of his voice said that he was a gringo; he belonged in public society. There were also the high, nasal notes of middle-class American speech — which I rarely am conscious of hearing today because I hear them so often, but could not stop hearing when I was a boy. Crowds at Safeway or at bus stops were noisy with the birdlike sounds of *los gringos*. I'd move away from them all — all the chirping chatter above me.

My own sounds I was unable to hear, but I knew that I   11
spoke English poorly. My words could not extend to form complete thoughts. And the words I did speak I didn't know well enough to make distinct sounds. (Listeners would usually lower their heads to hear better what I was trying to say.) But it was one thing for *me* to speak English with difficulty; it was more troubling to hear my parents speaking in public: their high-whining vowels and guttural consonants; their sentences that got stuck with "eh" and "ah" sounds; the confused syntax; the hesitant rhythm of sounds so different from the way gringos spoke. I'd notice, moreover, that my parents' voices were softer than those of gringos we would meet.

I am tempted to say now that none of this mattered. (In   12
adulthood I am embarrassed by childhood fears.) And, in a way, it didn't matter very much that my parents could not speak English with ease. Their linguistic difficulties had no serious consequences. My mother and father made themselves understood at the county hospital clinic and at government offices. And yet, in another way, it mattered very much. It was unsettling to hear my parents struggle with English. Hearing them, I'd grow nervous, and my clutching trust in their protection and power would be weakened.

There were many times like the night at a brightly lit gaso-   13
line station (a blaring white memory) when I stood uneasily hearing my father talk to a teenage attendant. I do not recall

what they were saying, but I cannot forget the sounds my father made as he spoke. At one point his words slid together to form one long word — sounds as confused as the threads of blue and green oil in the puddle next to my shoes. His voice rushed through what he had left to say. Toward the end, he reached falsetto notes, appealing to his listener's understanding. I looked away at the lights of passing automobiles. I tried not to hear any more. But I heard only too well the attendant's reply, his calm, easy tones. Shortly afterward, headed for home, I shivered when my father put his hand on my shoulder. The very first chance that I got, I evaded his grasp and ran on ahead into the dark, skipping with feigned boyish exuberance.

But then there was Spanish: *español*, the language rarely   14
heard away from the house; *español*, the language which seemed to me therefore a private language, my family's language. To hear its sounds was to feel myself specially recognized as one of the family, apart from *los otros*. A simple remark, an inconsequential comment could convey that assurance. My parents would say something to me and I would feel embraced by the sounds of their words. Those sounds said: *I am speaking with ease in Spanish. I am addressing you in words I never use with los gringos. I recognize you as someone special, close, like no one outside. You belong with us. In the family. Ricardo.*

At the age of six, well past the time when most middle-class   15
children no longer notice the difference between sounds uttered at home and words spoken in public, I had a different experience. I lived in a world compounded of sounds. I was a child longer than most. I lived in a magical world, surrounded by sounds both pleasing and fearful. I shared with my family a language enchantingly private — different from that used in the city around us.

Just opening or closing the screen door behind me was an   16
important experience. I'd rarely leave home all alone or without feeling reluctance. Walking down the sidewalk, under the canopy of tall trees, I'd warily notice the (suddenly) silent neighborhood kids who stood warily watching me. Nervously, I'd arrive at the grocery store to hear there the sounds of the gringo, reminding me that in this so-big world I was a foreigner. But if

leaving home was never routine, neither was coming back. Walking toward our house, climbing the steps from the sidewalk, in summer when the front door was open, I'd hear voices beyond the screen door talking in Spanish. For a second or two I'd stay, linger there listening. Smiling, I'd hear my mother call out, saying in Spanish, "Is that you, Richard?" Those were her words, but all the while her sounds would assure me: *You are home now. Come closer inside. With us.* "*Sí*," I'd reply.

Once more inside the house, I would resume my place in the family. The sounds would grow harder to hear. Once more at home, I would grow less conscious of them. It required, however, no more than the blurt of the doorbell to alert me all over again to listen to sounds. The house would turn instantly quiet while my mother went to the door. I'd hear her hard English sounds. I'd wait to hear her voice turn to soft-sounding Spanish, which assured me, as surely as did the clicking tongue of the lock on the door, that the stranger was gone.

Plainly it is not healthy to hear such sounds so often. It is not healthy to distinguish public from private sounds so easily. I remained cloistered by sounds, timid and shy in public, too dependent on the voices at home. And yet I was a very happy child when I was at home. I remember many nights when my father would come back from work, and I'd hear him call out to my mother in Spanish, sounding relieved. In Spanish, his voice would sound the light and free notes that he never could manage in English. Some nights I'd jump up just hearing his voice. My brother and I would come running into the room where he was with our mother. Our laughing (so deep was the pleasure!) became screaming. Like others who feel the pain of public alienation, we transformed the knowledge of our public separateness into a consoling reminder of our intimacy. Excited, our voices joined in a celebration of sounds. *We are speaking now the way we never speak out in public — we are together*, the sounds told me. Some nights no one seemed willing to loosen the hold that sounds had on us. At dinner we invented new words that sounded Spanish, but made sense only to us. We pieced together new words by taking, say, an English verb and giving it Spanish endings. My mother's instructions at bedtime would be lac-

17

18

quered with mock-urgent tones. Or a word like *sí,* sounded in several notes, would convey added measures of feeling. Tongues lingered around the edges of words, especially fat vowels, and we happily sounded that military drum roll, the twirling roar of the Spanish *r.* Family language, my family's sounds: the voices of my parents and sisters and brother. Their voices insisting: *You belong here. We are family members. Related. Special to one another. Listen!* Voices singing and sighing, rising and straining, then surging, teeming with pleasure which burst syllables into fragments of laughter. At times it seemed there was steady quiet only when, from another room, the rustling whispers of my parents faded and I edged closer to sleep.

Supporters of bilingual education imply today that students   19
like me miss a great deal by not being taught in their family's language. What they seem not to recognize is that, as a socially disadvantaged child, I regarded Spanish as a private language. It was a ghetto language that deepened and strengthened my feeling of public separateness. What I needed to learn in school was that I had the right, and the obligation, to speak the public language. The odd truth is that my first-grade classmates could have become bilingual, in the conventional sense of the word, more easily than I. Had they been taught early (as upper middle-class children often are taught) a "second language" like Spanish or French, they could have regarded it simply as another public language. In my case, such bilingualism could not have been so quickly achieved. What I did not believe was that I could speak a single public language.

Without question, it would have pleased me to have heard   20
my teachers address me in Spanish when I entered the classroom. I would have felt much less afraid. I would have imagined that my instructors were somehow "related" to me; I would indeed have heard their Spanish as my family's language. I would have trusted them and responded with ease. But I would have delayed — postponed for how long? — having to learn the language of public society. I would have evaded — and for how long? — learning the great lesson of school: that I had a public identity.

Fortunately, my teachers were unsentimental about their re-   21
sponsibility. What they understood was that I needed to speak
public English. So their voices would search me out, asking me
questions. Each time I heard them I'd look up in surprise to see a
nun's face frowning at me. I'd mumble, not really meaning to
answer. The nun would persist. "Richard, stand up. Don't look
at the floor. Speak up. Speak to the entire class, not just to me!"
But I couldn't believe English could be my language to use. (In
part, I did not want to believe it.) I continued to mumble. I resisted the teacher's demands. (Did I somehow suspect that once I
learned this public language my family life would be changed?)
Silent, waiting for the bell to sound, I remained dazed, diffident,
afraid.

Because I wrongly imagined that English was intrinsically a   22
public language and Spanish was intrinsically private, I easily
noted the difference between classroom language and the language at home. At school, words were directed to a general audience of listeners. ("Boys and girls . . . ") Words were meaning-
fully ordered. And the point was not self-expression alone, but
to make oneself understood by many others. The teacher
quizzed: "Boys and girls, why do we use that word in this sentence? Could we think of a better word to use there? Would the
sentence change its meaning if the words were differently arranged? Isn't there a better way of saying much the same thing?"
(I couldn't say. I wouldn't try to say.)

Three months passed. Five. A half year. Unsmiling, ever   23
watchful, my teachers noted my silence. They began to connect
my behavior with the slow progress my brother and sisters were
making. Until, one Saturday morning, three nuns arrived at the
house to talk to our parents. Stiffly they sat on the blue living-
room sofa. From the doorway of another room, spying on the
visitors, I noted the incongruity, the clash of two worlds, the
faces and voices of school intruding upon the familiar setting of
home. I overheard one voice gently wondering, "Do your children speak only Spanish at home, Mrs. Rodriguez?" While another voice added, "That Richard especially seems so timid and
shy."

That Rich-heard!   24

With great tact, the visitors continued, "Is it possible for you   25
and your husband to encourage your children to practice their
English when they are home?" Of course my parents complied.
What would they not do for their children's well-being? And
how could they question the Church's authority which those
women represented? In an instant they agreed to give up the language (the sounds) which had revealed and accentuated our
family's closeness. The moment after the visitors left, the change
was observed. "*Ahora*, speak to us only *en inglés*," my father and
mother told us.

At first, it seemed a kind of game. After dinner each night,   26
the family gathered together to practice "our" English. It was
still then *inglés*, a language foreign to us, so we felt drawn to it as
strangers. Laughing, we would try to define words we could not
pronounce. We played with strange English sounds, often over-
anglicizing our pronunciations. And we filled the smiling gaps of
our sentences with familiar Spanish sounds. But that was cheat-
ing, somebody shouted, and everyone laughed.

In school, meanwhile, like my brother and sisters, I was re-   27
quired to attend a daily tutoring session. I needed a full year of
this special work. I also needed my teachers to keep my attention from straying in class by calling out, "*Rich-heard*" — their
English voices slowly loosening the ties to my other name, with
its three notes, *Ri-car-do*. Most of all, I needed to hear my
mother and father speak to me in a moment of seriousness in
"broken" — suddenly heartbreaking — English. This scene was
inevitable. One Saturday morning I entered the kitchen where
my parents were talking, but I did not realize that they were
talking in Spanish until, the moment they saw me, their voices
changed and they began speaking English. The gringo sounds
they uttered startled me. Pushed me away. In that moment of
trivial misunderstanding and profound insight, I felt my throat
twisted by unsounded grief. I simply turned and left the room.
But I had no place to escape to where I could grieve in Spanish.
My brother and sisters were speaking English in another part of
the house.

Again and again in the days following, as I grew increasingly   28
angry, I was obliged to hear my mother and father encouraging

me: "Speak to us *en inglés*." Only then did I determine to learn classroom English. Thus, sometime afterward it happened: One day in school, I raised my hand to volunteer an answer to a question. I spoke out in a loud voice and I did not think it re- markable when the entire class understood. That day I moved very far from being the disadvantaged child I had been only days earlier. Taken hold at last was the belief, the calming assur- ance, that I *belonged* in public.

Shortly after, I stopped hearing the high, troubling sounds   29 of *los gringos*. A more and more confident speaker of English, I didn't listen to how strangers sounded when they talked to me. With so many English-speaking people around me, I no longer heard American accents. Conversations quickened. Listening to persons whose voices sounded eccentrically pitched, I might note their sounds for a few seconds, but then I'd concentrate on what they were saying. Now when I heard someone's tone of voice — angry or questioning or sarcastic or happy or sad — I didn't distinguish it from the words it expressed. Sound and word were thus tightly wedded. At the end of each day I was of- ten bemused, and always relieved, to realize how "soundless," though crowded with words, my day in public had been. An eight-year-old boy, I finally came to accept what had been tech- nically true since my birth: I was an American citizen.

But diminished by then was the special feeling of closeness   30 at home. Gone was the desperate, urgent, intense feeling of be- ing at home among those with whom I felt intimate. Our family remained a loving family, but one greatly changed. We were no longer so close, no longer bound tightly together by the knowl- edge of our separateness from *los gringos*. Neither my older brother nor my sisters rushed home after school any more. Nor did I. When I arrived home, often there would be neighborhood kids in the house. Or the house would be empty of sounds.

Following the dramatic Americanization of their children,   31 even my parents grew more publicly confident — especially my mother. First she learned the names of all the people on the block. Then she decided we needed to have a telephone in our house. My father, for his part, continued to use the word gringo, but it was no longer charged with bitterness or distrust. Stripped of any emotional content, the word simply became a name for those Americans not of Hispanic descent. Hearing him, some-times, I wasn't sure if he was pronouncing the Spanish word *gringo*, or saying gringo in English.

There was a new silence at home. As we children learned more and more English, we shared fewer and fewer words with our parents. Sentences needed to be spoken slowly when one of us addressed our mother or father. Often the parent wouldn't understand. The child would need to repeat himself. Still the parent misunderstood. The young voice, frustrated, would end up saying, "Never mind" — the subject was closed. Dinners would be noisy with the clinking of knives and forks against dishes. My mother would smile softly between her remarks; my father, at the other end of the table, would chew and chew his food while he stared over the heads of his children.

My mother! My father! After English became my primary language, I no longer knew what words to use in addressing my parents. The old Spanish words (those tender accents of sound) I had earlier used — *mamá* and *papá* — I couldn't use any more. They would have been all-too-painful reminders of how much had changed in my life. On the other hand, the words I heard neighborhood kids call their parents seemed equally unsatisfactory. "Mother" and "father," "ma," "papa," "pa," "dad," "pop" (how I hated the all-American sound of that last word) — all these I felt were unsuitable terms of address for *my* parents. As a result, I never used them at home. Whenever I'd speak to my parents, I would try to get their attention by looking at them. In public conversations, I'd refer to them as my "parents" or my "mother" and "father."

My mother and father, for their part, responded differently, as their children spoke to them less. My mother grew restless, seemed troubled and anxious at the scarceness of words ex-changed in the house. She would question me about my day when I came home from school. She smiled at my small talk. She pried at the edges of my sentences to get me to say some-thing more. ("What . . . ?") She'd join conversations she over-heard, but her intrusions often stopped her children's talking. By contrast, my father seemed to grow reconciled to the new

32

33

34

quiet. Though his English somewhat improved, he tended more and more to retire into silence. At dinner he spoke very little. One night his children and even his wife helplessly giggled at his garbled English pronunciation of the Catholic "Grace Before Meals." Thereafter he made his wife recite the prayer at the start of each meal, even on formal occasions when there were guests in the house.

Hers became the public voice of the family. On official busi-   35
ness it was she, not my father, who would usually talk to strangers on the phone or in stores. We children grew so accustomed to his silence that years later we would routinely refer to his "shyness." (My mother often tried to explain: Both of his parents died when he was eight. He was raised by an uncle who treated him as little more than a menial servant. He was never encouraged to speak. He grew up alone — a man of few words.) But I realized my father was not shy whenever I'd watch him speaking Spanish with relatives. Using Spanish, he was quickly effusive. Especially when talking with other men, his voice would spark, flicker, flare alive with varied sounds. In Spanish he expressed ideas and feelings he rarely revealed when speaking English. With firm Spanish sounds he conveyed a confidence and authority that English would never allow him.

The silence at home, however, was not simply the result of   36
fewer words passing between parents and children. More profound for me was the silence created by my inattention to sounds. At about the time I no longer bothered to listen with care to the sounds of English in public, I grew careless about listening to the sounds made by the family when they spoke. Most of the time I would hear someone speaking at home and didn't distinguish his sounds from the words people uttered in public. I didn't even pay much attention to my parents' accented and ungrammatical speech — at least not at home. Only when I was with them in public would I become alert to their accents. But even then their sounds caused me less and less concern. For I was growing increasingly confident of my own public identity.

I would have been happier about my public success had I   37
not recalled, sometimes, what it had been like earlier, when my family conveyed its intimacy through a set of conveniently pri-

vate sounds. Sometimes in public, hearing a stranger, I'd hark back to my lost past. A Mexican farm worker approached me one day downtown. He wanted directions to some place. "*Hijito,* . . . " he said. And his voice stirred old longings. Another time I was standing beside my mother in the visiting room of a Carmelite convent, before the dense screen which rendered the nuns shadowy figures. I heard several of them speaking Spanish in their busy, singsong, overlapping voices, assuring my mother that, yes, yes, we were remembered, all our family was remembered, in their prayers. Those voices echoed faraway family sounds. Another day a dark-faced old woman touched my shoulder lightly to steady herself as she boarded a bus. She murmured something to me I couldn't quite comprehend. Her Spanish voice came near, like the face of a never-before-seen relative in the instant before I was kissed. That voice, like so many of the Spanish voices I'd hear in public, recalled the golden age of my childhood.

Bilingual educators say today that children lose a degree of "individuality" by becoming assimilated into public society. (Bilingual schooling is a program popularized in the seventies, that decade when middle-class "ethnics" began to resist the process of assimilation — the "American melting pot.") But the bilingualists oversimplify when they scorn the value and necessity of assimilation. They do not seem to realize that a person is individualized in two ways. So they do not realize that, while one suffers a diminished sense of *private* individuality by being assimilated into public society, such assimilation makes possible the achievement of *public* individuality. 38

Simplistically again, the bilingualists insist that a student should be reminded of his difference from others in mass society, of his "heritage." But they equate mere separateness with individuality. The fact is that only in private — with intimates — is separateness from the crowd a prerequisite for individuality; an intimate "tells" me that I am unique, unlike all others, apart from the crowd. In public, by contrast, full individuality is achieved, paradoxically, by those who are able to consider themselves members of the crowd. Thus it happened for me. 39

Only when I was able to think of myself as an American, no longer an alien in gringo society, could I seek the rights and opportunities necessary for full public individuality. The social and political advantages I enjoy as a man began on the day I came to believe that my name is indeed *Rich-heard Road-ree-guess*. It is true that my public society today is often impersonal; in fact, my public society is usually mass society. But despite the anonymity of the crowd, and despite the fact that the individuality I achieve in public is often tenuous — because it depends on my being one in a crowd — I celebrate the day I acquired my new name. Those middle-class ethnics who scorn assimilation seem to me filled with decadent self-pity, obsessed by the burden of public life. Dangerously, they romanticize public separateness and trivialize the dilemma of those who are truly socially disadvantaged.

If I rehearse here the changes in my private life after my Americanization, it is finally to emphasize a public gain. The loss implies the gain. The house I returned to each afternoon was quiet. Intimate sounds no longer greeted me at the door. Inside there were other noises. The telephone rang. Neighborhood kids ran past the door of the bedroom where I was reading my schoolbooks — covered with brown shopping-bag paper. Once I learned the public language, it would never again be easy for me to hear intimate family voices. More and more of my day was spent hearing words, not sounds. But that may only be a way of saying that on the day I raised my hand in class and spoke loudly to an entire roomful of faces, my childhood started to end.

40

QUESTIONS ON MEANING

1. Rodriguez's essay is both memoir and argument. What is the thrust of the author's argument? Where in the essay does he set it forth?

2. How did the child Rodriguez react when, in his presence, his parents had to struggle to make themselves understood by "*los gringos*"?

3. What does the author mean when he says, "I was a child longer than most" (paragraph 15)?
4. According to the author, what impact did the Rodriguez children's use of English have on relationships within the family?
5. Contrast the child Rodriguez's view of the nuns who insisted he speak English with his adult view.

QUESTIONS ON WRITING STRATEGY

1. How effective an INTRODUCTION is Rodriguez's first paragraph?
2. Several times in his essay Rodriguez shifts from memoir to argument and back again. What is the EFFECT of these shifts? Do they strengthen or weaken the author's stance against bilingual education?
3. Twice in his essay (in paragraphs 1 and 40) the author mentions schoolbooks wrapped in shopping-bag paper. How does the use of this detail enhance his argument?
4. What AUDIENCE probably would not like this essay? Why would they not like it?

QUESTIONS ON LANGUAGE

1. Consult the dictionary if you need help defining these words: counterpoint (paragraph 8); polysyllabic (10); guttural, syntax (11); falsetto, exuberance (13); inconsequential (14); cloistered, lacquered (18); diffident (21); intrinsically (22); incongruity (23); bemused (29); effusive (35); assimilated (38); paradoxically, tenuous, decadent (39).
2. In Rodriguez's essay, how do the words *public* and *private* relate to the issue of bilingual education? What important distinction does the author make between *individuality* and *separateness* (paragraph 39)?
3. What exactly does the author mean when he says, "More and more of my day was spent hearing words, not sounds" (paragraph 40)?

SUGGESTIONS FOR WRITING

1. Write a brief personal history of your efforts to change your language habits.
2. Set forth a case in favor of the use of black English or of Spanish in public schools, contrary to Rodriguez's argument.

3. Try to define the distinctive quality of the language spoken in your home when you were a child. Explain any ways in which this language differed from what you heard in school. How has the difference mattered to you? (This language need not be a foreign language; it might include any words used in your family but not in the world at large: a dialect, slang, ALLUSIONS, sayings, FIGURES OF SPEECH, or a special vocabulary.)

Richard Rodriguez on Writing

For *The Bedford Reader*, Richard Rodriguez has described the writing of "Aria":

"From grammar school to college, my teachers offered perennial encouragement: 'Write about what you know.' Every year I would respond with the student's complaint: 'I have nothing to write about . . . I haven't done anything.'" (Writers, real writers, I thought, lived in New York or Paris; they smoked on the back jackets of library books, their chores done.)

"Stories die for not being told. . . . My story got told because I had received an education; my teachers had given me the skill of stringing words together in a coherent line. But it was not until I was a man that I felt any need to write my story. A few years ago I left graduate school, quit teaching for political reasons (to protest affirmative action). But after leaving the classroom, as the months passed, I grew desperate to talk to serious people about serious things. In the great journals of the world, I noticed, there was conversation of a sort, glamorous company of a sort, and I determined to join it. I began writing to stay alive — not as a job, but to stay alive.

"Even as you see my essay now, in cool printer's type, I look at some pages and cannot remember having written them. Or else I can remember earlier versions — unused incident, character, description (rooms, faces) — crumbled and discarded. Flung from possibility. They hit the wastebasket, those pages, and yet, defying gravity with a scratchy, starchy resilience, tried to re-open themselves. Then they fell silent. I read certain other sentences now and they recall the very day they were composed — the afternoon of rain or the telephone call that was to come a few moments after, the house, the room where these sentences were composed, the pattern of the rug, the wastebasket. (In all there were about thirty or forty versions that preceded this final 'Aria.') I tried to describe my experiences exactly, at once to discover myself and to reveal myself. Always I had to write against the fear I felt that no one would be able to understand what I was saying.

"As a reader, I have been struck by the way those novels and essays that are most particular, most particularly about one other life and time (Hannibal, Missouri; one summer; a slave; the loveliness of a muddy river) most fully achieve universality and call to be cherished. It is a paradox apparently: The more a writer unearths the detail that makes a life singular, the more a reader is led to feel a kind of sharing. Perhaps the reason we are able to respond to the life that is so different is because we all, each of us, think privately that we are different from one another. And the more closely we examine another life in its misery or wisdom or foolishness, the more it seems we take some version of ourselves.

"It is, in any case, finally you that I end up having to trust not to laugh, not to snicker. Even as you regard me in these lines, I try to imagine your face as you read. You who read 'Aria,' especially those of you with your theme-divining yellow felt pen poised in your hand, you for whom this essay is yet another assignment, please do not forget that it is my life I am handing you in these pages — memories that are as personal for me as family photographs in an old cigar box."

FOR DISCUSSION

1. What seems to be Rodriguez's attitude toward his AUDIENCE? Do you think he writes chiefly for his readers, or for himself? Defend your answer.
2. Rodriguez tells us what he said when, as a student, he was told, "Write about what you know." What do you think he would say now?

· Mark Hunter ·

MARK HUNTER, critic and journalist, was graduated from Harvard in 1975 with a B.A. in American history and literature. Before and during college, he worked as a rock musician. Currently he lives in Paris, where he writes of cultural events for the *International Herald Tribune*, an American daily newspaper published in Europe. He has contributed to *Esquire*, *Harper's*, *Mother Jones*, *American Health*, *Cosmopolitan*, *New West*, and other magazines, and in 1988 published a collection of his essays, interviews, and reporting.

The Beat Goes Off:
How Technology Has Gummed Up
Rock's Grooves

Mark Hunter's lament for rock attracted attention when first published in *Harper's* in 1986. It was included in Hunter's new book, which observes several aspects of America in the 1980s: work, stress, leisure, love, and relationships. In "The Beat Goes Off," the author examines rock music from its beginnings to 1986 and comes to some startling and controversial conclusions about what happened along the way.

Not long ago I borrowed a car, loaded it with 211 phonograph albums that had been sent to me by record companies over the past three years, and drove to a secondhand record store, where I sold them for about $150. This was illegal; the albums were plainly marked "demonstration — not for sale" (though every record company knows that many of the critics on its mailing list derive a sizable share of their income by selling these albums). I didn't set out to break the law; but I'd offered a dozen or so people as many records as they could carry away, and I'd gotten no takers. Selling the records seemed somehow better than simply dumping them in the street — or keeping them.

Of the roughly 500 albums I've received in the past five   2
years, maybe thirty were worth keeping. It's not easy for me to say that. Since the age of thirteen — that's twenty-one years ago — I have lived with and for rock-and-roll. I have spent incalculable hours around stereos and in rock clubs, listening, dancing, performing, falling in and out of love. I believed, as a California dance-hall queen told me once, that "rock-and-roll will keep you young." That the music itself would one day grow old was beyond imagining. Yet from what I hear, and I have heard an awful lot, the great creative period of this music is over.

What has aged rock music isn't merely or mainly laziness or   3
a lack of imagination — though there has been more than enough of that. The overwhelming problem is the new technology behind the backbeat and the changes it has set in motion, changes that demand an entirely different approach to music from the one that initially made rock a fresh and exciting form. Technology, in music as in every other field, has its imperatives as well as its possibilities. For rock, the imperatives have proved deadly.

I am fully aware that most rock fans, let alone most critics,   4
could care less about the technology involved in making records. But given the extraordinary extent to which rock music has penetrated our lives — a number-one pop hit today could be defined as a song that nearly everyone in the world will hear at least once — one might well take an interest in how it was recorded, and how this in turn shapes the kind of music being made. The fact is that what might be called the *content* of rock — the songs, the sound — follows to a great extent from formulas *imposed* by recording techniques. And these formulas are giving us music that is murderously dull.

The worldwide rock explosion began in 1963 when the Bea-   5
tles set off what would become, within a decade, a doubling of global record and tape sales (to about $2 billion worth). The Beatles represented something new in pop music, but it was not their beat that was new so much as the fact that they were a self-

contained composing, arranging, and performing unit. In this way they were quite different from the stars of the 1950s, who recorded material written by pop composers and arranged by record label "A&R" (artist and repertoire) directors. The great bands of the "British Invasion" of the mid-1960s — the Who, the Animals, the Rolling Stones — were similarly self-reliant, as were the literally thousands of rock bands that sprang up in England and the United States in the wake of their success.

The Beatles and the other great British bands arrived on the scene just ahead of a profound change in recording techniques — the move from monophonic taping, in which all the instruments used in a composition are recorded simultaneously on the entire width of the tape, to "multitracking," in which each instrument is recorded on a separate band of tape and then "mixed down" into the final product. The shift to multitracking took time, and its progress was reflected in the argot of the recording studio. In the 1960s, when a recording artist or engineer spoke of a "track," he meant an entire song (as in the Stones' Keith Richards's famous description of a typical pop album as "a hit single and ten tracks of shit"). Since the mid-1970s, "track" has been used to describe *one* instrumental or vocal part of a composition. 6

In the monophonic era, recording a song meant gathering an ensemble in a room, putting out one or more microphones, and recording the music in one "take," live. If you didn't like the take, you did it over, period. This was how Elvis Presley's epochal first recordings for the Sun label were made in the early fifties, and it remained the standard technique (there were some exceptions) through the mid-sixties. 7

The advantage of this method, in retrospect — at the time, engineers and producers simply had no other methods available — was that players could inspire one another to the kind of extra effort that comes only in ensemble work. If you have ever played in a good group, you know what those moments are like: Suddenly, each musician seems to be hearing the music *before it is played.* That's what happens on Elvis's "Mystery Train"; Scotty Moore (on guitar) and Elvis (singing) anticipate each other's phrases, arriving together just ahead of where the ear would 8 expect the beat to fall, driving the song toward a mounting excitement. There is no drummer on "Mystery Train," but that doesn't keep you from dancing to it.

The disadvantages of this method were considerable, however, and evident even at the time — in particular, the difficulty in getting a distinct sound color, or timbre, for each instrument, and in capturing a performance in which every musician and singer was at a peak. Producers went crazy when one verse on a take was poorly sung but the rest were superb, because there was no way to cut out the bad and keep the good. Engineers went crazy trying to keep the sounds of drums and amplified guitars from ending up in the singer's microphone. It could be done, but it was hard, and it became even harder in the 1960s, when the electric bass came into wide use and made possible a rhythm-section sound of extraordinary power.

Engineers developed techniques that ameliorated these problems, but they could not solve them entirely. By recording the instruments first, for example, and then rerecording this tape onto another, simultaneously with a live take of the singer, the problem of instruments fouling up a brilliant vocal could be eliminated. Unfortunately, every time sounds are transferred from one tape to another, there is a loss in quality. Producers tried to get as much of the sound on tape in a single take as possible, and to limit the number of times they made additions to the original performance. That is why Phil Spector introduced bigger rhythm sections to pop, and why he used such innovations as "massed pianos" on the sessions he produced for the Crystals in 1961 and 1962. The only way to achieve orchestral depth was to record an orchestra.

All this changed with the invention of stereo machines with three recording heads (or "capstans") in the early sixties. Now an engineer could not only record the vocals and instruments on separate tracks. He could "punch in" a performer at a given moment on a recording, and then "punch out" in confidence that the new, punched-in sounds would be in sequence with the rest of the composition. Simply put, it was no longer necessary to record a song from beginning to end. "Synchronization" opened the way to true multitrack recording.

The pop album that most profoundly signaled this shift was   12
the Beatles' *Sgt. Pepper's Lonely Hearts Club Band*, released in
1967. The album was recorded on a four-track machine, the best
then available, and the shock it caused when it was released, for
rock musicians and listeners alike, was manifold.

To start with, all the lyrics are comprehensible on first lis-   13
tening — this was a rock rarity in 1967. Moreover, by recording
the various parts — bass, drums, vocals, horns, guitars — on
separate tracks, stopping periodically for "premixes" in order to
combine several parts on one track, then "mixing down" to the
final stereo product, the Beatles achieved a precision and clarity
of each instrument and effect that was unprecedented in pop.
When next you hear that album, note how McCartney's bass
line on "Being for the Benefit of Mr. Kite!" is distinct from the
rest of the sound; on the Beatles' earlier records, the bass blends
in with the drums and rhythm guitars, an angry roar at the bottom of the sound.

In essence, the techniques used to make *Sgt. Pepper* allowed   14
the Beatles to *compose* an album, instead of performing it as they
would onstage. When it soared to number one on the charts,
those techniques became a commercial imperative. (Think of
the Stones, who rushed onto the market the slipshod *Their Sa-
tanic Majesties Request* — a hash of psychedelic effects and
chopped-up song structures.) In the wake of *Sgt. Pepper*, rock
performance and rock recording became sharply divided do-
mains. Eventually, that gap became the gulch where rock ran
dry.

With multitracking, all the musicians involved in making a   15
record no longer had to be present at the same time (a point un-
derlined by the Beatles in 1969 in the making of *Abbey Road*;
rarely were all of them in the studio together). Once the bass
line was on tape, the bass player could go home. Conversely, if
one player made a mistake, only his part needed to be re-
recorded. Moreover, thanks to the process of overdubbing,
which allows the engineer to record over selected portions of a
track, the performance of a given player on a song no longer had
to be continuous. If one verse was no good, the singer could re-

take it. And the engineer could "treat" the sounds electronically during recording or mixing to alter their timbre.

These techniques all but eliminated what had always been 16 an essential element in rock, the concept of ensemble spontaneity. Cream's marvelous recording of Robert Johnson's "Crossroads," for example, contains some notes that might as well not have been played, but one hardly notices them because the three musicians (Eric Clapton on guitar, Jack Bruce on bass, and Ginger Baker on drums) adapt their individual intensity and attack to one another's work, moving in and out of the lead as the moment demands. In multitrack work, where musicians take turns recording their parts, it is nearly impossible for an individual player to alter the ensemble's direction in this manner. A mistake will sound like a mistake, instead of a cue for the rest of the ensemble to incorporate an accident into a large effect.

Multitracking also changed the dynamic flow of individual 17 performances. All music achieves its effects through contrast; soft moments set up the tough ones, which in turn give way, relax. This follows naturally from performing a song in its entirety. In the version of "Try a Little Tenderness" that Otis Redding and his backup band, the Bar-Kays, recorded in the mid-sixties, Redding keeps a certain power in reserve until the final measures, when he pleads outright with the listener to "love her, please her, never leave her," while the band rises behind him to a frenzied crescendo. In the multitrack era, when a musician will cut an entire track and then go back to "correct" certain passages, often phrase by phrase, performances tend to settle at a single dynamic level. Vocalists in particular seem to lose a sense of overall dynamic flow. Listen to Madonna's "Material Girl": the final chorus sounds just like the first.

Along with this loss of dynamism there is, on an over- 18 whelming number of records, an absence of rhythmic invention. On one disc after another there is the "boom-BOOM" of a thudding bass drum followed by a snare enveloped in reverberation — a "handclap" effect. Part of the reason for this awful sameness is that multitracking has led musicians and producers to think of rhythm as a domain unto itself, which it decidedly is not. When you listen to the records Marvin Gaye made for Motown in the monophonic era, records like "Ain't That Peculiar," you can't help but notice that piano, bass, guitar, and drum sounds blend into a single timbre. It is practically impossible to hear the sound of the bass drum separately from the sound of the bass guitar on this record, which is no doubt why the drummer chose to rely on his sharply percussive snare drum to set the beat. The way the timbres of their instruments would eventually come through on tape forced the musicians to think of rhythm as being the domain of no one instrument, but rather as an element emerging from a dynamic equilibrium among the members of the ensemble.

When multitracking made it possible to record the bass and   19
drums separately, and to hear them distinctly even at high volumes, the role of rhythm musicians was deeply altered. Their sound was no longer far back in a percussive cloud, but could be moved right to the front of the mix — which works just fine in discos and dance clubs, where you listen mostly with your feet, but not at home in front of the stereo. You can hear the difference on a collection of "never before released masters" recorded by Gaye in the mid-sixties and early seventies and put on the market last year under the title *Motown Remembers Marvin Gaye*. Some remembrance: On nearly every song new bass and drum parts have been added through multitrack overdubs and mixed into the forefront. You can follow the beat more easily — even a deaf person could feel the impact of the bass drum — but its texture has been impoverished, cut off from the rest of the sound.

Before multitracking came along, a "groove" meant the   20
sense of swing inherent in an entire arrangement. On Wilson Pickett's "Midnight Mover," for example, the bass guitar opens with a four-measure pattern, constantly shifting in accent, that first descends an octave, then holds firm around the root chord while the rhythm guitar knocks out a two-bar phrase that counterpoints both halves of the bass line, in time and harmonically. Today, bass and drums are typically recorded first, and are thus obliged to play in a way that will not complicate the recording of subsequent tracks. A groove now means a two-bar phrase of bass and drum notes (often "played" by an electronic drum box) that repeats without changing, as on David Bowie's tiresome

single "Let's Dance." Rhythm, once the backbone, has simply become the flat bottom.

Multitracking has flattened rock in other ways. For one thing, it cut short a revolution in the creative politics of the music industry. The people who rose to the top of the industry in the sixties, people like Clive Davis of Columbia, believed in letting rock bands "do their own thing" in the studio. That made sense when what counted on a record was the ensemble creation. It no longer made sense with multitrack machines.

Aside from the fact that the entire ensemble is no longer needed to finish a record, multitracking has made bands more dependent on producers and engineers, who understand the new techniques better than most musicians do. Moreover, anyone who has recorded both monophonically and multitrack will tell you that it takes far longer to make a record one sound at a time. In the studio, time is money, and in the multitrack era time costs more money than ever: Studios have to update their equipment constantly to remain competitive, and the price of the investment is passed on to musicians and their record companies. In the early sixties, the cost of recording a typical "commercial" album — that is, one whose sound quality appeals to radio programmers and the average record buyer — was a few thousand dollars; the cost rose to $100,000 in the mid-seventies, and now often reaches twice that figure. With that much money at stake, most contracts now specify that the record company has the right to choose the producer; and, to an extent unmatched since the pre-Beatles days, those producers tend to impose proven commercial styles on artists.

An exception here proves the rule: In 1979, when the Police made their first and, in terms of dynamic variation, perhaps their best album, *Outlandos d'Amour*, they recorded each song as an ensemble, overdubbing only vocals and a few lead parts. In an attempt to retain control of their sound and hold down costs the group recorded the songs in a sixteen-track studio. (The standard number of tracks is now twenty-four; Yoko Ono has actually recorded on ninety-six tracks.) In effect, the Police made a multitrack record by a monophonic method. (By contrast, consider the fate of the Humans, an idiosyncratic Santa Cruz band whose first — twenty-four-track — album, *Happy Hour*, has a flat, compressed sound quite unlike the group's roaring surf-meets-psychedelia live sound, but quite like their producer's last hit. Not surprisingly, it bombed, taking the Humans down with it.)

Multitrack technology long ago altered the terms of live performance as well as audience expectations. In the sixties, rock bands typically amplified each instrument individually; this was true whether you were talking about the neighborhood garage band or the Jimi Hendrix Experience. The result was a charged, erratic, stormy sound. But when multitracking took hold, the rock public began to demand that live concerts sound as "clean" as studio recordings, and so stage amplification moved in the direction of complex live-mixing systems that could faithfully reproduce studio sound. These mixing systems sent the cost of concert production through the roof. And, in doing so, they drove a wedge between the thousands of local groups that constitute the amateur base of the rock movement and its better-heeled professional practitioners, who are the only ones who can afford the new equipment. 24

The punk movement of the mid-seventies angrily attempted to restore sonic amateurism to rock. When you listen to the Sex Pistols' *Never Mind the Bollocks*, it is like having hot metal poured over your head. But punk didn't sell — not much, anyway — and the New Wave music that followed (and drew on punk) confirmed the takeover of the technicians. New Wave, above all, was a clean-sounding music. 25

And as went music, so went the clubs where it was played. Rock club owners began to realize that their expensive sound systems could be amortized — without the hassles and expense of hiring musicians — simply by using them to play records for people who didn't care how the sound was made, so long as they could dance to the beat. The result was that the club scene sharply declined. Today, no major city boasts more than a few live-rock clubs of any distinction. And almost all rockers now mix records for dance clubs, which have become a crucial promotional route. The most pronounced sound on these "disco mixes" is the monotonous domination of bass and drums. 26

The decline of the club scene has wiped out the major training ground for rock musicians, and destroyed whatever claims rock had to the status of modern-day folk music. Folk music is, above all, local music, made by musicians playing their own arrangements of a broad standard repertoire as well as their own compositions. That is precisely how the Beatles, the Rolling Stones, or Bruce Springsteen, for that matter, got their start. These artists began by copying songs from records, then changed the arrangements to suit their own ideas and talents. A good example is the way the Band rearranged "Mystery Train," substituting Rick Danko's stuttering bass for the guitar that drives Elvis's classic. By the time these musicians started writing their own material, they had already developed large repertoires and coherent, instantly recognizable ensemble styles. And they had been able to refine their styles over time before live audiences.

In the mid-1980s, such an apprenticeship is no longer possible for new bands. With club space reduced to a few showcases in major cities, most bands don't have the opportunity to play four sets a night in the same club for a week. They have to play forty-five minutes' worth of music — enough to prove to any record company executives in the audience that they can make an album. When Spandau Ballet, one of the aurally anonymous "New Romantic" English bands of the early 1980s, was awarded its first recording contract, the members of the group had been playing together for six months, and knew one set of material. (Not coincidentally, instead of touring, the group promoted the album with disco singles.)

It should not surprise us, then, that we have "rock bands" today that are made up of as many machines — synthesizers and drum boxes — as young men and women, or that the audience for rock *watches* their favorites on TV.

Many recent rock movements, like the New Romantics, have been based not on a distinct musical style or, better yet, the ability to create new styles — the Beatles were masters at this — but on a *look*, in the fashion sense of the term. There is even a term for this, "visual bands." No one would deny, of course, that the visual aspect has always been crucial to a pop star's success; that was true for the young Frank Sinatra as well as for the Beatles. But these artists' visual presence served mainly to dramatize their music, rather than to distract from its hollowness.

Close your eyes the next time you watch an MTV video,   31 and you'll realize that the band could be anyone, which is to say *no one*. What rock video has confirmed is that rock music no longer requires ,an emotional — let alone physical — engagement on the part of its audience. It is merely something one watches, passively, without noticing its constituent elements. It is no longer worth *listening* to.

QUESTIONS ON MEANING

1. In your own words, state Hunter's THESIS. Do you agree or disagree with it?
2. According to the author, what was the chief advantage of the recording techniques used in the monophonic era? What were the disadvantages? How did the sound engineers cope with them?
3. What does Hunter see as the positive contributions multitracking has brought to rock music? What faults does he find with multitracking?
4. In what ways, according to Hunter, has the high cost of multitracking influenced present-day rock music?
5. What connection does the author perceive between multitracking technology and live performers?
6. What is Hunter's opinion of MTV?

QUESTIONS ON WRITING STRATEGY

1. Roughly what proportion of this essay is devoted to giving EVIDENCE in support of Hunter's view? Which of his supporting material do you find most convincing?
2. How much do you need to know about music to make sense of Hunter's essay?
3. Which members of Hunter's AUDIENCE might be expected to disagree with him? Which ones would most likely agree with the author's views?

4. What is the chief function of paragraphs 5–14?
5. Where in his essay has Hunter made expert use of TRANSITIONS? In each case, what makes the transition successful?

QUESTIONS ON LANGUAGE

1. With the aid of your dictionary, if necessary, define the following words: incalculable (paragraph 2); imperatives (3); repertoire (5); argot (6); epochal (7); ameliorated (10); manifold (12); unprecedented (13); conversely (15); crescendo, dynamic (17); reverberation, domain, equilibrium (18); percussive, impoverished (19); inherent (20); idiosyncratic, compressed (23); amortized (26); aurally (28); constituent (31).
2. What is a *backbeat* (paragraph 3)? If you don't know, can you figure it out from its context?
3. To what extent does Hunter rely on musical JARGON to get his ideas across?
4. In paragraphs 14, 20, and 25, the author uses vivid FIGURES OF SPEECH. What do they contribute to the essay's impact?

SUGGESTIONS FOR WRITING

1. Write a defense of present-day rock music against Mark Hunter's attack. Perhaps you might argue that spontaneity is not dead, or cite evidence to show that multitrack recording and other studio techniques sometimes help — not hurt — rock music. From your knowledge of current singers, musicians, and groups, give examples to support your claim.
2. Following Mark Hunter's lead, write a statement of your own opinion about a popular art form (other than rock music). Be sure to include enough evidence to persuade your readers that your views are worth paying attention to.

Mark Hunter on Writing

Asked how he went about writing his incisive essay on rock, Mark Hunter supplied this comment for *The Bedford Reader.* " 'The Beat Goes Off' began with the misadventure recounted in the first paragraph," he recalled. "I couldn't give my records away. But behind that incident were twenty-odd years as a rock musician, recording artist, and critic for numerous publications.

"Rock criticism, in general, is a poor genre — part celebrity journalism, part puff, and virtually no solid musical analysis. The latter failing became apparent to me after I moved to Paris in 1982 and began studying movements in contemporary composition. I saw that sound is sound, whoever makes it; and that the making is the hearing. I wanted to apply that insight to rock music, and after cutting a record in a multitrack studio with my own band, I found that the direction began to fall into place.

"Suddenly the diverse phenomena I had noticed as a critic and lover of rock music — the decline of clubs, the hundreds of bands working on 'demo tapes' instead of their stage acts, the falling quality of the music on the records — seemed part of the same underlying phenomenon. . . . It was as though I had noticed a rock falling into a pond; when the splash died away, I followed the ripples as they spread from the studio, through the industry, and into the club scene. I went back through my files — hundreds of interviews with artists ranging from Mick Jagger to Taj Mahal — and put in a call to engineers and artists whose work I knew about. When I had my facts nailed down, I started writing.

"The *final* version of this article is, in fact, an edited version of a longer draft, which *Harper's* asked for after seeing a first, shorter version. Like most published work in popular magazines, it represents a compromise of time (deadlines) and space. A longer version of this article will figure in a book that I have tentatively entitled *Harmonies of Noise,* which will relate changes in popular music to movements in jazz and contemporary composition — another long-overdue task. This is one world, and in the end, all musics add up to one Music."

FOR DISCUSSION

1. For what purpose did Hunter apparently write his essay? What central insight did he want to put into words?
2. What research went into Hunter's preparation for writing? What life experience?
3. What do you understand from the author's closing statement?

· William F. Buckley, Jr. ·

WILLIAM FRANK BUCKLEY, JR., was born in 1925, the son of a millionaire. Soon after his graduation from Yale, he wrote *God and Man at Yale* (1951), a memoir with a bias in favor of conservative political values and traditional Christian principles. With the publication of *McCarthy and His Enemies* (1954), a defense of the late Senator Joseph McCarthy and his crusade against Communists, Buckley and his coauthor L. Brent Bozell infuriated liberals. He has continued to outrage them ever since, in many other books (including *Up from Liberalism*, 1959), in a syndicated newspaper column, and in the conservatively oriented magazine he founded and still edits, *The National Review*. A man of a certain wry charm, Buckley has been a successful television talk-show host on the program "Firing Line." In 1965 he ran for mayor of New York as a candidate of the Conservative Party. Lately he has written *Atlantic High*, a celebration of sailing (1983), *Airborne: A Sentimental Journey* (1984), *Right Reason* (1985), and *High Jinx* (1987) and *Mongoose R.I.P.* (1988), the latest in a series of novels about the exploits of Blackford Oakes, an urbane spy for the CIA.

Why Don't We Complain?

Most people, riding in an overheated commuter train, would perspire quietly. For Buckley, this excess of warmth sparks an indignant essay in which he takes to task both himself and his fellow Americans. Does the essay appeal mainly to reason or to emotion? And what would happen if everyone were to do as Buckley urges?

It was the very last coach and the only empty seat on the entire train, so there was no turning back. The problem was to breathe. Outside, the temperature was below freezing. Inside the railroad car the temperature must have been about 85 degrees. I took off my overcoat, and a few minutes later my jacket, and noticed that the car was flecked with the white shirts of the passengers. I soon found my hand moving to loosen my tie. From one end of the car to the other, as we rattled through Westchester County, we sweated; but we did not moan.

I watched the train conductor appear at the head of the car. "Tickets, all tickets, please!" In a more virile age, I thought, the passengers would seize the conductor and strap him down on a seat over the radiator to share the fate of his patrons. He shuffled down the aisle, picking up tickets, punching commutation cards. *No one addressed a word to him.* He approached my seat, and I drew a deep breath of resolution. "Conductor," I began with a considerable edge to my voice. . . . Instantly the doleful eyes of my seatmate turned tiredly from his newspaper to fix me with a resentful stare: What question could be so important as to justify my sibilant intrusion into his stupor? I was shaken by those eyes. I am incapable of making a discreet fuss, so I mumbled a question about what time we were due in Stamford (I didn't even ask whether it would be before or after dehydration could be expected to set in), got my reply, and went back to my newspaper and to wiping my brow.

The conductor had nonchalantly walked down the gauntlet of eighty sweating American freemen, and not one of them had asked him to explain why the passengers in that car had been consigned to suffer. There is nothing to be done when the temperature *outdoors* is 85 degrees, and indoors the air conditioner has broken down; obviously when that happens there is nothing to do, except perhaps curse the day that one was born. But when the temperature outdoors is below freezing, it takes a positive act of will on somebody's part to set the temperature *indoors* at 85. Somewhere a valve was turned too far, a furnace overstocked, a thermostat maladjusted: something that could easily be remedied by turning off the heat and allowing the great outdoors to come indoors. All this is so obvious. What is not obvious is what has happened to the American people.

It isn't just the commuters, whom we have come to visualize as a supine breed who have got on to the trick of suspending their sensory faculties twice a day while they submit to the creeping dissolution of the railroad industry. It isn't just they who have given up trying to rectify irrational vexations. It is the American people everywhere.

A few weeks ago at a large movie theatre I turned to my wife 5
and said, "The picture is out of focus." "Be quiet," she answered. I obeyed. But a few minutes later I raised the point again, with mounting impatience. "It will be all right in a minute," she said apprehensively. (She would rather lose her eyesight than be around when I make one of my infrequent scenes.) I waited. It was *just* out of focus — not glaringly out, but out. My vision is 20-20, and I assume that is the vision, adjusted, of most people in the movie house. So, after hectoring my wife throughout the first reel, I finally prevailed upon her to admit that it *was* off, and very annoying. We then settled down, coming to rest on the presumption that: a) someone connected with the management of the theatre must soon notice the blur and make the correction; or b) that someone seated near the rear of the house would make the complaint in behalf of those of us up front; or c) that — any minute now — the entire house would explode into cat-calls and foot stamping, calling dramatic attention to the irksome distortion.

What happened was nothing. The movie ended, as it had 6
begun *just* out of focus, and as we trooped out, we stretched our faces in a variety of contortions to accustom the eye to the shock of normal focus.

I think it is safe to say that everybody suffered on that occa- 7
sion. And I think it is safe to assume that everyone was expecting someone else to take the initiative in going back to speak to the manager. And it is probably true even that if we had supposed the movie would run right through the blurred image, someone surely would have summoned up the purposive indignation to get up out of his seat and file his complaint.

But notice that no one did. And the reason no one did is be- 8
cause we are all increasingly anxious in America to be unobtrusive, we are reluctant to make our voices heard, hesitant about claiming our rights; we are afraid that our cause is unjust, or that if it is not unjust, that it is ambiguous; or if not even that, that it is too trivial to justify the horrors of a confrontation with

Authority; we will sit in an oven or endure a racking headache before undertaking a head-on, I'm-here-to-tell-you complaint. That tendency to passive compliance, to a heedless endurance, is something to keep one's eyes on — in sharp focus.

I myself can occasionally summon the courage to complain, but I cannot, as I have intimated, complain softly. My own instinct is so strong to let the thing ride, to forget about it — to expect that someone will take the matter up, when the grievance is collective, in my behalf — that it is only when the provocation is at a very special key, whose vibrations touch simultaneously a complexus of nerves, allergies, and passions, that I catch fire and find the reserves of courage and assertiveness to speak up. When that happens, I get quite carried away. My blood gets hot, my brow wet, I become unbearably and unconscionably sarcastic and bellicose; I am girded for a total showdown.

Why should that be? Why could not I (or anyone else) on that railroad coach have said simply to the conductor, "Sir" — I take that back: that sounds sarcastic — "Conductor, would you be good enough to turn down the heat? I am extremely hot. In fact, I tend to get hot every time the temperature reaches 85 degr — " Strike that last sentence. Just end it with the simple statement that you are extremely hot, and let the conductor infer the cause.

Every New Year's Eve I resolve to do something about the Milquetoast in me and vow to speak up, calmly, for my rights, and for the betterment of our society, on every appropriate occasion. Entering last New Year's Eve I was fortified in my resolve because that morning at breakfast I had had to ask the waitress three times for a glass of milk. She finally brought it — after I had finished my eggs, which is when I don't want it any more. I did not have the manliness to order her to take the milk back, but settled instead for a cowardly sulk, and ostentatiously refused to drink the milk — though I later paid for it — rather than state plainly to the hostess, as I should have, why I had not drunk it, and would not pay for it.

So by the time the New Year ushered out the Old, riding in on my morning's indignation and stimulated by the gastric juices of resolution that flow so faithfully on New Year's Eve, I rendered my vow. Henceforward I would conquer my shyness, my despicable disposition to supineness. I would speak out like a man against the unnecessary annoyances of our time.

Forty-eight hours later, I was standing in line at the ski re-   13
pair store in Pico Peak, Vermont. All I needed, to get on with my skiing, was the loan, for one minute, of a small screwdriver, to tighten a loose binding. Behind the counter in the workshop were two men. One was industriously engaged in servicing the complicated requirements of a young lady at the head of the line, and obviously he would be tied up for quite a while. The other — "Jiggs," his workmate called him — was a middle-aged man, who sat in a chair puffing a pipe, exchanging small talk with his working partner. My pulse began its telltale acceleration. The minutes ticked on. I stared at the idle shopkeeper, hoping to shame him into action, but he was impervious to my telepathic reproof and continued his small talk with his friend, brazenly insensitive to the nervous demands of six good men who were raring to ski.

Suddenly my New Year's Eve resolution struck me. It was   14
now or never. I broke from my place in line and marched to the counter. I was going to control myself. I dug my nails into my palms. My effort was only partially successful.

"If you are not too busy," I said icily, "would you mind   15
handing me a screwdriver?"

Work stopped and everyone turned his eyes on me, and I ex-   16
perienced that mortification I always feel when I am the center of centripetal shafts of curiosity, resentment, perplexity.

But the worst was yet to come. "I am sorry, sir," said Jiggs   17
deferentially, moving the pipe from his mouth. "I am not supposed to move. I have just had a heart attack." That was the signal for a great whirring noise that descended from heaven. We looked, stricken, out the window, and it appeared as though a cyclone had suddenly focused on the snowy courtyard between the shop and the ski lift. Suddenly a gigantic army helicopter materialized, and hovered down to a landing. Two men jumped out of the plane carrying a stretcher, tore into the ski shop, and lifted the shopkeeper onto the stretcher. Jiggs bade his companion goodby, was whisked out the door, into the plane, up to the

heavens, down — we learned — to a near-by army hospital. I looked up manfully — into a score of man-eating eyes. I put the experience down as a reversal.

As I write this, on an airplane, I have run out of paper and [18] need to reach into my briefcase under my legs for more. I cannot do this until my empty lunch tray is removed from my lap. I arrested the stewardess as she passed empty-handed down the aisle on the way to the kitchen to fetch the lunch trays for the passengers up forward who haven't been served yet. "Would you please take my tray?" "Just a *moment*, sir!" she said, and marched on sternly. Shall I tell her that since she is headed for the kitchen *anyway*, it could not delay the feeding of the other passengers by more than two seconds necessary to stash away my empty tray? Or remind her that not fifteen minutes ago she spoke unctuously into the loudspeaker the words undoubtedly devised by the airline's highly paid public relations counselor: "If there is anything I or Miss French can do for you to make your trip more enjoyable, *please* let us — " I have run out of paper.

I think the observable reluctance of the majority of Ameri- [19] cans to assert themselves in minor matters is related to our increased sense of helplessness in an age of technology and centralized political and economic power. For generations, Americans who were too hot, or too cold, got up and did something about it. Now we call the plumber, or the electrician, or the furnace man. The habit of looking after our own needs obviously had something to do with the assertiveness that characterized the American family familiar to readers of American literature. With the technification of life goes our direct responsibility for our material environment, and we are conditioned to adopt a position of helplessness not only as regards the broken air conditioner, but as regards the overheated train. It takes an expert to fix the former, but not the latter; yet these distinctions, as we withdraw into helplessness, tend to fade away.

Our notorious political apathy is a related phenomenon. [20] Every year, whether the Republican or the Democratic Party is in office, more and more power drains away from the individual to feed vast reservoirs in far-off places; and we have less and less say about the shape of events which shape our future. From this alienation of personal power comes the sense of resignation with which we accept the political dispensations of a powerful government whose hold upon us continues to increase.

An editor of a national weekly news magazine told me a few years ago that as few as a dozen letters of protest against an editorial stance of his magazine was enough to convene a plenipotentiary meeting of the board of editors to review policy. "So few people complain, or make their voices heard," he explained to me, "that we assume a dozen letters represent the inarticulated views of thousands of readers." In the past ten years, he said, the volume of mail has noticeably decreased, even though the circulation of his magazine has risen. 21

When our voices are finally mute, when we have finally suppressed the natural instinct to complain, whether the vexation is trivial or grave, we shall have become automatons, incapable of feeling. When Premier Khrushchev first came to this country late in 1959 he was primed, we are informed, to experience the bitter resentment of the American people against his tyranny, against his persecutions, against the movement which is responsible for the great number of American deaths in Korea, for billions in taxes every year, and for life everlasting on the brink of disaster; but Khrushchev was pleasantly surprised, and reported back to the Russian people that he had been met with overwhelming cordiality (read: apathy), except, to be sure, for "a few fascists who followed me around with their wretched posters, and should be horsewhipped." 22

I may be crazy, but I say there would have been lots more posters in a society where train temperatures in the dead of winter are not allowed to climb to 85 degrees without complaint. 23

QUESTIONS ON MEANING

1. How does Buckley account for his failure to complain to the train conductor? What reasons does he give for not taking action when he notices that the movie he is watching is out of focus?

2. Where does Buckley finally place the blame for the average American's reluctance to try to "rectify irrational vexations"?
3. By what means does the author bring his argument around to the subject of political apathy?
4. What THESIS does Buckley attempt to support? How would you state it?

QUESTIONS ON WRITING STRATEGY

1. Buckley includes five stories in his essay, four of them taken from personal experience. Which support his thesis?
2. In taking to task not only his fellow Americans but also himself, does Buckley strengthen or weaken his charge that, as a people, Americans do not complain enough?
3. Judging from the vocabulary displayed in this essay, would you say that Buckley is writing for a highly specialized AUDIENCE, an educated but nonspecialized audience, or an uneducated general audience, such as most newspaper readers?
4. As a whole, is Buckley's essay an example of appeal to emotion or of reasoned argument? Give EVIDENCE for your answer.

QUESTIONS ON LANGUAGE

1. Define the following words: virile, doleful, sibilant (paragraph 2); supine (4); hectoring (5); unobtrusive, ambiguous (8); intimated, unconscionably, bellicose (9); ostentatiously (11); despicable (12); impervious (13); mortification, centripetal (16); deferentially (17); unctuously (18); notorious, dispensations (20); plenipotentiary, inarticulated (21); automatons (22).
2. What does Buckley's use of the capital A in *Authority* (paragraph 8) contribute to the sentence in which he uses it?
3. What is Buckley talking about when he alludes to "the Milquetoast in me" (paragraph 11)? (Notice how well the ALLUSION fits into the paragraph, with its emphasis on breakfast and a glass of milk.)

SUGGESTIONS FOR WRITING

1. Write about an occasion when you should have registered a complaint and did not; or, recount what happened when you did in fact protest against one of "the unnecessary annoyances of our time."

2. Write a paper in which you take issue with any one of Buckley's ideas. Argue that he is wrong and you are right.
3. Think of some disturbing incident you have witnessed, or some annoying treatment you have received in a store or other public place, and write a letter of complaint to whomever you believe responsible. Be specific in your evidence, be temperate in your language, and be sure to put your letter in the mail.

William F. Buckley, Jr., on Writing

Speaking of his friend, a fellow columnist, Buckley has recalled, "George Will once told me how deeply he loves to write. 'I wake in the morning,' he explained to me, 'and I ask myself: Is this one of the days I have to write a column? And if the answer is yes, I rise a happy man.' I, on the other hand, wake neither particularly happy nor unhappy, but to the extent that my mood is affected by the question whether I need to write a column that morning, the impact of Monday-Wednesday-Friday" — the days when he must write a newspaper column — "is definitely negative. Because I do not like to write, for the simple reason that writing is extremely hard work, and I do not 'like' extremely hard work."

Still, in the course of a "typical year," Buckley estimates that he produces not only 150 newspaper columns, but also a dozen longer articles, eight or ten speeches, fifty introductions for his television program, various editorial pieces for the magazine he edits, *The National Review*, and a book or two. "Why do I do so much? . . . It is easier to stay up late working for hours than to take one tenth the time to inquire into the question whether the work is worth performing." (From *Overdrive: A Personal Documentary* [Garden City: Doubleday, 1983], pp. 76–78.)

Recently, Buckley made news by composing an entire children's book in about three hours. "I have discovered, in sixteen years of writing columns," he once declared, "that there is no observable difference in the quality of that which is written at very great speed (twenty minutes, say), and that which takes three or four times as long. . . . Pieces that take longer to write sometimes, on revisiting them, move along grumpily." (Introduction to *A Hymnal: The Controversial Arts* [New York: Putnam, 1975], p. 16.) This belief, you'll find, is radically different from that of most writers.

FOR DISCUSSION

1. What attitude toward writing does Buckley share with Marie Winn, the author of "The End of Play"? (See p. 388 in Chapter 8.) On what point do the two writers disagree?

· Garrison Keillor ·

GARRISON KEILLOR, writer and broadcaster, was born in 1942 in Anoka, Minnesota, and is a University of Minnesota graduate. A successful writer of humorous pieces for *The New Yorker* and other magazines, Keillor won a large and devoted radio audience with his Saturday evening program, *Prairie Home Companion*, featuring his own monologues, recitations of verse, tongue-in-cheek news notes, and commercials for businesses in the semifictional Midwestern small town of Lake Wobegon. The program thrived on PBS radio from 1974 until 1987, when Keillor stopped the series to live in Denmark and devote himself to writing. His books are *Happy To Be Here* (1982), *Lake Wobegon Days* (1985), and *Leaving Home: A Collection of Lake Wobegon Stories* (1987).

Shy Rights: Why Not Pretty Soon?

This essay was published in Keillor's first book, *Happy To Be Here*, a collection of humorous and satiric essays. Setting forth a modest — even shy — proposal for a mild-mannered revolution, Keillor touches on some truths that may stick with you.

Recently I read about a group of fat people who had organized to fight discrimination against themselves. They said that society oppresses the overweight by being thinner than them and that the term "overweight" itself is oppressive because it implies a "right" weight that the fatso has failed to make. Only weightists use such terms, they said; they demanded to be called "total" people and to be thought of in terms of wholeness; and they referred to thin people as being "not all there."

Don't get me wrong. This is fine with me. If, to quote the article if I may, "Fat Leaders Demand Expanded Rights Act, Claim Broad Base of Support," I have no objections to it whatsoever. I feel that it is their right to speak up and I admire them for doing so, though of course this is only my own opinion. I could be wrong.

Nevertheless, after reading the article, I wrote a letter to President Jimmy Carter demanding that his administration take action to end discrimination against shy persons sometime in the very near future. I pointed out three target areas — laws, schools, and attitudes — where shy rights maybe could be safeguarded. I tried not to be pushy but I laid it on the line. "Mr. President," I concluded, "you'll probably kill me for saying this but compared to what you've done for other groups, we shys have settled for 'peanuts.' As you may know, we are not ones to make threats, but it is clear that if we don't get some action on this, it could be a darned quiet summer. It is up to you, Mr. President. Whatever you decide will be okay by me. Yours very cordially."

I never got around to mailing the letter, but evidently word got around in the shy community that I had written it, and I've noticed that most shy persons are not speaking to me these days. I guess they think the letter went too far. Probably they feel that making demands is a betrayal of the shy movement (or "gesture," as many shys call it) and an insult to shy pride and that it risks the loss of some of the gains we have already made, such as social security and library cards.

Perhaps they are right. I don't claim to have all the answers. I just feel that we ought to begin, at least, to think about some demands that we *might* make if, for example, we *had* to someday. That's all. I'm not saying we should make fools of ourselves, for heaven's sake!

Shut Up (A Slogan)

Sometimes I feel that maybe shy persons have borne our terrible burden for far too long now. Labeled by society as "wimps," "dorks," "creeps," and "sissies," stereotyped as Milquetoasts and Walter Mittys, and tagged as potential psychopaths ("He kept pretty much to himself," every psychopath's landlady is quoted as saying after the arrest, and for weeks thereafter every shy person is treated like a leper), we shys are desperately misunderstood on every hand. Because we don't "talk out" our feelings, it is assumed that we haven't any. It is assumed that we never exclaim, retort, or cry out, though naturally we do on occasions when it seems called for.

Would anyone dare to say to a woman or a Third World   7
person, "Oh, don't be a woman! Oh, don't be so Third!"? And yet people make bold with us whenever they please and put an arm around us and tell us not to be shy.

Hundreds of thousands of our shy brothers and sisters (and   8
"cousins twice-removed," as militant shys refer to each other) are victimized every year by self-help programs that promise to "cure" shyness through hand-buzzer treatments, shout training, spicy diets, silence-aversion therapy, and every other gimmick in the book. Many of them claim to have "overcome" their shyness, but the sad fact is that they are afraid to say otherwise.

To us in the shy movement, however, shyness is not a dis-   9
ability or disease to be "overcome." It is simply the way we are. And in our own quiet way, we are secretly proud of it. It isn't something we shout about at public rallies and marches. It is Shy Pride. And while we don't have a Shy Pride Week, we do have many private moments when we keep our thoughts to ourselves, such as "Shy is nice," "Walk short," "Be proud — shut up," and "Shy is beautiful, for the most part." These are some that I thought up myself. Perhaps other shy persons have some of their own, I don't know.

A "Number One" Disgrace

Discrimination against the shy is our country's number one   10
disgrace in my own personal opinion. Millions of men and women are denied equal employment, educational and recreational opportunities, and rewarding personal relationships simply because of their shyness. These injustices are nearly impossible to identify, not only because the shy person will not speak up when discriminated against, but also because the shy person almost always *anticipates* being denied these rights and doesn't

ask for them in the first place. (In fact, most shys will politely decline a right when it is offered to them.)

Most shy lawyers agree that shys can never obtain justice   11
under our current adversary system of law. The Sixth Amendment, for example, which gives the accused the right to confront his accusers, is antishy on the face of it. It effectively denies shy persons the right to accuse anyone of anything.

One solution might be to shift the burden of proof to the de-   12
fendant in case the plaintiff chooses to remain silent. Or we could create a special second-class citizenship that would take away some rights, such as free speech, bearing arms, and running for public office, in exchange for some other rights that we need more. In any case, we need some sort of fairly totally new concept of law if we shys are ever going to enjoy equality, if indeed that is the sort of thing we could ever enjoy.

A Million-Dollar Ripoff

Every year, shy persons lose millions of dollars in the form   13
of overcharges that aren't questioned, shoddy products never returned to stores, refunds never asked for, and bad food in restaurants that we eat anyway, not to mention all the money we lose and are too shy to claim when somebody else finds it.

A few months ago, a shy friend of mine whom I will call   14
Duke Hand (not his real name) stood at a supermarket checkout counter and watched the cashier ring up thirty fifteen-cent Peanut Dream candy bars and a $3.75 copy of *Playhouse* for $18.25. He gave her a twenty-dollar bill and thanked her for his change, but as he reached for his purchases, she said, "Hold on. There's something wrong here."

"No, really, it's OK," he said.   15

"Let me see that cash register slip," she said.   16

"No, really, thanks anyway," he whispered. Out of the cor-   17
ner of his eye, he could see that he had attracted attention. Other shoppers in the vicinity had sensed that something was up, perhaps an attempted price-tag switch or insufficient identification, and were looking his way. "It's not for me," he pleaded. "I'm only buying this for a friend."

Nevertheless, he had to stand there in mute agony while she   18
counted all the Peanut Dreams and refigured the total and the
correct change. (In fairness to her, it should be pointed out that
Duke, while eventually passing on each copy of *Playhouse* to a
friend, first reads it himself.)

Perhaps one solution might be for clerks and other business   19
personnel to try to be a little bit more careful about this sort of
thing in the first place. OK?

How About Shy History?

To many of us shys, myself included, the worst tragedy is   20
the oppression of shy children in the schools, and while we
don't presume to tell educators how to do their work, work that
they have been specially trained to do, we do feel that schools
must begin immediately to develop programs of shy history, or
at the very least to give it a little consideration.

History books are blatantly prejudiced against shyness and   21
shy personhood. They devote chapter after chapter to the ac-
complishments of famous persons and quote them at great
length, and say nothing at all, or very little, about countless others who had very little to say, who never sought fame, and
whose names are lost to history.

Where in the history books do we find mention of The Lady   22
in Black, Kilroy, The Unknown Soldier, The Forgotten Man,
The Little Guy, not to mention America's many noted recluses?

Where, for example, can we find a single paragraph on   23
America's hundreds of scale models, those brave men of average
height whose job it is to pose beside immense objects such as
pyramids and dynamos so as to indicate scale in drawings and
photographs? The only credit scale models ever received was a
line in the caption — "For an idea of its size, note man (arrow,
at left)." And yet, without them, such inventions as the dirigi-
ble, the steam shovel, and the swing-span bridge would have
looked like mere toys, and natural wonders such as Old Faithful, the Grand Canyon, and the giant sequoia would have been
dismissed as hoaxes. It was truly a thankless job.

Shys on "Strike"

The scale models themselves never wanted any thanks. All they wanted was a rope or device of some type to keep them from falling off tall structures, plus a tent to rest in between drawings, and in 1906, after one model was carried away by a tidal wave that he had been hired to pose in front of, they formed a union and went on strike.

Briefly, the scale models were joined by a contingent of shy artists' models who had posed for what they thought was to be a small monument showing the Battle of Bull Run only to discover that it was actually a large bas-relief entitled "The Bathers" and who sat down on the job, bringing the work to a halt. While the artists' models quickly won a new contract and went back to work (on a nonrepresentational basis), the scale models' strike was never settled.

True to their nature, the scale models did not picket the work sites or negotiate with their employers. They simply stood quietly a short distance away and, when asked about their demands, pointed to the next man. A year later, when the union attempted to take a vote on the old contract, it found that most of the scale models had moved away and left no forwarding addresses.

It was the last attempt by shy persons to organize themselves anywhere in the country.

Now Is the Time, We Think

Now is probably as good a time as any for this country to face up to its shameful treatment of the shy and to do something, almost anything, about it. On the other hand, maybe it would be better to wait for a while and see what happens. All I know is that it isn't easy trying to write a manifesto for a bunch of people who dare not speak their names. And that the shy movement is being inverted by a tiny handful of shy militants who do not speak for the majority of shy persons, nor even very often for themselves. This secret cadre, whose members are not known even to each other, advocate doing "less than nothing." They believe in tokenism, and the smaller the token the better. They seek only to promote more self-consciousness: that ultimate shyness that shy mystics call "the fear of fear itself." What is even more terrifying is the ultimate goal of this radical wing: They believe that they shall inherit the earth, and they will not stop until they do. Believe me, we moderates have our faces to the wall.

Perhaps you are saying, "What can *I* do? I share your concern at the plight of the shy and wholeheartedly endorse your two- (or three-) point program for shy equality. I pledge myself to work vigorously for its adoption. My check for ($10 $25 $50 $100 $——) is enclosed. In addition, I agree to (circulate petitions, hold fundraising party in my home, write to congressman and senator, serve on local committee, write letters to newspapers, hand out literature door-to-door during National Friends of the Shy Drive)."   29

Just remember: You said it, not me.   30

QUESTIONS ON MEANING

1. What PARADOX is inherent in the idea of shy people's demanding their rights?
2. At what or at whom is Keillor's humor directed? Is he making fun of fat people? Blacks, women, or other minorities? Citizens of the Third World? Shy people?
3. Does Keillor make any serious points in his essay? Is so, what are they?
4. What objections might be raised to the suggestions Keillor makes in paragraphs 11 and 12 concerning the Bill of Rights?
5. In sum, exactly what does the author propose in this essay?

QUESTIONS ON WRITING STRATEGY

1. Where does Keillor's INTRODUCTION end and the body of his essay begin?
2. What role do exaggeration and oversimplification play in Keillor's essay?

3. Where in his essay does the author make effective use of UNDER-STATEMENT?

4. How does the TONE of Keillor's plea for shy rights differ from the one we have come to expect from groups who make demands? By what means does the author achieve his tone? What does it contribute to the essay's impact?

5. What strategies does Keillor appropriate from journalists who set out to expose society's evils? (See particularly the section called "A Million-Dollar Ripoff.")

QUESTIONS ON LANGUAGE

1. Explain the ALLUSION to "Milquetoasts and Walter Mittys" (paragraph 6).

2. From what other crusades for justice has Keillor borrowed words, phrases, and slogans, even CLICHÉS?

3. With the aid of your dictionary, if necessary, define the following words: psychopaths, leper (paragraph 6); adversary (11); blatantly (21); recluses (22); contingent (24); manifesto, cadre, tokenism (27).

4. What does Keillor mean by *silence-aversion therapy* (paragraph 8)?

SUGGESTIONS FOR WRITING

1. In the voice of one of Keillor's shy people, write a response to William F. Buckley's "Why Don't We Complain?" (p. 570).

2. Write a brief essay in which you propose, seriously or otherwise, your own solution for the problems of shy people. Or, if you prefer, take issue with Keillor's notion that shy people represent a minority in need of special understanding.

Garrison Keillor on Writing

For a long time, Garrison Keillor told an interviewer, he felt torn between radio and his other writing — "radio being kind of like a warm bath and writing being like a cold shower." For radio, on his *Prairie Home Companion* shows, he developed the form of a monologue fifteen or twenty minutes in length. "For me, the monologue was the favorite thing I had done in radio. It was based on writing, but in the end it was radio. It was standing up and leaning forward into the dark and talking, letting words come out of you.

"A monologue just has to have some clear places in it, some clear images, some definite people, some definite action. And then, once you have that, even if it's very slack, then the monologue can begin anyplace. If you feel the urgency of a story, the style and the phrasing of it is really not that important.

"It's just the opposite from sitting down and writing a story. In the written story, every word has to be right. When I tell stories on the radio, people are focused on my voice, so there's the sound of the human voice to sort of carry them over the imperfections. But in writing on the page, you have to create that voice artificially." (Interview with Mervyn Rothstein, the *New York Times*, August 20, 1985, p. 20.)

FOR DISCUSSION

1. What difference does Keillor find between writing for his radio show and writing for publication? What makes the one more difficult than the other?

· Martin Luther King, Jr. ·

MARTIN LUTHER KING, JR., (1929–1968) was born in Atlanta, the son of a Baptist minister, and was himself ordained in the same denomination. Stepping to the forefront of the civil rights movement in 1955, King led blacks in a boycott of segregated city buses in Montgomery, Alabama; became first president of the Southern Christian Leadership Conference; and staged sit-ins and mass marches that helped bring about the Civil Rights Act passed by Congress in 1964 and the Voting Rights Act of 1965. He received the Nobel Peace Prize in 1964. In view of the fact that King preached "nonviolent resistance," it is particularly ironic that he was himself the target of violence. He was stabbed in New York, pelted with stones in Chicago; his home in Montgomery was bombed; and finally in Memphis he was assassinated by a hidden sniper. On his tombstone near Atlanta's Ebenezer Baptist Church are these words from the spiritual he quotes at the conclusion of "I Have a Dream": "Free at last, free at last, thank God almighty, I'm free at last." Martin Luther King's birthday, January 15, is now a national holiday.

I Have a Dream

In Washington, D.C., on August 28, 1963, King's campaign of nonviolent resistance reached its historic climax. On that date, commemorating the centennial of Lincoln's Emancipation Proclamation freeing the slaves, King led a march of 200,000 persons, black and white, from the Washington Monument to the Lincoln Memorial. Before this throng, and to millions who watched on television, he delivered this unforgettable speech.

Five score years ago, a great American, in whose symbolic   1
shadow we stand, signed the Emancipation Proclamation. This momentous decree came as a great beacon light of hope to millions of Negro slaves who had been seared in the flames of with-

ering injustice. It came as a joyous daybreak to end the long night of captivity.

But one hundred years later, we must face the tragic fact   2
that the Negro is still not free. One hundred years later, the life of the Negro is still sadly crippled by the manacles of segregation and the chains of discrimination. One hundred years later, the Negro lives on a lonely island of poverty in the midst of a vast ocean of material prosperity. One hundred years later, the Negro is still languishing in the corners of American society and finds himself an exile in his own land. So we have come here today to dramatize an appalling condition.

In a sense we have come to our nation's capital to cash a   3
check. When the architects of our republic wrote the magnificent words of the Constitution and the Declaration of Independence, they were signing a promissory note to which every American was to fall heir. This note was a promise that all men would be guaranteed the unalienable rights of life, liberty, and the pursuit of happiness.

It is obvious today that America has defaulted on this prom-   4
issory note insofar as her citizens of color are concerned. Instead of honoring this sacred obligation, America has given the Negro people a bad check; a check which has come back marked "insufficient funds." But we refuse to believe that the bank of justice is bankrupt. We refuse to believe that there are insufficient funds in the great vaults of opportunity of this nation. So we have come to cash this check — a check that will give us upon demand the riches of freedom and the security of justice. We have also come to this hallowed spot to remind America of the fierce urgency of *now*. This is no time to engage in the luxury of cooling off or to take the tranquilizing drugs of gradualism. *Now* is the time to make real the promises of Democracy. *Now* is the time to rise from the dark and desolate valley of segregation to the sunlit path of racial justice. *Now* is the time to open the doors of opportunity to all of God's children. *Now* is the time to lift our nation from the quicksands of racial injustice to the solid rock of brotherhood.

It would be fatal for the nation to overlook the urgency of   5
the moment and to underestimate the determination of the Ne-

gro. This sweltering summer of the Negro's legitimate discontent will not pass until there is an invigorating autumn of freedom and equality. 1963 is not an end, but a beginning. Those who hope that the Negro needed to blow off steam and will now be content will have a rude awakening if the nation returns to business as usual. There will be neither rest nor tranquillity in America until the Negro is granted his citizenship rights. The whirlwinds of revolt will continue to shake the foundations of our nation until the bright day of justice emerges.

But there is something that I must say to my people who stand on the warm threshold which leads into the palace of justice. In the process of gaining our rightful place we must not be guilty of wrongful deeds. Let us not seek to satisfy our thirst for freedom by drinking from the cup of bitterness and hatred. We must forever conduct our struggle on the high plane of dignity and discipline. We must not allow our creative protest to degenerate into physical violence. Again and again we must rise to the majestic heights of meeting physical force with soul force. The marvelous new militancy which has engulfed the Negro community must not lead us to a distrust of all white people, for many of our white brothers, as evidenced by their presence here today, have come to realize that their destiny is tied up with our destiny and their freedom is inextricably bound to our freedom. We cannot walk alone.

And as we walk, we must make the pledge that we shall march ahead. We cannot turn back. There are those who are asking the devotees of civil rights, "When will you be satisfied?" We can never be satisfied as long as the Negro is the victim of the unspeakable horrors of police brutality. We can never be satisfied as long as our bodies, heavy with the fatigue of travel, cannot gain lodging in the motels of the highways and the hotels of the cities. We cannot be satisfied as long as the Negro's basic mobility is from a smaller ghetto to a larger one. We can never be satisfied as long as a Negro in Mississippi cannot vote and a Negro in New York believes he has nothing for which to vote. No, no, we are not satisfied, and we will not be satisfied until justice rolls down like waters and righteousness like a mighty stream.

I am not unmindful that some of you have come here out of   8
great trials and tribulations. Some of you have come fresh from
narrow jail cells. Some of you have come from areas where your
quest for freedom left you battered by the storms of persecution
and staggered by the winds of police brutality. You have been
the veterans of creative suffering. Continue to work with the
faith that unearned suffering is redemptive.

Go back to Mississippi, go back to Alabama, go back to   9
South Carolina, go back to Georgia, go back to Louisiana, go
back to the slums and ghettos of our northern cities, knowing
that somehow this situation can and will be changed. Let us not
wallow in the valley of despair.

I say to you today, my friends, that in spite of the difficulties   10
and frustrations of the moment I still have a dream. It is a dream
deeply rooted in the American dream.

I have a dream that one day this nation will rise up and live   11
out the true meaning of its creed: "We hold these truths to be
self-evident; that all men are created equal."

I have a dream that one day on the red hills of Georgia the   12
sons of former slaves and the sons of former slaveowners will be
able to sit down together at the table of brotherhood.

I have a dream that one day even the state of Mississippi, a   13
desert state sweltering with the heat of injustice and oppression,
will be transformed into an oasis of freedom and justice.

I have a dream that my four little children will one day live   14
in a nation where they will not be judged by the color of their
skin but by the content of their character.

I have a dream today.   15

I have a dream that one day the state of Alabama, whose   16
governor's lips are presently dripping with the words of interposition and nullification, will be transformed into a situation
where little black boys and black girls will be able to join hands
with little white boys and white girls and walk together as sisters
and brothers.

I have a dream today.   17

I have a dream that one day every valley shall be exalted,   18
every hill and mountain shall be made low, the rough places will
be made plain, and the crooked places will be made straight, and

the glory of the Lord shall be revealed, and all flesh shall see it together.

This is our hope. This is the faith with which I return to the 19 South. With this faith we will be able to hew out of the mountain of despair a stone of hope. With this faith we will be able to transform the jangling discords of our nation into a beautiful symphony of brotherhood. With this faith we will be able to work together, to pray together, to struggle together, to go to jail together, to stand up for freedom together, knowing that we will be free one day.

This will be the day when all of God's children will be able 20 to sing with new meaning

> My country, 'tis of thee,
> Sweet land of liberty,
>   Of thee I sing:
> Land where my fathers died,
> Land of the pilgrims' pride,
> From every mountain-side
>   Let freedom ring.

And if America is to be a great nation this must become 21 true. So let freedom ring from the prodigious hilltops of New Hampshire. Let freedom ring from the mighty mountains of New York. Let freedom ring from the heightening Alleghenies of Pennsylvania!

Let freedom ring from the snowcapped Rockies of Colorado! 22

Let freedom ring from the curvaceous peaks of California! 23

But not only that; let freedom ring from Stone Mountain of 24 Georgia!

Let freedom ring from Lookout Mountain of Tennessee! 25

Let freedom ring from every hill and molehill of Mississippi. 26 From every mountainside, let freedom ring.

When we let freedom ring, when we let it ring from every 27 village and every hamlet, from every state and every city, we will be able to speed up that day when all of God's children, black men and white men, Jews and Gentiles, Protestants and Catholics, will be able to join hands and sing in the words of the old Negro spiritual, "Free at last! free at last! thank God almighty, we are free at last!"

QUESTIONS ON MEANING

1. What is the apparent PURPOSE of this speech?
2. What THESIS does King develop in his first four paragraphs?
3. What does King mean by the "marvelous new militancy which has engulfed the Negro community" (paragraph 6)? Does this contradict King's nonviolent philosophy?
4. In what passages of his speech does King notice events of history? Where does he acknowledge the historic occasion on which he is speaking?
5. To what extent does King's personal authority lend power to his words?

QUESTIONS ON WRITING STRATEGY

1. What examples of particular injustices does King offer in paragraph 7? In his speech as a whole, do his observations tend to be GENERAL or SPECIFIC?
2. Explain King's ANALOGY of the bad check (paragraphs 3 and 4). What similarity do you find between it and any of the parables in the Bible, such as those of the lost sheep, the lost silver, and the prodigal son (Luke 15: 1–32)?
3. What other analogy does King later develop?
4. What indicates that King's words were meant primarily for an AUDIENCE of listeners, and only secondarily for a reading audience? To hear these indications, try reading the speech aloud. What use of PARALLELISM do you notice?
5. Where in the speech does King acknowledge that not all of his listeners are black?
6. How much EMPHASIS does King place on the past? On the future?

QUESTIONS ON LANGUAGE

1. In general, is the language of King's speech ABSTRACT or CONCRETE? How is this level appropriate to the speaker's message and to the span of history with which he deals?
2. Point to memorable FIGURES OF SPEECH.
3. Define momentous (paragraph 1); manacles, languishing (2); promissory note (3); defaulted, hallowed, gradualism (4); inextricably (6); mobility, ghetto (7); tribulations, redemptive (8); interposition, nullification (16); prodigious (21); curvaceous (23); hamlet (27).

SUGGESTIONS FOR WRITING

1. Has America (or your locality) today moved closer in any respects to the fulfillment of King's dream? Discuss this question in an essay, giving specific examples.
2. Argue in favor of some course of action in a situation that you consider an injustice. Racial injustice is one possible area, or unfairness to any minority, or to women, children, the old, ex-convicts, the handicapped, the poor. If possible, narrow your subject to a particular incident or a local situation on which you can write knowledgeably.

· Jonathan Swift ·

JONATHAN SWIFT (1667–1745), the son of English parents who had settled in Ireland, divided his energies among literature, politics, and the Church of England. Dissatisfied with the quiet life of an Anglican parish priest, Swift spent much of his time in London hobnobbing with men of letters and writing pamphlets in support of the Tory Party. In 1713 Queen Anne rewarded his political services with an assignment the London-loving Swift didn't want: to supervise St. Patrick's Cathedral in Dublin. There, as Dean Swift, he ended his days — beloved by the Irish, whose interests he defended against the English government.

Although Swift's chief works include the remarkable satires *The Battle of the Books* and *A Tale of a Tub* (both 1704) and scores of fine poems, he is best remembered for *Gulliver's Travels* (1726), an account of four imaginary voyages. This classic is always abridged when it is given to children because of its frank descriptions of human filth and viciousness. In *Gulliver's Travels* Swift pays tribute to the reasoning portion of "that animal called man," and delivers a stinging rebuke to the rest of him.

A Modest Proposal

*For Preventing the Children of Poor People in Ireland
from Being a Burden to Their Parents or Country,
and for Making Them Beneficial to the Public*

Three consecutive years of drought and sparse crops had worked hardship upon the Irish when Swift wrote this ferocious essay in the summer of 1729. At the time, there were said to be 35,000 wandering beggars in the country: Whole families had quit their farms and had taken to the roads. Large landowners, of English ancestry, preferred to ignore their tenants' sufferings and lived abroad to dodge taxes and payment of church duties. Swift writes out of indignation and out of impatience with the many proposals to help the Irish offered in England without result.

Although printed as a pamphlet in Dublin, Swift's essay is clearly meant for English readers as well as Irish ones. When circulated, the pamphlet caused a sensation in both Ireland and England and had to be reprinted seven times in the same year. Swift is an expert with plain, vigorous English prose, and "A Modest Proposal" is a masterpiece of irony. (If you are uncertain what Swift argues for, see the discussion of *Irony* in Useful Terms.) The dean of St. Patrick's had no special fondness for the Irish, but he hated the inhumanity he witnessed.

It is a melancholy object to those who walk through this great town[1] or travel in the country, when they see the streets, the roads, and cabin doors, crowded with beggars of the female sex, followed by three, four, or six children, all in rags and importuning every passenger for an alms. These mothers, instead of being able to work for their honest livelihood, are forced to employ all their time in strolling to beg sustenance for their helpless infants, who, as they grow up, either turn thieves for want of work, or leave their dear native country to fight for the Pretender in Spain, or sell themselves to the Barbados.[2]

I think it is agreed by all parties that this prodigious number of children in the arms, or on the backs, or at the heels of their mothers, and frequently of their fathers, is in the present deplorable state of the kingdom a very great additional grievance; and therefore whoever could find out a fair, cheap, and easy method of making these children sound, useful members of the commonwealth would deserve so well of the public as to have his statue set up for a preserver of the nation.

But my intention is very far from being confined to provide only for the children of professed beggars; it is of a much greater

[1]Dublin. — Eds.

[2]The Pretender was James Stuart, exiled in Spain; in 1718 many Irishmen had joined an army seeking to restore him to the English throne. Others wishing to emigrate had signed papers as indentured servants, agreeing to work for a number of years in the Barbados or other British colonies in exchange for their ocean passage. — Eds.

extent, and shall take in the whole number of infants at a certain age who are born of parents in effect as little able to support them as those who demand our charity in the streets.

As to my own part, having turned my thoughts for many   4
years upon this important subject, and maturely weighed the several schemes of other projectors,[3] I have always found them grossly mistaken in their computation. It is true, a child just dropped from its dam may be supported by her milk for a solar year, with little other nourishment; at most not above the value of two shillings, which the mother may certainly get, or the value in scraps, by her lawful occupation of begging; and it is exactly at one year that I propose to provide for them in such a manner as instead of being a charge upon their parents or the parish, or wanting food and raiment for the rest of their lives, they shall on the contrary contribute to the feeding, and partly to the clothing, of many thousands.

There is likewise another great advantage in my scheme,   5
that it will prevent those voluntary abortions, and that horrid practice of women murdering their bastard children, alas, too frequent among us, sacrificing the poor innocent babes, I doubt, more to avoid the expense than the shame, which would move tears and pity in the most savage and inhuman breast.

The number of souls in this kingdom being usually reckoned   6
one million and a half, of these I calculate there may be about two hundred thousand couples whose wives are breeders; from which number I subtract thirty thousand couples who are able to maintain their own children, although I apprehend there cannot be so many under the present distress of the kingdom; but this being granted, there will remain an hundred and seventy thousand breeders. I again subtract fifty thousand for those women who miscarry, or whose children die by accident or disease within the year. There only remain an hundred and twenty thousand children of poor parents annually born. The question therefore is, how this number shall be reared and provided for, which, as I have already said, under the present situation of affairs, is utterly impossible by all the methods hitherto proposed.

[3]Planners. — EDS.

For we can neither employ them in handicraft or agriculture; we neither build houses (I mean in the country) nor cultivate land. They can very seldom pick up a livelihood stealing till they arrive at six years old, except where they are of towardly parts;[4] although I confess they learn the rudiments much earlier, during which time they can however be looked upon only as probationers, as I have been informed by a principal gentleman in the country of Cavan, who protested to me that he never knew above one or two instances under the age of six, even in a part of the kingdom so renowned for the quickest proficiency in that art.

I am assured by our merchants that a boy or a girl before twelve years old is no salable commodity; and even when they come to this age they will not yield above three pounds, or three pounds and half a crown at most on the Exchange; which cannot turn to account either to the parents or the kingdom, the charge of nutriment and rags having been at least four times that value. 7

I shall now therefore humbly propose my own thoughts, which I hope will not be liable to the least objection. 8

I have been assured by a very knowing American of my acquaintance in London, that a young healthy child well nursed is at a year old a most delicious, nourishing, and wholesome food, whether stewed, roasted, baked, or boiled; and I make no doubt that it will equally serve in a fricassee or a ragout.[5] 9

I do therefore humbly offer it to public consideration that of the hundred and twenty thousand children, already computed, twenty thousand may be reserved for breed, whereof only one fourth part to be males, which is more than we allow to sheep, black cattle, or swine; and my reason is that these children are seldom the fruits of marriage, a circumstance not much regarded by our savages, therefore one male will be sufficient to serve four females. That the remaining hundred thousand may at a year old be offered in sale to the persons of quality and fortune through the kingdom, always advising the mother to let them 10

---

[4]Teachable wits, innate abilities. — EDS.
[5]Stew. — EDS.

suck plentifully in the last month, so as to render them plump and fat for a good table. A child will make two dishes at an entertainment for friends; and when the family dines alone, the fore or hind quarter will make a reasonable dish, and seasoned with a little pepper or salt will be very good boiled on the fourth day, especially in winter.

I have reckoned upon a medium that a child just born will weigh twelve pounds, and in a solar year if tolerably nursed increaseth to twenty-eight pounds.   11

I grant this food will be somewhat dear, and therefore very proper for landlords, who, as they have already devoured most of the parents, seem to have the best title to the children.   12

Infant's flesh will be in season throughout the year, but more plentiful in March, and a little before and after. For we are told by a grave author, an eminent French physician,[6] that fish being a prolific diet, there are more children born in Roman Catholic countries about nine months after Lent than at any other season; therefore, reckoning a year after Lent, the markets will be more glutted than usual, because the number of popish infants is at least three to one in this kingdom; and therefore it will have one other collateral advantage, by lessening the number of Papists among us.   13

I have already computed the charge of nursing a beggar's child (in which list I reckon all cottagers, laborers, and four-fifths of the farmers) to be about two shillings per annum, rags included; and I believe no gentleman would repine to give ten shillings for the carcass of a good fat child, which, as I have said, will make four dishes of excellent nutritive meat, when he hath only some particular friend or his own family to dine with him. Thus the squire will learn to be a good landlord, and grow popular among the tenants; the mother will have eight shillings net profit, and be fit for work till she produces another child.   14

Those who are more thrifty (as I must confess the times require) may flay the carcass; the skin of which artificially[7] dressed   15

---

[6]Swift's favorite French writer, François Rabelais, sixteenth-century author; not "grave" at all, but a broad humorist. — EDS.

[7]With art or craft. — EDS.

will make admirable gloves for ladies, and summer boots for fine gentlemen.

As to our city of Dublin, shambles[8] may be appointed for this purpose in the most convenient parts of it, and butchers we may be assured will not be wanting; although I rather recommend buying the children alive, and dressing them hot from the knife as we do roasting pigs. 16

A very worthy person, a true lover of his country, and whose virtues I highly esteem, was lately pleased in discoursing on this matter to offer a refinement upon my scheme. He said that many gentlemen of his kingdom, having of late destroyed their deer, he conceived that the want of venison might be well supplied by the bodies of young lads and maidens, not exceeding fourteen years of age nor under twelve, so great a number of both sexes in every county being now ready to starve for want of work and service; and these to be disposed of by their parents, if alive, or otherwise by their nearest relations. But with due deference to so excellent a friend and so deserving a patriot, I cannot be altogether in his sentiments; for as to the males, my American acquaintance assured me from frequent experience that their flesh was generally tough and lean, like that of our schoolboys, by continual exercise, and their taste disagreeable; and to fatten them would not answer the charge. Then as to the females, it would, I think with humble submission, be a loss to the public, because they soon would become breeders themselves; and besides, it is not improbable that some scrupulous people might be apt to censure such a practice (although indeed very unjustly) as a little bordering upon cruelty; which, I confess, hath always been with me the strongest objection against any project, how well soever intended. 17

But in order to justify my friend, he confessed that this expedient was put into his head by the famous Psalmanazar,[9] a native of the island Formosa, who came from thence to London above 18

---

[8]Butcher shops or slaughterhouses. — Eds.

[9]Georges Psalmanazar, a Frenchman who pretended to be Japanese, author of a completely imaginary *Description of the Isle Formosa* (1705), had become a well-known figure in gullible London society. — Eds.

twenty years ago, and in conversation told my friend that in his country when any young person happened to be put to death, the executioner sold the carcass to persons of quality as a prime dainty; and that in his time the body of a plump girl of fifteen, who was crucified for an attempt to poison the emperor, was sold to his Imperial Majesty's prime minister of state, and other great mandarins of the court, in joints from the gibbet, at four hundred crowns. Neither indeed can I deny that if the same use were made of several plump young girls in this town, who without one single groat to their fortunes cannot stir abroad without a chair, and appear at the playhouse and assemblies in foreign fineries which they never will pay for, the kingdom would not be the worse.

Some persons of a desponding spirit are in great concern   19
about that vast number of poor people who are aged, diseased, or maimed, and I have been desired to employ my thoughts what course may be taken to ease the nation of so grievous an encumbrance. But I am not in the least pain upon that matter, because it is very well known that they are every day dying and rotting by cold and famine, and filth and vermin, as fast as can be reasonably expected. And as to the younger laborers, they are now in almost as hopeful a condition. They cannot get work, and consequently pine away for want of nourishment to a degree that if any time they are accidentally hired to common labor, they have not strength to perform it; and thus the country and themselves are happily delivered from the evils to come.

I have too long digressed, and therefore shall return to my   20
subject. I think the advantages by the proposal which I have made are obvious and many, as well as of the highest importance.

For first, as I have already observed, it would greatly lessen   21
the number of Papists, with whom we are yearly overrun, being the principal breeders of the nation as well as our most dangerous enemies; and who stay at home on purpose to deliver the kingdom to the Pretender, hoping to take their advantage by the absence of so many good Protestants, who have chosen rather to leave their country than to stay at home and pay tithes against their conscience to an Episcopal curate.

Secondly, the poorer tenants will have something valuable 22
of their own, which by law may be made liable to distress,[10] and
help to pay their landlord's rent, their corn and cattle being already seized and money a thing unknown.

Thirdly, whereas the maintenance of an hundred thousand 23
children, from two years old and upwards, cannot be computed
at less than ten shillings a piece per annum, the nation's stock
will be thereby increased fifty thousand pounds per annum, besides the profit of a new dish introduced to the tables of all gentlemen of fortune in the kingdom who have any refinement in
taste. And the money will circulate among ourselves, the goods
being entirely of our own growth and manufacture.

Fourthly, the constant breeders, besides the gain of eight 24
shillings sterling per annum by the sale of their children, will be
rid of the charge of maintaining them after the first year.

Fifthly, this food would likewise bring great custom to tav- 25
erns, where the vintners will certainly be so prudent as to procure the best receipts for dressing it to perfection, and consequently have their houses frequented by all the fine gentlemen,
who justly value themselves upon their knowledge in good eating; and a skillful cook, who understands how to oblige his
guests, will contrive to make it as expensive as they please.

Sixthly, this would be a great inducement to marriage, 26
which all wise nations have either encouraged by rewards or enforced by laws and penalties. It would increase the care and tenderness of mothers toward their children, when they were sure
of a settlement for life to the poor babes, provided in some sort
by the public, to their annual profit instead of expense. We
should see an honest emulation among the married women,
which of them could bring the fattest child to the market. Men
would become as fond of their wives during the time of their
pregnancy as they are now of their mares in foal, their cows in
calf, or sows when they are ready to farrow; nor offer to beat or
kick them (as is too frequent a practice) for fear of a miscarriage.

Many other advantages might be enumerated. For instance, 27
the addition of some thousand carcasses in our exportation of

[10]Subject to seizure by creditors. — EDS.

barreled beef, the propagation of swine's flesh, and improvements in the art of making good bacon, so much wanted among us by the great destruction of pigs, too frequent at our tables, which are no way comparable in taste or magnificence to a well-grown, fat, yearling child, which roasted whole will make a considerable figure at a lord mayor's feast or any other public entertainment. But this and many others I omit, being studious of brevity.

Supposing that one thousand families in this city would be   28
constant customers for infants' flesh, besides others who might have it at merry meetings, particularly weddings and christenings, I compute that Dublin would take off annually about twenty thousand carcasses, and the rest of the kingdom (where probably they will be sold somewhat cheaper) the remaining eighty thousand.

I can think of no one objection that will possibly be raised   29
against this proposal, unless it should be urged that the number of people will be thereby much lessened in the kingdom. This I freely own, and it was indeed one principal design in offering it to the world. I desire the reader will observe, that I calculate my remedy for this one individual kingdom of Ireland and for no other that ever was, is, or I think ever can be upon earth. Therefore let no man talk to me of other expedients: of taxing our absentees at five shillings a pound: of using neither clothes nor household furniture except what is of our own growth and manufacture: of utterly rejecting the materials and instruments that promote foreign luxury: of curing the expensiveness of pride, vanity, idleness, and gaming in our women: of introducing a vein of parsimony, prudence, and temperance: of learning to love our country, in the want of which we differ even from Laplanders and the inhabitants of Topinamboo:[11] of quitting our animosities and factions, nor acting any longer like the Jews, who were murdering one another at the very moment their city was taken:[12] of being a little cautious not to sell our country and

---

[11]District of Brazil inhabited by primitive tribes. — Eds.
[12]During the Roman siege of Jerusalem (A.D. 70), prominent Jews were executed on the charge of being in league with the enemy. — Eds.

conscience for nothing: of teaching landlords to have at least one degree of mercy toward their tenants: lastly, of putting a spirit of honesty, industry, and skill into our shopkeepers; who, if a resolution could now be taken to buy only our native goods, would immediately unite to cheat and exact upon us in the price, the measure, and the goodness, nor could ever yet be brought to make one fair proposal of just dealing, though often and earnestly invited to it.

Therefore I repeat, let no man talk to me of these and the like expedients, till he hath at least some glimpse of hope that there will ever be some hearty and sincere attempt to put them in practice.

But as to myself, having been wearied out for many years with offering vain, idle, visionary thoughts, and at length utterly despairing of success, I fortunately fell upon this proposal, which, as it is wholly new, so it hath something solid and real, of no expense and little trouble, full in our own power, and whereby we can incur no danger in disobliging England. For this kind of commodity will not bear exportation, the flesh being of too tender a consistence to admit a long continuance in salt, although perhaps I could name a country which would be glad to eat up our whole nation without it.

After all, I am not so violently bent upon my own opinion as to reject any offer proposed by wise men, which shall be found equally innocent, cheap, easy, and effectual. But before something of that kind shall be advanced in contradiction to my scheme, and offering a better, I desire the author or authors will be pleased maturely to consider two points. First, as things now stand, how they will be able to find food and raiment for an hundred thousand useless mouths and backs. And secondly, there being a round million of creatures in human figure throughout this kingdom, whose sole subsistence put into a common stock would leave them in debt two millions of pounds sterling, adding those who are beggars by profession to the bulk of farmers, cottagers, and laborers, with their wives and children who are beggars in effect; I desire those politicians who dislike my overture, and may perhaps be so bold to attempt an answer, that they will first ask the parents of these mortals whether they would not at this day think it a great happiness to have been sold for food at a year old in this manner I prescribe, and thereby have avoided such a perpetual scene of misfortunes as they have since gone through by the oppression of landlords, the impossibility of paying rent without money or trade, the want of common sustenance, with neither house nor clothes to cover them from the inclemencies of the weather, and the most inevitable prospect of entailing the like or greater miseries upon their breed forever.

I profess, in the sincerity of my heart, that I have not the   33
least personal interest in endeavoring to promote this necessary work, having no other motive than the public good of my country, by advancing our trade, providing for infants, relieving the poor, and giving some pleasure to the rich. I have no children by which I can propose to get a single penny; the youngest being nine years old, and my wife past childbearing.

QUESTIONS ON MEANING

1. On the surface, what is Swift proposing?
2. Beneath his IRONY, what is Swift's argument?
3. What do you take to be the PURPOSE of Swift's essay?
4. How does the introductory paragraph serve Swift's purpose?
5. Comment on the statement, "I can think of no one objection that will possibly be raised against this proposal" (paragraph 29). What objections can you think of?

QUESTIONS ON WRITING STRATEGY

1. Describe the mask of the personage through whom Swift writes.
2. By what means does the writer attest to his reasonableness?
3. At what point in the essay did it become clear to you that the proposal isn't modest but horrible?
4. As an essay in argument, does "A Modest Proposal" appeal primarily to reason or to emotion?

5. How does "A Modest Proposal" resemble Garrison Keillor's "Shy Rights: Why Not Pretty Soon?" (p. 580)? In what essential ways do the two essays differ?

QUESTIONS ON LANGUAGE

1. How does Swift's choice of words enforce the monstrousness of his proposal? Note especially words from the vocabulary of breeding and butchery.
2. Consult your dictionary for the meanings of any of the following words not yet in your vocabulary: importuning, sustenance (paragraph 1); prodigious, commonwealth (2); computation, raiment (4); apprehend, rudiments, probationers (6); nutriment (7); fricassee (9); repine (14); flay (15); scrupulous, censure (17); mandarins (18); desponding, encumbrance (19); per annum (23); vintners (25); emulation, foal, farrow (26); expedients, parsimony, animosities (29); disobliging, consistence (31); overture, inclemencies (32).

SUGGESTIONS FOR WRITING

1. Consider a group of people whom you regard as mistreated or victimized. (If none come immediately to mind, see today's newspaper — or write, less seriously, about college freshmen.) Then write either:

   a. A straight argument, giving EVIDENCE, in which you set forth possible solutions to their plight.

   b. An ironic proposal in the manner of Swift. If you do this one, find a device other than cannibalism to eliminate the victims or their problems. You don't want to imitate Swift too closely; he is probably inimitable.

Jonathan Swift on Writing

Though surely one of the most inventive writers in English literature, Swift voiced his contempt for writers of his day who bragged of their newness and originality. In *The Battle of the Books*, he compares such a self-professed original to a spider who "spins and spits wholly from himself, and scorns to own any obligation or assistance from without." Swift has the fable-writer Aesop praise that writer who, like a bee gathering nectar, draws from many sources.

> Erect your schemes with as much method and skill as you please; yet if the materials be nothing but dirt, spun out of your own entrails (the guts of modern brains), the edifice will conclude at last in a cobweb. . . . As for us Ancients, we are content, with the bee, to pretend to nothing of our own beyond our wings and our voice, that is to say, our flights and our language. For the rest, whatever we have got has been by infinite labor and search, and ranging through every corner of nature; the difference is, that, instead of dirt and poison, we have rather chosen to fill our hives with honey and wax, thus furnishing mankind with the two noblest of things, which are sweetness and light.

Swift's advice for a writer would seem to be: Don't just invent things out of thin air; read the best writers of the past. Observe and converse. Do legwork.

Interestingly, when in *Gulliver's Travels* Swift portrays his ideal beings, the Houyhnhnms, a race of noble and intelligent horses, he includes no writers at all in their society. "The Houyhnhnms have no letters," Gulliver observes, "and consequently their knowledge is all traditional." Still, "in poetry they must be allowed to excel all other mortals; wherein the justness of their description are indeed inimitable." (Those very traits — striking comparisons and detailed descriptions — make much of Swift's own writing memorable.)

In his great book, in "A Modest Proposal," and in virtually

all he wrote, Swift's purpose was forthright and evident. He wrote, he declared in "Verses on the Death of Dr. Swift,"

> As with a moral view designed
> To cure the vices of mankind: . . .
> Yet malice never was his aim;
> He lashed the vice but spared the name.
> No individual could resent,
> Where thousands equally were meant.
> His satire points at no defect
> But what all mortals may correct.

FOR DISCUSSION

1. Try applying Swift's parable of the spider and the bee to our own day. How much truth is left in it?
2. Reread thoughtfully the quotation from Swift's poem. According to the poet, what faults or abuses can a satiric writer fall into? How may these be avoided?
3. What do you take to be Swift's main PURPOSE as a writer? In your own words, summarize it.

1. Write a persuasive essay in which you express a deeply felt opinion. In it, address a particular person or audience. For instance, you might direct your essay:

   To a friend unwilling to attend a ballet performance (or a wrestling match) with you on the grounds that such an event is for the birds

   To a teacher who asserts that more term papers, and longer ones, are necessary

   To a state trooper who intends to give you a ticket for speeding

   To a male employer skeptical of hiring women

   To a developer who plans to tear down a historic house

   To someone who sees no purpose in studying a foreign language

   To a high-school class whose members don't want to go to college

   To an older generation skeptical of the value of "all that noise" (meaning current popular music)

   To an atheist who asserts that religion is a lot of pie-in-the-sky

   To the members of a library board who want to ban a certain book

2. Write a letter to your campus newspaper, or to a city newspaper, in which you argue for or against a certain cause or view. Perhaps you may wish to object to a particular feature, column, or editorial in the paper. Send your letter and see if it is published.

3. Write a short letter to your congressional or state representative, arguing in favor of (or against) the passage of some pending legislation. See a news magazine or a newspaper for a worthwhile bill to champion. Or else write in favor of some continuing cause: for instance, saving whales, reducing (or increasing) armaments, or providing more aid to the arts.

4. Write an essay in which you argue that something you feel strongly about be changed, removed, abolished, enforced, repeated, revised, reinstated, or reconsidered. Be sure to propose some plan for carrying out whatever suggestions you make. Possible topics, listed to start you thinking, are:

   The drinking age

   Gun laws

The draft
Low-income housing
Graduation requirements
The mandatory retirement age
ROTC programs in schools and colleges
The voting age
Movie ratings (G, PG, PG–13, R, X)
School prayer
Fraternities and sororities
Dress codes
TV advertising

5. On the model of Maire Flynn's three-part condensed argument on page 504, write a condensed argument in three paragraphs demonstrating data, warrant, and claim. For a topic, consider any problem or controversy in this morning's newspaper and form an opinion on it.

FOR FURTHER READING

Three Writers in Depth

GEORGE ORWELL · E. B. WHITE · JOAN DIDION

· George Orwell ·

GEORGE ORWELL was the pen name of Eric Blair (1903–1950). For a biographical note and another Orwell essay, "A Hanging," see page 39.

Shooting an Elephant

If you have read Orwell's unforgettable "A Hanging" in Chapter 1, you are acquainted with the author and his experiences as a British police officer in Burma. Here is another, still more famous memoir of life in the Indian Imperial Police. Taken from Orwell's *Shooting an Elephant and Other Essays* (1950), it is a rare combination of personal experience and piercing insight. Today, as much as when first published, Orwell's recollections have much to tell about the nature of oppressive government — and the individual hireling holding the gun.

In Moulmein, in Lower Burma, I was hated by large numbers of people — the only time in my life that I have been important enough for this to happen to me. I was subdivisional police officer of the town, and in an aimless, petty kind of way anti-European feeling was very bitter. No one had the guts to raise a riot, but if a European woman went through the bazaars alone somebody would probably spit betel juice over her dress. As a police officer I was an obvious target and was baited whenever it seemed safe to do so. When a nimble Burman tripped me up on the football field and the referee (another Burman) looked the other way, the crowd yelled with hideous laughter. This happened more than once. In the end the sneering yellow faces of young men that met me everywhere, the insults hooted after me when I was at a safe distance, got badly on my nerves. The young Buddhist priests were the worst of all. There were several thousands of them in the town and none of them seemed to

1

have anything to do except stand on street corners and jeer at Europeans.

All this was perplexing and upsetting. For at that time I had   2
already made up my mind that imperialism was an evil thing and the sooner I chucked up my job and got out of it the better. Theoretically — and secretly, of course — I was all for the Burmese and all against the oppressors, the British. As for the job I was doing, I hated it more bitterly than I can perhaps make clear. In a job like that you see the dirty work of Empire at close quarters. The wretched prisoners huddling in the stinking cages of the lockups, the grey, cowed faces of the long-term convicts, the scarred buttocks of the men who had been flogged with bamboos — all these oppressed me with an intolerable sense of guilt. But I could get nothing into perspective. I was young and ill-educated and I had had to think out my problems in the utter silence that is imposed on every Englishman in the East. I did not even know that the British Empire is dying, still less did I know that it is a great deal better than the younger empires that are going to supplant it. All I knew was that I was stuck between my hatred of the empire I served and my rage against the evil-spirited little beasts who tried to make my job impossible. With one part of my mind I thought of the British Raj[1] as an unbreakable tyranny, as something clamped down, in *saecula saeculorum*,[2] upon the will of prostrate peoples; with another part I thought that the greatest joy in the world would be to drive a bayonet into a Buddhist priest's guts. Feelings like these are the normal by-products of imperialism; ask any Anglo-Indian official, if you can catch him off duty.

One day something happened which in a roundabout way   3
was enlightening. It was a tiny incident in itself, but it gave me a better glimpse than I had had before of the real nature of imperialism — the real motives for which despotic governments act. Early one morning the subinspector at a police station the other end of town rang me up on the phone and said that an elephant

[1]British imperial government. *Raj* in Hindi means "reign," a word similar to *rajah*, "ruler." — EDS.

[2]Latin, "world without end." — EDS.

was ravaging the bazaar. Would I please come and do something about it? I did not know what I could do, but I wanted to see what was happening and I got on to a pony and started out. I took my rifle, an old .44 Winchester and much too small to kill an elephant, but I thought the noise might be useful *in terrorem*.[3] Various Burmans stopped me on the way and told me about the elephant's doings. It was not, of course, a wild elephant, but a tame one which had gone "must." It had been chained up, as tame elephants always are when their attack of "must" is due, but on the previous night it had broken its chain and escaped. Its mahout,[4] the only person who could manage it when it was in that state, had set out in pursuit, but had taken the wrong direction and was now twelve hours' journey away, and in the morning the elephant had suddenly reappeared in the town. The Burmese population had no weapons and were quite helpless against it. It had already destroyed somebody's bamboo hut, killed a cow and raided some fruit stalls and devoured the stock; also it had met the municipal rubbish van and, when the driver jumped out and took to his heels, had turned the van over and inflicted violences upon it.

The Burmese subinspector and some Indian constables were waiting for me in the quarter where the elephant had been seen. It was a very poor quarter, a labyrinth of squalid bamboo huts, thatched with palmleaf, winding all over a steep hillside. I remember that it was a cloudy, stuffy morning at the beginning of the rains. We began questioning the people as to where the elephant had gone and, as usual, failed to get any definite information. That is invariably the case in the East; a story always sounds clear enough at a distance, but the nearer you get to the scene of events the vaguer it becomes. Some of the people said that the elephant had gone in one direction, some said that he had gone in another, some professed not even to have heard of any elephant. I had almost made up my mind that the whole story was a pack of lies, when we heard yells a little distance away. There was a loud, scandalized cry of "Go away, child! Go

[3]Latin, "to give warning." — EDS.
[4]Keeper or groom, a servant of the elephant's owner. — EDS.

away this instant!" and an old woman with a switch in her hand came round the corner of a hut, violently shooing away a crowd of naked children. Some more women followed, clicking their tongues and exclaiming; evidently there was something that the children ought not to have seen. I rounded the hut and saw a man's dead body sprawling in the mud. He was an Indian, a black Dravidian coolie, almost naked, and he could not have been dead many minutes. The people said that the elephant had come suddenly upon him round the corner of the hut, caught him with its trunk, put its foot on his back and ground him into the earth. This was the rainy season and the ground was soft, and his face had scored a trench a foot deep and a couple of yards long. He was lying on his belly with arms crucified and head sharply twisted to one side. His face was coated with mud, the eyes wide open, the teeth bared and grinning with an expression of unendurable agony. (Never tell me, by the way, that the dead look peaceful. Most of the corpses I have seen looked devilish.) The friction of the great beast's foot had stripped the skin from his back as neatly as one skins a rabbit. As soon as I saw the dead man I sent an orderly to a friend's house nearby to borrow an elephant rifle. I had already sent back the pony, not wanting it to go mad with fright and throw me if it smelled the elephant.

The orderly came back in a few minutes with a rifle and five   5
cartridges, and meanwhile some Burmans had arrived and told us that the elephant was in the paddy fields below, only a few hundred yards away. As I started forward practically the whole population of the quarter flocked out of the houses and followed me. They had seen the rifle and were all shouting excitedly that I was going to shoot the elephant. They had not shown much interest in the elephant when he was merely ravaging their homes, but it was different now that he was going to be shot. It was a bit of fun to them, as it would be to an English crowd; besides they wanted the meat. It made me vaguely uneasy. I had no intention of shooting the elephant — I had merely sent for the rifle to defend myself if necessary — and it is always unnerving to have a crowd following you. I marched down the hill, looking and feeling a fool, with the rifle over my shoulder and

an ever-growing army of people jostling at my heels. At the bottom, when you got away from the huts, there was a metalled road and beyond that a miry waste of paddy fields a thousand yards across, not yet ploughed but soggy from the first rains and dotted with coarse grass. The elephant was standing eight yards from the road, his left side towards us. He took not the slightest notice of the crowd's approach. He was tearing up bunches of grass, beating them against his knees to clean them and stuffing them into his mouth.

I had halted on the road. As soon as I saw the elephant I knew with perfect certainty that I ought not to shoot him. It is a serious matter to shoot a working elephant — it is comparable to destroying a huge and costly piece of machinery — and obviously one ought not to do it if it can possibly be avoided. And at that distance, peacefully eating, the elephant looked no more dangerous than a cow. I thought then and I think now that his attack of "must" was already passing off; in which case he would merely wander harmlessly about until the mahout came back and caught him. Moreover, I did not in the least want to shoot him. I decided that I would watch him for a little while to make sure that he did not turn savage again, and then go home.

But at that moment, I glanced round at the crowd that had followed me. It was an immense crowd, two thousand at the least and growing every minute. It blocked the road for a long distance on either side. I looked at the sea of yellow faces above the garish clothes — faces all happy and excited over this bit of fun, all certain that the elephant was going to be shot. They were watching me as they would watch a conjuror about to perform a trick. They did not like me, but with the magical rifle in my hands I was momentarily worth watching. And suddenly I realized that I should have to shoot the elephant after all. The people expected it of me and I had got to do it; I could feel their two thousand wills pressing me forward, irresistibly. And it was at this moment, as I stood there with the rifle in my hands, that I first grasped the hollowness, the futility of the white man's dominion in the East. Here was I, the white man with his gun, standing in front of the unarmed native crowd — seemingly the leading actor of the piece; but in reality I was only an absurd puppet pushed to and fro by the will of those yellow faces behind. I perceived in this moment that when the white man turns tyrant it is his own freedom that he destroys. He becomes a sort of hollow, posing dummy, the conventionalized figure of a sahib. For it is the condition of his rule that he shall spend his life in trying to impress the "natives," and so in every crisis he has got to do what the "natives" expect of him. He wears a mask, and his face grows to fit it. I had got to shoot the elephant. I had committed myself to doing it when I sent for the rifle. A sahib has got to act like a sahib; he has got to appear resolute, to know his own mind and do definite things. To come all that way, rifle in hand, with two thousand people marching at my heels, and then to trail feebly away, having done nothing — no, that was impossible. The crowd would laugh at me. And my whole life, every white man's life in the East, was one long struggle not to be laughed at.

But I did not want to shoot the elephant. I watched him   8
beating his bunch of grass against his knees, with that preoccupied grandmotherly air that elephants have. It seemed to me that it would be murder to shoot him. At that age I was not squeamish about killing animals, but I had never shot an elephant and never wanted to. (Somehow it always seems worse to kill a *large* animal.) Besides, there was the beast's owner to be considered. Alive, the elephant was worth at least a hundred pounds; dead, he would only be worth the value of his tusks, five pounds, possibly. But I had got to act quickly. I turned to some experienced-looking Burmans who had been there when we arrived, and asked them how the elephant had been behaving. They all said the same thing: He took no notice of you if you left him alone, but he might charge if you went too close to him.

It was perfectly clear to me what I ought to do. I ought to   9
walk up to within, say, twenty-five yards of the elephant and test his behavior. If he charged, I could shoot; if he took no notice of me, it would be safe to leave him until the mahout came back. But also I knew that I was going to do no such thing. I was a poor shot with a rifle and the ground was soft mud into which one would sink at every step. If the elephant charged and I

missed him, I should have about as much chance as a toad under a steamroller. But even then I was not thinking particularly of my own skin, only of the watchful yellow faces behind. For at that moment, with the crowd watching me, I was not afraid in the ordinary sense, as I would have been if I had been alone. A white man mustn't be frightened in front of "natives"; and so, in general, he isn't frightened. The sole thought in my mind was that if anything went wrong those two thousand Burmans would see me pursued, caught, trampled on, and reduced to a grinning corpse like that Indian up the hill. And if that happened it was quite probable that some of them would laugh. That would never do. There was only one alternative. I shoved the cartridges into the magazine and lay down on the road to get a better aim.

The crowd grew very still, and a deep, low, happy sigh, as of 10 people who see the theatre curtain go up at last, breathed from innumerable throats. They were going to have their bit of fun after all. The rifle was a beautiful German thing with cross-hair sights. I did not then know that in shooting an elephant one would shoot to cut an imaginary bar running from ear-hole to ear-hole. I ought, therefore, as the elephant was sideways on, to have aimed straight at his ear-hole; actually I aimed several inches in front of this, thinking the brain would be further forward.

When I pulled the trigger I did not hear the bang or feel the 11 kick — one never does when a shot goes home — but I heard the devilish roar of glee that went up from the crowd. In that instant, in too short a time, one would have thought, even for the bullet to get there, a mysterious, terrible change had come over the elephant. He neither stirred nor fell, but every line of his body had altered. He looked suddenly stricken, shrunken, immensely old, as though the frightful impact of the bullet had paralyzed him without knocking him down. At last, after what seemed a long time — it might have been five seconds, I dare say — he sagged flabbily to his knees. His mouth slobbered. An enormous senility seemed to have settled upon him. One could have imagined him thousands of years old. I fired again into the same spot. At the second shot he did not collapse but climbed with desperate slowness to his feet and stood weakly upright, with legs sagging and head drooping. I fired a third time. That was the shot that did for him. You could see the agony of it jolt his whole body and knock the last remnant of strength from his legs. But in falling he seemed for a moment to rise, for as his hind legs collapsed beneath him he seemed to tower upward like a huge rock toppling, his trunk reaching skywards like a tree. He trumpeted, for the first and only time. And then down he came, his belly towards me, with a crash that seemed to shake the ground even where I lay.

I got up. The Burmans were already racing past me across the mud. It was obvious that the elephant would never rise again, but he was not dead. He was breathing very rhythmically with long rattling gasps, his great mound of a side painfully rising and falling. His mouth was wide open. I could see far down into caverns of pale pink throat. I waited a long time for him to die, but his breathing did not weaken. Finally I fired my two remaining shots into the spot where I thought his heart must be. The thick blood welled out of him like red velvet, but still he did not die. His body did not even jerk when the shots hit him, the tortured breathing continued without a pause. He was dying, very slowly and in great agony, but in some world remote from me where not even a bullet could damage him further. I felt I had got to put an end to that dreadful noise. It seemed dreadful to see the great beast lying there, powerless to move and yet powerless to die, and not even to be able to finish him. I sent back for my small rifle and poured shot after shot into his heart and down his throat. They seemed to make no impression. The tortured gasps continued as steadily as the ticking of a clock. 12

In the end I could not stand it any longer and went away. I heard later that it took him half an hour to die. Burmans were bringing dahs and baskets even before I left, and I was told they had stripped his body almost to the bones by the afternoon. 13

Afterwards, of course, there were endless discussions about the shooting of the elephant. The owner was furious, but he was only an Indian and could do nothing. Besides, legally I had done the right thing, for a mad elephant has to be killed, like a mad dog, if its owner fails to control it. Among the Europeans opin- 14 ion was divided. The older men said I was right, the younger men said it was a damn shame to shoot an elephant for killing a coolie, because the elephant was worth more than any damn Coringhee coolie. And afterwards I was very glad that the coolie had been killed; it put me legally in the right and it gave me sufficient pretext for shooting the elephant. I often wondered whether any of the others grasped that I had done it solely to avoid looking a fool.

· George Orwell ·

For a biographical note, see page 39.

Politics and
the English Language

In Orwell's novel, *1984*, a dictatorship tries to replace spoken and written English with Newspeak, an official language that limits thought by reducing its users' vocabulary. (The words *light* and *bad*, for instance, are suppressed in favor of *unlight* and *unbad*.) This concern with language and with its importance to society is constant in George Orwell's work. (See "George Orwell on Writing," p. 47.) First published in 1946, "Politics and the English Language" still stands as one of the most devastating attacks on muddy writing and thinking ever penned. Orwell's six short rules for writing responsible prose are well worth remembering.

Most people who bother with the matter at all would admit 1
that the English language is in a bad way, but it is generally assumed that we cannot by conscious action do anything about it. Our civilization is decadent and our language — so the argument runs — must inevitably share in the general collapse. It follows that any struggle against the abuse of language is a sentimental archaism, like preferring candles to electric light or hansom cabs to airplanes. Underneath this lies the half-conscious belief that language is a natural growth and not an instrument which we shape for our own purposes.

Now, it is clear that the decline of a language must ulti- 2
mately have political and economic causes: It is not due simply to the bad influence of this or that individual writer. But an effect can become a cause, reinforcing the original cause and producing the same effect in an intensified form, and so on indefinitely. A man may take to drink because he feels himself to be a

failure, and then fail all the more completely because he drinks. It is rather the same thing that is happening to the English language. It becomes ugly and inaccurate because our thoughts are foolish, but the slovenliness of our language makes it easier for us to have foolish thoughts. The point is that the process is reversible. Modern English, especially written English, is full of bad habits which spread by imitation and which can be avoided if one is willing to take the necessary trouble. If one gets rid of these habits one can think more clearly, and to think clearly is a necessary first step towards political regeneration: so that the fight against bad English is not frivolous and is not the exclusive concern of professional writers. I will come back to this presently, and I hope that by that time the meaning of what I have said here will have become clearer. Meanwhile, here are five specimens of the English language as it is now habitually written.

These five passages have not been picked out because they are especially bad — I could have quoted far worse if I had chosen — but because they illustrate various of the mental vices from which we now suffer. They are a little below the average, but are fairly representative samples. I number them so that I can refer back to them when necessary: 3

(1) I am not, indeed, sure whether it is not true to say that the Milton who once seemed not unlike a seventeenth-century Shelley had not become, out of an experience ever more bitter in each year, more alien [*sic*] to the founder of that Jesuit sect which nothing could induce him to tolerate.
Professor Harold Laski (Essay in *Freedom of Expression*).

(2) Above all, we cannot play ducks and drakes with a native battery of idioms which prescribes such egregious collocations of vocables as the Basic *put up with* for *tolerate* or *put at a loss* for *bewilder*.   Professor Lancelot Hogben (*Interglossa*).

(3) On the one side we have the free personality: By definition it is not neurotic, for it has neither conflict nor dream. Its desires, such as they are, are transparent, for they are just what institutional approval keeps in the forefront of consciousness; another institutional pattern would alter their number and intensity; there is little in them that is natural, ir-

reducible, or culturally dangerous. But *on the other side*, the social bond itself is nothing but the mutual reflection of these
self-secure integrities. Recall the definition of love. Is not this
the very picture of a small academic? Where is there a place in
this hall of mirrors for either personality or fraternity?

> Essay on psychology in *Politics* (New York).

(4) All the "best people" from the gentlemen's clubs, and
all the frantic fascist captains, united in common hatred of
Socialism and bestial horror of the rising tide of the mass revolutionary movement, have turned to acts of provocation, to
foul incendiarism, to medieval legends of poisoned wells, to le-
galize their own destruction of proletarian organizations, and
rouse the agitated petty-bourgeoisie to chauvinistic fervor on
behalf of the fight against the revolutionary way out of the
crisis.   Communist pamphlet.

(5) If a new spirit *is* to be infused into this old country,
there is one thorny and contentious reform which must be
tackled, and that is the humanization and galvanization of
the B.B.C. Timidity here will bespeak cancer and atrophy of
the soul. The heart of Britain may be sound and of strong
beat, for instance, but the British lion's roar at present is like
that of Bottom in Shakespeare's *Midsummer Night's Dream* —
as gentle as any sucking dove. A virile new Britain cannot
continue indefinitely to be traduced in the eyes or rather ears,
of the world by the effete languors of Langham Place, brazenly
masquerading as "standard English." When the Voice of Britain is heard at nine o'clock, better far and infinitely less ludicrous to hear aitches honestly dropped than the present prig-
gish, inflated, inhibited, school-ma'amish arch braying of
blameless bashful mewing maidens!

> Letter in *Tribune*.

Each of these passages has faults of its own, but, quite apart   4
from avoidable ugliness, two qualities are common to all of
them. The first is staleness of imagery: The other is lack of precision. The writer either has a meaning and cannot express it, or
he inadvertently says something else, or he is almost indifferent
as to whether his words mean anything or not. The mixture of
vagueness and sheer incompetence is the most marked characteristic of modern English prose, and especially of any kind of
political writing. As soon as certain topics are raised, the con-

crete melts into the abstract and no one seems to think of turns of speech that are not hackneyed: Prose consists less and less of *words* chosen for the sake of their meaning, and more and more of *phrases* tacked together like the sections of a prefabricated hen-house. I list below, with notes and examples, various of the tricks by means of which the work of prose-construction is habitually dodged:

Dying Metaphors. A newly invented metaphor assists 5 thought by evoking a visual image, while on the other hand a metaphor which is technically "dead" (e.g., *iron resolution*) has in effect reverted to being an ordinary word and can generally be used without loss of vividness. But in between these two classes there is a huge dump of worn-out metaphors which have lost all evocative power and are merely used because they save people the trouble of inventing phrases for themselves. Examples are: *Ring the changes on, take up the cudgels for, toe the line, ride roughshod over, stand shoulder to shoulder with, play into the hands of, no axe to grind, grist to the mill, fishing in troubled waters, rift within the lute, on the order of the day, Achilles' heel, swan song, hotbed.* Many of these are used without knowledge of their meaning (what is a "rift," for instance?), and incompatible metaphors are frequently mixed, a sure sign that the writer is not interested in what he is saying. Some metaphors now current have been twisted out of their original meaning without those who use them even being aware of the fact. For example, *toe the line* is sometimes written *tow the line*. Another example is *the hammer and the anvil*, now always used with the implication that the anvil gets the worst of it. In real life it is always the anvil that breaks the hammer, never the other way about: A writer who stopped to think what he was saying would be aware of this, and would avoid perverting the original phrase.

Operators or Verbal False Limbs. These save the trouble of 6 picking out appropriate verbs and nouns, and at the same time pad each sentence with extra syllables which give it an appearance of symmetry. Characteristic phrases are: *render inoperative, militate against, make contact with, be subjected to, give rise to, give grounds for, have the effect of, play a leading part (role) in, make it-*

self felt, take effect, exhibit a tendency to, serve the purpose of, etc., etc. The keynote is the elimination of simple verbs. Instead of being a single word, such as *break, stop, spoil, mend, kill,* a verb becomes a *phrase,* made up of a noun or adjective tacked on to some general-purpose verb such as *prove, serve, form, play, render.* In addition, the passive voice is wherever possible used in preference to the active, and noun constructions are used instead of gerunds (*by examination of* instead of *by examining*). The range of verbs is further cut down by means of the *-ize* and *de-* formation, and the banal statements are given an appearance of profundity by means of the *not un-* formation. Simple conjunctions and prepositions are replaced by such phrases as *with respect to, having regard to, the fact that, by dint of, in view of, in the interests of, on the hypothesis that;* and the ends of sentences are saved from anticlimax by such resounding commonplaces as *greatly to be desired, cannot be left out of account, a development to be expected in the near future, deserving of serious consideration, brought to a satisfactory conclusion,* and so on and so forth.

Pretentious Diction. Words like *phenomenon, element, individual* (as noun), *objective, categorical, effective, virtual, basic, primary, promote, constitute, exhibit, exploit, utilize, eliminate, liquidate,* are used to dress up simple statements and give an air of scientific impartiality to biased judgments. Adjectives like *epoch-making, epic, historic, unforgettable, triumphant, age-old, inevitable, inexorable, veritable,* are used to dignify the sordid processes of international politics, while writing that aims at glorifying war usually takes on an archaic color, its characteristic words being: *realm, throne, chariot, mailed fist, trident, sword, shield, buckler, banner, jackboot, clarion.* Foreign words and expressions such as *cul de sac, ancien régime, deus ex machina, mutatis mutandis, status quo, gleichschaltung, weltanschauung,* are used to give an air of culture and elegance. Except for the useful abbreviations *i.e., e.g.,* and *etc.,* there is no real need for any of the hundreds of foreign phrases now current in English. Bad writers, and especially scientific, political, and sociological writers, are nearly always haunted by the notion that Latin or Greek words are grander than Saxon ones, and unnecessary words like *expedite, amelio-*

rate, predict, extraneous, deracinated, clandestine, subaqueous and hundreds of others constantly gain ground from their Anglo-Saxon opposite numbers.[1] The jargon peculiar to Marxist writing (hyena, hangman, cannibal, petty bourgeois, these gentry, lackey, flunkey, mad dog, White Guard, etc.) consists largely of words and phrases translated from Russian, German, or French; but the normal way of coining a new word is to use a Latin or Greek root with the appropriate affix and, where necessary, the -ize formation. It is often easier to make up words of this kind (deregionalize, impermissible, extramarital, nonfragmentatory, and so forth) than to think up the English words that will cover one's meaning. The result, in general, is an increase in slovenliness and vagueness.

Meaningless Words. In certain kinds of writing, particularly 　8
in art criticism and literary criticism, it is normal to come across long passages which are almost completely lacking in meaning.[2] Words like romantic, plastic, values, human, dead, sentimental, natural, vitality, as used in art criticism, are strictly meaningless in the sense that they not only do not point to any discoverable object, but are hardly ever expected to do so by the reader. When one critic writes, "The outstanding feature of Mr. X's work is its living quality," while another writes, "The immediately striking thing about Mr. X's work is its peculiar deadness," the reader accepts this as a simple difference of opinion. If words like black and white were involved, instead of the jargon words

---

[1]An interesting illustration of this is the way in which the English flower names which were in use till very recently are being ousted by Greek ones, snapdragon becoming antirrhinum, forget-me-not becoming myosotis, etc. It is hard to see any practical reason for this change of fashion: It is probably due to an instinctive turning-away from the more homely word and a vague feeling that the Greek word is scientific.

[2]Example: "Comfort's catholicity of perception and image, strangely Whitmanesque in range, almost the exact opposite in aesthetic compulsion, continues to evoke that trembling atmospheric accumulative hinting at a cruel, an inexorably serene timelessness. . . . Wrey Gardiner scores by aiming at simple bull's-eyes with precision. Only they are not so simple, and through this contented sadness runs more than the surface bitter-sweet of resignation." (Poetry Quarterly.)

dead and *living*, he would see at once that language was being used in an improper way. Many political words are similarly abused. The word *Fascism* has now no meaning except in so far as it signifies "something not desirable." The words *democracy, socialism, freedom, patriotic, realistic, justice,* have each of them several different meanings which cannot be reconciled with one another. In the case of a word like *democracy,* not only is there no agreed definition, but the attempt to make one is resisted from all sides. It is almost universally felt that when we call a country democratic we are praising it: Consequently the defenders of every kind of regime claim that it is a democracy, and fear that they might have to stop using the word if it were tied down to any one meaning. Words of this kind are often used in a consciously dishonest way. That is, the person who uses them has his own private definition, but allows his hearer to think he means something quite different. Statements like *Marshal Pétain was a true patriot, The Soviet Press is the freest in the world, The Catholic Church is opposed to persecution,* are almost always made with intent to deceive. Other words used in variable meanings, in most cases more or less dishonestly, are: *class, totalitarian, science, progressive, reactionary, bourgeois, equality.*

Now that I have made this catalogue of swindles and perversions, let me give another example of the kind of writing that they lead to. This time it must of its nature be an imaginary one. I am going to translate a passage of good English into modern English of the worst sort. Here is a well-known verse from *Ecclesiastes:*

> I returned and saw under the sun, that the race is not to the swift, nor the battle to the strong, neither yet bread to the wise, nor yet riches to men of understanding, nor yet favor to men of skill; but time and chance happeneth to them all.

Here it is in modern English:

> Objective consideration of contemporary phenomena compels the conclusion that success or failure in competitive activities exhibits no tendency to be commensurate with in-

9

nate capacity, but that a considerable element of the unpredictable must invariably be taken into account.

This is a parody, but not a very gross one. Exhibit (3), above, for instance, contains several patches of the same kind of English. It will be seen that I have not made a full translation. The beginning and ending of the sentence follow the original meaning fairly closely, but in the middle the concrete illustrations — race, battle, bread — dissolve into the vague phrase "success or failure in competitive activities." This had to be so, because no modern writer of the kind I am discussing — no one capable of using phrases like "objective consideration of contemporary phenomena" — would ever tabulate his thoughts in that precise and detailed way. The whole tendency of modern prose is away from concreteness. Now analyze these two sentences a little more closely. The first contains forty-nine words but only sixty syllables, and all its words are those of everyday life. The second contains thirty-eight words of ninety syllables: eighteen of its words are from Latin roots, and one from Greek. The first sentence contains six vivid images, and only one phrase ("time and chance") that could be called vague. The second contains not a single fresh, arresting phrase, and in spite of its ninety syllables it gives only a shortened version of the meaning contained in the first. Yet without a doubt it is the second kind of sentence that is gaining ground in modern English. I do not want to exaggerate. This kind of writing is not yet universal, and outcrops of simplicity will occur here and there in the worst-written page. Still, if you or I were told to write a few lines on the uncertainty of human fortunes, we should probably come much nearer to my imaginary sentence than to the one from *Ecclesiastes*.

As I have tried to show, modern writing at its worst does not consist in picking out words for the sake of their meaning and inventing images in order to make the meaning clearer. It consists in gumming together long strips of words which have already been set in order by someone else, and making the results presentable by sheer humbug. The attraction of this way of writing is that it is easy. It is easier — even quicker once you have the habit — to say *In my opinion it is a not unjustifiable assumption that* than to say *I think*. If you use ready-made phrases, you not only don't have to hunt about for words; you also don't have to bother with the rhythms of your sentences, since these phrases are generally so arranged as to be more or less euphonious. When you are composing in a hurry — when you are dictating to a stenographer, for instance, or making a public speech — it is natural to fall into a pretentious, Latinized style. Tags like *a consideration which we should do well to bear in mind* or *a conclusion to which all of us would readily assent* will save many a sentence from coming down with a bump. By using stale metaphors, similes, and idioms, you save much mental effort, at the cost of leaving your meaning vague, not only for your reader but for yourself. This is the significance of mixed metaphors. The sole aim of a metaphor is to call up a visual image. When these images clash — as in *The Fascist octopus has sung its swan song, the jackboot is thrown into the melting pot* — it can be taken as certain that the writer is not seeing a mental image of the objects he is naming; in other words he is not really thinking. Look again at the examples I gave at the beginning of this essay. Professor Laski (1) uses five negatives in fifty-three words. One of these is superfluous, making nonsense of the whole passage, and in addition there is the slip *alien* for akin, making further nonsense, and several avoidable pieces of clumsiness which increase the general vagueness. Professor Hogben (2) plays ducks and drakes with a battery which is able to write prescriptions, and, while disapproving of the every-day phrase *put up with*, is unwilling to look *egregious* up in the dictionary and see what it means. (3), if one takes an uncharitable attitude towards it, is simply meaningless: Probably one could work out its intended meaning by reading the whole of the article in which it occurs. In (4), the writer knows more or less what he wants to say, but an accumulation of stale phrases chokes him like tea leaves blocking a sink. In (5), words and meaning have almost parted company. People who write in this manner usually have a general emotional meaning — they dislike one thing and want to express solidarity with another — but they are not interested in the detail of what they are saying. A scrupulous writer, in every sentence that he writes, will ask himself at least four questions, thus: What am I trying to say?

What words will express it? What image or idiom will make it clearer? Is this image fresh enough to have an effect? And he will probably ask himself two more: Could I put it more shortly? Have I said anything that is avoidably ugly? But you are not obliged to go to all this trouble. You can shirk it by simply throwing your mind open and letting the ready-made phrases come crowding in. They will construct your sentences for you — even think your thoughts for you, to a certain extent — and at need they will perform the important service of partially concealing your meaning even from yourself. It is at this point that the special connection between politics and the debasement of language becomes clear.

In our time it is broadly true that political writing is bad writing. Where it is not true, it will generally be found that the writer is some kind of rebel, expressing his private opinions and not a "party line." Orthodoxy, of whatever color, seems to demand a lifeless, imitative style. The political dialects to be found in pamphlets, leading articles, manifestos, White Papers, and the speeches of under-secretaries do, of course, vary from party to party, but they are all alike in that one almost never finds in them a fresh, vivid, home-made turn of speech. When one watches some tired hack on the platform mechanically repeating the familiar phrases — *bestial atrocities, iron heel, bloodstained tyranny, free peoples of the world, stand shoulder to shoulder* — one often has a curious feeling that one is not watching a live human being but some kind of dummy; a feeling which suddenly becomes stronger at moments when the light catches the speaker's spectacles and turns them into blank discs which seem to have no eyes behind them. And this is not altogether fanciful. A speaker who uses that kind of phraseology has gone some distance towards turning himself into a machine. The appropriate noises are coming out of his larynx, but his brain is not involved as it would be if he were choosing his words for himself. If the speech he is making is one that he is accustomed to make over and over again, he may be almost unconscious of what he is saying, as one is when one utters the responses in church. And this reduced state of consciousness, if not indispensable, is at any rate favorable to political conformity.

In our time, political speech and writing are largely the de-   13
fense of the indefensible. Things like the continuance of British
rule in India, the Russian purges and deportations, the dropping
of the atom bombs on Japan, can indeed be defended, but only by
arguments which are too brutal for most people to face, and
which do not square with the professed aims of political parties.
Thus political language has to consist largely of euphemism, ques-
tion-begging and sheer cloudy vagueness. Defenseless villages are
bombarded from the air, the inhabitants driven out into the
countryside, the cattle machine-gunned, the huts set on fire with
incendiary bullets: This is called *pacification*. Millions of peasants
are robbed of their farms and sent trudging along the roads with
no more than they can carry: This is called *transfer of population* or
rectification of frontiers. People are imprisoned for years without
trial, or shot in the back of the neck or sent to die of scurvy in
Arctic lumber camps: This is called *elimination of unreliable elements*. Such phraseology is needed if one wants to name things
without calling up mental pictures of them. Consider for instance some comfortable English professor defending Russian totalitarianism. He cannot say outright, "I believe in killing off
your opponents when you can get good results by doing so."
Probably, therefore, he will say something like this:

"While freely conceding that the Soviet régime exhibits cer-   14
tain features which the humanitarian may be inclined to deplore,
we must, I think, agree that a certain curtailment of the right to
political opposition is an unavoidable concomitant of transitional periods, and that the rigors which the Russian people have
been called upon to undergo have been amply justified in the
sphere of concrete achievement."

The inflated style is itself a kind of euphemism. A mass of   15
Latin words fall upon the facts like soft snow, blurring the outlines and covering up all the details. The great enemy of clear language is insincerity. When there is a gap between one's real and
one's declared aims, one turns as it were instinctively to long
words and exhausted idioms, like a cuttlefish squirting out ink. In
our age there is no such thing as "keeping out of politics." All issues are political issues, and politics itself is a mass of lies, evasions,
folly, hatred, and schizophrenia. When the general atmosphere is

bad, language must suffer. I should expect to find — this is a guess which I have not sufficient knowledge to verify — that the German, Russian, and Italian languages have all deteriorated in the last ten or fifteen years, as a result of dictatorship.

But if thought corrupts language, language can also corrupt   16
thought. A bad usage can spread by tradition and imitation, even among people who should and do know better. The debased language that I have been discussing is in some ways very convenient. Phrases like *a not unjustifiable assumption, leaves much to be desired, would serve no good purpose, a consideration which we should do well to bear in mind*, are a continuous temptation, a packet of aspirins always at one's elbow. Look back through this essay, and for certain you will find that I have again and again committed the very faults I am protesting against. By this morning's post I have received a pamphlet dealing with conditions in Germany. The author tells me that he "felt impelled" to write it. I open it at random, and here is almost the first sentence that I see: "(The Allies) have an opportunity not only of achieving a radical transformation of Germany's social and political structure in such a way as to avoid a nationalistic reaction in Germany itself, but at the same time of laying the foundations of a co-operative and unified Europe." You see, he "feels impelled" to write — feels, presumably, that he has something new to say — and yet his words, like cavalry horses answering the bugle, group themselves automatically into the familiar dreary pattern. This invasion of one's mind by ready-made phrases (*lay the foundations, achieve a radical transformation*) can only be prevented if one is constantly on guard against them, and every such phrase anesthetizes a portion of one's brain.

I said earlier that the decadence of our language is probably   17
curable. Those who deny this would argue, if they produced an argument at all, that language merely reflects existing social conditions, and that we cannot influence its development by any direct tinkering with words and constructions. So far as the general tone or spirit of a language goes, this may be true, but it is not true in detail. Silly words and expressions have often disappeared, not through any evolutionary process but owing to the conscious action of a minority. Two recent examples were *ex-*

plore every avenue and *leave no stone unturned*, which were killed by the jeers of a few journalists. There is a long list of flyblown metaphors which could similarly be got rid of if enough people would interest themselves in the job; and it should also be possible to laugh the *not un-* formation out of existence,[3] to reduce the amount of Latin and Greek in the average sentence, to drive out foreign phrases and strayed scientific words, and, in general, to make pretentiousness unfashionable. But all these are minor points. The defense of the English language implies more than this, and perhaps it is best to start by saying what it does *not* imply.

To begin with it has nothing to do with archaism, with the   18
salvaging of obsolete words and turns of speech, or with the setting up of a "standard English" which must never be departed from. On the contrary, it is especially concerned with the scrapping of every word or idiom which has outworn its usefulness. It has nothing to do with correct grammar and syntax, which are of no importance so long as one makes one's meaning clear, or with the avoidance of Americanisms, or with having what is called a "good prose style." On the other hand it is not concerned with fake simplicity and the attempt to make written English colloquial. Nor does it even imply in every case preferring the Saxon word to the Latin one, though it does imply using the fewest and shortest words that will cover one's meaning. What is above all needed is to let the meaning choose the word, and not the other way about. In prose, the worst thing one can do with words is to surrender to them. When you think of a concrete object, you think wordlessly, and then, if you want to describe the thing you have been visualizing you probably hunt about till you find the exact words that seem to fit. When you think of something abstract you are more inclined to use words from the start, and unless you make a conscious effort to prevent it, the existing dialect will come rushing in and do the job for you, at the expense of blurring or even changing your meaning. Probably it is better to

---

[3]One can cure oneself of the *not un-* formation by memorizing this sentence: *A not unblack dog was chasing a not unsmall rabbit across a not ungreen field.*

put off using words as long as possible and get one's meaning as clear as one can through pictures or sensations. Afterwards one can choose — not simply *accept* — the phrases that will best cover the meaning, and then switch round and decide what impression one's words are likely to make on another person. This last effort of the mind cuts out all stale or mixed images, all prefabricated phrases, needless repetitions, and humbug and vagueness generally. But one can often be in doubt about the effect of a word or phrase, and one needs rules that one can rely on when instinct fails. I think the following rules will cover most cases:

   (i) Never use a metaphor, simile, or other figure of speech which you are used to seeing in print.

   (ii) Never use a long word where a short one will do.

  (iii) If it is possible to cut a word out, always cut it out.

  (iv) Never use the passive where you can use the active.

   (v) Never use a foreign phrase, a scientific word or a jargon word if you can think of an everyday English equivalent.

  (vi) Break any of these rules sooner than say anything outright barbarous.

These rules sound elementary, and so they are, but they demand a deep change in attitude in anyone who has grown used to writing in the style now fashionable. One could keep all of them and still write bad English, but one could not write the kind of stuff that I quoted in those five specimens at the beginning of this article.

I have not here been considering the literary use of language, but merely language as an instrument for expressing and not for concealing or preventing thought. Stuart Chase and others have come near to claiming that all abstract words are meaningless, and have used this as a pretext for advocating a kind of political quietism. Since you don't know what Fascism is, how can you struggle against Fascism? One need not swallow such absurdities as this, but one ought to recognize that the present political chaos is connected with the decay of language, and that one can probably bring about some improvement by starting at the verbal end. If you simplify your English, you are freed from the worst follies of orthodoxy. You cannot speak any of the necessary dialects, and when you make a stupid remark its stupidity will be obvious, even to yourself. Political language — and with variations this is true of all political parties, from Conservatives to Anarchists — is designed to make lies sound truthful and murder respectable, and to give an appearance of solidity to pure wind. One cannot change this all in a moment, but one can at least change one's own habits, and from time to time one can even, if one jeers loudly enough, send some worn-out and useless phrase — some *jackboot, Achilles' heel, hotbed, melting pot, acid test, veritable inferno*, or other lump of verbal refuse — into the dustbin where it belongs.

· E. B. White ·

For a biographical note on E. B. WHITE (1889–1985) and another of his essays, "Once More to the Lake," see page 110.

A Boy I Knew

In writing about your own childhood, it is evidently a difficult
task to step outside the first person and to resee the world
with any detachment at all. In "A Boy I Knew," E. B. White
tries, and (we believe) succeeds beautifully. This remarkable
essay, touching on White's childhood struggles with fear and
melancholy, was contributed to the series "My Most Unforgettable Character" in the *Reader's Digest* (June 1940).
White never reprinted it in book form, and we are happy and
proud to blow the dust off it.

I am quite sure that the character I'm least likely to forget is   1
a boy I grew up with and nowadays see little of. I keep thinking
about him. Once in a while I catch sight of him — down a lane,
or just coming out of a men's washroom. Sometimes I will be
gazing absently at my own son, now nine years old, and there in
his stead this other boy will be, blindingly familiar yet wholly
dreamlike and unapproachable. Although he enjoys a somewhat doubtful corporality, and occurs only occasionally, like a
stitch in the side, without him I should indeed be lost. He is the
boy that once was me.

The most memorable character in any man's life, and often   2
the most inspiring, is the lad that once he was. I certainly can
never forget him, and, at rare intervals when his trail crosses
mine, the conjunction fills me with elation. Once, quite a while
ago, I wrote a few verses which I put away in a folder to ripen.
With the reader's kind permission I will exhume these lines now,
because they explain briefly what I am getting at:

> In the sudden mirror in the hall
> I saw not my own self at all,

> I saw a most familiar face:
> My father stood there in my place,
> Returning, in the hall lamp's glare,
> My own surprised and watery stare.
> In thirty years my son shall see
> Not himself standing there, but me.

This bitter substitution, or transmigration, one generation   3
with another, must be an experience which has disturbed men
from the beginning of time. There comes a moment when you
discover yourself in your father's shoes, saying his say, putting
on his act, even looking as he looked; and in that moment everything is changed, because if you are your father, then your
son must be you. Or something like that — it's never quite clear.
But anyway you begin to think of this early or original self as
someone apart, a separate character, not someone you once
were but someone you once knew.

I remember once taking an overnight journey with my son   4
in a Pullman compartment. He slept in the lower berth, handy
to the instrument panel containing fan and light controls; I slept
in the upper. Early in the morning I awoke and from my vantage
point looked down. My boy had raised the shade a few inches
and was ingesting the moving world. In that instant I encountered my unforgettable former self: It seemed as though it were I
who was down there in the lower berth looking out of the train
window just as the sky was growing light, absorbing the incredi-
ble wonder of fields, houses, bakery trucks, the before-breakfast
world, tasting the sweetness and scariness of things seen and
only half understood — the train penetrating the morning, the
child penetrating the meaning of the morning and of the future.
To this child the future was always like a high pasture, a little
frightening, full of herds of steers and of intimations of wider
prospects, of trysts with fate, of vague passionate culminations
and the nearness to sky and to groves, of juniper smells and
sweet-fern in a broiling noon sun. The future was one devil of a
fine place, but it was a long while on the way.

This boy (I mean the one I can't forget) had a good effect on   5
me. He was a cyclist and an early riser. Although grotesque in
action, he was of noble design. He lived a life of enchantment;

virtually everything he saw and heard was being seen and heard by him for the first time, so he gave it his whole attention. He took advantage of any slight elevation of ground or of spirit, and if there was a fence going his way, he mounted it and escaped the commonplace by a matter of four feet. I discovered in his company the satisfactions of life's interminable quest; he was always looking for something that had no name and no whereabouts, and not finding it. He either knew instinctively or he soon found out that seeking was more instructive than finding, that journeys were more rewarding than destinations. (I picked up a little of that from him, and have found it of some use.)

He was saddled with an unusual number of worries, it seems to me, but faith underlay them — a faith nourished by the natural world rather than by the supernatural or the spiritual. There was a lake, and at the water's edge a granite rock upholstered with lichen. This was his pew, and the sermon went on forever. 6

He traveled light, so that he was always ready for a change of pace or of direction and was in a position to explore any opportunity and become a part of any situation, unhampered. He spent an appalling amount of time in a semidormant state on curbstones, pier-heads, moles, stringpieces, carriage blocks, and porch steps, absorbing the anecdotes, logic, and technique of artisans. He would travel miles to oversee a new piece of construction. 7

I remember this boy with affection, and feel no embarrassment in idealizing him. He himself was an idealist of shocking proportions. He had a fine capacity for melancholy and the gift of sadness. I never knew anybody on whose spirit the weather had such a devastating effect. A shift of wind, or of mood, could wither him. There would be times when a dismal sky conspired with a forlorn side street to create a moment of such profound bitterness that the world's accumulated sorrow seemed to gather in a solid lump in his heart. The appearance of a coasting hill softening in a thaw, the look of backyards along the railroad tracks on hot afternoons, the faces of people in trolley cars on Sunday — these could and did engulf him in a vast wave of depression. He dreaded Sunday afternoon because it had been deliberately written in a minor key. 8

He dreaded Sunday also because it was the day he spent   9
worrying about going back to school on Monday. School was
consistently frightening, not so much in realization as in antici-
pation. He went to school for sixteen years and was uneasy and
full of dread the entire time — sixteen years of worrying that he
would be called upon to speak a piece in the assembly hall. It
was an amazing test of human fortitude. Every term was a nightmare of suspense.

The fear he had of making a public appearance on a plat-   10
form seemed to find a perverse compensation, for he made frequent voluntary appearances in natural amphitheaters before
hostile audiences, addressing himself to squalls and thunder-
storms, rain and darkness, alone in rented canoes. His survival
is something of a mystery, as he was neither very expert nor very
strong. Fighting natural disturbances was the only sort of fighting he enjoyed. He would run five blocks to escape a boy who
was after him, but he would stand up to any amount of punishment from the elements. He swam from the rocks of Hunter's Island, often at night, making his way there alone and afraid
along the rough, dark trail from the end of the bridge (where the
house was where they sold pie) up the hill and through the silent
woods and across the marsh to the rocks. He hated bathing
beaches and the smell of bathhouses, and would go to any
amount of trouble to avoid the pollution of undressing in a stall.

This boy felt for animals a kinship he never felt for people.   11
Against considerable opposition and with woefully inadequate
equipment, he managed to provide himself with animals, so that
he would never be without something to tend. He kept pigeons,
dogs, snakes, polliwogs, turtles, rabbits, lizards, singing birds,
chameleons, caterpillars, and mice. The total number of hours
he spent just standing watching animals, or refilling their water
pans, would be impossible to estimate; and it would be hard to
say what he got out of it. In spring he felt a sympathetic vibra-
tion with earth's renascence, and set a hen. He always seemed to
be under some strange compulsion to assist the processes of in-
cubation and germination, as though without him they might
fail and the earth grow old and die. To him a miracle was essentially egg-shaped. (It occurs to me that his faith in animals has

been justified by events of recent years: Animals, by comparison with men, seem to have been conducting themselves with poise and dignity.)

In love he was unexcelled. His whole existence was a poem of tender and heroic adoration. He harbored delusions of perfection, and with consummate skill managed to weave the opposite sex into them, while keeping his distance. His search for beauty was always vaguely identified with his search for the ideal of love, and took him into districts which he would otherwise never have visited. Though I seldom see him these days, when I do I notice he still wears that grave inquiring expression as he peers into the faces of passersby, convinced that some day he will find there the answer to his insistent question.

As I say, I feel no embarrassment in describing this character, because there is nothing personal in it — I have rather lost track of him and he has escaped me and is just a strange haunting memory, like the memory of love. I do not consider him in any way unusual or special; he was quite ordinary and had all the standard defects. They seem unimportant. It was his splendor that matters — the unforgettable splendor. No wonder I feel queer when I run into him. I guess all men do.

· E. B. White ·

For a biographical note, see page 110.

Death of a Pig

"Death of a Pig" was E. B. White's response to an invitation
to contribute to the ninetieth anniversary issue of *The Atlantic Monthly* (January 1948). At the time, writing the essay di-
verted him from a preoccupation with his own health. Scott
Elledge, White's biographer, has observed, "If White had not
himself been sick at the time the pig fell ill, there would have
been no story. . . . The animal had become precious to him
for having 'suffered in a suffering world,' and as he watched it
die he experienced first the same terror, then the same healing
purgation that is evoked in an audience watching the performance of a classic tragedy." (*E. B. White: A Biography* [New
York: Norton, 1985], p. 271.) Readers have cherished "Death
of a Pig" as one of White's finest, most touching essays.

I spent several days and nights in mid-September with an 1
ailing pig and I feel driven to account for this stretch of time,
more particularly since the pig died at last, and I lived, and
things might easily have gone the other way round and none left
to do the accounting. Even now, so close to the event, I cannot
recall the hours sharply and am not ready to say whether death
came on the third night or the fourth night. This uncertainty af-
flicts me with a sense of personal deterioration; if I were in decent health I would know how many nights I had sat up with a
pig.

The scheme of buying a spring pig in blossomtime, feeding it 2
through summer and fall, and butchering it when the solid cold
weather arrives, is a familiar scheme to me and follows an antique pattern. It is a tragedy enacted on most farms with perfect
fidelity to the original script. The murder, being premeditated, is
in the first degree but is quick and skillful, and the smoked ba-

con and ham provide a ceremonial ending whose fitness is seldom questioned.

Once in a while something slips — one of the actors goes up 3 in his lines and the whole performance stumbles and halts. My pig simply failed to show up for a meal. The alarm spread rapidly. The classic outline of the tragedy was lost. I found myself cast suddenly in the role of pig's friend and physician — a farcical character with an enema bag for a prop. I had a presentiment, the very first afternoon, that the play would never regain its balance and that my sympathies were now wholly with the pig. This was slapstick — the sort of dramatic treatment that instantly appealed to my old dachshund, Fred, who joined the vigil, held the bag, and, when all was over, presided at the interment. When we slid the body into the grave, we both were shaken to the core. The loss we felt was not the loss of ham but the loss of pig. He had evidently become precious to me, not that he represented a distant nourishment in a hungry time, but that he had suffered in a suffering world. But I'm running ahead of my story and shall have to go back.

My pigpen is at the bottom of an old orchard below the 4 house. The pigs I have raised have lived in a faded building that once was an icehouse. There is a pleasant yard to move about in, shaded by an apple tree that overhangs the low rail fence. A pig couldn't ask for anything better — or none has, at any rate. The sawdust in the icehouse makes a comfortable bottom in which to root, and a warm bed. This sawdust, however, came under suspicion when the pig took sick. One of my neighbors said he thought the pig would have done better on new ground — the same principle that applies in planting potatoes. He said there might be something unhealthy about that sawdust, that he never thought well of sawdust.

It was about four o'clock in the afternoon when I first no- 5 ticed that there was something wrong with the pig. He failed to appear at the trough for his supper, and when a pig (or a child) refuses supper a chill wave of fear runs through any household, or ice-household. After examining my pig, who was stretched out in the sawdust inside the building, I went to the phone and cranked it four times. Mr. Dameron answered. "What's good for a sick pig?" I asked. (There is never any identification needed on a country phone; the person on the other end knows who is talking by the sound of the voice and by the character of the question.)

"I don't know, I never had a sick pig," said Mr. Dameron, 6 "but I can find out quick enough. You hang up and I'll call Henry."

Mr. Dameron was back on the line again in five minutes. 7 "Henry says roll him over on his back and give him two ounces of castor oil or sweet oil, and if that doesn't do the trick give him an injection of soapy water. He says he's almost sure the pig's plugged up, and even if he's wrong, it can't do any harm."

I thanked Mr. Dameron. I didn't go right down to the pig, 8 though. I sank into a chair and sat still for a few minutes to think about my troubles, and then I got up and went to the barn, catching up on some odds and ends that needed tending to. Unconsciously I held off, for an hour, the deed by which I would officially recognize the collapse of the performance of raising a pig; I wanted no interruption in the regularity of feeding, the steadiness of growth, the even succession of days. I wanted no interruption, wanted no oil, no deviation. I just wanted to keep on raising a pig, full meal after full meal, spring into summer into fall. I didn't even know whether there were two ounces of castor oil on the place.

Shortly after five o'clock I remembered that we had been in- 9 vited out to dinner that night and realized that if I were to dose a pig there was no time to lose. The dinner date seemed a familiar conflict: I move in a desultory society and often a week or two will roll by without my going to anybody's house to dinner or anyone's coming to mine, but when an occasion does arise, and I am summoned, something usually turns up (an hour or two in advance) to make all human intercourse seem vastly inappropriate. I have come to believe that there is in hostesses a special power of divination, and that they deliberately arrange dinners to coincide with pig failure or some other sort of failure. At any rate, it was after five o'clock and I knew I could put off no longer the evil hour.

When my son and I arrived at the pigyard, armed with a 10 small bottle of castor oil and a length of clothesline, the pig had emerged from his house and was standing in the middle of his yard, listlessly. He gave us a slim greeting. I could see that he felt uncomfortable and uncertain. I had brought the clothesline thinking I'd have to tie him (the pig weighed more than a hundred pounds) but we never used it. My son reached down, grabbed both front legs, upset him quickly, and when he opened his mouth to scream I turned the oil into his throat — a pink, corrugated area I had never seen before. I had just time to read the label while the neck of the bottle was in his mouth. It said Puretest. The screams, slightly muffled by oil, were pitched in the hysterically high range of pig-sound, as though torture were being carried out, but they didn't last long: It was all over rather suddenly, and, his legs released, the pig righted himself.

In the upset position the corners of his mouth had been turned down, giving him a frowning expression. Back on his feet again, he regained the set smile that a pig wears even in sickness. He stood his ground, sucking slightly at the residue of oil; a few drops leaked out of his lips while his wicked eyes, shaded by their coy little lashes, turned on me in disgust and hatred. I scratched him gently with oily fingers and he remained quiet, as though trying to recall the satisfaction of being scratched when in health, and seeming to rehearse in his mind the indignity to which he had just been subjected. I noticed, as I stood there, four or five small dark spots on his back near the tail end, reddish brown in color, each about the size of a housefly. I could not make out what they were. They did not look troublesome but at the same time they did not look like mere surface bruises or chafe marks. Rather they seemed blemishes of internal origin. His stiff white bristles almost completely hid them and I had to part the bristles with my fingers to get a good look. 11

Several hours later, a few minutes before midnight, having dined well and at someone else's expense, I returned to the pighouse with a flashlight. The patient was asleep. Kneeling, I felt his ears (as you might put your hand on the forehead of a child) and they seemed cool, and then with the light made a careful examination of the yard and the house for sign that the oil had worked. I found none and went to bed. 12

We had been having an unseasonable spell of weather — hot, close days, with the fog shutting in every night, scaling for a 13 few hours in midday, then creeping back again at dark, drifting in first over the trees on the point, then suddenly blowing across the fields, blotting out the world and taking possession of houses, men, and animals. Everyone kept hoping for a break, but the break failed to come. Next day was another hot one. I visited the pig before breakfast and tried to tempt him with a little milk in his trough. He just stared at it, while I made a sucking sound through my teeth to remind him of past pleasures of the feast. With very small, timid pigs, weanlings, this ruse is often quite successful and will encourage them to eat; but with a large, sick pig the ruse is senseless and the sound I made must have made him feel, if anything, more miserable. He not only did not crave food, he felt a positive revulsion to it. I found a place under the apple tree where he had vomited in the night.

At this point, although a depression had settled over me, I didn't suppose that I was going to lose my pig. From the lustiness of a healthy pig a man derives a feeling of personal lustiness; the stuff that goes into the trough and is received with such enthusiasm is an earnest of some later feast of his own, and when this suddenly comes to an end and the food lies stale and untouched, souring in the sun, the pig's imbalance becomes the man's, vicariously, and life seems insecure, displaced, transitory. 14

As my own spirits declined, along with the pig's, the spirits of my vile old dachshund rose. The frequency of our trips down the footpath through the orchard to the pigyard delighted him, although he suffers greatly from arthritis, moves with difficulty, and would be bedridden if he could find anyone willing to serve him meals on a tray. 15

He never missed a chance to visit the pig with me, and he made many professional calls on his own. You could see him down there at all hours, his white face parting the grass along the fence as he wobbled and stumbled about, his stethoscope dangling — a happy quack, writing his villainous prescriptions and grinning his corrosive grin. When the enema bag appeared, and the bucket of warm suds, his happiness was complete, and he managed to squeeze his enormous body between the two lowest rails of the yard and then assumed full charge of the irriga- 16 tion. Once, when I lowered the bag to check the flow, he reached in and hurriedly drank a few mouthfuls of the suds to test their potency. I have noticed that Fred will feverishly consume any substance that is associated with trouble — the bitter flavor is to his liking. When the bag was above reach, he concentrated on the pig and was everywhere at once, a tower of strength and inconvenience. The pig, curiously enough, stood rather quietly through this colonic carnival, and the enema, though ineffective, was not as difficult as I had anticipated.

I discovered, though, that once having given a pig an enema there is no turning back, no chance of resuming one of life's more stereotyped roles. The pig's lot and mine were inextricably bound now, as though the rubber tube were the silver cord. From then until the time of his death I held the pig steadily on the bowl of my mind; the task of trying to deliver him from his misery became a strong obsession. His suffering soon became the embodiment of all earthly wretchedness. Along toward the end of the afternoon, defeated in physicking, I phoned the veterinary twenty miles away and placed the case formally in his hands. He was full of questions, and when I casually mentioned the dark spots on the pig's back, his voice changed its tone.

"I don't want to scare you," he said, "but when there are spots, erysipelas has to be considered."

Together we considered erysipelas, with frequent interruptions from the telephone operator, who wasn't sure the connection had been established.

"If a pig has erysipelas can he give it to a person?" I asked.

"Yes, he can," replied the vet.

"Have they answered?" asked the operator.

"Yes, they have," I said. Then I addressed the vet again. "You better come over here and examine this pig right away."

"I can't come myself," said the vet, "but McFarland can come this evening if that's all right. Mac knows more about pigs than I do anyway. You needn't worry too much about the spots. To indicate erysipelas they would have to be deep hemorrhagic infarcts."

"Deep hemorrhagic what?" I asked.

"Infarcts," said the vet.

"Have they answered?" asked the operator.   27

"Well," I said, "I don't know what you'd call these spots, ex-   28
cept they're about the size of a housefly. If the pig has erysipelas I
guess I have it, too, by this time, because we've been very close
lately."

"McFarland will be over," said the vet.   29

I hung up. My throat felt dry and I went to the cupboard   30
and got a bottle of whiskey. Deep hemorrhagic infarcts — the
phrase began fastening its hooks in my head. I had assumed that
there could be nothing much wrong with a pig during the
months it was being groomed for murder; my confidence in the
essential health and endurance of pigs had been strong and
deep, particularly in the health of pigs that belonged to me and
that were part of my proud scheme. The awakening had been violent and I minded it all the more because I knew that what
could be true of my pig could be true also of the rest of my tidy
world. I tried to put this distasteful idea from me, but it kept recurring. I took a short drink of the whiskey and then, although I
wanted to go down to the yard and look for fresh signs, I was
scared to. I was certain I had erysipelas.

It was long after dark and the supper dishes had been put   31
away when a car drove in and McFarland got out. He had a
girl with him. I could just make her out in the darkness —
she seemed young and pretty. "This is Miss Owen," he said.
"We've been having a picnic supper on the shore, that's why I'm
late."

McFarland stood in the driveway and stripped off his jacket,   32
then his shirt. His stocky arms and capable hands showed up in
my flashlight's gleam as I helped him find his coverall and get
zipped up. The rear seat of his car contained an astonishing
amount of paraphernalia, which he soon overhauled, selecting a
chain, a syringe, a bottle of oil, a rubber tube, and some other
things I couldn't identify. Miss Owen said she'd go along with us
and see the pig. I led the way down the warm slope of the orchard, my light picking out the path for them, and we all
climbed the fence, entered the pighouse, and squatted by the pig
while McFarland took a rectal reading. My flashlight picked up
the glitter of an engagement ring on the girl's hand.

"No elevation," said McFarland, twisting the thermometer in 33
the light. "You needn't worry about erysipelas." He ran his
hand slowly over the pig's stomach and at one point the pig
cried out in pain.

"Poor piggledy-wiggledy!" said Miss Owen. 34

The treatment I had been giving the pig for two days was 35
then repeated, somewhat more expertly, by the doctor, Miss
Owen and I handing him things as he needed them — holding
the chain that he had looped around the pig's upper jaw, holding the syringe, holding the bottle stopper, the end of the tube,
all of us working in darkness and in comfort, working with the
instinctive teamwork induced by emergency conditions, the pig
unprotesting, the house shadowy, protecting, intimate. I went
to bed tired but with a feeling of relief that I had turned over
part of the responsibility of the case to a licensed doctor. I was
beginning to think, though, that the pig was not going to live.

He died twenty-four hours later, or it might have been forty- 36
eight — there is a blur in time here, and I may have lost or
picked up a day in the telling and the pig one in the dying. At
intervals during the last day I took cool fresh water down to him
and at such times as he found the strength to get to his feet he
would stand with head in the pail and snuffle his snout around.
He drank a few sips but no more; yet it seemed to comfort him
to dip his nose in water and bobble it about, sucking in and
blowing out through his teeth. Much of the time, now, he lay
indoors half buried in sawdust. Once, near the last, while I
was attending him I saw him try to make a bed for himself but
he lacked the strength, and when he set his snout into the dust
he was unable to plow even the little furrow he needed to lie
down in.

He came out of the house to die. When I went down, before 37
going to bed, he lay stretched in the yard a few feet from the
door. I knelt, saw that he was dead, and left him there: His face
had a mild look, expressive neither of deep peace nor of deep
suffering, although I think he had suffered a good deal. I went
back up to the house and to bed, and cried internally — deep
hemorrhagic intears. I didn't wake till nearly eight the next

morning, and when I looked out the open window the grave was already being dug, down beyond the dump under a wild apple. I could hear the spade strike against the small rocks that blocked the way. Never send to know for whom the grave is dug, I said to myself, it's dug for thee. Fred, I well knew, was supervising the work of digging, so I ate breakfast slowly.

It was a Saturday morning. The thicket in which I found the 38 gravediggers at work was dark and warm, the sky overcast. Here, among alders and young hackmatacks, at the foot of the apple tree, Lennie had dug a beautiful hole, five feet long, three feet wide, three feet deep. He was standing in it, removing the last spadefuls of earth while Fred patrolled the brink in simple but impressive circles, disturbing the loose earth of the mound so that it trickled back in. There had been no rain in weeks and the soil, even three feet down, was dry and powdery. As I stood and stared, an enormous earthworm which had been partially exposed by the spade at the bottom dug itself deeper and made a slow withdrawal, seeking even remoter moistures at even lonelier depths. And just as Lennie stepped out and rested his spade against the tree and lit a cigarette, a small green apple separated itself from a branch overhead and fell into the hole. Everything about this last scene seemed overwritten — the dismal sky, the shabby woods, the imminence of rain, the worm (legendary bedfellow of the dead), the apple (conventional garnish of a pig).

But even so, there was a directness and dispatch about ani- 39 mal burial, I thought, that made it a more decent affair than human burial: There was no stopover in the undertaker's foul parlor, no wreath nor spray; and when we hitched a line to the pig's hind legs and dragged him swiftly from his yard, throwing our weight into the harness and leaving a wake of crushed grass and smoothed rubble over the dump, ours was a businesslike procession, with Fred, the dishonorable pallbearer, staggering along in the rear, his perverse bereavement showing in every seam in his face; and the postmortem performed handily and swiftly right at the edge of the grave, so that the inwards that had caused the pig's death preceded him into the ground and he lay at last resting squarely on the cause of his own undoing.

I threw in the first shovelful, and then we worked rapidly ⁴⁰ and without talk, until the job was complete. I picked up the rope, made it fast to Fred's collar (he is a notorious ghoul), and we all three filed back up the path to the house, Fred bringing up the rear and holding back every inch of the way, feigning unusual stiffness. I noticed that although he weighed far less than the pig, he was harder to drag, being possessed of the vital spark.

The news of the death of my pig traveled fast and far, and I ⁴¹ received many expressions of sympathy from friends and neighbors, for no one took the event lightly and the premature expiration of a pig is, I soon discovered, a departure which the community marks solemnly on its calendar, a sorrow in which it feels fully involved. I have written this account in penitence and in grief, as a man who failed to raise his pig, and to explain my deviation from the classic course of so many raised pigs. The grave in the woods is unmarked, but Fred can direct the mourner to it unerringly and with immense good will, and I know he and I shall often revisit it, singly and together, in seasons of reflection and despair, on flagless memorial days of our own choosing.

For a biographical note on JOAN DIDION (born in 1934), see
page 8. Another of her essays, "In Bed," appears on page 10.

On Keeping a Notebook

In this example-filled essay, Joan Didion characterizes herself
as a compulsive keeper of notebooks. By revealing what kinds
of entries she puts into her notebooks, and why she does it,
she provides her readers with a fascinating glimpse into the
mind of one of America's foremost essayists and fiction writers. "On Keeping a Notebook" first appeared in *Holiday* magazine in 1966 and was later collected in Didion's widely acclaimed book of essays, *Slouching Toward Bethlehem* (1968).

"'That woman Estelle,'" the note reads, "'is partly the rea- 1
son why George Sharp and I are separated today.' *Dirty crêpe-de-
Chine wrapper,*[1] *hotel bar, Wilmington RR, 9:45 a.m. August Monday morning.*"

Since the note is in my notebook, it presumably has some 2
meaning to me. I study it for a long while. At first I have only
the most general notion of what I was doing on an August Monday morning in the bar of the hotel across from the Pennsylvania Railroad station in Wilmington, Delaware (waiting for a
train? missing one? 1960? 1961? why Wilmington?), but I do remember being there. The woman in the dirty crêpe-de-Chine
wrapper had come down from her room for a beer, and the bartender had heard before the reason why George Sharp and she
were separated today. "Sure," he said, and went on mopping the
floor. "You told me." At the other end of the bar is a girl. She is
talking, pointedly, not to the man beside her but to a cat lying
in the triangle of sunlight cast through the open door. She is

---

[1]Robe of light crinkly silk or rayon fabric. — EDS.

wearing a plaid silk dress from Peck & Peck, and the hem is coming down.

Here is what it is: The girl has been on the Eastern Shore, 3
and now she is going back to the city, leaving the man beside
her, and all she can see ahead are the viscous summer sidewalks
and the 3 A.M. long-distance calls that will make her lie awake
and then sleep drugged through all the steaming mornings left
in August (1960? 1961?). Because she must go directly from the
train to lunch in New York, she wishes that she had a safety pin
for the hem of the plaid silk dress, and she also wishes that she
could forget about the hem and the lunch and stay in the cool
bar that smells of disinfectant and malt and make friends with
the woman in the crêpe-de-Chine wrapper. She is afflicted by a
little self-pity, and she wants to compare Estelles. That is what
that was all about.

Why did I write it down? In order to remember, of course, 4
but exactly what was it I wanted to remember? How much of it
actually happened? Did any of it? Why do I keep a notebook at
all? It is easy to deceive oneself on all those scores. The impulse
to write things down is a peculiarly compulsive one, inexplicable
to those who do not share it, useful only accidentally, only secondarily, in the way that any compulsion tries to justify itself. I
suppose that it begins or does not begin in the cradle. Although
I have felt compelled to write things down since I was five years
old, I doubt that my daughter ever will, for she is a singularly
blessed and accepting child, delighted with life exactly as life
presents itself to her, unafraid to go to sleep and unafraid to
wake up. Keepers of private notebooks are a different breed altogether, lonely and resistant rearrangers of things, anxious malcontents, children afflicted apparently at birth with some presentiment of loss.

My first notebook was a Big Five tablet, given to me by my 5
mother with the sensible suggestion that I stop whining and
learn to amuse myself by writing down my thoughts. She returned the tablet to me a few years ago; the first entry is an account of a woman who believed herself to be freezing to death in
the Arctic night, only to find, when day broke, that she had
stumbled onto the Sahara Desert, where she would die of the

heat before lunch. I have no idea what turn of a five-year-old's mind could have prompted so insistently "ironic" and exotic a story, but it does reveal a certain predilection for the extreme which has dogged me into adult life; perhaps if I were analytically inclined I would find it a truer story than any I might have told about Donald Johnson's birthday party or the day my cousin Brenda put Kitty Litter in the aquarium.

So the point of my keeping a notebook has never been, nor   6
is it now, to have an accurate factual record of what I have been doing or thinking. That would be a different impulse entirely, an instinct for reality which I sometimes envy but do not possess. At no point have I ever been able successfully to keep a diary; my approach to daily life ranges from the grossly negligent to the merely absent, and on those few occasions when I have tried dutifully to record a day's events, boredom has so overcome me that the results are mysterious at best. What is this business about "shopping, typing piece, dinner with E, depressed"? Shopping for what? Typing what piece? Who is E? Was this "E" depressed, or was I depressed? Who cares?

In fact I have abandoned altogether that kind of pointless   7
entry; instead I tell what some would call lies. "That's simply not true," the members of my family frequently tell me when they come up against my memory of a shared event. "The party was *not* for you, the spider was *not* a black widow, *it wasn't that way at all.*" Very likely they are right, for not only have I always had trouble distinguishing between what happened and what merely might have happened, but I remain unconvinced that the distinction, for my purposes, matters. The cracked crab that I recall having for lunch the day my father came home from Detroit in 1945 must certainly be embroidery, worked into the day's pattern to lend verisimilitude; I was ten years old and would not now remember the cracked crab. The day's events did not turn on cracked crab. And yet it is precisely that fictitious crab that makes me see the afternoon all over again, a home movie run all too often, the father bearing gifts, the child weeping, an exercise in family love and guilt. Or that is what it was to me. Similarly, perhaps it never did snow that August in Vermont; perhaps

there never were flurries in the night wind, and maybe no one else felt the ground hardening and summer already dead even as we pretended to bask in it, but that was how it felt to me, and it might as well have snowed, could have snowed, did snow.

How it felt to me: that is getting closer to the truth about a notebook. I sometimes delude myself about why I keep a notebook, imagine that some thrifty virtue derives from preserving everything observed. See enough and write it down, I tell myself, and then some morning when the world seems drained of wonder, some day when I am only going through the motions of doing what I am supposed to do, which is write — on that bankrupt morning I will simply open my notebook and there it will all be, a forgotten account with accumulated interest, paid passage back to the world out there: dialogue overheard in hotels and elevators and at the hat-check counter in Pavillon[2] (one middle-aged man shows his hat check to another and says, "That's my old football number"); impressions of Bettina Aptheker[3] and Benjamin Sonnenberg[4] and Teddy ("Mr. Acapulco") Stauffer;[5] careful *aperçus* about tennis bums and failed fashion models and Greek shipping heiresses, one of whom taught me a significant lesson (a lesson I could have learned from F. Scott Fitzgerald, but perhaps we all must meet the very rich for ourselves)[6] by asking, when I arrived to interview her in her orchid-filled sitting room on the second day of a paralyzing New York blizzard, whether it was snowing outside.

I imagine, in other words, that the notebook is about other people. But of course it is not. I have no real business with what one stranger said to another at the hat-check counter in Pavil-

---

[2] Fashionable and expensive New York restaurant. — EDS.

[3] American Marxist writer and lecturer (born in 1944), who came to prominence in 1964–65 as a leader of the Free Speech Movement, an organization of student protesters at the University of California, Berkeley. — EDS.

[4] New York publicist and public relations executive (1901–1978). — EDS.

[5] Millionaire jet-setter. — EDS.

[6] In a famous anecdote, Fitzgerald, author of *The Great Gatsby* and other fiction set in high society, remarked to his friend Ernest Hemingway, "The very rich are different from us." "Yes," said Hemingway, "they have more money." — EDS.

lon; in fact I suspect that the line "That's my old football number" touched not my own imagination at all, but merely some memory of something once read, probably "The Eighty-Yard Run." Nor is my concern with a woman in a dirty crêpe-de-Chine wrapper in a Wilmington bar. My stake is always, of course, in the unmentioned girl in the plaid silk dress. *Remember what it was to be me:* That is always the point.

It is a difficult point to admit. We are brought up in the 10 ethic that others, any others, all others, are by definition more interesting than ourselves; taught to be diffident, just this side of self-effacing. ("You're the least important person in the room and don't forget it," Jessica Mitford's governess[7] would hiss in her ear on the advent of any social occasion; I copied that into my notebook because it is only recently that I have been able to enter a room without hearing some such phrase in my inner ear.) Only the very young and the very old may recount their dreams at breakfast, dwell upon self, interrupt with memories of beach picnics and favorite Liberty lawn dresses and the rainbow trout in a creek near Colorado Springs. The rest of us are expected, rightly, to affect absorption in other people's favorite dresses, other people's trout.

And so we do. But our notebooks give us away, for however 11 dutifully we record what we see around us, the common denominator of all we see is always, transparently, shamelessly, the implacable "I." We are not talking here about the kind of notebook that is patently for public consumption, a structural conceit for binding together a series of graceful *pensées*;[8] we are talking about something private, about bits of the mind's string too short to use, an indiscriminate and erratic assemblage with meaning only for its maker.

And sometimes even the maker has difficulty with the 12 meaning. There does not seem to be, for example, any point in my knowing for the rest of my life that, during 1964, 720 tons of

[7]Mitford had an aristocratic British upbringing. (See biographical note on p. 249.) — EDS.

[8]Thoughts. — EDS.

soot fell on every square mile of New York City, yet there it is in my notebook, labeled "Fact." Nor do I really need to remember that Ambrose Bierce liked to spell Leland Stanford's name "£eland $tanford"[9] or that "smart women almost always wear black in Cuba," a fashion hint without much potential for practical application. And does not the relevance of these notes seem marginal at best?:

> In the basement museum of the Inyo County Courthouse in Independence, California, sign pinned to a mandarin coat: "This MANDARIN COAT was often worn by Mrs. Minnie S. Brooks when giving lectures on her TEAPOT COLLECTION."

> Redhead getting out of car in front of Beverly Wilshire Hotel, chinchilla stole, Vuitton bags with tags reading:

> > MRS LOU FOX
> > HOTEL SAHARA
> > VEGAS

Well, perhaps not entirely marginal. As a matter of fact, 13 Mrs. Minnie S. Brooks and her MANDARIN COAT pull me back into my own childhood, for although I never knew Mrs. Brooks and did not visit Inyo County until I was thirty, I grew up in just such a world, in houses cluttered with Indian relics and bits of gold ore and ambergris and the souvenirs my Aunt Mercy Farnsworth brought back from the Orient. It is a long way from that world to Mrs. Lou Fox's world, where we all live now, and is it not just as well to remember that? Might not Mrs. Minnie S. Brooks help me to remember what I am? Might not Mrs. Lou Fox help me to remember what I am not?

But sometimes the point is harder to discern. What exactly 14 did I have in mind when I noted down that it cost the father of someone I know $650 a month to light the place on the Hudson in which he lived before the Crash? What use was I planning to make of this line by Jimmy Hoffa:[10] "I may have my faults, but

---

[9]Bierce, satirist and short story writer, was poking fun at Stanford, wealthy railroad-builder and founder of Stanford University. — EDS.
[10]President of the Teamsters' Union (1913–1975?). — EDS.

being wrong ain't one of them"? And although I think it interesting to know where the girls who travel with the Syndicate[11] have their hair done when they find themselves on the West Coast, will I ever make suitable use of it? Might I not be better off just passing it on to John O'Hara?[12] What is a recipe for sauerkraut doing in my notebook? What kind of magpie keeps this notebook? *"He was born the night the Titanic went down."* That seems a nice enough line, and I even recall who said it, but is it not really a better line in life than it could ever be in fiction?

But of course that is exactly it: not that I should ever use the line, but that I should remember the woman who said it and the afternoon I heard it. We were on her terrace by the sea, and we were finishing the wine left from lunch, trying to get what sun there was, a California winter sun. The woman whose husband was born the night the *Titanic* went down wanted to rent her house, wanted to go back to her children in Paris. I remember wishing that I could afford the house, which cost $1,000 a month. "Someday you will," she said lazily. "Someday it all comes." There in the sun on her terrace it seemed easy to believe in someday, but later I had a low-grade afternoon hangover and ran over a black snake on the way to the supermarket and was flooded with inexplicable fear when I heard the checkout clerk explaining to the man ahead of me why she was finally divorcing her husband. "He left me no choice," she said over and over as she punched the register. "He has a little seven-month-old baby by her, he left me no choice." I would like to believe that my dread then was for the human condition, but of course it was for me, because I wanted a baby and did not then have one and because I wanted to own the house that cost $1,000 a month to rent and because I had a hangover.

It all comes back. Perhaps it is difficult to see the value in having one's self back in that kind of mood, but I do see it; I think we are well advised to keep on nodding terms with the people we used to be, whether we find them attractive company or not. Otherwise they run up unannounced and surprise us,

15

16

---

[11]Consorts of the bosses of organized crime. — Eds.
[12]Novelist and story writer (1905–1970). — Eds.

come hammering on the mind's door at 4 A.M. of a bad night and demand to know who deserted them, who betrayed them, who is going to make amends. We forget all too soon the things we thought we could never forget. We forget the loves and the betrayals alike, forget what we whispered and what we screamed, forget who we were. I have already lost touch with a couple of people I used to be; one of them, a seventeen-year-old, presents little threat, although it would be of some interest to me to know again what it feels like to sit on a river levee drinking vodka-and-orange-juice and listening to Les Paul and Mary Ford and their echoes sing "How High the Moon"[13] on the car radio. (You see I still have the scenes, but I no longer perceive myself among those present, no longer could even improvise the dialogue.) The other one, a twenty-three-year-old, bothers me more. She was always a good deal of trouble, and I suspect she will reappear when I least want to see her, skirts too long, shy to the point of aggravation, always the injured party, full of recriminations and little hurts and stories I do not want to hear again, at once saddening me and angering me with her vulnerability and ignorance, an apparition all the more insistent for being so long banished.

It is a good idea, then, to keep in touch, and I suppose that 17
keeping in touch is what notebooks are all about. And we are all on our own when it comes to keeping those lines open to ourselves: Your notebook will never help me, nor mine you. "*So what's new in the whiskey business?*" What could that possibly mean to you? To me it means a blonde in a Pucci bathing suit sitting with a couple of fat men by the pool at the Beverly Hills Hotel. Another man approaches, and they all regard one another in silence for a while. "So what's new in the whiskey business?" one of the fat men finally says by way of welcome, and the blonde stands up, arches one foot and dips it in the pool, looking all the while at the cabana where Baby Pignatari[14] is talking on the telephone. That is all there is to that, except that several

[13]Hit record of 1951, on which Paul and Ford, an electric guitarist and a singer, multiplied their sounds by overdubbing. — Eps.
[14]Socialite and fashion designer. — Eps.

years later I saw the blonde coming out of Saks Fifth Avenue in New York with her California complexion and a voluminous mink coat. In the harsh wind that day she looked old and irrevocably tired to me, and even the skins in the mink coat were not worked the way they were doing them that year, not the way she would have wanted them done, and there is the point of the story. For a while after that I did not like to look in the mirror, and my eyes would skim the newspapers and pick out only the deaths, the cancer victims, the premature coronaries, the suicides, and I stopped riding the Lexington Avenue IRT because I noticed for the first time that all the strangers I had seen for years — the man with the seeing-eye dog, the spinster who read the classified pages every day, the fat girl who always got off with me at Grand Central — looked older than they once had.

It all comes back. Even that recipe for sauerkraut: Even that brings it back. I was on Fire Island when I first made that sauerkraut, and it was raining, and we drank a lot of bourbon and ate the sauerkraut and went to bed at ten, and I listened to the rain and the Atlantic and felt safe. I made the sauerkraut again last night and it did not make me feel any safer, but that is, as they say, another story. 18

· Joan Didion ·

For a biographical note, see page 8.

Miami: The Cuban Presence

Destined to form part of Joan Didion's book *Miami* (1987),
this self-contained section first appeared in the *New York Review of Books* for May 28, 1987. Didion begins by poking fun
at the assumption (of some local white Anglo-Saxon historians) that Hispanic people in Miami are an insignificant minority. With facts and statistics, she demonstrates the vital
Cuban presence in Dade County. A faithful reporter, Didion
chronicles some clashes and resentments between the newcomers and long-time Florida residents. The result is a deeper
and more true-to-life view of a city than we obtain from "Miami Vice."

On the 150th anniversary of the founding of Dade County,   1
in February of 1986, the Miami *Herald* asked four prominent
amateurs of local history to name "the ten people and the ten
events that had the most impact on the county's history." Each
of the four submitted his or her own list of "The Most Influential People in Dade's History," and among the names mentioned
were Julia Tuttle ("pioneer businesswoman"), Henry Flagler
("brought the Florida East Coast Railway to Miami"), Alexander Orr, Jr. ("started the research that saved Miami's drinking
water from salt"), Everest George Sewell ("publicized the city
and fostered its deepwater seaport"). . . . There was Dr. James
M. Jackson, an early Miami physician. There was Napoleon
Bonaparte Broward, the governor of Florida who initiated the
draining of the Everglades. There appeared on three of the four
lists the name of the developer of Coral Gables, George Merrick. There appeared on one of the four lists the name of the
coach of the Miami Dolphins, Don Shula.

On none of these lists of "The Most Influential People in   2
Dade's History" did the name Fidel Castro appear, nor for that
matter did the name of any Cuban, although the presence of
Cubans in Dade County did not go entirely unnoted by the
Herald panel. When it came to naming the Ten Most Important
"Events," as opposed to "People," all four panelists mentioned
the arrival of the Cubans, but at slightly off angles ("Mariel
Boatlift of 1980" was the way one panelist saw it), and as if this
arrival had been just another of those isolated disasters or innovations which deflect the course of any growing community, on
an approximate par with the other events mentioned, for example the Freeze of 1895, the Hurricane of 1926, the opening of the
Dixie Highway, the establishment of Miami International Airport, and the adoption, in 1957, of the metropolitan form of
government, "enabling the Dade County Commission to provide urban services to the increasingly populous unincorporated
area."

This set of mind, in which the local Cuban community was   3
seen as a civic challenge determinedly met, was not uncommon
among Anglos to whom I talked in Miami, many of whom persisted in the related illusions that the city was small, manageable, prosperous in a predictable broad-based way, southern in a
progressive Sunbelt way, American, and belonged to them. In
fact 43 percent of the population of Dade County was by that
time "Hispanic," which meant mostly Cuban. Fifty-six percent
of the population of Miami itself was Hispanic. The most visible
new buildings on the Miami skyline, the Arquitectonica buildings along Brickell Avenue, were by a firm with a Cuban
founder. There were Cubans in the board rooms of the major
banks, Cubans in clubs that did not admit Jews or blacks, and
four Cubans in the most recent mayoralty campaign, two of
whom, Raul Masvidal and Xavier Suarez, had beaten out the in-
cumbent and all other candidates to meet in a runoff, and one
of whom, Xavier Suarez, a thirty-six-year-old lawyer who had
been brought from Cuba to the United States as a child, was by
then mayor of Miami.

The entire tone of the city, the way people looked and   4
talked and met one another, was Cuban. The very image the

city had begun presenting of itself, what was then its newfound glamour, its "hotness" (hot colors, hot vice, shady dealings under the palm trees), was that of prerevolutionary Havana, as perceived by Americans. There was even in the way women dressed in Miami a definable Havana look, a more distinct emphasis on the hips and décolletage, more black, more veiling, a generalized flirtatiousness of style not then current in American cities. In the shoe departments at Brudine's and Jordan Marsh there were more platform soles than there might have been in another American city, and fewer displays of the running shoe ethic. I recall being struck, during an afternoon spent at La Liga Contra el Cancer, a prominent exile charity which raises money to help cancer patients, by the appearance of the volunteers who had met that day to stuff envelopes for a benefit. Their hair was sleek, of a slightly other period, immaculate pageboys and French twists. They wore Bruno Magli pumps, and silk and linen dresses of considerable expense. There seemed to be a preference for strictest gray or black, but the effect remained lush, tropical, like a room full of perfectly groomed mangoes.

This was not, in other words, an invisible 56 percent of the population. Even the social notes in *Diario Las Americas* and in *El Herald*, the daily Spanish edition of the *Herald* written and edited for *el exilio*, suggested a dominant culture, one with money to spend and a notable willingness to spend it in public. La Liga Contra el Cancer alone sponsored, in a single year, two benefit dinner dances, one benefit ball, a benefit children's fashion show, a benefit telethon, a benefit exhibition of jewelry, a benefit presentation of Miss Universe contestants, and a benefit showing, with Saks Fifth Avenue and chicken *vol-au-vent*, of the Adolfo (as it happened, a Cuban) fall collection.

One morning *El Herald* would bring news of the gala at the Pavillon of the Amigos Latinamericanos del Museo de Ciencia y Planetarium; another morning, of an upcoming event at the Big Five Club, a Miami club founded by former members of five fashionable clubs in prerevolutionary Havana: a *coctel*, or cocktail party, at which tables would be assigned for yet another gala, the annual "Baile Imperial de las Rosas" of the American Cancer Society, Hispanic Ladies Auxiliary. Some members of the community were honoring Miss America Latina with dinner dancing at the Doral. Some were being honored themselves, at the Spirit of Excellence Awards Dinner at the Omni. Some were said to be enjoying the skiing at Vail; others to prefer Bariloche, in Argentina. Some were reported unable to attend (but sending checks for) the gala at the Pavillon of the Amigos Latinamericanos del Museo de Ciencia y Planetarium because of a scheduling conflict, with *el coctel de* Paula Hawkins.

Fete followed fete, all high visibility. Almost any day it was 7 possible to drive past the limestone arches and fountains which marked the boundaries of Coral Gables and see little girls being photographed in the tiaras and ruffled hoop skirts and maribou-trimmed illusion capes they would wear at their *quinces*, the elaborate fifteenth-birthday parties at which the community's female children came of official age. The favored facial expression for a *quince* photograph was a classic smolder. The favored backdrop was one suggesting Castilian grandeur, which was how the Coral Gables arches happened to figure. Since the idealization of the virgin implicit in the *quince* could exist only in the presence of its natural foil, *machismo*, there was often a brother around, or a boyfriend. There was also a mother, in dark glasses, not only to protect the symbolic virgin but to point out the better angle, the more aristocratic location. The *quinceanera* would pick up her hoop skirts and move as directed, often revealing the scuffed Jellies she had worn that day to school. A few weeks later there she would be, transformed in *Diario Las Americas*, one of the morning battalion of smoldering fifteen-year-olds, each with her arch, her fountain, her borrowed scenery, the gift if not exactly the intention of the late George Merrick, who built the arches when he developed Coral Gables.

Neither the photographs of the Cuban *quinceaneras* nor the 8 notes about the *coctel* at the Big Five were apt to appear in the newspapers read by Miami Anglos, nor, for that matter, was much information at all about the daily life of the Cuban majority. When, in the fall of 1986, Florida International University offered an evening course called "Cuban Miami: A Guide for Non-Cubans," the *Herald* sent a staff writer, who covered the classes as if from a distant beat. "Already I have begun to make some sense out of a culture, that, while it totally surrounds us, has remained inaccessible and alien to me," the *Herald* writer was reporting by the end of the first meeting, and, by the end of the fourth:

> What I see day to day in Miami, moving through mostly Anglo corridors of the community, are just small bits and pieces of that other world, the tip of something much larger than I'd imagined. . . . We may frequent the restaurants here, or wander into the occasional festival. But mostly we try to ignore Cuban Miami, even as we rub up against this teeming, incomprehensible presence.

Only thirteen people, including the *Herald* writer, turned up 9 for the first meeting of "Cuban Miami: A Guide for Non-Cubans" (two more appeared at the second meeting, along with a security guard, because of telephone threats prompted by what the *Herald* writer called "somebody's twisted sense of national pride"), an enrollment which suggested a certain willingness among non-Cubans to let Cuban Miami remain just that, Cuban, the "incomprehensible presence." In fact there had come to exist in South Florida two parallel cultures, separate but not exactly equal, a key distinction being that only one of the two, the Cuban, exhibited even a remote interest in the activities of the other. "The American community is not really aware of what is happening in the Cuban community," an exiled banker named Luis Botifoll said in a 1983 *Herald* Sunday magazine piece about ten prominent local Cubans. "We are clannish, but at least we know who is whom in the American establishment. They do not." About another of the ten Cubans featured in this piece, Jorge Mas Canosa, the *Herald* had this to say:

> He is an advisor to US Senators, a confidant of federal bureaucrats, a lobbyist for anti-Castro US policies, a near unknown in Miami. When his political group sponsored a luncheon speech in Miami by Secretary of Defense Caspar Weinberger, almost none of the American business leaders attending had ever heard of their Cuban host.

The general direction of this piece, which appeared under 10 the cover line "THE CUBANS: *They're ten of the most powerful men in Miami. Half the population doesn't know it,*" was, as the *Herald* put it,

to challenge the widespread presumption that Miami's Cubans are not really Americans, that they are a foreign presence here, an exile community that is trying to turn South
Florida into North Cuba. . . . The top ten are not separatists;
they have achieved success in the most traditional ways. They
are the solid, bedrock citizens, hard-working humanitarians
who are role models for a community that seems determined
to assimilate itself into American society.

This was interesting. It was written by one of the few Cu-   11
bans then on the *Herald* staff, and yet it described, however un-
wittingly, the precise angle at which Miami Anglos and Miami
Cubans were failing to connect: Miami Anglos were in fact interested in Cubans only to the extent that they could cast them
as aspiring immigrants, "determined to assimilate," a "hard-
working" minority not different in kind from other groups of
resident aliens. (But had I met any Haitians, a number of Anglos
asked when I said that I had been talking to Cubans.) Anglos
(who were, significantly, referred to within the Cuban community as "Americans") spoke of cross-culturalization, and of what
they believed to be a meaningful second-generation preference
for hamburgers, and rock-and-roll. They spoke of "diversity,"
and of Miami's "Hispanic flavor," an approach in which 56 percent of the population was seen as decorative, like the Coral Gables arches.

Fixed as they were on this image of the melting pot, of immi-   12
grants fleeing a disruptive revolution to find a place in the
American sun, Anglos did not on the whole understand that assimilation would be considered by most Cubans a doubtful goal
at best. Nor did many Anglos understand that living in Florida
was still at the deepest level construed by Cubans as a temporary
condition, an accepted political option shaped by the continuing dream, if no longer the immediate expectation, of a vindica-
tory return. *El exilio* was for Cubans a ritual, a respected tradition. *La revolución* was also a ritual, a trope fixed in Cuban
political rhetoric at least since José Martí, a concept broadly interpreted to mean reform, or progress, or even just change.
Ramón Grau San Martín, the president of Cuba during the autumn of 1933 and from 1944 until 1948, had presented himself

as a revolutionary, as had his 1948 successor, Carlos Prío. Even Fulgencio Batista had entered Havana life calling for *la revolución*, and had later been accused of betraying it, even as Fidel Castro was now.

This was a process Cuban Miami understood, but Anglo Miami did not, remaining as it did arrestingly innocent of even the most general information about Cuba and Cubans. Miami Anglos for example still had trouble with Cuban names, and Cuban food. When the Cuban novelist Guillermo Cabrera Infante came from London to lecture at Miami-Dade Community College, he was referred to by several Anglo faculty members to whom I spoke as "Infante." Cuban food was widely seen not as a minute variation on that eaten throughout both the Caribbean and the Mediterranean but as "exotic," and full of garlic. A typical Thursday food section of the *Herald* included recipes for Broiled Lemon-Curry Cornish Game Hens, Chicken Tetrazzini, King Cake, Pimiento Cheese, Raisin Sauce for Ham, Sauteed Spiced Peaches, Shrimp Scampi, Easy Beefy Stir-Fry, and four ways to use dried beans ("Those cheap, humble beans that have long sustained the world's poor have become the trendy set's new pet"), none of them Cuban.

This was all consistent, and proceeded from the original construction, that of the exile as an immigration. There was no reason to be curious about Cuban food, because Cuban teenagers preferred hamburgers. There was no reason to get Cuban names right, because they were complicated, and would be simplified by the second generation, or even by the first. "Jorge L. Mas" was the way Jorge Mas Canosa's business card read. "Raul Masvidal" was the way Raul Masvidal y Jury ran for mayor of Miami. There was no reason to know about Cuban history, because history was what immigrants were fleeing.

Even the revolution, the reason for the immigration, could be covered in a few broad strokes: "Batista," "Castro," "26 Julio," this last being the particular broad stroke that inspired the Miami Springs Holiday Inn, on July 26, 1985, the thirty-second anniversary of the day Fidel Castro attacked the Moncada Barracks and so launched his six-year struggle for power in Cuba, to run a bar special on Cuba Libres, thinking to attract local Cubans by commemorating their holiday. "It was a mistake," the manager said, besieged by outraged exiles. "The gentleman who did it is from Minnesota."

There was in fact no reason, in Miami as well as in Minnesota, to know anything at all about Cubans, since Miami Cubans were now, if not Americans, at least aspiring Americans, and worthy of Anglo attention to the exact extent that they were proving themselves, in the *Herald's* words, "role models for a community that seems determined to assimilate itself into American society"; or, as George Bush put it in a 1986 Miami address to the Cuban American National Foundation, "the most eloquent testimony I know to the basic strength and success of America, as well as to the basic weakness and failure of Communism and Fidel Castro." 16

The use of this special lens, through which the exiles were seen as a tribute to the American system, a point scored in the battle of the ideologies, tended to be encouraged by those outside observers who dropped down from the northeast corridor for a look and a column or two. George Will, in *Newsweek*, saw Miami as "a new installment in the saga of America's absorptive capacity," and Southwest Eighth Street as the place where "these exemplary Americans," the seven Cubans who had been gotten together to brief him, "initiated a columnist to fried bananas and black-bean soup and other Cuban contributions to the tanginess of American life." George Gilder, in *The Wilson Quarterly*, drew pretty much the same lesson from Southwest Eighth Street, finding it "more effervescently thriving than its crushed prototype," by which he seemed to mean Havana. In fact Eighth Street was for George Gilder a street that seemed to "percolate with the forbidden commerce of the dying island to the south . . . the Refrescos Cawy, the Competidora and El Cuño cigarettes, the *guayaberas*,[1] the Latin music pulsing from the storefronts, the pyramids of mangoes and tubers, gourds and plantains, the iced coconuts served with a straw, the new theaters showing the latest anti-Castro comedies." 17

There was nothing on this list, with the possible exception 18

[1]Short, lightweight Cuban jackets. — EDS.

of the "anti-Castro comedies," that could not most days be found on Southwest Eighth Street, but the list was also a fantasy, and a particularly *gringo* fantasy, one in which Miami Cubans, who came from a culture which had represented western civilization in this hemisphere since before there was a United States of America, appeared exclusively as vendors of plantains, their native music "pulsing" behind them. There was in any such view of Miami Cubans an extraordinary element of condescension, and it was the very condescension shared by Miami Anglos, who were inclined to reduce the particular liveliness and sophistication of local Cuban life to a matter of shrines on the lawn and love potions in the *botanicas*, the primitive exotica of the tourist's Caribbean.

Cubans were perceived as most satisfactory when they appeared most fully to share the aspirations and manners of middle-class Americans, at the same time adding "color" to the city on appropriate occasions, for example at their *quinces* (the *quinces* were one aspect of Cuban life almost invariably mentioned by Anglos, who tended to present them as evidence of Cuban extravagance, i.e., Cuban irresponsibility, or childishness), or on the day of the annual Calle Ocho Festival, when they could, according to the *Herald*, "samba" in the streets and stir up a paella for two thousand (ten cooks, two thousand mussels, two hundred and twenty pounds of lobster, and four hundred and forty pounds of rice), using rowboat oars as spoons. Cubans were perceived as least satisfactory when they "acted clannish," "kept to themselves," "had their own ways," and, two frequent flash points, "spoke Spanish when they didn't need to" and "got political"; complaints, each of them, which suggested an Anglo view of what Cubans should be at significant odds with what Cubans were.

This question of language was curious. The sound of spoken Spanish was common in Miami, but it was also common in Los Angeles, and Houston, and even in the cities of the Northeast. What was unusual about Spanish in Miami was not that it was so often spoken, but that it was so often heard: In, say, Los Angeles, Spanish remained a language only barely registered by the Anglo population, part of the ambient noise, the language spoken by the people who worked in the car wash and came to trim the trees and cleared the tables in restaurants. In Miami Spanish was spoken by the people who ate in the restaurants, the people who owned the cars and the trees, which made, on the socio-auditory scale, a considerable difference. Exiles who felt isolated or declassed by language in New York or Los Angeles thrived in Miami. An entrepreneur who spoke no English could still, in Miami, buy, sell, negotiate, leverage assets, float bonds, and, if he were so inclined, attend galas twice a week, in black tie. "I have been after the *Herald* ten times to do a story about millionaires in Miami who do not speak more than two words in English," one prominent exile told me. "'Yes' and 'no.' Those are the two words. They come here with five dollars in their pockets and without speaking another word of English they are millionaires."

The truculence a millionaire who spoke only two words of   21
English might provoke among the less resourceful native citizens of a nominally American city was predictable, and manifested itself rather directly. In 1980, the year of Mariel, Dade County voters had approved a referendum requiring that county business be conducted exclusively in English. Notwithstanding the fact that this legislation was necessarily amended to exclude emergency medical and certain other services, and notwithstanding even the fact that many local meetings continued to be conducted in that unbroken alternation of Spanish and English which had become the local patois ("I will be in Boston on Sunday and *desafortunadamente yo tengo un compromiso en* Boston *que no puedo romper y yo no podre estar con Vds.*," read the minutes of a 1984 Miami City Commission meeting I had occasion to look up. "*En espíritu, estaré, pero* the other members of the commission I am sure are invited . . ."),[2] the very existence of this referendum was seen by many as ground regained, a point made. By 1985 a St. Petersburg optometrist named Robert Melby was launching his third attempt in four years to have English de-

---

[2]Didion illustrates the mingling of both languages in Miami speech. Rendered entirely in English, the statement would read: "I will be in Boston on Sunday and unfortunately I have an appointment in Boston that I can't break and I won't be able to be with you. In spirit, I will be, but the other members of the commission I am sure are invited . . ." — EDS.

clared the official language of the state of Florida, as it would be in 1986 of California. "I don't know why your legislators here are so, how should I put it? — spineless," Robert Melby complained about those South Florida politicians who knew how to count. "No one down here seems to want to run with the issue."

Even among those Anglos who distanced themselves from such efforts, Anglos who did not perceive themselves as economically or socially threatened by Cubans, there remained considerable uneasiness on the matter of language, perhaps because the inability or the disinclination to speak English tended to undermine their conviction that assimilation was an ideal universally shared by those who were to be assimilated. This uneasiness had for example shown up repeatedly during the 1985 mayoralty campaign, surfacing at odd but apparently irrepressible angles. The winner of that contest, Xavier Suarez, who was born in Cuba but educated in the United States, a graduate of Harvard Law, was reported in a wire service story to speak, an apparently unexpected accomplishment, "flawless English."

A less prominent Cuban candidate for mayor that year had unsettled reporters at a televised "meet the candidates" forum by answering in Spanish the questions they asked in English. "For all I or my dumbstruck colleagues knew," the *Herald* political editor complained in print after the event, "he was reciting his high school's alma mater or the ten Commandments over and over again. The only thing I understood was the occasional *Cubanos vota Cubano* he tossed in." It was noted by another *Herald* columnist that of the leading candidates, only one, Raul Masvidal, had a listed telephone number, but: ". . . if you call Masvidal's 661-0259 number on Kiaora Street in Coconut Grove — during the day, anyway — you'd better speak Spanish. I spoke to two women there, and neither spoke enough English to answer the question of whether it was the candidate's number."

On the morning this last item came to my attention in the *Herald* I studied it for some time. Raul Masvidal was at that time the chairman of the board of the Miami Savings Bank and the Miami Savings Corporation. He was a former chairman of the Biscayne Bank, and a minority stockholder in the M Bank, of which he had been a founder. He was a member of the Board of Regents for the state university system of Florida. He had paid $600,000 for the house on Kiaora Street in Coconut Grove, buying it specifically because he needed to be a Miami resident (Coconut Grove is part of the city of Miami) in order to run for mayor, and he had sold his previous house, in the incorporated city of Coral Gables, for $1,100,000.

The Spanish words required to find out whether the num- 25 ber listed for the house on Kiaora Street was in fact the candidate's number would have been roughly these: *"¿Es la casa de Raul Masvidal?"* The answer might have been *"Sí,"* or the answer might have been *"No."* It seemed to me that there must be very few people working on daily newspapers along the southern borders of the United States who would consider this exchange entirely out of reach, and fewer still who would not accept it as a commonplace of American domestic life that daytime telephone calls to middle-class urban households will frequently be answered by women who speak Spanish.

Something else was at work in this item, a real resistance, a 26 balkiness, a coded version of the same message Dade County voters had sent when they decreed that their business be done only in English: WILL THE LAST AMERICAN TO LEAVE MIAMI PLEASE BRING THE FLAG, the famous bumper stickers had read the year of Mariel. "It was the last American stronghold in Dade County," the owner of the Gator Kicks Longneck Saloon, out where Southwest Eighth Street runs into the Everglades, had said after he closed the place for good the night of Super Bowl Sunday, 1986. "Fortunately or unfortunately, I'm not alone in my inability," a *Herald* columnist named Charles Whited had written a week or so later, in a column about not speaking Spanish. "A good many Americans have left Miami because they want to live someplace where everybody speaks one language: theirs." In this context the call to the house on Kiaora Street in Coconut Grove which did or did not belong to Raul Masvidal appeared not as a statement of literal fact but as shorthand, a glove thrown down, a stand, a cry from the heart of a beleaguered raj.[3]

---

[3]Compare George Orwell's use of this same word in "Shooting an Elephant." (p. 615). — EDS.

1. What insights into the nature of imperialism does George Orwell provide? To write on this subject, you might compare and contrast the attitudes expressed in "Shooting an Elephant" with those in "A Hanging" (in Chapter 1). Or, you might define the nature of imperialism, drawing your evidence from both Orwell essays.

2. From browsing in current newspapers and magazines, find a few passages of writing as bad as the ones George Orwell quotes and condemns in "Politics and the English Language." Try to analyze what you find wrong with them.

3. Like Orwell, who in "Politics and the English Language" deliberately worsens a verse from Ecclesiastes, take a passage of excellent prose and try rewriting it in words as abstract and colorless as possible. For passages to work on, try paragraph 2 from Thoreau's "The Battle of the Ants" in Chapter 7, paragraph 12 from Martin Luther King's "I Have a Dream" in Chapter 10, or any other passage you admire. If you choose an unfamiliar passage, supply a copy of it along with your finished paper. What does your experiment demonstrate?

4. What light does E. B. White's "A Boy I Knew" cast upon his essay "Once More to the Lake" (in Chapter 2)? In "A Boy I Knew," see especially paragraph 3 ("There comes a moment when you discover yourself in your father's shoes . . .") and paragraph 4, the memory of the train journey with his son.

5. As E. B. White does in "A Boy I Knew" and Joan Didion does in "Keeping a Notebook" (para. 16), write a portrait of your younger self. Try to write with detachment, admiring strong points and admitting to shortcomings.

6. Inspired by E. B. White's "Death of a Pig," write a narrative account of a painful experience you have witnessed, in which you try to empathize with another person (or, as White does, with an animal).

7. Sum up whatever useful suggestions for your own writing you derive from Joan Didion's "On Keeping a Notebook." Or else, like Didion, write an account of your own favorite method of writing or studying.

8. After reading Joan Didion's "Miami: The Cuban Presence," write

a paragraph contrasting Didion's view of Miami with your previous idea of it.

9. An alternative, after you have read Didion's essay on Miami,
   would be to write a short essay on a town or city you know well. In
   your own essay, try to show the importance of a certain group of
   people. Perhaps they are citizens of a certain neighborhood, members of an age group or ethnic group, or members of a community
   organization. What have they contributed to the life and culture
   of their city?

USEFUL TERMS

Abstract and **Concrete** are names for two kinds of language. Abstract words refer to ideas, conditions, and qualities we cannot directly perceive: *truth, love, courage, evil, wealth, poverty, progressive, reactionary*. Concrete words indicate things we can know with our senses: *tree, chair, bird, pen, motorcycle, perfume, thunderclap, cheeseburger*. The use of concrete words lends vigor and clarity to writing, for such words help a reader to picture things. See *Image*.

Writers of expository essays tend to shift back and forth from one kind of language to the other. They often begin a paragraph with a general statement full of abstract words ("There is *hope* for the *future* of *motoring*"). Then they usually go on to give examples and present evidence in sentences full of concrete words ("Inventor *Jones* claims his *car* will go from *Fresno* to *Los Angeles* on a *gallon* of *peanut oil*"). Beginning writers often use too many abstract words and not enough concrete ones.

Allusion refers a reader to any person, place, or thing in fact, fiction, or legend that the writer believes is common knowledge. An allusion (a single reference) may point to a famous event, a familiar saying, a noted personality, a well-known story or song. Usually brief, an allusion is a space-saving way to convey much meaning. For example, the statement "The game was Coach Johnson's Waterloo" informs the reader that, like Napoleon meeting defeat in a celebrated battle, the coach led a confrontation resulting in his downfall and that of his team. If the writer is also showing Johnson's character, the allusion might further tell us that the coach is a man of Napoleonic ambition and pride. To observe "He is our town's J. R. Ewing" concisely says several things: that a leading citizen is unscrupulous, deceptive, merciless, rich, and eager to become richer — perhaps superficially charming and promiscuous as well. To make an effective allusion, you have to be aware of your audience. If your readers are not likely to recognize the allusion, it will only confuse. Not everyone, for example, would understand you if you alluded to a neighbor, to a seventeenth-century Russian harpsichordist, or to a little-known stock car driver.

Analogy is a form of exposition that uses an extended comparison based on the like features of two unlike things: one familiar or easily understood, the other unfamiliar, abstract, or complicated. See Chapter 7. For *Argument by Analogy* see the list of *Logical Fallacies* on pages 506–508.

Argument is one of the four principal modes of writing, whose function is to convince readers. See Chapter 10.

Audience, for a writer, means readers. Having in mind a particular audience helps the writer in choosing strategies. Imagine, for instance, that you are writing two reviews of the French movie *Jean de Florette*: one for the students who read the campus newspaper, the other for amateur and professional filmmakers who read *Millimeter*. For the first audience, you might write about the actors, the plot, and especially dramatic scenes. You might judge the picture and urge your readers to see it — or to avoid it. Writing for *Millimeter*, you might discuss special effects, shooting techniques, problems in editing and in mixing picture and sound. In this review, you might use more specialized and technical terms. Obviously, an awareness of the interests and knowledge of your readers, in each case, would help you decide how to write. If you told readers of the campus paper too much about filming techniques, you would lose most of them. If you told *Millimeter*'s readers the plot of the film in detail and how you liked its opening scene, probably you would put them to sleep.

You can increase your awareness of your audience by asking yourself a few questions before you begin to write. Who are to be your readers? What is their age level? Background? Education? Where do they live? What are their beliefs and attitudes? What interests them? What, if anything, sets them apart from most people? How familiar are they with your subject? Knowing your audience can help you write so that your readers will not only understand you better, but more deeply care about what you say.

Cause and Effect is a form of exposition in which a writer analyzes reasons for an action, event, or decision, or analyzes its consequences. See Chapter 8.

Claim is the proposition that an argument demonstrates. Stephen Toulmin favors this term in his system of reasoning. See page 501. In some discussions of argument, the term *thesis* is used instead.

Classification is a form of exposition in which a writer sorts out plural things (contact sports, college students, kinds of music) into categories. See Chapter 6.

Cliché (French) is a name for any worn out, trite expression that a writer employs thoughtlessly. Although at one time the expression may have been colorful, from heavy use it has lost its luster. It is now "old as the hills." In conversation, most of us sometimes use clichés, but in writing they "stick out like sore thumbs." Alert writers, when they revise, replace a cliché with a fresh, concrete expression. Writers who have trouble recognizing clichés generally need to read more widely. Their problem is that, so many expressions being new to them, they do not know which ones are full of moths.

Coherence is the clear connection of the parts in a piece of effective writing. This quality exists when the reader can easily follow the flow of ideas between sentences, paragraphs, and larger divisions, and can see how they relate successively to one another.

In making your essay coherent, you may find certain devices useful. Transitions, for instance, can bridge ideas. Reminders of points you have stated earlier are helpful to a reader who may have forgotten them — as readers tend to do sometimes, particularly if your essay is long. However, a coherent essay is not one merely pasted together with transitions and reminders. It derives its coherence from the clear relationship between its thesis (or central idea) and all its parts.

Colloquial Expressions are those which occur primarily in speech and informal writing that seeks a relaxed, conversational tone. "My favorite chow is a burger and a shake" or "This math exam has me climbing the walls" may be acceptable in talking to a roommate, in corresponding with a friend, or in writing a humorous essay for general readers. Such choices of words, however, would be out of place in formal writing — in, say, a laboratory report or a letter to your senator. Contractions (*let's, don't, we'll*) and abbreviated words (*photo, sales rep, TV*) are the shorthand of spoken language. Good writers use such expressions with an awareness that they produce an effect of casualness.

Comparison and Contrast, two writing strategies, are usually found together. They are a form of exposition in which a writer examines the similarities and differences between two things to reveal their natures. See Chapter 4.

Conclusions are those sentences or paragraphs that bring an essay to a satisfying and logical end. They are purposefully crafted to give a sense of unity and completeness to the whole essay. The best conclusions evolve naturally out of what has gone before and convince the reader that the essay is indeed at an end, not that the writer has run out of steam.

Conclusions vary in type and length depending on the nature and scope of the essay. A long research paper may require several paragraphs of summary to review and emphasize the main points. A short essay, however, may benefit from a few brief closing sentences.

In concluding an essay, beware of diminishing the impact of your writing by finishing on a weak note. Don't apologize for what you have or have not written, or cram in a final detail that would have been better placed elsewhere.

Although there are no set formulas for closing, the following list presents several options:

1. Restate the thesis of your essay, and perhaps your main points.

2. Mention the broader implications or significance of your topic.

3. Give a final example that pulls all the parts of your discussion together.

4. Offer a prediction.

5. End with the most important point as the culmination of your essay's development.

6. Suggest how the reader can apply the information you have just imparted.

7. End with a bit of drama or flourish. Tell an anecdote, offer an appropriate quotation, ask a question, make a final insightful remark. Keep in mind, however, that an ending shouldn't sound false and gimmicky. It truly has to conclude.

Concrete: See *Abstract and Concrete.*

Connotation and **Denotation** are names for the two types of meanings most words have. Denotation is the explicit, literal, dictionary definition of a word. Connotation refers to the implied meaning, resonant with associations, of a word. The denotation of *blood* is "the fluid that circulates in the vascular system." The word's connotations range from *life force* to *gore* to *family bond*. A doctor might use the word *blood* for its denotation, and a mystery writer might rely on the rich connotations of the word to heighten a scene.

Because people have different experiences, they bring to the same word different associations. A conservative Republican's emotional response to the word *welfare* is not likely to be the same as a liberal Democrat's. And referring to your senator as a statesman evokes a different response, from him and from others, than if you were to call him a baby-kisser, or even a politician. The effective use of words involves knowing both what they mean literally and what they are likely to suggest.

Data, another name for *Evidence*, is a term favored by logician Stephen Toulmin in his system of reasoning. See page 501.

Deduction is the method of reasoning from general to specific. See page 505.

Definition may refer to a statement of the literal and specific meaning or meanings of a word (*short definition*), or to a form of expository writing (*extended definition*). In the latter, the writer usually explains the nature of a word, a thing, a concept, or a phenomenon; in doing so the writer may employ narration, description, or any of the expository methods. See Chapter 9.

Denotation: See *Connotation and Denotation*.

Description is a mode of writing that conveys sensory evidence. See Chapter 2.

Diction is a choice of words. Every written or spoken statement contains diction of some kind. To describe certain aspects of diction, the following terms may be useful:

Standard English: words and grammatical forms that native speakers of the language use in formal writing.

Nonstandard English: words and grammatical forms such as *theirselves* and *ain't* that occur mainly in the speech of people of a particular social background.

Slang: certain words in highly informal speech or writing.

Colloquial expressions: words and phrases from conversation. See *Colloquial Expressions* for examples.

Regional terms: words heard in a certain locality, such as *spritzing* for raining in Pennsylvania Dutch country.

Dialect: a variety of English based on differences in geography, education, or social background. Dialect is usually spoken, but may be written. Maya Angelou's essay in Chapter 1 transcribes the words of dialect speakers: people waiting for the fight broadcast ("He gone whip him till that white boy call him Momma").

Technical terms: words and phrases that form the vocabulary of a particular discipline (*monocotyledon* from botany), occupation (*drawplate* from die-making), or avocation (*interval training* from running). See also *Jargon*.

Archaisms: old-fashioned expressions, once common but now used to suggest an earlier style, such as *ere*, *yon*, and *forsooth*. (Actually, *yon* is still current in the expression *hither and yon*; but if you say "Behold yon glass of beer!" it is an archaism.)

Obsolete diction: words that have passed out of use (such as the verb *werien*, "to protect or defend," and the noun *isetnesses*, "agreements"). *Obsolete* may also refer to certain meanings of words no longer current (*fond* for foolish, *clipping* for hugging or embracing).

Pretentious diction: use of words more numerous and elaborate than necessary, such as *institution of higher learning* for college, and *partake of solid nourishment* for eat.

To be sure, archaisms and pretentious diction have no place in good writing unless a writer deliberately uses them for ironic or humorous effect: H. L. Mencken has delighted in the hifalutin use of *tonsorial studio* instead of barber shop. Still, any diction may be the right diction for a certain occasion: The choice of words depends on a writer's purpose and audience.

Division is a form of expository writing in which the writer separates a single subject into its parts. See Chapter 6.

Effect, the result of an event or action, is usually considered together with *cause* as a form of exposition. See the discussion of cause and effect in Chapter 8. The term *effect* may also refer to the impression a word, sentence, paragraph, or entire work makes on its audience.

Emphasis is stress or special importance given to a certain point or element to make it stand out. A skillful writer draws attention to what is most important in a sentence, paragraph, or essay by controlling emphasis in any of the following ways:

Proportion: Important ideas are given greater coverage than minor points.

Position: The beginnings and ends of sentences, paragraphs, and larger divisions are the strongest positions. Placing key ideas in these spots helps draw attention to their importance. The end is the stronger position, for what stands last stands out. A sentence in which less important details precede the main point is called a *periodic sentence*: "Having disguised himself as a guard and walked through the courtyard to the side gate, the prisoner made his escape." A sentence in which the main point precedes less important details is a *loose sentence*: "Autumn is orange: gourds in baskets at roadside stands, the harvest moon hanging like a pumpkin, and oak and beech leaves flashing like goldfish."

Repetition: Careful repetition of key words or phrases can give them greater importance. (Careless repetition, however, can cause boredom.)

Mechanical devices: Italics (underlining), capital letters, and exclamation points can make words or sentences stand out. Writers sometimes fall back on these devices, however, after failing to show significance by other means. Italics and exclamation points can be useful in reporting speech, but excessive use sounds exaggerated or bombastic.

Essay refers to a short nonfiction composition on one central theme or subject in which the writer may offer personal views. Essays are sometimes classified as either formal or informal. In general, a *formal essay* is one whose diction is that of the written language (not colloquial speech), serious in tone, and usually focused on a subject the writer believes is important. (For example, see Carl Sagan's "The Nuclear Winter.") An *informal essay*, in contrast, is more likely to admit colloquial expressions; the writer's tone tends to be lighter, perhaps humorous, and the subject is likely to be personal, sometimes even trivial. (See James Thurber's "University Days.") These distinctions, however, are rough ones: An essay such as Judy Syfers's "I Want a Wife" may use colloquial language and speak of personal experience, though it is serious in tone and has an undeniably important subject.

Evaluation is judging merits. In evaluating a work of writing, you suspend personal preference and judge its success in fulfilling the writer's apparent purpose. For instance, if an essay tells how to tune up a car and you have no interest in engines, you nevertheless decide how clearly and effectively the writer explains the process to you.

Evidence is the factual basis for an argument or an explanation. In a courtroom, an attorney's case is only as good as the evidence marshaled to support it. In an essay, a writer's opinions and generalizations also must rest upon evidence, usually given in the form of facts, statistics, examples, and expert testimony. See Chapter 10.

Example, also called *exemplification*, is a form of exposition in which the writer illustrates a general idea. See Chapter 3. An example is a verbal illustration.

Exposition is the mode of prose writing that explains a subject. Its function is to inform, to instruct, or to set forth ideas. Exposition may call various methods to its service: example, comparison and contrast, process analysis, division, classification, analogy, cause and effect. Expository writing exposes information: the major trade routes in the Middle East, how to make a dulcimer, why the United States consumes more energy than it needs. Most college writing is exposition, and most of the essays in this book (those in Chapters 3 through 9) are expository.

Figures of Speech occur whenever a writer, for the sake of emphasis or vividness, departs from the literal meanings (or denotations) of words. To say "She's a jewel" doesn't mean that the subject of praise is literally a kind of shining stone; the statement makes sense because its connotations come to mind: rare, priceless, worth cherishing. Some figures of speech involve comparisons of two objects apparently unlike. A *simile* (from the Latin, "likeness") states the comparison directly, usually connecting the two things using "like," "as," or "than": "The moon is like a snowball," "He's lazy as a cat full of cream," "My feet are flatter than flyswatters." A *metaphor* (from the Greek, "transfer") declares one thing *to be* another: "A mighty fortress is our God," "The sheep were bolls of cotton on the hill." (A *dead metaphor* is a word or phrase that, originally a figure of speech, has come to be literal through common usage: "the *hands* of a clock.") *Personification* is a simile or metaphor that assigns human traits to inanimate objects or abstractions: "A stoop-shouldered refrigerator hummed quietly to itself," "All of a sudden the solution to the math problem sat there winking at me."

Other figures of speech consist of deliberate misrepresentations. *Hyperbole* (from the Greek, "throwing beyond") is a conscious exaggeration: "I'm so hungry I could eat a horse and saddle," "I'd wait for you a thousand years." Its opposite, *understatement*, creates an ironic or humorous effect: "I accepted the ride. At the moment, I didn't much feel like walking across the Mojave Desert." A *paradox* is a seemingly self-contradictory statement that, on reflection, makes sense: "Children are the poor man's wealth." (Wealth can be monetary, or it can be spiritual.)

Focus is the narrowing of a subject to make it manageable. Beginning with a general subject, you concentrate on a certain aspect of it. For instance, you may select crafts as a general subject, then decide your main interest lies in weaving. You could focus your essay still further by narrowing it to operating a hand loom. You can also focus your writing according to who will read it (*Audience*) or what you want it to achieve (*Purpose*).

General and **Specific** refer to words and describe their relative degrees of abstractness. General words name a group or class (*flowers*); specific words limit the class by naming its individual members (*rose, violet, dahlia, marigold*). Words may be arranged in a series from general to specific: *clothes, pants, jeans, Levis.* The word *cat* is more specific than *animal,* but less specific than *tiger cat,* or *Garfield.* See also *Abstract and Concrete.*

Generalization refers to a statement about a class based on an examination of some of its members: "Lions are fierce." The more members examined and the more representative they are of the class, the sturdier the generalization. Insufficient or nonrepresentative evidence often leads to a hasty generalization. The statement "Solar heat saves homeowners money" would be challenged by homeowners who have yet to recover their installation costs. "Solar heat can save homeowners money in the long run" would be a sounder generalization. Words such as *all, every, only,* and *always* have to be used with care. "Some artists are alcoholics" is more credible than "Artists are always alcoholics." Making a trustworthy generalization involves the use of *inductive reasoning* (discussed on pages 505–506).

Hyperbole: See *Figures of Speech.*

Illustration is another name for the expository method of giving examples. See Chapter 3.

Image refers to a word or word sequence that evokes a sensory experience. Whether literal ("We picked two red apples") or figurative ("His cheeks looked like two red apples, buffed and shining"), an image appeals to the reader's memory of seeing, hearing, smelling, touching, or tasting. Images add concreteness to fiction — "The farm looked as tiny and still as a seashell, with the little knob of a house surrounded by its curved furrows of tomato plants" (Eudora Welty in a short story, "The Whistle") — and are an important element in poetry. But writers of essays, too, find images valuable in giving examples, describing, comparing and contrasting, and drawing analogies.

Induction is the process of reasoning to a conclusion about an entire class by examining some of its members. See pages 505–506.

Introductions are the openings of written works. Often they state the writer's subject, narrow it, and communicate an attitude toward it (*Tone*). Introductions vary in length, depending on their purposes. A research paper may need several paragraphs to set forth its central idea and its plan of organization; on the other hand, a brief, informal essay may need only a sentence or two for an introduction. Whether long or short, good introductions tell us no more than we need to know when we begin reading. Here are a few possible ways to open an essay effectively:

1. State your central idea, perhaps showing why you care about it.

2. Present startling facts about your subject.

3. Tell an illustrative anecdote.

4. Give background information that will help your reader understand your subject, or see why it is important.

5. Begin with an arresting quotation.

6. Ask a challenging question. (In your essay, you'll go on to answer it.)

Irony is a manner of speaking or writing that does not directly state a discrepancy, but implies one. *Verbal irony* is the intentional use of words to suggest a meaning other than literal: "What a mansion!" (said of a shack); "There's nothing like sunshine" (said on a foggy morning). If irony is delivered contemptuously with intent to hurt, we call it *sarcasm*: "Oh, you're a real friend!" (said to someone who refuses to lend the speaker a dime to make a phone call). Certain situations also can be ironic, when we sense in them some incongruity, some result contrary to expectation, or some twist of fate: Juliet regains consciousness only to find that Romeo, believing her dead, has stabbed himself.

Jargon, strictly speaking, is the special vocabulary of a trade or profession; but the term has also come to mean inflated, vague, meaningless language of any kind. It is characterized by wordiness, abstractions galore, pretentious diction, and needlessly complicated word order. Whenever you meet a sentence that obviously could express its idea in fewer words and shorter ones, chances are that it is jargon. For instance: "The motivating force compelling her to opt continually for the most labor-intensive mode of operation in performing her functions was consistently observed to be the single constant and regular factor in her behavior patterns." Translation: "She did everything the hard way." For more specimens of jargon, see the examples George Orwell gives in "Politics and the English Language" (For Further Reading).

Metaphor: See *Figures of Speech.*

Narration is the mode of writing that tells a story. See Chapter 1.

Nonstandard English: See *Diction.*

Objective and **Subjective** are names for kinds of writing that differ in emphasis. In objective writing, the emphasis falls on the topic; in subjective writing, it falls on the writer's view of the topic. Objective writing occurs in factual reporting, certain kinds of process analysis (such as recipes, directions, and instructions), and logical arguments in which the writer attempts to omit personal feelings and opinions. Subjective writing sets forth the writer's feelings, opinions, and interpretations. It occurs in friendly letters, journals, editorials, by-lined feature stories and columns in newspapers, personal essays, and arguments that appeal to emotion. Very few essays, however, contain one kind of writing exclusive of the other.

Paradox: See *Figures of Speech*.

Paragraph refers to a group of closely related sentences that develop a central idea. In an essay, a paragraph is the most important unit of thought because it is both self-contained and part of the larger whole. Paragraphs separate long and involved ideas into smaller parts that are more manageable for the writer and easier for the reader to take in. Good paragraphs, like good essays, possess unity and coherence. The central idea is usually stated in the topic sentence, often found at the beginning of the paragraph. All other sentences in the paragraph relate to this topic sentence, defining it, explaining it, illustrating it, providing it with evidence and support. Sometimes you will meet a unified and coherent paragraph that has no topic sentence. It usually contains a central idea that no sentence in it explicitly states, but that every sentence in it clearly implies.

Parallelism, or **Parallel Structure**, is a name for a habit of good writers: keeping ideas of equal importance in similar grammatical form. A writer may place nouns side by side ("*Time* and *tide* wait for no man") or in a series ("Give me *wind, sea,* and *stars*"). Phrases, too, may be arranged in parallel structure ("*Out of my bed, into my shoes, up to my classroom* — that's my life"); or clauses ("Ask not what your country can do for you; ask what you can do for your country").

Parallelism may be found not only in single sentences, but in larger units as well. A paragraph might read: "Rhythm is everywhere. It throbs in the rain forests of Brazil. It vibrates ballroom floors in Vienna. It snaps its fingers on street corners in Chicago." In a whole essay, parallelism may be the principle used to arrange ideas in a balanced or harmonious structure. See the famous speech given by Martin Luther King, Jr. (Chapter 10), in which each paragraph in a series (paragraphs 11 through 18) begins with the words "I have a dream" and goes on to describe an imagined future. Not only does such a parallel structure organize ideas, but it also lends them force.

Paraphrase is putting another writer's thoughts into your own words. In writing a research paper or an essay containing evidence gathered from your reading, you will find it necessary to paraphrase — unless you are using another writer's very words with quotation marks around them. In paraphrasing, you rethink what the other writer has said, decide what is essential, and determine how you would say it otherwise. (Of course, you still acknowledge your source.) The purpose of paraphrasing is not merely to avoid copying word for word, but to adapt material to the needs of your own paper.

Although a paraphrase sometimes makes material briefer, it does not always do so; in principle, it rewrites and restates, sometimes in the same number of words, if not more. A condensation of longer material that renders it more concise is called a *summary*: for instance, a statement of the plot of a whole novel in a few sentences.

Person is a grammatical distinction made between the speaker, the one spoken to, and the one spoken about. In the first person (*I*, *we*), the subject is speaking; in the second person (*you*), the subject is being spoken to; in the third person (*he, she, it*), the subject is being spoken about. The *point of view* of an essay or work of fiction is often specified according to person: "This short story is told from a first person point of view." See *Point of View*.

Personification: See *Figures of Speech*.

Persuasion is a function of argument. See Chapter 10.

Point of View, in an essay, is the physical position or the mental angle from which a writer beholds a subject. Assuming the subject is starlings, the following three writers have different points of view. An ornithologist might write about the introduction of these birds into North America. A farmer might advise other farmers how to prevent the birds from eating seed. A bird-watcher might describe a first glad sighting of an unusual species. Furthermore, the *person* of each essay would probably differ. The scientist might present a scholarly paper in the third person; the farmer might offer advice in the second; the bird-watcher might recount the experience in the first. See *Person*.

Premise is a name for a proposition that supports a conclusion. In a *syllogism* we reason deductively from the major and minor premises to the conclusion that necessarily follows. See *Deduction*. In expository writing, premises are the assumptions on which an author bases an argument.

Prewriting generally refers to that stage or stages in the process of composition before words start to flow. It is the activity of the mind before setting pen or typewriter keys to paper, and may include evoking ideas, deciding on a topic, narrowing the topic, doing factual reading and research, defining your audience, planning and arranging material. An important stage of prewriting usually comes first: *invention*, the creation or discovery of ideas.

Invention may follow from daydreaming or meditation, reading, keeping a journal, or perhaps carefully ransacking your memory.

As composition theorist D. Gordon Rohman has observed, prewriting may be defined as "the stage of discovery in the writing process when a person assimilates his subject to himself." In practice, the prewriting stage sometimes doesn't neatly end with the picking up of paper; reading, research, taking into account your audience, and further discovery may take place even while you write.

Process Analysis is a form of exposition that most often explains step by step how something is done or how to do something. See Chapter 5.

Purpose is a writer's reason for writing; it is whatever the writer of any work tries to achieve. To achieve unity and coherence, a writer often identifies a purpose before beginning to write. The more clearly defined the purpose, the better the writer can concentrate on achieving it.

In trying to define the purpose of an essay you read, ask yourself, Why did the writer write this? or What was this writer trying to achieve? Even though you cannot know the writer's intentions with absolute certainty, an effective essay generally makes some purpose clear.

Rhetoric is the study (and the art) of using language effectively. Often the modes of prose discourse (narration, description, exposition, and argument) and the various methods of exposition (exemplification, comparison and contrast, and the others) are called rhetorical forms.

Rhetorical Question indicates a question posed for effect, one that requires no answer. Instead, it often provokes thought, lends emphasis to a point, asserts or denies something without making a direct statement, launches further discussion, introduces an opinion, or leads the reader where the writer intends. Sometimes a writer throws one in to introduce variety in a paragraph full of declarative sentences. The following questions are rhetorical: "When will the United States learn that sending people to the moon does not feed them on earth?" — "Shall I compare thee to a summer's day?" — "What shall it profit a man to gain the whole world if he lose his immortal soul?" Both reader and writer know what the answers are supposed to be. (1. Someday, if the United States ever wises up; 2. Yes; 3. Nothing.)

Satire is a form of writing that employs wit to attack folly. Unlike most comedy, the purpose of satire is not merely to entertain, but to bring about enlightenment — even reform. Frequently, satire will employ irony — as in Jonathan Swift's "A Modest Proposal" (Chapter 10).

Sentimentality is a quality sometimes found in writing that fails to communicate. Such writing calls for an extreme emotional response on the part of an audience, although its writer fails to supply adequate reason for any such reaction. A sentimental writer delights in waxing teary over certain objects: great-grandmother's portrait, the first stick of chewing gum baby chewed (now a shapeless wad), an empty popcorn box saved from the World Series of 1952. Sentimental writing usually results when writers shut their eyes to the actual world, preferring to snuffle the sweet scents of remembrance.

Simile: See *Figures of Speech*.

Slang: See *Diction*.

Standard English: See *Diction*.

Strategy refers to whatever means a writer employs to write effectively. The methods set forth in each chapter of this book are strategies; but so are narrowing a subject, organizing ideas clearly, using transitions, writing with an awareness of your reader, and other effective writing practices.

Style is the distinctive manner in which a writer writes; it may be seen especially in the writer's choice of words and sentence structure. Two writers may write on the same subject, even express similar ideas, but it is style that gives each writer's work a personality.

Suspense is often an element in narration: the pleasurable expectation or anxiety we feel that keeps us reading a story. In an exciting mystery story, suspense is constant: How will it all turn out? — Will the detective get to the scene in time to prevent another murder? But there can be suspense in less melodramatic accounts as well.

Syllogism is a name for a three-step form of reasoning that employs deduction. See page 505 for an illustration.

Symbol is a name for a visible object or action that suggests some further meaning. The flag suggests country, the crown suggests royalty — these are conventional symbols familiar to us. Life abounds in such relatively clear-cut symbols. Football teams use dolphins and rams for easy identification; married couples symbolize their union with a ring.

   In writing, symbols usually do not have such a one-to-one correspondence, but evoke a whole constellation of associations. In Herman Melville's *Moby-Dick*, the whale suggests more than the large mammal it is. It hints at evil, obsession, and the untamable forces of nature. Such a symbol carries meanings too complex or elusive to be neatly defined.

More common in fiction and poetry than in expository writing, symbols can be used to good purpose in exposition because they often communicate an idea in a compact and concrete way.

Thesis is the central idea in a work of writing, to which everything else in the work refers. In some way, each sentence and each paragraph in an effective essay serve to support the thesis and to make it clear and explicit to an audience. Good writers, before they begin to write, often set down a *thesis sentence* or *thesis statement* to help them define their purpose.

Tone refers to the way a writer regards subject, audience, or self. It is the writer's attitude, and sets the prevailing spirit of whatever he or she writes. Tone in writing varies as greatly as tone of voice varies in conversation. It can be serious, distant, flippant, angry, enthusiastic, sincere, or sympathetic. Whatever tone a writer chooses, usually it informs an entire essay and helps a reader decide how to respond.

Topic Sentence is a name for the statement of the central idea in a paragraph. Often it will appear at (or near) the beginning of the paragraph, announcing the idea and beginning its development. Because all other sentences in the paragraph explain and support this central idea, the topic sentence is a way to create unity.

Transitions are words, phrases, sentences, or even paragraphs that relate ideas. In moving from one topic to the next, a writer has to bring the reader along by showing how the ideas are developing, what bearing a new thought or detail has on an earlier discussion, or why a new topic is being introduced. A clear purpose, strong ideas, and logical development certainly aid coherence, but to ensure that the reader is following along, good writers provide signals, or transitions.

To bridge paragraphs and to point out relationships within them, you can use some of the following devices of transition:

1. Repeat words or phrases to produce an echo in the reader's mind.

2. Use parallel structures to produce a rhythm that moves the reader forward.

3. Use pronouns to refer back to nouns in earlier passages.

4. Use transitional words and phrases. These may indicate a relationship of time (*right away, later, soon, meanwhile, in a few minutes, that night*), proximity (*beside, close to, distant from, nearby, facing*), effect (*therefore, for this reason, as a result, consequently*), comparison (*similarly, in the same way, likewise*), or contrast (*yet,*

but, nevertheless, however, despite). Some words and phrases of transition simply add on: *besides, too, also, moreover, in addition to, second, last, in the end*.

Understatement: See *Figures of Speech*.

Unity is the quality of good writing in which all parts relate to the thesis. (See *Thesis*.) In a unified essay, all words, sentences, and paragraphs support the single central idea. Your first step in achieving unity is to state your thesis; your next step is to organize your thoughts so that they make your thesis clear.

Warrant, the thinking that leads from data to claim, is a term favored in Stephen Toulmin's system of reasoning. See pages 501–505.

ESSAYS ARRANGED
BY SUBJECT

CHILDREN AND FAMILY

THE CONDUCT OF LIFE

CONTEMPORARY ISSUES

DEATH

ENVIRONMENT

HISTORY

HUMOR AND SATIRE

THE NATURAL WORLD

OTHER COUNTRIES, OTHER PEOPLES

PSYCHOLOGY AND BEHAVIOR

READING, WRITING, AND LANGUAGE

SCHOOL AND COLLEGE

SCIENCE AND TECHNOLOGY

SELF-DISCOVERY

SPORTS AND LEISURE

WARFARE AND WEAPONS

WOMEN

for Ignoring Audience." From *College English*, Volume 49, Number 1. Copyright © 1987 by the National Council of Teachers of English. Reprinted by permission of the publisher and the author.

Joseph Epstein, "What Is Vulgar?" Reprinted from *The American Scholar*, Volume 51, Number 1, Winter, 1981–82. Copyright © 1981 by the author. Reprinted by permission of the publisher.

Paul Fussell, "Notes on Class." From *The Boy Scout Handbook and Other Observations* by Paul Fussell. Reprinted by permission of Oxford University Press, Inc.

Stephen Jay Gould, "Sex, Drugs, Disasters, and the Extinction of Dinosaurs" and an excerpt from the prologue reprinted from *The Flamingo's Smile: Reflections in Natural History* by Stephen Jay Gould, by permission of W.W. Norton & Company, Inc. Copyright © 1985 by Stephen Jay Gould.

Jeff Greenfield, "The Black and White Truth about Basketball." Reprinted by permission of the Sterling Lord Agency, Inc. Copyright © 1988 by Jeff Greenfield.

Ernest Hemingway, "Hills Like White Elephants." From *Men Without Women*. Copyright 1927 Charles Scribner's Sons; copyright renewed © 1955 Ernest Hemingway. Reprinted with the permission of Charles Scribner's Sons. Excerpt from "Indestructible." Reprinted by permission; © 1947, 1975 The New Yorker Magazine, Inc. Excerpt from "An Afternoon with Hemingway" by Edward Stafford. Reprinted with permission of *Writer's Digest*. Excerpt from *The Green Hills of Africa*. Copyright 1935 Charles Scribner's Sons; copyright renewed © 1963 Mary Hemingway. Reprinted with the permission of Charles Scribner's Sons, an imprint of Macmillan Publishing Company. From the interview with Ernest Hemingway by George Plimpton in *Writers at Work: The Paris Review Interviews*, Second Series, edited by George Plimpton. Copyright © 1963 by The Paris Review, Inc. Reprinted by permission of Viking Penguin Inc. Excerpt from *Conversations with Hemingway*. Reprinted by permission.

Banesh Hoffmann, "My Friend, Albert Einstein." Reprinted with permission from the January 1968 *Reader's Digest*. Copyright © 1967 by The Reader's Digest Association, Inc.

Mark Hunter, "The Beat Goes Off: How Technology Has Gummed Up Rock's Grooves." Copyright © 1987 by *Harper's Magazine*. All rights reserved. Reprinted from the May issue by special permission.

H. W. Janson, Excerpt from *History of Art*. Reprinted from the book *History of Art* by H. W. Janson, 3rd edition, published by Harry N. Abrams, Inc., NY, 1986. All rights reserved.

Garrison Keillor, "Shy Rights: Why Not Pretty Soon?" From *Happy to Be Here*. Copyright © 1982 Garrison Keillor. Reprinted with the permission of Atheneum, an imprint of Macmillan Publishing Company. Excerpt

ries, edited by George Plimpton. Copyright © 1981 by The Paris Review, Inc. Reprinted by permission of Viking Penguin Inc.

Alice Walker, "In Search of Our Mothers' Gardens." From *In Search of Our Mothers' Gardens,* copyright 1967 by Alice Walker. Reprinted by permission of Harcourt Brace Jovanovich, Inc. "Women." Copyright © 1970 by Alice Walker. Reprinted from her volume *Revolutionary Petunias & Other Poems* by permission of Harcourt Brace Jovanovich, Inc. Excerpt from "Telling the Black Woman's Story" by David Bradley. Originally published in the January 8, 1984 issue of the *New York Times Magazine.* Reprinted by permission.

E. B. White, "Once More to the Lake." From *Essays of E. B. White.* Copyright 1941 by E. B. White. Reprinted by permission of Harper & Row, Publishers, Inc. "A Boy I Knew." Reprinted with permission from the June 1940 *Reader's Digest.* "Death of a Pig." From *Essays of E. B. White.* Copyright 1947 by E. B. White. Reprinted by permission of Harper & Row, Publishers, Inc. Pages 84–85, 649–650 from *Letters of E. B. White,* collected and edited by Dorothy Lobrano Guth. Copyright © 1976 by E. B. White. Reprinted by permission of Harper and Row, Publishers, Inc.

Marie Winn, "The End of Play." From *Children Without Childhood,* by Marie Winn. Copyright © 1981, 1983 by Marie Winn. Reprinted by permission of Pantheon Books, a Division of Random House, Inc.

Tom Wolfe, "Pornoviolence." From *Mauve Gloves and Madmen, Clutter & Vine* by Tom Wolfe. Copyright © 1967, 1976 by Tom Wolfe. Reprinted by permission of Farrar, Straus and Giroux, Inc. From "Sitting up with Tom Wolfe" by Joe David Bellamy. Copyright © 1974 by The Trustees of the University of Illinois. Reprinted by permission of the University of Illinois Press.

To the Student

We regularly revise the books we publish in order to make them better. To do this well we need to know what instructors and students think of the previous edition. At some point your instructor will be asked to comment on *The Bedford Reader*, Third Edition; now we would like to hear from you.

Please take a few minutes to complete this questionnaire and send it to Bedford Books of St. Martin's Press, 29 Commonwealth Avenue, Boston, Massachusetts 02116. We promise to listen to what you have to say. Thanks.

School _____

School location (city, state) _____

Course title _____

Instructor's name _____

Please rate the selections.	Liked a lot	Okay	Didn't like	Didn't read
Didion, *In Bed*	—	—	—	—
Angelou, *Champion of the World*	—	—	—	—
Orwell, *A Hanging*	—	—	—	—
Thurber, *University Days*	—	—	—	—
Trillin, *It's Just Too Late*	—	—	—	—
Hemingway, *Hills Like White Elephants*	—	—	—	—
Dillard, *Singing with the Fundamentalists*	—	—	—	—
White, *Once More to the Lake*	—	—	—	—
O'Connor, *King of the Birds*	—	—	—	—
Senturia, *At Home in America*	—	—	—	—
Lawrence, *Snake*	—	—	—	—

	Liked a lot	Okay	Didn't like	Didn't read
Dickinson, *A narrow Fellow in the Grass*	___	___	___	___
Rosenblatt, *Oops! How's That Again?*	___	___	___	___
Staples, *Black Men and Public Space*	___	___	___	___
Hoffmann, *My Friend, Albert Einstein*	___	___	___	___
Walker, *In Search of Our Mothers' Gardens*	___	___	___	___
Greenfield, *The Black and White Truth about Basketball*	___	___	___	___
Britt, *Neat People vs. Sloppy People*	___	___	___	___
Catton, *Grant and Lee: A Study in Contrasts*	___	___	___	___
Rosenthal, *No News from Auschwitz*	___	___	___	___
Mitford, *Behind the Formaldehyde Curtain*	___	___	___	___
Elbow, *Desperation Writing*	___	___	___	___
Quammen, *Is Sex Necessary? Virgin Birth and Opportunism in the Garden*	___	___	___	___
Saukko, *How to Poison the Earth*	___	___	___	___
Syfers, *I Want a Wife*	___	___	___	___
Davies, *A Few Kind Words for Superstition*	___	___	___	___
Sheehy, *Predictable Crises of Adulthood*	___	___	___	___
Fussell, *Notes on Class*	___	___	___	___
Ehrlichs, *The Rivet Poppers*	___	___	___	___
Thoreau, *The Battle of the Ants*	___	___	___	___
Thomas, *The Attic of the Brain*	___	___	___	___

	Liked a lot	Okay	Didn't like	Didn't read
Vidal, *Drugs*	___	___	___	___
Winn, *The End of Play*	___	___	___	___
Gould, *Sex, Drugs, Disasters, and the Extinction of Dinosaurs*	___	___	___	___
Sagan, *The Nuclear Winter*	___	___	___	___
Oates, *On Boxing*	___	___	___	___
Wolfe, *Pornoviolence*	___	___	___	___
Ehrlich, *About Men*	___	___	___	___
Epstein, *What Is Vulgar?*	___	___	___	___
Le Guin, *Why Are Americans Afraid of Dragons?*	___	___	___	___
Mencken, *The Penalty of Death*	___	___	___	___
Ehrenreich, *Hope I Die before I Get Rich*	___	___	___	___
Rodriguez, *Aria: A Memoir of a Bilingual Childhood*	___	___	___	___
Hunter, *The Beat Goes Off: How Technology Has Gummed Up Rock's Grooves*	___	___	___	___
Buckley, *Why Don't We Complain?*	___	___	___	___
Keillor, *Shy Rights: Why Not Pretty Soon?*	___	___	___	___
King, *I Have a Dream*	___	___	___	___
Swift, *A Modest Proposal*	___	___	___	___
Orwell, *Shooting an Elephant*	___	___	___	___
Orwell, *Politics and the English Language*	___	___	___	___

	Liked a lot	Okay	Didn't like	Didn't read
White, *A Boy I Knew*	___	___	___	___
White, *Death of a Pig*	___	___	___	___
Didion, *On Keeping a Notebook*	___	___	___	___
Didion, *Miami: The Cuban Presence*	___	___	___	___

Are there any writers not included you would like to see added? _____

_____

_____

Did you read the comments by the writers on writing? _____

Were they useful? _____

_____

Any general comments or suggestions? _____

_____

_____

_____

_____

_____

_____

_____

Name _____

Mailing address _____

Date _____